GHOST AND GUARDIAN

SANAN KOLVA

ISBN: 978-1-7325872-8-1

PART ONE

LORD

LORD

"Hold still, Cylin. I'll make this quick." Pryor crouched on the hard, barren dirt. His smile was almost sympathetic. "We all have to make sacrifices sometimes."

"No! Let go of me!" Cylin struggled against the hands pinning her on the ground.

Jael caught her short blond hair, his thick fingers scraping her scalp. "She has lovely skin. Shame to slice it to shreds," he mourned. "Bone men pay good coin for young skin like that."

Cylin bared her teeth and tried to bite his hand, but couldn't get the right angle. "Let go of me!" she shouted again. She couldn't break free of Pryor's thugs. Alger sat on her legs while Hakon pinned her arms and Jael held her head still. Each of them outweighed her by at least fifty pounds.

"Consider it a payment toward your debt. You're lucky. I could be selling a lot more, but we just need a piece," Pryor said. "You know I'll patch you up right after, just like I did for Alger."

Alger grunted in agreement, glancing to his left hand and the two missing fingers.

"The bone men are waiting, and they aren't the sorts to

wait forever." Pryor's head jerked toward the road. Somewhere hidden by the night, the bone men waited for their piece of flesh as payment for safe passage. "You won't miss an ear," he promised, drawing his knife and wiping it clean on his pant leg.

The knife flashed toward her face. Cylin shrieked and jerked her head aside. The blade opened a gash on her right cheek and nicked her ear. She shrieked again. Hot blood ran down her skin.

Pryor cursed. "Hold her *still*, you fall-brained oaf!" He glared first at Jael, then at Cylin. His eyes narrowed. The flickering light of the campfire gave his features deeper menace than usual, and his voice grew hard. "I can sell a piece to the bone men now, or I can give you to them whole. I promise you *they* will take far more than I will when they skin you. Now hold still, girl, while I still think you're worth more to my team alive."

Her heart raced. Fear shook her.

Gods of my father's hearth, if I've ever found favor with you, don't let Pryor do this.

Cylin squeezed her eyes shut as the knife cut toward her face again. She felt a sting as the blade broke skin, then it was gone. Pryor shouted in surprise and pain. Cylin's eyes snapped open to see the knife spin out of his hand, glinting in the firelight. Pryor jumped to his feet, grabbing his pistol. The hands holding Cylin relaxed as the other men searched for the source of danger.

She sucked in a deep gulp of air. Had her family's hearth gods actually answered her desperate prayer?

"Release the girl." The low voice came from the darkness, cold with promise of dire consequences.

"Who in a scavenger's bones are you?" Pryor demanded, aiming into the night.

"Release her," the voice repeated. It sounded male, but Cylin didn't recognize it. *Who is this? A drifter? We would have heard a vehicle miles away. Why would anyone be walking the wasteland this late? There's no shelter for hours.*

"She's mine," Pryor growled. "And if I want to sell her piece by piece to the bone men, that's my business, not yours. Who do you think you are, some would-be lawman? A hero?" He spat the last word with scorn.

"A ghost."

Steps crunched on the ground, scattering pebbles across the bare dirt. Pryor aimed toward the sound. As if pulled by a string, his hands jerked up and the bullet fired harmlessly into the sky.

"What the--," Pryor began, but he got no further. A figure rushed into the light, slamming into Pryor and sending the muscular man sprawling to the dirt.

The three holding Cylin sprang to their feet, grabbing weapons. Cylin scrambled back, eyes wide. She pushed to her feet as the men focused on the intruder.

"Ah, there you go. See, that wasn't so hard, was it?" A flash of white as the intruder grinned, his tone mocking. "Now we can all go about our business."

Alger yelled in fury and lunged. The stranger sprang aside with lithe grace. He was shorter than Alger, barely as tall as Cylin, easily ducking under Alger's grab. Cylin's gaze darted around the camp. Pryor climbed to his feet, face twisted with rage. Jael and Hakon moved to flank the stranger.

I could run while they're focused on him. No one's watching me. She cast a look into the darkness, then back at the camp. *I might be able to grab my pack, but food and water are in the truck, and Pryor has the key.* She wouldn't get far without water, and her bag contained only enough purification tablets for a day. Pryor didn't trust her with more than that.

The dancing fire cast light onto the stranger's face. His hair was black as night, and his skin so smooth that any bone man would pay twice a standard rate for it—though what bone men did with skin, Cylin didn't want to know. He held no visible weapon. His mouth curled in a feral, confident grin, fearless even when unarmed and surrounded.

He's crazy. He's got to be crazy. Pryor's going to carve him to bits. She swallowed hard. *I guess a hearth god doesn't have much power these days. But if one unarmed lunatic is all the rescue I get, I'd better use it.*

She glanced to the truck, into the darkness, and finally back to the stranger. *Do I take my chances in the night, hope I don't run into the bone men or whatever mutated creatures lurk in the dark? Or do I take my chances with a madman who has no reason to defend me?*

Giving herself no time to reconsider, Cylin lunged for the pistol she knew Jael kept tucked in the holster at his back.

Jael turned when he felt her hands. "Hey! What you think you doin?"

She was amazed her hands didn't shake as she pointed the gun at his chest. *Not the head, Father always said. Aim for the largest target.* Cylin squeezed the trigger. The pistol jumped in her hands. A sharp crack echoed in the night. Jael staggered, then toppled, blood staining his shirt.

In that moment of distraction, the stranger attacked. Cylin shook her head as her eyes and mind played tricks on her. She could almost have said the man flew, and that he didn't even touch Alger when he sent the man crashing into the truck. Pryor raised his gun again, and the stranger eyed him.

"I wouldn't, if I were you," he warned in a low, calm voice. "Count your losses and leave."

Pryor leveled the pistol, eyes locking with the stranger's. Whatever he saw, he slowly lowered the weapon. "You think you can take what's mine without consequence?"

"You can give the bone men their due, pay your passage. Best take him before anything starts to spoil." The stranger jerked a nod toward Jael's corpse.

Pryor glared at Cylin, all calm gone from his face. "You still owe me, Cylin. I will collect."

"Carve off someone else's face, Pryor," she spat. "I don't owe you a damned thing."

Hakon helped Pryor lift Alger into the truck cab, then they dragged Jael's body into the back. The stranger watched, silent. Cylin did as well, though her heart pounded so hard she thought it would burst. At any moment, she expected Pryor to shoot them both, but he didn't. The truck rumbled to life and roared down the road, leaving her standing in their camp with only an empty pistol, her pack, and the stranger who'd rescued her.

Her breath came quick and shallow. *Pryor really intended to take my skin. I didn't think he would. He threatened a few times, but I didn't believe he'd actually do it.* The betrayal stung as fiercely as the cut on her face. *He could easily have sold a few trinkets in the last town. They would have covered the bone men's toll. Instead he did… this.*

The stranger turned, amber eyes fixed on her. "Where's Chance?"

Her hands ached from her grip on the pistol. "What?"

"Chance. Is Chance here?"

"Mister, I don't know who or what 'Chance' is, so I doubt it. You looking for a person, or a place?"

"He's my cousin." The hard edge in the stranger's eyes softened, and he stepped toward her. "Are you all right? That cut looks nasty. Come over to the light."

The right side of her face burned. Cylin cautiously moved closer to the fire, never taking her eyes off the man and not loosening her grip on the pistol. It was empty, but he didn't need to know that. She turned so the light hit the long slash. The stranger moved to her side and touched the cut gently. Cylin hissed and jerked back.

"It doesn't look deep, but it might scar."

"Great, that'll make one side of my face not fit for the bone men," she said tightly. "Maybe I should carve up the other cheek myself."

The stranger stiffened sharply. "Don't say that. There's more to life than avoiding the attention of the bone men."

"Yeah, I'm sure. I'll let you know when I find out what."

The stranger offered her a hand. Now that he stood still, she saw an angular face with high cheekbones and large, slightly slanted amber eyes. Cylin stared into them until she finally blinked and tore her gaze away. In the depth of his eyes she saw deep pain and loss. He didn't look older than twenty-five, yet at the same time he looked ageless, as if time had forgotten to mark his years. By some trick of the light and shadows, his ears looked elongated and pointed. "You should have someone take a look at that cut," he said.

Cylin frowned. "You just did."

"Someone like a doctor," he told her, still offering his hand. "I'll take you to one. Or you can go your own way, if you prefer."

Cylin waited, but no catch followed, no threats, no indication that he expected favors of any sort in return. "Who are you? Why did you attack Pryor and his men?"

"Because I heard you scream."

Cylin's eyebrows rose. "You attacked them because I screamed?"

He waved at the barren land. "There's nothing for miles. No settlements, no one on the road except the bone men. Noises like that are more likely to attract abominations than aid. A scream out here isn't a plea for help or sympathy, it's a vocalization of pain that won't be denied."

She eyed him, wary. "And that's a reason to jump into a fray for someone you don't know?"

"I will never stand by when someone is trying to hurt a youth, no matter who they are."

She was almost insulted to be called a youth, but Cylin

restrained the impulse to take offense. "I… well… thanks." She accepted his hand.

"The man who held the knife—was he your father?"

"Pryor? Oh good gods, no! He bought my debt a couple of years ago, when he needed someone thin and light enough to get into tight spaces to add to his scavenger crew." The question was oddly gratifying. Most people in her experience assumed she was either Pryor's plaything or the camp whore. And men who thought that got mad when she refused to let them have a piece of the action.

Maybe the hearth gods knew what they were doing after all. Or they got lucky. Probably just got lucky.

She changed the subject. "You know a doctor?" *What am I thinking? I can't pay a doctor. I have nothing to offer.*

"In my village. It's a bit of a walk, if you're up for it."

"Anywhere is a bit of a walk from here," she countered. That was why the bone men ruled this area of wasteland, demanding tribute from those who passed through. There was no one to drive them off, no one to enforce what passed for laws. "Who are you?"

The stranger laughed. "It's not as far as you might think. My name's Lucian. You?" He picked up scattered bits of gear around the camp, quickly and efficiently looting anything of worth.

"Cylin." She snatched up her pack before Lucian could.

He offered her a rag. "Hold that to your face, Cylin. It'll stop the bleeding." Lucian considered the campfire. "Let it burn out. Nothing out here to catch fire." He started walking. Cylin followed, with only the triplet moons lighting their way. "Cylin…" Lucian murmured, repeating her name as if to taste it. "That's pretty. My wife's name was Cilvi."

"Your wife? You're married?" Cylin asked. That was encouraging. A wife meant someone who might object if Lucian took an unwanted interest in her.

"I was," Lucian answered, voice distant. "She died."

"I'm sorry." She didn't know anything else to say. People died. They died from starvation, they died from raiders and thieves, they died from the toxins seeping from the poisoned ground.

Lucian's head jerked in a nod. He fell silent, and Cylin didn't ask any more questions. The only sounds were their feet crunching over the barren ground.

They walked through the night. Lucian didn't seem to tire, and Cylin's feet kept moving, one after the other. As morning brought light, though, she asked, "What in poison rain is *that*?" Her arm shook wearily as she pointed toward the vast wall of green ahead of them.

"That," Lucian told her, "is a forest. My home. My village is there."

A chill ran down her spine. She'd heard of a forest somewhere in the wastes. Rumors said the trees were tainted and corrupt, that they could move on their own and attack people. Those who dared enter the shadow of its boughs never left. She turned a hard look on Lucian. "You *have* to be kidding me. No one goes in *there*."

"Oh? Then I must be no one," Lucian said.

"Well, you did call yourself a ghost when you attacked Pryor. So maybe you don't have to worry about poisoned, corrupted forests that eat people."

"The forest won't harm you, Cylin," Lucian promised. "If people don't leave, it's because they chose not to. Oh, and bandits don't leave either, but you're not a bandit. Unlike this waste, the land within the forest is fertile. No toxins, no poisons." He rested a hand on her arm. "Come on, I'll show you."

Cylin flinched from the touch, and Lucian withdrew his hand immediately. "Sorry," she said. "Sorry, just, please don't." Usually she could suppress the reaction, but she was exhausted and hurting. "I'm sorry. I need to rest. Just a couple of hours. Then I'll be ready to keep going and find your village."

When Lucian didn't argue, Cylin sat down. She didn't have a coat, and her blanket had been in Pryor's truck, so she curled up on the bare ground. Lucian sat beside her, a presence she could sense, but that didn't feel threatening. She closed her eyes and let sleep come. As she slid into dreams, Cylin's last memory was a feeling like she was floating, rocking gently back and forth.

She woke expecting the stink of diesel mixed with sweat. Instead, she breathed in the lingering smell of bleach, and beyond it, a sneaking scent of bacon. Cylin lay on a mattress, covered by a blanket. Her eyes fluttered open, and her confusion increased, bordering on panic. She lay in a small, unfamiliar room with simple furnishings. The bed frame was metal, and the chair and side table were wood. A wash basin sat on the side table, and a hazy mirror hung on the wall over it. Shelves on the far wall held boxes with bottles and what looked like rolls of gauze. She found her bag on the floor beside the bed, still laced shut. The mattress sagged as Cylin sat. Under the blanket, she was fully clothed, which reassured her a little. She pulled her bag onto the bed beside her.

The right side of her face itched. Cylin reached for the spot and found cloth. She stopped short, then stumbled over to the mirror above the water basin. A strip of gauze covered the gash, a light crust of dried blood holding it in place. Someone had washed her face; she saw no dried blood down her cheek or neck, though the collar of her shirt sported stains. She started to peel the gauze back, but hissed in pain at the pull on her scabs, and left the gauze alone.

A knock sounded on her door. "Young lady? If you are awake, breakfast is ready."

Cylin jumped. "Who are you and where am I?" She cautiously opened the door.

The man on the other side was sixty-five if he was a day. His gray hair was cut short, and he sported a trimmed beard streaked with silver. He stood with an air of dignity, as if he expected respect as his due. "I am Doctor Kinnel, and you are in my infirmary. Lord Lucian brought you here yesterday and asked me to tend to your injury."

"Yesterday? I wasn't asleep *that* long… wait, *Lord* Lucian?" she burst. "He's a *lord?*" *That's not right—it can't be. That man was a lord? What sort of lord wanders the wastes alone in the middle of the night?*

"He is the leader of our village," Doctor Kinnel answered. "We call him Lord Lucian. Now come. Breakfast is getting cold."

Numb, Cylin followed the older man into his kitchen. He motioned her to a chair, and Cylin sat. A moment later, he set a plate in front of her with a pile of scrambled eggs and three thick strips of bacon, still sizzling from the stove.

"Do you take tea?" Doctor Kinnel asked.

"Yes, please," Cylin said reflexively. Tea? She hadn't drunk tea in years. Pryor hadn't thought it worth the expense.

She devoured her eggs and the slices of meat before the doctor set a steaming mug beside her plate. Cylin lifted the mug and breathed in the scent of mint. She'd been told once that tea was meant to be savored, and she tried to take her time. Doctor Kinnel sat across the table with his own steaming mug.

As she scanned the room, she realized that the lights on the walls glowed with illumination too steady to be candle flames. "This place has… electricity?"

"We do. A series of generators small enough to be powered by the faster streams here. The output is more than enough for our modest needs."

He spoke like the idea was… normal. "How long did I sleep?" she asked.

"A day and a half. You woke briefly yesterday, but went right back to sleep after eating a little soup. You needed the rest." The doctor sipped his tea. "Lord Lucian said that the sight of the forest alarmed you."

"The… forest," Cylin repeated. She swallowed hard and glanced around. "Am I… in the forest? I've heard stories and… none of them are good." *Can I even leave this house? Is it safe to step outside, or am I trapped here?*

Doctor Kinnel chuckled softly. "No, I imagine not. Dire rumors discourage bandits, raiders, and other unsavory sorts. The rumors protect our village. We call it Forest Town—not the most imaginative name, but it suits."

"But… how? How is there a forest here at all? Anything that grows in the wastes is corrupted and filled with poison," Cylin demanded.

To that, the doctor shook his head. "I'm neither botanist nor chemist. I don't know the means, but this area is free of toxins. The ground sustains healthy life, and the water is clean. We grow crops and raise animals without fear that we poison ourselves. You don't even have to purify the water to drink it."

"And… people live here," Cylin said.

Doctor Kinnel nodded. "Lord Lucian dwelt here first. Over time, other people trickled in, forming a village."

"So Forest Town isn't very old, then," Cylin said. "If he was the first person here."

"Ah… no. I arrived here forty years ago, and already the foundations of the village existed, several handfuls of people. Now we have well over one hundred residents." He watched her face and chuckled with wry humor. "And yes, Lord Lucian was here when I first arrived. He looked the same then as he does now. No older, no younger."

"What? How?"

"You'll have to ask him yourself," he answered. "I don't

want to taint your opinions with my own before you hear his answer."

Maybe he'd been mutated by the radiation or biological weapons. She'd never heard of one that made a person stop aging, but everyone heard stories about unnatural results from too much exposure. Most people just died, but some… changed. In whispers, people claimed that the bone men used the flesh they bought to experiment, then extract the essences to sell to those who were willing to pay.

"Lord Lucian will be glad to know you're awake and well," Doctor Kinnel said. "If you're feeling up to it, I'll ask someone to show you around. Also, one of the women left a change of clothes for you."

"I can't pay you," Cylin said, a knot of dread in her stomach. How much did she owe this time? How was she going to settle the debt? A doctor's care wasn't cheap.

"I don't charge anyone for care, and the clothes are a gift." He collected the dishes and set them in the sink.

She hated being in debt. Pryor had used her debt far too often. "I can take care of the dishes."

"No need, young lady. You are a guest and injured." He poured water into the sink from a bucket. Doctor Kinnel smiled gently. "You owe no debt to me, Miss Cylin. You may find Forest Town strange, but I assure you, all offers of assistance are genuine. We were all newcomers once."

"So I'm expected to stay here?" Cylin asked cautiously. "What's the catch?"

"You are *welcome* to stay," the doctor said, "but no one demands it, should you decide not to do so."

"And you don't charge for care," she repeated. Her eyes narrowed. "Are you *really* a doctor?"

He laughed. "Yes, young lady, I really am. Would you care to see my diploma from medical school? I had the distinction of belonging to one of the final graduating classes before the bombing of the universities."

He was at least sixty-five, then, if not older. "Um, no, that's all right."

"Ancients only know why I still keep the thing," Doctor Kinnel said. "Now, might I ask a personal question?"

"Sure, I guess," Cylin said.

"You are a young lady, and Lord Lucian said that you were traveling in the company of brutish men. Is there a possibility that you might be pregnant?"

She blinked several times before making sense of the question. Anger spiked, but it faded after a moment. He wasn't asking if she was a whore yet. "No possibility," she said firmly, trying to imitate the stern tone her mother had used so long ago to indicate that a question was quite unacceptable.

Doctor Kinnel was not intimidated. "You're more fortunate than many young women who find their way here, then."

"What would you do if I said I was or might be?" Cylin asked.

"Offer you vitamins and care in the hopes that you could bear a healthy child. And if your circumstances were such that you did not wish to raise the child yourself, I would offer you opportunity to meet couples who would adopt the infant."

She wasn't sure what to think. His attitude ran at odds with most villagers she'd met or lived around. Like he actually cared about her opinions. "Pryor, the man who owned my debt... he believed that a girl was off-limits until she turned eighteen. I don't know why he picked that age, but he held to it, and wouldn't let any of his men cross that line either. So I just... didn't mention it when I turned eighteen, and they kept on not bothering me." She shrugged. "Probably one reason I didn't try to run off. Most warlords or village leaders don't care how old a girl is if they want her."

Doctor Kinnel nodded slowly. "Rest assured, no one in

Forest Town will bother you. And if anyone does, inform me or Lord Lucian immediately."

So even the lord of this place doesn't force himself on anyone who strikes his fancy? Most lords just take whatever and whoever they want.

Unsure what to think, Cylin returned to her room. A pile of folded cloth she'd mistaken for linens proved to be a waist-length tunic of soft deep blue wool and a pair of leather trousers. Whoever had left them had thoughtfully included a belt. The pants hung the right length, or nearly so, but were too large at the waist. Cylin cinched the belt to the tightest notch. The former owner clearly ate better than she had.

If this land really grows safe crops, they might even eat two meals every day!

She hefted her bag over her shoulder. Everything she owned nestled inside it, and though it wasn't much, it was hers. Leaving the room, Cylin followed the hall into a large room that appeared to be the main part of the infirmary. Doctor Kinnel was cutting cloth into long strips for bandages. A woman in her early thirties sat in one of the chairs. Her brown hair was looped in braids around her head, and her skin was tan. Her face was weathered, but the lines told of smiles more than frowns. Seeing Cylin, her face brightened in a welcome that shone all the way to her eyes.

"Oh, it looks like they fit you! I'm glad. I had to guess at your size. Lord Lucian can say 'she's about your height and thinner' all he wants, but that's hardly enough to guess someone's measurements."

Cylin started, blinked, and asked, "You brought the clothes? Thanks."

"Cylin, this is Myra. She's one of the best tailors in the village," Doctor Kinnel said. "Myra, meet Cylin."

Myra beamed at Cylin. "It's a pleasure. Welcome to Forest Town. I'm sure you must be ready to get outside a bit and stretch your legs after a good long rest."

"Um, I guess so," she agreed, unsure how else to respond.

Cylin followed Myra outside. Her first impression of Forest Town was of trees, towering trees circling a wide clearing. Patchy grass sprouted around the edges of the open area, but most of the ground was packed dirt worn bare by feet. A scattering of leaves added dots of color. The stone walking paths seemed redundant, winding from the trunks of trees around to the well in the middle.

Cylin shivered, eyeing the behemoths, though if she didn't have many places to run should branches reach down to grab her. When nothing showed any aggressive movements, she peered around more carefully, seeing no houses, and only a few larger buildings tucked between trees, mostly hidden by the undergrowth.

"We work down on the ground," Myra told her. "Most days, I'm weaving in there." She pointed to one of the buildings. "It's also where we spin thread and card wool. Tanning and dying are both done outside the village, because of the smell."

Cylin wrinkled her nose and nodded in understanding. "I've done a little of that before. But… where do people live?"

Myra pointed up. Cylin turned her gaze to the tree branches, seeing nothing until what she had taken for a tangle of vines swayed back and forth as someone ran across it. A bridge? Finally she picked out platforms among the thick branches and glimpsed people walking about. "Up *there*?" she gasped.

"It's safe," Myra assured her. "The branches are thick and the houses stand against the trunks, even in the trunks sometimes. You see the paths? They lead to stairs up to the branches."

Cylin gulped, not eager to put her faith in trees. Especially trees rumored to eat people. To her eyes, the platforms looked crude, not inspiring confidence, and she imagined the houses as rough huts, like those she saw in most villages. "Why the stone paths?" she asked.

"Winter and spring turn the ground into a mud pit. It's not a problem now, when everything's dry, but once it soaks in the water, you're liable to lose a boot walking across the bare ground. That's another advantage to living up above!" Her expression sobered. "The last, of course, is that it hides us from attackers, when they risk entering the forest."

"Bandits?" Cylin asked. Then she shook her head. "Of course you'd have to worry about bandits. You have crops, animals, clean water… drifter's bones, you have a *doctor*. Anyone would want that."

"And that's the truth," Myra agreed. "But Lord Lucian protects us. We've never lost a single person to raids."

Cylin remembered the man who'd fought Pryor alone and with utter confidence of success. "What about when he leaves, though?"

"Oh, he doesn't leave the forest all that often," Myra said. "And when he does, he puts someone in charge in case of an emergency. He's never gone more than a couple of days. Sometimes he brings someone back with him, like you. Other times it's supplies, or moonshine, or nothing at all." Myra gazed at Cylin. "But I can tell you, no matter what he might have had in mind when he left, if he sees someone in trouble, he acts, no questions asked. Especially young people. He doesn't expect anything in return."

"What, there's a lord anywhere who doesn't expect 'favors' from women?" Cylin muttered. She felt guilty saying it. The man *had* saved her from Pryor, and he hadn't tried to claim anything from her afterwards. He'd even stopped when she'd flinched away from him.

A flush of anger colored Myra's cheeks, then faded. "Lord Lucian isn't like that. I don't know what you've seen or what sorts you've met, but he's not looking to bed anyone against their wishes. We have laws here, and one of those laws is that rape is a capital offense. I've… heard stories about someone who tried and Lord Lucian's reaction. He won't tolerate it from anyone, man or woman, and he absolutely will not take someone against their will." Myra walked to the well and drew up a bucket of water. "The rest of the rules are fairly basic. Don't steal. Don't kill each other. If a dispute can't be resolved, Lord Lucian judges it." She scooped up a drink, then offered the bucket to Cylin. "Best water you've ever tasted. It's totally safe, right from the ground. And it's free."

Cylin hesitantly scooped up a drink in her hand. The water was shockingly cold and tasted of minerals. "It's good! But… free? Are you sure?" *There's got to be a catch somewhere. No one has this sort of wealth and just gives it away to anyone.*

"Sure as I can be after living here ten years!" Myra assured her cheerfully. "Most things here work on barter. Some people, like me and Doctor Kinnel, work in the trades we learned before we came here, but most others rotate through other jobs until they settle on one they like: working the fields, hunting, scouting, sentries, watching the livestock, that sort of thing. We even have a school. We know everybody hits rough times, but if someone's slacking off and not pulling their weight with no good reason, they hear about it quick. We're small enough for news to travel fast." She smiled at Cylin. "But if you decide to stay, don't worry about that yet. Except for some of the children, we were all newcomers here at one time or another. We know it takes time to find your niche."

"My niche?" Cylin's head swam, and she had trouble keeping up with everything she saw and heard. "How am I supposed to know that?"

"You don't have to worry about it yet. You're a guest." Myra led her up one of the paths between trees. "Lord Lucian's home is over here. This trail also leads to the fields."

The path was graveled, with a slight slope that Cylin soon

felt in her legs. The path split at a far sharper slope, one branch climbing the side of a steep, rocky hill, the other curving away and around. Myra pointed up the hill to a shadowed indentation. "Lord Lucian lives in the cave. If you're up for it, I'm sure he'd be glad to see you."

Cylin considered the path climbing the slope, drew a deep breath, and let it out. "Sure, I'm up for it."

Myra gave her an encouraging smile and offered her a hand. Cylin declined, starting the ascent unaided. Sweat trickled down her face and made the gauze itch like mad. She was almost glad that she needed both hands to keep her balance, because it kept her from scratching at the gash. The stones along the sides of the path were worn smooth, offering handholds without cutting her skin.

At the top of the path, Cylin was startled to see a young man, sixteen or seventeen years old. He sat near the cave entrance, whittling, though he looked up when she approached. Cylin stared for a long moment, saying nothing, her hand rising to the gauze on her cheek. He had brown eyes and brown hair, but the feature that caught and held her eyes was his scar. The jagged cut ran from his hairline, down his cheek to his jaw, and from there, down the side of his neck to vanish under his shirt. She swallowed hard. Whoever had carved him, they hadn't intended to just take an ear.

"You must be Cylin," the young man said, breaking the silence. "Lord Lucian told me about you. I'm Devin." He held out a hand, and Cylin was relieved to see that the scar at least did not run *that* far.

She shook his hand, and his grip was firm and steady. "Yeah, I'm Cylin."

"You're here to see Lord Lucian," Devin said.

Cylin nodded, only just noticing that Myra hadn't joined her. She looked over her shoulder for the woman, but Myra sat down on a rock and waved her in. "Go ahead. I'll wait here. Devin will show you in."

"Is that your job?" Cylin asked.

Devin nodded. "Lord Lucian didn't have anyone as a doorkeeper, so I took it on."

He slid from his perch. He walked with a mild limp, and she noticed a cane resting beside his rock. He left the cane and pushed a thick hide away from the mouth of the cave. The covering was dyed mottled gray like the rock around it, creating the illusion of a shallow indent rather than an extensive cave. The air inside was cooler, and when Devin let the hide fall closed, Cylin stood in darkness until her eyes found a faint glow of light ahead. Devin touched her shoulder.

"Straight ahead until you can see clearly. You shouldn't trip on anything." His steps shuffled beside her.

The light came from stripes of luminescent rock running through the walls. As the light grew stronger, Cylin also noticed the air warming to a comfortable temperature. She ran a hand along the wall and found the stone smooth and seamless, as polished as a marble floor. No signs of chisel marks. The rock might simply have flowed away of its own accord, leaving a smooth tunnel in its wake. She shivered.

"Lord Lucian!" Devin called.

"I'm here," a voice called back. "Come in."

Devin turned right at a branch of the tunnel and following it until it opened into a wide room lit both by the glowing stone and lanterns. Tables filled the room, piled with scrap metal, wires, and enough clutter to make a magpie jealous. A man sat at a table, his back to them, intent on some task. Cylin saw black hair pulled back in a short braid at the nape of his neck. Hearing their steps, he turned and greeted them with a smile.

"Good to see you, Cylin! You're looking better. I trust Doctor Kinnel took good care of you."

Despite what the doctor and Myra had said, Cylin had

expected to see someone other than her rescuer. Someone older. "*You* are the *lord* of this place?"

He laughed. "I did tell you I would take you to my village."

"I didn't think you meant that you *ran* it!" Cylin protested.

His laugh was warm and his eyes danced. "You didn't ask, either."

Is this really the same man who faced Pryor? Cylin didn't find the cold anger she'd seen when he rescued her, though pain lurked behind the smile in his eyes. "I didn't know I had to," she countered.

"Come in and make yourself comfortable," Lucian invited. "Sit down if you can find a place. There are chairs somewhere. And I have something to return to you." He searched around his table for a moment. "Now where is it… ah!"

Devin lifted a chunk of machinery off a chair and sat, but Cylin stayed where she was. Lucian walked to her, and Cylin was startled to be reminded that he was barely as tall as her. In her memory, he had gained at least a foot. He held a pistol to her, butt first. Cylin took it and stared in surprise at Jael's gun.

"I don't see that style often, and wanted to take a look at it. A good gun. I cleaned it for you and found bullets." In his other hand, Lucian held an ammo pouch.

"It was Jael's. I shot him with it," Cylin said quietly.

"It's yours now," Lucian told her.

She accepted the ammo pouch with a strange sensation in her gut. She'd never had a gun of her own. Pryor wisely hadn't trusted her with one. "Thanks."

Lucian shook his head. "All I did was clean *your* gun," he told her, the careful emphasis enforcing the idea that he was returning her property rather than granting her some lordly dispensation.

"Are you *really* the lord of this village? Doctor Kinnel claimed that you founded this place more than forty years ago." Cylin watched him carefully.

"Closer to fifty when people started venturing into the forest," he told her easily.

"You're not fifty years old," Cylin said flatly.

"No, I'm not. But you wouldn't believe me if I told you how old I *really* am," Lucian said.

"Try me," she challenged.

"When I was your age, one of my father's friends had a pet razorclaw."

"A… what?"

"Razorclaw." Lucian held up a hand to almost shoulder height. "About this tall, bipedal reptile with front talons that could rip through steel. There might be some still alive in the deep jungles, but most places in the world, they went extinct millennia ago."

"That's ridiculous!" Cylin said sharply. "No one lives that long!" She glanced at Devin, searching for some sign that this was a prank, an outlandish tale told to every newcomer.

"No human lives that long," Lucian corrected.

"What, you aren't human?" *This has to be an elaborate joke.*

"I am an elf." Lucian brushed black hair back to emphasize pointed ears.

She sputtered. "Elves aren't real! Are you going to claim that the mutated monsters out in the wastelands are ancient spirits too?"

"You accept the existence of whatever fanciful mutations someone claims to have seen, yet believe elves aren't real?" Lucian asked, one brow quirking in amusement.

"People have *seen* the mutations! Everyone knows *those* are real," Cylin snapped. "You're laughing at me! Either this is a bad joke, or you're crazy!"

Devin sucked in his breath in a sharp gasp and jumped to his feet. "Don't say that!"

Lucian's eyes narrowed. The humor vanished, replaced by a cold, hard gaze. Cylin flinched back. This was the man who'd faced down Pryor, the dangerous shadow in the night. "I do not joke about such things, and I am *not* insane."

Cylin edged back, heart pounding.

Devin grabbed her arm and pulled her back further. "Lord Lucian, it's all right." His words were quick and tense. "It's all right."

Lucian closed his eyes and turned his back to them. "Go."

Devin pulled Cylin out of the room. "I'm sorry," he said in a low, rushed voice. "I should have warned you. I didn't think about it."

"What just happened?" Cylin demanded in a whisper. "What was that?"

Devin shook his head quickly. "Some things… some things upset him. People calling him crazy… that's one of them."

"Oh. Great. The crazy guy flips out when someone calls him crazy. Sure, that goes a long way to proving that he's perfectly sane." Cylin fought back a laugh that tasted of fear.

"Just come on before you make things worse," Devin said.

He rushed her out of the cave and back into daylight. Cylin stood blinking for several moments before her eyes adjusted.

"Is everything all right?" Myra asked in concern.

"Your lord thinks he's an *elf*?" Cylin burst. "And apparently gets upset when someone doesn't think that's something that a normal, stable person says."

"Oooh." Myra drew out the word into a sound of understanding. "Devin, is Lord Lucian all right?"

"He'll be okay. I think it was just… so soon after him having gone Ghost, it was easy to hit another trigger. I should have warned Cylin," Devin let out a breath.

"Oh." Myra's hand rose to her mouth. "I didn't even think about that."

"Think about *what*?" Cylin cut in. "Telling me that your

lord is cr— that he looks like he's about to kill someone when they call him mad?"

"Well… yes," Myra told her. "I apologize, Cylin. And he won't hurt you. Even when he's like that, he won't hurt you."

Devin sank down on a rock. "We… well, Lord Lucian calls it 'going Ghost.' He gets really cold and distant, and it's like every emotion other than anger gets pushed down. I don't know why he uses that term. Myra's right, though. He won't hurt you, even when he's gone Ghost. Well, if you were trying to murder someone, he'd probably hurt you, but not if you're not doing anything wrong."

She looked between Devin and Myra. "Your lord thinks he's some kind of ancient spirit out of a bedtime story, but I should be okay with that because he's *probably* not going to hurt me? And that's supposed to inspire me with confidence and reassure me that this is a good place to stay? Maybe he's not the only crazy one around here."

"He is *not* crazy," Devin snapped.

"Don't tell me you actually believe him," Cylin scoffed. "You look old enough to have outgrown fairy tales."

Devin's face darkened. "Are you always a bitch when someone helps you? Lord Lucian didn't *have* to rescue you! He could have just kept on going and ignored you like anyone else. He could have kept looking for the people he's actually *trying* to find. You'd rather he left you to the bone men?"

"I'd rather live somewhere with a lord who's not completely delusional!"

"Yeah? Like where?" Devin retorted. "One of those walled towns on the poison plains, where the local lord thinks he owns you because you're female? At least Lord Lucian cares what happens to people. He protects us, takes care of us, and he doesn't ask anything in return, even when he rescues ungrateful cynics who throw his kindness out the door like it's nothing! If you don't like it, why don't you just leave and go find one of those 'not delusional' lords. See how *that* works out for you."

"Hey, that's enough," Myra cut in. "We're going to bother Lord Lucian if you keep yelling."

Cylin bit back a sharp retort and just jerked her head in a nod. "Fine."

Devin glowered at her, but picked up his whittling without another word.

Myra took Cylin's arm and led her back down toward the trees. Cylin looked over her shoulder. "Well that was a warm and encouraging welcome." *Is there something in the water or the air that makes people delusional here? I should be getting out of here as fast as my legs will carry me.*

"Devin is quite devoted," Myra said. "Lord Lucian rescued him as well. I know this is a lot to take in on your first day. Why don't you come back to my house, have lunch, and rest a bit?"

"Lunch?" Cylin asked.

"Midday meal." Myra tsked. "You don't usually eat lunch? No wonder you're so skinny!"

Thoughts of fleeing the village ran headlong into the idea of eating *three* times a day. "I didn't usually get *two* meals a day," Cylin responded, letting herself be led back into the clearing.

Myra tutted and climbed one of the stairs up to the branches. Cylin followed uncertainly. To her great relief, Myra didn't cross any of the swaying rope and vine bridges, but entered a compact wooden house that looked sturdier than Cylin had feared. "Come in and make yourself comfortable. I'll warm some stew. Just you and me for lunch today. My husband, Searel, is hunting and my little girl is in her lessons."

Cylin looked around the house and relaxed, finding it refreshingly normal. Colorful hangings in abstract patterns decorated the walls. Plump cushions softened the carved wood furniture. Several dolls lay haphazardly on the floor, their worn clothes and patchy string hair telling of much love and much play. She set her bag down in a corner. "What's your daughter's name?"

"Leesa," Myra answered. "She's six, going on seven now. The light of our lives, and a bundle of endless energy. We always wanted a child, Searel and I, but until we found Forest Town, it wasn't safe. All respect to the women who can manage it, but I knew I wouldn't be able to care for a child while on the run."

Cylin started. "You were fugitives?" She tried to imagine the cheerful woman living as a vagabond or a criminal, and failed.

"The lord of the place we came from… well, he was of the opinion that everything in his domain was his to take and use as he pleased. Searel and I disagreed with him on that." Myra didn't expound further, but Cylin didn't need her to.

"And you ended up here?" Cylin asked instead.

"We heard rumors about a forest, and a village where people didn't live in fear, and a lord who took care of his people. It sounded too good to be true, but we didn't have anywhere else to go. Now, here we are." She smiled. "And it's everything that the stories claimed." Myra gazed at Cylin and her expression grew serious. "I know it's a lot to accept, Lord Lucian claiming to be an ancient, ageless elf. But I can say he doesn't look a day older than when I met him. And I've seen him… do things. Things that a normal person can't do." She waved Cylin to the kitchen. "Could you set the table?"

"Sure." Relieved to be of some help, Cylin set bowls on the table, then spoons and cups. "Is it a mutation? An effect of radiation, or something from the war?" Everyone heard stories about such things.

"That's possible," Myra allowed. "But I don't know… personally, I'd rather think that Lord Lucian's one of the ancient spirits here to protect us. Searel and I have always had leanings toward the Old Ways."

Once, people had worshiped the ancient spirits. The idea that her hostess actually gave that deep of devotion to Lucian unsettled Cylin. "What's he think of that?"

"Oh, he prefers that we don't honor him as a god, so we keep our prayers private," Myra said, as if it were a small matter.

She served soup for lunch. The hot food settled comfortably in Cylin's stomach, and was followed by weariness.

"Would you like to rest for a while?" Myra asked. "You look worn out."

"Yeah. Guess I'm more tired than I thought."

Myra showed her to a small bedroom. The bed was neatly made, and didn't look as if it had been slept in at all. "This is the guest room. Make yourself comfortable."

Cylin set her bag by the bed, kicked off her shoes, and lay down atop the covers. Her eyes closed, and sleep followed.

She woke when someone knocked on the door. Cylin raised her head, looking around in muzzy disorientation. "Yes?"

"Mama said to tell you that dinner's almost ready!" called a young, high-pitched voice from the other side.

"Oh... Thanks." She shook her head to clear the fog of sleep. The smell of roasted meat permeated the house. She ran fingers through her hair, working out the worst of the tangles before she left the room and slung her bag over her shoulder. Cylin opened the door to be greeted by a girl of six or seven, with dark hair looped in braids around her head, much like Myra's.

"Hi!" the girl greeted. "Are you Cylin? Mama said you're new and that Lord Lucian brought you. I'm Leesa!"

"Uh, hi Leesa. Yes, I'm Cylin." Cylin marveled that the child showed no fear of a stranger.

Leesa caught Cylin's hand. "Come on. We have to wash for dinner! Daddy brought home a deer."

Cylin let the girl pull her to the washroom. A basin sat on the counter, and Leesa pulled out a stepstool to reach it. She splashed her hands into the water, rubbed soap on them, then splashed again. Cylin recalled her own mother telling her to wash before dinner. It had been years since she'd had easy access to both soap and enough clean water to have the luxury of washing her hands before a meal. The water was lukewarm, and she added more from a pitcher to make up for Leesa's splashing before scrubbing her hands with the soap. Dirt caked the lines of her skin, and didn't come off easily, but the surface grit washed loose.

I wonder if I could take a bath. How long has that been?

She could have figured out the answer if she'd tried. She'd stopped worrying about bathing once Pryor took her in, hoping it would discourage him from taking advantage of her. Only later had she realized that his interest in her body had nothing to do with sex. He liked his women older. Girls were livestock to sell to the bone men.

Still, I thought he valued me for more than that. I thought being useful to him would protect me. She touched the gauze on her cheek, a stark reminder of that betrayal.

Pulling her thoughts away from Pryor, Cylin dried her hands and walked with Leesa back to the open dining area and kitchen. Myra was pulling something from the oven. A man stood beside her chopping leafy greens and arranging them in a serving bowl. His skin was darker than Myra's, and his face had similar lines of wear.

He turned at the sound of their footsteps. "Good evening and welcome to our home. Myra told me that you'd be joining us this evening. It's our pleasure to have you join us, Cylin. I am Searel, and you've met our daughter, Leesa."

"Um, hi. Thanks," Cylin answered. Everyone was so...

cheerful, like they were actually pleased at her presence, and not suspicious of a stranger. Her stomach growled loudly. "Sorry!"

"No need," Searel assured her. "We have plenty, and it's our honor to share with you. Sit, please. The food will be ready shortly."

Leesa proudly directed Cylin to her seat at the table. Cylin sat and finally glanced around a little. "Is that a wood stove? Is that safe up here?" She'd seen villages after a fire. How much worse would it be when the houses sat in trees?

"There's always some danger of fire," Myra admitted. "But the stoves are sturdy, and we haven't had any serious fires in all the time we've been here."

"Where does the metal come from?" Cylin asked. "Do you have a smith here as well?'

"We do. Lord Lucian supplies the metal from his cave," Searel answered. "I understand that he brought you to our village."

"I… yes, he did," she said, hesitant to say more.

"I like Lord Lucian!" Leesa told her. "He'll play with me sometimes when he comes out to the village. But he spends lots of time in his cave, and I'm not supposed to go up there alone."

"No, you're not," Myra agreed, carrying a steaming platter to the table. "I don't want you getting lost in Lord Lucian's caves again."

"I wasn't lost!" Leesa protested. "I just didn't know which way was out."

Searel set the bowl of greens on the table. "And that is why you aren't to go there by yourself. Did you wash your hands?"

"Yes, Daddy!" Leesa climbed into her chair.

Through dinner, Cylin watched her hosts for prompts as to the meal etiquette. It was hard to pay much attention to the subtler details, though, when the food was so good. She didn't know most of the spices used on the meat, and the idea of eating fresh greens without at least boiling them first was mildly unsettling. Both Myra and Searel ate heartily and encouraged Cylin to have her fill.

After the meal, as Cylin helped clear the table, Myra said, "Won't you stay the night with us, Cylin? Forest Town doesn't have an inn, but the guest room is yours for as long as you would like."

"Are you sure?" Cylin asked. "I don't want to be in the way." She hadn't thought about where she would spend the night. And she certainly wasn't going to venture into the forest in the dark. Even if the trees didn't assault people during the day, who knew what came out after dark.

Ghosts, her mind whispered, calling up the image of Lucian darting through Pryor's camp.

"We're sure," Searel told her. "It's been too long since we last hosted anyone."

"Please?" Leesa asked, bouncing on the balls of her feet. "Please please? The last woman didn't stay." She heaved a sigh. "I liked her."

"I know you did, dear," Myra told her daughter. "But if someone doesn't want to stay, we won't make them."

"The last woman?" Cylin asked.

"Many families open their homes to newcomers," Searel explained. "So people can get their feet under them without worrying about where they'll sleep or get food. It gives them time to decide if they want to stay or if this is just a place to stop for a little while on their journey."

Cylin thought about that. "Was that something that Lord Lucian set up?"

"As I understand it, yes," Myra answered. "When we came, we stayed a few months with another couple. Their daughter is one of Leesa's best friends."

Leesa nodded in happy agreement. "We sit next to each other in studies!"

Cylin smiled. "Well, it'd be nice to have somewhere to stay for a while. Thanks."

"Yay!" Leesa bounced, bubbling with excitement. The girl happily talked at Cylin for the rest of the evening, showing off a collection of toys and dolls, most of them worn and old, probably once belonging to Myra. After the girl was finally in bed, Cylin settled in the sitting room with Myra and Searel, all of them sipping tall glasses of cool water. No one spoke at first, and the silence was comfortable. Searel finally spoke. "Might I ask what you think of Lord Lucian so far?"

Cylin shifted and toyed with her glass. Lucian's cold, hard eyes haunted her memory. "I don't want to offend you after you've been so kind," she said.

"Ah… He told you that he's an elf, then?" Searel asked.

"Is it *that* obvious?" Cylin asked in consternation, glad to seize on that detail rather than Lucian's reaction when she called him mad.

Searel smiled. "Well, it wasn't as stunning to Myra and I as it is to some people, but hearing a man declare himself to be an ancient spirit is a bit of a shock, whether you follow the Old Ways or not. I think that every wanderer who has come here has questioned his claim, wondered over it, and decided whether it was enough to make them turn away from the refuge this village offers."

Cylin considered that. "Is he why some people don't stay?"

"Not the only reason, but he is one," Searel said. "Some just don't find Forest Town suited to their liking, and take offense that we won't change our way of life to suit their whims. Others have trouble settling down and staying in one place. No one has to stay, no matter the circumstances of their arrival."

"Honestly, if someone doesn't want to be here, then they

shouldn't stay," Myra said. "I certainly agree with Lord Lucian on that."

Do I want to stay here? I don't know—I don't know enough to say. "At the moment, being somewhere where I can eat three meals a day and drink clean water is a strong draw." Her mouth twitched in a wry smile. "Thinking of clean water, is there somewhere I can take a bath?"

"Absolutely!" Myra assured her. "I'll take you there first thing in the morning. It's a little late tonight."

"Thank you," Cylin told her sincerely.

"Rest well, Cylin, and welcome to Forest Town," Searel said.

～

Cylin lay on the bed, staring at the ceiling. *Do I stay or do I go? Lucian rescued me when he didn't have to, and brought me here when he could have left me on my own. But he's delusional enough to think that he's an elf, and has actually convinced other people too.*

Still, they have clean water and fertile ground. They eat three meals a day. So far, everyone says Lucian is a good lord who mostly leaves people alone. How many places can say that?

She rolled on her side. *Having a bed is nice. Having access to a doctor is amazing. Is a delusional lord that big a deal? They all tend to be at least a little crazy, and the next one I meet might be worse, just like Devin said.*

She sighed. *I can stay here a little while, at least. If things get too weird, I can always grab my stuff and leave then.* Reaching over the edge of the bed, she touched the top of her bag, reassured that it was ready should she need to bolt.

～

Morning began with breakfast, then Myra left her husband in charge of getting Leesa ready for the day and led Cylin down to the bath house. The building was set a little distance from the rest of the village. Steam flowed into the brisk morning air when Myra opened the door and entered. Two doorways led from the entry room, each with a symbol above the door.

"The right side is for women, the left for men," Myra explained, walking in the right doorway.

Cylin heard the chatter of voices before they entered the dressing room. A handful of women ranging from her age to white-haired grandmothers stood in various stages of undress. Those coming from the bath wore towels wrapped around their bodies, those heading in didn't bother covering up. When Cylin entered, she instantly became the center of attention. She tensed, unsure whether she'd be met with hostility or welcome.

"You must be the young lady Lord Lucian found! Do come in! Myra, dear, it's good to see you. I'm glad you brought your guest. What's your name?"

"Cylin," she answered, trying to keep track of all the people talking to her.

Myra shooed the other women back. "Let Cylin get a bath! Ione, do we still have any of that lavender oil? And a good scrub?"

The other women rushed to accommodate, fetching soaps, oils, and towels. Cylin undressed and hung her clothes and bag on one of the hooks, though she was uneasy to let them out of her sight. She touched the gauze on her cheek. "Do you think this will be all right, Myra?"

"It should be fine," Myra assured her. "Later today, check in with Doctor Kinnel. He'll want to make sure it doesn't need special care."

Cylin followed her into the next room and climbed into the wide tub of steaming, warm water. The other women helped her wash her hair and scrub away layers of grit and grime from her skin. Cylin welcomed their help, and doubly welcomed their scented soaps and the oils they worked through her hair until it shone. By the end of the bath, she could barely get out of the tub, and allowed the other women to help her into the dressing room. They toweled her dry and helped her dress, then made sure she got safely back to Myra's house. Once inside, Cylin stumbled to the guest room and lay down for a long, dreamless nap.

When she woke, Cylin listened for sounds in the house. Wood creaked softly on occasion, but no steps thumped across the wooden floors, and no boards squeaked from the passage of feet. The house felt empty, though the scent of bread lingered from the morning. Dull aches ran through her body when she sat. She stretched to work them out.

A sheet of parchment lay on the table beside her bed. Cylin picked it up, but the script didn't match any of the letters her parents had taught her in her childhood. Next to the note, she found a hairbrush with a polished wood handle and stiff bristles. Cylin ran it through her damp hair until it was finally free of tangles and rat nests, though it felt like she pulled out half her hair in the process. Letting her hair hang loose, she ventured outside.

The pleasantly warm air promised a comfortable summer day. Birds sang in the trees, and the scent of maples hung in the air, reminding her of the towering tree that had survived in the yard of her parents' house. Cylin carefully walked across the platform, less certain of her footing without Myra's confident presence beside her. She found one of the staircases that wrapped around the tree trunk and stepped onto the first step. It creaked underfoot, but didn't shift or move like a step on the verge of giving way. She'd explored and scavenged enough buildings to feel the difference between a sturdy step and one that would snap the moment she put her weight on it. Pryor had always sent her down first, as the smallest and lightest of them.

The open air to her right was unsettling, as was the long drop to the ground. Looking up as she walked, Cylin realized that the steps were not visibly bolted onto the trunk. They almost seemed to have grown out of the tree itself, though that was improbable.

Once she reached ground, her gaze swept the village. *If I need shelter, what's closest?* Unlike the barren plains, Forest Town offered a wealth of hiding places—trees, rocks, hollows, and of course the houses, if she had enough time to reach the branches. Pryor had often asked her the most efficient escape route when they entered a town or ruin. She, in turn, had always told him her second-best route, saving the first strictly for herself, in case he proved to be the one she had to escape.

Didn't help when he did come after me.

One hand brushed the gauze on her cheek. Cylin found the infirmary. The walls were mostly wood, but cut stones outlined the doorway, and the door was painted a blue the color of the sky. Cylin knocked, and the doctor's voice invited her inside.

"Hello Doctor Kinnel," she greeted.

"Ah, Cylin, good. Come in, young lady. Here for a check-up?" He set aside an instrument he'd been polishing.

"Myra said you would want to take a look at the cut," she said.

"Have a seat." He waved her to one of the chairs, and Cylin sat. Doctor Kinnel carefully peeled back the gauze. "Do you have any other concerns? Anything out of the ordinary?"

"I've been sleeping," Cylin answered. "Lots more than usual—nearly every chance that I get, it seems. I took a bath this morning, and I could barely get back to the house before I fell asleep. And yesterday, the same thing. After lunch, I was nodding off."

He didn't seem surprised. "How long has it been since you were last someplace where you felt safe, Cylin? Not anytime recently, I would wager."

"No," she said, puzzled by the question. "Though I don't know if I would say I feel that way here yet either."

"Your body feels differently. Your unconscious mind and your body are in agreement that Forest Town is far safer than anywhere you have been in a long time. You've been living in a constant state of fear and alertness, and doing so takes a toll on you. Given the chance to recover, your body is seizing the opportunity while it can. You will probably notice an increase in appetite as well."

Cylin laughed. "I've eaten three meals in one day. If that's normal here, I won't worry about my appetite as long as it can keep up!"

"Ahh." Doctor Kinnel swabbed cool cream over her cheek. "How many did you normally eat in a day, and how often did you get meat in your diet?"

"One meal, sometimes two. We might get meat once a week. Otherwise it depended what we scavenged," Cylin told him. She felt comfortable talking to this man, though she couldn't say why. "How is the cut looking?"

"It's healing," Doctor Kinnel answered. "You will probably carry the scar, though."

Scars reminded her of the young man outside Lucian's cave, Devin. "Can I ask what happened to Devin?" she asked. "I met him when I spoke to Lucian, and I saw his scar."

"Then I think you already know what happened to him," Doctor Kinnel said mildly. Cylin flushed and opened her mouth, but he continued. "It's not my place to say who tried to skin him, but I know Lord Lucian rescued the boy. Devin was perhaps twelve at the time. Lord Lucian brought him to me, both of them covered in Devin's blood and Lord Lucian frantic to save him. I wasn't sure I could. The cut ran from his scalp to the bottom of his ribs. Devin was still conscious, amazingly. He clung to Lord Lucian with all his might, and even while I fought to save his life, Devin held on to Lord Lucian's hand." Doctor Kinnel sat down beside Cylin. "If ever in my life I have seen a miracle, it was that Devin survived."

"Does he believe that Lucian is an elf?" Cylin asked.

"With all his heart and soul," the doctor said. "Once he recovered, he took on the duty of attendant and gatekeeper for Lord Lucian."

"Is Lucian insane?" Cylin asked. "Does he really think that he's an elf?"

If her blunt question offended him, his face gave no sign. "I don't think that's the correct question," Doctor Kinnel told her.

Cylin frowned, head cocked to one side. "Why not? What should I be asking?"

"The real question is 'does it matter?'"

She stiffened. "Of course it matters!"

"Regardless of what he might or might not be, what he might or might not think he is, Lord Lucian survives. Regardless of whether he caused this forest to grow, or found it already here, he is here, and he allowed the foundation of Forest Town. He protects the people here. He survives, he thrives, and he leads, and as long as the rest of us cling to his coattails and ride in his wake, we too will survive, even thrive and grow strong. Does this belief of an inhuman origin make him strong? Perhaps, and if it does, I will not seek to undermine that which keeps us safe." His gaze fixed on Cylin. "Will you?"

Cylin opened her mouth, searching for a response, but she found none. "I… don't know."

"I won't tell you what to believe, Cylin. That's up to you.

But those who choose to stay here do so because of Lord Lucian, not in spite of him." Doctor Kinnel applied fresh gauze to her cut. "Now, get plenty of rest, and come see me if you have any questions or concerns, or notice any unusual reactions."

Cylin's mind swam with questions as she returned to Myra's house. Her cheek felt raw and tender after being cleaned, tended, and poked. Her mind was distracted from the discomfort, though, as she pondered Doctor Kinnel's question. Did it matter whether Lucian was crazy? She thought it should, but she was less confident in that answer than she had been.

At dinner, she listened to Myra, Searel, and Leesa tell her about their days, and asked questions as she thought of them. When asked about her own day, she talked about the bath, and how wonderful it felt to be clean. *Like I finally washed away the touch of their hands on me. Like I finally washed away Pryor's hold.*

"Tomorrow, I'd like to learn some of the jobs people do here," Cylin said, diverting her thoughts and the conversation.

"Of course!" Myra told her. "Anyone would be happy to have you shadow them."

"Thanks." *I don't know whether I'm staying, but I'll pull my weight while I'm here. I'm not going to be locked in debt to anyone again.*

She went to her room and lay down, but sleep didn't come. In the darkness and quiet, questions tumbled over and over.

Is this place really safe? Everything that people say just seems too good to be true. What's the catch? What do they expect in return? Lucian claims to be an elf, but what does that mean? What sort of tribute do the people of Forest Town pay him? People are adamant that he doesn't expect sex. And clearly the town has children, so the child-sacrifice stories probably don't apply. Obviously people work, but they'd do that whether they're here or somewhere else.

She rolled over on the soft bed. *This is so comfortable. I could have a bed, a place to live, enough food. I can stay here. Just for a little while. Appreciate the comforts at least until I find out what they really cost.*

~

Cylin followed a young woman up the slope, out of the shelter of the trees into a vast cleared stretch of fields. Myra had introduced her to Cylin as Aya, and she was just a few months over twenty years old. Aya kept a steady stream of talk as she walked, though most of the names flowed past Cylin without context. At least she didn't expect much response from Cylin, happy simply having an audience to her enthusiastic monologues.

"Have you worked on a farm before, Cylin? Lots of people haven't, so don't worry! This is straightforward work, just weeding and checking for signs of insects. And it smells better than tending the animals."

"A little," Cylin murmured.

"You have? Oh, even better! Come on, the tools are kept in these sheds. Just return them at the end of the day, so the next person can use them tomorrow." Aya pointed to a row of three small sheds. "You can put your bag over here with the rest, if you want."

Cylin's hand gripped one of her bag straps as if Aya might snatch it from her. "I'd rather keep it."

Aya shrugged. "Okay. If you change your mind later, that's fine too. No one's going to steal it, I promise."

But if I need to leave in a hurry, I might not have time to reach it. "Thanks. I'd still prefer to keep it."

Aya didn't argue, at least. She introduced Cylin to a few other young women as they all set to work. The work proved monotonous, and conversation with others relieved some of the creeping boredom. Aya and her friends had lived in Forest

Town between four to seven years. When she asked them about Lucian, most of the girls just shrugged.

"Most of the time he's just... there," Aya said. "I mean, I know he's incredibly good looking, but after a while it stops being so remarkable and becomes... Lord Lucian. I've never really talked to him, and haven't had any problems serious enough to take to him. Still, I know I could if I needed to. He'll listen to any problem someone brings to him, even if they're just a child."

"Really?" Cylin asked. "That's... pretty unusual."

"Is it?" another girl asked. "I thought lords were supposed to take care of their people and listen to them."

"Yeah, that's... not usually how that works in other towns," Cylin told her. "Most lords only care about helping when there's something in it for them." *So what's in it for Lucian?*

The girls collectively shivered. "Glad we don't live somewhere like that!"

Is that true? Or is he fooling you all?

Days passed faster than Cylin realized, sliding into a full month. She learned the many different kinds of edible plants grown in Forest Town. She'd not imagined the varieties available—grains, vegetables, fruits, and more. She learned how to tend chickens, goats, and rabbits. She learned some of the basics of gathering fibrous plants to process for textiles, and a little about making thread and cloth. She learned a little about maintaining the water-powered generators that provided Forest Town with electricity. She even gained confidence navigating the swaying rope bridges without fearing she was about to fall off or tip them over.

She also learned to shoot the pistol she'd stolen from Jael. No one questioned her right to own the weapon, and both men and women in Forest Town offered her lessons in its use. They even offered her ammunition when she expressed concern over wasting her limited supply on practice.

"Don't worry about it! Practice as much as you need. Just collect the spent brass and give it to Devin, or return it to Lord Lucian's cave. He'll take care of it," promised Myra.

"Take care of it?" Cylin repeated. "He has the tools to reload?"

"Seems that way," Myra said. "No one really knows what all he has in the depths of his caves. Or if they do, they aren't telling. I don't think even Devin knows."

Lucian remained an enigma. He spent the majority of his time in his caves, but sometimes he walked through the village, speaking with people, and more importantly, listening to them. When he saw Cylin, he always asked how she was doing, if she was settling in well, if she needed anything. She always told him that she was fine, though sometimes she wondered what he would do if she said anything else.

When she wasn't working, Cylin wandered around the village or into the forest. She walked along the edge of Forest Town, appreciating her day off when Leesa dashed up to her. The girl carried something bundled in her shirt, cradled carefully.

"Cylin! Mama's busy. Will you come with me?"

"Sure. Where to?" Cylin asked, taking the girl's free hand.

"Lord Lucian's cave. I found a baby bird that got attacked by a fox. I chased off the fox but the bird is hurt. Lord Lucian can make it better!" Leesa tugged Cylin toward the path leading to Lucian's cave.

"A bird? Leesa, I don't think that--," Cylin began.

"He can make it better!" Leesa insisted.

Cylin opened her mouth to argue, but closed it. The girl's faith in Lucian was absolute, and Cylin hesitated to shatter her illusions. Together they made their way up the path to the mouth of the cave. Cylin frowned as she looked around. "Where's Devin? He's usually here, isn't he?"

"I think he had an errand," Leesa told her. "I saw him

going to the fields. But it's okay! We can still visit Lord Lucian!" Without hesitation, Leesa pushed aside the hide covering the doorway and called "Lord Lucian! Are you here?"

The echoes had barely faded when Cylin heard footsteps on the stone and a gently chiding voice. "Leesa, you aren't supposed to come here on your own."

"I'm not alone! Cylin's here too!" Leesa assured him. She didn't venture further into the cave, though, instead waiting for Lucian to come to them.

"Ah, that's good." He stepped outside and squinted against the light, then smiled down at the girl. "What can I do for you, Leesa?"

Leesa carefully unwrapped her shirt. "I found a baby bird, and it's hurt! You have to make it better!" She held out a lump of feathers. The bird's chest rapidly rose and fell, whether because of pain or fear Cylin didn't know.

Lucian took the bird gently from Leesa. It twittered weakly, and Lucian made a soothing noise. "Easy there, easy…" He ran his fingers lightly over the bird, smoothing rumpled feathers. Cylin watched him, wondering in spite of herself if he really could make the injured bird whole. Lucian met Leesa's intent gaze. "I can't heal the bird, Leesa."

"But you *have* to!" she insisted. "You're an elf! You have magic!"

Cylin tensed, a knot of tension in her gut.

"Not all elves have the same magic, Leesa. We have our own talents. You know that your mother is very good at sewing, but she doesn't draw?"

Leesa nodded hesitantly.

"Elves are like that too. Some can heal, and others can make stone or plants move, but just because an elf can do one of those things doesn't mean they can do all the other things." His voice was gentle.

"But it's hurt!" she protested.

"I know." Lucian cupped the injured bird in his hand. "That's why we're going to take this little bird to Doctor Kinnel. He'll do what he can for it."

Leesa's large, watery eyes stayed on him. "Will you come with me?"

"Of course," Lucian told her. "Cylin and I will go to the infirmary with you. Won't we?" He glanced at Cylin.

"Of course!" Cylin said quickly, shaking off her thoughts. "Yes, absolutely."

Lucian carried the bird. Leesa clung to his free hand with one hand, and Cylin's hand with the other, though the path wasn't wide enough for three abreast, and she had to release Lucian on the descent. Once they reached the bottom, the girl latched onto him again. Some people looked askance at the three of them, but refrained from asking questions.

At the infirmary door, Lucian knocked, then returned the bird to Leesa. "Go on in and tell him about the bird. If he can help, he will."

Leesa nodded, eyes wide and watery. Cylin opened the door for her, and moved to follow her inside, but Lucian put a hand on her shoulder to stop her. "Let her do this herself," he said quietly.

Cylin heard Leesa speaking, heard the moment when the girl's voice broke and she started to cry even with the door closed. She fixed a sharp glower on Lucian. "Can't you hear how upset she is? You could have reassured her."

"I could have lied to her," Lucian said. "I won't do that."

"Lied? Telling a crying child that things will be all right is a lie?"

Lucian turned, facing her. His face was hard. "Do *you* think that bird will live?"

"Well… probably not," Cylin admitted.

"Exactly. That bird might suffer less than it would if she hadn't found it, but I won't pretend that should comfort a child who hopes for a miracle. Is that 'reassurance'? Claiming it will be 'all right' *is* a lie, and I won't lie to a child. It does far more harm than good. Even those lies that people call 'innocent' falsehoods. One day, the child realizes all the lies told them, and must wonder what *other* lies they believed."

She eyed him dubiously. "And you would know?"

"Yes, I would." His amber eyes bore into hers. "Do you still think me crazy, Cylin?"

"Uh…" What should she say? Would he fall into that cold fury again if she said yes? "I don't know. Maybe. But… I don't know if it matters, does it? Most lords of towns are at least a little off, and it seems to work well enough here."

The intense gaze did not relent. "*Does* it matter? Only you can say. It mattered to you before. It mattered to you now that I offered no comforting platitudes to Leesa. Is that the most on which you will take a stand?"

Cylin blinked. "Wait, are you saying you *want* me to disagree with you and say I think you're crazy?"

"I am saying that you should know what you believe and what matters to you. Know where you will take a stand. Because if you don't care enough to hold to something, you'll meet someone to whom it *does* matter, who will seek to force their way of thinking and seeing on you. Do you know where you'll hold firm and where you will bend?"

"Most people tell me to shut up and stay in line, not argue with them," Cylin said.

"I am not most people."

"I won't dispute that." Cylin met the intense gaze. "I don't think you're an elf, Lucian. And even if I did think you some fairy tale ancient magic being, I wouldn't worship you."

"Good. We were never gods, no matter what some thought."

"Some humans, or some elves?" She couldn't resist asking.

"Both," Lucian answered, voice dark. "Don't trust anyone

who tells you they're a god, Cylin. Even if they're right, if they have to tell you, they're not worth following."

Cylin let out a faint laugh. "Well, I guess it's safe to say *you* aren't Shironak."

He frowned. "Not who?"

He definitely wasn't Shironak, if he hadn't even heard the name before. "Half a year ago, when I was still with Pryor, we were in a town, and this drifter was standing at the town well, preaching and calling for people to join in calling on an 'ancient spirit' he called Shironak. Pryor's men entertained themselves by heckling the fellow, but some of the locals seemed pretty interested. I'd mostly forgotten about it until now."

Lucian frowned. "I don't know the name. But if you hear anyone making such claims here, tell me at once. Please." He paused. "Thank you, Cylin."

"For what?"

"For taking a stand." With that, he turned and vanished into the depths of the forest.

Against all predictions, the injured bird recovered, though one wing didn't heal properly, and it couldn't fly more than a short, awkward flutter. The little brown ball of feathers became a common sight around the village, joining the chickens in pecking up seeds and bugs on the ground or perching on the stairs up into the trees. It could hop up the steps, albeit slowly, but more often than not someone saw it and carried it the rest of the way. Leesa's faith in Lucian was entirely unshaken by his inability to heal the little thing. She happily told anyone who would listen how Lucian had told her to take it to the doctor, and how Doctor Kinnel had performed a miracle, saving the bird's life. The tale grew in the telling, of course, but the sparrow became another refugee to find a home in Forest Town.

Cylin grew more at ease with the forest. While at first the trees had felt foreign and unnatural, she grew accustomed to them, and came to appreciate the shade and shelter they offered. On her free days, she packed a meal and explored.

Picking a direction she hadn't gone, Cylin wandered until she heard water. Finding a stream splashing and dancing down the slope, she followed it upstream and walked along the bank. She didn't notice how long she walked, looking instead at the plants along the way and identifying as many as she could. The stream tumbled down the side of a rock face. When Cylin found her way to the top of the rock, she found a deep, wide pool carved in it. The stream poured down from another rock wall, feeding into the pool. Lichen and algae coated the rim of the stone basin, but no green slime clouded the water, and neither did plants. A few leaves floated on the surface of the water, but the bottom of the pool was unnaturally clean. The smooth sides of the pool and the width of it both struck Cylin as unnatural—something made rather than something formed by the water alone.

"And I thought all the way out here, I wouldn't have anyone coming to enjoy the view."

Cylin jumped at the voice, looking all around before finally looking up. Lucian, wearing nothing but a loincloth, stood at the top of the rock wall above the pool, grinning at her.

"What? You… I… the view?" Cylin stammered, staring at him. He was lean, muscles toned and defined, his skin lightly tan. The grin lighting his face seemed to lift years from him. His hair was tied back in a short tail, clearly exposing his abnormally long and pointed ears.

Still grinning, Lucian dove from the rock into the pool. Cylin yelped and jumped back as a wave of cold water washed up on her legs. "Hey!"

Lucian surfaced, treading water lazily. "Coming in? The water's fine."

"Fine?! The water's cold as a statue's balls!" she countered.

"Warmer than glacial melt," he assured her, then ducked back under the surface and swam the length of the pool and back. His movements were smooth and confident, gliding through the water like a fish. Coming up again, he asked, "Are you sure?"

"Quite sure!" Cylin said. "I like my baths hot, thank you very much. And even if I was interested, I have nothing to swim in."

"Just take off whatever you don't want getting wet," Lucian said easily. Her face must have told her thoughts on that idea, because his expression sobered. Lucian pulled himself out of the water at the opposite end of the pool, letting it lie between them. "I won't touch you, Cylin. If you like, I won't even get in the water while you swim. You have my word on it."

"But you'd stay there and watch," she countered.

"Yes, I would. I don't know how well you swim. I won't leave when someone might drown in my pool." There was nothing licentious in his gaze or his voice, only calm practicality.

"I don't swim. Please, don't let me stop you," Cylin said finally.

Lucian studied her. "Are you sure?"

"You looked like you were having fun. Don't stop for my sake. Please."

Lucian climbed back up to the top of the rock face, dripping water as he went. The playful joy from his first dive was absent, and his second dive sliced into the water with barely a splash. He came up, treading water again. "What's on your mind?"

"Do other people come out here?" Cylin asked. "I've never heard about this pool."

Lucian shook his head. "No. This is one of my secrets, a place I come to relax. I don't mind that you've found it. You're not the first to do so. But I would prefer that you not mention it to anyone else, aside from Devin or Doctor Kinnel. They know how to find it, in case either needs me."

"Where did you learn to swim?" Cylin asked. "Most places I've been don't have enough clean water for something like this." She waved at the pool.

"My father taught me. He swam every day that he could, and even in places that didn't have easy access to water, he would make some. He shaped a lot of pools in caves. Sometimes in the open, like this."

"He shaped them?" Cylin interrupted. "What do you mean?"

"Magic," Lucian said easily. "My father's one of the most skilled elves I know in the art of shaping and manipulating stone. His pools were often deeper and wider than this. And with higher cliffs to jump from." He smiled. "When you came out here, you reminded me of our morning swims when I was young. The women of the clan used to come out to watch. They called it 'enjoying the view'."

"Enjoying the view?" Cylin paused, then realized that "scenery" being admired probably had nothing to do with the landscape, and everything to do with muscular men wearing nothing but loincloths. Heat flushed her cheeks. "Oh. Do you and your father look alike?"

"We do. His hair is auburn, and he tends to keep it long. Some people say he's better looking than me, more like some statues of an ancient hero." His mouth twitched in a smile. "Not that I have anything to complain about in that regard. Our morning swims… those are some of my best memories, times when my father was truly happy. Or at least, I think he was. Swimming was one of the few times that he wasn't in constant fear of my mother finding us, a time when he could put that fear out of his mind. I didn't know it back then. I didn't know a lot of things when I was young."

"A lot of things that you should have known?" Cylin hazarded.

"A lot of things that I should have known," he agreed quietly. "A lot of things about which I was lied to in an effort to protect me from the truth."

"Your parents lied to you?" Cylin asked.

"My entire clan did. Damned by good intentions. My father was determined not to taint me against my mother. He thought it would be better for me to grow up innocent of the truth."

Cylin considered whether she should ask the question that his words raised. "What truth were they protecting you from?"

He climbed out of the water and up the rocks once again. "The truth that she was the most evil, sick, twisted, sadistic person to ever live on this world."

"Your mother?" Cylin repeated. "That is... well... um... That's... quite a claim."

At the top of the rock wall, he sat rather than diving again. "Have you ever heard of the Black Witch?"

Cylin nodded. Between historical tales and fairy tales, nearly anyone must have heard of the Black Witch. "She supposedly brought kingdoms to their knees, and people lived in absolute terror of her. Are you saying that your mother was worse than her?"

"No. My mother *was* her."

"What? But... but she was human."

Lucian shook his head. "She made herself look human, but she was not. Her name was Willow." He spat the word with venom, eyes gleaming with hate.

"The stories say she was one of the cruelest, most evil rulers ever to gain power. They also say she died seven hundred years ago."

"Your stories got that much right, on both counts. They're pretty much all wrong about *how* she died, but they are right that she died then. I would know. I was there. She was more than evil. She was *vile*."

"Wait, 'vile' is *worse* than 'evil'?" Cylin asked, seizing on a subject that seemed less fraught.

A faint smile tugged at the corners of Lucian's mouth, easing the tension in his lean form. "Oh yes. The worst possible insult, according to my cousin's wife. If she called someone 'vile,' you knew they were the worst sort of scum. The only person I regularly heard her call 'vile' was my mother."

"Was she nice? Your cousin's wife, I mean. And your cousin?" He'd mentioned a name, hadn't he? When he rescued her from Pryor. "Chance?"

Lucian nodded. "Her name was Ahmea, and she was an incredibly kind and gentle person. Wonderful cook. I don't think anyone could have been a better match for Chance." Lucian gazed into the pool. "She died in the war."

Cylin almost protested that the war had ended six decades ago, but didn't. Maybe there was something to his claims, or maybe it was all a delusion, but right now, she wanted to listen more than she wanted to argue. "You can't use magic to find your cousin?" she asked instead.

He eyed her, trying to guess whether she was serious. "Not safely. Something happened when the bombs poisoned the land. They poisoned the spirit world as well, and it's not safe anymore to leave my body and wander out there searching for Chance." His hands clenched into fists. "If I could, I'd be gone in an instant. I would find him." He let out a shaky breath. "I know Chance is alive. I'd know if he were dead. But I can't reach him, and I can't find him. So... so I'm here, waiting for him to find me."

She didn't have to know Chance to see that he was deeply

important to Lucian, a friend on whom he relied. "I am sure that he will. If he's alive and he's worthy of the faith you have in him, then I'm sure he'll find you." *Unless he's holed up somewhere else, waiting for Lucian to find him.*

"Thank you." Lucian bowed his head. "If you don't mind, I'd like to be alone now."

"Right, sorry." Cylin nodded and retreated.

Her walk back to the village was quiet as her thoughts turned over each other. When he'd been talking, she hadn't doubted him. Hadn't doubted that he had been alive long enough for his mother to be the Black Witch. Hadn't doubted that he was everything he claimed to be. It had bothered her more that he talked about the war as if it were a recent event than when he spoke of events that even history books called ancient.

Why?

~

When Cylin returned to Forest Town, she climbed the slope to Lucian's cave. Devin sat at his post, whittling patterns into a piece of wood. She hadn't talked to him more than the briefest of polite pleasantries since her first day in Forest Town, and he'd made no effort to talk to her.

He eyed her warily as she approached. "Lord Lucian's not available," he said, voice curt.

"I need to talk to you," Cylin said.

Devin blinked, startled, then he frowned. "Why? Trying to convince me that Lord Lucian's crazy? That I'm crazy for believing him?"

"I figure that you know more about him than most," Cylin said. *Why am I here? Why do I even care about whatever insane past Lucian has concocted?* "I want to know."

"Why?" Devin repeated. "You don't believe him. You've

made no secret of that while you've been here. I figured you'd have left as soon as you stocked up. Or are you trying to swindle someone out of their goods?"

Cylin stiffened indignantly. "I am not a thief! If anyone's a swindler around here, it's not *me*. And what's it to you whether I stay or go? You might have noticed, I'm actually *working* while I'm here."

"Instead of sitting on my ass on a rock," Devin finished in a mocking imitation of her voice. "That's what you're thinking, isn't it? That I just sit here and do nothing while everyone else works."

Cylin shrugged. "You said it, not me."

He spat on the rocky ground. "Well unlike the guy who sliced you, my father didn't plan to stop with an ear when he carved me up. He didn't want me running off either, and I guess the bone men don't care all that much if a few bones are smashed up."

Cylin glanced at Devin's legs. They looked whole as far as she could see, but pants and shoes could hide plenty of scars. He walked with a limp, but he made the trek up here daily, and if he didn't usually walk fast, few people in Forest Town were in a hurry. "You seem to get around all right now."

He scowled at her. "Short distances, with plenty of time to rest." His gaze challenged her. "So, aren't you going to ask why Lord Lucian hasn't fixed it?"

Cylin shook her head. "He told Leesa that he can't heal when she brought him that bird. If he can't heal birds, I expect he can't heal people either."

That gave Devin a moment of pause. "So you do listen to him."

"The fact that he admits he *can't* do one of the things legends claim about elves certainly doesn't prove that he *can* do anything else."

Devin rolled his eyes. "Of course not. Why do you refuse to consider that he might be exactly who he claims to be?"

Cylin swept her arm in a gesture to encompass the entire world. "Look at this place. Not Forest Town—everything outside it. The world has gone to utter shit out there, Devin. Seriously, if there are magical people with all those legendary powers, why in drifters' bones would they let this happen? Why did they let the war destroy everything? Why didn't they stop the bioweapons and the bombs? Why do we have bone men and wastelands and mutated monstrosities?"

Devin's shoulders slumped. "Lord Lucian said... that not all the elves like us very much. Some would be happy if every human died. He even told me once that... that he thought some of the destruction in the war was *caused* by elves. That their influence might have been the reason things actually got as bad as they did."

"Seriously?" She tried to put a twist of scorn into her voice, but somehow, it came out quizzical and curious instead. "That's like... pissing in your own well to wreck your neighbor's crops, isn't it?"

"Maybe they thought they could fix it after we all died. Maybe they can all do things like whatever Lord Lucian did to make the forest grow here. Maybe they didn't care. I don't know. Lord Lucian didn't say. I don't think he knows either."

"So elves don't just know where each other are all the time or anything?" Cylin asked.

He gave her a long, dubious look that said it was a stupid question. "Of course not. And they don't all look alike, they don't all act alike, and they don't all have the same kinds of magic. They're *people*, Cylin, not just flat characters from old legends. Lord Lucian is a person."

"He is," she acknowledged. "A possibly crazy person, but he's a person."

"He is *not*—" Devin surged to his feet.

"Devin, he claims his mother is the Black Witch. That doesn't do much to refute my doubts of his sanity."

Devin froze, color draining from his face. "Who told you that?"

She didn't expect the sudden change, nor the alarm in Devin's eyes. "Um, he did. Earlier today. I was walking and came across him swimming."

"What did he tell you?" Devin's voice quavered slightly.

"That she was his mother, that she was an elf, and that she was, how did he put it, 'the most evil, sick, twisted, sadistic person to ever live on this world.' Oh, and that she was vile, and that vile is worse than evil."

"No details?" Devin asked, cautious.

"No, I didn't ask for details. When someone describes a person like that, I can guess that I don't really *want* the details." Cylin watched Devin, frowning. "What's it to you?"

Devin let out a shaky breath and sank back down on his rock. "If he'd actually told you details, and you were still walking around and talking about it like it didn't bother you, I'd be thinking that *you* were the crazy one."

Cylin's eyebrow rose. "So do you know particulars?"

He shuddered. "More than I want to. I know that she did... horrible things, and when Lord Lucian was young, his father and the rest of their clan spent a lot of time running away from her. They... spent a lot of time running away from her or hiding from her until her death, really." His gaze moved to her face, warily searching for signs that she was laughing at him.

She couldn't summon scorn. Devin's stance proclaimed his belief in everything he said. "I've met some pretty nasty people. And so have you." She nodded toward his scars. "She was worse than that?"

"She was worse than that," Devin said, no doubt in his voice. "I don't want to talk about it anymore."

That didn't mean Lucian was an elf. Plenty of humans had

horrible families. Maybe he'd told Devin real things from his own past, weaving them into part of his story of being an elf.

Or maybe there really is truth in Lucian's claim.

Two handfuls of days passed quietly after her meeting with Lucian at the pool. Cylin continued to work shifts in the fields. It was hot, sweaty work, exhausting in the summer sun, but no one yelled at her or mocked her for not working as quickly as them. No one even tracked quotas, and when she took breaks for water or shade, no one penalized her for it.

When everyone finished for the day and returned their tools to the sheds, Cylin walked back to Forest Town with Aya and her friends. The girls accepted Cylin into their number easily, and didn't seem to mind that she listened more than she talked. As much as they chattered, she wasn't sure they even noticed her quiet.

They passed the path to Lucian's cave. Cylin paused, frowning and wondering if she only imagined a faint vibration in the ground.

Aya glanced back to her. "Something wrong? Did you forget something back at the fields?"

A ridiculous question. Cylin never left her belongings where she couldn't grab them at a moment's notice. "No, just- -"

A scream echoed from the cave. Cylin's head snapped toward the slope. The other girls skittered back as if something might tear down the path to attack.

"What was that?" Cylin demanded, hurrying toward the path.

Aya grabbed her arm. "Wait! Cylin, don't."

"What do you mean, wait?" She jerked free. "Who was that?" *Someone's in Lucian's cave. Who? Why?* She'd almost dismissed her initial fears that some sinister secret hid in Forest Town's apparent peace. Now they all rushed back to her.

Devin scrambled down the path, breathless and pale. He stumbled to a stop when he saw them. "Go on home. Nothing you can do here."

"What's going on?" Cylin demanded, stepping close and looking him in the eye, the way Pryor did when he wanted answers.

"It's all right, don't worry, it's all right," he said rapidly. His flushed, sweat-streaked face, wild eyes, and shaking voice belied the words.

"Answer me!"

Another scream rent the air. Devin threw up an arm to block Cylin as she moved toward the path. "Don't! It's… Lord Lucian is… he sometimes…"

"Lord Lucian's… having an episode," Aya said.

Devin's head jerked in a nod. "I think it's going to be a bad one."

"An 'episode'?" Cylin interrupted. "What in drifter's bones does *that* mean?"

Aya answered before Devin could. "It's… well… an episode. He doesn't know where he is or who anyone is. He thinks he's somewhere else." She shifted uncomfortably. "Somewhere… unpleasant, I guess. They start like this, with him screaming loud enough that we hear it outside."

"You mean that's *Lucian*?" Cylin looked from Aya to Devin. "And you just leave him alone like this?"

"We can't do anything to help him. Doctor Kinnel's tried drugging him, but even that doesn't work." Devin swallowed hard. "Cylin, he doesn't know who any of us are. He thinks we're…" He shook his head quickly, cutting himself off. "You should go home. It'll run its course, and things will be quiet again."

Aya tugged on Cylin's sleeve. "Come on."

"Go ahead without me," Cylin told her.

Aya hesitated, but the sounds from the cave obviously bothered her. She ran back to Forest Town to catch up with her friends.

Cylin fixed her gaze on Devin. "Lucian thinks we're what?"

"Um..." Devin swallowed hard again. "Thinks we're pawns of his mother. Thinks we're here to torment him. He wouldn't hurt anyone intentionally, but when he's like this... he's not himself."

"You're saying he's dangerous."

"When he doesn't know who you are, and thinks you're his enemy? When he thinks that he's defending himself from torture? You'd be dangerous too," Devin said. "I *want* to help him, but I *can't*! I've tried, and... and after the last time I tried, he ordered me not to, because he doesn't want to hurt me in the midst of one of these."

Cylin looked at the path again. "Did he order you to stop other people from going up there?"

"No..." Devin said. "But--"

"Then step aside, Devin."

"It's not safe!"

"I'll take that risk," Cylin told him. She stepped around Devin and started up the slope.

"Why?"

She paused. "He asked me what I was willing to take a stand for. I guess I'm willing to take a stand for not leaving him alone with... whatever is going on. Maybe it won't make a difference. But I know how to defend myself." *And I need to know, to really, truly know, what's happening in there.*

Devin didn't say anything, and he didn't follow her.

When Cylin reached the top of the path, she cast a look over her shoulder. Villagers hurried past, heading for their homes with the haste of people avoiding something unpleasant. Only Devin lingered, shoulders slumped. Cylin wasn't sure whether she would rather he stayed there or followed her. Either way, she didn't think he would go home or sleep tonight.

The darkness at the cave entrance hung like an oppressive weight. She felt her way along the wall until the stripes of glowing rock lit the tunnel. At the first side passage, she peered into the workroom, where Lucian had been on her first visit. The room was empty, and the cries rose from deeper in the cave. To her relief, the unnaturally smooth, even tunnel had few branches from the main tunnel, and none of them went far before opening into rooms.

The screams died down to mumbled words, occasionally rising to a shout. Cylin finally found Lucian's living space. Fur rugs covered the floor of the roomy cavern and glowing rocks provided steady light. Polished stone reflected the light around the room, showing chairs overturned, hides and cushions flung about, and Lucian standing with his back pressed against a wall. His hair hung loose and wild, his eyes darted about. His breath came in rapid pants, and sweat gleamed on his skin. His shirt hung unlaced and untucked.

"Lucian?" Cylin asked, moving toward him.

His amber eyes snapped to her, and Cylin froze, stunned by the raw hate and fear in his gaze. "I am not playing this game. Do you hear me? Not this time."

"What game? Lucian, I want to help you," Cylin told him.

He laughed, a hard, mocking sound far worse than his screams. "Help? Oh, I'm *sure* you do. So Mother's letting you play this time, Ayliad? I *know* what *your* help looks like. Going to 'help' me just like you have Chance?" He pushed away from the wall, stalking toward her like a prowling cat.

"Lucian, I don't know who Ayliad is, or what game you think she's playing. I'm Cylin. Cylin, from Forest Town. You rescued me from Pryor, remember?" The closer he drew, the more aware she grew of the threat he posed.

"Don't you?" Lucian retorted. "Then you are just one of

her constructs. A mindless minion, here to do your job. You're here to lead me out? Draw me into the trap?"

"Lucian, I don't understand!" Cylin burst. "Just *tell* me! What will it hurt to do that?"

His eyes narrowed. "It will convince you that I'm crazy. Then you'll call in others to imprison me, for my own safety of course. After that, my dear, sweet, loving, oh so worried sister will come visit me as often as she can. You'll already disbelieve anything I say. You'll call it all part of my delusions, and pity me when I tell you what she does when no one is watching."

"What... what does she do?" Cylin asked, edging back several steps from Lucian.

"She does whatever she wants," Lucian hissed. "Just like Mother taught her. She knows how to force a man against his will. She's had all too much practice."

Cylin blanched. "Your *sister* would try to rape you?"

"Not try." Lucian's voice was stone cold. "She would. She has. She did. And she does it again, and again, and again in these mind-fucks that are Mother's games." He screamed at the ceiling. "I *know* you're doing this! I won't play any longer! Fuck yourself, bitch! I hate you! Do you hear me? I won't be your tool!"

A chair flew from the floor and smashed into the wall, breaking all four legs. Cylin ducked as another followed, sharp fear in her throat. "Lucian, stop! You don't have to! You don't have to play her games. She's not here!"

He eyed her with sharp suspicion. "You're just a construct. This, all this is in my head, her game, the playground she made for herself in my soul. I know where I *really* am: chained to a wall in my cell, where she tortures us to draw my father into her net." Lucian's eyes narrowed. "So why would one of her constructs tell me not to follow her rules?"

"Perhaps it means that I'm not one of her constructs," Cylin replied.

She meant that he was not in some dream or hallucination, but Lucian interpreted the words differently. "Not hers? Then… you're one I created?"

"I'm not a construct, not anyone's tool, Lucian. I'm your friend," Cylin said. Cautiously, she held her hand out to him.

He jerked back as if she offered a venomous snake. "You're in my head. You're a healer? I don't know you. How did you get here? You shouldn't be here. If any of them find you…" He shuddered. "Get out now, while you can." His gaze was fiercely intent. "You have to find the others. Chance, Dash, and the others. She's holding them captive as well. Get them out."

One name she knew, one she did not. "Lucian." When he didn't draw back, she cautiously set a hand on his shoulder. "I'm here to help you."

He shook his head. "She'll find you."

"That's a risk I'm willing to take," Cylin said. "All right?" She gave him a gentle push toward the one couch that still had a few cushions. "Sit down. Tell me what's happening."

He let himself be steered to the couch, but sat on the floor instead of the cushions. Cylin sat as well, leaving a healthy space between them. "Why are you sure this isn't real?"

"That cell is the only place I know is real," Lucian said flatly. "Everywhere else is part of her game, and anything that happens in them serves her in some way. And I know that in every one of them, I will lose."

She couldn't imagine what that would be like to so deeply believe that everything was a twisted mind-game and that nothing was real. *Does Lucian really go through each and every day waiting for a trap to spring? Waiting for his world to come crashing down?* She recalled her own four years in Pryor's company, always alert, always on edge. *I have some idea how that feels.*

"Is Chance safe?" he asked softly. "Did you reach him? Did you get him away from her? You have to keep him safe. She hates him."

"Who does? Ayliad?" Cylin asked.

"No. No, Ayliad just wants to fuck every man she can find whether they want it or not. Mother. Willow. *She* wants to destroy him, because he dared stand against her." He closed his eyes, rocking slightly. "She's hurt him so much, so many times, and he keeps fighting back. He keeps refusing to bow to her." Lucian's eyes snapped open. "I have to find him."

"You will," Cylin told him. "I believe you. But not right now. You need to rest."

Lucian shook his head, pushing to his feet. "No, I have to find Chance! He needs my help! You must know where he is." He looked at Cylin. "Please! Tell me!"

"I don't know, Lucian," she admitted. "He's not here." She braced for another outburst of anger.

Lucian sucked in a sharp breath, eyes growing wide. "Chance isn't here? She doesn't have hold of him? Then he escaped!" Tension fled his body and he slumped onto the couch. "No wonder she's furious. Chance got away from her, so she's taking it out on me." Lucian cradled his head in his hands. "The bitch."

"Then you had better be prepared," Cylin told him. "Rest. Try to get some sleep, Lucian."

His head jerked up, and his gaze once again grew wary. "I sleep alone."

"I wasn't implying anything else!" she said quickly. She understood far better than she wanted to. If his own sister had actually assaulted Lucian like that, Cylin could forgive him for the sharp reaction to the idea of being unaware and defenseless with someone else in his room. "I'll stay over here. I swear that I will not touch you while you sleep."

Lucian kept one eye on her as he edged to the bed at the far end of the room. Cylin remained seated on the floor. Lucian settled on the edge of the bed, then, before Cylin's eyes, stone tendrils rose from the floor, weaving around each other as they climbed to the ceiling and anchored themselves to it, forming a lattice around the bed with Lucian inside. Only then did he finally lie down. Cylin stared at the rock barrier, numb. She had just seen magic worked before her very eyes, yet it failed to amaze her. The horrors implied by Lucian's words wouldn't be banished by simply proving he could work magic.

Lucian slept, or appeared to sleep. Eventually Cylin climbed onto the couch and dozed.

She started awake when Lucian stirred. He sat up and blinked at the lattice, then at her. "So, there's a woman in my room, and apparently my response last night was to hide in the corner with a wall between us?"

His voice sounded steady and very much present. Cylin rubbed her eyes. "You don't remember? Last night was… not a good night."

"Judging from the state of the room, I can guess that I had what the people of Forest Town call 'an episode.' If that's what you mean by 'not a good night,' no, I don't remember. I never do. Though I'm told that during them, I tend to talk about my family. And given that I felt a need to raise this barrier, I can even guess who I was talking about." Lucian rested a hand on the lattice, and it sank back into the floor like liquid.

Cylin sat up, rolling her shoulders. "Lucian, I hope you don't mind me saying this, but if even half of what you said last night was true, your family is completely f--" She caught the word, recognizing the double meaning. "Has serious issues."

He gave her a sharp, hard smile. "Completely fucked up? Up, down, and sideways. I won't ask what parts I brought up. I prefer not to know which delights of my past I relived."

Cylin opened her mouth, then closed it again.

"I've told Devin to leave me alone when these happen. I could hurt someone. I have hurt people, in the past. Did I harm you at all? Anything?"

She shook her head quickly. "No, I'm not hurt. Shaken up, but not hurt. Devin warned me."

He stood, but didn't approach her. "And you came in spite of that. I hope your aversion to rules and authority isn't so severe that it overpowers your survival instincts."

She met his eyes. Sane eyes, now, unlike the previous night. "You asked me what I believed and said that only I can choose what I'll stand up for. I decided that I needed to come here and find out for myself whether I could or could not help you. And I decided that I wasn't going to leave you up here alone when you were screaming loud enough to be heard in the village."

Lucian was silent for a long moment. Finally he asked, "Did you help?"

"I… don't know," she admitted. "I think I might have, a little. Something I said calmed you, and you were willing to lie down and go to sleep." The more she thought about his ravings during the night, the more amazed she was that Lucian had been willing to sleep with her present, rock barrier or not.

He ran a hand through his black hair and sat on the bed. "I need rest and time alone. You undoubtedly need sleep. Would you tell Devin that I want no visitors today?"

"Are you sure?" Cylin asked. "Shouldn't someone stay here?"

"I want to be alone. No one would appreciate my company today. I'll sleep most of the day anyway. Go. Please."

She hesitated, then pushed to her feet. "If you're sure. I hope your rest is peaceful, Lucian."

"So do I." Those quiet words followed her out of the room. Then, quieter still, "Cylin… thank you."

She picked her way back to the cave entrance. Pushing aside the hide, Cylin shivered as brisk early morning air rushed over her. She hadn't noticed the warmth or stuffiness of the cave until fresh air hit her. Rubbing her hands on her arms to warm them, she looked down from the vantage of the top of the path.

Forest Town slept. The sun barely colored the sky, not yet peering over the horizon. At the base of the path, Cylin saw a figure sitting hunched against a rock, wrapped in a blanket. When her feet sent stones clattering down the path, Devin raised his head and turned to her.

He didn't say anything until she had reached the bottom, where he waited, but then the words rushed out in a torrent. "Cylin, are you all right? Is Lord Lucian all right? I stayed here--I thought you might come out during the night and I didn't want you to be alone if you did."

She rested a hand on his shoulder. "Lucian knows where he is and who I am now, and he's resting. He said he doesn't want any visitors today."

Devin nodded. "That's normal. Episodes exhaust him. Sometimes he'll let Doctor Kinnel come in if he hurt himself, but most of the time he wants to be alone. How are you? Are you all right?"

"Shaken up," she admitted. She saw the worry and fear in Devin's eyes. *He's seen these before. He knows what they're like. He knows the things Lucian says.* "He was talking about… games that his mother played."

Devin cringed. "I hate those. They're some of the worst episodes. Did he... think that you were anyone?"

"At first he accused me of being his sister," Cylin said.

Devin shuddered, and she knew she didn't have to explain any more on *that* subject.

"Then he thought that I was some kind of 'construct,' he called it. A part of the 'game' under his mother's control."

"Did he attack you?" Devin asked.

She shook her head. "Something I said convinced him I wasn't what he thought I was. Then I kind of stumbled on saying that Chance isn't here. I expected that to make things worse, but it actually calmed him. A lot."

Devin's eyes widened. "Oh. Because he thought he was held captive by his mother, so if Chance *wasn't* there, that would mean Chance was out of reach of Lucian's mother."

"Well, I'm glad that makes sense to you, and made sense to him," Cylin said dryly. She sobered. "Is Lucian's family really as messed up as all that sounded?"

"Actually, it's way worse than that."

For a moment, she hoped he was making a joke, but Devin was dead serious. "All right, how much worse does it get than his mother torturing him and his sister raping him?"

"The fact that Lord Lucian *had* a sister wasn't his father's idea," Devin told her. "And... Chance has two sons by Ayliad, and they weren't his idea either. Their family tree doesn't always branch in the right directions. Lord Lucian's uncle, Chance's father, made some things worse too." He shuddered. "I... learned a lot more than I wanted to from some of his episodes."

"So are they... some of those elves who would rather see us all dead?" she asked.

Devin shook his head. "Not them. Well, maybe they did, but Willow and Chance's father died before the war."

"Are you *sure*?"

"Lord Lucian is sure, and he'd know." Devin's head drooped, and he caught himself, jerking up. "Sorry. I kept jumping at sounds in the dark, and I couldn't rest knowing you were up there."

"Get some sleep, Devin." *Did he stay up for Lucian's sake, or for mine?*

"You're probably going to leave Forest Town, aren't you?" His gaze fell to the ground. "Now you've proven to yourself that Lord Lucian's crazy."

"All leaders are crazy. It's not a job for a sane person. But I can live with Lucian's style of crazy, now that I actually know what it is."

Devin frowned at her. "Why?"

"What?"

"Why is this enough for you?" He waved toward the cave. "Why did *that* convince you to *stay*?"

Why was learning what Lucian's mother and sister had done an argument in favor of staying? Why wasn't she fleeing for the wasteland after his episode of screaming at the walls? "Because I understand it, Devin, that's why." *And because, understanding it, maybe I have some way to help.* "Get some sleep. I'll still be in Forest Town tomorrow. Not like I got much sleep either."

Devin looked at her for a long moment, then shook his head. "I should be watching the cave."

"Nope. You should be sleeping." Cylin caught his arm before he took more than a step onto the path. "Come on. You have to have a house here somewhere, right?" She tugged him toward Forest Town.

"But—"

"Devin, is *anyone* going to expect to talk to Lucian today?"

"I—no, I don't think so."

"Then you can get some sleep and go up there later." She pulled him after her.

Devin stopped protesting and followed her into the village. He pointed. "My house is there. I can get there without help."

Devin wearily climbed to his home. Cylin started toward Myra's house, but turned when she glimpsed someone walking to the well. Doctor Kinnel raised a hand in greeting to her.

"Good morning," he greeted. "How is Lord Lucian?"

Cylin blinked, surprised by the question. "He's... tired," she answered finally.

"I know he had an episode last night, and I know that you entered his cave while it was in progress. Devin was frantic with worry when he told me." The doctor's gaze was serious. "How are you? Are you hurt in any way?"

She shook her head. "Lucian didn't harm me. He scared me, but he didn't hurt me. This morning, he didn't remember any of it." She lowered her voice. "So what *are* these episodes, really?"

Doctor Kinnel filled a bucket with water and gestured for Cylin to follow him to the infirmary. "I've sat through a few of them," he said, unlocking the door. "Please, come in. I'll make tea."

Cylin closed the door after herself. "Do you know why he has them?"

"I know some of the triggers that can lead to one, but even without those, sometimes one simply happens, like last night."

"Triggers? Like what?" she interrupted.

He filled the kettle and set it on the stove to heat. "One that quite often put him on the edge was any sort of prolonged, open debate with him regarding whether or not he actually was an elf. Primarily, I believe, because those very often fell into the other person or people questioning his sanity."

Cylin had started to take mugs from the shelf, but stopped. "Uh... I did that. The first day I was here. Is that why Devin reacted so strongly at the time?"

"It's undoubtedly why he didn't let you linger to continue the argument," Doctor Kinnel said. "But if you're concerned that your words back then are responsible for his episode last night, don't be. The time lapse is long enough that it's unlikely to be a contributing factor. Another trigger is discussing sexual assault or abuse with him."

She nodded, understanding that well enough from what he'd said.

"We've eliminated as many of the triggers as possible, but I think that trauma of the mind does not heal as easily as that of the body, and that separation from his support system may have reopened wounds that had appeared to have healed," Doctor Kinnel said finally.

"His… support system?" Cylin asked. She set the mugs on the table and sat. "Do you mean people like Chance?"

"And the rest of his clan," the doctor agreed. "Lucian was separated from some of his clan during the chaos of the wars, but not all of them. The rest, such as his wife, died to violence, sickness, or poisons, and he couldn't save them. Each loss wounded his spirit." He shook his head. "I'm no psychologist, Cylin. I studied to be a surgeon, before the world fell to pieces. I can't heal Lucian's mind; I can only try to minimize the damage."

Cylin finally realized something. "You believe him. You believe he's an elf."

"I would be hard pressed not to believe him something other than human," he answered, pouring boiling water into the mugs. "But to be honest, I never doubted him all that much."

Cylin eyed him curiously. "I thought people who studied sciences in the old world were supposed to be skeptics about magic and myths. That's what I heard, anyway."

He chuckled softly. "Oh, no doubt we were *supposed* to be. I'm sure many of my colleagues doubted anything and every-thing about magic. But Lord Lucian is not the first elf I've seen."

Cylin straightened. "He's not?"

The doctor sipped tea and leaned back. "When I was a child, my parents took a research post studying a tribe of people living deep in the southern jungle. The idea was to bring them modern medicine, modern tools… offer them the trappings of civilization. But at the same time, learn about their unique culture. These people followed an ancient religion that worshiped a spirit who was lord over savage jungle beasts. I know that a number of people in Forest Town have fallen back on the old faiths, worshiping the 'ancient spirits,' but at that time, it was rare for any 'civilized' person to admit to following those ways."

"And by 'ancient spirits', you mean they worship Lucian," Cylin cut in.

"Yes, whether he likes it or not. The spirit that the jungle tribe revered was said to be fearsome, dangerous, but also benevolent to those who worshiped him. Most importantly, he was said to never harm a child. Any child, whether human, spirit, or animal. The villagers chose one child from their number to bring their offerings for the spirit. And one time, their priest allowed me to accompany the chosen child."

"Did you see anything?" Cylin asked.

He nodded. "I saw him. Not much taller than I was—I remember that clearly. I was lanky, ten years old, and the 'spirit' was eye level with me. He had a wild, feral look to him." He smiled faintly. "The fact that he was followed by three of the most terrifying creatures I've ever seen might have influenced that impression. I described them to Lord Lucian once, and he called them razorclaws—an apt name. The guardian spirit and his beasts all looked straight at me, then took the offerings and disappeared into the jungle. I never saw him again, but I've never forgotten that moment." Doctor Kinnel set down his mug and rested his elbows on the table. "It wasn't until much later that I finally realized that the jungle spirit I saw and the elves of legends and fairy tales bore stark similarities. So when I met Lord Lucian, I knew what he was. That jungle elf protected his people from anything that threatened them. He watched over them and kept them safe. Lord Lucian does the same thing. He guards us, and no matter what horrors he carries in his past, I believe he will do anything to protect the people who matter to him."

Cylin nodded in somber agreement. "I think... I understand that feeling."

Lucian's episode passed with little comment from the people of Forest Town. When Cylin pressed, most people tried to pretend it never happened, as if not talking about it could erase the event altogether. They didn't want to think that their lord was as damaged as any of them.

Lucian didn't speak of the incident either. After several days in his cave, he resumed his wanderings of Forest Town, smiling and laughing as if nothing had happened. He did seek her out when he was roaming, though he rarely said anything beyond small pleasantries. After nearly a week, she finally stopped him at the edge of the fields.

"All right, Lucian, what is it?"

"What is what?" he asked.

Cylin folded her arms. "You've been coming out every day for the last six days, going around the village until you find me, but once you do, you just say hello and move on. So, what is it?"

"Ah. Not as subtle as I thought I was."

"I'm jumpy. I notice things like that." Cylin glowered at him. "Do you want to ask me something or not?"

"Just making sure you're still here," Lucian said.

A sarcastic response died on her lips. "You… oh. Why?"

"A lot of people leave after they experience one of my episodes—people who have no idea what I might be doing, only hearing the screams in the village. You actually came in, heard my ravings. You did something to calm me. But I don't imagine it's an experience you'd want to go through again. So…" He stopped, shaking his head. "I'm not saying this well. Wish I could just mind-speak it to you instead, but that only works with other elves. What I'm trying to say is that I would very much *like* you to stay in Forest Town, but I wouldn't be surprised if you grabbed your bag and fled for the hills instead."

"I'm still here."

"Obviously. But that doesn't mean you'll still be here tomorrow, or the day after."

"You think I would leave without saying goodbye?" Cylin asked.

Lucian raised an eyebrow. "And risk someone trying to stop you or talk you out of it? If you decided to leave, yes, I think you'd do so without warning and without saying goodbye."

He was right. "I'd... leave a note or something. Draw a stick figure waving goodbye to a bunch of trees."

He laughed softly at that, then grew serious. "*Are* you going to leave, Cylin? I won't stop you or try to dissuade you if you are."

She glanced over her shoulder to the fields, then met Lucian's eyes. He looked tired, worn, and resigned. He expected her to say yes, expected that his hallucinations drove her away. "Well, I'm not going to promise that I'll absolutely live the rest of my life here and never set foot outside the forest again, but I'm not planning to take off anytime soon. I know what I'm getting into now. I'd rather know than be guessing what dark secrets keep this place functional."

He didn't say anything at first, like he was waiting for her to laugh and say she'd lied to his face. "You're going to stay?"

She gave him an annoyed look. "That's what I said. Yes, I'm going to stay. So you don't have to lurk around just to make sure I'm still here. If I'm leaving, I'll tell you."

"Then I will have something for you tomorrow," Lucian said. "First thing in the morning."

"What sort of thing?" she asked.

He shook his head. "You'll see. I'll be waiting for you outside Myra's house tomorrow."

What could he possibly have for me? Cylin frowned as he left, and thought about the mysterious promise through the rest of the day.

She woke early in the morning, before Myra and her family rose. Cylin crept through the house, stepping lightly to avoid waking anyone. Outside, the platform glistened with dew. The morning was pleasantly cool. She looked around, not seeing anyone else about yet. She turned around and jumped with a startled squeak. Lucian had somehow appeared beside her. He grinned and touched a finger to his lips for silence.

She followed him along the platforms and across a bridge to a small residence. The platform on which it stood commanded a good view of Forest Town. She could see both the path that led to the fields and the main entry road to Forest Town, depending which direction she looked.

"What's this, Lucian?" she asked.

His eyes gleamed like a boy showing off a new treasure. "It's yours."

"Mine?" She looked at him in confusion.

He opened the door to the residence. "It's yours. Your house. Your space. No other homes on this platform—it's all yours."

She looked inside, then hesitantly stepped over the threshold. She flipped the light switch, and illumination filled the room. The main room held a table and two chairs, a kitchen nook, and a worn but serviceable sofa. A mantle hung over the fireplace, ready to host her family gods. She opened the closed door, and found a bedroom with a dresser, closet, and a single-person bed. Another chair rested in the corner, and a small table stood beside the bed. One more door let into a small bathroom.

This is... mine? All of it?

Lucian waited for her in the main room. "Do you like it? Is it large enough? If it's too small, I can—"

"This is for me?" she interrupted.

"It is. It's your home, for as long as you want it."

Her eyes stung. She wiped them quickly, hoping he didn't notice. She swallowed hard. "No one's ever..." *No one's ever invited me to stay. Never offered me a place all to myself.*

Lucian seemed to understand the words she didn't say. "If no one's ever offered you a place of your own, they were obviously idiots."

That startled a laugh from her. "Idiots, huh? All of them?"

"All of them," Lucian said. "And that's my opinion as leader of Forest Town."

If she thought long about this gift, she was going to break down, and she refused to break down in front of Lucian. "So do you just have a bunch of extra homes tucked away in the trees for people, or something?"

"Nope. I make them as we need them. I thought you'd like this spot, where you can keep an eye on things."

"You... make them." Looking around, she saw seamless wood floor and walls. No boards or nails. *And he chose this spot just for me. A spot where I can see someone coming, and they can't sneak up on me.* "You mean, with magic?"

He nodded.

"So, you can make trees into houses overnight, and make rock walls appear and disappear at will."

"I can also mind-speak with other elves and fly," Lucian told her.

"Wait, you can *fly*?" Cylin demanded.

He shrugged. "Well, I can make objects float, and that includes myself. Or other people."

She stared at him, then shook her head with a laugh. "I think it might be faster for you to tell me what you can't do than what you can!"

Lucian didn't laugh. "I can't heal. I don't have any ability to locate people or things. I can't read minds or shapeshift. And while

I can shape plants, metal, and stone, I can't do anything with synthetic materials like plastic. I know how to work glass, but only the normal way, no magic involved. I can't shape bone or coral."

"Bone's pretty brittle," Cylin said. "And we're a long way from anywhere with coral. That *is* an ocean thing, right?"

"It is. Bone can be reinforced with magic to strengthen it. And coral…" He stopped. "Willow's lair lay in the ocean. She called it the Coral Palace. No rock. No metal. Nothing I could use." His voice grew very soft on the last sentences.

"So she could manipulate those, but you can't?" Cylin wasn't sure if she was moving the conversation in a safer direction.

Lucian nodded. "Some abilities run in families, but that doesn't mean that every child will have every ability. The only ones that seem to be universal are mind-speech and an ability to sense where another had worked magic. And even those aren't strong with every elf."

"So you being able to do all this isn't normal, even for an elf?"

"No. Some elves have one or two abilities beyond those we all share, in varying strengths. But me…" He sighed. "I am my father's son."

"And that's not a good thing?"

"My father is incredibly powerful magically and very attractive. That sort of person draws attention, and not all of it is welcome. Like my mother, and others who saw him as someone to manipulate, control, and use, or they saw him as a threat to their own position, a rival, even though he didn't want what they had. Power is a trap. You never have enough. Someone else always has more. Like my father, I have enough to be dangerous. Enough to be a threat, but too often, not enough to protect the people and things that matter." He leaned against the wall, eyes distant. Then he straightened, shaking his head. "But I didn't come here to whine. I came here to show you your new house!"

He didn't want to talk more about his past. She forced the rest of her questions back, though he hadn't really answered her. She was once again confronted by the overwhelming fact that this was *hers*. "It's… I don't know what to say about this, Lucian, except… thank you."

He smiled. "You don't have to say anything, Cylin. That's my job. My job to tell you 'Welcome home.'"

At first, Cylin thought she only imagined subtle shifts in the attitudes of the people of Forest Town toward her. They'd always been welcoming and friendly, but once she moved into her own home, they accepted her as one of them. She only recognized the slight caution, the hesitation to form too close of ties to her once it was gone. A house made her part of the community rather than a wandering transient who might vanish like the morning dew.

People whose names she barely knew took the time to ask what she needed to be ready for winter. Fellow field workers chatted with her about the weather, or the coming harvest. They invited her to make preserves with them. They brought housewarming gifts and laughed off her protests that she didn't have anything to offer in return.

After a week of her new status as a member of Forest Town, Cylin sought out Devin at his house, first thing in the morning. His residence sat on a lower branch than most, giving him fewer steps to climb. The house looked about the same size as hers. When she knocked, she heard a surprised, "Come in?"

She opened the door and stepped into a house that looked very little like her own. She wasn't sure why she expected that it ought to. His walls held shelves lined with wood carvings such as she'd seen him whittling. A cane rested in a stand by the door, though she'd rarely seen him use it. Several cushioned chairs provided seating. Devin sat at the table, a steaming mug before him.

He blinked at her in surprise. "Cylin? Something wrong?"

"I need to ask you something." She spoke quickly, wanting to get the question out before she second-guessed it.

"About Lord Lucian?" he asked. He waved at the table. "Sit down? Want something to drink?"

She sat across the table from him and waved off the offer of a drink. "Not about Lucian. About Forest Town. And it probably sounds like a stupid question."

"Uh, okay…" Devin said uncertainly. "What is it?"

She rested her elbows on the table and looked at him intently. "Is this all some weird setup, or are people acting like this for real?" At his puzzled expression, she added, "People here in Forest Town. They act like they are actually pleased that I decided to stay. Is that for real, is that an act, or is it a ploy to get me to relax so everyone can have a laugh at the idea that I'd think they *want* me here?"

Devin's expression passed from surprised, to indignant, to unexpectedly sympathetic. "It's genuine. People really do want you to stay. They just… kind of forget what it was like to be suspicious of everything."

"You can *forget* that?" Cylin asked, dubious.

"Yeah, you can. Eventually. Until someone reminds you." After a pause, Devin said, "For the first couple of years here, I didn't trust anyone except Lord Lucian, and maybe Doctor Kinnel. I figured anyone else would sell me to the bone men, given half a chance."

And from what he'd implied, he would have difficulty running away if someone did try to drag him away. At least she knew she could fight someone off. "Is that why you decided to become the door guard for Lucian? So that if you needed help, he'd be close enough to hear?"

He considered. "I don't think I thought of it quite like that, but I guess so. One reason, at least. Wasn't like I could work in the fields or be a good scout, in any case. I know Lord Lucian doesn't really *need* someone up there, but other people seem to feel like it makes things more… dunno, official to have a gate-keeper. Like they think it's how things ought to be."

"Huh." She considered that. "So, maybe they also think that welcoming in strangers and newcomers is also 'how things ought to be,' so they do it because they want it to be 'normal' instead of weird and suspicious."

"Kind of, except that they don't remember that to some people, it *is* weird and suspicious to be treated like we're… one of them, and not a resource they can sell to the bone men in a pinch."

A deep boom, as much felt as heard, interrupted them. Cylin started, for one terrifying instant fearing an earthquake. Devin jerked to his feet. He nearly fell, and clung to the table for support. "That's the alarm drum!"

For a moment, his words made no sense. Then Cylin grabbed toward her waist. With a jolt and a cold sinking in her gut, she realized she'd left both her pistol and her bag in her house. She would never have let such a lapse happen even a month ago.

Devin scrambled for the door at a limping run. She followed, heart racing.

Outside, people poured onto the walkways in various states of dress or undress, caught in the midst of their morning ritu-als. Cylin's gaze swept the ground for the source of the alarm. She saw someone beating a mallet against a massive hide drum, and the sound vibrated through the trees.

Lucian sprinted into the village. Cylin wasn't certain his feet actually touched the ground. The sentry let the mallet drop, and eerie silence fell over Forest Town. The sentry drew a deep breath, and even from where she stood, Cylin could see that he was shaking.

"Lord Lucian, bandits in the forest. Coming toward the village. I counted twelve armed men from two trucks. I think the leader is a bone man!"

Lucian's expression grew grim. "Thank you. Get to shelter." He looked up to the trees. His gaze found Cylin and Devin, and though he addressed his words to everyone, Cylin was sure he was speaking to her. "Stay in the trees and out of sight. I'll take care of this."

Cylin opened her mouth to protest. "But--" *Could I make it to my house before the bandits arrive? If I can get my gun...*

Devin's hand gripped her arm. "Don't."

"What?" She spun to face him. "He's not going to face them alone!"

"Yes, he is." Devin kept hold of her arm. "Trust him. Lord Lucian can handle them."

"Twelve armed bandits? Alone?" She looked to the other platforms. Some people had gone inside and shut their doors tight. Others had retrieved weapons, but no one lined up to form a defensive firing line or take advantage of their height and concealment to prepare a killing field. Doctor Kinnel and others covered the doors that were at ground level, and when they pulled them closed, the buildings seemed to vanish even when she knew what to look for.

They really do think Lucian can handle this alone. Have they forgotten how to protect themselves? Her jaw tightened. *Gods of my family, protect Lucian. Please.*

Lucian strode to the center of the village and stood in front of the well. His back was to Forest Town and his gaze fixed on the forest. On the walkways, parents comforted their children, holding them close and whispered reassurances or ushered them inside. Stillness hung over the village as everyone waited.

Cylin found herself counting heartbeats, but her pulse raced too fast to offer any sense of time.

I could still get back to my house. Get my gun.

The crash of breaking branches interrupted the stillness. Figures gathered at the edge of the clearing, then advanced, guns trained on Lucian.

Cylin stiffened. "What the fuck is he doing here?"

Devin glanced over at her sharp whisper. "Who?"

She pointed to the brute walking beside the apparent leader. "That's Hakon. He was one of Pryor's thugs. I don't see Pryor or Alger, though. What's he doing with these guys?"

Devin shivered. "Don't know, but that guy in the middle is definitely a bone man. He's got that weirdly perfect face."

Cylin focused on the leader and understood what Devin meant. The man's handsome features were as smooth as if they'd been molded in plaster. Something about his face was just a little off—not enough for her to pinpoint exactly what was wrong, but enough to give her the creepy sensation that she was looking at someone wearing a human face like a mask.

I have a perfect shot at him from here. Dammit, how could I have been so stupid as to leave my gun in the house?

Hakon glowered at Lucian and glanced to the bone man. "That's him. The guy who ran off with the girl we was gonna give you."

Lucian plucked an insect off the rim of the well and watched it creep across his fingers. Without even looking back at the intruders, he asked. "What business do you have here?"

"You took somethin' that didn't belong to you, and we're gonna take it back," Hakon sneered.

"Should I remember you?" Lucian asked, dismissive. "I've seen enough scum in my days, why would you matter to me?"

The bone man spoke. "You took a girl before the promised tribute could be paid. The debt remains, and we have come to collect it."

Hakon laughed. "If you haven't sold her off yourself. Hmm, nah, you probably got *other* uses for pretty young girls. And pretty young boys as well, if rumors is true."

Devin stiffened beside Cylin.

If Hakon expected anger, Lucian disappointed him. "Ah. You're one of the slimeballs who tried to carve Cylin's face to sell to the bone men. I told you that you'd be wise to leave me alone. Clearly, you're no smarter than you look."

While Hakon fumbled for a response, the bone man laughed. "You have hidden well, lord of the forest. The tales claim you have hidden an entire village under these boughs. I seek only the one promised us. The underlings will no doubt expect some of the conquerors' share from the rest of the village, but if you comply, I will ensure their lusts are restrained."

Lucian didn't flinch. His voice was cold and hard. "You won't leave here alive."

"That is your answer? A pity." The bone man nodded to the thugs. "Aim for something not fatal. We shall make use of him."

Cylin gasped as the crack of gunfire erupted. Devin gripped her shoulder tightly.

Lucian didn't move. The two thugs who'd circled to either side of him fell on the ground, writhing and bleeding. Lucian looked to one side, then the other, then back to the bone man. "I'm not good at 'not fatal' when someone shoots at me."

The remaining men gaped at him, then began firing. Lucian strode toward them, bullets veering and curving around him. In a pause while they frantically reloaded, Lucian spoke, voice tight with fury. "You think I'll allow you to attack my home, threaten my people, and succeed? You will take nothing from here. Not even your lives."

In a sudden burst of movement, he rushed one of the men. Grabbing the barrel of the man's rifle, Lucian bent it up and back so that it pointed at its wielder. "Did you think the rumors about me were lies and foolishness? Or did you listen to them at all?"

The man's mouth opened and closed without sound, like a fish out of water. Lucian raised a hand, fingers curled like claws as if he intended to tear the man's eyes out. When he'd rescued Cylin from Pryor, Lucian had been calm, cold, calculating. What she saw now was pure, raw fury.

The man dropped his ruined gun and scrambled back, babbling incoherently. Lucian finally lowered his hand and straightened. Something in his stance changed, as if he shed the fury and donned a calmer, if no less angry, demeanor. Around his feet, blades of fresh grass sprouted out of the ground. The trees seemed to lean closer, looming over the intruders.

Never taking her eyes off Lucian, Cylin whispered, "Has he gone 'Ghost'?"

Tension radiated from Devin. "No. No, this isn't the Ghost at all. I'm... not sure what it is."

Men backed away from Lucian. Hakon glared at them and pointed his handgun at Lucian. "Fucking cowards! He's just one nutcase with some cheap tricks!"

"How many children have you murdered?" Lucian demanded, voice cold and hard. He stepped toward Hakon. "How many have you raped? Sold to the bone men? Ripped from their parents, their families, their homes? How many have you carved up piece by piece? We find those you leave behind, the broken pieces that you abandon, forgotten and lost. We give them life and hope, and we will never let you touch Cylin or any of our people."

Hakon squeezed the trigger. His gun exploded. He screamed, falling to his knees and clutching the bloody mess of his hand. His face bled from dozens of cuts and gashes from flying shards of metal. Lucian loomed over him. The ground trembled. Cylin gripped a railing.

"Devin, what's happening?"

"I don't know," Devin whispered, his voice quavering.

A crack opened beneath Hakon. Even the bone man scrambled away from him. Hakon's head jerked up, and Cylin saw his mouth move, but she couldn't hear his words over the cracking and shaking of the ground. He grabbed at Lucian, but Lucian stepped out of reach. Hakon scrabbled for a hold on the dirt, but the crack opened wide and the earth crumbled under his hand. Cylin saw hate, fear, and pain on his face as he fell into the darkness. A thick green vine coiled out of the crack and snatched the retreating bone man's ankle before he could escape. He shouted in fear and alarm as it dragged him into the dark opening in the earth. The edges of the crack slammed together over him, cutting off his final shout of rage. Cylin clung to the railing, her eyes wide, forgetting even to breathe.

She couldn't see Lucian's face, but his stance betrayed nothing as he turned toward the remaining men, who stood frozen in shock as the ground swallowed their leader. Lucian's voice carried clearly in the sudden silence.

"Run."

Three men shouted in rage or fear and charged at him. The rest bolted for the forest.

None of them made it.

The ground cracked again, but this time it did not swallow the men. Plants burst through the packed dirt, tangles of vines and saplings that swarmed after the men like a starving pack of wolves to lame elk. Cylin saw a branch impale one man through the gut. Another was swept off his feet by vines. She had a glimpse of his limbs being torn apart before the mass of plants swallowed him and his horrified screams. She couldn't move and couldn't look away as the men who had come to take revenge on her and on Lucian were slaughtered. The leaves of the plants were dyed red and the thorns dripped blood.

"We will not allow you to harm our people." Lucian's voice seemed to echo, as if more than one person spoke. "You are nothing but food for our roots, useless and forgotten."

The plants sank back into the ground, dragging with them the mangled bodies of men who Cylin sincerely hoped were dead. Lucian turned to face the village, and the burning fury in his eyes belied his calm voice. On one of the platforms, a child whimpered and began to wail. Lucian's gaze flew toward the sound even as the mother tried to hush her son. Cylin tensed, not sure what to do if he interpreted the sound as a threat.

He spoke. "They are gone. Do not fear them."

Cylin licked her lips and spoke. "I don't think that it's those men that he's afraid of, Lucian."

Her voice wasn't loud, but Lucian turned to her. "The danger is gone. We have removed it."

"You're frightening him, Lucian. Drifter's bones, you're frightening most of us." Cylin swallowed hard.

Lucian cocked his head to one side, considering her words. "We apologize. We are... not as skilled as our host in using words to calm or sooth. We ask your assistance in doing so in our absence. We... must rest."

"Who is 'we'?" Cylin demanded. *And what in drifters' bones does he mean by 'host'?*

"We are the Guardian. We are the Tree. We are this forest. We will not harm any of our own. You have our most fervent vow on that." He looked over the throng watching him from above. "But we distress you, and for that, we are sorry. Devin, Cylin, please care for the things that need done. We will rest, and our host will return."

He left the silent village. Only after he had vanished into his cave did a cacophony of voices burst forth. Cylin didn't try to listen to them. Their questions were the same as hers. "Guardian? Devin, do you know anything about… this?"

Devin shook his head in quick denial. "Lord Lucian's said things about 'the Tree,' but I don't understand any of it. I… I don't know, Cylin." He was shaking. "He just… ripped those men to pieces."

She gripped his shoulder. "Right now, we have a lot of frightened, confused people, and they need us to help them. All right? There could be more bandits in the forest. And we should search their vehicles for anything we can use."

"Right," Devin said, but he didn't move.

No one knows what to do. No one's taking charge. They don't know what to do without Lucian. Cylin looked around quickly, then raised her voice. "Searel. Gather scouts and check the forest around the village for any more bandits."

Myra's husband started when he heard his name, then jerked his head in a nod and tapped the shoulder of a man near him, waking the other from his daze. Cylin pointed at a cluster of people on the next walkway over. "You there. Head down to the bandits' trucks. Bring back anything we can use, and watch for any sentries." The villagers obeyed, relieved to have someone giving instructions and providing an illusion of confidence. "Devin, get Doctor Kinnel and have him make sure no one got hurt when the ground started shaking."

Devin nodded. "And… what are you going to do?"

She bit her lip. "I'm going to talk to Lucian."

He wanted to argue, but after a moment of silence, just nodded. "Please be careful."

"I will."

She scrambled up the slope to Lucian's cave faster than she'd ever done before, not caring about the scrapes the rocks and brush dealt to her hands and arms. She checked each room until finally she found Lucian at the very end of the cave, sitting at the edge of a tiny pool. He turned slightly toward her.

"We are here. Is there need of us outside?"

"No, we have things under control." She kept her gaze on him, cautious. "But what's this 'we' business?"

"We are the Guardian," he repeated, as if that explained everything.

"Yep, you said that already. Doesn't tell me much, Lucian."

"We are with Lucian, but we are not Lucian. We are a part of the Tree." He considered her. "And that, too, means nothing to you. Forgive us. We do not often try to speak to humans."

"Well maybe you should. You might make more sense if you did," Cylin said.

Lucian shook his head. "We are a fragment of magic born into Lucian, but we are not an elf."

"What's 'the Tree'?" Cylin asked, hoping that might offer a little more context.

His lips twitched in a smile. "We think Lucian can explain more clearly than we can. And now that you are safe, the danger is removed, and Lucian is more calm, we will return to our rest."

"That makes even less sense than what you said before, and I didn't think that was possible," Cylin said.

Lucian rubbed his face and let out a long breath, shoulders hunching. "It means that the Guardian is done talking. Dammit." His head jerked up. "Are you all right, Cylin?"

"Um, yeah, I'm fine. So is everyone else, just shaken up and unsettled." She eyed him. "You're back to being you?"

He nodded.

"What happened?"

He closed his eyes and leaned against the wall. "I didn't recognize that man at first. Then he said he was here for you, and I knew he was with the one who cut you." His hands clenched in fists. "I wanted him to suffer. The Guardian... intervened. You might be unsettled by the Guardian's methods, but if it had been left to me, that man wouldn't be dead yet. He'd just wish he was."

"I… Lucian… I'm just glad to know he's gone. He's dead. That's enough for me," Cylin said.

"But not enough for me, it seems." Lucian turned and met her eyes. "Anyone who hurts my friends deserves to suffer. I don't have many now who I would call friends. And of any of them here, you're the only one who never calls me 'Lord.'"

Heat rushed to Cylin's face. "I'm sorry. I just never…"

"Don't. Don't start now. I'd rather just be Lucian. Just Lucian, who keeps his friends safe."

She remembered the crack that swallowed Hakon. The thorns and vines that ripped men apart. *He did that because of me. To… protect me. And he would have done worse to them.*

"I've lost too many friends," Lucian whispered. "I don't want to lose any more."

"If you're sure you want a smart-mouthed, contrary human as a friend, I… I'm still not planning to run off and leave in the middle of the night," she blurted. It sounded better in her head than aloud.

A thin laugh from Lucian. "I realize it isn't as obvious when I'm the one in charge, but I'm a pretty authority-averse, irreverent little shit myself. I'm in charge because I'm not about to let someone else give me orders. But sometimes I need someone who's not afraid to call me on my crap. Most people here won't. Most people here *worship* me." He shuddered. "Devin certainly would never admit I've done anything wrong. Doctor Kinnel does, sometimes, but he'd rather not."

"For an authority-averse, irreverent little shit, you do pretty good as a leader," Cylin said.

His lips quirked in a faint smile. "When the target for being a 'good leader' is that people have food, shelter, and security, and I'm not raping anyone, hitting that goal isn't as much of an accomplishment as you imply."

"Then why can't anyone else manage it?" she countered.

"Because most of them lack the moral fortitude of a turd." He let out a heavy sigh. "How badly did the Guardian scare everyone?"

"Well, they were pretty alarmed, but no open panic in the trees," Cylin told him. "They'd probably feel better to see you back to yourself." *Just like they do after you have an episode.*

He nodded and slowly pushed to his feet. She couldn't see him clearly in the dim light of the cave, but once they got outside, the pallor of his skin became obvious, as did the lines of exhaustion.

"Lucian, are you all right?"

"The Guardian used a lot of magic. It's just… draining."

"So, what *is* the Guardian? Or the Tree? The answer I got earlier didn't explain much."

Lucian looked down to the trees, as if deciding whether he'd rather face the villagers or answer her. Finally, he sat on a smooth stone. "The Tree was... is an entity formed by magic gone wrong."

"Magic can 'go wrong'?" Cylin asked, casting an uneasy look at the forest.

"Not often. And it's rarely catastrophic. But when it is, the results are never pleasant. The Tree became entwined with my father and its magic infected him. That's been passed on to his descendants. In some of us, the Tree magic has developed a personality of sorts, reflecting aspects of its host's character. Mine calls itself the Guardian. It shares my personality, my memories, and my goals, but it is still, fundamentally, a plant-mind, not an elf. That's why the plural, the 'we.' It's a part of a whole. My brother embraced his Tree aspect so completely that it's no longer a separate entity like the Guardian, but really a part of him." His gaze grew distant. "I don't know whether or not he survived the wars. If he did... this blighted land would be a constant torture to him."

"Couldn't he make trees grow, like you did here?" Cylin asked.

Lucian shook his head. "Mirrors of our personalities. Like me, the Guardian fights. When I came here, it altered the trees so that they break down the poisons in the ground and purify the land. That isn't what my brother, Dash, would do. The Guardian alters the world to conform to its will. Dash alters himself to survive the world. The Guardian purifies the poisons to fix what it perceives as the wrongs. Dash would make himself able to drink the poisons to survive in the world as it is."

"I think I like the Guardian's idea better," Cylin admitted. "The things that have been twisted by the poisons are not things I want to see stick around."

Lucian gazed into the trees. "Everything's been touched by poisons. Some just hide it better."

Cylin followed his gaze, but didn't see anything out of the ordinary. "Lucian, does Forest Town have any defenses other than... well... you?"

"We have sentries watching the road. The terrain slows down bandits, and the paths aren't obvious when you don't know what to look for. But if you're asking whether the village has any plan for what to do if I'm... unavailable, the answer is that we do in theory, but I doubt anyone other than Doctor Kinnel knows it by now. And he knows it because he wrote it."

Cylin gave him a long, pointed look. "That's a crappy plan."

"No, it's a good plan that's had crappy implementation." Lucian turned to her. "I'll put you in charge of teaching people to follow it."

"Right, I'm sure that's a good idea," Cylin retorted. "Put the new person in charge of that sort of thing."

His gaze showed no humor or teasing. "You still remember how to take care of yourself. I can't think of anyone better."

They reached the village as the scouts returned. People tensed when they saw Lucian, and watched him cautiously. He smiled wearily. "I'm sorry to have frightened everyone earlier."

"Don't worry about it, Lord Lucian!" a scout said quickly. "It's been a long time since anyone tried to attack. We... weren't expecting this, is all."

Around him, others nodded in hasty agreement, murmuring assent.

Even when he acknowledges that he made a mistake, did something he shouldn't have done, they won't accept that he did anything wrong. They really do hold Lucian up like he's some mythical figure, a god among us. Cylin glanced at Lucian, saw the strain in his eyes. *And he hates it.*

"We brought the salvage to Doctor Kinnel to inventory," the scout continued. "Guns and other weapons were in good shape. Bedding and clothes are probably salvageable. And it looked like they raided a distillery or something recently, because one truck was loaded with crates of hard alcohol."

"I'm sure we can put that to good use." Lucian gave a thin smile. "Any more bandits lurking in the woods?"

"No sir, not even sentries by their trucks." A pause. "Um... what should we do about their trucks, Lord Lucian?"

"I think most of you have a better idea what to do with a truck than I do," Lucian answered. "Do whatever you think best."

"If they're in good working order, I'd suggest parking them somewhere, keeping up on whatever maintenance they need, and having them available in case we ever need them," Cylin said.

People looked at her as if she'd started speaking another language. "Why would we need them?" someone asked.

"Transporting people, goods, animals. Any time we need to move something large, or need to get somewhere faster than on foot. They probably have a few spare fuel tanks on the trucks, right?"

"Well, yes, but…" The sentry who spoke looked truly puzzled by the idea that reliable transportation might be important.

How about a way to move people around? Get children to safety if someone attacks again?

"What do you think, Lord Lucian?"

Just take a few steps to protect yourselves! Cylin fought not to snap the words aloud.

"I don't need the scrap metal for anything. If you want to keep the vehicles, I'll make a sheltered space to park them," Lucian said.

"Yes sir." The sentry nodded firmly as if Lucian had declared they were keeping the trucks.

Cylin didn't go down to the road with Lucian and the sentries. She found herself walking around the village common. At first she skirted the areas where the plants had ripped through the ground, but finally she made herself walk to the spot where the earth swallowed Hakon. The hole was gone, leaving only a rough seam of uneven ground. A scar on Forest Town.

Her fingers brushed the scar on her cheek. *Did you send him, Pryor? Hope you aren't expecting him back. I'm not yours any longer. I hope you think about that and choke.*

~

Barely a week after the bandit attack, harvest arrived in a flurry of long days and late nights. Once things finally settled back into the normal routine, Lucian followed through on his threat to put Cylin in charge of organizing Forest Town's defenses.

Many long-term residents accepted Lucian's proclamation

without complaint, but responded to Cylin's efforts with patronizing indulgence, indicating that they would participate, but didn't see a real need for the effort. Those newer to Forest Town took part more readily, driven by their own survival instincts. No one directly spoke of the Guardian, but Cylin felt the memory lurking in people's thoughts.

She recruited Doctor Kinnel to teach basics of wound care and what he called "first aid." The experienced sentries worked with people on concealment. The hunters taught tracking and foraging.

By the time the first snow fell, training had become a habit. Some people still complained that it was unnecessary, but the grumbling lost most of its strength.

Winter had always been Cylin's least favorite season: a time of cold, hunger, and death. Last winter, with Pryor, she'd spent huddled in the back of a drafty truck, buried under thin blankets and praying to her family gods that she wouldn't get frostbite and lose fingers or toes. In Forest Town, winter could be a time of beauty, and even fun. She had a thick, warm coat. Myra knitted her a new hat and gloves. She even had fur-lined, hole-free boots that fit comfortably.

Glad for the warm clothes, Cylin stood beside Devin as Doctor Kinnel scooped a sample of snow into a glass jar, then added several drops of colored liquid from a vial. She leaned over to Devin and whispered, "So, what is this supposed to prove?"

"He's testing whether the snow is safe, or if it's tainted and we shouldn't let the children play in it," Devin whispered back. "Didn't the people you were with test the snow and rain?"

She shook her head. "Pryor assumed nothing was safe to consume unless it was filtered and boiled."

Doctor Kinnel studied the jar, then announced, "Contaminant levels are low this year. I'd recommend boiling before using it as drinking water, though."

In a chorus of cheers, children broke away from their parents and darted down the stairs to the ground. Cylin watched in bemusement and mild alarm as they sprang on the thin, wet snow and began rolling it in balls and stacking them. She cast a questioning look to Devin.

"What?" he asked, puzzled. "Didn't you ever play in the snow?"

"Uh, no, not when everyone told me it was probably toxic and might kill me," Cylin told him.

"Oh." Devin considered that. "Well, there's not enough snow yet to do much with, but next time, I'll show you how to build a snow person."

"Is that what they're doing?" She nodded toward the children.

"I think so." Devin grinned. "Kind of hard to tell when some kids are trying to build and others are trying to start a snowball fight."

The first snow melted by the end of the day, leaving the village common a muddy swamp. The next week brought a stronger storm and a steady fall of fat flakes. The trees broke the howling wind, robbing the storm of its fury as it passed over Forest Town.

Devin was showing Cylin how to build crude figures from snow when Lucian joined them. Almost at once, laughing children bundled in coats and gloves jumped on him, knocking him into a pile of snow. Laughing with them, Lucian picked himself up, white snow dusting his black hair.

"All right, whose idea was that?" He scooped up one of the boys. "Yours?"

The giggling boy squirmed, denying the accusation until Lucian set him down and caught another child. The second one managed to grab a handful of snow and threw it at Lucian's chest. Lucian staggered as if dealt a fierce blow. "What? This one came armed! You know what *that* means!"

The children scattered, squealing in delight. Lucian scooped a handful of snow into a loose ball and tossed it at one of the fleeing children. That, evidently, was a signal to the rest. Devin ducked behind the questionable shelter of their snow figures as everyone around them began flinging snow in every direction. Cylin imitated him.

"What in drifters' bones is this?" she asked.

"This is Lord Lucian starting a snowball fight." Devin grinned. "He does this a lot in winter. Wants to make sure everyone has some happy memories of the season. If you want to join, just start tossing snowballs at someone. Even Lord Lucian—he doesn't mind."

"Oh, believe me, if I start throwing snowballs at anyone, he is definitely my target," Cylin said.

"I heard that!" Lucian called. "Come on, Cylin! Give me your best shot!"

"If you start throwing snowballs, you become a target too," Devin warned. "The rules are that you don't target non-combatants, you don't pack a ball so hard that you'll hurt someone, and if you join the fight, you're in it until it's either over or you go upstairs to the trees. And if someone gets hurt or starts crying, the game stops immediately."

"Good to know. Thanks." Cylin scooped snow into a ball, stepped out of shelter, and tossed her missile at Lucian.

She hit him solidly in the chest. He grinned, and half a dozen snowballs from all directions flew at her as the children welcomed their new target.

By the time the snowball fight wound down, Cylin lost count of how many times she was hit, or how many she had thrown. Snow matted her gloves and caked her coat. When she stopped moving, the chill seeped through her clothes.

"All right!" Lucian called. "Everyone, to the bath house! Warm up, then dry off!"

Cylin paused just outside the bath house. "I don't have any dry clothes here."

Leesa caught her hand. "It's okay, Cylin! My mama will bring some for you."

Cylin cast a look toward the trees and her house, but the warmth of the bath house called to her. Deciding that one way or another, dry clothes would be a worry for later, she headed in.

Fortunately, Leesa was right, and Myra brought a spare set of clothes for Cylin. One more instance of Forest Town hospitality. She wasn't certain she would ever get used to it, and she sincerely hoped she never took it for granted.

Cylin slept deeply that night. She woke before dawn by habit to perform her morning rituals and prayers. Her coat and boots were still damp from the play in the snow, so she pulled on a thick sweater and a jacket and slipped on her regular shoes before stepping outside.

From her ledge, she looked over the sleeping village. Her breath rose in a cloud, but the cold didn't bite too fiercely. Almost no one was up this early. Just her, a few forest animals, and someone entering the village common from the forest.

She froze. The figure wore a heavy coat and a thick hat, and didn't carry themselves like anyone she recognized.

Who is that? How did they get here? Did they sneak past the sentries? They should have an escort if they're a stranger. What if they're a bandit spy? Dammit, we talked about this! Am I the only one who cares about protecting Forest Town?

She darted inside, buckled on her pistol belt, and rushed back outside. The stranger crossed the village common and followed the path toward Lucian's cave. Cylin rushed down the steps. Her feet sank in the snow and she silently cursed that her boots were too wet to wear.

"Hey you!" she called, running after the stranger. One

hand stayed near her gun and she prepared to drop to the snow if the other brandished a weapon.

The other turned and gave her a charming smile. "Oh, hello. Sorry, am I trespassing?"

He was slim with slanted amber eyes, a straight nose, and a boyish smile. Cylin guessed him to be seventeen or eighteen years old. He exuded more good cheer than any stranger in the middle of winter reasonably should. And somehow, his feet barely dented the snow, while her steps sank not quite to her ankles.

"Who are you?" Cylin asked warily. "Why are you here?"

"My name's Tammin. I'm looking for someone, and I'm pretty sure they're somewhere in this forest. Do you live here? Do you know of other people in the area?"

"Yes, I live here," Cylin told him. She didn't want to tell him more than necessary about Forest Town, but neither did she want him to think her alone. "So do other people. And some of them really ought to have noticed you coming, and made sure you had a proper escort."

"There's more people here?" Tammin asked. "Wow. I didn't expect that, though maybe I should have." He peered into the trees, then looked up, and his expression brightened. "Oh! The houses are in the trees. That's smart. Keeps random weirdos from wandering in."

"Well, *usually* it does," Cylin said, eyeing him. "Come on. People will be waking up by now. You can see if the person you're looking for is here."

"Erm." Tammin didn't move. "I'm actually pretty sure that the person I'm looking for is further this way." He gestured toward Lucian's cave. "Does anyone live up there?"

Cylin's eyes narrowed. "Does the person you're looking for have a name?"

"Well, sure. His name's Lucian. Do *you* have a name?"

"You're looking for Lucian." She fixed a long look on him. "What's your business with him?"

Tammin frowned. "He's my uncle. Is there some kind of problem?"

Lucian's only spoken of two siblings: Dash and Ayliad. If Tammin IS his nephew, which side of the family is he from, and why is he looking for Lucian? "Come with me, Tammin. We'll give you a place to warm up and something to eat while I check whether Lucian is available."

Tammin considered that, then shrugged. "All right. A hot meal does sound pretty good right now. Thanks."

Amiably, he followed her back into Forest Town. Cylin knocked on Doctor Kinnel's door, knowing he was one of the first to rise. When the doctor opened the door, one of his eyebrows rose in surprise at Tammin.

"A new arrival? Come in."

"Tammin, this is Doctor Kinnel. Doctor, this is Tammin. I found him wandering through the village unescorted. He says he's looking for Lucian." Cylin ushered Tammin inside.

"I didn't actually know other people lived here until my as-of-yet-unnamed escort stopped me," Tammin added. He pulled off a glove and stuck out his hand. "Nice to meet you."

Doctor Kinnel shook Tammin's hand gravely. "And is your name one Lucian would recognize, Tammin?"

The young man paused and chewed his lip a moment. "He's more likely to know me by my nickname." He turned to Cylin. "When you check if he's available, would you please tell him that Quicksilver is looking for him?"

Both Doctor Kinnel's eyebrows rose in surprise, but he didn't look alarmed by the name. Tammin shed his coat and hat, revealing a mop of silver hair at contrast with his apparent youth. He gestured at it. "It's always been this color—thus the nickname."

"I see." Cylin eyed him, then looked to Doctor Kinnel.

The doctor nodded. "Go see if Lucian is up. I'll see that Tammin gets breakfast."

If Tammin means to cause trouble, leaving him alone with our only doctor is a bad idea. But leading him straight to Lucian could be a worse one.

Still debating the wisdom of letting Tammin out of her sight, Cylin left the infirmary and slogged back through the snow. Snow and ice made the path up to Lucian's cave treacherous, and she couldn't climb as fast as she wanted. Finally reaching the mouth of the cave, she stopped to catch her breath before venturing inside.

Behind the thick hide covering the entrance, the cave was nearly warm, and a pleasant relief from the morning chill. "Lucian, are you up?" Cylin called.

She waited, and finally heard movement and Lucian's voice in return. "Cylin? Something wrong? Come in."

She found him in one of the rooms, sitting beside a stove. "Morning," she greeted him. "A young man wandered into the village alone this morning, and said he's looking for you."

Lucian straightened from his casual slouch. "Who?"

"He gave me the name Tammin, but said you'd be more likely to recognize him by the nickname Quicksilver."

Lucian sprang to his feet, a grin spreading across his face. "What? Quick's here? Where is he?"

"Um, I left him with Doctor Kinnel, since I wasn't sure if he was trouble or not," Cylin told him. "Though I'm guessing… he isn't?"

Lucian chuckled. "Oh, Quick's always trouble, but not the bad sort. I haven't seen him since… the war." He strode for the door. Cylin hurried after him, catching up when Lucian paused to pull on a coat and hat. Excitement radiated from Lucian as he hurried down to the village.

At the infirmary, Doctor Kinnel and Quicksilver had been joined by Devin, who eyed Quicksilver cautiously. When

Lucian entered, Quicksilver jumped to his feet. "Lucian! There you are!"

"Well hello to you too." Lucian's grin grew even wider.

Quicksilver grabbed Lucian in a fierce hug. "We've been worried about you! Had no idea where you were! We didn't even know for sure that you were alive!"

Lucian returned the hug. "I've been here."

Quicksilver stepped back. "You've been here a while. I can tell. But you weren't easy to find. I had no idea even where to start looking, and I couldn't just set off with no direction." He dropped into a chair and swallowed a gulp of tea.

"So how did you find me now?" Lucian pulled another chair and sat.

"Well, I--" Quicksilver stopped, glancing to Cylin, Devin, and Doctor Kinnel. "Um."

Lucian frowned and followed his gaze, puzzled. Then his expression cleared with understanding. "You can answer honestly, Quick. Everyone in the room knows we're elves. Or at least they know I'm an elf, and have probably guessed that you are too."

"Really?" Quicksilver's expression became surprised. "You mean you actually found a group of humans who both believe you're an elf and don't think we're responsible for the end of the world? You have all the luck."

"Not luck," Doctor Kinnel said. "People who can't respect Lord Lucian or his rules don't stay here. Now, regardless of that, you found your way here somehow."

Quicksilver nodded. He still looked uncomfortable, but said, "I followed my arm."

"Ah." Lucian nodded as if that made perfect sense.

Before any of the humans could ask for clarification, Quicksilver turned to them. "So, magic has a 'feel' to it that's individual to each elf. Like, before I even got in sight of this forest, I knew it was Lucian's doing. Some elves are better than others at picking apart the details of who did what when. That's not my strength. I can just pick out a few people I know, and not from long distances. But a few months ago, I felt this *immense* burst of magic."

Lucian cocked his head to one side. "The Guardian?"

Quicksilver nodded. "Don't know what you or the Guardian were doing, but to me, it felt like in addition to whatever was going on, the Guardian also decided to reach out, shake me, and yell 'Get over here already!'" Quicksilver rubbed his left arm. "Lucian, do they know about the Guardian?"

"A little," Lucian answered. "Quicksilver is my nephew. He has the Tree magic as well, though it's not manifested in any particular way."

"Yep, I'm a Sapling," Quicksilver said. "According to the Guardian, at least, who likes assigning names to all the other people who carry Tree magic." He pushed up his left sleeve to reveal either a birthmark or a tattoo of vines winding up his arm. "This is where that magic… 'lives,' for lack of a better term. So, I just had to follow the Guardian's tug, and that led me here."

Devin still eyed Quicksilver warily. "You said 'we' earlier. Who came with you?"

"No one. I was really hoping to find Lucian before winter hit, because travel in winter is a stupid idea, and I know how stubborn he can be. And I know that he's going to want to take off as soon as I say I've been helping Eria take care of Chance."

Lucian burst to his feet. "Where's Chance?"

Quicksilver flinched slightly. "A couple months' travel from here in good weather, Lucian. He's comatose. Eria's caring for him."

"Eria" wasn't a name Cylin knew, but a glance to Devin didn't indicate any strong negative associations. Lucian barely seemed to hear Quicksilver's response. His eyes narrowed and he stepped toward Quicksilver, looming over him. "Where's Chance?"

Quicksilver jumped to his feet. "He's nearly *three months* away! You cannot leave now to find him."

"Why not?" Lucian growled.

"Because if we leave right now, in the middle of winter, *we will die*, Lucian. All right? We'll die. I don't care how strong your magic is, or how stubborn you are, winter out there *will* kill you!" Quicksilver stepped back, putting the chair between himself and Lucian.

"And Chance is out there." Lucian's gaze never left Quicksilver.

"Chance is comatose. He's not 'out' anywhere. He's lying on a bed, in shelter, with plenty of food, water, and heat, under the extremely competent care of his daughter the healer. *Chance* is as fine as he can possibly *be*, Lucian!"

Lucian closed his eyes and slowly let out his breath. "Chance is safe?"

"Chance is safe." Quicksilver cast a look around the room. "And from the looks of things, you're safe too, and you have people who are going to worry about you and might object a little to you taking off without warning or explanation."

"I need to find Chance. That's explanation," Lucian countered.

Quicksilver's jaw tightened. "Did you not hear the 'leave now and we will die' part?"

The trouble, Cylin realized, was that Quicksilver was trying to argue with logic, and logic was clearly the last thing Lucian cared to hear. She stepped in front of Lucian and planted her hands on her hips. "What do you think's going to happen to Chance if you freeze or starve somewhere before you reach him, Lucian? You think he'd just wake up and be okay? Or would he blame himself for you doing something so stupid?"

Lucian stopped and gave her a hard look.

Cylin met his gaze and held her ground.

He scowled at her. "What? Should I do nothing? Pretend I don't *finally* have a way to find him?"

"You should make actual *plans*, Lucian. Like how to get there with all your fingers and toes, and how to make sure Forest Town can survive for months without you," she retorted.

Devin glanced aside. "Assuming you come back here at all."

That finally snapped Lucian firmly back to the present. "Of course I'll come back."

"Why would you?" Devin said. "You'll have Chance and the rest of your people. You won't need some crippled human hanging around." His tone was hard, bitter, and he refused to meet Lucian's eyes.

"This is my home and you are my friend, not 'some cripple'," Lucian said. "I *will* come back, and I'll bring Chance, Eria, and anyone else we find."

Quicksilver watched Devin. "Lucian, I'm sure that sounded good in your head, but I don't think it's quite as reassuring as you think it is."

Devin's afraid that Lucian will leave forever.

"I won't abandon anyone, Devin. Not Chance, not you, and not Forest Town," Lucian promised.

"And if bone men or bandits attack while you're gone?" Devin demanded.

"Then you'll deal with them without me. Isn't that what Cylin has been teaching the last couple months?"

Is this why he was so quick to take up the idea of me teaching people to protect themselves? How long has Lucian been planning his departure?

Devin's jaw tightened and he still didn't meet Lucian's gaze. "Fine. You're going to go find Chance. Guess that's all that really matters anyway." He turned and limped out of the infirmary without another word.

Silence filled the room in his absence. Quicksilver finally

broke it. "Hey, Lucian, I don't know anything about that guy, or any of his history, but I'm pretty sure that somehow, in some way, you just fucked up."

Lucian cast him a glare. "Thank you so much for that astute observation, Quicksilver."

Cylin waited, but Lucian didn't move. "So. Are you going to talk to Devin or not?"

"Most people like a little space when they're upset," Lucian said.

"Yeah, well, most people aren't thinking they're a temporary replacement for your real friends, either."

"Devin is not a 'temporary replacement' for anyone!"

Cylin didn't blink. "Not me you have to convince, Lucian."

His jaw tightened. Without a word, Lucian left the room in a storm cloud of frustration and anger.

Quicksilver watched him go. "Wow. Uncanny. He looked *just* like his father right then."

Doctor Kinnel cleared his throat. "Cylin, it appears that Quicksilver will be staying in Forest Town for the winter. Would you mind showing him around?"

Cylin cast the doctor a look. "Yeah, I kind of would mind right now."

"I can look around on my own," Quicksilver offered. "As long as no one's going to shoot at me."

Doctor Kinnel gave Cylin a pointed look. She heaved a sigh. "Fine."

As they stepped outside, Quicksilver spoke in a quiet, apologetic voice. "I really didn't mean to make trouble."

"Well, you've succeeded pretty well in doing so," Cylin told him.

"I didn't expect to find Lucian living with humans. Are Cilvi, Tash, and Sun here as well?"

"Who?" She eyed Quicksilver.

"Cilvi is Lucian's wife. Tash is a close friend of his, and Sun is Tash's wife." He paused and closed his eyes a moment. "But I guess you asking the question answers mine."

"Lucian told me that Cilvi died. The other names I don't know," Cylin said.

Quicksilver's face pinched. "If they were here, I'm sure you'd know. Since they aren't... they're probably dead." He drew a deep breath and let it out slowly. "I knew it was possible, but all of them..."

They walked a little way. Quicksilver looked up to the trees and finally broke the silence with an obvious change of subject. "So... how many people live here?"

"About a hundred and fifty, give or take," Cylin said. "The number fluctuates depending on how often new people come, and if they stay."

"Well, it's not the easiest place to find, but if it's safe, sheltered, and has clean land and water—and I know the Guardian wouldn't settle for less—it seems like an ideal place to stay," Quicksilver said. "Why do they leave?"

She raised an eyebrow. "You're related to Lucian, and you're asking that?"

"Oh." Quicksilver considered that. "So, I'm guessing he's pretty open about being an elf?"

"He told me on my first day here. I thought he was insane."

"But you stayed," he said.

"I decided three meals a day was worth hanging around for a little while. Then a little while became longer and longer. Some other stuff happened, and I finally settled on staying," Cylin said.

"Other stuff?" Quicksilver asked.

"Yes, 'other stuff.' That's personal."

"Ah, sorry."

She eyed him. "Sorry that you asked, or sorry that I won't tell you?"

Quicksilver smiled. "I don't really see it as an either/or sort of answer."

"So, sorry that I won't tell you," Cylin said.

"Sorry that we have clearly gotten off on the wrong foot," Quicksilver said. "Really. I am sorry about that. If there's anything I can do…"

Cylin made a sound of irritation, and Quicksilver cut himself short. She gave him a long, hard look. "Forest Town has been here for decades, with Lucian in charge. He *is* the lord of Forest Town, and people have gotten pretty damned used to knowing that they're safe, and that if something bad happens, or bandits show up, Lucian will take care of it. You have no idea how absolutely terrifying and devastating it will be to them here to find out that he plans to *leave*, and won't be back for months, even a year or more. Given that your arrival is the trigger for that decision, are you prepared to be a target when they want someone to blame?"

"Oh." Quicksilver considered the question. "Well, I can't really fault them if they do." He eyed her. "Is that why you don't like me?"

"No, I don't like you because you remind me of every pompous twit I've ever met. The ones who strut around like they own the place because their father is someone important, so they act all fake-friendly with everyone and collect fawning followers who tell them how wonderful they are."

Quicksilver blinked at her. "I remind you of *that*? Well… shit." He paused. "Um, if you don't mind my asking, Cylin, how many *genuinely* friendly people have you met?"

"People your age? Not many before I came here," she answered.

Quicksilver quickly stifled a laugh. "Sorry. Just I, uh, hope you haven't actually met that many people my age. But I'll assume you mean the age I look, instead. Please, ask Lucian to confirm this, but I'm not one to fake friendliness. I much prefer to be genuinely nice. I'm not trying to get anything out of it, although it does help me not get shot at, most of the time." He looked around. "So, your infirmary is back there, the town well is here, houses are in the trees, and Lucian lives somewhere up that way... what else should I know about Forest Town?"

She remembered that she was supposed to be showing him around. "Bath house is over there, where you see the steam."

"Bath house? Oh, *that* sounds nice," Quicksilver said, perking up. "Though I really shouldn't be surprised to find one in a place where Lucian lives."

"Oh, are you also one of the 'swims wherever possible' elves?" Cylin asked.

"It seems to be in the blood," he said. "Yeah, I am, though not as devoted to it as Lucian or his father. And I've been traveling for months straight. A bath sounds really, really nice. And a hot bath, even better. I know Lucian will swim in glacial melt, but I prefer water that won't turn my toes blue."

"Weavers and tailors work over there," Cylin told him, pointing. "We also have fields and animals further up the trail, past Lucian's cave."

"What about shops? Stores? A trading post?" Quicksilver asked.

"Not really." Which, when she thought about it, was a little strange. "People trade and barter with each other, mostly."

"Huh. I suppose when you don't have any outside sources of supplies, that makes the most sense."

"Anything with metal, and most things with wood, Lucian makes," Cylin added.

Quicksilver pursed his lips. "Right. I can see why that will make his departure a challenge for everyone."

Lucian emerged from Devin's house. He looked worn and tired, serious. Descending the steps to the ground, he nodded to Cylin and Quicksilver. "Cylin, would you mind checking on Devin later? Not right now—he needs some time."

"Sure, Lucian. I can do that."

"Come up to the cave with me, Quick. Tell me everything that's happened."

Quicksilver nodded quickly. "Of course." He turned to Cylin with a smile of apology. "If you have any questions for me, just ask."

Lucian raised an eyebrow at him. "Flirting already?"

"Nope! I think Cylin would shoot me if I tried. Just trying to negotiate a truce," Quicksilver answered. He followed Lucian up the path toward the cave.

Cylin watched them go, then finally climbed back to her own home to warm up and mull the implications of this new arrival. And of Lucian's coming departure.

By afternoon, everyone knew about Quicksilver, and rumors ran rampant through the branches. Every sentry who'd been on duty in the early morning hours reported to Cylin to apologize for their failure to notice his approach, promising to be more attentive. The thought that someone malicious could have easily slipped by them finally reinforced the ideas she'd been trying to instill since taking charge of the village defenses.

She found Devin still at home. He opened the door when she knocked, and didn't look surprised to see her. He also looked exhausted, and let her in without a word.

"He's going to come back," Cylin said, closing the door behind her.

Devin's shoulders slumped. "He says he will, but why would he?"

"Because it's his home, Devin. And seriously, if he won't tell a crying child 'it's going to be okay' to comfort her, do you really think he would lie about something *this* important? Have you *ever* caught Lucian lying?"

"No," Devin admitted. "But he might not think it's a lie right now. What if Chance convinces him not to return?" He sat in a chair and waved Cylin toward the other.

She sat. "Then I expect Lucian will pick him up by the collar and carry him back here in an attempt to convince him of how good it is."

Despite himself, Devin laughed. "I... yeah, I could see Lord Lucian doing that."

"He won't abandon his friends. Even if we are human."

Devin bit his lip, then burst, "But what does Lord Lucian really *know* about living outside the forest? He's never been gone longer than a week in *forty years*! We know his quirks, but out there? What happens when he runs into a warlord and objects to the local rules? Or comes to a place where the bone men work openly? When he casually uses magic in front of someone?" He swallowed hard. "What happens when he has an episode out there?"

That was a horrifying thought, but watching Devin's eyes, she realized there was more. For the first time, Devin faced the realization that Lucian was not invincible or infallible. What could she say to that? "Did you tell him that?"

Devin shook his head. "Of course not."

"Of course not," Cylin sighed. "Devin, would you really rather he think you believe he would abandon his home and his friends? Is that actually better than telling him that you're worried about him?"

"I... no. But how can I tell him that after I... well... said some things I shouldn't have said?"

"Well, first, you give yourself some time to rest and think about it," Cylin said. "Which means you don't try to talk to him until tomorrow, after you've slept. And then you walk up to the cave and say something like 'Hey, Lucian, can I talk to you?'"

"I don't want to talk about this around Quicksilver," Devin said.

"Then tell Quicksilver to leave. Tell him I have questions for him." She didn't know that she wanted to subject herself to more of Quicksilver, but Devin needed to have this talk with Lucian.

Devin cast her a sidelong look. "*Do* you have questions for him?"

"Plenty of them. Though he might call it more of an interrogation than a friendly chat. What do you know about him?"

"Not a whole lot. He's Lord Lucian's nephew, and he never comes up when Lord Lucian is having an episode, so he doesn't seem to have any connection to... that. He and Chance's daughter are good friends. I don't remember Lord Lucian saying anything particularly bad about him."

Cylin nodded. "I guess that's good. At least, better than someone who's going to create trouble with Lucian. I don't trust him, but I'll try to give him a fair chance."

"All right. Then... tomorrow morning, I'll go talk to Lucian." Devin didn't look happy with the idea, but he agreed to it, and that was sufficient for Cylin.

The sun was barely risen and Cylin was still nursing a mug of tea when someone knocked on her door. When she opened it, she found Quicksilver standing on the landing, smiling pleasantly.

"Good morning! Devin wants to talk to Lucian without any spying ears around, so I got tossed out of a nice warm bed and into the cold with instructions that you want to talk to me."

He was fully dressed, with thick coat and hat, so clearly he'd had *some* time between getting up and leaving the cave. Cylin stepped aside. "Come in, then. You're letting the heat out."

He entered and shed his winter gear. Underneath, he wore a long-sleeved woven shirt and denim pants. His shoes were utterly impractical for slogging through snow, but appeared perfectly dry.

"Do you want tea?" Cylin asked. "The water's hot."

"If it's no trouble," Quicksilver said. "Even just plain hot water would be fine."

"I can offer mint, ginger, or juniper tea," Cylin said. "What's your preference?"

"Mint, please." He sat at the table while she fixed a mug for him.

After a moment, something occurred to Cylin. She set the mug of tea in front of Quicksilver, frowning. "Did Lucian tell you where my house was?"

"Kind of. He told me to look for one of the most recent ones, only one in its tree, with a view of the entrances. I narrowed it down pretty quickly from that description."

"How would you know what houses are more recent than others?" Cylin sat again.

"The magic feels fresher," Quicksilver said. Seeing her expression, he shrugged. "I don't have good words to explain it. Magic is like... an extra sense, and trying to describe it is kind of like trying to describe light to a blind person. It's just *there*, and it's always been there, but you don't have the refer- ence points I can use. But this house definitely feels fresher and newer to my sense of magic. More so than the rest of the village, or even the forest in general."

"The forest in general has a feel?" Cylin asked.

"Oh, sure! It's nice; really familiar. I like being back surrounded by the... essential Lucian-ness of it."

"The essential 'Lucian-ness' of this forest?" Cylin repeated.

"Sorry, I'm not very good at describing metaphysical concepts," Quicksilver said.

"And what *are* you good at describing?" she asked.

"Breasts."

"*Excuse* me?!"

"I tend to think I'm very good at describing them, and I've never gotten any complaints from any woman who's let me study hers, and... and that's *definitely* not the answer you were looking for."

"No, it isn't," she agreed dryly.

"Sorry." Quicksilver looked abashed. "Right, anyway, where were we? Metaphysical conversation about the essence of Lucian and how it permeates this forest, right? Right."

"And it's familiar."

Quicksilver nodded. "Lucian's magic is stronger than a lot of elves, and he certainly has more abilities than most. Like, sure, I can fly, and manipulate plants, but shaping rock or metal? That's nothing I can do. Lucian gets it from his father. And... well, and from his mother, too." He paused. "Um... do you know much of Lucian's family history?"

"Some," she replied cautiously. "I know he and Chance are very close. He was married to a woman named Cilvi, who died after the war."

Quicksilver shook his head. "Yeah, no, that's not really the part I mean. Um, how about this: would it mean anything to you if I said that my mom is Lucian's sister?"

"*What?*" Cylin slammed her mug down hard enough to spill Quicksilver's tea.

"Right, *that's* the part I wondered if you knew," he said.

Her voice dropped to a hiss. "Your mother is *Ayliad?*"

"It wasn't *my* idea! I definitely did not ask for an incestuous nymphomaniac for a mother." He pushed back from the table as if worried she might lunge at him.

"Then who's your father?" Cylin demanded.

"Someone unrelated, thank the Tree. One of her harem of pretty boys." He gave her a tight, wry smile. "Obviously, you know some of the messy side of the family story."

"I know about Ayliad, and a little about Willow."

Quicksilver winced. "Yeah, dear old Grandmother. She

was..." He shuddered. "It's a good thing she's dead. She hurt a lot of people, especially in our family."

"I got that impression, yeah," Cylin said.

"Did you know I have two half-brothers?" Quicksilver asked.

"No. From which side?"

"Oh, I have no idea if my father spawned any other offspring. My mother had twins, years before I was born." He paused and swallowed hard. "Their father is Chance."

She remembered Lucian's ravings during his episode. "I'm going to take a wild guess here that Chance's wishes weren't considered in the matter."

"That's got to be one of the politest ways of saying it I've ever heard. And from everything I know, Chance's wishes were about the last thing she cared about. Being told 'no' just made her more determined." Quicksilver shivered. "Yeah, our family is so messed up. I should just be glad I'm not my own uncle or something."

"Your own... how would that even..."

"Don't ask. Just don't even ask," Quicksilver said. "Because if I think too hard about it, I could figure out who my mother could have fucked to make that happen, and that's not something I want to ponder."

"Lucian knows this, right?"

"That I'm Ayliad's child? Yes, absolutely. He's known for a long time. Things were pretty unpleasant when he first found out, but he worked it out. Probably helped that I was younger than you are at the time. And I mean, actual age, which is really young for an elf. We don't consider someone an adult until they're at least a hundred years old." He shifted uncomfortably. "So is this something Lucian actually talks about? Family and all that entails?"

Does he know about Lucian's episodes? If he doesn't, how much would Lucian want me to say? "No, not usually. Only when he's having… a bad day."

She saw no look of understanding, no acknowledgment that he knew just how bad a "bad day" could be. "That sounds ominous. Is that something I'll need to worry about while we're traveling?"

"I don't know," Cylin told him. "Maybe. You should ask him about it. It's his business to tell, not mine."

Quicksilver looked like he wanted to argue, but held his tongue. "All right. I'll ask him."

Cylin finished her tea. "So, did you get that bath you were lusting over yesterday?"

"Not yet. Is it all right if I go down there? Do you have more questions for me first?"

"You can go," Cylin told him. "Try not to make trouble."

"I rarely *try* to make trouble," he protested. "It finds me all on its own." He sipped the last of his tea. "Thank you for the tea, and for not shooting me yesterday. Lucian told me you're in charge of the village defenses, so I do realize you could have done so when you saw me wandering into the village without alerting any of your sentries."

Cylin frowned. "Did you see them?"

He hesitated, then nodded. "Yeah, I noticed them, and avoided them. I thought they might belong to a bandit camp or something."

"Did you encounter many on your way here?" She knew she was delaying him from going to the bath house, but her interest was piqued now.

Quicksilver grimaced. "Bandits, plenty of petty warlords, a few near misses with bone men. The world's a lot uglier than it used to be. But you know that already."

"I do, but Lucian hasn't been far from the forest since he arrived," Cylin said. "He *doesn't* know what it's like out there—not as much as he probably thinks he does."

"Oh." Quicksilver pursed his lips. "That's... good to know. I'll have to rethink our return route. As you might have noticed, subtlety isn't one of Lucian's strongest skills."

"I have noticed that, yes," Cylin agreed. "Obviously you know about the Guardian—do you know about the Ghost?"

Quicksilver had started to stand, but froze partway up. "The Ghost? You mean when Lucian hits an emotional flatline so he can take care of whatever needs done, and damn the consequences?"

"I would have described it more as muting most emotions except those needed in the immediate moment," Cylin said. "But you do know about it."

"Yeah." Quicksilver shivered. "The times I've seen him go Ghost were, by and large, terrifying. He doesn't make a habit of that, does he?"

Cylin shook her head. "I haven't seen it often."

"Well, that's a relief." Quicksilver smiled. He stood and pushed in the chair. "I'm going to run off to the bath now, before something else comes up. But if you need anything from me, I'll do my best to oblige."

He left her home and made his way to the bath house, cheerfully greeting townspeople as if they were old friends.

He hasn't been here two days, and he's making friends faster than I have my whole time in Forest Town. By the time he's done in the bath house, he'll probably have every teenage boy in town mimicking him. She considered. *Maybe my comparison of Quicksilver to some warlord's son isn't that far off after all. He has the same air that attracts a lot of people.*

And his mother is one of Lucian's worst nightmares.

~

No fresh disasters befell Forest Town during the afternoon. Quicksilver set about befriending everyone he could, as if chatting with strangers came naturally to him.

To Cylin's surprise, despite her initial impression, the usually open and welcoming people of the town remained cautious of his overtures, responding politely, but not warmly. For his part, Quicksilver appeared undeterred by the less than enthusiastic welcome. When she thought about it, Cylin realized that even a lukewarm Forest Town welcome was still more friendly than a lot of places would be. She wondered whether Quicksilver could tell that he was being snubbed.

Cylin's afternoon training session, primarily meant for those involved in town defense, but open to anyone, got more attendees than she'd seen since she first took charge of Forest Town defenses. At first she wondered why Quicksilver's arrival triggered the resurgence in caution. But when she listened to the talk between others, the answer became more clear. Opinions about Lucian's nephew ran that while he acted friendly enough, neither Cylin nor Devin trusted him, and that was enough to make the rest of Forest Town uneasy.

When did my opinion become important enough that an entire town questions a newcomer because of it?

When dusk fell, she knocked on Devin's door. She hadn't noticed him return from Lucian's cave, but lights were on inside, and he answered the door. "Hi Cylin. Come in."

"Hey. Wanted to check on you. How did your talk with Lucian go?" She stepped inside and closed the door.

Devin shrugged. "It... went. I think he listened when I told him I was worried, and about the dangers outside the forest. And... I apologized for what I said yesterday. I know he'll come back." He sighed. "Just, when I think about him leaving, a part of me wonders whether someone's going to try to sell me to the bone men again without him to stop them."

"That won't happen," Cylin said firmly. "I'll shoot anyone who tries."

He blinked, startled. "You would?"

"I will. And as much as the rest of the town respects you

and me, I think most anyone else would do the same. Fuck, they're ready to distrust Quicksilver just because we don't like him."

Devin blinked again. "Oh." Then, "Really? Are you sure?"

"Well, I don't know what sensible person thinks I'm a good judge of character, but yeah, I'm sure. People were talking about it all day." Cylin laughed softly. "So does that sound as weird to you as it does to me?"

He just nodded. After a long moment, he said, "If that's true, does that mean that people will also expect us to take charge when Lord Lucian is gone?"

"Gods of my father's hearth, I hope not!" Cylin said quickly. But once the thought began to take shape, she couldn't dismiss it. "I think Doctor Kinnel would be better. Although you've been around Lucian more than most people. I could see them thinking you'd have a good idea what decisions he'd make."

"And you're in charge of the village defenses," Devin said. "I think we'd better at least think about it."

"Not tonight," Cylin told him. "If I think about it tonight, I might just run off and never come back."

Devin finally smiled. "Take me with you if you do."

She held out her hand. "All right. It's a deal. If I run off in the middle of the night, you can come too."

He took her hand and they shook on it.

~

Lucian came down to Forest Town the following morning. As if drawn by instinct, people paused in their work, emerging from houses and buildings to gather around him. Cylin stood on her balcony, leaning on the railing and watching him. Lucian cast a look up her direction and waved in greeting. She waved back, but didn't join the throng on the ground. Her perch offered a better view.

Lucian smiled at the people gathered around him. "I'm sure you've all heard that my nephew, Quicksilver, got here a few days ago. And I'm sure you're wondering why, and how things are going to change. Rest assured, right now you'll notice very little difference. Maybe some more activity at times, and I'll need to consult with people on various matters, finalize some plans."

"Plans for what?" someone asked uncertainly.

Lucian's smile widened. "Plans for other surviving members of my family to join us in Forest Town."

People murmured in surprise and excitement. Cylin leaned on the railing, catching snatches of the conversations. Lucian stood calm and smiling amid the crowd.

She felt a light vibration on her platform. Cylin spun, reaching toward her gun. Quicksilver stood on the platform, although she stood between him and the stairs to the ground.

"Sorry to trespass," he apologized. "May I join you?"

"How did you get here?" she demanded. "Fly?"

"Yes?" He answered tentatively, as if unsure she would believe him.

"Figures." Cylin scowled, then sighed. "Well, you're here, so I guess you can stay."

"Thanks."

Below, Lucian continued. "I know I'll be asking a lot of everyone, to welcome more elves among us. But most of all, I will be asking your patience, even when things seem chaotic and confused."

People quickly shouted their agreement, their unquestioning devotion to Lucian. He bowed to them and withdrew back toward his cave.

"No mention of a months-long absence, I notice," Cylin said under her breath.

Quicksilver watched Lucian leave and frowned. "What is he up to?"

"What do you mean?" she asked. "What did you hear that I didn't?"

"It's not what he said so much as how he said it," Quicksilver answered. He paused to glance around, as if someone might have snuck up to spy on them. "I think Lucian's going to do something reckless and stupid." He cupped his hands over his mouth and blew on them.

Cylin motioned for him to follow her. The wind blowing through the trees had a bite to it, and she didn't fancy lingering in it. Once they were sheltered in the warmth of her home, Cylin asked, "Reckless how? What sort of thing would Lucian do?"

"I don't know! I don't see very many things he could do here, but we're talking about Lucian, so I *know* he'll find something, and if I can't predict it, I have no idea how to prepare for it. There are no 'sensible' limits when we're talking about Lucian trying to find Chance."

Cylin hung her coat on a peg. "So... what, should I expect the forest to uproot itself and start walking toward wherever Chance is, Forest Town and all?"

"Stars above, *please* don't suggest that to Lucian! I'm not sure if he or the Guardian *could* do that, but he'd try." Quicksilver ran a hand through his silver hair. "I just hate not knowing what he's going to attempt. Any chance you could try to get the answer out of him?"

"Me?" Cylin blinked. "Why do you think I would be able to if you can't?"

"Well, you seem to be close to him, and he trusts you." Quicksilver hesitated. "Um, can I ask a personal and kind of inappropriate question?"

I should have known this was coming. "The answer to your question is no," Cylin said.

He blinked. "Don't I get to ask it first?"

She folded her arms. "You were going to ask if I'm having sex with Lucian. The answer to that question is no. But if I'm wrong, and you have some *other* personal and invasive question, go ahead and ask."

He blinked again. "Uh... no, that was the one. Sorry." He paused. "How did you know?"

"I've been asked that before, by other people in town. Honestly, some have been pretty disappointed when I said no. Like they think everything would be better if he just got laid."

A startled laugh from Quicksilver. "They might be right, you know. Elves tend to be more open about sex than humans. But actually, the reason I thought you might be is because you treat him differently than everyone else does. You're much more relaxed when talking to him or about him. You are the *only* person I've heard who doesn't call him 'Lord Lucian', you know."

"I know," she said. "I also don't worship him. I have my hearth gods; I don't need to start following the worship of 'ancient spirits'."

"Worshiping?" Quicksilver repeated. "People do that?"

"Didn't you notice, outside when he was talking?" she countered. "Yeah, people worship him."

"That must drive him nuts."

"It does. Most try to keep it out of his face." Cylin walked to the kitchen and set the kettle on the stove. "Now I have something to ask you."

"Well after my question to you, I'm a little worried, but ask away."

She turned to face him. "How old are you?"

His eyebrows in surprise. "Real answer?"

"Real answer."

"I am one thousand, six hundred, and fifty-seven years old."

"And you look seventeen."

He shrugged. "I don't understand the science of it. I'm pretty sure that the rules as humans know them don't exactly apply to us elves. We grow up, but we don't... get *old* like humans do. It's more like... we physically mature to our 'ideal' age and appearance—when that is varies by individual—and just... stop. So yeah, I've looked like this for most of my life. Lucian too. He's looked about the age he appears now for as long as I've known him."

Cylin gazed at him, trying to guess whether or not he was lying. "How does that even work?"

"I have no idea, honestly. I didn't go to college or anything like that, so I just know what I picked up through life. Chance and Lucian took some time to attend one of the universities, though."

"Really?" Cylin frowned, wondering why a thousand-year-old elf would bother. "Wasn't that supposed to be expensive?"

Quicksilver chuckled. "When you can pull gold straight out of the rocks, money isn't really a problem. It was Chance's idea. He wants to know everything—he did something like a triple major." Seeing Cylin's puzzled expression, he explained, "Three different fields of study, at the same time. Lucian took a slightly less overachieving route with one major field of study and two minor ones, but he also competed in a couple sports."

"Swimming?" Cylin asked.

"Of course." Quicksilver chuckled. "I don't remember what the other one was."

She filled the kettle with water. "You want tea?"

Quicksilver lounged in one of the living room chairs. "Sure, that sounds—what the *fuck*?!" He launched out of the chair, nearly hit the ceiling, and apparently forgot that he was supposed to come back to the ground.

Cylin dropped the kettle in the sink and raced to him. "What?"

Quicksilver's head turned as if he was watching something beyond the walls of her house. Color drained from his face. "Shit. What is he... shit."

Cylin grabbed Quicksilver's arm and jerked him down eye level with her. "Quicksilver, what did Lucian do?"

He swallowed hard. "He... he did... something really stupid." Quicksilver glanced around, then scrambled to the door and grabbed both his coat and Cylin's. He tossed her to her. "We... um... we better get up there."

Cylin caught her coat and pulled it on, checked that the stove wasn't going to burn her house down, and hurried outside. She started toward the stairs, but Quicksilver caught her arm. "No time for that, Cylin. I'll get us there faster."

She had just a moment to be confused by his words, then her feet left the ground. Cylin yelped, then bit her lip to stop a more forceful objection. Quicksilver's hold on her arm was firm, but not restrictive. She fought an impulse to pull away, not sure whether he required the contact to hold her aloft. They rose over the railing and flew toward Lucian's cave. Cylin glanced down and immediately regretted it. Her legs hung over empty air, the ground much too far below. Wind whipped in her face.

We're flying. Shit, we're actually flying. Flying very fast, and it's a long way down. Her stomach twisted into knots.

Quicksilver landed in front of Lucian's cave. Devin, sitting just inside the mouth of the cave, jumped to his feet with startled obscenities and stared at them.

"Sorry, no time for courtesies!" Quicksilver told him. "Where's Lucian?"

Devin's mouth opened and closed twice before he managed to answer. "Inside. He said he was going to take care of a few things and didn't want to be disturbed."

"Dammit, Lucian," Quicksilver snarled. "No time for explanation. Lucian just did something really stupid and dangerous, and I need to stop him." He rushed past Devin into the cave.

Devin glanced to Cylin. She shook her head. "I don't know what happened either, but if Lucian's doing something, we might need to interrupt it."

Devin bit his lip, then nodded. "All right. But I'm going with you."

They trailed Quicksilver deeper into the cave, finally catching up with him at Lucian's bedroom.

Cylin hadn't been in this room since Lucian's episode. It stood in order now, no sign of the chaos that had dominated it then. The furniture was neat and whole. Clothes hung on hooks in the wall. Lucian lay on the bed, a single cover drawn over him, eyes closed and chest moving in the slow, deep rhythm of sleep. Cylin glanced to Devin, then Quicksilver.

"If all this fuss and worry is over Lucian taking a nap, I'm going to be pretty mad at you, Quicksilver," Cylin warned.

Quicksilver gave her a tight smile. "If this is just a nap, I'll happily accept you being mad at me." He crossed the room to Lucian and shook his shoulder. "Hey, Lucian, wake up."

Lucian didn't respond. His breathing didn't even change. Cylin and Devin joined Quicksilver around the bed.

Quicksilver pulled one of Lucian's eyelids up. Instead of being rolled back in sleep, Lucian's eyes stared blankly, an empty, hollow gaze.

Quicksilver stood perfectly still for a long moment, then cursed rapidly in languages Cylin didn't recognize.

"Lord Lucian?" Devin shook Lucian's shoulder, as if he could succeed where Quicksilver had not. He turned sharply to Quicksilver. "What did he do?"

"Shit." Quicksilver sank down on the floor. He let out a heavy breath. "Shit. Lucian sent his essence into the spirit realm."

"Wait, wait, he did *what*?!" Cylin interrupted. "How? No,

never mind, don't try to answer that. I'm sure it's some elf magic thing."

"Most elves can't either," Quicksilver said quietly. "That's limited to the most powerful. I can barely see the edges of the spirit realm when I really try; I'm certainly not able to separate my spirit from my body to go wander around out there." He shuddered. "It was dangerous to do even before the war tore things to shreds. Now that place is filled with monsters and twisted souls of tormented dead elves and worse. Things lurking out there can shred a soul to pieces, and they're always hungry. Lucian's powerful enough that he's like a giant beacon in the middle of the night. *Everything* will go racing toward that, and he's there alone! If something attacks him out there, hurts him badly enough, he might not come back!"

Devin stared at Lucian, as pale as Quicksilver. "Is he..." He gulped, then spun to Cylin. "Doctor Kinnel! You have to get him! He'll know what to do!"

Quicksilver shook his head. "I don't know what a human doctor could do—"

"He can!" Devin insisted. "Cylin, please."

"Right. I'll get him." She had no more idea than Quicksilver what Doctor Kinnel could do to help Lucian, but she needed to do *something*.

The trip from Lucian's cave to the infirmary passed in a blur. She walked quickly without quite breaking into run, as much to avoid attracting attention as to avoid slipping. Cylin rushed inside and breathed a sigh of relief to find the waiting area empty. "Doctor Kinnel?"

He emerged from the kitchen, a mug of tea in hand. "Is someone injured, Cylin? Did someone fall?"

She shook her head, glancing around again to confirm they were alone. "Something's wrong with Lucian."

"What? He appeared fine when he was down here earlier.

An episode? No, you wouldn't come to me for that." Doctor Kinnel motioned her to follow him. "Tell me more."

She entered the small kitchen, but didn't sit. "Quicksilver said that Lucian sent his mind into the spirit realm."

"That idiot!" Doctor Kinnel slammed his mug down on the table. "Lucian knows better!"

She'd never heard him speak of Lucian without the honorific before. Cylin blinked. "So you... know something about this?"

"Describe his state," Doctor Kinnel ordered.

"He looked like he was sleeping, but when Quicksilver opened his eyes, Lucian was staring off at nothing. He didn't stir at all."

"That idiot," Doctor Kinnel repeated. He began opening cupboards and pulling out jars and bottles. "Fetch the gray duffel from the infirmary. It's on the top shelf of the tall metal cabinet with doors."

Only one metal cabinet in the infirmary had doors. Cylin found the gray bag and pulled it down, disturbing a cloud of dust. It was heavier than she expected, and clanked like it contained pieces of metal. She brushed some of the dust off and brought it into the kitchen.

"This one? What's inside?" She laid the duffel on the kitchen table.

"The tools I used *last* time he did this." Doctor Kinnel set a collection of small bottles on the table, holding each one up to the light to check its contents. "How long ago did he leave?"

"Less than an hour," she told him. "Do you know how to bring him back? Quicksilver said he couldn't do it."

The doctor carefully slid each bottle into loops on his belt. He gave her a faint smile. "I told you that my parents and I lived for a time in the jungle. After I saw the elf who was guardian of the village, the high priest took it on himself to teach me a great deal of very, very old lore about the 'ancient spirits'. I was the first outsider initiated into their arts. Much of it was rituals for appeasing angry spirits, or asking for blessings, but the teachings also included ailments suffered by spirits and how to treat them. Lucian has proven that the tales carry truth. Fortunately for him." Doctor Kinnel pulled on his coat and hefted his gear. Cylin followed him out of the infirmary.

To Cylin's relief, no one expressed concern at seeing the doctor leave, and people gave little attention to his route. The last thing Cylin wanted was for rumors to begin about Lucian falling ill. She offered the doctor a steadying hand up the slick slope, much as she wanted to urge him faster. Just inside the cave, Devin met them, shifting restlessly from foot to foot.

"You can bring Lucian back, can't you Doctor?" Devin asked in a rush.

"I'll do my best," Doctor Kinnel said. "Lucian is in his room, I assume? Good. Devin, fill a gallon bucket with snow, and another with warm water."

"Yes sir!" Devin scrambled to obey.

In Lucian's room, Quicksilver paced. He greeted the doctor with a quick nod. "No changes. He's still… out there somewhere."

"Do you know of any narcotics, alcohol, or other drugs in the caves?" Doctor Kinnel asked him.

Quick blinked. "Uh… he's got some whiskey stashed away in the back."

"Bring a bottle." The doctor set his bag down on the floor beside a small stone table.

Quicksilver's eyebrows rose in question, but he left the room. Cylin looked to Lucian, as if he might have woken in the brief time no one was watching him. He still lay in apparent slumber.

Doctor Kinnel pulled a chair to the table and sank into it with a tired grunt. He opened the duffel and pulled out metal rods. Cylin watched him assemble a tripod. A blackened metal pan at the base seemed meant to hold a small fire. The doctor pulled a brass bowl the size of his cupped hands from the bag and held it to her.

"When Devin returns, wash this twice in the warm water, then once with snow."

A faint sheen of residue clung to the insides of the bowl. Around the outside, she could barely distinguish figures cast in the worn metal. Some danced, others knelt and raised their arms in supplication to looming forms. "What's this?"

"A sacred ritual bowl, passed down for generations from priest to priest," Doctor Kinnel said. "It was given to me upon completion of my training."

Cylin stopped. "You're a *priest* of a faith that calls Lucian and Quicksilver gods?"

"I am," he said simply. "And that training has served me well over the years. Though I do not call either of our resident elves 'gods', nor offer them worship." He continued assembling the tripod.

Devin entered, pulling two large buckets on a wheeled dolly. He brought them to the table and stopped, panting. Steam rose from one, and the other was piled high with snow. "Is this enough? I can get more."

Doctor Kinnel turned and nodded approval. "That's plenty. Thank you. Sit and rest."

Cylin looked at the buckets. "Am I supposed to dunk this in the water, or use a cloth or something to wash it?"

The doctor fished a square of cloth from his pocket. "Use this. And fully immerse the bowl when you wash it."

The water in the steaming bucket was pleasantly warm, not too hot. Cylin used the kerchief to remove the residue during the first and second wash. It clung to the cloth and bowl both, and she scrubbed hard to clean it off. The snow, now turning to slush, melted faster when she set the warm bowl in it. Heat rapidly leached away, and her fingers stung with cold when she set the clean bowl on the table.

Quicksilver returned carrying one of the bottles scavenged from the bandits' trucks. "Sorry! Took longer than I thought to find them." He paused and eyed Doctor Kinnel's setup. "What's this?"

Doctor Kinnel motioned for Quicksilver to set the bottle on the table. "It is the Ritual of Waking, to be administered to spirits who become lost while Dreamwalking."

"I'm pretty sure I never heard of *that* being taught in medical school," Quicksilver said. "Even at the ones that were pretty... out there."

The doctor poured careful drops of liquid from his vials into the bowl. "No, I learned this ritual when I was initiated as a priest of the Calinao faith at the age of fifteen."

Quicksilver's mouth formed a silent "oh."

Uncertain silence filled the room as Doctor Kinnel added ingredients to the bowl, then set it atop the tripod. He emptied a small bag of compact pellets into the burner pan and lit them with a hand-held lighter. As the mixture heated, he murmured soft words in a language Cylin didn't know. When steam rose from the bowl, he opened the whiskey bottle and poured a shot into a measuring glass, then carefully added that to the mixture. The sharp tang of alcohol joined less familiar scents, like a market filled with exotic spices.

Devin shifted restlessly, and finally sat in a chair. Quicksilver watched Doctor Kinnel with rapt attention. Cylin glanced over to Lucian and wondered just how a bowl of hot whiskey and scented oils was supposed to bring him back.

Doctor Kinnel said it worked before. And I don't have any better ideas.

The doctor's words more clearly became a chant. She could almost hum their cadence. The doctor lifted the bowl by its edges and stood. Cylin followed him to Lucian's bed and, without thinking about it, held out her hands in silent offer.

He gave her the briefest nod of thanks and rested the bowl in her hands. It was uncomfortably warm, but not burning hot. Doctor Kinnel dipped his fingers in the liquid and applied the mixture to Lucian's face. It left rust colored streaks on Lucian's tan skin. First, three straight lines on his forehead, then half-circles under his eyes. Two straight lines on either cheek, another down his nose. The doctor continued chanting, and when the first lines dried, he applied more. Cylin caught herself whispering the most frequently repeated words in the chant, though she had no idea what they meant.

What's this supposed to do? Is this a waste of time? Cylin looked to Doctor Kinnel. Though his chant held steady, sweat dripped down his face, and his expression was strained. His hand trembled when he began a fresh application of the lines. *What's he doing, and what's it doing to him?*

As the doctor began a fourth application, Lucian's cheek twitched, and he turned his head away from the doctor's hand. Quicksilver jerked to his feet with a startled yelp.

Doctor Kinnel let his stained hand fall, and his chant faded out in a long breath. "He's back."

Cylin caught him with an arm as he wavered. Devin scrambled over and took the bowl so she could guide Doctor Kinnel to a chair.

"Back and extremely not happy about it," Quicksilver said.

"Well that's his own damned fault for taking off without warning in the first place," Cylin snapped. "Are you okay, Doctor Kinnel?"

He raised a shaking hand to wave off her concern. "Such a ritual is better left to the young and hale. It's draining." He closed his eyes. "Set the bowl over the fire pan again. Let it boil dry. The fumes will prevent him from attempting to leave again for a time." He grabbed the whiskey bottle and gulped down a deep swallow.

Devin complied quickly. A moment of silence fell over the room. Then, Lucian's eyes snapped open.

He rolled from his bed to fall in a graceless sprawl on the floor. Quicksilver, Devin, and Cylin all started toward him, but Doctor Kinnel raised his hand. "Wait."

"What? But--" Devin began.

"If my experience from the previous time holds true, he will be disoriented and confused," the doctor said. "Allow him a chance to recover."

Lucian pushed up on his hands and knees, breathing hard. He raised his head, turning toward their voices. His gaze showed no recognition, like when he'd been in the throes of an episode. His lips curled back and he growled in the back of his throat.

"Lord Lucian?" Devin asked.

Lucian's gaze cleared briefly. "Out," he snarled.

Devin started toward the doorway, but paused when no one else followed. "Um…"

"I am not leaving until the bowl is empty," Doctor Kinnel said. "Come, sit down, Devin."

Devin hesitated, then returned and sat. Cylin kept an eye on Lucian, half-expecting him to use his magic to somehow force them all to leave. However, his eyes already glazed over. Abandoning his efforts to stand, Lucian lay down on the stone floor and closed his eyes again.

Quicksilver let out a breath and joined them at the table. "Whatever you did, it must have drained his magic. He should sleep for a while. Maybe until tomorrow morning."

Cylin eyed him curiously. "You're not familiar with this ritual?"

"Nope! I have no idea how it could even work. Didn't know any humans could do something like that. If another elf is powerful enough and has the right skills, they can catch someone who's gone off into the spirit realm, even drag them back to their body, but you, sir, are definitely not an elf."

Doctor Kinnel chuckled. "That I certainly am not. And I can offer you little insight as to how the rituals work, only that they seem to do so."

"Are you sure that the ritual is what brought him back?" Devin asked uncertainly. "Couldn't Lord Lucian have been coming back anyway, and it was coincidence?"

Quicksilver shook his head emphatically. "No, the ritual definitely forced him back to his body. If he'd been on his way back on his own, he wouldn't have been half as outraged as he was." He sighed and looked to Lucian. "Might be better if the rest of you aren't up here when he wakes."

"It may well be best if no one is here when he wakes," Doctor Kinnel said. "Last time, it triggered an episode."

"A what?" Quicksilver asked. "I've heard that term used once or twice, but no one wants to explain it."

"When Lucian has an 'episode', he thinks that everything and everyone is part of some mind-game his mother is playing on him," Cylin said.

Color drained from Quicksilver's face. His eyes grew wide. "He… that's…" He swallowed hard. "I… I heard that he… used to have instances of that, but… but he'd healed from that long before I ever met him, probably before I was even born. Does this… happen often?" He sounded genuinely frightened by the idea.

"Once in the time I've been here," Cylin told him. "Which has been less than a year."

Doctor Kinnel cleared his throat. "They aren't frequent, but are more likely to occur in times of high stress."

"But what do you do? How do you treat them?" Quicksilver asked.

"We wait them out, mostly," the doctor said. "Sometimes, he's willing to talk during them, but it's often safer simply to allow one to run its course. Although Cylin succeeded in calming him somewhat, when she witnessed one." He checked the bowl atop the tripod, and nodded in satisfaction. "This should suffice." He dipped a cup into the bucket of water and used it to extinguish the flame in the fire pan. "Cylin, Devin, help me pack all this back into my bag. Spirits willing, I won't need these tools a third time."

Quicksilver fidgeted. "I think it'd be better not to leave him completely alone in this cave. I'll stay in one of the other rooms, but I'm still going to be here when he wakes up."

"That choice is yours," Doctor Kinnel said. He pushed to his feet with a grunt.

"Lucian won't wake for a while, right?" Cylin asked. When both Doctor Kinnel and Quicksilver nodded, she continued, "Then you can take Doctor Kinnel back to the infirmary, Quicksilver. Devin and I will stay here until you return."

Quicksilver blinked. "Me? Why?"

"Because you can take him down the same way you brought me up here, and save him a long walk," she said.

"Oh! Right, I can do that." He turned to the doctor. "If you don't mind, that is, and aren't afraid of heights."

"Ah, you mean flying," Doctor Kinnel said. "These weary bones would not object."

Quicksilver cast a long look at Lucian, then left the room with the doctor and his gear. Cylin stood, pulled a blanket off the bed, and draped it over Lucian.

"Cylin, do you think Doctor Kinnel could teach someone how to do that ritual he did?" Devin asked.

She gave him a long, speculative look. "You want to learn it?"

"Well, he did say it's work for someone younger, and you saw how drained he was." Devin rose. "And maybe he knows other things that will help Lord Lucian, but that he doesn't have the time or materials to do. I could do something useful."

"Ask Doctor Kinnel," she told him. "If he can teach you, he'll tell you, and if he can't, at least you'll know."

He nodded. They both sat again and waited in silence.

Quicksilver found them still there when he returned. "You guys can go if you want. But if you want to stay, I don't mind that either." His tone was cheerful, but his eyes were more serious than Cylin had seen before. "In either case, though, we should leave Lucian's room and let him sleep."

Cylin glanced to Devin. "I'd rather stay in the cave until he's awake. Devin?"

"I'll stay as well." Devin climbed to his feet. "The sitting room is more comfortable, though."

They left the bedroom and followed another branch of the cave to a room furnished with five stuffed chairs, a fireplace with no chimney, and several low tables. Swaths of fabric on the walls added bright splashes of colors around the room. Warmth radiated from the fireplace, though no fire glowed in it. They each settled into a chair around the fireplace.

Quicksilver finally broke the silence. "I hate waiting around doing nothing but staring at the wall. Do either of you know how to play Shadow Ladies?"

"Play what?" Cylin asked. "Never heard of it." She glanced at Devin, who shook his head in answer.

Quicksilver grinned and fished a deck of cards out of a pocket. "Perfect. Get comfortable, and I'll teach you."

Several hours later, Cylin was convinced that Quicksilver could either read minds, or was excellent at sleight of hand and stacking decks. Given that he was an elf, both could be true. But she was catching the hang of the card game, and enjoying it, especially when she or Devin shuffled instead of Quicksilver.

She dealt six cards to each of them. "Question for you, Quicksilver."

"Oh?" He checked his cards, then turned his attention to her. Devin frowned at his own hand, reordering the cards.

"I know Lucian's mother is dead. Is his father too?" Cylin asked.

"Lonewind?" Quicksilver laughed. "No, it would take a lot to kill Lonewind."

"Something like the destruction of most of civilization and the corruption of huge stretches of the world?" Cylin asked dryly.

"Oh, well, sure, that might have been a danger to him, if he'd been here," Quicksilver allowed.

"Is he out wandering through the spirit world like Lucian?" Cylin asked.

Quicksilver shook his head. "About two centuries ago, he made a craft that could withstand the vacuum of space and left this planet with most of our clan's older generation."

Cylin just stared at him. Finally she glanced to Devin to see if he already knew this story. He opened and closed his mouth, struggling to form words. "He... what... How? Why?"

Quicksilver smiled wryly. "You know how Lucian can be stubborn and really intense sometimes? Imagine that ten times stronger. Lucian is a powerful, impressive man. Lonewind is a force of nature. Fortunately, he also has people who anchor him. Lucian going Ghost is creepy, but I would take the Ghost any day over seeing Lonewind lose control and let loose the Demon." He shuddered.

"And that relates to him leaving?" Cylin asked.

"Our clan lived in a remote region, well away from humans, but technology was advancing. Lonewind realized that a time would come when elves wouldn't be able to count on remaining hidden away and unseen. He didn't want to make the necessary adaptations to live among humans, and he didn't want to pretend to be less than he was. So, he decided the alternative was to leave. Also, he'd fallen into a funk, lost interest in most things, and even his best friend couldn't pull him out of it. When he first started on the idea of a spaceship, most of us were just glad he'd finally found something that energized him again. It took me at least a decade to realize he was actually serious about leaving. Though I'm sure some people figured it out much sooner."

"And he did this a full century before any human began developing space flight?" Cylin asked. Her parents had taught her about such fantastical achievements as sending people into orbit and even landing on the largest moon.

"He thinks outside the box. Or the planet," Quicksilver said.

"And he didn't see any middle ground between 'adapt to living around humans' and 'leave the solar system'? We've got three moons! He could have just moved to one."

"The moons were the first place humans went when they figured out how to get up there without dying," Quicksilver pointed out. "Besides, there's no air on the moons."

"There's no air in space, either," Devin argued.

"Yeah, but he planned to find a new planet where he and the rest of the clan could live," Quicksilver said. "Apparently, that's not as easy as it sounds, because last I heard, they hadn't found one."

"Why didn't he take Lucian, you, and the others with him?" Cylin asked. *Did Lucian's father abandon him?*

"He wanted to!" Quicksilver assured her quickly. "Lonewind loves Lucian with everything he has. Lucian stayed because he chose to. And because he stayed, Chance, Tash, and their wives all stayed too." He shifted uncomfortably. "If they'd gone, I'd have gone too, but I was actually glad for an excuse not to. The ship was large and all, as such things go, but it would still have gotten pretty claustrophobic for me. I don't do well with confined spaces." He shook his head. "But, at least until the war, we still heard from them regularly. Spirit-walking makes distance a lot less of an issue, even between stars."

She sensed a lot of history hidden behind his explanation.

Perhaps if Quicksilver tried less hard to convince them that a bunch of elves completely leaving the planet was "no big deal," she might have accepted it more readily.

She started to ask another question, but Quicksilver abruptly jumped to his feet, tossing his cards on the table and turning in the direction of Lucian's bedroom. "Well what the stars did you expect, Lucian?!"

Devin jumped at the unexpected outburst. Cylin set down her cards. "So, Lucian's awake?"

Quicksilver glanced to her and nodded. "Thought he'd sleep longer."

"Does he know where he is?" Devin asked, cautious.

Quicksilver fell silent a moment, then said, "He knows he's in his room, in his cave, in Forest Town, and that his head feels like someone's been hitting it with a hammer. Which is actually a tempting idea."

"Good. If he knows where he is, he's not having an episode." Devin's shoulders relaxed.

"How long has he been asleep?" Cylin looked around the room for a clock.

"It's been four and a half hours. If he was Lonewind, he'd have slept until noon tomorrow." Quicksilver settled back into his chair, apparently not about to rush back up the hall to check on Lucian in person. "Maybe that ritual works differently than just draining an elf's magic. But then, I've seen Lonewind run himself dry more often than I have Lucian, so I don't exactly know how long it takes him to recover."

Devin looked toward the doorway. "Should someone see if he's all right?"

"He's all right," Quicksilver said. "Pissed, and his head's hurting strongly enough to come through his mind-speech, but he's all right. Reminding me of his extensive and creative vocabulary of profanity. I'd tell him to go back to sleep, but he won't listen to me."

"You are weirdly open about all this," Devin said.

Quicksilver frowned, confused. "About what?"

Devin waved a hand in a gesture to encompass the entire situation. "About... elves, magic, Lord Lucian, your clan, and all of this."

Quicksilver grew serious. "Did Cylin tell you about my parents?"

"No, I didn't," Cylin answered, while Devin looked puzzled.

"Ayliad's my mother," Quicksilver told Devin.

Devin grew pale.

"My grandmother, Willow, and my mother, Ayliad, caused the clan a lot of pain. They used lies and secrets to twist and pervert everyone around them. I saw the results, the damage they did to people dear to me, and I vowed that I would never be like that. Sure, I'll lie and pickpocket with the best around strangers, when needed, but within the clan, I don't deceive, and I don't hide information."

"Within the clan," Cylin repeated. "Fine, but what does that have to do with us, right now? Lucian's here, but the rest of your clan is not."

He blinked at her, as if the answer was clear. "You, Devin, Doctor Kinnel, you guys are part of the clan."

Cylin and Devin both stared at him. "We're humans," Devin said, stating the obvious.

"You're Lucian's friends. You're the people who support him, help him, the people who he counts on. Of *course* you're part of the clan!" He turned toward the doorway. "Right?"

Cylin and Devin both followed his gaze. Lucian leaned against the doorway, drawn and pale. Streaks from the ritual still marked his face. His amber eyes lingered on each of them for a long moment before he answered. "Of course they are."

Devin jumped to his feet. "Lord Lucian! You shouldn't be up."

Lucian waved a trembling hand, brushing aside the concern. He slowly made his way to them and dropped into an empty chair.

"Did you find him?" Cylin asked.

Lucian's head jerked up at her voice, and he immediately winced at the sharp motion. "Yes. I found Chance. I tried to wake him. I don't know whether or not I did." He glowered at Quicksilver. "Since I got dragged back before I could be sure."

"And how many wraiths took bites out of you on the way there?" Quicksilver demanded. "How many did you have to fend off? How much of your energy did you spend just trying to stop one of them from making a snack out of you, Lucian? Ten? Twenty? Or did you bother to keep track?"

Lucian's jaw tightened. "Too many."

"Was it worth it?" Cylin asked.

He gave her a long, unreadable look. "Yes."

"Good. I'd hate to think you did something that stupid, throwing yourself into danger, scaring Quicksilver, and forcing Doctor Kinnel to perform a ritual that knocked him on his ass, if it wasn't actually worth it."

Lucian sat in silence for a long moment. "It's been a long time since I was out there. I forgot just how bad it really is in the spirit realm. But not all the ghosts are malicious. Some were... familiar. They knew why I'd come, and guided me."

"Well I hope you thanked them for helping you to not join them." Now that she was sure Lucian was safe, Cylin's worry turned into anger at him and his reckless disregard for... everything. "You could have died! And what if Doctor Kinnel hadn't been able to pull you back? What if that ritual had killed him instead?"

"I didn't ask anyone to drag me back!" Lucian snapped. "And now I don't even know if I succeeded in waking Chance or not! You could have just—"

"I could have just not done what I believed was right,"

Cylin interrupted, standing. "Is that what you're saying? I should put aside my beliefs when they inconvenience you? Hypocritical asshole."

Their eyes locked, neither of them willing to yield. Lucian said nothing.

After a long, tense moment of silence, Cylin said, "You're welcome for hauling your spirit ass back, Lucian. I'm going home."

No one stopped her as she left the sitting room and strode up the long hall and out of the cave.

She intended to go straight home, but before she got there, Dion, one of the sentries, rushed into town. Seeing Cylin, he rushed to her, panting for breath. She caught his shoulders to steady him.

"What's wrong?"

"Bandits headed for the village." He paused a moment to catch his breath. "Ten men, big guys."

Bandits now? Dammit! Lucian's in no shape to deal with that. "Alert the village. We've practiced this. Everyone should know where to go."

Dion looked up the hill toward Lucian's cave. "What about—"

"Report up there after you've alerted the village," Cylin said firmly.

Dion hesitated, then said in a quiet voice, "Cylin, one of the men said your name."

She froze. "What? Describe him!"

"Tall, hair turning a little gray, about fifty, I think? Seemed to be in charge. He wore a long leather duster with some kind of symbols on it."

Pryor. Pryor is here. She swallowed hard, but kept her voice mostly steady. "Do what I told you. I'm going to scout these guys out."

Dion gulped and nodded quickly. Cylin ran back to her house and belted on her gun. Her gaze fell on her backpack. She no longer kept it on a hook beside the door, but it was still close at hand, packed with a stash of supplies if she had to leave in an emergency. She hesitated, debating whether to take or leave it.

Pryor would expect me to have it, if he saw me. He'd never believe I'd settle down anywhere.

She slung it over her shoulders and headed into the forest, silently cursing Lucian for being a reckless idiot.

The forest was still and quiet under a blanket of snow. She moved carefully around the deeper drifts and tried to place her feet where her tracks could most easily be mistaken for natural breaks in the snow.

Why is Pryor coming here now? It's been months since Hakon and the bone man attacked us. If Pryor wanted me that badly, he wouldn't have waited this long.

It took at least half an hour to work her way quietly toward the road. She stopped when she heard steps trudging through the snow. Ducking behind a tree, she waited to get a look at the intruders.

Six figures dressed in heavy winter furs worked their way through the forest, military-grade automatic weapons held at the ready. She didn't see Alger or Pryor among them, and Dion had spoken of a larger force.

Shit, are they splitting up to attack Forest Town from multiple points? I'd better get back.

A heavy and far too familiar hand gripped her shoulder. "Ah, Cylin. I thought I might find you here."

She turned slowly, hand sinking to her gun. Pryor loomed over her with an arrogant smile. Beside him, Alger stood with his gun casually aimed at her gut. A little behind them, several more men trudged through the snow.

I didn't even hear them coming. Some scout I am. "I don't owe you a damned thing, Pryor. Go fuck yourself."

Pryor chuckled. "Don't flatter yourself, girl. You're not worth that much. No, I got myself a lead on a bounty around here. Someone's willing to pay a pretty price for that freak who attacked us."

A chill ran up her spine. Cylin tried to project an air of disinterest. "Really? Who'd want him?"

"The leader of the bone men, apparently." Pryor grinned. "Oh, don't worry too much. They were very specific in wanting him alive and intact." He lowered his voice conspiratorially. "I know you know where he is, Cylin. You show me the way, and I'll cut you in on the reward. Trust me, even with a fair split, you'll be living well for a long time. Might even buy yourself a nice little town somewhere to call yourself lord of."

"You're so full of shit, Pryor."

He shook his head. "I'm being one hundred percent straight with you, girl. No debts. A reward you can live on for decades, just for one man."

"One man who kicked your ass without breaking a sweat."

Anger flashed in his eyes. Once, she'd lived in terror of that look, and shadows of that fear crept through her. "I'm being reasonable here, Cylin, but you're in no position to bargain. The boys are getting impatient for some plunder. I could step back right now, and every one of them will fuck you until you don't know which way's up. Or you can work with me, get yourself a nice payout, and move on." His lip curled. "It's not like you don't have everything you need in that bag. I know you, girl. You've got no loyalties to him or this place, just whatever debts you owe. And I know full well that if someone had offered to pay off your debt in exchange for my head, you'd have taken the deal without looking back."

"Yeah, but you're not this guy. You have no idea what you're trying to screw with, Pryor." It didn't matter that she was still mad at Lucian. She wasn't about to let anyone come after him while he was weak. Especially not Pryor.

"Don't I?" He chuckled. "Some mutated freak with a few tricks."

"Yeah, that's what Hakon thought too when you sent him here with that bone man." She raised her voice, and several of the thugs turned to listen. "The forest ate him."

Pryor snorted. "Don't try to be pretty about saying he's dead, girl. It doesn't suit you."

"Oh, I wasn't trying to be pretty, Pryor. I mean that the forest ate him. Opened a crack under his feet. The vines came out of it and dragged him down screaming." She made sure the other men could hear her. "Every last one of them died like that. Saw one guy get all four limbs ripped off before the plants tore his head off his neck." Cylin looked Pryor in the eyes. "You still want to call *that* 'a few tricks'?"

"Shut it, you stupid bitch," Alger growled.

"Hah! I'm not the one leading a bunch of dumb thugs into a haunted forest to attempt to capture an ancient spirit."

Behind Pryor, the men exchanged uneasy looks. Pryor sneered. "I know you don't believe that shit, Cylin."

"Uh, boss…," Alger said, looking past Cylin. "Where'd the rest of the guys go?"

Cylin fought the urge to look over her shoulder. She was just buying time for the rest of the village to muster defenses, and couldn't imagine what might have happened to the other group. If Quicksilver and Doctor Kinnel were right, Lucian shouldn't have much, if any, magic to protect the village.

But Quicksilver's an elf too, and he has plant magic.

She gave Alger a knowing smile. "Guess they were lucky. They got to go quietly."

Pryor grabbed her and jerked her around in front of him

like a shield, pinning her arms. Cylin felt the cold, hard press of a muzzle against her neck. "Show yourself, scumbag, or I'll feed *her* head to your damned trees."

"No you won't." Lucian's voice whispered through the shadows. Snow spilled to the ground as tree branches leaned toward the men. The forest creaked and groaned as it shifted.

Someone fired wildly at the trees. Pressed against Pryor, Cylin couldn't turn far enough to see who, or why. The sound abruptly ceased. She also felt the muzzle of Pryor's gun warp and bend. She twisted against him and kicked at his shin. Pryor cursed and tightened his hold on her.

Alger raised his gun to aim into the forest, then gaped as a branch slapped it out of his hand. The men around them shouted in alarm. From the crashing, some decided to run.

Lucian appeared from the shadows, clearly floating above the snow. To Cylin's eyes, he still looked exhausted, and she wondered how he had the strength to fly. He also looked like he was ready to rip Pryor apart with his bare hands.

"You think I'm going to stand by and let shit like you in my home?" Lucian snarled.

"I think if you want the girl safe, you'll shut up and come along quietly," Pryor said. Cylin could hardly believe the sheer brazen idiocy of his threat. He shifted his hold on Cylin, attempting to get something from his pocket. "I know how to deal with freaks like you."

Cylin jerked forward, then threw herself back against Pryor. She was sure she felt a little extra push, enough to knock Pryor off balance. He slipped in the snow and fell, Cylin landing on him as hard as she could, elbows bent in the hopes of driving them into somewhere painful. She heard him grunt with lost breath, and his hold on her relaxed.

She scrambled to her feet. Alger was making strangled noises. A quick glance showed him trying to pry a branch off his neck as his face turned purple.

"Little bitch!" Pryor thrashed back to his feet. "You'll pay for that!"

"This is one tab you'll never collect, Pryor." Cylin darted back, ducking under Alger's reach.

Her gun was in her hand before she remembered drawing it. Months of target practice guided her aim as Pryor lunged at her. Cylin squeezed the trigger. Pryor staggered, blood spreading across his chest. He bared his teeth and grabbed for her.

Then she was in the air, flying above his reach. Pryor screamed in fury and threw something, but it fell short of either her or Lucian. They landed beside Quicksilver on a thick branch. Lucian's nephew shot her a tight, nervous grin.

"Sorry we were a little late. You okay?"

"I'm fine," she said.

Below, Pryor staggered through the snow, one hand pressed to his wound. Cylin raised her gun to finish him off, but Lucian pushed the barrel down. "Waste of bullets. He's dead, just doesn't know it yet." His voice was heavy with weariness.

"Yeah? Well I'm not waiting until he figures it out." She shifted the weapon out of his reach and fired.

Pryor crumpled with a cry of pain and anger, then he was still.

Lucian winced. "That wasn't necessary."

She looked him straight in the eyes. "Yes, Lucian, it was. And how did you manage to do *any* of that when you're about ready to fall out of this tree?"

"I just had to deal with the guns. And that one." He nodded at Alger. "Quick handled the rest."

"I hate fighting, and I hate killing people, but I'll do it when I must," Quicksilver said quietly, looking away.

Lucian's gaze moved to her backpack and lingered there. "When Dion said you'd gone ahead, I thought…"

"If you say you thought I was going to abandon Forest Town, I will punch you off this branch, Lucian."

He shook his head. "No. But I thought you might try to convince Pryor to take you if he'd leave the village alone."

"He wasn't looking for me. He was looking for you, so even if I'd considered that, it wouldn't have worked." She looked at Quicksilver. "Can you put me back on the ground?"

"Sure."

By the time the Forest Town defenders found the site of the confrontation, Lucian and Quicksilver were gone, but she was sure she could still feel Lucian watching her. Guarding her.

~

When Cylin left her house the following morning, Lucian was sitting on her platform, staring west, away from Forest Town. He didn't turn.

"Quicksilver said I ought to make you a plaque to commemorate your joining the not-insignificant ranks of people who I've pissed off badly enough to send storming off at one time or another. I decided jewelry would be better for you. Easier to pack."

He raised his hand. A silver bracelet floated from his hand to hang in front of Cylin. A gap in the solid metal band allowed it to slide onto a wrist. Vine-like patterns ran around the rim, and script swirled across the face, delicate and elegant.

"What does it say?" Cylin didn't take it.

"'Welcome to the fucking family'."

She raised a dubious eyebrow at his back. "Really?"

"Really."

The script looked too fine, with its swoops and looping letters, for the message. Cylin took the bracelet and ran a finger over the words. "How much of your family have you pissed off that badly?"

"Most of them, at some point. Sometimes there's yelling and cursing involved." Lucian finally looked over his shoulder at her. "I'm not sorry that I went out to find Chance. I am sorry that I wasn't prepared for Pryor."

"I'm not sorry I called you an idiot." Cylin folded her arms across her chest. "And I'm not sorry that we dragged you back. But… thanks for the help with Pryor. It's cold out here. Come inside."

Lucian slowly climbed to his feet. His eyes were bloodshot and his walk unsteady. Though she didn't smell the reek of booze on him, Cylin asked the first thought to come to mind. "Are you drunk?"

He snorted something like a laugh. "I wish. No. That can trigger an episode. I am, however, exhausted and dealing with a throbbing headache that refuses to go away."

It occurred to Cylin, belatedly, that Lucian's magic had been drained to the dregs yesterday. Assuming the bracelet was new, Lucian must have used whatever little magic he'd recovered to make the jewelry, then come down here. "Did you sleep at all?"

"I decided that might not be wise. Wasn't sure where I'd be when I woke up." Lucian followed her inside.

"You'd be in Forest Town, at wherever you went to sleep. Or do you mean something else?" Cylin asked.

Lucian dusted snow off his pants. "Physically, I'd be here. Mentally, who knows."

She eyed him. "So, are we testing whether 'not enough sleep' triggers an episode?"

"It hasn't yet, and I've put that to the test plenty of times." Lucian flopped gracelessly into a chair.

Cylin shook her head and poured him a mug of hot water from the kettle. "You want tea?"

"I want my family and friends safe. I want a world that isn't screwed up. I want to be able to do normal things without wondering what's about to go catastrophically wrong."

"Well, all I can offer is tea. You want some or not?"

"Sure. As long as it's not lavender or chamomile."

Cylin studied her shelf. "Mint or juniper, then." She chose mint and handed him the mug while the tea steeped. "If getting drunk can trigger an episode, why did you have that whiskey from the bandits' truck?"

"Because I have shitty risk assessment." Lucian swirled his tea in the mug. "And because it felt like an appropriate 'fuck you' to them."

Cylin fixed a fresh mug of tea for herself and sat across from him in the cozy living room. A fire burned in the hearth. On the mantle over the fire, her trio of hearth gods gazed over the house, as they had the homes of her ancestors for generations. "Are you going to wait until spring?"

"I don't have much choice." Lucian scowled into his mug, then sipped. "Quick refuses to consider setting out before then, and winter will be over before I'm fit to head back into the spirit realm."

"Now that's an answer to inspire confidence," Cylin muttered.

"Chance *needs* my help!" Lucian leaned forward. "I might have been able to wake him, but I don't know. I touched his mind, and it was in a very dark place. Someone has to pull him out of it, and I might be the only person still alive on this planet who *can*."

"How dark a place?" Cylin asked.

"As dark of one as I am in during an episode."

She shuddered. "Does he have episodes too?"

Lucian shook his head. "No, but he was the target of much of my mother's wrath. He stood up to her, defied her, and fought her, and for that, she wanted to destroy him."

That single statement explained so much about Lucian's

reactions during his episode, and why telling him of Chance's absence had been a relief to him rather than a source of distress. "If you're the one who can bring him back, you'd better be damned careful, and at least *try* not to be completely careless."

Lucian waved a hand wearily. "Yeah, I heard it from Quick already." He barked a hard laugh. "He told me he needs me alive, sane, and stable. I don't think he liked me telling him that the only one of those I could promise with any confidence was 'alive'."

Cylin stood and walked to the hearth. She picked up the middle god from the mantle—a squat figure with a benevolent expression, a knife in one hand, and a bundle of grain in the other. *It's a small house. It surely doesn't need the watch of three gods. So you can watch over Lucian instead.* She turned to Lucian and held the god to him. "I want you to have this. For protection. When... you leave."

Lucian blinked in surprise, staring at it. He took it from her hand. "Your hearth god?"

I don't even know what elves worship. Do they have gods? What if giving him a hearth god is an insult, or offends whatever power he follows? "I..." She fought the urge to snatch it back.

"Cylin, this is precious to you. One of your family gods. Are you certain you want to give it to me?" Lucian asked. He handled the god with more respect than she expected.

"I'm sure." She put confidence into the words. "That is Ficgesh, a god of protection, and... I'd feel better knowing you had a little more protection, since I can't go with you myself."

"Thank you, Cylin," Lucian said quietly. "I'm honored."

She shifted uncomfortably. "Maybe it will help... remind you of us here in Forest Town. And anyway, if I'm part of the family, that makes these your hearth gods too, so it's only right that one of them go with you." She bit back further words, knowing she would just babble.

Lucian chuckled softly. "I'm surprised you aren't demanding to come with me yourself."

"I would, if you hadn't dumped half the responsibilities for Forest Town on my shoulders! And don't say you haven't; you know full well who people will look to while you're gone. And since the *other* half of those duties will be on Devin and Doctor Kinnel, I'm not about to leave them scrambling to figure out the village defenses on top of everything else."

Lucian raised an eyebrow.

She scowled at him. "It's true and you know it."

"Of course I do. But I wasn't sure whether you did, or whether that mattered."

"You're such an idiot, Lucian."

"Already established," he agreed easily.

She folded her arms across her chest. "This is my home too. If all the competent people leave, who's going to keep things running?"

"They'd manage, one way or another, if they had to," Lucian said. "I won't demand that anyone stay against their wishes."

She rolled her eyes. "Did you not fucking *hear* me, Lucian? Forest Town *is my home*. I haven't had one of those since my parents died when I was eight, and the village leaders sold off everything in their house, including me. I'm not staying here because anyone is going to *make* me do so. I'm staying because this is my *home!*"

"I heard you," he said quietly. "But I wanted to be sure I understood you." He sipped his tea. "When I was younger, I spent so long looking for a place to call home that I realized I might not recognize it when I found it. What does home feel like to you, Cylin?"

"A place to stop running. A place where I can just... be, without wondering who I owe debts to, who I need to watch my back around, or who's going to sell me to the bone men."

She paused. "Wow, that sounds as eye-roll-worthy as some of the worst drivel I've heard in fireside tales. Sorry."

"Don't be. Anyone who would mock you deserves to be punched in the face. And you have my unquestioning permission to deliver that punch to any who you think have earned it." Lucian stood, hearth god cradled in the crook of one arm. "I know it's going to be hard here while I'm gone, and I can't prepare for every possibility. But I know Forest Town will be in good hands with you, Devin, and Doctor Kinnel." He gave her a deep, oddly formal bow. "Welcome home, and... welcome to the fucking family."

INTERLUDE ONE: AWAKENING

The ground shook with the force of a blast, and choking dust filled the air. Heat burst through the walls as the world erupted in flames. Chance staggered, trying to see, trying to breathe.

Lucian yelled to him, and he followed that voice, running down a street choked with burning debris. He stumbled over something – a charred corpse. Ahmea helped him up, telling him through mind-speak that Quicksilver had gotten Eria to safety, and they had to follow. But smoke and fire filled the air, and he couldn't see.

Lucian called again from somewhere distant. He reached for that call.

Maji appeared beside them. The tall, pale elf grabbed Chance's arm in a firm grasp, telling him that they had to go. A new wave of attacks was imminent. Before he could protest, Maji teleported, carrying the three of them away from the rain of burning rubble. They landed in a narrow scrap of shelter. Chance coughed in the smoky air, one hand resting on Ahmea's shoulder, and he shouted for Lucian.

The world exploded as a blast shattered their shelter, flinging him into the air. He grasped for Ahmea, but his hand caught only the edge of her skirt. His magic was drained and exhausted. He couldn't stop her when she smashed into a wall, her head cracking against the stone. She dropped limply to the ground. He screamed in helpless anguish as he felt her die.

Bones broke as he crashed into a smoldering pile of rubble. He screamed again, then welcomed the darkness that promised the end of pain.

Somewhere, despairing, Lucian called to him.

The darkness spat Chance out once more. He cradled Ahmea in his arms, as if his magic could return her spirit to her broken body. Cold laughter echoed around him. Raising his head, horror and dread seized him. He sat on the polished marble floor of a throne room. Willow sat on her throne, gazing down on him with a cruel smile playing on her lips.

"Ah, Chance, you poor thing," she purred. "You're all alone now. Ahmea can't help you any longer. Such a pity. Your folly has killed your mate. Tsk. And after I warned you that you always hurt those you love. Now look what you've done."

Blood stained his hands. He frantically tried to wipe it away, but it clung to his skin. Willow smiled and rose, walking deliberately down the steps. He shrank back, clutching Ahmea against him.

Willow laughed again. In her hand, she carried a jeweled collar. "You forgot your place, slave. You are mine, and your futile attempts to deny it only bring pain to anyone you have left."

He could only watch her and cower in fear. Once, he could have fought her, but now…

Suddenly, he was no longer alone. Lucian, eyes burning with golden fire, stood beside him. Willow stopped, shocked by the intrusion.

"You won't touch him!" Lucian's hand shot up, and Willow flew back to crash against the wall. She crumpled.

Ignoring her, Lucian crouched. "Chance, come with me."

He looked down at Ahmea. "She's gone, Lucian. Ahmea is dead. I couldn't save her. I couldn't protect her."

"I know. I'm sorry, Chance. But she wouldn't want you to stay trapped here forever. Come back."

"What's left, Lucian?" he asked in despair.

Lucian just held out his hand. Even as he offered it, he began to fade from sight.

He grabbed at Lucian's outstretched hand. "No! Don't leave!"

"Come back, Chance." Even the words were fading. "I'll be waiting."

"Lucian! Don't leave me! Come back! Lucian!"

Lucian was gone, but something remained. Something that called him away from the darkness. Trembling, he rose, and step by stumbling step, he followed.

PART TWO

VAGABOND

VAGABOND

Rain fell in a steady drizzle, coating the broken asphalt and turning the ground beyond to thick mud. Lucian and Quicksilver floated just above the ground, avoiding the worst of the muck, but not even hats and oiled coats could keep them dry.

Spring rain should have been a herald of new life and fresh growth, but the barren wasteland only drank the water, polluted it, and spread its poisons further. Fifty years ago, this had been farmland, before fire rained from the sky and weapons forged by human science and elven magic released toxins into the ground. They were three days out of Forest Town, and Lucian could no longer sense even a hint of his forest.

Lucian pulled off his hat and tilted his head back, letting water fall on his face and his short black braid. Quicksilver cast him a sidelong look. "Is that safe?"

"I'm not going to drink it," Lucian said. "And it isn't the rain that's making the Guardian all thorny."

"Is it bad?" Quick asked. "I keep my sense of magic wrapped pretty tight these days."

"I've sensed worse, but it's not good." Lucian rubbed his forehead, where an ache had been pulsing for the last two and a half days. "The Guardian is definitely feeling thorny, and would really rather I either let it out to consume and destroy all the corrupted magic in the ground, or go back to Forest Town." Neither of which Lucian would do. The first would knock him unconscious for days and leave his body completely under the control of the symbiotic magical entity that lived within him. The second would mean turning back. He was not going to give up now, when he finally had the means to find his cousin, Chance, and reuniting with the remaining members of their clan.

Chance had been in a coma since the bombings that killed Ahmea, his wife, fifty years ago. Those same bombings had separated Lucian from him. Although Lucian knew with his entire being that Chance lived, he didn't know where to find his cousin. He'd ventured out of his body and into the spirit world twice in an attempt to reach Chance, but the crazed and twisted spirits of elves and other beings warped by corrupted magic made such ventures even more dangerous than crossing the wastelands of the physical world. If not for the arrival of his nephew Quicksilver in Forest Town, he still might not know how to find Chance.

"You know, this is one of those times I'm glad my Tree magic never developed its own personality. I'm okay with being a Sapling." Quick considered, shrugged, then pulled off his own hat, freeing a mop of silver hair.

"As far as I know, only the Guardian developed its own distinct persona. It just names all the rest of you as it sees you," Lucian told him.

"Oh, I know, but if your piece of Tree magic can do it, any of them could, potentially," Quick said.

Lucian's father, Lonewind, had been infected with the Tree magic a century before Lucian's birth, and the magic had been passed on to each of his descendants. Lucian's aspect of the Tree had first woken and taken on its personality several thousand years ago in combat against a pocket of corrupted magic that attempted to infest Lucian. The Guardian had never relinquished that instinctual desire to purge any source of tainted magic that it sensed. And this land oozed that corruption from every rock.

Quicksilver's aspect of the Tree had never taken any particular strong traits, and the Guardian had dubbed him a Sapling. Quick's mother Ayliad, on the other hand, had gained the name the Fruit. As Lucian understood it, the original Tree, when it was still a living plant, had produced a fruit that was sweet, attractive, and dangerously addictive. Lucian knew all too well how accurately that described his sister. Fortunately, Quicksilver took after his father in his looks, and his personality bore no resemblance to either his mother or grandmother, Willow.

The drizzle continued through the day. Lucian and Quicksilver camped in the ruins of an old farmhouse and set out bowls and bottles to capture rainwater. It needed to be boiled before drinking, but it helped stretch out the supplies they'd carried from Forest Town. They found enough dry wood and tinder to make a small fire.

After they ate, Lucian sat in the circle of warmth and light, toying with the squat figure of a hearth god, turning it around in his hand and admiring the craftsmanship. Cylin had given it to him, a gift to watch over him in his travels. The idol held no magic, no power, but he half wondered if he should say some sort of prayer to it anyway. He didn't believe in the human gods, and elves were more likely to revere their ancestors than any higher power. But the hearth god reminded him of Cylin and the other humans in Forest Town. He missed Cylin, Devin, Doctor Kinnel, and the rest of the people there. He missed the structure and predictability of living there. He missed being the person everyone looked to for answers, whether he had them or not. And he missed being free of the damned headache.

"Can I ask you something, Lucian?" Quicksilver asked, settling across the fire and hanging a pot of water to boil. "It's something I kept wondering about while I was in Forest Town, but I wasn't sure how best to bring it up."

"Go ahead," Lucian said.

"I wasn't expecting to find you alone with humans. What happened? Cilvi was with you, so were Tash and Sun, from that last brief contact we had before things really went to shit."

Lucian had known the question would come, but he couldn't prepare for it, or for the surge of raw pain and grief the memory brought. One moment, his wife had been at his side, the next... "Cilvi died in an ambush almost a year after we were separated from you. Soldiers came out of the shadows, firing before we could stop them. We tried to stop the bleeding, but she was hurt too badly. Too many bullets, too fast." The soldiers had died in agony, but it had already been too late. He stared into the fire rather than watching Quicksilver's expression of grief and pain. "Tash got sick. Toxins in the water or the ground. He and Sun both." "Sick" sounded far better than describing the sight of skin rotting off his friends, or their screams of agony, or his increasingly desperate attempts to ease their pain in any way possible. The point when memory simply stopped was a relief—a gaping dark hole of unawareness.

He was quiet for a moment, then continued. "I don't remember much after that. I must have continued on. I hope I buried them. From there, eventually, I came to the place where my forest is now. Why the Guardian decided that was the right place, I can't tell you. I wasn't aware of what happened. I woke up in a forest, with a cave waiting to be called 'home,' and I knew that I needed to stay there, because I couldn't find Chance in the state I was in."

"You wandered a long time to end up there," Quicksilver said. "We're hundreds of miles from the city where we lived when the bombings separated us." He gazed at Lucian. "That must have taken a toll on you."

"I suppose. I don't remember. I was exhausted, hadn't been eating, and had no idea how I got where I was. Once I'd been there a bit, I tried to send my spirit out to find Chance."

"I'm sure you did!" Quicksilver said quickly. "I have no doubt that you tried to find us, Lucian. I also know the spirit world is horribly dangerous now. I can feel those *things* sometimes."

"They're the twisted and corrupted souls of elves," Lucian told him. "Some of them… try to talk to me when I leave my body. They're insane, and the things they want…" He shuddered and shook his head.

"Don't tell me. I don't want to know." Quicksilver held up a hand to ward off any more images. He let out a long breath. "I'm sorry about Cilvi, Tash, and Sun, Lucian. I don't know if you knew, but Ahmea died as well."

"I know. I felt Chance's pain when he lost her." He'd felt echoes of that pain still when he touched Chance's sleeping mind.

Quicksilver just nodded, and silence fell over their camp.

Ten more days brought them to the first signs of human life. The patchwork remains of the asphalt led into a ruined city. Lucian eyed it dubiously. Rubble had been assembled into a rough outer wall topped with wire. Lucian glimpsed shapes moving atop the wall. Outside, tall fences ringed areas that contained either livestock or attempts at plant growth.

Quicksilver grimaced. "Town's called New Haven. It's not a pleasant place. I traded with them, but the local lord is a pain, and he caters to bone men. They can't grow much of anything, so most of their food is imported, and that adds up quickly."

"Do we need to stop?" Lucian asked. "We still have several hours of light."

Quicksilver frowned, shaking his canteen. "We could use fresh water, but there's a more hospitable town a few more days on. As long as we conserve, we should be all right."

"I don't want to stop here," Lucian said. The place made his skin crawl.

Quick shrugged. "Fine by me."

Hostile eyes watched from the walls as they bypassed the city. Instinct told Lucian that letting himself be caught inside those walls would invite disaster. He could feel the poisons in the land, and the Guardian's restless reaction to them. But more importantly, he knew his temper was frayed, and it would not take much of a push to break it.

When it became obvious they weren't going to enter New Haven, several shouts, too distant to understand, came from the walls. Figures rushed back and forth.

Quicksilver eyed the figures uneasily. "Wonder what that's all about."

"My best guess, they're not happy to be losing out on whatever money they'd get from us." Lucian watched the activity for a long moment. "Let's go, before they mobilize and come after us."

Quick's eyes widened in alarm. "Why would they... Is a token tribute really *that* important to them? If their lord's ego needs stroked that badly, he must seriously be overcompensating."

I hate to think that this scum lurks less than two weeks travel from Forest Town. Lucian's jaw tightened. He forced himself to walk away from the town before he gave in to the desire to wipe it off the face of the earth. "Let's see how much distance we can put between us and them before nightfall."

"Sure." Quicksilver scrambled after him. "Just so you know, though, their walls are tall for a reason, and that reason comes out when the sun sets. We'll need some kind of shelter, unless you want to shape one for us."

"I don't even want to *touch* this rock with magic. The taint runs deep. Any magic I give it is likely to be warped into something neither of us would like," Lucian told him.

Quicksilver glanced to the sky. "We'd better hurry, then. About two hours to nightfall. I remember seeing some kind of old house on my way to find you. Didn't look very sturdy, but better than nothing, right?"

"We'll see. Lead the way."

Quicksilver set a quick pace. New Haven faded in the distance, but the prickling sense on the back of Lucian's neck persisted, only growing stronger. It crept down his spine like a thousand ants.

The sun hung just above the horizon when they reached the farm. The barn roof had caved in, dragging sections of the walls with it. Those that remained listed and bowed. The house was marginally better; the walls still stood, though no windows remained, and only patches of the roof beams stood exposed. Odd tracks marked the dirt leading toward the structures, clawed feet more humanoid than animal. Lucian stepped closer to examine them, passing a pair of crude totems made from debris and animal hide.

Pain stabbed through his skull as the Guardian roared in fury. Lucian dropped to one knee, fingers curling like claws and breath hissing between his teeth. Corrupted magic pulsed from the ground before him like a heartbeat.

"Lucian!" Quicksilver grabbed his shoulder, then sucked his breath sharply between his teeth and pulled Lucian back.

The moment he crossed back over the division line marked by the totems, the assault ceased. Lucian drew a deep breath and forced his fingers to uncurl. Every hair on the back of his neck stood on end.

Quick shuddered. "What was that? I didn't feel anything until I reached for you, but as strong as that was, we should have been sensing it for miles."

Lucian warily eyed the totems. "Those seem to be blocking our ability to sense the magic, somehow. I don't know if it's to conceal or contain, and I really don't know how bits of stick, fur, and twine could hold any power."

Quick frowned uneasily. "Sounds more like a human fairy tale than real magic as we know it. Could it be some odd effect of whatever happened here? Whatever caused this pocket of bad magic?"

"Maybe." Lucian was dubious, but had no better explanation. He pointed to the tracks. "But something lives here. I don't want to meet it, whether it made the totems or something else did." He eyed the crumbling structures, searching for signs of anything about to rush out and attack. He felt eyes on him, but nothing made itself known.

Quick shivered again, then looked over his shoulder. "We better get going, then. If New Haven grunts really are following us, we still need shelter."

"Feet on the ground," Lucian told him. "No magic. This is a bomb waiting for a spark."

"Right." Quicksilver eyed the farm again, shivered, and set off away from both it and the community of New Haven.

Half an hour later, only twilight lit the sky. The cracked and pitted road made difficult walking, but Lucian wasn't willing to relent yet and fly. The back of his neck itched, as if something watched them. He looked over his shoulder.

"New Haven is damned determined. Light behind us."

"Light?" Quicksilver repeated. "New Haven is full of idiots, then. You don't turn on lights unless you want attention." He turned. "Hmm, that light's not moving."

Lucian frowned, looking again. The glow was too pale to be a fire, but Quick was right that it remained stationary. "A trap?"

"Maybe, but for who? Setting it behind us isn't likely to do New Haven much good if we're the target." Quick frowned and looked to Lucian. "You intend to go back and find out anyway, don't you?"

"I want to know what's on our tail." Lucian closed his eyes, letting his sense of magic probe the land around them. "We should be safe to fly."

"Good, because I'm sure not *walking* back there." Quicksilver rose a foot off the ground. "I saw the hide and claws of a nightbeast during my previous visit to New Haven, and I never want to meet a live one."

Flying was as natural as breathing to Lucian. He floated up to an easy twenty feet. The growing darkness would conceal him, and should some monster prove unexpectedly able to leap high enough to threaten him, moving higher took no effort. Quicksilver rose quickly to his height and added another five for good measure. The beacon of light drew them cautiously back the way they'd come.

Lucian saw movement. Six men spread out in the pool of light, searching the ground. The light source proved to be a tall outdoor flood lamp converted to charge on solar power, mounted on a folding frame. Several of the men examined the lamp with envy.

"Damn fine light. They'd be stupid to leave it behind, but I don't see much else. We sure this is the travelers' camp?" one man grunted.

"What else you think it would be?" countered another. "This light sure ain't one of ours, and it's gotta be worth at least a couple weeks of meals. Boss will wanna know where they got it."

"Think they're worth much else? Looked like any old vagabonds to me," said a third.

The second man just shrugged. "Everybody's worth something when the bone men come to town."

Lucian's eyes narrowed. Quick had mentioned that New Haven had dealings with bone men, but he hadn't expected to hear their pursuers speak openly of selling passing travelers to the dealers of flesh and blood. Even slave traders were better than bone men. Slave traders at least didn't skin their victims alive.

Whispers of sound caught his ear. Had they been in his forest, Lucian would have assumed the noises the calls of insects, but in this place, he'd neither seen nor heard insects. The whispers were just on the edge of his hearing, rising and falling like speech, though he couldn't tell if the sounds made words. A shiver ran down his spine.

Below, the men's heads jerked up and their eyes searched the darkness, but the bright lamp left them night-blind. All drew weapons and stepped closer to the shadows, finally realizing the dangers of the light.

Lucian glimpsed movement in the darkness. A humanoid shape darted between rocks, followed by another, and another. Their skin was rough and thick like armor, and they wore scraps that made a passing attempt at clothing. In the dark, Lucian couldn't pick out fine details, but their forms and movements reminded him of... something. Something he couldn't place. The lead figure paused, head cocked, then it looked up directly at Lucian. Slitted eyes like a cat studied him. He looked back at it, wondering in spite of himself whether it really could spring into the air and grab him. Then the other bowed, breaking gaze with him, and sprang forward.

It snatched one of the humans before the man knew he

was under attack. His frightened scream cut short in a gurgle. The other humans trained their weapons on the spot where he'd been and unleashed rapid bursts of gunfire. The other two stalkers attacked from either side.

Quicksilver winced. *They're going to be slaughtered.* His mental voice was tight.

Lucian glanced at him. *Since they were just talking about selling us to bone men, my sympathy is limited.*

Yeah, but still... Quick trailed off. *Okay, no, you're right. I can't feel sorry for them either.*

More screams from below, then sudden silence. The light flickered and went dark. Lucian looked down again. Three figures stood around the lamp, and all looked up to Lucian and Quicksilver.

"The Raven flies tonight." The voice was a gravelly female. "Do he and the Silver come to steal out feast?"

*They *talk*?! I have no idea what that means, but I don't think I like it,* Quick told Lucian.

Raven? Silver? He remembered the speaker looking up at him before the attack, and her unexpected little bow to him. *Am I the Raven?* "Why would the Raven want your... feast?" Lucian retorted, eyes never leaving the trio.

"The Raven and the Silver lured the prey here. Perhaps we stole their prey. Perhaps the Raven is like Shiranak, unwilling to share, though surely there is plenty." The speaker sounded almost apologetic.

Didn't Cylin mention Shiranak? An elf who's promoting himself to godhood? "I'm not Shiranak," Lucian said. "And we're more interested in the gear carried by those men than in any... feast."

A pause, then a rough laugh. "The Raven thinks we mean to eat our prey."

One of the other figures shifted restlessly and said, "The Raven is right."

The main speaker cuffed the other. "No. This is bad meat. Not for eating." She turned her gaze back to Lucian. Moonlight glittered in her eyes. "The Raven will take all? Or will he leave some for us?"

Lucian's eyes narrowed. *Can I trust her—trust them? Why would they let us loot the men they killed?*

The leader still watched him, but the other two cowered back, hunching low and looking away from him.

Are they scared of us? Quicksilver asked in mind-speech. *After they took out those men without breaking a sweat?*

"I want half their weapons and ammunition," Lucian said. "And half their water. Also their money, if they have any."

"And we… may claim the rest?" she asked.

"You can have the rest," Lucian agreed, not without reservations.

She bowed to the ground. "The Raven is most generous." She jabbed her companions. "Go! Collect the Raven's share."

They scrambled to obey as if their lives depended on it, hastily looting the corpses bare. They spread out the bounty, such as if was, for Lucian's inspection. He knew it could still be a trap, but as quick as they were to cower before him, he didn't think so. Lucian floated down to the ground.

Guns, knives, canteens, clothing, and a few handfuls of trinkets summed up the worldly goods of the men of New Haven. Lucian picked the weapons he thought the best quality, three canteens, and two money purses. "I'll take these. The rest is yours."

The female bowed low again. "The Raven is benevolent. We will take the rest to our lair."

"I have a question for you," Lucian said. "What's the purpose of the totems at the farm back there?"

She considered him, then said, "They hide our lair from Shiranak's eyes. From the eyes of his servants. His gaze sees to all shadows, but the totems hide us from him."

Lucian raised an eyebrow. "You've met Shiranak?"

"We were… not always as we are," she admitted. "His anger fell upon us and changed us. We escaped, hid, found our lair. We do not follow Shiranak." She paused. "Does the Raven require our fealty?"

"No!" Lucian said quickly. "I don't require anyone's fealty. Just… don't hinder my travels."

"As you wish, Raven." All three bowed as if before a lord… or a god.

Unsettled and uncomfortable, Lucian collected the gear he'd claimed and flew back up to join Quicksilver and leave the ambush far behind.

Sunrise found them still flying. Lucian didn't have any trouble maintaining levitation through the night, but Quicksilver visibly drooped. Dark circles ringed his eyes, and his voice was thick and weary. "Hey, Lucian, how safe does the ground feel here?"

Solid, barren stone lay below them, and Lucian didn't feel any high concentrations of poison near the surface. "Good enough. And you need to rest before you fall out of the sky."

Quicksilver sank to the ground, stumbled, and caught himself. "Right. Yeah. Sorry."

"For needing sleep? Don't worry about it." Lucian landed beside him. Drawing on his reserves of magic, he shaped a small cave in the rock.

Quick raised an eyebrow at him. "Stars above, Lucian, you still have enough magic to do that?"

"Are you complaining about a sheltered place to sleep? I could probably keep going for a while, but this feels like a decent place to catch some rest."

"You could keep going for a while." Quick snorted. "You're

Lonewind's son, no doubt about that." He stepped into the shelter, dragged a blanket from his pack, and lay down.

Lucian didn't comment on the remark about his father. He remembered occasions when Lonewind had, for one reason or another, exhausted all his magic in a violent burst, then slept for two days straight. The thought made him wonder how long he would be unconscious if he were to do the same. Lucian pushed the question aside. He had no wish to leave himself so exposed and defenseless. He lay down beside Quicksilver and drew a thin shell of stone, pocked with ventilation holes, over their shelter.

Sleep was deep and without dreams that he remembered. Lucian roused to Quicksilver lightly shaking his shoulder. He groaned and blinked in the darkness.

"Sorry to wake you, Lucian, but could you open the rock? I really, *really* need to step outside for a minute," Quicksilver said.

"Sure, sorry," Lucian mumbled, sitting up.

Rock flowed back, creating an opening. Both he and Quicksilver listened for any sounds that would indicate something lurked outside before Quicksilver slipped out. Lucian let his head rest on the ground again, but now that he was awake, his own body made its needs known. Reluctantly, he rose and stepped outside into daylight. Chill air washed over him, making him realize how stuffy the shelter had grown. He guessed the time to be midafternoon.

Once necessities were dealt with, Lucian pulled their gear from the cave and smoothed the stone back to its natural form. Quicksilver raised an eyebrow.

"Not going to leave it?"

Lucian shook his head. "It clearly wasn't a natural formation. No need to leave it for people to ask questions."

Quick looked through his pack. "I've got some jerky and a couple of really old snack bars in here. You want one, Lucian?"

"Save the snack bars. Those things last for centuries,"

Lucian told him. "I have dried fruit and hardtack from my village. We should eat those first."

The bread was stale and dry, and the fruit leathery. Both served to rouse his thirst as they walked, though Lucian tried to conserve his water. The hard stone offered little shelter from sun or wind, and the spring air was still crisp and cool. Lucian looked to the sky, glad to see no clouds. Rain here would be miserable, and possibly dangerous if they were on low ground.

"What do you know of Shiranak?" he asked Quick.

"Not much. I heard the name a few times on my way to find you, but once I was certain it didn't refer to either you or Lonewind, I steered clear. Most of the folks I heard invoking his name acted like rabble-rousing fanatics, and I wanted nothing to do with that." He eyed Lucian. "You're thinking about last night?"

Lucian nodded. "Those three remind me of something, but I can't pin down what, exactly."

"Hmm." Quick considered. "Lynx, maybe?"

Lucian paused. "Lynx?"

"They moved a lot like him," Quick said. "I don't think any of them were blind, so not exactly like him, but they had that same predatory look to them. And, you know, the claws and armor."

Lynx was Quick's older half-brother by Ayliad. He and his twin, Echo, were also half-brothers to Chance's daughter Eria. The pair had been raised to serve their mother and grandmother as tools. Echo possessed a particularly powerful mind-reading ability, and Lynx served as his anchor and protector, pulling Echo back to himself when the voices in his head grew too strong. Lynx's greatest loyalty proved to be to his brother, and he had eventually been convinced that turning against his mother and joining Chance was in his brother's best interests.

That hadn't made his integration into the clan simple or easy. For Lynx, protecting Echo took priority over everything and everyone else. He'd gone so far as to allow one of the clan's most powerful enemies to magically alter him, giving him thick, armor-like hide and deadly claws and fangs. That particular enemy was long dead, but the comparison between Lynx and the figures they'd seen the previous night unsettled Lucian.

"If someone else is experimenting and finding ways of twisting elves and humans into monsters, they may well end up with something that resembles Lynx," Lucian finally said. "If Shiranak is playing with those powers, I definitely want nothing to do with him."

"Yeah." Quick shivered. "We don't need to deal with yet one more megalomaniac nutcase."

Conversation lapsed into silence. Lucian spent the rest of the day pondering the matter of the three escapees from Shiranak, but found no answers to his questions. The three days that followed took them through the rocky landscape and back into land that should have been fertile and full of spring growth, but supported only the heartiest of shrubs and weeds.

A low, restless anxiety lurked in the back of his mind and though it never fully formed, it never relented either. He missed Forest Town, most especially the simple predictability of the days. Here he had no Devin to offer him a schedule, or tell him when someone needed his help, no reports on the fields and the livestock. No distractions from his thoughts and no structure to his day.

The fourth day after New Haven, they reached another settlement. A wall surrounded a collection of houses and buildings. Quicksilver pointed at the wall. "This is a pretty good place. Not built on any ruins or anything. Some people found good water, and saw that plants would grow here, so they made a town. Independent. They've held off being taken over by any warlords so far, and are more than willing to run off people who make trouble or who they don't like."

"What are their opinions of bone men?" Lucian asked.

"They think bone men should be killed, burned, and used to fertilize the fields. Bone men are really not popular here, especially after the town's run-ins with New Haven people."

Lucian nodded. He could sense poisons in the ground, but they were less concentrated. "You want to stop here?"

"We need water," Quicksilver told him. "Unless you feel like delving into the ground and finding it yourself."

"No, I don't think that I should," Lucian said. "Can we pay for it?"

"I can pay; don't worry about that," Quicksilver assured him. He fussed with his mop of hair, arranging it to conceal his ears.

The action reminded Lucian that he couldn't walk openly into this town and expect immediate respect and acceptance. His short black hair didn't fall in a way that would hide distinctively elven ears, but a bandana served as temporary concealment.

They followed the road to the town gate. Quick cupped his hands around his mouth and called, "Hey there! Anyone in?"

"Who's there?" a gruff male voice answered.

"My name's Tammin. I was through here last year, late fall, and got supplies. I have a friend with me."

"Tammin." Sounds of movement came from the other side of the wall. Lucian waited impatiently. He'd forgotten what it was like to be around humans who didn't know him and who didn't fall over themselves to accommodate him. The gate creaked open. "All right, we don't have record of you making any trouble, Tammin. Make sure that doesn't change."

"No problem!" Quicksilver responded lightly. He nodded to the bearded man as they walked inside.

Tammin? Lucian asked.

*Yeah… It sounds more like a human name than Quicksilver does. So, I use it. And it *is* my name.*

A collection of children ran around a packed dirt court-yard. The gatekeeper, a bearded man aged beyond his years by toil and sickness, nodded at the two elves as they passed. Quicksilver flashed the man a disarming grin. The man smiled back and waved them on. The children paused in their play to look curiously at the newcomers. Lucian nodded to them and offered a smile. Several children waved, another hid shyly, while the rest stared openly at him.

"Come on, Lucian." Quicksilver pointed to a large building with solar panels on the roof. "They sell fresh water over here. Distilled, boiled, and purified to make it as clean as they are able."

Quicksilver continued talking, but Lucian only heard him peripherally. His gaze moved over the village, watching the people watching him. They weren't hostile, but they didn't trust him either. Patches of green grew around the bases of build-ings, and a smile touched the edges of Lucian's mouth.

Quicksilver noticed. "What's up?"

"Those are the first healthy plants I've seen since we left the forest. I've missed them," Lucian answered. The Guardian wanted to feed magic into the plants, to transform them into something that could further purify the land.

"Oh. Yeah, I miss seeing green as well. There is some around the area where Eria, Chance, and I have been living." Quicksilver motioned for Lucian to follow. "Come on, we should get our supplies and keep going."

The building proved to be the store as well as the source for fresh water. The shelves held a hodge podge of tools, weapons and ammunition in locked cases, cans of food decades past their "best by" date, but possibly still edible, as well as fresh produce and meat in the small coolers. Electricity powered the entire building. Quicksilver began bartering for water. Lucian handed him two packages of freeze-dried mixed fruit to add to their tab, which Quick accepted without even a pause in his bargaining.

Lucian left the interactions with people to his nephew. Being around humans, he kept expecting to hear familiar voices or feel the surrounding, soothing presence of the forest. Lacking those, he struggled to stay focused. A young woman in the aisle asked if he was all right, to which Lucian smiled politely.

"I'm fine, thank you."

If Devin had been present, he would have recognized the warning signs and suggested Lucian retire to his cave, where it was quiet and he could rest. Lucian could almost hear the young man's voice, and cast a look over his shoulder in search of him.

Lucian? Quicksilver's worried voice touched his mind, pulling Lucian's focus back to his surroundings.

We need to leave soon. Before something happens.

*Before *what* happens, Lucian? Do you sense something dangerous near?*

Yes. Me.

Almost done. Just have to pay for this. You can hang on that long, can't you? We need these supplies so we can go on and get to Chance, Quicksilver told him.

Find Chance. Yes, that's what I'm doing. That's why we're here. Lucian closed his eyes and drew a long, deep breath. *We are going to Chance.*

In the midst of the growing maelstrom of his thoughts, that was a solid point. Lucian clung to it as Quicksilver quickly wrapped up the haggling and accepted the fresh jugs of water. Lucian carried two jugs when Quick handed them to him, and followed when Quick led him out of the village with only a few rushed farewells to the locals.

Lucian walked in a blank haze. Quicksilver spoke to him, but he didn't know whether he answered. He thought he did sometimes, but Quicksilver only looked more distressed and anxious.

As the sky grew dark with night, Quicksilver made camp. Lucian sat, the world fading in and out around him. Quicksilver spoke his name, but Lucian didn't answer. He heard worry in Quick's voice, but it came from a distance.

If I sleep now, will I wake up outside of this dream? Dream? No, not a dream. Another game. She's toying with my mind again. Tremors of anger danced over his skin. *Why are you doing this, bitch? What sadistic joy do you take in torturing your own son?*

"I hate you." The whisper slipped from his lips.

Quicksilver turned. "What was that, Lucian? Did you say something?"

Lucian sneered. "What a lovely twist for you, Mother. Using Ayliad's son to lead me into your trap."

Quicksilver's eyes opened wide and he flinched back from the gleam in Lucian's eyes. "Lucian, I don't understand what you're saying. We're going to find Chance, remember? I came to bring you to Chance."

"Chance." When all else failed, when nothing made sense anymore, there was one thing she could never take from him. Lucian drew up his legs, wrapping his arms around them. "I have to find Chance. Where is he? Where did she take him?"

"Chance is with Eria, Lucian. He's safe, and I'm going to help you reach him," Quicksilver soothed. "But first, we have to rest. You need to sleep. Can you do that?"

Sleep? Weariness lingered around the edges of his mind. "I can sleep," he said.

"Good. Just lie down and sleep," Quicksilver said. He pulled a blanket over Lucian's shoulders. "Get some rest."

Lucian closed his eyes.

He woke with morning's light, exhausted and bleary. Quicksilver sprang to his side as he began to stir. His nephew's eyes were rimmed with heavy, dark lines and brimmed with worry. Lucian tried to sift through his memory, but the fragments he caught proved too shattered to tell him anything. Lifting his head, he saw only barren land. "Where are we? I thought we stopped in a village to get supplies. Did we?"

"You don't remember?" Quicksilver asked.

"I remember the village, I think. We did stop in one, didn't we?"

Quicksilver nodded. "Yeah, and we bought supplies. I thought about staying the night, but you were looking kind of off, and then you told me that we needed to leave before anything happened."

Lucian rolled stiff shoulders. "It was a bad night, then. I don't usually remember much about those." More honestly, he didn't remember anything other than fragments of the very beginning. "Did I say anything?"

Quicksilver hesitated, shifting uncomfortably. "Mostly you screamed a lot. And... well, said some stuff about Ayliad."

Lucian let out a long breath and ran his hands through his hair. "I'm sorry, Quick. I… this happens sometimes. I lose track of what's really going on. I don't know what I say."

"You don't have to apologize, Lucian," Quicksilver said quietly. "I know the stuff you said about her was true. I don't like to hear it, but I know it's true." He turned and busied himself with breakfast, leaving any further details of the night unsaid. "Did being in town set this off?"

"I don't think so," Lucian answered wearily. "I don't know what sets it off. It would happen in Forest Town, too. My people called them 'episodes'." He closed his eyes and tried to bring some semblance of order to his raging mind.

"Cylin, Devin, and Doctor Kinnel warned me about them, but I didn't realize they were... quite that bad." Quick shifted self-consciously. "I really should have listened to them. Here—have breakfast."

He shoved a plate with meat and reconstituted scrambled

eggs into Lucian's hands. Lucian ate without tasting anything. Pain and exhaustion, as always, followed on the wake of an episode, as if he had once again experienced all the torture he relived. Despite the bone-deep weariness, he looked to Quicksilver. "Up for walking today?"

"Tired, but I'll get by. Walking sounds safer than flying. Less distance to fall if I pass out," Quicksilver answered. "What about you? Pardon me for saying it, but you look like crap."

"I need to be moving," Lucian told him.

Quicksilver nodded and helped him to his feet. "Let's go, then."

Lucian didn't know how he got through the day. One foot went in front of the other, time after time, and he had no thoughts to give the empty landscape. They stopped late in the day, and Lucian lay down immediately. Quicksilver had to rouse him to get him to eat dinner. As soon as his plate was empty, Lucian lay back down and slipped into darkness. His last fleeting thought was a hope that he would not dream.

Laughter rang through the air, whimsical and teasing. A shudder raced down Lucian's spine. He spun around, searching for the source. Looking down, he saw that he stood on a hill, and the ground under him was covered with green.

He would have liked it if the growth had been any plant other than morning glory.

Vines clung to his legs. Lucian jerked away from their touch. "Where are you, bitch?"

"Such language, Lucian! I would think you didn't want to see me."

He spun to find her standing behind him. Soft blue eyes undressed him with their gaze, the petite mouth curved into a flirtatious smile, and the long blond hair flowed to the ground behind her. Vines of morning glory clung to her naked body, doing nothing more than teasing at covering her.

"Don't you have anything kinder to say to your own sister? Or your former lover, for that matter? You used to be better at pillow talk, Lucian."

Lucian swung at her smug, beautiful face. Ayliad easily avoided the blow, then flashed him a serpent's smile. "Such temper! It's always getting you into trouble." She laughed. "No, I take that back. Your temper is always getting OTHER people into trouble. People like Chance."

Lucian screamed in fury and lunged at her, but the vines seized him. "You have no right to talk about Chance! You're the one who hurt him, you and your mother!"

"And Mother's perfect Prince had nothing to do with it?" Ayliad laughed. "Really, Lucian, you know better." She pushed him back, and the vines dragged him down to the ground, pinning his limbs. "You never did anything to drive his actions? You never forced him into harm's way to protect you?"

Lucian thrashed against the hold of the vines. Ayliad licked her lips. With deliberate leisure, she unlaced his shirt. Lucian screamed in rage and refusal, ripping at the vines.

Overhead, the blue sky became black as clouds of poison rolled across it. Ayliad looked up and laughed as poison rained down on them. Black vines burst from the ground and swallowed her in their embrace. The black taint spread through the vines of morning glory, corrupting everything it touched. Vines dug into Lucian's left arm, invading his body with their taint. He screamed and fought to break free.

Ayliad pressed her mouth to his. "Join me, dear brother."

"No!"

The Guardian surged up in response, lashed back to purify the poison and drive the invading vines from him.

*Someone screamed in pain and rage, someone beyond the edges of the dream. Fury exploded in his mind. *We are not done. You will be MINE!**

The Guardian lashed out again, severing the black vines, and everything fell into darkness.

Sun poured down on his face when Lucian woke, the cry echoing in his mind. He blinked, trying to shake off the haze. The light in the sky seemed wrong, too bright.

"Lucian, are you awake?" Quicksilver scrambled to his

side. "I was worried. You wouldn't wake up when I tried to rouse you."

"How long did I sleep?" Lucian asked, rubbing his eyes.

Quicksilver hesitated. "Well… you've been out for a day and a half, give or take. Some of it I wouldn't really call resting, but you weren't awake."

"What?" Lucian sat up, then stopped, feeling something softer than stone under his hand. He started at the ground. "What… what is this?"

Quicksilver licked his lips. "You started screaming. I tried to wake you, or calm you down, but something set off the Guardian, and…" He gestured at the patch of grass surrounding Lucian. "And that happened."

Lucian's fingers curled in the grass. He could feel it working into the toxins already, breaking them down into nutrients. It was the Guardian's work without question. But why?

"Someone call to me in the dream." Lucian shuddered, fiercely hoping the call he'd heard had nothing to do with the person who invaded his nightmare. He looked to Quicksilver as if his nephew might have some answer.

Quick sat back on his heels. "And the Guardian reacted. I certainly felt that happen."

Lucian nodded. "But I don't understand why the Guardian would react to a dream. It knows the difference." Much as he might wish the Guardian could drive Ayliad out of his nightmares.

Quicksilver pursed his lips, thinking. "Maybe it didn't react to the dream. Maybe it reacted to whoever was calling to you."

Lucian frowned. "But why would the Guardian do that?" He remembered the cry of pain, then the fury from the other voice, and rubbed his head, trying to shake off the sensation of vines crawling over his skin… then under it. Stiffly, he climbed to his feet. "We should keep going. Chance is waiting."

"Is it all right to just leave those?" Quicksilver nodded at the plants.

"If they survive, they'll break down the poisons, just as the trees in my forest do. I know the poisons will eventually break down on their own, but the corrupted magic might not. These will deal with both." Lucian gestured at the plants. "We should go. I'm ready."

Quicksilver offered no arguments. "All right."

Another day passed. Exhaustion continued to nip at Lucian's heels, but he kept moving, more afraid of what his mind would conjure if he stopped.

"Do you think that Lonewind knows what happened here?"

Quicksilver's question came without preamble as they trekked along the edge of a deeply pitted road. Lucian stared into the distance, though he saw little but more wasteland and a collection of hills. "The last time I spoke to him, things hadn't hit the fan yet. He talked about the last world they'd found—not fit to live on, but weird and beautiful with active volcanoes and constant eruptions, lava spraying through the air. He said he'd visit again after the next planet. But if he's tried to come since this place went to crap, I don't know. If he did, he wasn't able to reach me through the spirit world." Lucian shuddered. "If he called, I'm not sure I would be able to hear him through all the chaos and screams out there."

"So he might not even know," Quicksilver said.

"I'd be surprised if he doesn't," Lucian said. "He doesn't visit every year on my birthday anymore, but he certainly doesn't go fifty years without saying hello. He worries about us too much to do that." He smiled as he said it. His relationship with his father had been sometimes rocky, sometimes outright antagonistic, but time had healed many wounds and mended many rifts. "Last time he passed on a message from Jayde asking when Cilvi and I were going to start having children.

And from the incredible blush Tash got after Lonewind spoke to him, I suspect her message to her son was more detailed." Tash's mother had never been shy about her desire for children and grandchildren.

Quicksilver laughed. "I remember that. Always looked forward to Lonewind's visits."

"So did Chance," Lucian said. "He was always glad to hear the news of everyone—including his sons."

"I'm surprised Lonewind still agreed to take Lynx and Echo with him when you and Chance decided to stay," Quicksilver said.

"He offered the choice to everyone, even if he didn't like them. Lynx decided leaving the planet was better for Echo, so off they went," Lucian said. "I was more surprised that you decided to stay." He looked at his nephew. Quicksilver had been one of the last members of the tribe to give his decision, and he'd never publicly offered a reason for his final choice to remain instead of joining Lonewind in the stars, even in the intervening two hundred years. Up until the moment when Quicksilver gave his decision, Lucian had always thought his nephew more likely to go than stay.

"Lonewind understood my reason," Quicksilver said, giving no more answer than before. "Besides, we weren't planning on this being permanent, once Lonewind and the others found a new world. Or I wasn't, at least. I miss everyone, though. Especially now."

"Even Lynx and Echo?" Lucian asked in a gentle tease to lighten the mood.

"Are you kidding?" Quicksilver asked. "I would *love* to have Lynx here now. I might not have Echo's 'favored brother' status, but I'm still entitled to some protections as a sibling. Even if Lynx does look like a walking lizard." He let out a long breath. "Echo, on the other hand… Echo's better off not being here. All that mess in the spirit world, with *his* abilities? I… don't think even Lynx would be able to keep him sane."

Lucian nodded slowly in understanding. Some elves could read minds. Most knew how to turn the ability off and only used it at need. Echo listened to everything and everyone, all the time. From the moment his skill had manifested, Ayliad, Willow, and Lonewind's brother Moonfire had taught him to take it all in, looking into every mind, delving into every secret, to the point where he could completely reflect and take on the personalities of the people whose minds he'd explored.

His twin brother, Lynx, had been charged with controlling and protecting Echo. Brain and brawn, some might have said, but Lynx was the dominant twin, claiming both roles. Echo was like a permanent child, eternally surrounded by all the playmates anyone could want and more within his own head, stunting his mental and emotional development. Like a child, he could throw a tantrum when denied what he wanted. Unlike a child, he could manipulate the minds of others to achieve his goals. And unlike a child, he sometimes was over-whelmed by the more forceful personalities he'd absorbed, mirroring that other person. Lucian had more than once seen Echo mirroring him, and it was truly disconcerting.

He looked to the empty blue sky. *I hope everyone out there is safe, wherever they are now.*

~

Days blended together as Lucian found a new routine in travel. They walked or flew and watched for creatures, bone men, bandits, and other dangers. They visited settlements for supplies when necessary, but only entered those Lucian deemed safe, where the poison levels were low enough to not rile the Guardian. Somehow, Quicksilver always had enough money to pay for their needs, and always in the local currency. Their purchases were simple—water and food, sometimes a piece of gear when something wore out, though Lucian could fix anything metal that broke. He did notice when Quicksilver bought a long scarf of lightweight cloth in one town, and after they left, he asked about it.

Quicksilver handed it to him. "A head wrap. Start wearing it before we get close to the next city." He dug a similar wrap from his bag and wound it around his head. "Lots of people wear them around here, and they're the best way to hide pointed ears."

Lucian frowned as he tried to imitate Quicksilver. He'd made some effort to conceal his more identifiably elven features in other towns, but hadn't prioritized the disguise. "That hasn't been much of an issue before. Why now?"

"The people around here are kind of... weird on the matter of elves, so I don't want to make it an issue."

"They don't believe in elves?" Lucian asked.

"No, they do. That's the problem," Quicksilver said uncomfortably. "At least some of the people in charge hold to the philosophy that elves are demons, and we're the source of all that's wrong with the world today. Those people butt heads with the ones who hold to the idea that elves are the ancient spirits or gods to be honored, respected, and stayed the hell away from. Officially, people worship family gods or practice pseudo-animism."

Lucian considered that as he followed Quicksilver. "Tell me more about this place."

"You'll know we're getting close because you'll see the smoke plumes. Before the war, it was a factory town, and it still is, though I don't know what they were making before or how they escaped being bombed to oblivion. They maintain as much technology as they can, and they produce good quality stuff. I didn't buy any—it's expensive, as you might guess, and even my fingers aren't *that* light. But Lucian, I had *ice cream* there last time.

"It's not a place I want to linger, though. I got pretty uncomfortable senses from the town and the people. Felt like a city on the brink of a revolt, if you know what I mean. And having seen the guards, I don't think I'd put money on the rebels succeeding. The city leader's a ruthless woman."

"You are not making me look forward to this visit," Lucian told him.

Quicksilver let out a long breath. "I'm tempted to suggest you wait outside, but to be honest, I'd feel safer going in there with someone rather than alone."

"All right," Lucian allowed. "We'll stick together, and won't stay long."

Late afternoon of the following day, they reached the city gates. Thick steel doors, marked with only small patches of rust, loomed balefully over them. Lucian suppressed the urge to walk up to one and metal-shape a hole through one. Guards carrying military rifles stood at the gates, and he glimpsed movement from the top of the wall.

"Identify yourselves," one guard ordered.

"Travelers in need of supplies, sir," Quicksilver said. "My name's Tammin, and this is Lucian."

"Hmm." The guard's eyes narrowed and he flipped through a ledger. "You were through here last year, Tammin."

"Yes sir."

The guard flipped pages again, studied something, then studied Quicksilver. "Looks like you were here and gone before the seditionists started preaching."

"Um, the what?" Quicksilver asked, openly surprised. "Seditionists?"

"Fellow claiming to be a missionary, spreading the worship of ancient spirits in the name of 'Shiranak.' Caused a lot of trouble. We're not admitting anyone who came to the city during that period. However, you seem to be in the clear. Stay out of trouble, Tammin. And your friend as well."

"Absolutely, sir," Quicksilver said quickly. "Thank you!"

"We're still searching your bags before letting you in," the guard told them.

Quicksilver opened his mouth to protest, but swallowed the words back with a visible effort. "I didn't have to do that last time," he said, reluctantly relinquishing his pack.

"Smugglers bringing in black market goods," the guard told him curtly. "What weapons are you carrying?"

"My knife, and there's a pistol in the bag," Quicksilver said. "Family heirloom." The tension in his voice said he wouldn't give up the weapon without protest.

The human unpacked all Quicksilver's gear, checking everything, including the gun, before finally nodding. "Nothing that requires confiscation," he said, leaving it all for Quicksilver to pack away again. The man turned to Lucian, waiting.

Lucian silently allowed the man to take his bag. The guard began unloading the contents. When he found a small bundle wrapped in cloth, he unwound the cloth and looked with dubious distaste at the worn wooden figurine. "What sort of trash is this?"

Lucian drew an indignant breath, standing tall and glaring at the guard. "By what right do you insult the god of my hearth?" he demanded, voice chill.

The guard jerked as if stung. "What? God?" He looked at the statue in his hand as if only now really seeing it. His eyes grew wide. "My deepest apologies. I did not realize… I would not insult any man's gods."

Lucian's stormy scowl did not relent. "Ficgesh has watched over my family for countless generations and guarded our travels. Now you dare mock my god?"

The guard grew pale. "Sir, I offer my deepest apologies for my ignorant words. Tonight, I will offer libations for the offense

I have given your god. Forgive me. I'll detain you no longer." He quickly wrapped the figurine and placed it back in Lucian's bag, then waved for Lucian to collect the items that had been unpacked—not even half the contents of his bag.

Lucian nodded curtly as he repacked. "I hope not everyone within these walls speaks so carelessly."

The guard bowed again. "No, sir. Please forgive me. We have had many heretics seeking to enter and undermine the faithful, but clearly, you are no such man."

He was tempted to needle the man just one more time, but they had access to the city, and starting a fight wouldn't get them supplies. He simply gave the guard a dark scowl and shouldered his bag. The gates shuddered open with a clatter of chains and gears. As they walked through the entry passage, Lucian glanced up, noting the murder holes along the way.

Quicksilver glanced at him. *Um, Lucian, since when do you carry a hearth god?*

Cylin gave it to me. For protection. Seems like it worked. I was worried I'd have to hypnotize him to keep him from poking too deep into my bag.

From Cylin? Remind me to thank her when we get back, Quicksilver said.

Another armed guard awaited them at the far end, opening the gate to allow them into the city. "You're entering Gerto Sher. Curfew is at sunset, strictly enforced. You are allowed access to the market and lower-level residential areas. Factory areas are restricted. Rabble-rousing will be suppressed with extreme prejudice."

"Understood," Quicksilver said quickly. "We're here for supplies, and then will be on our way."

"Good. Even the factories don't need fresh workers at the moment." The guard waved them past.

What is that supposed to mean? Lucian asked Quicksilver.

Quick cast a glance over his shoulder. *It means they've had enough trouble in town that the factories are filled with people either in slavery or indentured servitude as punishment for their crimes.*

Lucian's eyes narrowed, but he said nothing.

That's what the rumors said, at least. I don't know for sure; didn't go poking around to find out. Quicksilver nodded to the main street and spoke aloud. "The market is down this way."

The buildings stood two or three stories, packed together with narrow alleys between. Built of brick or covered with metal siding, they were uniformly drab and gray with soot from the factories. The smell of coal smoke and metal hung in the air. Lucian searched for any break in the monotonous dulled hues, but even the people wore drab clothes. Most covered their heads with wraps like those he and Quicksilver wore.

How do they live here? There's no color!

Those who can afford it brighten the insides of their homes with decorations, I'm told, Quicksilver answered. *The rest make do with what they can.*

A shout echoed from further down the street, followed by a low but steady rumble of voices, not clear enough to under-stand the words. Lucian frowned. "Sounds like a chant. Do they hold assemblies?"

A woman hurrying up the street paused, hearing him. "Those crazy disciples of Shiranak are gathered at the statue again for prayers. Rumor is the watch is coming with explosives to blast the damned thing to pieces this time, but they won't risk it with all the people there. Not yet, at least. This keeps up, though, and who knows what'll come of it."

"What statue?" Quicksilver asked. "There weren't any monuments in the square last time I was here."

"*The* statue," she said sharply. "Shiranak. That crazy

fanatic called it out of the ground. Go see for yourself if you don't believe me."

Lucian didn't need Quicksilver to direct him toward the square. The street led straight to it. Crowds of people jammed the area, congregating around a marble statue at least twenty feet tall.

"The faithful will be blessed!" A man stood on the statue's pedestal, shouting at the crowd. "But those who deny Lord Shiranak will feel his wrath! Brothers and sisters, join us. Pray with us! Call upon Lord Shiranak to judge the unfaithful and cleanse this land! Call upon him to bring us justice, and cast down those who oppress the weak, who steal our children, who cast us into chains, darkness, and death!"

Some people cheered, others screamed insults and taunts. Guards stood around the perimeter of the square, but none moved to break up the assembly, though several twitched and gripped their weapons tightly at the man's call for justice against oppressors. Lucian read worry in the stances of the people closest to him. The situation was not a riot yet, but it wouldn't take much of a spark to start one.

Lucian turned his attention to the statue itself. Offerings, mostly food and coin, littered the pedestal on which it stood. The figure was tall, both majestic and imposing. His form was slender and graceful, dressed in an elegant, archaic styled pants and tunic, with a long cloak of feathers covering one shoulder and hanging down his back. His features were sharp and angular, his expression stern, but somehow hinting at an air of benevolence. He held one hand out as if in a greeting or to bestow a blessing. His hair hung loose, tucked behind clearly pointed ears.

"Damn," Quicksilver breathed in awe. "How did someone get away with making something like that?"

"No one 'made' it," a man said sharply, hearing him. "The prophet Nasser came to our city to proclaim Shiranak. When the people rejected him, he prayed to Shiranak to give us a sign. Lord Shiranak granted his prayer, raising this statue fully formed from the depths of the earth." The man glared at Quicksilver and Lucian. "Are you here to worship, or to join the unbelievers in their mockery?"

"We're here to buy supplies," Lucian retorted. "If you want to worship ancient spirits, go right ahead. Just point me to a store."

The adherent continued to scowl, but jabbed a finger toward a building. "You may not make your choice today, strangers, but the time draws near. Soon, all must decide whether to stand with Shiranak or against him."

Okay, note to self, don't say things like that out loud around here, Quicksilver glanced to Lucian. *What do you think of that thing?*

Lucian gave the statue another long look as they walked toward the store. *Decent work, a little rushed. The stone on the surface isn't the best for this sort of thing, so he had to pull pretty deep underground to get something good to work with. He left some flaws in the stone, but not critical ones, so they aren't likely to weaken it enough that it will fall over before someone takes a sledgehammer or explosives to it. Whoever did this was a decent rock shaper, and the image is pretty much an idealized elf. I'm glad the figure is male. If it was female, I might suspect that someone was trying to establish a cult around the worship of Mother.*

Quick blanched at the thought, then frowned. *That statue was made with rock shaping? So this 'prophet' was an elf?*

Ready-made miracles on call, Lucian said. *Either he was an elf or he had an accomplice who was. Might even be more effective that way, especially if the prophet was truly a believer. Then if he were arrested, he couldn't give away any secrets.*

Sneaky. So, Shiranak. Anyone you recognize?

Lucian answered with a quick shake of his head as he stepped around a cluster of people. *Stylized. Maybe someone from Willow's era, but could as easily be from somewhere else entirely. Maybe someone we've never encountered. Shiranak is probably smart enough not to put his own face on his statues. But it seems likely he's old blood, whoever he is.*

I'm honestly not sure whether I'd be happier finding out it's someone we've never met or not. Stars know the old blood produced more than its share of narcissistic megalomaniacs. Quicksilver pushed open the shop door. "Anyone here?"

The voice of a bored teenager answered. "Yeah, we're open. Whaddaya want?" Lucian saw a brown-haired young man slouched at the counter. He straightened a little when he saw that his visitors weren't familiar faces. "Sorry. Uh, can I help you? Dried food's down the second aisle, water jugs are by the cooler."

"Thanks," Quicksilver said.

Lucian paused to close the door and take in the store. Shelves sagged under the weight of cans of food, the electric lights shone with a steady illumination, and in the back of the store, coolers hummed. Lucian slowly walked down an aisle, seeing goods he'd not found since the war, fresh from the local factories. The wire rack at the front of the store even held a meager assortment of magazines and prints. At least half of them were pornographic, and another quarter devoted to either decrying or promoting the worship of Shiranak.

Can we afford any of this, Quicksilver? Lucian asked.

As long as we don't buy too much. Essentials first, then we can see about extras. Quicksilver was examining the prices on the jugs of water.

"Quite the tense situation outside. What's with all that?" Lucian asked the cashier, nodding toward the door.

The youth studied Lucian before answering. "You guys aren't from around here, are you?"

"Nope," Lucian agreed, giving the youth a disarming smile. "This is the first I've heard of Shiranak. What's the big deal?"

"Yeah, well, it's been going strong since the prophet came through. I didn't care at first; figured the guards would have him strung up or run out of town pretty quick. But then he raised that statue in the middle of town, and no one knew what to do about it all. Some of the officials pretty well went nuts trying to explain it away."

"Is the prophet still in town?" Lucian asked.

The youth shook his head. "Naw, moved on once he taught some folk the prayers and such. They even sing sometimes. My dad thinks they're going to be the ruin of the city, but I don't know. You aren't from around here, so maybe you can't tell, but this city's a pretty crappy place if you're not rubbing elbows with the upper crust. You get in debt, and before you know it you're stuck in the factory, working 'til you drop. If Shiranak actually brings change or whatever, is it really going to be worse than how things are right now? My sister died of the black cough after working in a factory because she couldn't buy the medicine for it."

Lucian nodded in sympathetic understanding and went to help Quicksilver carry several large jugs of water. They collected an assortment of dried food, and the cashier added up their total. Quicksilver paid, though he grimaced at the price. Outside, the noise of the crowd continued steadily.

"I don't think we're going to make it out of town before sunset," Quicksilver said. Turning to the young man, he asked, "Where can we stay for the night where we won't get mugged or harassed?"

Lucian almost protested, but he swallowed his objections to staying the night. Quick was right, with the press of people and the addition of their supplies, they wouldn't easily make the gate before sunset, no matter how much this city set him on edge.

The young man considered the question. "Depends. You lean more towards the side that's with Shiranak, or the side that's against him?"

"Is there a side that's still 'keep our heads down until we're sure which way the wind's going to blow'?" Quicksilver asked.

"Honestly, not much of one. Head south from the market and try the Bronze Turtle," the young man said. "Probably the closest you're going to get."

Lucian carried the jugs of water, and Quicksilver took the rest of the supplies. They skirted the edges of the square, Quick in the lead, and found the Bronze Turtle as the sky was growing dark. Along the way, they mysteriously acquired enough money to pay for a room and dinner, though Quicksilver haggled with the proprietor before settling on a price. They carried their gear up to the room—two beds, no lice, and a small bathroom was all they could expect. Lucian opened the window and breathed in the evening air. Lights glowed around the statue of Shiranak, and he heard the voices of people in the courtyard despite the curfew. Restless people. Angry people.

A handful of patrons sat in the dining room, but no one talked much. People nodded in silent greeting to Lucian and Quicksilver when they sat, and a pair of young women whispered, giggled softly, and blushed, heads bent together. The food was tolerable, if overcooked. Lucian didn't linger, returning to the room once he'd finished the meal. Quicksilver stayed downstairs for a little longer, but he came up before too long.

"No one's chatty tonight. It's too quiet," he told Lucian.

"Only in here," Lucian replied. He sat at the window, listening to the growing sounds of unrest. "Things are going to get ugly tonight in the square."

"Shit," Quicksilver cursed. "If they have riots in the city, no one's leaving tomorrow. Including us."

"Oh, we're leaving," Lucian said. "Not until it gets later and darker, but we're leaving tonight. Get some rest. I'll wake you when it's time."

Quicksilver nodded, grim. "You got it."

Quick lay down and appeared to drop into sleep immediately. Lucian kept his post at the window, listening to the crowd. He sensed outward with his rock-shaping magic, feeling the tread of feet on the streets, the movement of people around the statue.

He stiffened, sensing magic manipulating the statue. Lucian watched, feeling the working of the magic as he realized what must be happening. Someone, or a group of people, were physically assaulting the statue, trying to bring it down. A rock-shaper was repairing their damage as it happened. Lucian's eyes sank closed as he shut out distractions and focused on the statue. It was a difficult reach, on the very edge of his range of manipulation, but he tweaked one of the weak points in the statue's torso. Not enough that anyone watching would notice anything. Only someone who was attuned to magic, or someone who was actively shaping the stone, would notice Lucian's touch.

Who's there? The mental voice was sharp and tight, and in it Lucian read shocked alarm. The other had thought himself the only elf in the city, or at the very least, the only rock-shaper.

A traveler passing through. No one you need worry about, unless your actions tonight force me to delay my plans to leave, Lucian answered.

Who in the Ancients are you? You're not a servant of Shiranak. I would have been told if another was here. Certainly if it was someone of your power.

Just a traveler, Lucian repeated. *I have no part of Shiranak. All I'm looking to do is leave town by midnight. So I politely ask if you can refrain from starting a riot before then?*

A long silence, then the other answered. *I… will try.* Another pause. *Shiranak could use your assistance. There is much to be gained from joining his cause.*

I have my own cause and my own business, Lucian answered curtly. *I'm not looking for an alliance right now.*

Then perhaps later. I hope to speak to you again sometime. Perhaps face to face, next time.

"I doubt it," Lucian muttered aloud. He pulled back his senses and rested, listening for any sign that the trouble outside had escalated.

Near midnight, the other elf's voice touched his mind. *If you have not yet left, friend, you should do so soon. The anger of the repressed will not remain restrained for much longer.*

Understood. Lucian said nothing more. Climbing stiffly to his feet, he shook Quicksilver's shoulder. "Time to go."

Quicksilver yawned and stretched. "Skipping out in the middle of the night… That's not going to make us welcome if we show up again."

"I doubt that'll be a concern," Lucian said. "Rioting will start any minute now and I don't want to be here when it does."

"It's that bad?" Quicksilver asked. He rose and pulled on his pack. "And I bet I can't even head downstairs and get our money back."

Lucian shrugged. "You pickpocketed it from other people on the way here. It's not that much of a loss, is it?"

"Hey!" Quicksilver objected. "I worked hard for it."

"And you can work just as hard next time, in the next town," Lucian told him, hefting the jugs of water and stabilizing them with a touch of levitation. He dropped the room key on the table and opened the window.

Quicksilver cast a final, sorrowful look at the bed, then followed Lucian out. "Next place probably won't have clean, comfortable beds," he said with a sigh.

Something crashed in the square, and voices rose in anger. A small explosion rocked the ground. Quicksilver shut his mouth on his complaints and levitated alongside Lucian. *I'm done griping,* he promised. *We can go.*

They glided over the wall in silence, well over the heads of the guards. Had any of them looked up, they would have glimpsed two figures flying above them, then vanishing into the night.

Keeping his mental voice focused just to Quicksilver, Lucian said, *Be careful when we talk. There's at least one other elf in the city, a follower of Shiranak. I spoke with him briefly, but didn't mention that I wasn't alone.*

Someone was there? Quicksilver asked in surprise. *What did he say?*

He made a token effort to recruit me, but he wasn't expecting anyone to be in the city, so he wasn't prepared, and when I declined, he let it go. Mentioned that someone of my power would be useful to Shiranak. He didn't give me any clues as to Shiranak's identity, though. I didn't ask, either. Didn't want to sound like I was actually interested.

What was he doing there, though? Quicksilver asked, voice as focused as Lucian's.

I sensed him manipulating the statue, so I assume it was under attack and he was repairing it. I strongly suspect he was also inciting the rioters.

Shit... Well, that will be a mess no matter who wins. And if the city officials realize that a real, actual 'ancient spirit' was in the city, rioting the people, it might never be safe for us to return there. Quicksilver shot a scowl over his shoulder. *And avoiding Gerto Sher doesn't leave many other options for resupplying around here. A few villages, but their prices run twice those of the city, at least for strangers.*

That assumes the local authorities win, Lucian said. *Unless Shiranak is sacrificing one of his on-hand prophets, pushing this to the breaking point implies an expectation of success.*

Quicksilver considered that and grimaced. *Hard to say which idea I like less, honestly. Especially if Shiranak deals with dissent by turning people into creatures like those we encountered near New Haven.*

They kept to the air for most of the night. Lucian was worn, but had no desire to put himself on the ground anywhere near the city, where a patrol might come across them. They came to ground an hour before sunrise and walked on for a time. When finally they found an abandoned house, they took shelter inside, disguised their presence as best they could, and dropped into exhausted sleep.

By the time Lucian roused, a fire burned in the stove, a kettle of water boiling merrily. Just for a moment, he expected to hear Ahmea in the kitchen, making breakfast, and to feel Cilvi snuggled up against him. He reached toward the spot where she would lie, but only empty air and cold floor met his searching hand.

"Morning, Lucian," Quicksilver said. He sat at the rickety table, carefully perched on a chair with only three legs as he sipped a steaming mug of tea.

"Morning, Quick." Lucian crawled from his nest of blankets, raked fingers through his black hair, and made himself tea. The smell of mint reminded him of Forest Town, gently pushing back the phantoms of older memories.

They ate a breakfast of dried meat from Gerto Sher. Lucian could swear he tasted ash and acrid smoke in the meat. He wondered whether he actually wanted to know what animal it came from. He sniffed it, but smelled nothing out of the ordinary.

"Something wrong with it?" Quick asked.

Lucian shook his head. "Probably not. Unless it tastes odd to you."

Quicksilver took another bite, chewing thoughtfully. "No, seems pretty normal to me. Maybe a little bit of 'industry smoke' in the background."

"Perhaps that's it," Lucian said. He finished his piece of meat and packed his gear. "I want more distance from that city. I feel like it's still clinging to my skin." He rubbed his arm as if he could wipe away the sensation. "How much further to Chance?"

"At least a month," Quick said. "Longer if we run into trouble."

"Only if that trouble slows us down," Lucian retorted. *And I won't stop until I find Chance.*

They shouldered their gear and took to the road. Lucian cast a look over his shoulder toward the city they'd left, now long out of sight.

Who is Shiranak? What's his goal? Growing up, Lucian had met many powerful elves, both enemies and allies. A few had respected his father's desire to just be left alone, and hadn't tried to draw their clan into plots and power struggles, and an even rarer few had understood that desire. The rest saw only a threat to their power and a tool to further their ambitions.

As human technology advanced, the most powerful elves found ways to conceal themselves, leave the planet, or disappear. Lucian and the rest of the clan who didn't leave with Lonewind worked to blend in with the humans. Had Shiranak done the same? Put aside pride and allowed himself to be mistaken for a mere mortal, a powerless human? Few of the ancient elves, those powerful enough to have survived millennia, could manage that.

Without preamble or explanation, Lucian said, "If Shiranak has actually been passing as a human until recently, he's more capable of humility than most old-blood elves."

Quicksilver raised an eyebrow in surprise, but followed the thread of Lucian's thoughts. "That's true. I can't think of any we've met outside the clan who could give up that arrogant superiority and act like a human."

Lucian chuckled. "Even *in* our clan, the only really powerful elf who I think could do so would be Arrel." The elf had been a good friend of Lonewind's, an equal to Lonewind's magic, but one of the least proud people Lucian knew, with an insatiable curiosity.

Quicksilver burst out laughing.

Lucian gave him a puzzled look. "What?"

Quick wiped his eyes, still laughing. "Lucian, *you* passed as human for *years*."

"Well, sure, but—"

"You are one of the most powerful elves in the clan. Seriously. Who's stronger than you? Lonewind, Arrel, who else? You and Chance are pretty evenly matched, and neither of you are slouches as magic goes."

"I'm not old blood." Lucian folded his arms across his chest.

"Your parents are Lonewind and Willow. You're older than probably two-thirds of the elves on the planet. You count as 'powerful,' like it or not."

"I am not *that* old," Lucian protested.

Quicksilver cast him a long, dubious look.

"Okay, yes, I've been around a while, but I'm not *old*. Old isn't about years. It's about adaptability. That's the problem the old-blood elves have. They can't or won't adjust and adapt to the world; they expect it to adapt to them.'"

"Old is no longer adaptable, huh?" Quicksilver pondered that. After nearly half an hour of silent walking, he spoke again. "What if Shiranak isn't old blood?"

"Why do you say that?" Lucian asked.

"Well, we already assume he didn't put his own face on that statue—it's an idealized image. We never heard of this cult of Shiranak before the war, so it's relatively new. An adaptation to the way things are now." Quicksilver waved a hand in a sweeping gesture. "Pretend for a minute that I decided to start a cult to worship elves. I wouldn't set myself up as the god. Who'd follow that? But if I built it around, say, Lonewind, present him as the ideal, people would follow that. Stars, if I tried, I bet I could build one around you, Lucian."

Lucian held up his hands as if to ward off attack. "No. Oh no. Don't even suggest that. It's bad enough having the people of Forest Town worshiping me."

"I wouldn't *do* it, Lucian! But you and Lonewind would be far easier to present as gods. You have the looks, the power. I would just be the humble servant, proclaiming your will rather than promoting myself. The messenger, who controls access to the words of the gods."

Lucian shivered, following that idea far too easily. "So the image could be a figurehead, and Shiranak could be anyone, man or woman. And we have no idea what they want."

"True. And they still might be someone we know. There are even elves who used to be part of the clan and split off to go their own ways. But I prefer that idea to that of a new, crazed, overly powerful megalomaniac."

"I don't," Lucian said grimly. "Fanatics and true believers can be far more dangerous than a single person, even one with strong magic. *Ideas* hold more power than people do, Quick. And I don't like any idea that sets us up as gods."

Quicksilver didn't have an answer to that. They walked on through the day.

What would happen if Shiranak found Forest Town? Would he back off from another elf's people, or would he try to convert them? How would my people react? A thin, humorless smile found Lucian's lips. *Cylin would probably just shoot the messenger. And if she did... I wouldn't blame her in the least.*

Concern for Forest Town nagged at the back of his thoughts, much as he assured himself that the humans could deal with whatever trouble might find them. He briefly considered venturing into the spirit realm to check on them, but one look at the teeming hordes of hungry, angry wraiths reminded him how stupid that would be. The worry never completely relented through the following days of travel, and taunted his dreams. Something more lurked in those dreams, a whispering voice telling him that he was too far from the protection of his home. It eluded him when he tried to capture it, slipping away like water through his fingers.

They followed the remains of roads where they found them, and otherwise used the sun and stars for navigation. Sometimes they passed listing light posts, or the blasted remains of road signs. Most were illegible, destroyed by blasts, wind, and the caustic rain, but on occasion Lucian or Quicksilver picked out logos of once-famous restaurants, or announcements of odd tourist destinations. The days were hot, and the nights chill. Most days, they traveled from dusk until a few hours after dawn, then found shelter where they could to sleep out the heat of the day.

Lucian jerked awake from a dream of fire and screams, his heart racing. He sucked in rapid gulps of air, both confused and relieved to find them free of smoke. The stone where he laid felt of his magic, but it wasn't his cave, and he didn't feel the forest anywhere near.

Where am I? Why am I here? Why does the land feel dead? Where is my forest?

"Breakfast, Lucian." Quicksilver poked his head into the shelter, then frowned. "Are you all right?"

"Uh… Sure," Lucian managed as the world settled into focus. "Thanks." Confusion still clung to him, but he remembered he'd been traveling with Quicksilver for something very important.

He ate, then followed when Quicksilver started walking. Night crept across the sky, bringing cool air. Stars sprinkled the expanse. The larger moon was waning, and the smaller two shone only as slivers above.

Flickers of movement distracted Lucian as they walked, the trackless path of ghosts around them. Every time he tried to look at one, it vanished, but if he didn't focus, he could see them from the corner of his eye: elves walking about, talking to one another, or sometimes, screaming in silent agony.

Quicksilver commented about the night. Lucian made a sound of agreement, though he wasn't sure what Quicksilver had said. The flickering forms danced around them, but they didn't seem to concern Quick, who only talked about unrelated matters. He kept glancing at Lucian from the corner of his eye with an air of concern that inexplicably grated on Lucian's nerves.

He made yet another attempt to drag Lucian into conversation. "You seem off tonight. Are you feeling okay?"

"Your guess is as good as mine."

"Lucian!" Quicksilver stopped, hands planted on his hips. "I'm serious!"

"So am I." Lucian walked past him.

An exasperated sigh. "Lucian! Dammit, how hard is it to actually answer at least *one* question tonight?"

Lucian spun, eyes flashing. "I *did* answer. Your guess," he jabbed a finger at Quick's chest, "is as good as mine. How am I doing? Do I 'feel okay'? Why don't *you* try answering that, because I *do not know the fucking answer*. Ask the damned ghosts— maybe they know!"

Quicksilver stumbled back a step when Lucian's voice rose to a shout, eyes wide. He blinked, then cautiously asked, "The... ghosts?"

"Yes, the ghosts!" Lucian snapped. "You know, the ones that have been hanging around us all evening?"

Quick's eyes swept their surroundings then returned to Lucian. "I don't see any ghosts, Lucian."

Around them, ghosts threw back their heads in silent laughter at the absurd statement.

Quicksilver shivered, looking around again. "What do they look like? Anyone we know?"

"They look like elves. Screaming."

"And you *see* them?" Quicksilver repeated.

"*Yes*, I see them. And they see us."

Quick pulled his coat more tightly around himself. "Are you… sure we should be traveling tonight, Lucian? We can stop here. There's a little shelter up ahead." He pointed to a shadow from a broken slab of pavement jutting over the road.

"Afraid of ghosts?" Lucian sneered.

"Afraid of the sorts of ghosts most likely to gather around you," Quick said in a low voice. "I'd… be more comfortable if we stopped until you aren't seeing them."

There was a reason they shouldn't stop, a pressing, important, vital reason to keep going, but it hung just beyond Lucian, taunting. Quicksilver's face pinched with concern. Finally, Lucian acquiesced. "All right."

Quicksilver led the way to the slab and set about making camp and lighting a small fire. Lucian sat in the shelter of the slab and gazed across the wasteland. He leaned back on his elbows. Something stung his arm, like thorns nipping his skin. He brushed at it distractedly, feeling a vine wind around his arm. Something about that wasn't right, but he couldn't focus on the reason why. His eyes lost focus, and the ghosts grew more daring, creeping closer. Some took on familiar features. Chance's demented father, Moonfire, smirked at him. Tash laughed at some unheard joke. Cilvi blew Lucian a kiss and crooked a finger to beckon him to follow her.

Willow slipped up behind Lucian and whispered in his ear. "It's time, my perfect son. It's time you learned to obey your mother." She rested her hands on his skull even as he wrenched away from her.

Knives drove through his mind and into his soul. Lucian jerked, then screamed.

~

Chains shaped of bone held his wrists and ankles to the wall, holding him upright in his underwater prison. Lucian knew this place, this room, all too well. His pulse spiked. Adrenaline raced through his body. When the games reached their end, when she wanted to start the tortures again, Willow pulled him back here. Back to her Coral Palace. Back to hell.

He strained against the chains, but they didn't yield. They never did.

"So here you are, my dear brother."

Fear, then fury seared through him. Ayliad appeared before him, long golden hair flowing across her shoulders and down her back. She wore a halter top and a wrap skirt, both doing more to accentuate her body than to conceal anything. She pressed herself against him, blocking his scream of rage with her mouth. She broke the kiss, her mouth so close he felt her breath stir the water across his face, smelling of something sweet, seductive, enticing. Her fingers ran through his short black hair. "Hush now, Lucian. There's no one to hear you here. You're mine—all mine."

"Never!" He lunged at her, trying to bite, to claw, anything to hurt her, drive her back.

She laughed, stepping out of reach. "My dear, beautiful brother, will you never learn? What I want, I take. And I want you. You and Chance."

"I won't let you touch him!" Lucian screamed, thrashing against his restraints.

Her smile widened. She looked around the room, taking in every detail. "Is this the place that truly haunts you the most,

Lucian? I must say, it holds so many fond memories for me. I wonder, did Chance ever tell you about the bargain he made with me?"

Lucian still strained, fingers curling as if he could wrap them around her smooth, flawless neck.

"Trapped and alone, separated from everyone, he still thought he could do something to protect you. He offered himself to me, that he would give himself to me willingly if doing so would spare you. A pity for you that he's not here now, isn't it?"

Lucian screamed in wordless rage. Ayliad smiled and rested a hand on his bare chest. Her fingers traced the definition of his muscles, moving down his abdomen, sliding ever lower. Her eyes never left his, gleaming with lust and malice.

A single, snarled word rose in his throat. "No."

She grinned. "You always know just what to say to put me in the mood, Lucian."

Her healing magic tingled across his skin like a thousand centipedes. His hands clenched, but he could not stop her from stimulating his body to her desires. Her mouth pressed against his again as she shoved him back against the wall and forced herself on him.

When she was done, he hung in the chains, breathless and drained. His lips curled back in a snarl against the shame and humiliation. "I… hate… you."

She licked her lips, looking at him through her long lashes. "And you can't do anything about it."

Ayliad pressed her hand to his chest. Pain ripped through him like razors. Lucian screamed, thrashing.

Vines rose from the floor to wind around him. They teased loose his shackles and dragged him down to the floor as Ayliad poured a twisted perversion of healing magic through his body, wracking him with blinding agony. The vines pinned him spread-eagle. Ayliad straddled him, smiled at his screams, and raped him again.

When she finally allowed the torment to end, tears stung Lucian's eyes. He stared unseeing at the ceiling, with its jagged knobs of living coral, the silent witnesses to his humiliation.

She lay beside him, tracing her finger down his cheek. Her breath was hot against his ear. "I can take the pain away, Lucian. All of it—the loss, the fear, the confusion. You don't have to think. You don't have to feel. Just close your eyes and let go."

"No." His voice, raw from screaming, wavered. "I can't. I won't."

She tenderly stroked his hair. "You don't have to hurt anymore. I will take it all away. Let go."

"No." He twisted his face away from her, turning toward the wall.

"Nothing you do will bring back what you've lost, Lucian. The memories consume you. The loss will devour you." Her hand traced the tip of his ear. "I can make you forget. I can even be your precious Cilvi, if that's what you want."

He shuddered. Ayliad, pretending to be his beloved wife… the thought was too horrifying to bear. But despite himself, her whispered promise of oblivion tempted.

If I just… forget, will the pain really be gone? I…

Ayliad kissed him, and he flinched. "I know what you want, Lucian," she whispered. "What you don't admit even to yourself. Let go."

"No!" A new voice shattered the seductive web of Ayliad's words. "I won't let you take him!"

"Well, well. This is a surprise," Ayliad purred.

Lucian jerked, straining anew at the restraining vines as his gaze snapped to the source of the shout. "Chance! No, get away!" *I can't let her reach Chance. I can't let her hurt him again!*

A surge of strength flooded him. The vines holding his

arms yielded. Lucian tore free, gasping in pain. He lunged for Ayliad as she moved toward Chance. Lucian's hand closed tight around her arm and flung her toward the far wall.

She staggered, but caught herself, looking not at Lucian, but at Chance. "You cannot stop me, Chance. Look at you—so weak you can barely stand. You think *you* will stand in my way?"

"Maybe not." Chance's voice was tight and angry. "But I can give Lucian the strength to banish you back into whatever dark pit of his soul you crawled from."

Lucian pushed up to his knees and glared at her. "I don't want your 'forgetting' or your 'peace.' Get away from me, bitch."

She just smiled, pursing her lips and blowing a kiss at both him and Chance. "Until next time, my dear brother."

Then she was simply… gone. Lucian panted. His chest burned, and he couldn't draw a full breath. Chance bolted to his side. Lucian gripped his cousin's arm. "You shouldn't be here."

"Neither should you, Lucian," Chance retorted. "So get us somewhere else."

Lucian looked at him and blinked without comprehension.

Chance shook his shoulders. "Lucian! Listen to me. We are inside your head. This is your mind, your soul. Do you understand?"

"No," he admitted in a whisper.

"You can take us somewhere else, Lucian. I know you can do this. Just trust me," Chance said. Though his voice was steady, his eyes kept darting around the room, as if expecting Ayliad, or worse, Willow, to appear at any moment. "Please."

"I always trust you, Chance." Lucian swallowed hard. Somewhere… anywhere but here.

The walls melted away around them, becoming dark stone, a chamber in a cave, furnished with chairs and a bed. That too faded into a forest. Then it was the chamber again. Lucian squeezed his eyes closed as the scene flickered between the two.

Chance made a sound of pain. "Just... pick one, Lucian."

Lucian opened his eyes, and they were in the cave, sitting on the stone floor. Chance rested his hand on Lucian's shoulder and healing magic ran through him, warm and familiar. The constriction in his chest eased, and he could breathe again. It felt real. But Ayliad's magic had felt real too.

Lucian gripped Chance's arm, looking into his cousin's grey eyes. "Tell me you're real. You're not some figment I dreamed up to stop her."

"I'm real, Lucian," Chance told him. He was gaunt, the shadows deep in his hollow cheeks and weary eyes. "I'm real, and I'm here with you, inside your head."

Lucian gripped his cousin's shoulders and embraced him. "But how?"

Chance held him tightly. "Later, Lucian. It can wait. What matters is that I *am* here, and I need your help. But first, you have to wake up. I cannot lose you to the demons haunting your soul. Especially not... that one."

"We're inside my head," Lucian repeated in a whisper. "But... how much?" His gaze grew intense. "How much, Chance? Has this all been in my head? Is... is everyone really still alive?"

Chance looked away. "No. You didn't imagine that. Ahmea is dead. You're the only pillar I have left to cling to."

Everyone is dead. Cilvi, Tash, Sun, Ahmea... they're all dead. Lucian bowed his head and nodded, tears stinging in his eyes again. "And you'll be there when I wake."

"I will, I promise." Chance gripped his hand. "Now, rest. I'll stay here with you until you fall asleep."

He wanted to protest. He didn't want to close his eyes for fear that Chance would disappear. But Chance offered his shoulder to lean on. Reassured by the presence beside him, Lucian closed his eyes and slept.

Lucian jerked awake with sudden, sharp panic. He lay in the shadowed shelter of the pavement slab. Frayed metal cables hung overhead like serpents. The air smelled of dust.

Where am I? Where's Chance? This isn't my cave. I don't feel the forest anywhere. It's not the Coral Palace. Where's Chance?

Lucian looked around urgently, panic rising. Then relief flooded him and the knot in his chest loosened. Chance lay curled beside him, back pressed against the wall of the shelter.

He is here. That was real.

Lucian lifted his arm, intending to rest it on Chance's shoulder. Something slid from his bare skin. He glanced down and froze, dread racing down his spine.

A desiccated black vine crumbled to dust, leaving only a handful of needle-sharp thorns on the stone. Barely a whisper of magic hung to the remains, faint enough that he could almost believe he imagined it. He touched his arm, and felt tender welts where the thorns had pierced. Lucian shuddered, pulling his arm close against his body.

That wasn't an episode last night. It was an attack. His breath came faster, his chest tight. *Ayliad attacked me. I don't know how she found me, or how she connected herself to this vine, but somehow, she used it to touch me and get into my head.*

Few elves with healing magic ever learned, or had reason to learn, how to use their magic to project their consciousness into someone else's mind. Soul healers, they were called, at least when they used that ability to help others. Those like Willow and Ayliad, who used it to torture and abuse, had no title Lucian knew except "fucked up psychopath."

He looked at Chance again, and a new chill struck.

However Chance had found him and gotten here, he'd gone diving into Lucian's mind. Chance had been within Ayliad's reach and not known it. If she hadn't withdrawn, but had pressed her attack, what could have happened?

She's hurt Chance too many times. I won't let her do so again. Ever. He closed his eyes and drew a deep breath. *I can't allow her to get in my head again. I must find a way to keep her away, drive her back. I won't put Chance in that position again. And it's better if he never knows that he actually faced her, and not some delusion spawned from the depths of my soul.*

What if she comes after him rather than me? How do I stop her?

Footsteps approached from outside. "Are you awake?" Quicksilver peered into the shelter, then crouched. He waited until Lucian met his eyes, and the tension in his shoulders eased. "You're back with us."

Lucian relaxed slightly, forcing his fear back behind a wall so he could pretend to be all right. "I'm awake. I *am* awake, right? This is real? Chance is here."

"You're awake," Quicksilver assured him. "This is real. Chance… well, Chance found us."

"What happened last night?"

Quicksilver hesitated. "Well, you were talking about seeing ghosts."

Lucian nodded. "I remember."

"You do? Okay. Well, you lay down, and things were quiet for a bit, until you started screaming." Quicksilver shuddered. "The last episode, you spent a lot of time screaming, but you would still respond. Usually by saying something horribly disturbing, but you did still *respond*. This time, I couldn't get anything from you. You didn't know I was here at all."

"This episode was… different," Lucian admitted. He shivered. "I also remember most of it."

"I tried to talk to you, rouse you, something. I couldn't do anything when you started to scream and convulse. It went on for… what felt like hours. Then suddenly, Snow appeared, with Chance clinging on his back. Snow let Chance down beside you and blinked off again before I could even ask him about Eria. Not that I'm sure Snow would have answered. He came around to check on us sometimes over the years, but he was always in his panther form."

Snow was an elf younger than Quicksilver with two rare talents: shapeshifting and teleportation, both inherited from his father. He favored the form of a large white panther, but when he spent too long in that form, he began to lose connection with his elven nature.

Lucian nodded in understanding and motioned for Quicksilver to continue.

"I asked Chance how he got here and what was going on. All he said was 'I'm saving Lucian.' Then he was in your head, and everything went creepily quiet. When he came back to himself, Chance just curled up and went to sleep. That was… about six hours ago." Quicksilver looked at Chance with a worried expression. "I've been trying to call to Eria through mind-speech, but she hasn't answered. I can't imagine her letting her father leave on his own, but… she must still be too far away for my magic to reach her. I really hope Chance didn't somehow set out without her. I don't know how long he's been awake from the coma, but he's not looking good."

Lucian looked back at Chance. Quicksilver was right. Chance was as gaunt as he'd been in Lucian's mind, and his skin was sallow. Dark shadows lined his face and hollow cheeks. Lucian rested a hand on his cousin's shoulder. Chance stirred slightly, then settled again.

"How far are we from the place where you and Eria lived?" Lucian asked.

"A couple of weeks still." Quicksilver pushed up to his feet. "Well, not much we can do until either Chance wakes or Eria answers me. Are you hungry? I've been stewing some meat, since I had far too much time and nothing to do with it but worry."

"I'll take some," Lucian agreed.

Quicksilver brought him a bowl and Lucian ate, not leaving Chance's side. Quicksilver made a few attempts to draw him into conversation, but gave up and left him alone after a little while. The sun rose high enough to cast light into the shelter, and Quicksilver joined them to escape the heat of the day.

Chance stirred. Lucian turned to him, tense and suddenly anxious, though he wasn't certain why. Chance shifted, then opened his eyes. He focused on Lucian, and his lips moved in a small smile.

You're awake.

I'm awake, Lucian agreed, relieved. He grabbed Chance in a tight hug. *You're really here. I can't believe it. You're here. You found me.* He released Chance and looked his cousin in the eyes. *How?*

You called me. Or something did. I knew that you needed help quickly. Chance looked past Lucian to Quicksilver. *Is Snow still here?*

Quicksilver jumped, as if he hadn't expected his presence to be acknowledged. "No, Snow left almost as soon as you hit the ground." He straightened. "Chance, where is Eria? How did you get here? When I left, you were still in a coma! Even if you woke up shortly after I left, how can you be strong enough to be out and traveling?"

Eria says it's been a few months since I woke, Chance said. *She doesn't think I should be traveling yet, but she agreed this is safer than if I travel through the spirit realm. I hope Snow has gone back to our camp to bring her and our gear.*

He tried to sit, and Lucian helped him up. Chance gripped his arm with more strength than his wasted form implied. He held Lucian's gaze. His mental voice was tight, meant only for

Lucian to hear. *I heard you call to me. I was dreaming, but you called me out of those dreams.*

Were they good dreams? Lucian asked, though he suspected the answer.

No, they were not. They were dreams I could not have escaped without your help, Lucian. I heard you.

Chance heard me, and he woke to answer me. *A few months ago, when it was still winter, I couldn't wait any longer. Quicksilver had promised he would lead me to you come spring, but I couldn't wait. I went into the spirit realm to search for you. I found you, but didn't know whether or not you heard me, and I was pulled back to my body before I could find out.* Lucian gazed at Chance. *I wasn't there when you woke. Chance… I'm sorry.*

Chance held his gaze. *Lucian, if you hadn't done that, as reckless as we both know it was, I would still be trapped in my own mind.* He glanced around the shelter. *And you might still be where you were, in your head.*

Lucian shivered. *I think if they had to, the Guardian or the Ghost would have found a way to drag me out.*

Chance frowned, eyes narrowing. *The Guardian I might believe, but the Ghost has not, in general, demonstrated a lot of skill in preserving your mental health.*

No, Lucian acknowledged. *But the Ghost hates Ayliad.* That was an easier answer, right now, than delving into how the Ghost had changed.

It wasn't enough to satisfy Chance. *That place, that room isn't somewhere I want to find your soul, Lucian. And I certainly don't want to leave your escape from it to "maybe the Ghost or the Guardian will notice something's wrong."*

I don't want to think about it right now, Chance. Let me be glad to see you for a little while before digging into everything that's wrong with my head!

Chance's eyes dropped to the ground. *I'm sorry, Lucian.*

Sorry. Didn't mean to snap at you, Lucian said, upset at himself for his reaction. Everything seemed sharper, somehow —his relief at finally reuniting with Chance, his need to see Chance somewhere safe, his fears about his own sanity.

Quicksilver sprang to his feet. "Someone's coming."

Lucian stood, tense, and Quicksilver reached for a weapon. Outside, pebbles shifted as light paws padded across stone, followed by a questioning "Mrrrow?"

"Dad, are you here? Uncle Lucian, Quick?"

"Eria!" Quicksilver said. "We're in here, out of the sun."

Lucian eased back down to the ground. Chance's daughter ducked into the shelter, followed by a large white panther. Eria's face was flushed and her short red-gold hair windblown. She gave Quicksilver a quick hug, then rushed over to Lucian and threw her arms around him. "Uncle Lucian! I'm so glad to see you!"

He embraced her. "It's good to see you, Eria." Even after so many centuries, sometimes he still thought of her as the golden-haired little girl who would gleefully scramble up trees rather than the mature adult who devoted herself to the life of a traveling healer.

She released him and stepped back, looking him over critically. "Dad demanded that Snow carry him last night, saying you needed help. Are you all right?"

"I am now," he answered. "And he was right."

She sighed. "Well, yeah, of course he was. He's pretty much always right when he says you need help. That's why I didn't try to stop him." Her gaze moved to Chance, and she sighed again. "And it's why we set out in the first place, despite it being a terrible idea. Dad's in no condition to be traveling and hasn't regained his strength yet. If not for Snow, we wouldn't have gotten far."

The panther raised his head, hearing his name. He greeted everyone with a throaty "Mrrow," then began grooming.

Lucian smiled. The world might have fallen into chaos and ruin, but at least some things remained constant.

Lucian, where's Tash? Chance asked. *What about Cilvi and Sun?*

"They're... gone." His throat tightened on the word. As youths, he, Chance, and Tash had been inseparable. Tash hadn't been nearly as powerful in magic as either Lucian or Chance, but he'd always been a steady presence, dependable and stable, ready to pull his friends back to the ground when they needed it.

Tash is dead? A mix of disbelief and grief filled Chance's mental voice and pinched his expression. *Sun and Cilvi too?*

Lucian nodded, silent.

You've been alone since then? Chance asked.

Lucian shook his head. "I've been living in a village with humans."

"You've been living with humans?" Eria repeated. "Is that safe? Some of the places we passed were pretty unpleasant and very unfriendly. I wouldn't want to stay in any of them."

"Forest Town is safe," Lucian promised. "It's my village. I'm the leader. It's in the middle of a forest created by the Guardian. We'll be safer there than most places."

Eria accepted his judgment, but Chance looked dubious. Speaking just to Lucian, he said, *I haven't seen as much of the lands as Eria since I woke, but 'safer than most places' seems a pretty low bar. How safe *is* this place, really?*

I trust the people there with our lives, Lucian answered.

Chance gave that long, silent thought. Finally, he just said, *I see.*

Eria searched through a pile of bags and handed one to Quicksilver. "I think I grabbed the most important things you left behind. I decided it was best to assume we wouldn't be heading back to the glade once we found you and Lucian."

Quicksilver looked in the bag and nodded. "Thanks. And

that seems likely. I spent the winter in Lucian's village, and it really is a nice place. Friendly people. They're protective of Lucian, too. But that's not too surprising, seeing as he's a better leader than at least ninety percent of the warlords in other communities. Nice lush forest, thanks to the Guardian. They have crops, livestock, all the trappings of a growing community."

Eria frowned. "Sounds like a ripe target for bandits."

"Sometimes," Lucian answered. "The Guardian uses them for fertilizer."

"But you… and the Guardian… aren't there now," she said.

"I left the village defenses in capable hands," he said.

Elven or human hands? Chance asked.

"Human. I'm the only elf there," Lucian said. "Until Quick arrived, I hadn't seen another elf since…" *Since Tash and Sun died.* "In years."

"Well, it sounds like the best place to head right now," Eria said. "But not for at least another day." She yawned and stretched. "I'm exhausted, and Snow must be too."

In response, Snow looked up, rose in a full-body stretch, then curled up in the sun to nap.

"Sounds like a good idea to me," Quicksilver agreed. "That was a long night. Lucian, you okay with keeping an eye on things?"

"Yeah. Get some rest," Lucian said. He settled back as comfortably as he could, molding the ground under him to be rid of a couple sharp rocks that jabbed into his back.

After Eria and Quicksilver went to sleep, the camp fell quiet. Outside, the wind tossed dirt and an occasional pebble. Lucian didn't even hear insects. In the shelter, he heard only the quiet sounds of sleepers. At first, he thought Chance was among them, but when he turned, he saw that his cousin's eyes were open, watching him with a gaze that sought to pierce into Lucian's soul.

How long have you been alone, Lucian? He might not have the strength or muscle to speak clearly aloud, but his mental voice was steady.

I haven't been alone. I've been living in my village.

You know what I mean. How long has it really been since you were last among elves?

Lucian let out his breath in a heavy sigh. *I don't know.*

Chance's eyes narrowed. *What happened?*

Lucian closed his eyes as he gathered his thoughts and his memories of the chaotic aftermath of the bombings. *It's been… fifty-some years since the war reached us and you went into a coma. Tash, Sun, Cilvi, and I got out of Briarhold City intact. We tried to find you and anyone else from the clan, but everything was chaos. So many people running, fighting, panicking. Outside the city was no better. Whoever attacked Briarhold, they used bombs that combined biological weaponry and corrupted magic. The poisons that were unleashed…* He shook his head. *The Guardian kept trying to take control. Cilvi kept me grounded enough to hold on, while Tash and Sun kept us moving until we got far enough away that I could push the Guardian back. A lot of those first months are hazy, but we got through them. Sometime early in the second year, soldiers ambushed us.*

With the words came the memories, images frozen in time. Men and women with guns, firing indiscriminately. Cilvi's scream of pain and anger. Blood rushing from the wound in her chest, flowing between her fingers. Lucian's hands hitting the ground, magic pouring into the earth. The soldiers writhing in agony, impaled on the rock spikes that radiated out from Lucian like an impact crater.

Chance inhaled sharply.

Lucian drew a deep, shaking breath. *Tash said I went

Ghost after that. He never said how long, but judging by the seasons, the gap in my memory is at least a month, probably longer.*

You don't remember anything? Chance interrupted. *In the past when you've gone Ghost, you still remember events, just from a detached, emotionless perspective.*

Lucian shook his head. *Nothing. When I did come out of it, I felt hollow. Empty. I… wanted to keep living in that haze, but Tash wouldn't let me. He kept pulling me further out of it. Things got better for a while. At least a year. We spent it looking for you and the others, sometimes joining with bands of human survivors for a while. That was about the time when we all started to realize that plants were dying when they should be growing, and that something was really, seriously wrong. Tash, Sun, and I discussed experimenting to see whether the Guardian could reverse the effects.*

Sounds dangerous, Chance said. *Letting the Guardian loose when corrupted magic is involved.*

The Guardian itself was a result of corrupted magic, and it was fiercely possessive of its host. It took offense to, and offensive action against, other sources of corruption. *I know. But nothing else was working. Tash and Sun were confident they could keep the Guardian under control and pull me back if needed.* Lucian swallowed hard. *Before we could try it, though, Sun got sick. Then Tash.* He looked at his hands rather than Chance, and spoke in a strained whisper, fearing to let the horrific images seep into his mind-speech. "I tried everything I could. Every medicine I could find, every plant I could grow." His voice cracked. "Everything… except give the end Tash begged me for… while he could still speak."

Chance's hand fell on Lucian's shoulder and squeezed. *It's not your fault, Lucian.*

Lucian jerked his head in a sharp shake. *No. There must have been something I could have done, some way I could have saved them. Maybe if we hadn't spent so long debating, and just let the Guardian out, it could have purified whatever killed them before it happened.* His eyes stung as he gazed at Chance. *Anything other than choosing between watching them die or ending their pain.*

Sometimes, nothing we can do will ever be enough, Chance said softly, and Lucian heard echoes of his pain at Ahmea's death.

For long moments, they sat in the silence of shared grief. Finally, Lucian said, *Sun died first, then Tash only hours after her. I remember hearing the last breath leave him. Seeing death claim his body. After that, nothing. I remember nothing at all until I woke in a cave in the heart of a forest, and it all felt like my magic. The Guardian made the forest, and the Ghost must have made the cave. I was exhausted, half-starved, and looked like I'd been trying to crawl up a cliff with my bare hands. It could have been months, could have been years since I lost Tash and Sun. No elves ever stumbled on my forest. Took humans a while before they began venturing into it either. Finally, some were bold or desperate enough to enter, despite trees that sometimes moved without wind.*

And you let them stay, Chance said.

Lucian shrugged. *Why not? Sometimes a little company was nice. As more came, I set some ground rules, and they started calling me 'lord.' That's how Forest Town started.*

Chance gazed at him in silence, his eyes trying to peer into the depths of Lucian's soul. Finally he said, *What about what happened last night? Has that happened in your village of humans?*

Lucian shifted uncomfortably. He'd hoped Chance would be distracted from questions about the previous night or Lucian's mental state. And he truly didn't want to speak of Ayliad or the thorny vine that had wrapped around his arm. He shuddered. *Things similar to it. I don't live in the village;

my home is in a cave just beyond the village. When I'm having… a bad day, I stay there. And when I have what the villagers call 'an episode,' I have it there, away from them.*

Do they know you're an elf?

I tell people up front that I am. Not all of them believe me, but many gradually accept the idea, over time.

Chance blinked, then shook his head with a sigh. *Only you, Lucian, would just tell everyone that you're an elf straight out and then expect them to be all right with that.*

Lucian's faint smile faded. *No, I don't expect them to be all right with it. I expect the ones who aren't all right with it to leave before they make trouble. And on that front, it's been quite successful.*

And how many worship you? Chance responded.

I don't ask. I've made it clear that I don't want their worship, and I'm no god, but I know some do so anyway.

Chance snorted. *They're more likely to get help from you than from some useless hearth god.*

Actually, I did get help from a hearth god, quite recently, Lucian told him, jumping on the change of topic.

Chance raised a dubious eyebrow.

Lucian told him about Gerto Sher, from the searching of their bags at the entrance, to the cult of Shiranak, to his departure with Quicksilver as the riots began.

I don't like the sound of this 'Shiranak.' Chance shifted positions with a wince. *Especially not if he's promoting himself to godhood.*

Yeah. And while my conversation with his elven follower was brief, I got the feeling that he was on board with the whole idea that Shiranak is more than the average elf. Lucian rose and paced around their shelter, relieving aching muscles.

The statue didn't look like anyone you knew?

Lucian shook his head. *No, that would have been too easy. But at least it was male. It wasn't… her.*

Chance shivered. *True.*

They both fell silent, and eventually Chance closed his eyes. Lucian left the shade of their shelter and climbed atop the slab of asphalt to survey the landscape. He found no familiar landmarks, nor any signs of human habitation. Just barren, rocky land and blowing dust.

Snow roused in the afternoon, climbed up to Lucian's perch, and demanded ear scratches. Lucian complied, listening to the massive cat's rumbling purr.

"Thanks for watching over everyone, Snow," Lucian said.

Snow rubbed his head against Lucian, nearly bowling him over. Then he climbed to his feet, stretched, and yawned wide, showing a mouthful of sharp teeth. Lucian scratched the panther's ears again, and received a throaty "Mrrow" in response. Snow jumped down to the ground and darted off, vanishing for an instant, to reappear fifty feet ahead. "Blinking," they'd called it within the tribe, before anyone knew the term "teleportation." Snow used the talent effortlessly, each leap carrying him further until he was gone from sight. Lucian drifted back down into the shade of their shelter and waited for the others to wake.

By dusk, Quicksilver, Eria, and Chance had all roused. Snow appeared beside the campfire with four plump rabbits in his mouth, which he deposited beside Eria. Lucian looked at the animals and raised an eyebrow.

"You didn't raid some poor farmer's hutch, did you Snow?" he asked.

Snow huffed, offended, and firmly shook his head.

Eria laughed softly. "Yeah, we have no idea where Snow finds game or how far he travels to get it, but he insists he never steals from anyone, and the animals are always healthy. Or, well, they were before he caught them."

Chance's wife Ahmea had been the best cook Lucian ever knew, and Eria was a close second. With a few seasonings from the depths of her bag, she transformed the rabbits into the best meal Lucian had eaten in years.

When nothing remained of dinner but bones picked clean of meat, Eria finally asked, "So, where are we going now? On to Uncle Lucian's Forest Town? Or somewhere else?"

Chance sat propped against a slab of rock. His eyes drooped wearily, but his mental voice was steady and clear. *Forest Town seems like the best idea. I'm curious to see the place and meet these humans he's collected.*

"It's got my vote too," Quicksilver added. "Besides, one of Lucian's friends there would probably hunt me down specifically to shoot me if Lucian *didn't* come back."

"I don't think Cylin would actually shoot you," Lucian said.

"I do!" Quicksilver countered. "I don't think she'd make it fatal—maybe just shoot me in the foot or something—but she'd make very sure I knew she wasn't happy."

Chance raised an eyebrow. *Who is Cylin?*

"A young woman I rescued from some thugs. They intended to sell her to bone men," Lucian answered. "She's now in charge of Forest Town's defenses."

What are bone men?

"Roaming groups who pay money for bodies and body parts. They're known for wanting them as fresh as possible, and offer more if the parts being sold are still attached to a living person. People of questionable moral character sometimes pay debts or buy passage through certain areas by providing them with non-essential extremities, like fingers, ears, that sort of thing." Lucian was quiet for a moment. "And some people give them far more than that."

Eria shuddered. "What do they do with the bodies and parts?"

"If anyone knows, they aren't talking," Lucian told her.

"I've heard plenty of theories, but none I'd believe without proof."

"Most settlements I've come across are either strongly opposed to the bone men, and will kill them on sight, or in league with them and willing to give them stray travelers when they can," Quicksilver put in. "Not much middle ground between the two."

"They sound utterly vile," Eria said.

Despite himself, Lucian smiled. "Vile" had been a word that Chance's wife, Ahmea, reserved for only the worst people, the irredeemably evil. Hearing it from her daughter reminded him of days long past, when their clan had still been whole. The moment passed, and he grew serious again. "They are vile, as are those who sell their own children to those bone men."

A collective shudder ran through the group around the fire.

Lucian finally broke the stillness. "We can't follow the same route back. I want to stay well away of Gerto Sher, no matter which way the uprising turned out. Do you have ideas of a good alternate route, Quick?" Of any of them, Quicksilver had the most reliable, unerring sense of direction.

"Yeah, I have an idea. It'll take us longer, and we might have trouble if we hit bad storms, but if we head west from here, we should reach the Bronze River. We can follow it upriver for a while, then turn back west toward Lucian's forest." Quicksilver sketched a crude map in the dirt. "We're likely to encounter more human settlements along the river, so we need to be careful. I don't know how the people of that area feel about elves, so we need to keep a low profile." He glanced to Lucian. "As low of one as we can, at least."

"I can keep a low profile," Lucian told him.

"Says the guy who unintentionally became lord and god of a human village," Quick countered.

Lucian started to protest, but stopped when he heard thin

but heartfelt laughter from Chance. Eria's startled but happy expression told Lucian that Chance had found few reasons to laugh since he woke. Finally, Lucian just shook his head. "I'll do my best, how about that?"

We all will, Chance said.

Eria gave him a stern look. "You need to work on talking out loud, Dad. Especially if we're going to be around humans."

Chance scowled with a sound of annoyance. "I know, I know." His voice scratched in his throat. The "I" came out as little more than a thin sigh, more sensed than heard. He slowly raised his arms in a series of stretches. Healing could do many things, but even magic could not completely stop muscle atrophy during a decades-long coma.

"Snow will attract too much attention in a town," Lucian said. "We'll need to get Chance a long robe or something like it so he can float without being obvious." He closed his eyes a moment. Quietly, he spoke. "You have no idea how good it is to be with you all again. How much I've missed everyone."

Eria stood up, circled around the fire, and hugged him tightly. "I've missed you too, Uncle Lucian."

Chance, though, gazed at Lucian, and spoke for Lucian's mind alone. *You may say that, but I think that, perhaps, I do know.*

Lucian didn't answer, and Chance offered no deeper insights.

~

Lucian stood in a forest clearing, the grass soft and green under his bare feet. A light wind stirred the branches of the trees, but otherwise, the forest stood quiet, lacking the sounds of birds or animals. The silence should have felt oppressive, but here, it was restful.

A figure separated from the trees and strode toward him, taking form *and features until Lucian faced a mirror of himself, except that the black hair was green and formed of leaves, while twigs and leaves sprouted from the other's limbs. Vines curled around the other's left forearm. His intense amber eyes held Lucian's.*

"We must return to the forest."

"I had to find Chance." Lucian scowled at the Guardian.

"We know. Of course you had to find him. Now he is found. Why is there any question of whether to return?"

"There's no question. We're leaving tomorrow, but travel still takes time," Lucian growled, irritated to have his rest interrupted to be lectured by a tree. "We'll be on our way, even if not as fast as I want to go. Deal with it."

The Guardian stepped closer. "Travel faster."

Lucian folded his arms. "Chance is weak. I'm not going to push him beyond what he can manage because you want some damned trees. Deal with it!"

The Guardian stopped, frowned, then shook his head. "We need to be there. YOU need to be there. Chance needs to be there. Our forest is protected. The Fruit cannot reach you there."

Lucian froze. The Fruit was the Guardian's name for Ayliad—beautiful, addictive, and dangerous. "What did you say?" He grabbed the Guardian by the shoulders and shook him. "What do you know? You… You knew she was out there. How? What do you mean, the forest is protected?"

The Guardian pushed Lucian's hands away. "During the Black Days, the time you do not remember, she sought to draw you to her. We battled and drove her away constantly, but she persisted."

Lucian's mouth twisted in disgust. "She thought I would go to her willingly?"

The Guardian gazed at him without blinking. "You would have. You were lost within grief and pain, and recognized only that she offered a means of easing both. Her magic drew you and fed your need. She would have corrupted you to her desires."

Lucian shook his head, but something in the Guardian's words rang true in his soul, an echo of the promises Ayliad had whispered to him when she invaded his mind. Could I really have been that lost? Could I really have considered turning to her?

"We needed a means of protecting you from her even when we were not in control. We created the forest and infused it with our essence. It will protect you from her, and it will protect Chance."

His jaw tightened. "She was in my head last night. Why didn't you stop her then?"

"The Fruit did not come alone. With her came another, shrouded in corruption. While we battled the corruption, the Fruit slipped past us." The Guardian's voice grew hard. *"You* must return. She knows that you are vulnerable, and that Chance is awake. She will try again."

Lucian's hands clenched in fists. "I won't let her touch Chance."

The Guardian nodded, satisfied. "Return to our forest, and he will be safe."

The figure walked back into the trees and vanished. Then the trees, too, disappeared, taking the dream with them.

～

As dawn lit the horizon, the elves packed their camp. Lucian debated whether to reshape the rock to swallow the traces of their presence, but decided it did little harm to leave the remains of a fire and some rabbit bones. Maybe such signs of life would encourage some other wandering vagabond.

Snow let Chance crawl onto his back, carrying him with little evident effort. Quicksilver took the lead, putting his back to the rising sun and setting off in the direction he claimed would lead them to the Bronze River. Lucian trusted Quicksilver's sense of direction far more than his own, and the wastes lacked recognizable landmarks.

As they walked, they traded stories, Eria and Quicksilver relating their life in a sheltered glade where they'd lived and cared for Chance. It wasn't a large place, but the ground could support plants, and a natural spring provided clean water. Its remote location protected it from discovery by most, and Quicksilver had manipulated the plants to make the access points look from the outside like nothing more than long-dead tangles of thorns and brambles.

Lucian, in turn, told them about Forest Town and its people. He reminisced about Doctor Kinnel's arrival. Forest Town had been less than twenty people then, and the prospect of having an actual *doctor* among them seemed too good to be true to the humans. Lucian had been more cautious; his own experiences with human doctors had rarely been productive, and he'd never heard one speak of elves as anything other than fairy tales and old superstition. When Lucian introduced himself, he declared himself to be both lord of the forest and an elf. Doctor Kinnel, still a young man then, simply looked him up and down, took in Lucian's declaration, and said, "I expect you'll make a better lord than most, then."

"Lucian, did you know that Doctor Kinnel is a priest of a faith that worships us 'ancient spirits'?" Quicksilver interrupted.

Lucian nodded. "The topic came up as I got to know him. And he proved that the rituals worked the first time he had to drag me back from a spirit-walk."

"And the second time," Quicksilver added under his breath.

That's not an ability I'd want in the hands of humans, Chance said.

"He doesn't use it except in need," Lucian said. "It's very taxing on him." More taxing than Lucian had realized, especially as the doctor grew older. Doctor Kinnel had been weary and drained for nearly a month after dragging Lucian back to his body. It was fortunate that no one had suffered a serious crisis during the winter while Doctor Kinnel was still recovering.

Things will be easier for him with Chance and Eria in Forest Town.

Maybe Doctor Kinnel can focus more on passing on his skills to train a new generation of doctors. Human lives are so short, and so much knowledge has already been lost.

The topic of conversation wandered into stories of the strangest quirks they'd encountered among humans, from people who insisted on touching both sides of a doorframe before stepping through a door, to those who never looked in a mirror, and meandered on from there, flowing easily between them.

In the pause, Lucian found himself lost in thought, brow creased in a frown. Snow paced up beside him, and Chance leaned over to elbow him. *You have a serious look on your face. What's on your mind?*

Lucian shook himself. "Just thinking, that's all."

About?

"Nothing bad. It's just that things seem so... ordinary right now. Normal. And that just feels weird," Lucian said finally.

Chance laughed. *Everything's normal, and that's weird. Ah, I have missed you, Lucian.*

"Hey!" He shot Chance a scowl. "But really... yes, it's weird to me to feel like things are the way they should be again. It's just... the years in Forest Town, I spent waiting. Waiting for something to happen, for someone to find me, for a glimpse of how to find you. But now the waiting is finally over, and things are right again."

Chance grew serious. *We still have a long trip ahead, Lucian.*

"I know. But that trip will be made with all of you, and not alone." He gave Chance a mock scowl. "And if you keep poking, I'm going to say something ridiculously maudlin and embarrassing."

So... normal, like you said.

"Hey!" Lucian laughed. "All right, all right, I walked into that one."

Chance just grinned, as if they were both still as young as they looked. Some of the weight lifted from Lucian's spirit, and he grinned back.

"You're going to have to rebuild muscle tone, Chance," Lucian said. "I can't race you to the next hill when you're this weak, and there's no way I'm trying to race Snow. He'd win even if he didn't blink over there."

Snow voiced a throaty purr and rubbed his massive head against Lucian's leg, nearly bowling him over.

"Yeah, yeah. Working on it," Chance rasped, forcing the words aloud. He climbed off Snow's back to walk for a while. *Though what I could really use is a pool to swim in. Not practical right now, I know, but it would still be nice.*

"I made a swimming spot in my forest," Lucian told him.

Chance chuckled. *Of course you did. I'd be more worried if you didn't find or make some way to swim. The more you talk about this place, though, the more I look forward to reaching it.*

The Guardian's warning in his dream still hung close, building on his increasing desire to be home. "So do I," Lucian agreed. "So do I."

Three days brought them to the muddy banks of the Bronze River. Once, it had been a lifeline for trade, moving ore and produce. The dams that had constrained it, producing electricity and protecting the surroundings from annual floods, had suffered catastrophic damage during the war, and the river ran wild again. Lucian saw evidence of flooding in the debris strewn across the rocks.

They found a path that could almost be called a road, though they didn't encounter other travelers on it. Hardy plants grew along the riverbank, giving bright spots of green to the brown landscape.

Another day of travel saw them to a village nestled on a high spot, above the watermark of the flood waters. A stone wall ringed the community. Snow and Chance hung back out of sight as Lucian, Quicksilver, and Eria approached the front gate.

A pair of men confronted them. "No room here," one said gruffly without preamble. "Keep moving."

Lucian raised an eyebrow at the curt greeting. "No supplies for sale?"

The men eyed him suspiciously. "We're not letting any refugees in town. Mayor's orders."

"Refugees?" Quicksilver repeated, tone puzzled. "We're travelers, sir, only looking to make a few purchases and be on our way."

The second man scowled deeply. "Travelers who just happen to be following the same route as every other scraggly clump of refugees? Yeah, sure. Not in our town."

Quicksilver's brow pinched in a worried frown, and he looked to Lucian and Eria, then back to the guards. "What if only one of us came into town? Just long enough to get the supplies we need? Then we can be on our way."

The two men consulted in low voices, then one tromped through the gate and into the town, presumably to consult with someone of higher authority. He returned some minutes later, still scowling. "One person, and you better be out of town before sunset."

Quicksilver nodded. "All right. You guys wait out here?"

"We'll wait here," Eria agreed.

The scowling men let Quicksilver through the gate, and one of them followed him inside. Lucian and Eria sat down at the side of the road under the wary gaze of the remaining guard.

"So, refugees from where?" Lucian asked.

The human eyed him like he was an idiot. "Either you're full of shit, or you been livin' under a rock."

Lucian waved toward the wasteland. "There's lots of rocks out there, you know. We're wanderers."

"Drifters." The guard spat in the dirt. "Near as bad as refugees, except at least you keep on drifting."

"The refugees?" Eria prompted.

"You heard of Shiranak while you been out there under the rocks?"

"The name's come up in other towns," Lucian said, a chill of apprehension running down his spine. "Those I hear talking about him say he's some ancient spirit and try to convert people to worship him."

The guard barked a laugh. "Well, guess the converting isn't happening fast enough for his liking. A month or two ago, we started seeing handfuls of people coming our way claiming to have escaped from towns that got overrun by Shiranak's army. Supposedly this army is full of mutated creatures under the ancient spirit's control. Not that anyone could really say what these monsters look like. Sounds like a lot of shit to me, but all the groups have said about the same thing."

"And they come here looking for shelter?" Eria asked.

The guard shrugged. "Most haven't got more than the clothes they're wearing, and no skills worth mentioning. They ain't going to find shelter here."

"No, I imagine not," Eria said. "They keep going upriver?"

"Yeah. Don't know if they con some other town into taking them, or if they get grabbed by bone men."

"You have problems with bone men in these parts?" Lucian asked.

"Who doesn't?" the man retorted. "I even heard they have a base somewhere along the river."

"Well that's great," Lucian muttered. "Thanks for the warning."

The guard just grunted. Lucian considered offering him something in return for the information, but if his attitude reflected that of the rest of the town, Lucian didn't care to reward it.

Quicksilver returned in less than an hour, carrying a relatively small bundle wrapped in cloth. "All right, done here."

"Get everything we need?" Lucian asked.

"Enough to get to our next stop," Quicksilver told him. He didn't say more until they returned to Chance and Snow's hiding place. Setting down the bundle, he unwrapped it. "So, I got a robe for you, Chance, and some water filter and purification kits. That's about it for what I could afford, unfortunately." He handed the cloth to Chance. "Everyone was pretty tense."

"The guard outside wasn't too friendly either," Eria said. "But he did tell us more about the refugees."

Chance raised an eyebrow in question at the exchange. Lucian summarized the visit and the information picked up from the guard.

Eria cast a dark look back toward the village. "He didn't act concerned about the fate of the refugees, even when he spoke of the bone men."

"Honestly, I can understand," Quicksilver said. "They have pretty much nothing there. There's no way their village could absorb a bunch of new people. Maybe one or two, but more than that and they wouldn't have enough food to go around. It's not that I couldn't afford to buy food there; they simply didn't have any to sell me. When it's down to that, they have to be heartless toward outsiders."

Regardless, now we know that Shiranak has some sort of army and is willing to conquer other settlements, Chance said. *And we know that the bone men have some presence in this area, though we don't know where this supposed base of theirs is.*

"If it exists," Lucian put in. "But refugees make ripe targets for bone men, so base or not, they'll have a presence." He let out a heavy breath and ran a hand through his short black hair. "Keep your eyes open for trouble. Let's keep moving."

In the next three days, they received similarly frosty receptions at two more settlements. One allowed Quicksilver to enter for supplies, the other flatly refused any access. The challenge of resupplying concerned Lucian less than the lack of information. The locals' clipped, rude orders to keep moving offered no insight into the surrounding land and allowed little opportunity for questions.

They saw signs of travelers before them—campsites, discarded items, indications of larger groups. Several times, they passed grave markers. They didn't encounter any people on the road, leaving Lucian to wonder just how far behind the refugees they were. From the signs they saw, the group had to be at least twenty people, and that size of group couldn't move very quickly.

Two more days of travel brought them in sight of a grove of stunted, hearty evergreen trees. Snow, at the lead of the group, stopped, sniffing the air intently. He nudged Chance's leg until Chance slid off his back, then blinked away. Lucian frowned, looking after the panther, then turned to Chance.

"Did he tell you anything?"

Chance shook his head. He was regaining strength and muscle, and could walk slowly. His magical strength had recovered far more quickly, especially as he used it to accommodate his physical weakness. *No, but something worried him.*

Eria peered at the trees. "I think I see something down there. Quick, do you?"

Quicksilver squinted. "Maybe? Hard to tell from here."

Snow blinked back to them and vocalized a low noise of

distress, then looked pointedly toward the trees. Lucian started down the slope toward the grove. Snow bounded ahead of him, looking back to make sure they followed.

As he got close, Lucian smelled something rotting. He waited for Chance, Eria, and Quicksilver to join him before he entered the grove. The tallest of the trees stood no more than ten feet, spindly branches dotted with needles. Nothing about them triggered the Guardian, and Lucian didn't sense any magic in them, so assumed they must be natural growth. That was an encouraging thought.

The sight within the grove, on the other hand, was anything but encouraging. Half a dozen human bodies sprawled around the trees, throats slit. Their blood, long dry, stained the dirt rusty red. Whoever killed them had stripped the bodies of anything useful, leaving them wearing only tattered and worn rags of clothing in a mockery of decency.

Quicksilver made a muffled sound of revulsion, one hand rising to pinch his nose shut. The stench of decay hung heavy around them, and the drone of flies disturbed the silence. Eria staunchly moved to the nearest body and crouched beside it, one hand extended to hang just over the rotting corpse.

I'd say they were killed three days ago, maybe four, she said. *This one, at least, was already weak from lack of food.* She turned to Lucian. *Do you think this the work of these 'bone men'?*

Lucian shook his head, grateful that mind-speech meant he didn't have to open his mouth. *I doubt it. The bone men take even the most starved victims, from all I've heard. They wouldn't just murder people and leave the corpses behind.*

Quicksilver shifted uneasily. *What if the bone men had already used them for... whatever they do, and this is how they dispose of--*

Lucian shook his head again. *People who accept chunks

of flesh as payment aren't going to waste usable parts. And these people were simply killed, not carved up.*

Chance spoke. *There are other tracks around. I'd say either bandits caught them, or a band of refugees decided to conserve their resources by getting rid of their weakest members. Judging by the state of the bodies and the lack of signs of struggle, I'm inclined toward the second possibility.*

Lucian looked over the grisly scene again and nodded slowly. None of the dead had been restrained, though if they were all as starved as Eria suggested, they might not have had the strength to fight regardless of whether or not they accepted their fates.

Can we at least bury them? Quicksilver asked.

If we can, we should, Eria said. She looked to Lucian.

The ground held little taint. Lucian focused on the bodies and reached out with his magic. The ground beneath the bodies shifted and pulled away, gently drawing the dead into the earth. The act felt oddly familiar, like a distant memory all but forgotten.

Did I bury Tash and Sun like this? I hope I did. I hope I didn't leave their bodies as the killers left these to rot.

The sensation faded, whatever memory he'd stirred sinking back into the darkness before it fully formed. Lucian said no words over the unmarked graves, only brushed the trees lightly with his magic, gifting them a touch of strength and health to continue their battle against the wasteland.

Solemn and subdued, they continued on.

Late in the afternoon of the following day, the dirt trail turned into a stone-paved road. With murmurs of surprise, they pressed on later than usual. As twilight colored the sky, they saw the city.

Lurking in the banks of the river, it was smaller than Gerto Sher. High stone walls surrounded the bulk of the city, and less sturdy, clearly more recent wooden walls abutted the south side of the wall, appearing to be an expansion of some sort. Snow vanished like a ghost when they came in sight of the city, keeping to the wilds and out of sight of humans. Lamps lit a gatehouse at the city entrance.

Lucian frowned slightly. "Quick, do we have any money?"

"Not much, but if we can get inside, I should be able to scrounge up enough to rent a room." Quicksilver considered the town ahead. "If they let us inside, at least."

"Are you thinking of going in there?" Eria asked.

"A town this size should have more information than the louts we've met along the way," he said. "And we might find a bathhouse."

"A bed and a bath would be welcome," Chance rasped. "I wouldn't mind having either for a couple nights."

"A town of this size might also have a market," Lucian said. Fresh supplies and real beds both sounded incredibly tempting.

They took a little time to check their head wraps, ensure that Chance's robe hung long enough to conceal that he floated several inches above the ground, and disguise any other signs they were more than average humans. Prepared to receive another frosty reception from people who wanted nothing to do with more "refugees," Lucian stood tall, as if he were back in Forest Town and about to address his people, and strode to the gate. The others followed.

A man and a woman stood at the gatehouse, both armed with guns and pikes. They waited until Lucian stood before them before the man spoke. "Fair evening to you. You've reached Springvale. How many are with you?" His gaze moved to Quicksilver, Eria, and Chance, lingering the longest on Chance. Chance gazed back at him from under the hood of the long robe. His magic lifted him just above the ground, and the long hem of the robe hid the fact that his feet did not touch the earth.

"Four of us in total," Lucian answered cautiously. "Why?"

"You've come to seek refuge, yes?" the woman asked.

Lucian hesitated. *Will they let us in if we say we're just passing through?*

Eria spoke before he decided how to answer. "You are offering shelter to refugees? We've not met with many friendly receptions on this road."

The woman nodded and pointed to the wooden barricade. "The city council decreed the construction of the outer annex to create a place where refugees might stay. Those who demonstrate resourcefulness and skill are offered the chance to prove themselves and earn citizenship among us." She studied them, much as her companion had, and like him, her gaze lingered on Chance.

Lucian eyed both the humans. "And what's the problem? You keep staring at my cousin."

The woman looked back to him. "We cannot allow anyone who is sick or a potential carrier of disease to enter."

Lucian's jaw tightened. "He's not ill."

"Any who enter must also be fit to work," the man said. "To that requirement, we can make no exceptions aside from the very young. And your cousin is no child."

"I can work," Chance said, his voice rasping in his throat.

The sound of it clearly did not convince the guards. Chance's gaze remained on them. Lucian felt a touch of magic in the air. The eyes of both guards took a glazed, glassy look for a moment. It cleared, and the woman spoke as if nothing had happened. "Come with me. I'll show you to the entrance."

All four elves followed her, and neither human questioned Chance's presence again. Lucian felt momentarily guilty about letting his cousin manipulate them with magic, but it passed quickly. They needed supplies, and they had no intentions of staying long enough for Chance's ability or inability to contribute to become an issue.

They passed through the main gate, then followed a street

along the inside of the wall to a second gate, this one already open, leading into the section enclosed by the wooden walls. The houses within were compact and bunched together, the streets narrow. People milled around, some turning to consider the newcomers, others paying them no heed.

The woman guided them to a long bunkhouse. "You can sleep here tonight. Tomorrow, get settled and look around. Someone will be available to provide an orientation."

"I know it's too late tonight, but I assume we can go into Springvale and purchase supplies and such," Quicksilver said.

She raised an eyebrow in surprise. "You have funds? You are welcome to look around the market and make purchases, as long as you don't neglect responsibilities within the camp."

She seems to think we plan to stay, Lucian observed to his friends.

You didn't exactly tell her otherwise, Uncle Lucian, Eria told him.

And I don't think I will, just yet. I'm not convinced they'd let us inside otherwise. "Thank you. We will get settled for the night," Lucian told the woman.

She nodded and strode back to her post, leaving them at the door of the bunkhouse. Lucian watched people entering houses, preparing for night, and wondered how the housing was determined. By need? By the value a person brought to the community? And who determined that?

The only exit from this little annex is back into Spring-vale, Chance said, interrupting his thoughts. *And they can cut that off by simply closing the gate.* He turned to Lucian. *I don't like this.*

Let's not make too many judgments until we talk to the people who live here already, Eria said. *We can rest a day or two, resupply, and be on our way.*

Lucian entered the bunkhouse. A single room ran the length of the building, lined with rows of beds. A string of electric lights buzzed on the ceiling. A thin man in faded plaid shirt sat at a small table by the nearest bed. He looked at them.

"Four o' you? Should be beds down the third row." He reached over to the end of the bed and tapped a sliding panel. "If this is red, the bed's claimed. If it's black, it's open."

"Thanks," Quicksilver told him.

"My name's Tate, and I'm in charge of the bunkhouse. You need anything, you come to me."

"Thanks, Tate," Lucian said. "I'm Lucian, and this is Tammin, Chance, and Eria."

"Go get settled in. Come dawn, come see me. I'll have assignments for you for the day, then you'll get breakfast." He flipped a ledger open. "Any of you read?"

Considering that we knew the elf who invented our written language, I should hope so, Chance quipped to Lucian.

Lucian tried not to laugh. "All of us do."

Tate's eyebrows rose in surprise. "Do you now? My, my. Fresh into town, and you already have a point in your favor." He noted something in the ledger.

"A point?" Eria repeated.

Tate nodded. "They told you at the gate that some earn citizenship in Springvale, based on the skills and talents they bring. We track that by points. Useful skills such as literacy count in your favor. Criminal activity, causing or taking part in disruptions, and failure to contribute all count against you."

"How many points does it take to earn citizenship?" Quicksilver asked, giving Tate a guileless smile.

Tate chuckled. "Afraid that's not for me to say, Tammin. But rest assured, it will be granted to those who prove worthy of it. Now, best you go get settled. It's almost lights-out."

As if in agreement with Tate, the lights overhead flickered and dimmed momentarily. Before they sought beds, though, Chance asked, "What's the cost for a night here?"

Tate smiled. "A day's work tomorrow. We like to keep things simple and accessible to all the refugees, regardless of their means or lack thereof."

"I see." Chance inclined his head in a nod and followed Lucian down the row of bunks.

The elves sought out a cluster of open beds, set the sliders to indicate occupation, and settled down in actual beds for the first time in months. Quicksilver made a sound of contentment and pulled the blankets around himself.

Lucian lay in the dark, listening to the sounds of people breathing around him. The bed was comfortable, the blankets warm, but sleep wasn't coming. Feeling oddly like a naughty child up past his bedtime, he rolled onto his side and whispered, "Chance?"

I'm awake, Chance answered.

Lucian continued in mind-speech rather than risk being overheard or disturbing anyone else. *Is it just me, or do things feel off here?*

*Do things feel off about a town that takes in people with vague promises of being allowed to stay, uses them as labor, and houses them in such a way that they can't easily leave? What do *you* think I'm going to say about that, Lucian?* Chance retorted. *Of course things feel off. What I don't know yet is their goal.*

It doesn't have to be our problem. We can resupply and keep moving. Lucian didn't really believe himself, but getting involved would be dangerous, especially knowing Chance's penchant to uncover secrets that others wanted to keep concealed. And the longer they stayed here, the more it delayed their return to Forest Town. *These people might have problems, but they aren't MY people. What if refugees are coming to Forest Town? What if Shiranak's people find it?*

He heard the eye-roll in Chance's mental voice. *You know as well as I do that it's already our problem, Lucian. We're here. If they don't want people to leave, it won't be a matter of simply buying supplies and walking out the gate. Did you notice that we're already in debt? We work tomorrow to pay for tonight. And tomorrow, we eat their food, use their supplies, and then we have to pay for those with another day's work.*

Perpetual debt, Lucian said. *And refugees who, for the most part, don't have any way to pay except to work more and hope they can reach whatever undefined goal earns them citizenship.* He thought about Forest Town, and how outsiders and refugees were welcomed without debt or obligation, and his jaw clenched. *And what about families? Do children have to work? Do their parents instead run up even greater debt to cover their needs?*

Good questions. Let's see what we find out tomorrow.

The morning wakeup was impossible to miss. Lights blazed on, shattering the darkness, and a loud, repeated buzzing filled the bunkhouse, like an alarm clock held to a microphone. Lucian jerked awake, disoriented by the unexpected blast of light and sound. A startled curse from Quicksilver, to his left, said he wasn't alone in his reaction.

Throughout the bunkhouse, people muttered and swore and crawled out of bed. The elves followed their examples, finding the washrooms and imitating others' morning rituals. They drew some curious looks, and people gave Chance cautious berth, but no one challenged them. Neither, Lucian noticed, did anyone offer them advice or assistance. People moved as if each dwelt in a private bubble of isolation from their neighbors, even as they exchanged brief, polite greetings.

At the entrance, Tate spoke briefly to each person as they left. Some, he gave scraps of parchment, others only received verbal instructions. When Lucian, Chance, Quicksilver, and Eria reached him, he greeted them with a smile. "Good morning. I trust you slept well. Assignments for you. Simple tasks, for today, so you have the chance to get settled, and we can learn something of your skills." He held scraps of parchment to each of them.

Lucian accepted his, but asked, "I didn't see any lockers or places to store out belongings securely. Where would we find such?"

Tate looked surprised, as if it never occurred to him that someone would want to ensure strangers didn't rifle through their belongings. "Your bags are safe enough here. But if you prefer, you can find lockers through this door, in the storage room." He gestured to a closed door against the wall.

"Thanks." Lucian gathered the party's gear and carried it into the room, followed by the other elves.

The storage room, a long, narrow room, held implements of cleaning, spare bedding and disassembled bed frames. In the shadows of the back wall, Lucian found the lockers—a row of cubbies with locking metal doors. The keys hung in the locks. He opened one and carefully stowed their gear inside.

Chance pulled the keys out of several doors, examining them, then swapping them and testing them in other locks. He shook his head. *They're all keyed identically.*

Of course they are, Lucian said. *After all, why would anyone actually want to keep their belongings secure?* He closed the locker door and turned the key. A light touch of magic on key and tumblers altered the lock. *And yet, what a surprise, I somehow found the one that's keyed differently.* He smirked and handed the key to Quicksilver. *Hang onto this.*

The key vanished into Quicksilver's pocket. *You got it.*

They rejoined the milling refugees and found their way to breakfast. The meal was simple but filling—eggs, sausage, and tubers that might or might not have been potatoes. Small pockets of conversation rose around the mess hall, but like in the bunk house, most people kept to themselves. Lucian, Chance, Quicksilver, and Eria looked over their assignments for the day while they ate. Lucian and Chance had been assigned to help in the construction of a building, while Quick-silver and Eria had mess hall duties.

"Be careful," Chance said quietly to his daughter and Quicksilver.

"You too, Dad," Eria said. "Keep Uncle Lucian out of trouble."

"Been trying to do that since before you were born," he told her with a small smile.

Lucian and Chance crossed the refugee quarter to their work site. The foreman eyed them with a grunt of irritation. "Just what I need, a pair of half-starved drifters." He jerked a thumb at a pile of tools. "Gear up."

Despite the foreman's misgivings, Lucian and Chance joined the crew on the new building, working as a team to build walls. Most of Chance's energy went to the task on hand and disguising his weakness, but Lucian drew a few of the other men into conversation. They had been living in Spring-vale for nearly a month, a team of three who'd come from a hamlet far down the Bronze River, driven out by Shiranak's advance. Lucian didn't learn much he couldn't already guess about Shiranak. They'd only seen his army, not the man himself or anyone claiming to be him.

Lucian spoke a little of their own journey to the city. When he told them about the bodies, all three humans nodded grimly.

"They don't let in folk who are sick or can't hold their own," one said. "Surprised your cousin there got in, but guess he must have been able to prove he could handle it. Some groups pick out who's most likely to keep them from being let in and, well…" He drew a finger across his throat. "Patrols find the graves sometimes, I hear. Poor sots, but better than being left to starve or get taken by the bone men." He shivered.

"Know anyone who's been admitted as a citizen?" Lucian asked.

"Nah, not yet, but we all got good marks going so far. Just a matter of time."

Another of the men spoke. "Seems harder the older you are. I hear a lot about kids being taken in."

"Oh?" Lucian asked curiously.

The man shrugged. "That's what I hear, at least. Seems to happen every week or so—kids are running around, then one of the officials comes through, and some of the kids are gone into the city the next day. Orphans, mostly, getting adopted by folk in Springvale. Glad for them. Kids need a good home."

"They do," Lucian murmured in agreement. "I notice it's all adults working. Do the children have duties as well?"

"Not that I've seen. Mostly they run around."

"I was wondering. When we arrived, we were told a day's work paid for the previous night's accommodations, and I was curious how that worked out for families."

The man shrugged. "Not sure on that. Have to ask someone with kids about it."

He and Chance worked until they were released in the late afternoon. Weary, they washed up and returned to the bunkhouse. Eria was already there, and smiled when she saw them.

"All done? Quick and I finished our jobs a while back. He went into town to get supplies."

Lucian smiled back. "Yeah, all done here. Could use a nap, though."

Chance lay down and closed his eyes. His mental voice was far more alert than the physical image he presented. *I want to know more about these "adopted" children.*

Lucian stretched, yawned, and lay down as well. *You and me both.* He gave Eria a quick rundown of their conversation with the construction workers.

I'll ask and see what I can find tomorrow, she said. *One

of the cooks took a liking to me and Quick. A motherly sort. She might tell me something.*

Quicksilver returned in about an hour carrying a large bag. "Hey Lucian, hey Chance." He set the bag on his bed. "You have to check out the market sometime. It's been ages since I saw one this nicely stocked."

Lucian sat up and considered the bag. "So you bought one of everything?"

Quicksilver laughed, shaking his head. "I wish. No, just staples and the stuff on our list." His voice was cheerful, but his gaze searched the room and its shadows.

Lucian rose and stretched. "Well, I'm ready to walk around a little. Why don't we take a stroll? You can tell us what you found."

"Sure." Quicksilver picked up the bag again.

Chance and Eria joined them. Tate nodded to the four as they headed outside again. Quicksilver began describing the market and the wide variety of goods he'd found there, especially food. When he was confident they were far enough from listening ears, he lowered his voice, eyes pinched and serious.

"I got a little hassle leaving the area, and I'm certain I was tailed the whole time. The market was good, but the whole experience was weird. Whenever I bought preserved food, I got subtle pushback from the vendor or an attitude like they were indulging me. Some talked like I was acting like a silly child, and they were just going along with the game. It got a little better when I started prefacing my purchases by saying I'd been on the road a long time and was more comfortable not relying completely on someone else for my necessities." He glanced around again, watchful. "I don't know what would happen if we announced we were leaving. The impression I got is that people don't *do* that."

"Did you see many children in town?" Lucian asked.

Quicksilver frowned. "Some, but not more than I'd expect. Why?"

"The population of children here among the refugees evidently diminishes weekly," Lucian told him. "The refugees believe they are being adopted by families in Springvale and given citizenship."

Quicksilver's frown deepened. "Then I'd expect to have seen more of them." He looked to Lucian. "You don't think they're in the town."

"I don't. Keep an eye out for anything else that seems out of place."

"The refugee district has electricity," Eria said.

Lucian, Chance, and Quicksilver turned to her, puzzled.

She gestured at the buildings around them. "They have electricity, even here in their new addition. I haven't seen any solar panels, so this must be an addition to whatever their existing power source is. And whatever that source is, it's producing enough power to supply this area—and they had the materials to run power to all these buildings. How many towns could do that? How many *would* do that for outsiders who they might not even intend to let stay?"

Now I wonder if powering the buildings isn't just a convenient side-effect of running wiring to power surveillance cameras, Chance said, eyes lifting to scan the buildings. "I don't see any, but I wouldn't be surprised."

Lucian started down the street at a slow walk. *If they are watching, standing around will draw more notice.* The hair on the back of his neck prickled at the thought of being spied on. Like Chance, he hadn't seen any cameras yet, but that didn't mean they weren't there. He watched the people as they walked. Heads hung and conversations were stilted and perfunctory. Compared to the vitality of Forest Town, Springvale's refugee annex oozed depression. Thoughts of Forest

Town roused a deep longing for the comforts of home. *We should leave. I want to reach my forest before harvest.*

Not yet, Chance said. *Not until I know what's really going on here.*

Chance, you've been awake from a coma for barely six months. Can't you wait at least a full year before digging into someone else's trouble? Lucian argued. He glanced to Eria and Quicksilver. *A little help here?*

I'm not touching this one, Lucian, Quicksilver said quickly. *Not for a pile of food and money ten feet high.*

Eria sighed. *Uncle Lucian, I'm not going to get into the question of who is more stubborn between you and Dad. And while I do worry that Dad will find trouble when he starts looking, if we can help these people, we should. Walking off and leaving them without doing so goes against everything I believe.*

Chance shot Lucian a smug look of triumph, but quickly grew serious. *Children are disappearing here, Lucian. Give me seven days. If I can't figure out what's going on and where the missing people are by then, we'll leave for your village.*

Lucian scowled, but knew Chance wouldn't budge. The only argument he could possibly make was to invoke Ayliad and the warning the Guardian had given him. For a moment, he considered it, but he wasn't ready to face the questions and the fear that doing so would bring. *Seven days from when we arrived. So you have five more until we leave.*

Chance just nodded, accepting that.

They finished the afternoon, ate in the dining hall, and finally retired for the night. Lucian lay awake a long time, and when he finally slept, his dreams were restless.

The following morning began much like the previous. However, when they compared assignments, none of them had been placed together, and no one worked in the same place that they had the previous day.

Chance frowned. "Determining our strengths, or just split-ting us up?"

"Hard to say, but laundry duty is about the last place I want to be," Quicksilver groaned.

With misgivings, they split up to their various tasks. Lucian spent the morning filling holes in the dirt street. He was part-nered with Tieln, a dark-haired young man who looked no older than seventeen, though he claimed to be twenty. He was thin, but the tone of his muscles gave Lucian reason to believe the young man could wield weapons as easily as he did a shovel. His clothes were worn and drab, like many things in this area of the city. Even in the heat of the day and the labor, he didn't roll his long sleeves up. Tieln didn't volunteer much initially, but Lucian drew him into conversation. Light probing revealed that Tieln had been in Springvale for almost three weeks, coming from a city nearly as large as this one. With a little more digging, Lucian learned that Tieln had been a guard in his home city. He admitted to Lucian that although he'd left the city with a group of fellow guards, he'd split off from them during the journey, and came to Springvale with a different group.

"Think you'll stay here?" Lucian asked, tamping down the dirt in the hole he'd filled.

Tieln hesitated. "I haven't decided yet, sir." He'd addressed Lucian with the honorific throughout the conversation, and it seemed a verbal reflex rather than a conscious decision. Another hesitation. "I... am not certain whether I will be given the choice. What of you?"

"My companions and I have another destination," Lucian said. "We stopped here primarily for supplies."

Tieln considered his words carefully. "If you plan to leave, sir, you should do so soon. And, if I might suggest... you do so without informing anyone of your intentions beforehand."

Lucian's attention peaked. "What do you know?"

Tieln shook his head quickly. "Nothing certain, sir. Only suspicions and an uneasy feeling. Please, forget I said anything." He focused on his work with determination, pretending not to hear Lucian.

Partway into the afternoon, Chance's voice reached Lucian. *I just saw half a dozen Springvale officials talking to a clump of boys—asking them whether they had families here, where they are staying, that sort of thing. The official in the back, keeping mostly out of view of the boys, was taking notes. I'm going to keep an eye on them.*

Be careful, Lucian told him. The scene described could be innocuous, but Chance's intuition rarely led him wrong, much as Lucian hoped it might this time.

The rest of the day passed with little of note. When the four elves regathered for dinner, they exchanged brief spoken accounts of their days, and kept the rest carefully to mind-speech.

I plan to keep an eye on those children who were approached today, Chance said. *If any of them disappear, I want to know where they go.*

The guy I worked with today warned me we shouldn't tell anyone if we're planning to leave. I got the feeling when we leave, we'd better go in the middle of the night and just disappear ourselves, Lucian said.

I didn't learn anything new today, I'm afraid, Eria said. *Except no one bothers to dust behind anything, and half the people just don't care if they do decent work or not.*

I'm on someone's watch list, Quicksilver said. *I know I said that everything was normal in the laundry, but it was almost... aggressively normal. Like everyone there was absolutely determined to prove to me that Everything is Fine, and There is Nothing to Worry About.* He glanced to Lucian. *Oh, and someone definitely tried to open our locker in the storage room, too. They didn't go as far as taking the door off its hinges, at least. And they didn't get in.*

Wonderful. Lucian sighed, poking a fork into a green blob pretending to be mashed peas. His gaze moved over the mess hall, and he saw Tieln enter.

The young man collected his food and strode toward a far corner of the room, away from others. On impulse, Lucian called him over as he passed.

"Tieln, you can join us if you like."

Tieln stopped, looking at Lucian in surprise. His eyes moved to the others around the table, then back to Lucian. "Thank you, sir, but I had better not. I don't want to cause you any trouble."

"What sort of trouble?" Chance asked.

Tieln didn't answer, continuing to an empty table for his solitary meal.

"Right, that's not concerning at all," Quicksilver muttered.

He's being watched and he knows it, Chance said. He glanced to Lucian. *You have the best chance of getting more from him.*

I'll follow him home tonight, Lucian said. *Still have a couple of hours until sunset.*

Following Tieln proved easier than Lucian expected. After dinner, the young man left the mess hall and made his way to a shack near the outer wall. Lucian trailed him, moving with the groups of people who drifted toward their homes.

Tieln's arrival at the shack was greeted with whoops and cheers, and a pack of children rushed outside to practically tackle him. For the first time, Lucian saw Tieln smile, and he looked even younger than the seventeen years that Lucian had guess him to be. The young man scooped up the smallest of the children, a boy probably six years old, and set him on his shoulders. Two girls not much older latched onto his pant legs.

The eldest of the children, a boy just into his teens, related the day's activities to Tieln.

"Some men from the city came and talked to us today," the boy said.

Lucian saw Tieln stiffen slightly. "Did they? What did they say?"

"Oh, just asked a bunch of questions, made sure no one was sick and we had enough food, that sort of thing," the boy answered, oblivious to Tieln's concern. "Updating their records or something."

"One of the other boys I play with said that sometimes they take kids into the city so families can adopt them," one of the younger girls piped up. "But I don't want to be adopted by someone else. Can you adopt us, Tieln?"

Tieln smiled tightly. "We'll see, Jade."

"Okay." She beamed at him, then looked up the street. Her eyes found Lucian, and she waved cheerfully. "Hi, mister!"

Tieln spun around quickly, one hand rising automatically to steady the boy on his shoulders, the other dropping to his belt in search of a weapon that wasn't there. He saw Lucian, and his wariness did not relent.

Lucian gave the children a friendly smile. "Good evening. I'm new to the city, just walking around to get my bearings."

"I worked with him today," Tieln added, eyes never leaving Lucian.

"Ohhh." The girl sighed. "This is grown-up stuff, isn't it?" Without waiting for an answer, she began herding the other children back into the shack.

Tieln lifted the boy from his shoulders and set him on the ground. The boy giggled and scampered inside after the others. Tieln stood between Lucian and the door. "There are more interesting areas of the city to see, sir."

"Any relation of yours?" Lucian asked, nodding toward the house.

Tieln gazed at him, tense and silent.

"Did you meet them on the road?" Lucian tried.

A nod. For a moment, it seemed Tieln would leave it at that, but he finally said, "The rest of the guards from my city wanted to..." He shook his head. "They weren't interested in helping children. I... parted ways with them."

His tone implied that the parting had been both permanent and violent. Lucian nodded his understanding. "And you brought the children here?"

"I intended only to stop for a brief stay," Tieln told him.

Lucian looked to the shack and lowered his voice. "Someone threatened the children if you tried to leave, didn't they?"

Tieln's shoulders tensed and his mouth tightened. The shadows of the buildings brought out the sharp angles of his features, an almost elven look to his face. "Sir, I think it would be better if you explored somewhere else now."

Lucian held his gaze and spoke quietly. "If we find a way out that you can take them through, I'll let you know. Good night, Tieln."

Tieln said nothing, and didn't move from his spot until Lucian was several blocks gone.

The third day brought yet another assortment of assignments. Lucian didn't like being separated from his friends, and the longer he spent with the refugees, the more his skin crawled. He didn't know if he was being watched or not, and his assignment for the day surrounded him with a ragged bunch of men and women who barely spoke at all and grunted in response to his attempts at conversation. Their task seemed to be nothing more than moving boxes from one stack to another for no reason Lucian could determine. Just... uselessly moving boxes. Even sorting trash, like Quicksilver, had *some* purpose.

He walked off his post without a comment to stretch his

legs. None of his supposed coworkers even looked up. On the off chance that a surveillance camera might be watching, Lucian flipped a rude gesture at the air.

I wonder how long I could be gone before someone noticed. Or cared.

Nearly five minutes after he left his assignment, Lucian heard the pound of running feet coming toward him. He paused, wondering if he was about to get his answer. The sound came from ahead, rather than from the direction of his work site. Lucian stepped to the side of the narrow street, half in shadows.

Tieln rounded a corner, dark hair plastered to his forehead. Sweat stained his shirt, and his face was a mask of determination.

Lucian blinked. "Tieln?"

The young man skidded to a stop before Lucian, sucking in deep breaths. He straightened, collecting himself, then seized Lucian's arm. "Sir, I need to ask you something."

In his surprise at being grabbed, Lucian didn't pull away. Tieln's brown eyes fixed on him intently, and Lucian met them. "Ask."

"Are you one of the ancient spirits? You or any of your companions?"

"What?" That was the *last* question Lucian expected, especially not with such intensity.

"Are you?" Tieln demanded.

Is he trying to hunt out disciples of Shiranak? "And if I am, what difference does it make?" Lucian snapped.

Tieln's grip tightened on his arm. "If you are, you *must* leave the city, now. You and the young woman and the boy with silver hair."

Lucian froze. Before he remembered moving, he'd grabbed Tieln and slammed him against the wall. "Where is Chance?"

"He's with the children I was guarding." Tieln swallowed hard. "Taken, like them."

"Taken where?" Lucian growled. The wooden wall at Tieln's back began to warp, spines forming on the boards.

"If I knew that, I would already be there trying to free them!" Tieln burst. "They *took the children!*"

Lucian stepped back, releasing Tieln. "How do you know they took Chance?" Even as he asked the question aloud, he called to his cousin. *Chance? Where are you?*

Chance did not answer. Lucian's hands clenched.

"I snuck off from my assignment to check on the children," Tieln said quickly, eyeing the spikes in the wall. "There's a spot where I can see their play area without interrupting them. When I reached it, Springvale guards had swarmed the spot. I ducked out of sight before they saw me. It wasn't hard—they were focused on someone else." He glanced at Lucian. "Your friend."

Lucian said nothing, his eyes not leaving Tieln.

"They'd caught him spying when they came to collect the children," Tieln continued. "I don't know if there was a struggle or they took him by surprise. He was unconscious when I saw him. They drugged him, said he'd be a valuable addition. Then I heard a lot of startled swearing, and someone said, 'He's one of *them*. One of the spirits!'"

Lucian's hands curled into fists. "And you don't know where they've taken him."

Tieln straightened. "I know how to find them. I'm going to find them and save the children—and your friend, and anyone else they have. But if your friend is a spirit, the officials will be coming for you and your other friends as well."

"Elves, not spirits," Lucian said. "I'm going with you."

Tieln opened his mouth to object, considered the spikes grown from the wall, and thought better of it. "Yes sir. Follow me."

Quick. Eria. Lucian sent his thoughts flying to them.

Drop whatever you're working on, get our gear if you can, and get out of town.

On it, Quicksilver answered with alacrity.

Is Dad with you, Uncle Lucian? I haven't heard from him in a couple of hours, Eria said.

He ran into some trouble. I'm going to get him out of it, Lucian told her.

Uh oh... Try not to raze the city, please?

Lucian's mental voice was tight. *If what I suspect is true, the city deserves it.*

Tieln gazed into the distance for a long moment, then set off at a jog. Lucian followed. Anger twisted and roiled, waiting for an excuse to break free. Lucian sensed the Ghost ready to seize control if the anger did. Mentally, he pushed the Ghost back.

I will be the one to rescue Chance, not you.

As they neared the gate to Springvale proper, Tieln slowed, then stopped before they came in sight of the gate. He turned to Lucian.

"We are both supposed to be at our assigned tasks, sir, and the guards will question our need to leave. They'll also report it up their chain of command."

And, as Chance noticed when we arrived, this is the only exit. "They took Chance and the children into the city?"

"Through the city. I believe they're outside it now," Tieln answered.

Lucian eyed him. "How do you know? You said you didn't know where they were taking them."

Tieln opened his hand, revealing a compact electronic device. The screen displayed several strings of numbers. "When I left my home city, I grabbed a number of things from the armory that I thought might be useful, among them half a dozen tracking devices and this receiver. I gave the tracking devices to several of the children, so if we were separated for any reason, I could find them. The devices are small, easily missed. Based on the distance displayed on the receiver, I believe they've been taken outside of the city."

That sort of technology was rare so long after the war, but Lucian knew the devices were designed to be sturdy, so it wasn't impossible that some still survived. "Then we don't need to go through Springvale at all; we need to get outside." He strode away from the gate, toward the outer wall.

Tieln trailed after him. "Scaling the wall will draw as much attention as trying to go through the city will, sir."

Lucian said nothing. Wooden walls surrounded the refugees' section of Springvale. He half wished they were stone. Stone was easier to work with, and didn't draw the Guardian's interest. Reaching the barrier, Lucian put his hand to the thick boards, then smiled slightly. Wooden boards, but iron nails and fasteners. The bits of metal yielded readily to his magic until a gentle push from his hand dislodged the boards.

Tieln stared at the opening. "What did you do?"

"Magic," Lucian said, curt. "Come on." He directed a mental call to Eria and Quicksilver. *Follow the sense of my magic. I'm leaving a hole in the wall.*

On my way, Eria said.

Thanks, Lucian, Quicksilver replied. *I was trying to decide how to head out without flying over someone's head. Also, got our gear. Caught Tate picking the lock. He's going to be confused and mad when he wakes up.*

He should be glad he's waking up at all. If I'd caught him, he wouldn't, Lucian said.

Um, Lucian, maybe tone down the murderous intent a little? Quicksilver suggested cautiously. *It's kind of scary.*

Lucian didn't reply. He followed Tieln through the gap in the wall and across a narrow patch of thin, yellow grass before the ground grew dry and desolate once more. The human glanced at him, and whatever he saw in Lucian's face made his tan skin grow pale. Tieln set a quick pace just short of a jog, but it wasn't fast enough for Lucian. Without offering warning or explanation, he reached out with his magic and lifted both himself and the human off the ground.

Tieln yelped in surprise and alarm, eyes wide. The ground flew past below them, faster than a human could run. Lucian fixed a sharp gaze on Tieln. "Is this the right direction?"

Tieln swallowed hard and consulted his device, clutching it tight and trying not to look down. "Turn two degrees to the north." Despite the fear in his eyes, his voice was steady. His hands, however, trembled.

A rocky ridge jutted from the ground ahead of them. The terrain offered no obstacle for Lucian, who simply lifted himself and Tieln up to the top of the sheer cliff.

"Sir!" Tieln said quickly, pointing to the road that had been concealed by the ridge.

Lucian stopped their flight abruptly and spat profanities. They'd traveled about a mile from Springvale. The tracks in the dirt told Lucian that at least one truck had driven the road recently, and he hadn't heard it. The wind was already beginning to sweep away the tire marks.

You cannot have Chance. I won't let you take him.

Lucian's eyes stayed on the road. "The children were taken that way?"

"Yes sir," Tieln said. A pause. "Can your magic move as fast as a truck?"

"No."

Tieln checked his device. "They're moving quickly away from us. This is the right direction."

"Good." Lucian's magic flung them back into motion, following the road.

The distraction from his anger and fear was too brief. Lucian searched for any hint that they were gaining on the truck, but saw only the bare dirt road stretching out ahead of them. He called to Chance, but still heard no answer.

Halfway into the second hour of their pursuit, Lucian sensed a flicker of distant magic. *Chance? Are you there? Chance!*

Still no answer came, from Chance or anyone else, leaving Lucian to wonder if he'd only imagined the flicker. They still followed the road. The terrain grew rocky, and the jagged slopes of mountains rose in the distance.

As they neared the fourth hour, Tieln checked his receiver. "We've been gaining on them, sir. They must have reached their destination."

"Good."

Tieln drew a sharp breath and pointed. "Sir!"

Lucian followed his gesture and saw the symbol painted on the bare metal of a long-faded road sign. Seven crimson lines curved off either side of a wide center line in a stylized, almost artistic depiction of a rib cage. Lucian's hands closed into fists, fingers digging into his palms. Fury burned through him. His eyes narrowed and he hissed, "Bone men."

Beside him, Tieln's mouth tightened and his eyes grew cold. "The rumors around the city were true, then. There *are* bone men in the hills."

Without another word, Lucian flew down the road, pushing as fast as he could go. He considered leaving Tieln behind, but a thin, rational corner of his mind insisted he might need the human's help.

They found the truck half an hour later, parked in a narrow canyon. Dry brush concealed the canyon entrance, but no one had considered a need to obscure the view from above. The vehicle was a dull dusty brown color, and Lucian might have missed it if not for the glint of sunlight in the side mirrors. It might have once been a military troop transport vehicle. A tan canopy covered the long truck bed. A single armed man patrolled around the truck, his stride and stance betraying boredom and a lack of attention. Not that many people thought to look up.

Chance! Lucian called.

A muddled response answered him, confused and laced with panic.

I'm coming, Chance. Just hang on.

Lucian plunged toward the sentry. The man either heard something or glimpsed movement from the corner of his eye and spun around in time to catch Lucian's feet in the face. The force of the impact knocked him to the ground, dazed. Lucian landed beside the sentry and punched him in the face until bone cracked and the man stopped moving. Lucian wiped blood from his knuckles and rose, breath hissing between his teeth.

When Lucian stepped away, Tieln stripped the sentry of his weapons and slit the man's throat. He pointed down the canyon. "They're further in, sir."

The canyon walls drew closer together as they progressed on foot. The natural funnel had Lucian searching for ambush points or additional sentries. None presented themselves, however. The canyon drew to a narrow point, then nothing more than a crack in the rock too thin for even a child to squeeze through.

Lucian spun to face Tieln, for a moment wondering whether the human had drawn him out here duplicitously. Tieln stared at the end of the canyon in confusion. "What is… there must be some other way further in." He looked to Lucian. "Can your magic do something, sir?"

Lucian drew a deep breath to find a hint of calm. He rested a hand on the wall of the canyon and searched for any concealed openings. He found a passage just to his left. Some sort of complex latch system connected to the door, complete with wires that probably connected to traps. Leaving the door alone, Lucian commanded the stone to yield. An opening spread from his hand into the canyon wall to meet the existing passage.

Tieln sucked in a sharp breath, his eyes wide. He tentatively touched the edge of the opening, as if expecting it to be hot.

Sweat beaded Lucian's brow. Though he could fly for hours on his own, carrying a second person drew more of his magic than he expected, and left him with less than he would have liked to deal with the bone men. He wiped moisture from his brow and plunged into the dark tunnel. Tieln hurried after him.

A few electric lights cast pale illumination down the passage, once Lucian's tunnel joined the main one. They were weak and widely spaced, not so much dispelling the darkness as adding shadows and depth to it. The floor was level and clean, the stone marked with slight indents where carts had been wheeled up and down the passage. The further they advanced, the more Lucian caught an odd scent in the air, one he couldn't identify.

A murmur of voices echoed to them. Lucian stopped a moment, then continued on more slowly, stepping lightly. He could have floated, but chose to save his magic until he knew what they faced. He heard four distinct voices—two male and two female.

"...best take we've had yet," one of the women said. "I hope the others can nab the spirit's companions. If *all* of them are spirits, think how much we'd bring home!"

"Probably too much to hope," a man responded. "Still, maybe at least one of them will be." He chuckled. "You know, sometimes I think I ought to thank Shiranak. All these refugees have our coffers overflowing."

Lucian's jaw tightened and his hands clenched in fists. Tieln touched his shoulder lightly and spoke in a low voice.

"Sir, how do you want to take them out? If I can get close enough, I can handle two of them."

Lucian glanced back at him. "But can you do it quietly?"

Tieln considered the question carefully. He carried a handgun scavenged from the sentry by the truck as well as a long, wicked-looking knife. "Maybe. Can you?"

Before he answered, Lucian moved forward a little more, finally getting a look at the speakers. They wore the uniforms of Springvale guards, and stood around a wheeled cart. None of the faces showed any hint of guilt or shame as they examined the goods for which they had traded the lives of children and Chance.

His hands clenched. Rage boiled over. His magic reached into the stone, coiled around it, shaping it into weapons. Slender rock spikes from the walls slammed into the humans like spears, driving through throats, eyes, between ribs to pierce hearts. Startled and pained gurgles began, then cut short. The spikes drew back into the walls. The guards crumpled into bloody heaps.

Tieln stared. "You... can do that?"

"They've sold countless people to the bone men. They took your charges, and they took Chance. They deserve far worse than this." He stepped over the bodies and looked into the cart. "And they did it for money and trinkets." Lucian's voice was flat and hard as he fought his desire to bring down the entire cavern. *If I knew where they have Chance and the children, I'd bring down the rest of the cave in a heartbeat.*

Tieln looked into the cart and blinked, surprised. "Radios, surveillance equipment, weapons, and... is that a generator?"

"Probably." Lucian glanced down at the equipment. "Water powered, I expect. Must be how Springvale maintains its technology. Convenient to have all these refugees handy to sell to the bone men when they need something new."

Tieln's grip tightened on the gun. "Lead the way, sir. I'd

like very much to remove that option from the people of Springvale."

Beyond the bodies of the guards, the passage ended in a heavy steel door. Lucian tested it and found it locked. He hesitated only a moment, then knocked.

A small panel slid open, spilling bright light into the passage. "You have word of the spirit's companions?" asked a male voice.

"We do," Lucian answered coolly. "Open up."

Apparently, the man on the other side didn't notice that Lucian's voice was unfamiliar, and couldn't see him clearly enough to know he wasn't one of the guards. Or else he didn't care. The lock released with a loud, heavy clunk and the door swung in.

Lucian flung the door open with a shove strengthened by magic. It slammed into the wall, clipping the man attending it. He staggered and blinked, confused to find strangers before him. Lucian grabbed him by the throat and shoved him against the wall.

"Where are the prisoners?"

The man's eyes cleared. He kicked at Lucian. One hand rose to pry at the grip on his throat, the other dropped to his waist. The light glinted on metal.

Tieln grabbed the man's hand and twisted the blade from his grasp. "Where are the children?" he demanded.

The man's lips curled in a smile too wide, a smile that never reached his eyes. His skin was smooth and flawless, like his features had been molded from plastic rather than flesh. "They serve."

Lucian's hand squeezed tighter on the man's neck. "Where?"

"Enter... and see." The smile never faltered, even as the man gasped for air.

"Very well." Lucian nodded to Tieln.

Tieln drove a knife between the man's ribs and into his heart without hesitation. When he couldn't feel the beat of the man's pulse, Lucian let him drop to the ground. Neither he nor Tieln spoke. Aside from the door they'd entered by, the room had only one exit, leading deeper inside.

The door opened into a well-lit room. Electric lights glowed in the ceiling, showing tables and benches arranged like a mess hall. Odors of cooked meat and cabbage lingered in the air. The room was empty, but could comfortably hold twenty. Lucian gave it a cursory scan and pressed on to the next door.

He heard voices before he turned the knob, and paused briefly. Looking to Tieln, he asked, "Are the guns loaded?"

Tieln double checked his weapons and nodded. "Yes sir."

"Are you a good shot?"

"A decent one, sir."

"Good. Shoot to kill." Lucian jerked the door open.

If not for the fact that no one had the equipment or facilities to make movies for fifty years, he would have thought he'd stepped onto the set of some second-rate, mad scientist film. Bookshelves and cabinets lined the walls. Liquids boiled and frothed inside beakers over burners on heavy wooden tables. Though well-lit, the room reeked of malevolent gloom. The stink of chemicals and pain stung his nose, and the high-pitched whine of machines set his nerves on end.

"What's this? More guests?" Down the length of the room, a dozen figures in gray laboratory coats turned from their beakers and test tubes to face the door. All of them smiled at Lucian and Tieln with the same too-wide plastic smile. All had the same too-perfect faces, like someone had cast them from identical molds. Rusty spatters of dried blood stained their coats.

"Where are they?" Lucian demanded, eyes flickering around the room in search of Chance or the children.

"What will you pay?" The closest man drew an obsidian blade from his belt. "An arm? A leg? A companion?"

The gun thundered in Tieln's hand, leaving Lucian's ears ringing. The man staggered, but didn't fall. Blood spread down the right side of his coat. His smile somehow spread wider. "In blood, then." He straightened, pulling a handgun of his own from under his coat.

Tieln fired again, and didn't wait to see whether the second shot stopped the bone man before turning his aim to another.

I don't have time for this. Lucian dropped to his knees and pressed his palms to the cool stone. *You're between me and Chance.*

The floor rippled, throwing bone men off balance and tossing glass beakers from tables and shelves. Rock spikes stabbed from the floor. Those who'd kept their feet dodged, but those who'd fallen were not so lucky.

"Another elf!" one of them shouted. "Subdue him, and he will be a gift to our lady!"

"I'm no one's gift to anyone," Lucian snarled. The bone man who'd shouted flew back, slamming into the wall with bone-shattering force.

The three remaining bone men aimed handguns at Lucian and Tieln and returned fire. Tieln ducked for cover, but Lucian smelled a sudden sharp tang of blood. Tieln took out another bone man, and didn't appear to be bleeding anywhere vital. Lucian nudged the trajectory of the bullets away from himself and Tieln and stood to glare at the final men.

"Where is Chance, and where are the children?" he demanded.

"The children have been prepared for our work. The elf awaits our lady's return, as you should." The bone man snatched something from the table and pointed it at Lucian. The missiles flew fast as bullets.

Lucian sprang into the air, though his magic was running dangerously low. One dart tore through the leg of his pants and grazed his leg, and the other lodged itself in his leather shoe. The tip of the dart pressed against his foot, not quite piercing all the way through to break skin, but dangerously close.

Tieln's next shot dropped that man, but after that, Lucian heard only the click of a weapon lacking ammunition. Lucian kicked off the shoe with the dart embedded in it and dove at the final bone man. The man saw Lucian coming, but only smiled. "The lady is waiting for you. She will bless us for bringing you to her."

"Fuck your 'lady'!" Lucian slammed into the bone man. The man gripped Lucian's left arm, and a sharp sting bit into his skin. The human smashed into a table, his head striking the corner with a sickening crunch. He did not rise.

Lucian's eyes swept the room for any sign of movement. He ran back to Tieln. "You hurt?"

Tieln winced as he stood. "I'll live, sir." Blood seeped through his shirt from a gash on his ribs. "Nothing that won't mend."

"Good." Lucian offered him a shoulder to lean on, but Tieln declined.

Lucian pulled up his sleeve to check his arm. Two small punctures bled and his arm tingled a little, but he didn't feel any swelling or heat that might indicate poison.

At the back of the room, they found a heavy iron door, locked and barred from their side. Together, they lifted the bar away. Lucian spent a little more magic removing the lock tumblers. The door swung open on silent hinges.

Lucian knew the scent of fear all too well. The room reeked of it. Cages large and small filled the space, giving the large room a crowded, claustrophobic feel. The walls were a sterile white, and the lights cold and harsh. In the cages nearest the door, eight children sat. Lucian recognized most of them from the pack at Tieln's home.

Tieln bolted to the cages and grabbed a door as if he could yank it open. "Lily!"

The girl inside the cage didn't respond. Her eyes stared blankly through Tieln, glassy and empty. None of the children even blinked when Tieln spoke their names.

Lucian looked past them. *Where is Chance?*

He saw a shift of movement in the corner, heard the clank of metal against metal. Lucian rushed to it and found a cage large enough for a man. Inside it, Chance slumped against the bars. His chest rose and fell in rapid, panicked breaths. His arms were chained to the bars on either side of him. Dried blood stained his left arm, but Lucian didn't see any wounds. That didn't wake nearly the blind fury in him as the other restraint did.

The bone men had locked a collar around Chance's neck. Like a slave. Like everything Willow had ever wanted to inflict on Chance.

"Chance!" Lucian hissed.

Chance's head jerked up. His eyes were wide and unfocused.

"Chance, do you hear me?" Judging from Chance's eyes, he'd been drugged.

Chance's gaze found Lucian and snapped into desperate, intense focus. *Help me.*

Please let me still have strength enough for this. Lucian called up his magic, knowing he stood on the edge of pushing too far. Sweat dripped down his face and his hands trembled with the effort of lifting them. *I have to get Chance out of here. I can't pass out now.*

The chains and collar fell away. The cage lock released. Lucian staggered under a wave of exhaustion and vertigo.

Chance crawled out of the cage and crumpled on the floor, clawing at his neck as if he could scrape away the lingering feel of the collar. He was breathing hard and sweat beaded his forehead. His captors had taken the concealing robe from him, leaving him wearing only a too-large shirt and worn pants.

Lucian dropped to his knees beside Chance. "Are you hurt? Do you know where you are?"

"Lucian?" Chance grabbed his arm. "We have to go. She knows where I am!" His voice rasped in his throat, but the fear came through clearly. "She was here. She wouldn't stop touching me, whispering…" He shuddered.

Cold dread ran down Lucian's spine. The chains, the collar… now Chance's whispered words. He pulled his cousin to his feet. "Who was here, Chance?" Offering the only reassurance he had, he added, "Willow is dead. She can't reach you now."

"Not Willow. Ayliad."

Lucian's blood froze. *She found him, and I wasn't here to protect him. I swore I wouldn't let her touch Chance again, and I failed him. Why did I let myself be convinced to stay in Springvale?*

He turned Chance to face him, pulling up one desperate hope. "Chance, you've been drugged. Is there a possibility— any at all, that it wasn't her? That it was someone else, and you hallucinated Ayliad?"

Chance's glazed eyes cleared, meeting Lucian's. His grip on Lucian's arm grew tighter, and he whispered, "I hope so."

"If she was here, she'd never pass up the opportunity to greet me," Lucian added darkly. *She would have been standing behind the bone men, taunting me with what she'd been doing to Chance.*

Chance said nothing to that, only shivered. Lucian helped him back to Tieln and the children. Tieln had found a key and gotten the children out of the cages, but they remained unresponsive. Tieln looked helplessly to Lucian.

"I don't know if they've been drugged, or poisoned, or what's wrong, sir!" He glanced to Chance and appeared relieved to not see the elf in the same state.

Chance lifted his arm off Lucian's shoulder and sank down

beside the closest child. He rested a hand on her arm. Lucian felt a brief pulse of magic. "Drugged." He grimaced. "Nasty stuff."

Another, longer sense of magic, Chance's healing running through the child's thin body. A moment later, she shifted positions slightly, Chance lifted his hand from her.

"Rish, do you hear me?" Tieln asked urgently.

The girl turned toward him, her movements slow and sleepy. She didn't answer, but smiled at Tieln.

"I can counter it enough to get them moving," Chance said. "The rest will wear off in time."

"Are you sure you're up for this?" Lucian asked in a low voice. Chance's hands were shaking and his breathing still held the quick edge of repressed panic.

"We can't carry them all and we can't leave them," Chance replied. He moved to the next child.

Lucian kept a careful eye on him. Chance often felt the effects of drugs more acutely than most, but if this one hindered his healing, he hid it well. He'd regained his magical strength far faster than his physical strength. Once he'd brought all eight children to a half-awake state, Chance turned to Tieln. "You're bleeding."

"It's not serious—" Tieln began.

Chance ignored him, pushed to his feet, and gripped Tieln's arm for balance. The young man voiced a startled yelp. "What was that?"

"Healing," Chance said. "And 'not serious' my ass. Would have needed stitches at the least. Let's go."

They herded the children through the laboratory. Seeing the grisly scene of blood and mangled corpses, Lucian was glad the children weren't aware enough to really see what lay around them. Chance's gaze swept over the room and his expression grew dark.

"I told them they'd regret this," he said in a low, hoarse voice.

Slowly, they made their way through the tunnels. The children didn't move quickly, and Lucian finally picked up one of the youngest who continued to straggle behind. Night had fallen by the time they finally got outside. The moons' pale illumination barely reached them.

"Where are we?" Chance asked. "Where are Eria and Quick?"

"We're about twenty miles from Springvale," Lucian told him. "I told Eria and Quick to get our gear and get out of town after Tieln told me you'd been abducted."

Chance frowned at Tieln.

"The spot you chose for observation is one I often used to check on the children," Tieln explained. "On my way there, I discovered you had been taken, and that they had revealed you were a spirit… an elf. And I learned that my charges had been abducted as well. I thought it best to warn Lucian of your fate before I set in pursuit."

Chance still frowned. "And how did you find us this far from the city?"

Tieln briefly raised the handheld device he'd been consulting. "I gave several of my charges beacons so I could use this to locate them if we were ever separated."

"Hmm." Clearly, Chance found something off about the explanation, but he didn't elaborate, nor share his suspicions with Lucian.

"The guards brought you all here by truck," Lucian said, too tired to press Chance to share his thoughts. "Presumably, that truck still has at least enough fuel to drive back to Springvale, or wherever they stored it."

"You're not going *back*, are you, sir?" Tieln burst, aghast.

"No," Lucian said. "But it will get us at least twenty miles in any *other* direction, too."

To his relief, the truck remained undisturbed. Lucian checked the cab and found the keys still in the ignition. Tieln lifted the children into the back and, after a moment's hesitation, climbed in after them.

"Do you know how to operate this vehicle, sir?" he asked Lucian.

Lucian chuckled. "I was alive long before humans invented automatic transmissions. I can drive a manual just fine."

"I meant… well… sorry, sir. Just… I don't know how to operate one at all." Tieln paused again, then got the children settled in the back of the truck.

Chance dragged himself into the passenger seat in the cab, letting Lucian drive. The truck growled to life and Lucian coaxed it into gear and backed out of the canyon. He forced himself to focus, though he wanted nothing more than to close his eyes and sleep. Neither of them spoke until he had the truck back onto what passed for a road.

"Lucian."

He glanced to Chance, keeping one eye on the road. "Yes?"

"Thank you."

Lucian frowned slightly. "For what?"

"For coming. For getting me out of there. And for tearing those twisted fuckers to pieces."

"Any time, Chance. Any time."

After a while, Chance spoke again. "Where are Eria and Quick now?" His voice was thick with exhaustion.

Lucian rubbed his eyes and rolled down the window to let in cool evening air. "I'm not sure. I haven't spoken to them since leaving the city. And right now, I'm not sure I have the magic to reach either of them."

Chance turned toward him sharply. "Stop the truck."

Lucian braked, slowing the vehicle, though he saw nothing outside to warrant concern. "Why?"

"Because if you are *that* drained, you definitely should *not* be driving. You should be sleeping."

"You're in no shape to drive, and Tieln already said he doesn't know how," Lucian countered.

"So we'll find a place to stop, and you will sleep," Chance said. "And so will I, and Tieln, and those children. When it's morning and we can see where we're going, we find Eria and Quick."

Lucian stepped on the accelerator again. "And when the Springvale guards come and find us while we're all asleep? Do you want to lay wagers on them having only one truck?"

"Turn left here," Chance told him.

Lucian complied, wincing as the tires bounced over rocks. "This isn't a road."

"No, it's a place to stop. Stop the truck, turn off the lights, and rest before you pass out, Lucian," Chance told him.

Lucian scowled at his cousin, but finally shut off the truck. "This is a bad idea."

"They won't find us," Chance told him. He reached over and pulled the keys out of the ignition. He closed his eyes, and Lucian sensed magic.

The truck swayed slightly as it rose off the ground. Lucian couldn't see the landscape, but felt the truck settle gently down on its shocks a moment later. Chance let out a heavy breath and let his head rest against the passenger side door.

"Humans won't find us here," he said quietly. "So sleep."

Lucian wanted to argue, but he was too worn. He leaned back in the driver's seat and closed his eyes. Sleep came faster than he expected.

He woke to sunlight on his face. Lucian groaned and raised an arm to shield his eyes. Every muscle ached. He blinked away sleep and turned to assure himself that Chance hadn't vanished.

To his relief, his cousin still slept, half curled on his seat, head resting against the window. He stirred when Lucian began to move and opened one eye.

Urgh. Sorry. Should have faced the truck away from the sun.

It made a good alarm clock, Lucian said. He fumbled the door open.

A wash of cool morning air hit him, intruding sharply into the stuffy warmth of the cab. Lucian muttered a curse and forced himself to step outside. Everything ached and a piercing headache pulsed behind his eyes. Thirst scratched at his throat. Lucian steadied himself against the truck. He didn't remember the last time he'd run his magic so dry, and he'd forgotten the muzzy hangover that doing so left. He steadied himself against the truck and waited for the pounding to subside.

The morning sun crept over the hills and threw long shadows behind Lucian and the truck. Lucian looked around, seeing a wide, flat stretch of rock atop a natural stone pillar, inaccessible by any road.

The other truck door closed. Feet crunched over loose stones, and Chance joined him. "Feeling better?" Chance asked quietly.

"Tired, but all right. You picked a good spot for us to stop last night."

"You weren't driving nearly as well as you thought you were," Chance told him. "Seemed the best option."

Lucian turned to his cousin. Chance's black hair lay in an unkempt rat's nest. His clothes hung rumpled and loose. His wrists were raw from the shackles, and bruises darkened his pale skin. Chance ran a trembling hand through his hair, then abandoned the effort when the tangles wouldn't yield.

"How are you doing?" Lucian asked him.

Chance looked to the horizon. "I just keep thinking about what happened. I should have been prepared, I should have taken more precautions. A century ago, I'd never have been that careless in my spying."

Lucian saw fear in Chance's eyes. Despite what he said, that wasn't where Chance's thoughts really lingered. "You're thinking about Ayliad."

Chance shuddered. "When you found me, you asked if the drugs had muddled my perception, and it might have been someone else. They didn't, and it wasn't. I wanted to believe it wasn't her, but she was there, Lucian, in spirit form. I felt her hands on me, and I couldn't push her away." He wrapped his arms around himself. "She whispered in my ear, saying how much she looked forward to picking up where she left off last time she had me."

Lucian's fists clenched. Neither of them had seen Ayliad in the flesh in centuries, yet the threat of her presence still flung them back into times better forgotten. She'd tracked the clan down at her mother's instructions and worked her way into their number. She'd seduced Lucian, knowing full well that he was her brother. She'd seduced her half-brother Dash, and set her sights on Chance as well. When Chance rejected her advances, Ayliad had done far worse than seduction.

Lucian rested a steadying hand on Chance's shoulder. "I won't let her touch you again."

His thoughts, however, carried none of the confidence his words did. *Ayliad never tormented us by spirit before. She was always confined to the physical. If she's discovered the ability to venture through the spirit realm...* He shivered. Ayliad in the flesh was bad enough, but at least she had some limits there.

The truck shifted as someone moved in the bed. Lucian and Chance both roused from their private thoughts and turned. Tieln emerged into the morning light.

"Good morning, sirs," the human greeted. "The children are still asleep and haven't stirred. Are they okay?"

"That's what I expected," Chance assured him.

Tieln was quiet for a moment, then straightened. "You are both spirits… elves. Are you with Shiranak?"

Lucian stiffened. "What?"

"We are with no one but ourselves," Chance said. He studied Tieln. "What would you have done if we were?"

"I would rethink my original rejection of Shiranak's tenets of faith," Tieln answered. "My mother followed the worship of the ancient spirits, but she was also… somewhat insane. However, you, sir," he looked at Lucian, "have done more for these children and me than any other man or god."

"We're not gods. I don't want anyone's worship, and Shiranak can piss off for all I care. I don't give a shit about the whole 'ancient spirit' crap he's pushing, and I *certainly* don't want to be part of it."

Some of the tension relaxed from Tieln's shoulders. "Yes, sir."

Lucian faced him. "What's with the 'sir' business?"

Tieln looked startled, then frowned, as if he hadn't realized he was using the title when he addressed Lucian. "Habit, I guess," he said finally. "You carry yourself like you expect to be respected, or like you're in charge. I'm sorry, sir." He caught himself. "Sorry."

Lucian waved one hand in dismissal. "Use it if you like."

Tieln walked to the edge of the table of rock, then jerked back in surprise when he realized how far they were from the ground. "You did this?"

"I did," Chance corrected. "But I assume you have some familiarity with magic."

Tieln shook his head. "Not before yesterday. I have never, to my knowledge, met elves before."

"Are you sure?" Chance asked in a mild tone that said he didn't believe Tieln.

Tieln shook his head emphatically. "I'm sure." He paused. "Why?"

Chance folded his arms across his chest. "Since I've never seen someone successfully use a handheld game system as a tracking device, you must have employed some other means of locating the children and me."

Lucian's eyebrows rose. "What?"

"I'm surprised you didn't recognize it, Lucian. You used to own one," Chance told him with a slight smile.

"I had more important matters on my mind," Lucian said. *But I should have paid more attention.* "Let me see it."

Tieln pulled the device from his pocket and held it up, but didn't release it. "It came from my mother."

Now that he could see it clearly, Lucian recognized the shape and style of the device. A handheld game player, the manufacturer's logos long worn away. "So how *did* you track the children?" *Humans don't have magic. Could he have already known where to find the bone men's lair? Had he tracked them before? If so, why not just say so?*

Tieln shifted uncomfortably. "I... don't know how to explain it, sir." He held the "tracking device" close against his chest as if one of them might wrestle it from him.

Chance's eyes narrowed. "How old are you?"

"Twenty," Tieln answered, cautious and puzzled at the shift in topic.

"Don't lie, Tieln," Chance said coolly.

Tieln started to respond, but stopped. "According to the city records, that is my age," he said stubbornly.

Chance didn't blink. "How old are you?"

Tieln looked from him to Lucian, then back. His gaze dropped to the ground, and he spoke quietly. "I'm... forty-eight years old."

"That's better," Chance said.

Lucian eyed his cousin, brows rising. "Given his looks, I assumed he was claiming to be older than he was, not younger."

Tieln swallowed hard. "It's the truth, sir. I don't know the reason I still look like I'm little more than a youth, if some mutation from the war is to blame, or—"

"One of your parents was an elf," Chance cut in. To Lucian, he added, "I sensed it when I healed him."

"An… elf?" Tieln repeated incredulously, staring at Chance. "But… that's…"

"It's possible," Lucian said slowly. "There have always been a few rumors, though rare. Our birth rates are low enough among our own kind, I can't imagine a viable pregnancy happens often between species. You're sure, Chance?"

"I'm sure," Chance said. He gazed at Tieln. "Just as I'm sure his ability to find the children had nothing to do with an electronic game, and everything to do with magic."

"I don't have magic!" Tieln protested quickly.

Both elves gazed at him with dubious expressions.

"I just have a… talent for knowing where things and people are. It's not magic!"

"Even when they are miles away?" Lucian asked. He shook his head. *Magic doesn't go away just because you don't want it, Tieln.*

"I never said I don't want it, sir! Only that it's not magic," Tieln objected.

Chance's eyebrows rose and he half-smiled. "Responding to words that were not spoken aloud doesn't support your case as much as you think it does."

Tieln looked between them. "What do you mean? I heard—"

"That is exactly what I mean. You heard." Chance gazed at him. *And you still hear, whether we are speaking aloud or using mind-speech.*

Tieln shook his head again, much like newcomers to Forest Town did when Lucian told them that he was an elf. And like them, he hadn't had enough time to process everything.

"Why don't you check on the kids, Tieln? Have you tried to contact Eria or Quick, Chance?" Lucian asked.

"Not yet." Chance's intent gaze finally left Tieln. "Did you check how much fuel we have?"

"Not yet," Lucian responded. He rolled his shoulders and stretched. "We'd better get the truck back down to the ground, too."

As his magic lifted the truck, Tieln, and himself, Lucian realized that he couldn't blame Tieln for not putting his own "finding" ability in the same category as flying and rock-shaping. The skills Lucian had demonstrated were far flashier than Tieln's. With no one to teach him, Tieln had drawn his own conclusions about who and what he was, and developed his magic to meet his own needs.

Chance floated down after them on his own, his gaze distant. Tieln climbed into the back of the truck to check on the children. Lucian climbed into the driver's seat, but didn't start the truck. He closed his eyes and leaned back.

Quick, you and Eria out there? He sent the thought in search of his nephew.

Lucian! Are you all right? Is Chance with you? Is everyone safe? Quicksilver responded immediately, his mental voice sharp with worry.

We're all right. Left a nest of dead bone men and a handful of dead Springvale guards behind us. Chance is safe, as are the children who were taken. Are you and Eria all right?

We had a few… hiccups getting out of the city, but we're out and safe. We decided to hunker down until we heard from you or Chance. We went upriver a couple of miles. Do you think you can find your way there?

I can find the river, and I'll head upriver of Springvale. You'll hear us coming. We requisitioned the truck the guards used to transport Chance and the kids.

We'll be waiting.

Several minutes later, Chance climbed into the truck and handed him the keys. "Eria said she and Quicksilver took shelter in a cave several miles upriver of Springvale. No serious efforts being made by Springvale to patrol the area."

"Why bother, when they have deals made with the biggest threat in the area?" Lucian said darkly. "Or rather, *had* deals with them." He started the truck. "We have about a third of a tank of fuel."

Lucian followed the road, such as it was, through the hills. Once they reached level ground, he turned off the road leading to Springvale. The truck bounced over the rough ground, but it was designed to withstand a certain amount of off-road driving. The shock absorbers, however, felt like they hadn't been replaced since before the war. He didn't push the truck too hard, though they still moved faster than they would have on foot.

Once they reached the river, Lucian found a passable road again, to the relief of his jostled bones. Half an hour later, Eria's mental voice nudged him.

I hear a vehicle. Is that you, Uncle Lucian?

I hope so. If not, someone else is driving along this road, and we might be in for an unpleasant meeting. Lucian tapped the truck horn in a quick honk. *Did you hear the horn?*

Yes, she said, relieved. *We'll be out in a minute.*

Lucian stopped the truck and got out. A moment later, Tieln cautiously looked out from the back of the truck. "Problem, sir?"

"No problem," Lucian assured him. "We're picking up Eria and Quicksilver."

Tieln remained cautious and watchful until the other two elves emerged and hurried to the truck. Eria threw her arms around Lucian in a fierce hug. "Thank you for bringing Dad back safely."

He wrapped his arms around her. "Always."

She released Lucian and hugged Chance, who'd also left the truck. Finally, Eria looked to Tieln. "Thank you for helping my father and Uncle Lucian. I understand that your wards were abducted as well. How are they? My name is Eria, and I'm a healer. I'll help however I can."

Tieln stared at her for a moment, then shook himself. "Thank you, ma'am. Your father checked on the children earlier, but if you would like to, please do. My name is Tieln, formerly of the city of Redcreek."

"A pleasure to meet you," Eria said. She considered the truck. "Is there room for our bags in there with you and the children?"

"Plenty of room," Tieln said. He looked past her to Quicksilver and the packs that floated behind him like ducklings. "Oh. Did you conceal your gear outside before you entered Springvale?"

"No, we brought them with us," Eria said. "Why?"

"The gate guards let you pass with them? When I arrived, my gear was confiscated with a promise that it would be returned once it was checked for any contraband or restricted items such as weapons." Tieln shook his head. "I was allowed to bring a personal kit with me, and the same for the children, but somehow no one got around to returning the rest of my belongings."

Lucian's eyebrow rose. He looked to Chance. "It sounds like when you convinced the gate guards to let us enter, you sidestepped a few other issues as well."

"Evidently," Chance said. "Though we wouldn't have entered if they'd insisted on taking our gear."

"Unfortunately, that option was not available to me," Tieln said. He considered for a moment, then addressed Lucian. "Sir, the children and I are indebted to you. I realize that this is a great deal to ask, but as we are lacking both supplies and transportation, could we accompany you for a time?"

It hadn't occurred to Lucian that they might *not* do so. He cast quick glances to his companions, checking for any objections. Finding none, he answered. "Of course you can. In fact, I'd encourage you to come with us the rest of the way to my village. It's a good, safe place with fertile ground. About a hundred fifty people."

Tieln's face pinched in unease. "A hundred fifty elves, sir?"

"No, humans," Lucian told him. "Everyone but us is human there. The children will be safe, and I promise, if someone offers to adopt one of your wards, they mean it, and no one will sell anyone to bone men."

"I'll consider it, sir. Thank you."

Quicksilver loaded the packs into the truck. "And speaking of your village, Lucian, we'd better hit the road again, before anyone from Springvale comes looking for this truck they so fortuitously loaned us."

Eria caught Chance's sleeve as he stepped toward the passenger door. "Dad, would you mind riding in the back with me? I'd like to know what you know about the children and their health."

"All right." Chance went with her into the back of the truck, trailed by Tieln.

Quicksilver intercepted Lucian. "You look exhausted. How about I drive for a while so you can grab a nap?"

"I'm sensing a conspiracy here, Quick," Lucian said.

Quicksilver gave him his most innocent smile. "I have no idea what you're talking about. But honestly, it doesn't take a mind-reader to guess that neither you nor Chance got enough sleep, and you're both too stubborn to admit you need a break. So, I'll drive, you'll take a nap, and no one will be the wiser. Fair?"

"All right, fair." Lucian shook his head and climbed into the passenger seat. "But for the record, I'm doing just fine."

"Duly noted!" Quicksilver hopped into the driver's seat. After a couple false starts, he got the truck in gear and in motion. "Damn, this thing is unwieldy."

"Especially compared to that speedster sports car you used to drive," Lucian said. "That thing did what, zero to two hundred in sixty seconds?"

"Two hundred and thirty was my best," Quicksilver said. "And you're one to talk, considering the cars you owned." He sighed. "I do miss the Silver Lightning, though. It was great for picking up girls. Though it wouldn't be much use now. Even if we had fuel, it only seated two."

"Can't have everything, I suppose." Lucian leaned against the door and closed his eyes. Chance was safe, and they were on their way back to Forest Town, where Ayliad couldn't reach them. Finally, he could rest.

INTERLUDE TWO: SHIRANAK

Tense silence hung over Forest Town. The buildings on ground level stood hidden under camouflage, the doors locked and barred. Residents sheltered in their houses, leaving only the town defense force stationed on the walkways, weapons loaded and ready. Cylin's gaze swept over the village. It would take a careful eye to even see Forest Town as anything more than a clearing in the trees.

Twice now since Lucian's departure, concealment had proved sufficient deterrent against bandits. These new arrivals, however, moved with purpose through the forest. They were a small band, ten people led by a red-haired man who looked too young to be any sort of warlord or bandit leader. However, the way he issued orders, he clearly expected obedience. The sentries had also reported that most of his men wore concealing, hooded robes that all too closely matched descriptions of members of Shiranak's army.

Newcomers to Forest Town in the last months had all brought similar stories: their towns and villages approached by someone claiming to bring the word of Shiranak. Not long after the would-be spokesman was tossed out, Shiranak's army attacked and overran the settlement. Those who survived were offered the choice to accept the new rule or be exiled. Cylin hadn't decided whether that was a better or worse option than "convert or die."

Below her perch, the men entered the village clearing. The leader walked forward, well out of cover, where Cylin had a clear shot at him. He stood there several minutes, looking around as if waiting for something.

What are you doing, asshole? Looking for something? Waiting for one of us to show ourselves? Well, keep right on waiting. And stay right there, so I can put a bullet between your eyes.

Finally he looked over his shoulder. "Ah well, it seems he really isn't here now. A pity. Let's see what we can find."

"Very well." The speaker was the only other unhooded man, with dull brown hair and a tendency to hunch, as if he might start running on all fours at any moment. "Starting with the cave?"

They can't even see Lucian's cave from here. How would they know about it?

"No, I think we should start with the houses in the trees," the young leader replied. "Find out just what we have here."

Cylin stiffened. She hadn't seen him looking up the trees. *I don't know who you are, but you are definitely trouble.* She lined her pistol sights on his head and squeezed the trigger.

The bullet veered off course and hit the dirt at the man's feet. He raised one eyebrow, looking up and fixing his gaze directly on her. "Really? Was that necessary?"

Shit. He's an elf. Cylin rose from her crouch. "I'm not impressed."

"Are you sure?" he countered.

"Lucian did it better." The words came almost without thought.

He considered, then shrugged. "Well, that's fair. But where *is* Lucian? I tried calling ahead, but he didn't answer."

Does he really know Lucian, or is he faking? "He's taking care of some business."

"Ah. That's a shame. I wanted to talk to him."

Cylin snorted dubiously. "You expect me to believe *that?* Coming here with a pack of twisted mutations, giving orders to search homes, and you claim you want to *talk?*"

"I take precautions when I travel. Followers of Shiranak sometimes face unfriendly reception."

"Yeah, I wonder why *that* is," Cylin muttered. "So who are you?"

He gave her a charming smile, as if greeting an old friend rather than the stranger who'd just tried to shoot him. "My name is Yazah. I grew up as part of the same clan as Lucian. And you, my dear?"

"I'm no one's 'dear'. Certainly not yours." Cylin scowled down at him. She didn't look to see where the rest of the village defenders were, but if they followed training, they should be positioning themselves to take out as many of Yazah's minions as possible, should this conversation turn bad. Not that Cylin thought it was particularly good at the moment.

"My apologies. You are in charge in Lucian's absence?"

The true answer was that she, Devin, and Doctor Kinnel divided the responsibilities of leadership between them, but she didn't want this follower of Shiranak looking for any more potential targets. "I am. What's your purpose here, Yazah?"

"My purpose? To bring the blessings of Shiranak to you all, if you will bow to him."

Cylin tensed, and sensed unease run through the branches of Forest Town. They'd all heard from refugees about what happened to towns that rejected Shiranak's "invitation." Cylin steeled herself. "So who is Shiranak? You?"

The question surprised Yazah, but he smiled. "No. I am his heir."

"And you seem familiar with Lucian. So, Yazah, what

makes you think we'd want to turn from our elf to yours? Because frankly, I know you have magic, but you aren't gods."

"You should consider it, my as-of-yet-unnamed lady, because you have undoubtedly heard tales of the fates of those who have refused my lord's offer," Yazah answered.

"Really?" Cylin imitated the tone he'd used when she shot at him. "I thought you came here to talk to Lucian. Still planning on having that chat with him?"

"Of course," Yazah said. The hooded figures still stood impassive and without any hint of emotion, but the unhooded man beside Yazah gazed around the clearing with cold, sharp eyes, as if picking out every hiding place, every shadow and shelter where someone might lurk.

Cylin holstered her gun and folded her arms across her chest. "Well then, Yazah, unless you really *want* to be dodging rock spikes while trying to have that conversation, I'd suggest that you don't fucking mess with his home. That sort of thing makes him cranky."

"Hmm." Yazah turned to the other man. "What do you think, Ravys?"

"I think Lord Shiranak will not approve of us remaining here indefinitely," the other answered.

"True, but he won't approve of us leaving without attaining our goal, either," Yazah replied. He stroked his chin. "An interesting quandary. Is it worth potentially upsetting Lucian to ensure that the meeting happens?"

Cylin's gaze never left the pair. *Yazah's not afraid of Lucian. Is he stupid, or does he have reason to be so confident? How powerful is Lucian compared to other elves? Quicksilver gave me the impression that Lucian's stronger than most, but maybe Yazah is too.* Her gaze moved to Ravys. She couldn't tell if he was human or elf. Maybe Yazah could afford to be confident because a group of elves could handle Lucian, even if individually they weren't as strong.

Of course, regardless of how he compares to Lucian, Yazah's stronger than us, and he can divert bullets. How do I prevent him from overrunning Forest Town?

Her gaze swept the trees, where nervous defenders clutched their weapons. The rest of the residents of Forest Town waited in their houses, anxiously awaiting word that it was safe to come out again.

Cylin ran her fingers over the bracelet Lucian had given her, and the elegant elven script in the metal. An inscription that was purely Lucian, and impeccably appropriate: "Welcome to the fucking family." *This is my home, and I'll be damned if I let some elf with delusions of grandeur lay one hand on any of these people.* "So, Yazah, does your boss expect you to meet Lucian here, or does he care where this chat happens?"

"The location isn't important. I was trying to be courteous and have it in Lucian's territory, but it can take place anywhere. Why? Do you know where I can find him?" Yazah asked.

"I know how to ensure he'll find you," she countered.

One of Yazah's eyebrow rose. "I'm listening."

"You and your… whatever they are go on your way and leave Forest Town and its people alone. I'll go with you. When Lucian comes back, he'll come find you." Cylin forced the words to sound more confident than she felt. *This is not the stupidest idea I've ever had. It might be close, but it's not the stupidest.*

The shocked faces of the rest of the village defenders turned toward her, but their training held, and no one exposed their position by giving voice to their protests. And she didn't need to hear them to know that every one of them wanted to do so.

"You're suggesting that you accompany us as an envoy?" Yazah asked. "A representative in Lucian's place, until he is available?"

That's not what I meant, and you know it as well as I do. Cylin gazed at the elf for a long moment before nodding. "Yeah."

"My lord Yazah…," Ravys began in disapproval.

Yazah waved him off. "Come now, Ravys, we can accommodate a guest. I would be delighted to host this young woman. And she can see for herself whether she and her fellow villagers would, in fact, find benefits in joining Shiranak." His gaze never left Cylin.

This is a bad idea, but I'm not going to let Shiranak's minions attack Forest Town. She strode down the steps set in the side of the tree, descending from the platform to the ground. "Name's Cylin. So, I guess we're all friends now, aren't we?" Cylin smiled coolly at Yazah and his followers.

Ravys's eyes narrowed. "Do not push your luck, girl."

"Wouldn't dream of it." She looked to Yazah. "We have a deal?"

He studied her. His eyes lingered on the long scar down her cheek, then moved to her eyes. In a low voice, Yazah asked, "Do you really think you're important enough that Lucian will come just for you, Cylin?"

She gave him a hard stare. "You told me you know Lucian. Do you really think he *wouldn't*?"

"What are you to Lucian?" Yazah pressed.

"His friend."

One of the elf's eyebrows rose. "His friend, or his 'friend'?"

Cylin's eyes narrowed and she scowled, an expression intended to convey disdain and some question as to Yazah's intelligence. "Lucian is *way* too old for me."

Yazah straightened, startled for a moment. Then he threw back his head and laughed. "I like your spirit, girl! We have a deal." He held his hand to her.

She gripped it and shook. "And since we're all friends now, you won't object to me being armed on this trip, of course."

Cylin could feel Ravys's eyes as if they could bore holes through her spine. Yazah, however, matched her even tone. "I could hardly object to that. But, of course, since we *are* all friends now, and you are our guest, I am duty-bound to protect you during our journey. So you won't object to bringing only one magazine for your gun."

Asshole. "Of course not," Cylin agreed.

"Then please, make whatever arrangements you need, and we will be on our way." Yazah looked up to the trees. "And please, no one attempt to follow us. I'll ensure Lucian can find our trail, and I would truly hate to be forced to supplement it with the blood of his people, especially when Cylin has so generously offered a solution that lets us avoid such… unpleasantness."

Yeah, he's definitely an asshole. An asshole who wants to talk to Lucian and is willing to do whatever necessary to make that happen. Don't know his reason, but I doubt it's good. Cylin drew a deep breath and let it out. *I survived Pryor. I can handle this guy. And when Lucian finds us, he can show Yazah why no one fucks with his friends.*

～

Lucian leaned against the body of the truck. Five days of travel were more than he had a right to expect from the vehicle, but he couldn't shake the faint sense that it had betrayed them by dying now.

Quicksilver shook a jug, then shook his head. "Sorry, Lucian. We are completely dry. Unless you sense a still anywhere in the next few miles, Tieln?"

The young man shook his head quickly. "No, I don't."

Tieln still insisted his "knack" for finding things wasn't magic, but he'd been willing to use his talent to aid their travels, mostly in locating stills and the grizzled moonshiners who operated them. Moonshine was not the ideal substitute for fuel, but it had kept the truck running, as long as no one cared too much about potential long-term damage to the engine. The owners of the stills were not always eager to welcome strangers, but the handful of gold nuggets Lucian offered in trade for their brew quickly smoothed negotiations.

"Well, we have half the day left, so we're on foot from here," Lucian announced.

Eight children clung close to Tieln. They were managing as well as could be expected, given the circumstances. Eria had won them over quickly, and Quicksilver's easy manner put them at ease, but they remained uncertain about Lucian and Chance. If they complained about the travel or conditions, they did so out of Lucian's hearing. The older children kept an eye on the younger ones without prompting.

How long did they wander as refugees alone before Tieln found them? They're young, but they're tough kids.

Quicksilver hopped up onto the roof of the truck and surveyed the land. "This looks like about the right point to leave the river and head west. I'm going to guess we are about…" He looked at the children, clearly adjusting his estimate to account for them. "About ten days' walk to Forest Town." He pointed west and floated back down.

Several of the children grinned and nudged each other, as they did every time any of the elves demonstrated visible magic. Elven magic, to them, was less a source of awe than one of endless fascination, and Lucian found himself more likely to use his abilities in front of an appreciative audience, even when a mundane method would work just as well.

They fell into a line with Quicksilver, Lucian, and Chance in the lead, the children in the middle, and Tieln and Eria bringing up the rear. Lucian suspected that Snow was somewhere in the area, but the white panther had stayed out of sight, only marking his presence with occasional tracks.

They walked mostly in silence for a while. The children whispered in hushed voices sometimes. Eventually the oldest boy, a thirteen-year-old named Emmer asked, "Do all elves fly?"

Lucian chuckled and looked back to him. "No, not all elves fly. Eria doesn't. Quite a few elves only have one or two magic abilities, and flying isn't really very common. It does run in my family, though."

"Sometimes it skips people," Quicksilver added. "Neither of my parents could fly."

Emmer frowned. He pointed to Lucian and Chance. "You and you are cousins, right? And Eria's your daughter."

Chance nodded. "Eria calls Lucian her uncle, but technically speaking, he isn't."

Emmer flushed. Lucian guessed that Chance was answering a question the children had whispered about, but not yet asked. The boy looked to Quicksilver. "Is that the same for you?"

Quicksilver shook his head. "No, Lucian actually is my uncle. All four of us are part of the same family."

Emmer frowned again. He looked to Lucian. "And you're in charge of the town we're going to?"

"I am," Lucian agreed.

"But… you're here." The idea seemed to confuse the boy. "And you don't have guards or servants or anything. Well, I guess maybe the other elves could be your guards, but they don't act like it."

"They aren't my guards. I don't have guards or servants in Forest Town, either," Lucian told him.

"The lord in our town never went anywhere without guards," Emmer told him. "He said he had to keep the peasants in their place."

Lucian scowled. "I wouldn't like the lord of your town. And he wouldn't like me, either."

Emmer shrugged. "He's dead now. Shiranak's people killed him. Are you like Shiranak?"

It seemed the floodgates of questions had opened. Lucian shook his head. "I've never met Shiranak, so I can't say for sure. But I think if we ever met, he would not like me any more than I would like him."

"Would you fight him? He has an army of monsters!" Emmer's eyes were wide.

Lucian remembered the three escapees from Shiranak that he and Quicksilver had met. "I know he does. But I'm not afraid of them. I'd be more concerned about any other elves he has on his side."

"The monsters don't scare you at all?" Emmer looked at him in awe. "You *must* be really strong."

Lucian smiled. "I also have friends who I know will help me if I get in trouble. Just like you do."

The boy considered that and nodded gravely. "Like how you and Tieln rescued us and your cousin."

"Exactly," Lucian assured him.

That seemed to satisfy Emmer. The boy fell back with the rest of the children, and they whispered softly among themselves.

As he walked, Lucian's senses searched for any hint of his

forest, though he knew they were still too far away. He hadn't told Chance about his dream or the Guardian's warning about Ayliad. It horrified him to think that during that forgotten period of time after Tash and Sun died, he'd been tempted to seek comfort from her.

You're thinking very hard about something. Chance's mental voice gave him a welcome change of focus.

Just thinking, Lucian answered. Knowing Chance wouldn't accept that, he added, *Thinking about what will come next, after we get back to Forest Town.*

If it's everything you say, it should at least be a good place to rest and finish recovering. Chance continued to regain his strength, but they both knew he still had a ways to go.

It's a safe place, Lucian told his cousin firmly. *The Guardian wouldn't have it any other way.*

Chance smiled slightly. *True. Your Tree magic is as over-protective as you are.*

Lucian started to respond, but paused, rethinking his words.

Chance watched him, and his eyes narrowed. *Lucian?*

He shook his head.

Lucian, what did the Guardian do? Chance pressed.

Apparently, the Guardian knew about Ayliad and didn't tell me, Lucian finally answered. *The Guardian has known about her for years, but only told me a little while ago.*

Chance drew a sharp breath. *What?*

The Guardian revealed it when telling me that the forest… my forest will protect us from her. At least in spirit form, she can't reach us there. Lucian took a long, deep breath and let it out.

Have you told this to anyone else? Chance demanded.

*Of course not! It's taken me this long to tell *you*, and you already know she's out there. You think I want to tell Quicksilver that his evil, nymphomaniac, incestuous mother is stalking us again?* Lucian retorted.

You'd rather he find out by her showing up instead? Chance countered.

It would save a lot of debate and discussion, Lucian said. *And I notice that you didn't bring up that she visited.*

Chance stiffened. After a moment, he conceded the point. *All right, neither of us want to talk about it. You believe the Guardian about your forest being protected?*

*I believe that if she'd had a way to get at me before now, she wouldn't have waited, so *something* interfered. And the Guardian hates her.*

They both fell quiet after that, each to his own thoughts.

Five more days of walking passed without incident. The land was barren and rocky with little growth, but the magical corruption in the earth wasn't strong enough to put the Guardian on edge. They rationed water carefully. If anyone lived in this wasteland, they left no traces.

Late in the morning of the sixth day, Lucian stopped abruptly. His gaze swept the monotonous landscape, settling on jagged rock formations and petrified tree stumps. The others stopped with him, wary. Lucian noticed their caution, and shook his head.

"It's not trouble. I recognize this area—I know where we are now. Still a couple of days to Forest Town, but I know this area."

"Glad to hear it," Quicksilver said. "I knew we were headed the right direction, but I wasn't… completely confident that I hadn't miscalculated."

Lucian raised an eyebrow at his nephew. Quicksilver just shrugged.

The mood of the group brightened. The children asked Lucian or, more often, Quicksilver questions about Forest Town. Lucian doubted any of them had even seen a forest before, and chuckled when their eyes grew huge at the idea of so many trees.

By the time they camped, Lucian could sense the siren call of the forest, distant though it was. The next day, he struggled to keep his pace to one the children could maintain.

When they stopped for the night, Tieln paced around the camp restlessly. Lucian finally asked, "What's bothering you?"

Tieln stopped. "I'm… not certain, sir. It's probably nothing."

"I doubt that," Lucian said. "What is it?"

"Just a… feeling. A sensation like something is tugging at my attention, but there's nothing there." Tieln shook his head.

Lucian glanced around the camp then, in open mind-speech to everyone who could hear it, he asked, *Who can sense the forest now?*

I can, Quicksilver answered immediately.

As can I, Chance said.

Not yet, Eria said. *But my range isn't as far as all the rest of you.*

Lucian still watched Tieln. The young man shifted from one foot to the other. His voice was quiet. "Sir, I do not have magic."

"You have the ability to sense magic," Lucian told him. "I suspect that's what you're feeling."

"But I did not feel this when we flew in pursuit of the children, or when you opened holes in the rocks," Tieln argued.

"Those were brief bursts," Lucian said. "My forest required far more magic to create, and is much larger."

Tieln frowned, but didn't argue. Eventually, he sat down, but he didn't look at ease, even when he finally went to sleep.

Watching Tieln, Lucian spoke to Chance. *I sympathize with him, and know that discovering he's half elf is probably making him question his identity, but at the same time, it's getting really annoying to have to argue with him every time magic comes up.*

You could try not forcing him to accept it, Chance said. *He might be happier pretending he doesn't have any magic for the rest of his life, however long that will be.*

Lucian gave him a dubious look. *Ignore it? Pretend he's just another normal human?*

What difference does it make, Lucian, whether he accepts the truth now or in a hundred years?

Lucian hesitated, questioning his own intentions. *It just seems a waste. He has an opportunity to learn and discover what other abilities he might have with people who can teach him. He might not have that in a hundred years.*

Lucian, Tieln is not a stray puppy you've adopted. He can decide for himself, Chance said. *So let him.*

Lucian tried to argue, but found he couldn't articulate his reasons. Much like Tieln trying to describe his "strange sensation," it was a feeling that gave little regard to logic. *It's… important,* he finally said. *But I don't know why.*

Chance's expression grew serious. *Is the Guardian telling you something about him? If, say, Dash was his father, it might recognize Tree magic in him.*

Lucian's brow knit in consideration. He hadn't considered that, but the idea that his younger brother, Dash, might have gotten a human woman pregnant was not impossible. Before the war, Dash had certainly found a niche in a segment of the human population devoted to living in harmony with nature. Not just because of their "free love" principles, but those certainly hadn't detracted from the group's appeal to Dash.

Lucian finally shook his head. *It's not the Guardian. I wish it *was* that easy to explain.* He sighed. *Sorry to bug you about it. It's probably my imagination. I'm going to get some sleep. Night.*

You're not bugging me, Lucian, Chance said. *And if

there is something related to Tieln that requires he understand his magic, we'll figure it out. Tell me if you figure out something more.*

Lucian didn't bring up the matter again, and he didn't press Tieln. The nagging sensation continued without explanation or resolution, and he tried to ignore it. He knew Chance was keeping one eye on him in unobtrusive concern, but neither of them spoke of it.

On the tenth day since they abandoned the truck, the forest became a dark blotch on the horizon, growing larger the closer they came. When human eyes could finally pick out details, the children exclaimed in surprise and excitement.

"Those are *trees*? They're huge!"

"How many are there?"

"Does it go forever? I can't see the edges."

"Are we going to live here? Are there monsters in there? Are they friendly monsters?"

Laughing, Lucian assured them that his forest was monster-free, and answered their questions as best he could. He didn't have any trouble urging everyone to walk a little faster. By late afternoon, they reached the edge of the forest and stepped under the shelter of the leafy canopy. His shoulders relaxed.

We're home. We're safe. She can't reach us here.

Eria smiled. "This is beautiful, Uncle Lucian. And the whole place feels like your magic. It's... protective." She turned to him. "Is that weird? I don't usually feel intent in magic, but this really feels protective. I didn't feel that when we were outside."

"It is protective," Lucian told her. "The forest is protective of anyone who comes in peace." He didn't mention the fates of those who did not come in peace. The children didn't need to hear about bandits turned to fertilizer. "Come on. This way to Forest Town."

He led the way along forest trails. The children and Tieln

gawked at the trees and plants, or jumped at the cries of birds and movement of animals. Lucian bit back his impatience and kept them moving.

As they neared the first sentry post, he listened for indications that they'd been spotted, but he didn't expect the sudden rush of sounds as someone scrambled from their post with no heed given to stealth.

"Lord Lucian! Lord Lucian! You've returned!" A wide-eyed hunter by the name of Mehr rushed from concealment.

"Easy, Mehr," Lucian said. "I'm back. What's wrong?" Fear ran icy fingers down his spine.

Mehr swallowed hard. "You'd… better head to the village. Doctor Kinnel can explain."

Doctor Kinnel? Is someone sick? Did Forest Town have an epidemic of some sort while I was gone? Lucian shot a look to Quicksilver. "Show everyone else the path." Without waiting for acknowledgment, he sprang into the air and flew toward the village. Peripherally, Lucian was aware that Chance followed him.

He reached Forest Town before the news of his arrival did. People in the village common froze, staring, then rushed toward him. "Lord Lucian! Lord Lucian!"

"Where's Doctor Kinnel?" Lucian demanded. "Or Devin and Cylin?"

Someone raced to the infirmary door to fetch the doctor. Lucian's gaze swept the village and fell on a single bullet on the ground. He took a step toward it, wondering why no one had picked it up.

"Lord Lucian!" Devin emerged from the infirmary at a limping run, with Doctor Kinnel close behind him. Lucian rushed to them, steadying Devin when he tripped. Devin clutched Lucian's arm as if he expected Lucian to vanish. "I'm sorry, Lord Lucian!"

"What happened?" Lucian demanded. "Someone tell me!"

Doctor Kinnel answered. "Forest Town was visited by disciples of Shiranak, led by an elf. He claimed to be looking for you."

The chill ran down Lucian's spine again. Behind it, rage flared to life.

"He claimed to know you," Devin said. "He said his name was Yazah."

He hadn't heard that name in centuries. Yazah, Snow's older brother, had once been Eria's lover, though their relationship had never been so formal as to commit to marriage. Yazah had split off from the rest of the clan centuries before Lonewind and the others set off into space. "Yazah? With disciples of Shiranak?" he asked, bewilderment muting his building anger. "What happened?"

"Cylin tried to shoot him, but that unfortunately did not work," Doctor Kinnel said. "When he decided you were not here, and none of us knew when you might return, he and his second-in-command openly debated the merits of conquering Forest Town and how that might or might not impede their efforts to arrange a meeting with you. A debate held right there, in the hearing of everyone in the town." He nodded to the spot where Lucian had seen the bullet.

"He did *what?*" Lucian's hands clenched. His voice was a dangerous growl. *You dared threaten my home, Yazah?*

"Cylin… volunteered to go with them," Devin said, voice choked. "On the condition that they leave everyone else alone." He bit his lip. "Yazah agreed, but he said that if any of us tried to follow them, he'd… use their blood to mark his trail. He said he'd leave a trail you could follow—"

Whatever else Devin said was lost in the fury that seared through Lucian like fire. "He took Cylin? He dared threaten my home, and he *took Cylin?*" The ground trembled under his feet.

"Lucian." Chance clamped a firm hand on his shoulder.

Lucian jerked away. Hands clenched, trembling with rage,

he snarled, "He violated my home. He *took* my *friend*." The trembling of the ground intensified. "I will tear him apart." Light dimmed and his vision narrowed to a tight, fierce tunnel.

Then the Ghost ripped control from him, and Lucian fell raging into darkness.

INTERLUDE THREE: FRUIT

Cylin scanned the restaurant. She sat with Yazah, Ravys, and Yazah's pack of minions, which Yazah aptly referred to as "Creatures". They had a table toward the middle of the room. While some people had hurriedly left upon seeing Yazah enter, most hadn't, and if conversations were more hushed, they weren't absent. The patrons seemed to take the arrival of the elf and his monstrous guards without batting an eye. Cylin received more curious looks than any of Yazah's party did.

"You come here a lot?" she asked Yazah.

"Often enough," Yazah answered. "It's a convenient stopover. We're in Shiranak's territory now, and tomorrow we'll reach our destination." He had been a surprisingly pleasant host during their seven days of travel, answering her questions and making sure she had what she needed. Ravys, on the other hand, rarely spoke to her, and never lost his scowl.

A tall woman with dark skin and dark hair brought plates to their table. "Welcome, Lord Yazah. An honor to host you tonight."

"It's always a pleasure, Shara. And please send my thanks

to your marvelous cooks as well." He handed the woman payment for their meal without any quibbling over the price or expectation that he should receive a discount. Once the woman had placed meals around the table and left, Yazah looked to Cylin and raised an eyebrow. "You have something else you'd like to ask?"

"Not really a question. Just noticing that you paid her," Cylin said. She picked up a fork and cautiously poked the pile of narrow white grains. They looked a little too much like maggots for her comfort.

"That's rice," Yazah told her. "It's safe to eat. And of course I paid. That is how business is conducted in civilized society."

"Lord Shiranak believes in rule of law," Ravys said. He sliced a bite from his thick steak. "I should think Lucian would do the same."

"Depends what that means," Cylin asked. "What's 'rule of law'?"

"It means that everyone follows the same laws. Those in authority have a responsibility to model correct behavior to those under them. If Lord Shiranak, or I as his heir, cannot obey the laws that we have made, how can we expect anyone else to do so?" Yazah answered.

Cylin looked between them. "Are you serious?"

"Completely." Yazah held her gaze. "Lord Shiranak believes that none are above the law, not even those who issue those laws."

"So what happens when someone screws up?" Cylin asked cautiously.

"Punishments are meted without distinction for class or rank," Ravys told her. "The severity depends on the crime. For the worst, that is their fate." He nodded to the Creatures around the table.

"You mean you... feed them to the Creatures?" Cylin asked, uneasy.

"No. I turn them *into* Creatures," Ravys told her, and his gaze hinted that he wished to inflict the same fate on her.

Cylin looked at the Creatures again, paling. *These twisted monstrosities used to be people.*

"This is hardly pleasant dinner conversation!" Yazah said. "Enough talk of punishments and torture. Enjoy your dinner."

You mentioned torture, not me. Cylin ate her food. Her appetite had deserted her, but years of privation had honed her instinct to eat food when it was provided, whether or not she was hungry.

The restaurant door opened. Ravys glanced toward it, as he had every other time it opened. For a moment, he went very still, then he scowled at Yazah. "You have a guest."

Cylin turned to look. A woman stepped through the door, every movement calculated to draw eyes. Her long golden hair flowed across her shoulders and down to her waist. Her dress shimmered in the muted lamp light and showed far more skin than it covered. She was lean, with long legs, flawless skin, and a bust that should have looked too large for her frame, yet somehow appeared perfectly proportional. She was easily the most stunning woman Cylin had ever seen. She had the angular features Cylin associated with elves, and jewels glittered along the length of her long, pointed ears. Her gaze swept over the room and found their table. Her lips curled in a smile.

Yazah looked, and smiled in return. "Now Ravys, she is an ally. We should embrace those who further Shiranak's goals."

"*You* would do well to embrace that one a little less enthusiastically, milord," Ravys muttered.

Yazah stood. The woman walked straight to him, pulled him close, and greeted him with a long, passionate kiss.

Ravys made a sound of disgust. "And straight to fondling his tonsils with her tongue."

The woman broke the kiss and gave Ravys a cold smile. "Oh, piss off, Ravys. No one cares what you think." She looked to Cylin. "Now, who is this? Have I been gone so long that you've been seeking comfort elsewhere, Yazah?" She didn't sound offended, but amused.

Yazah chuckled and sat. At his gesture, the Creatures rose and slunk outside. "No, this is Cylin. She's from Lucian's village of humans."

The woman settled beside Yazah, her leg touching his. Her eyebrows rose. "You found Lucian?"

"I found Lucian's village. He wasn't home, so Cylin kindly offered to come with me to facilitate a meeting."

"I see." The woman studied Cylin with new interest. Her gaze found the scar down the side of Cylin's face, and she frowned. "That's an unfortunate mark on such a lovely face, Cylin. How did you come by it?"

"Someone wanted to carve off a chunk of my face and sell it to the bone men," Cylin said curtly.

Yazah blinked in surprise and looked at her sharply, but whatever message he intended to convey was lost. The woman's smooth brow wrinkled in a frown. "What a horrible thought." Moving faster than Cylin expected, the woman caught hold of her chin with a firm grip, turning Cylin's head for a better look at the scar. She ran one long finger along Cylin's cheek.

An odd tingle ran through the scar, unpleasant but not quite uncomfortable. Cylin jerked free. "Hey! What…?"

The woman smiled and retrieved a folding hand mirror from… somewhere. She offered it to Cylin. Vine-like markings, either a birthmark or a tattoo, curled down her left arm. "See for yourself, my dear."

Cylin took the mirror warily and examined her face. The

scar was gone. She ran her finger down the line of Pryor's slice, and felt no puckering, no roughness. She looked at the woman. "What? How?"

The woman retrieved her mirror. "Better, isn't it? A pity Lucian couldn't do that for you himself, but alas, healing is one skill my dear brother lacks."

Cylin froze. "Lucian is your brother?" She glanced at the woman's left arm again. Those vine markings looked very much like those that adorned Quicksilver's arm. A mark of the Tree magic.

"Indeed, I am." She held her hand to Cylin. "I am Ayliad."

Cylin didn't reciprocate immediately. Ravys jabbed her sharply in the ribs. Cylin winced, then finally held out her hand in return. Again, Ayliad moved as swiftly as a striking serpent to grip Cylin by the wrist. "And who is Lucian to you, Cylin?"

Cylin met Ayliad's eyes without flinching. *What would you do if I claimed to be his lover?* "Lucian is my friend."

A tingle ran through Cylin's arm. Ayliad smiled. "Indeed. I'm glad to hear that." She released Cylin. "And so kind of you to facilitate Lucian coming here. I'd expected only to make a brief visit to meet with Yazah, but if Lucian is on his way, I think I should stay a little longer. Dash should be sufficiently fed on Tree magic to keep him until I return."

Yazah looked at her mildly. "Ayliad, have I ever told you that your obsession with your brothers is creepy?"

She waved a dismissive hand. "We all have our quirks. Besides, Dash is only my half-brother. And given the toxins in the soil and water alike, he would have spiraled into a far worse state without me feeding him."

"Still creepy," Yazah told her.

"Creepy enough that you're not interested in a little fun tonight?" she asked, smirking.

"Well, not *that* creepy."

Cylin glanced between them. She remembered that Dash was Lucian's younger brother, but she didn't understand what Ayliad meant about "feeding" him. From Yazah's response, though, Cylin was willing to bet that it involved sex.

Ayliad reached over and teased a lock of Yazah's red hair. "Thinking of people I look forward to seeing again, some of my men caught Chance a little while back. I visited—in spirit —to say hello. So good to see that he's finally awake."

Yazah straightened. "You are *not* bringing Chance *here*."

Ayliad's eyebrows rose. "Oh? You don't want to see him again?"

"I know what happens when someone—anyone—tries to imprison Chance, and I'm not interested in inviting that trouble here. You're not bringing Chance."

Ayliad waved a dismissive hand. "Don't worry. Even if I cared to, Lucian already found him. Left quite a mess in his wake. Dismembered my men and killed the guards. A pity. They had a profitable arrangement with the local town. Ah well… they were only humans."

Evidently, she felt no fear of Lucian's retribution. Yazah clearly didn't share her confidence on the matter. Which made Cylin wonder just what he expected to happen when Lucian came to find her.

Do you think that just because I'm human, and don't have thousands of years of history with Lucian, that he's going to bring any less trouble on you?

Ayliad looked to Cylin again. "But I shouldn't speak ill of humans. They may not have elven beauty, but they can still produce some quite attractive specimens. I brought some of mine with me. If you wish, Cylin, you can find them at the hut by the stables. They will all be eager to please you in any way you wish."

"Uh…" Cylin blinked, at a loss for words.

"Ah, you brought some of your harem?" Yazah asked.

"Of course," Ayliad told him. "But only from those who are trained and willing. I follow Shiranak's rules when I'm here."

"But you're… inviting another woman to, uh, use your harem?" Cylin asked.

"Of course, my dear. I am always willing to share them, and I believe that other women should gain the benefits of my expertise. As I said, they will be eager to please you in every way possible." Ayliad smiled and stood. Her fingers continued to run through Yazah's hair. "But right now, there's someone else's expertise that I would like to consult."

Yazah rose, smiling. "It would be my pleasure. Ravys, take care of whatever details need handled tonight. I'll see you tomorrow."

Once Yazah and Ayliad were gone, Ravys made a sound of disgust. Cylin raised an eyebrow at him. "What, she's not your type?"

He gave her a cold look. "I do not *have* a 'type.' I have no interest in such physical frivolities, and that woman's mother was once my lord's rival. Fortunately, Ayliad has none of her mother's interest in building an empire, only in fucking any man she deems attractive. And, should you be wondering, yes, she was indeed serious in offering you the use of her harem." He made a shooing motion.

Cylin rose. "Well, I'd bet they're more pleasant company than you." She walked outside. The idea of sex with someone belonging to Lucian's rapist sister didn't appeal at all. *Well, I suppose I could see if they have a deck of cards and know how to play Shadow Ladies. Ayliad DID say they would be willing to please me however I want.*

She shivered, glancing over her shoulder at the building. She touched her cheek where the scar had been. *Psycho bitch.*

PART THREE

GHOST

GHOST

E ria had lived for over a thousand years. She had persisted through a tumultuous youth plagued by repeated attacks from Lucian's depraved mother, Willow. She had seen her father's spirit shattered by Willow, then be slowly pieced back together by her mother, Ahmea, and by Lucian. She'd faced down enemies ten times more powerful than her. She had survived the annihilation of most of human civilization.

When the ground beneath her feet trembled, icy terror ran through her veins.

Beside her, the half-elf Tieln caught himself against a tree and steadied the closest of the children who clung to him. His eyes darted about the forest in alarm. "An earthquake?"

"No," Eria said, voice quiet to disguise the tremble in it. "Lucian."

Ahead of them, Quicksilver turned around, his face nearly as pale as his shock of white hair. His eyes met Eria's, and she could read his thoughts from his face, even without using mind-speech. The only times either of them sensed such fury from Lucian happened when someone hurt Eria's father, Lucian's cousin, Chance.

"This way!" Quicksilver bolted up the forest trail.

Eria started after him, then paused to make sure Tieln and the children followed. The children, all human refugees rescued by Tieln, stared with wide, frightened eyes, but they clung close when he hurried after Quicksilver and Eria. Eria didn't pay attention to the details of the forest, focused on the sense of Lucian's magic.

Dad, are you all right? she asked urgently in mind-speech.

I'm not hurt, he responded immediately. *Get up here fast.*

We're on our way. *If Dad is safe, what happened?*

Quicksilver led them between the trees until they opened into a wide clearing. Lucian stood with his back to the path, and Chance faced him. Two human men, one of them a teenager, the other in his sixties if not older, stood near them, tense. More humans watched from perches and balconies in the trees around the clearing. Lucian stood stiff and still in thinly restrained anger.

Quicksilver rushed to the gathering. "What happened?" He looked at Lucian, swallowed hard, and looked away, taking in the rest of the scene. "And... where is Cylin?"

"She was taken." Lucian's voice was flat and hard as steel.

The younger human spoke. "Cylin... volunteered to accompany the followers of Shiranak who came here looking for Lord Lucian. She went with them to protect everyone else."

"Oh shit," Quicksilver breathed. "Lucian...?"

Eria drew close enough to see Lucian clearly. He stood still as a statue, expressionless except for the anger burning in his amber eyes. He looked to Quicksilver, then to Eria, and spoke in a monotone. "Yazah led the disciples of Shiranak who came here."

Eria's breath caught in her throat. "Yazah?" She hadn't seen Yazah in decades, but the times they had crossed paths, more often than not the two of them spent more time rekindling their physical passions than engaging in philosophical conversation. "Yazah... with Shiranak? But why?" Even given Yazah's differences with the rest of the clan, she struggled to imagine him willingly joining someone who sought to build an elven-controlled empire from the ruins of human civilization.

"That was the name he gave, young lady," the older human said. "Though I am in no position to judge whether or not it was the truth."

"It was," Lucian said in that same monotone.

Eria shivered. She knew that tone and its meaning. She knew it meant that Lucian had gone "Ghost."

Lucian turned and started walking toward one of the paths out of the clearing. Chance grabbed his arm. He was still recovering from years spent comatose, and Eria knew that even at his best, her father couldn't have physically overcome Lucian. But at Chance's touch, Lucian stopped.

"Where are you going, Lucian?" Chance demanded.

"I'm going to bring Cylin back."

"You're going to do what Shiranak wants? You're going to walk into whatever trap he's laid?" Chance shook his head. "That is a stupid plan, Lucian."

"No." Lucian gazed at Chance. "'Stupid' would be allowing Lucian to do as *he* wishes right now."

Chance went very still. "You are Lucian."

"I am the Ghost."

"Which *is* part of Lucian!" Chance snapped, exhaustion and fear making his voice sharp.

Lucian held Chance's gaze. "Not in the way I once was."

"What's happening, Tieln?" one of the children whispered more loudly than she intended. "Why did the elf suddenly get all scary?"

Did I ever ask that question of my parents? Or did I just accept that sometimes, Uncle Lucian turned emotionless and scary, and I just needed to stay out of the way until it was over?

Lucian turned to gaze at the children, then looked at Tieln, and finally back to Chance. "This is not the place to talk. Doctor Kinnel will see to the children. Chance, Quicksilver, Eria, Tieln, come with me."

Several people began speaking at once. Lucian ignored all protests. His levitation magic snatched up those he'd called along with himself and carried them over the trees, up a slope, to a cave. The stones radiated Lucian's magic, and he strode inside with the confidence of familiarity. Eria glanced at the others uncertainly, then followed.

Footfalls behind her announced that the others came after her—Quicksilver's rapid steps, Chance's weary ones, and Tieln's hesitant ones. The walls of the cave were smooth and the floor even. Light glowed from the stones, growing stronger as their presence woke it. Lucian marched into a sitting room furnished with padded chairs around a fireplace with neither fire nor chimney.

Lucian stood in front of the fireplace and pointed at the chairs. "Sit."

"Woof?" Quicksilver said very softly as he paused beside Eria. If Lucian heard, he didn't respond. Quick settled into one of the chairs. He didn't like conflict, and tended to accommodate others' demands without open objection as much as possible.

Eria sat as well, as did Tieln. Chance did not. He stood facing Lucian, silent. Waiting.

Tieln finally broke the tense silence. "Sir, what is going on?"

"This place is a sanctuary that no one has desecrated and survived. Yet Shiranak, through Yazah, has brought his corruption into it, and dared abduct my friend." Still no emotion colored Lucian's monotone. "Shiranak made a critical error. He violated the sanctity of my home."

"That does not answer *my* question, Lucian." Chance fixed him with a piercing gaze.

Lucian didn't bat an eye. "The Guardian and I protect Lucian from himself. Right now, the Guardian restrains him until either he calms enough to be rational, or I bring him to the target of his wrath."

"The 'Ghost' is just a name *we* gave to the times when *you* shut down emotionally for long enough to take care of whatever needed taken care of, Lucian," Chance snapped. "The Guardian might be its own entity, but the Ghost is *not!*"

"The Ghost *was* not," Lucian corrected. "But the Ghost as it was could not have kept Lucian alive after Cilvi died, nor after Tash and Sun did."

Eria cleared her throat. "But this didn't happen when the bone men abducted Dad. Why was *this* enough to trigger the Ghost, when that wasn't?"

"It nearly was. Lucian held control only by his determination to free Chance himself. He believed that once we reached Forest Town, we would all be safe. As I said, this is a sanctuary, and his entire being clung to that belief. Shiranak shattered that hope and proved it to be nothing but illusion." Lucian gazed at Chance. "Now the only pillar of stability left to him is you."

"Ghost? Guardian?" Tieln asked uneasily. His eyes shifted toward the doorway, as if he considered his chances of escape.

The Guardian is the personification of Lucian's plant magic, Eria told him in mind-speech. She knew Tieln wasn't comfortable with magic or mind-speech, and hadn't learned how to use it himself, but it was the quickest means of answering his question, conveying not only the words, but the emotions and impressions that accompanied them. *The Ghost is the name we adopted to describe his mental state when Lucian shoved all his emotional responses into the background until he'd dealt with whatever crisis was immediately in front of him.*

Eria missed whatever her father said in response to Lucian… the Ghost's declaration. She didn't think it mattered, in the end. Her mother, Ahmea, had been one of the pillars that Chance relied on, but Chance and Lucian had always been the primary supports for each other. The Ghost was only saying what Chance already knew.

Chance glowered at the Ghost. "Bring Lucian back."

The Ghost didn't blink. "No."

"*Now*," Chance ordered.

"No," the Ghost repeated. "He is beyond reason right now. He would only carve a swath of destruction from here until he collapsed in pursuit of Yazah. He would harm the humans who dwell here, whether he intended to or not." He stepped closer to Chance, until they stood barely a foot apart. "He wants vengeance on Shiranak, no matter the cost. Step aside, so I can ensure he finds it."

Chance lifted a hand as if he meant to place it on Lucian's head. The Ghost caught his wrist. Chance glared. "If I have to go past you to reach Lucian, I will."

"Will you really dive into his mind now, while one of our own clan betrays us and now roams free?" the Ghost countered.

Eria jumped to her feet and placed a hand on each of their shoulders. "Dad… he's right. If Yazah really serves Shiranak, we need to stop him." She looked at the Ghost. "And once we do, you'll let Chance into your mind."

The Ghost inclined his head in agreement. "Lucian has far more need of a spirit healer than he admits. Perhaps more than he knows."

Elves with the magic to heal injuries to the body were not unusual. Far more rare were those who could also enter the mind to heal the spirit as well as the body. Eria knew only two: her father, and Cahron, closest friend of Lucian's father, Lonewind. Both had discovered the skill out of their own traumas, and both primarily applied that skill to one person. For Cahron, Lonewind, and for Chance, Lucian.

Chance looked from the Ghost to Eria. His jaw tightened, but finally he let his hand fall. "You know this should not wait."

"I know that if Shiranak tortures or kills Cylin, the wounds in Lucian's spirit will be far greater than if we retrieve her safely," the Ghost said. "Step aside."

Chance folded his arms. "Not a chance in hell. You're not leaving without me."

"Or me," Eria said quickly. "If I can talk to Yazah, maybe I can… convince him not to do this."

"I'm not staying behind," Quicksilver added. He looked to Tieln and smiled apologetically. "Sorry, this isn't what any of us expected we'd be dealing with when we got to Forest Town. But I know you and the children will be welcome, even when we're not here."

Tieln opened his mouth, then closed it again. He drew a deep breath and stood. "Sir."

The Ghost turned to him.

"Sir, I do believe the things you have said about this village. I believe that my wards will be cared for and treated well. I want them to stay, but I am going with you. I too have a matter to settle with Shiranak."

The Ghost studied him for a long, silent moment. Unexpectedly, a small smile, barely more than a twitch of the lips, broke his expressionless mask. "I would expect no less. Stubborn and foolhardy runs in the blood."

Everyone looked at him in confusion. "What… do you mean, sir?" Tieln asked.

"Show us your left arm," the Ghost ordered.

Tieln glanced down at the long-sleeved shirt he always wore. "I…"

Quicksilver paled. "Oh shi…" He pushed up his own left sleeve, exposing the twisting vine pattern on his skin. "Do you have *these*, Tieln?"

Tieln drew a sharp breath, eyes growing wide. He peeled back the edge of his cuff, showing the beginning of a similar pattern. "What do they mean?"

Chance looked sharply at the marks, then at the Ghost. "Lucian."

"They mean that the Guardian marked him." The Ghost looked at Chance, then at Tieln. "They mean he is my son."

For a moment, silence hung over the room. Chance opened his mouth, but Quicksilver spoke first. "Stars, Lucian, if you knew that, why didn't you tell us earlier?!"

Eria watched the Ghost. "Lucian doesn't know."

Her voice was soft, but the Ghost inclined his head toward her in confirmation. "He does not. He remembers nothing of the three years between the deaths of Tash and Sun, and waking here in these caves."

Tieln said nothing, only stared at the Ghost.

The Ghost turned to him. "Your mother had just lost her husband. I saw in her a despair as deep as Lucian's. I offered her hope and a reason to live a little longer. Though I doubted any pregnancy would result from our tryst, my hope was that in the months before her child, or lack of one, became clear, she would find more reasons to live."

Tieln swallowed hard. "But you didn't stay." His voice quavered.

"I did not. I guided her to a shelter with other humans, but Lucian's instability made it unsafe for me to remain."

"So you didn't know until now, and Lucian never knew," Eria whispered. Her heart ached for Tieln, growing up thinking himself some sort of freak, knowing nothing about his heritage. If he'd ever dreamed of finding his father, she was certain this was not how he had envisioned that meeting.

The Ghost waited for anyone else to speak, and when no one did, he said, "If you are coming with me to hunt Shiranak, I'm leaving now."

That pronouncement jerked their attentions back to the crisis at hand. The Ghost strode to the doorway. Chance followed on his heels. Eria glanced at Quicksilver, who just gave her a small, helpless shrug before joining the exodus.

Eria turned to Tieln. "Are you all right?"

Tieln blinked and started. "I... uh... I'm not sure."

"Do you still want to come with us to stop Shiranak?"

"Yes!" His head jerked in a sharp nod. "That hasn't changed. Even if everything else has."

She walked with him. "I'm sorry. I'm sure there was a better way for you to have learned about your father." Ahead, she could hear Chance's sharp voice. He wasn't taking Lucian's shift into the Ghost easily. She wasn't sure how much she could help, but she would do what she could.

Tieln voiced a short, sharp laugh. "Better way? I don't know... When I was old enough to understand, I figured that my mother was crazy. I thought she'd been raped, and that her insistence that she was blessed by an ancient spirit, who gave her a son, was how she coped with that. At least it meant that she loved me—I never doubted that. And I saw enough other children who were definitely products of rape, whose mothers raised them and supplied for their physical needs out of obligation, but never *loved* them."

Eria winced. "I... can't imagine that," she admitted. "Not that I don't believe you, but the idea of blaming a child for who their parent was is just inconceivable to me." She shook her head. "If Lucian had known about you, I have no doubt he would have done everything possible to find you and your mother. If *any* of us had known about you, we would have."

Tieln said nothing. They stepped out of the cave into the afternoon sun. Eria looked around, trying to get her bearings and find a route to the village that didn't require flight. She had inherited her father's healing magic, but levitation was not among her abilities. A well-worn path led down the slope, and Eria didn't see any other trails from the cave. She started down it, and Tieln followed. She didn't see the other three, but she hadn't seen or heard them in the cave any longer, so hoped they'd headed toward the village.

Quick, I'm outside the cave and heading down a path. Which way from there to get back to Forest Town?

Quicksilver answered immediately, and she sensed his apology for not waiting for her. *When you reach the bottom of the trail, turn left. That will bring you to Forest Town. Right will take you to the fields. We're in the commons by the well.*

Eria and Tieln quickly made their way back to Forest Town, and found Quicksilver waiting for them, alone. He pointed to a building tucked between two massive trees.

"Lucian and Chance just headed into the infirmary with Doctor Kinnel and Devin to get a more detailed explanation of what happened." He waved them to follow him. "And some of the residents have already taken the kids to get food, baths, and clean clothes, Tieln."

When they entered the infirmary, Eria paused a moment, startled by not only the cleanliness, but by the resemblance it bore to many clinics from before the war, even down to a framed copy of a medical school diploma hanging on the wall. Judging from the date, Doctor Kinnel had been in one of the last graduating classes before the war entirely disrupted higher education, making him even older than she'd thought.

Quicksilver headed into the kitchen, where the two humans and the two elves sat around a table. The Ghost listened, impassive, as the young man Devin described the arrival of Shiranak's forces.

"Two of them looked like men, the other nine were some sort of... twisted monsters. They hunched down when they walked, and had claws and fangs, and their skin..." Devin glanced to Doctor Kinnel for help.

"Bipedal, humanoid, with fangs and claws, as Devin said. They appeared to possess a form of natural armor covering their vitals, and to a lesser degree, their limbs," the doctor supplied. "From my limited observation, they didn't display great propensity toward independent thought, and obeyed orders immediately and without question."

Eria shivered. They sounded uncomfortably similar to her half-brother Lynx. Or rather, to Creatures, the magically twisted monstrosities created by the same elf who altered Lynx's appearance. But that one-time enemy of their clan, Karishan, was dead, and that was one death she celebrated, even in her hatred of fighting. Karishan had been a cunning, evil megalomaniac with a vision of uniting all elves under his rule, and to that end, he had on multiple occasions captured and tortured members of their clan.

"The man leading them looked young," Devin continued. "He had fiery red hair in a braid, straight nose, and wide mouth. He looked like he was always smiling... even when he was talking to the other man about searching the houses, or telling us that if we followed, he'd... mark a trail for you with our blood." He shuddered.

Eria didn't want to believe Yazah capable of such things. She thought of his cheerful, boyish grin and tried to imagine it coupled with threats of violence. *What have you done, Yazah?*

Rather than follow that thought further, she turned back to her comparison between Shiranak's minions and Creatures.

Shiranak. Karishan.

Eria stiffened, sucking a sharp breath between her teeth. Heads turned to her in concern, and Devin trailed off in his recitation. Eria flushed. "I'm sorry. I just… had an unnerving thought."

"Oh?" Chance asked.

Eria looked to Tieln, forcing her voice to be steady. "Do the descriptions Devin and Doctor Kinnel gave sound like the army that attacked your city?"

"Shiranak's army? The monstrous troops do, except there were many more of them. I don't remember seeing a red-haired man among them, though," he answered.

"Lucian and I encountered a couple escapees from Shiranak on our way back to you," Quicksilver put in. "They kind of resembled Lynx."

Eria shook her head. "Not Lynx. Creatures. Karishan's Creatures."

"Karishan is dead," the Ghost said with firm finality. "We all made certain of that."

Chance went very still. "We killed Karishan. But not Ravys."

Both Devin and Doctor Kinnel started. A sinking dread filled Eria even before Devin said, "That was the name Yazah called the other man."

"*Ravys* was here?" the Ghost demanded.

"He appeared to defer to Yazah," Doctor Kinnel said, showing no reaction to the Ghost's fury. "And Yazah referred to himself as Shiranak's heir."

Eria gripped the back of a chair to steady herself. *Yazah, Karishan's heir? Working alongside Ravys? He knows the torments they inflicted on me. He knows I had nightmares for years after. Stars, Yazah was captured by Karishan as well! He KNOWS what they did! How could he… how… why?*

A light touch of warmth and comfort ran through her, easing the tightness in her chest and helping her calm her rapid breathing. Her father's hand squeezed her shoulder, and his healing blunted the edge of her panic. She reached up and rested her hand atop his with a small nod. When she could speak again, Eria said, "If Yazah... and Ravys are trying to rebuild Karishan's empire..."

"We must assume they are doing just that," Chance said. "Though it remains to be seen whether Yazah is acting under his own free will, or being controlled and manipulated by Ravys." He spat the name with venom. "Ravys is almost as skilled at twisting and manipulating people as his master was."

Eria swallowed hard. *Ravys WAS almost as skilled as Karishan. But it's been hundreds of years since Karishan's death, and stars only know how much more skilled he's become.* Ravys wasn't the master of honeyed words that Karishan had been—there was always an edge to Ravys, an air that made others instinctually aware they faced a savage predator. Eria thought of Yazah again, the smile that could inspire anyone to trust him. Pair him with Ravys... She shivered.

"I know nothing about Karishan, but if he is Shiranak, and these men are acting in his name, we have little time to waste," Tieln said, looking around the room.

"I want to go with you," Devin said, pushing to his feet. He winced and caught himself on the edge of the table when his leg objected to the sudden movement.

"No," the Ghost said flatly.

"Lucian, they took Cylin!" Devin burst. "Let me come with you!"

"Sir, please allow me to go in your place," Tieln said, stepping forward.

Devin stopped and blinked. "What?"

"I have matters to settle with Shiranak as well. You have my word I will do everything in my ability to bring your friend back safely. If you can, only ensure the children who accompanied me here are kept safe." Tieln's gaze lingered on Devin's visible scars. "Though we rescued them from the bone men before any physical harm was done, they still fear someone will try to take them again."

Devin opened his mouth, then closed it and finally nodded. "Okay. All right. But keep Lord Lucian safe, and bring Cylin home."

"You have my word on it," Tieln said.

The Ghost turned to leave, but Doctor Kinnel spoke. "Lucian. Don't forget the trucks. Cylin insisted we should keep them for emergencies. I believe this qualifies."

The Ghost paused, then nodded. "Maintenance?"

"Monthly. And each is stocked with supplies, extra fuel, and weapons."

"Good."

Eria looked at the two humans, then the Ghost. *Would you mind giving me a moment before you head on to wherever we're going next?*

The Ghost glanced to her. *We do not have many moments to wait. What is it?*

Devin, Eria answered simply.

The Ghost's hard gaze softened slightly. *Ah. All right, I will give you that moment.*

The Ghost left the infirmary, and the rest of the group followed. Eria lingered behind.

"Do you need something, young lady?" Doctor Kinnel asked.

She almost laughed. Though her physical appearance might convey an impression of youth, the ages of every human in Forest Town combined would not be a quarter of her own. Rather than correct him, though, Eria turned to the focus of her attention. "Devin, I am afraid we didn't have a proper introduction earlier. I am Eria, Chance's daughter, and I am a healer."

Devin started when she spoke to him, and his expression grew confused. "Um, hello. I've... heard some about you. Oh, but I'm not hurt. I stumbled earlier, but that's an old injury." He self-consciously shifted his weight to his good leg and shook his hair to partially cover the jagged scar that ran down the side of his face and neck before disappearing under his clothes.

Eria gave him a gentle smile. "I know, but I can see that the old injury still troubles you. I have no doubt Lucian did everything he could to help you, but he doesn't have any sort of healing magic. I do."

Doctor Kinnel's brow furrowed. "Are you implying that elven healing magic can repair damage so long after it was inflicted?"

"It can't cause limbs to regrow, or restore something that was removed, but injuries that did not heal correctly, yes. I can repair at least some of the damage, if not always all of it," she told him. Turning to Devin, she added, "I will not, however, force you to accept it if you don't want it."

Devin started to speak, stopped, and tried again. "Lord Lucian needs to find Cylin and catch those men who took her. I don't want to slow anyone down."

"I already told Lucian that I was going to offer you my healing. For this, he's willing to wait a few minutes," Eria assured him. "It won't take long."

The young man hesitated again, then sat. "All right. If you promise it won't delay Lord Lucian from rescuing Cylin."

Eria rested a hand lightly on his shoulder. "I promise."

Healing magic came easily to her. Eria sent a trickle of power into Devin, seeking out the worst of the damage, assessing, studying. The wounds were at least five years old, and told a tale of someone intending to skin the youth. Devin's left ankle and leg had been broken roughly, presumably to prevent him from escaping. Though it was far from the worst injury she'd seen, it still made bile rise in her throat.

She focused on the leg, first numbing the nerves, then reshaping the bones to their proper forms, clearing away the effects of years of walking on a joint not shaped quite as it should be. It felt like hours within her healer's trance, but she knew mere minutes had passed. Removing the scar took only seconds, nearly an afterthought to the repair of his leg. Eria drew a slow, deep breath, and let her hand fall from his shoulder. She felt mildly winded, as if she'd just run up a slope.

"How does that feel?" she asked Devin.

He stared at her and blinked. Then he tentatively moved his left foot. His eyes widened in wonder as he rotated it. "It… doesn't hurt," he whispered. "You… did that?"

She nodded. "Be careful for a few days—give your body a chance to adjust. But you should be able to walk without limping."

He swallowed hard. "Thank you." Devin raised his head and met her gaze. "Please keep Lord Lucian safe."

"I will do everything I can," Eria promised. Before either Devin or Doctor Kinnel could question her further, she slipped outside.

The Ghost stood at the edge of the forest. Seeing her, he nodded curtly and strode into the trees. A few villagers called uncertain questions at him, but he ignored the humans. Eria hurried after him, Quicksilver and Tieln on her heels. Eria paused, glancing back to Chance.

Dad?

I'm coming. His mental voice was tight and tense. He was angry, and she wasn't sure if he quite knew who the target of his anger was, whether Lucian, the Ghost, Yazah, Karishan and Ravys, or something else. He caught up with them, floating inches off the ground to bypass the limitations of his still-weak body.

The Ghost followed a narrow path down to a concealed cave. Inside, two trucks awaited under heavy canvas covers. The paint was worn and faded, but any rust patches had been buffed out. Either vehicle could comfortably carry two people in the cab and at least eight in the back, more if they weren't worried about comfort or supplies.

The Ghost checked over the first truck, nodded briefly in satisfaction, and climbed into the driver's seat. "Get in."

Chance took the passenger seat, giving the Ghost a glare that dared him to argue. The Ghost did not. Eria climbed into the back. A bench on either side offered seating, and small lockers offered places to store personal goods. A window offered access between the cab and the back. As Quicksilver and Tieln scrambled in, the truck rumbled to life much more smoothly than their stolen Springvale truck had.

"Wow, I was not expecting this," Quicksilver said as the vehicle began to move. "I had no idea Lucian had these stashed away."

From the cab, the Ghost said, "The trucks belonged to bandits sent by the man who I rescued Cylin from. The first time we met, I let him go. If he'd been smart, he wouldn't have tracked her down a second time."

"This woman who was taken—is she his lover?" Tieln asked Quicksilver.

Quicksilver shook his head. "No, but she is his friend, and one of the few people in Forest Town who recognizes Lucian as a person, not a god."

Tieln considered that, frowning. "When the disciples of Shiranak attempted to convert my city, they proclaimed him superior to any hearth god. They called for people to put aside their 'blind idols' and turn their worship to one worthy of it, capable of working great wonders. I have seen a little of what Lucian is capable of, and that would be sufficient to convince me."

Eria shivered. "If the name Shiranak *does* refer to the elf named Karishan—and given the presence of Ravys, that seems far too likely—he may well have considered himself a god, even compared to other elves. He probably looked at humans as little more than animals."

"Who is, or was, Karishan?" Tieln asked.

Eria glanced to the window into the cab, but neither Chance nor the Ghost indicated that they heard or intended to answer. She turned back to the young half-elf.

"I'm going to preface this by saying our clan has been around for a long time. Quick and I are both over a thousand years old, and Lucian and Chance have centuries on either of us. Lucian's father," and Tieln's grandfather, she realized, "is Lonewind. He's the head of our clan, and very powerful." Hearing the words as she said them, they sounded entirely insufficient to explain Lonewind.

"Um. Lucian seems very powerful to me," Tieln said. He glanced toward the cab, then focused on her again.

"Oh, he is!" Quicksilver agreed, nodding vigorously. "But Lonewind is powerful more in a 'force of nature' sort of level. You just kind of have to get out of the way or hang on and hope for the best with Lonewind."

"Unfortunately, Lonewind's power also made him a target for other powerful elves," Eria continued. "One such was Lucian's mother, Willow. But Karishan was another such ambitious elf who set his sights on gaining control over and loyalty from other powerful elves. Our clan had three major conflicts with Karishan before I was born—one of them even before Lucian was born. Karishan was ancient and powerful *then*. He believed elves should be united under one leader, and we should build an empire with humans subject to our rule. He taught himself methods of psychological manipulation, which he combined with magical torture to convert his victims into loyal servants or, failing that, into monstrous, mindless slaves, simply called 'Creatures'." She shivered, pulling up her legs and wrapping her arms around her knees. "Karishan's methods were very effective. I witnessed… and experienced that first hand."

Tieln stiffened. "This elf hurt you?" His hand reflexively moved toward the gun at his side, as if a threat might materialize within the truck.

"He's hurt many members of our clan," Eria answered quietly. "And far too many outside our clan."

"Eria told you the clan had three encounters with Karishan before we were born. I know of two more that happened after Eria and I were both out of childhood," Quicksilver said. "In the first, Yazah was captured, as were my two older half-brothers, Lynx and Echo." He paused a moment, and Eria guessed he was debating how much to explain of the convoluted circumstances that surrounded Lynx and Echo. Apparently leaving that matter for another time, Quicksilver continued. "We knew Yazah had been tortured, but we thought he'd escaped traumatized, but overall okay in the long run. It seems… we might have been wrong."

Has Yazah followed Karishan that long? How could I have never known? Eria shivered. "The time I was taken, things escalated further than ever before," she told Tieln. "In addition to the mental and physical tortures, Karishan experimented in manipulating corrupted magic, and finding methods of using it to control other elves. Lucian's younger brother Dash was one of his victims. We couldn't simply escape. It became a war— our clan against Karishan and Ravys." She remembered only fragments of the battle, sharp bursts of stark terror. The image of Dash, his skin laced with black veins of corruption, calling the trees, the plants, the very earth to trap them all. The image of Lucian being taken over by something not himself—something that spoke of itself in the plural and offered as its name "Guardian." The two battling until the Guardian overwhelmed Dash and purged the corruption from him. Her fingers dug into her skin. Eria drew a slow, deep breath. "In the end, Ravys escaped, but Karishan was killed." *And I thank whatever divine powers might exist that he is dead.*

Tieln shifted uncomfortably. "Even if he is dead, does that truly mean that he is gone? If tales of elf magic are true, what about those of ghosts and restless spirits?"

"That's a terrifying thought," Quicksilver said softly. "And not just because of Karishan, either."

A chill ran down Eria's spine. If Karishan's spirit still lingered, what about Willow's? "That's a thought sure to give me nightmares."

The Ghost's mental voice, cool but firm and echoing with deadly conviction, answered her. *I will not allow Karishan to harm you again. Even if he is a spirit, if he touches you, I will tear him into shreds.*

She swallowed hard. *But what will you do if he's not the only specter from our past? What if we meet Ayliad's spirit, or Willow's?*

Ayliad isn't dead, the Ghost told her. *She is already seeking us. And if Willow's spirit still lingers… then I will step back, and cede control once more to Lucian. What I will do to Karishan is nothing compared to what Lucian would do to Willow.*

Ayliad isn't dead. And she's looking for us. Eria bit her lip. Her own encounters with Lucian's sex-obsessed, incestuous sister had been blessedly few, but she knew more than she wanted from her half-brothers, Lynx and Echo, and from far too many hushed conversations she shouldn't have been eavesdropping on. *Does Dad know? About Ayliad?*

He knows. The Guardian's power in this forest blocks her from reaching anyone within. That is one reason Lucian wished so strongly to reach it, and why he so fiercely needed to believe it would always remain a place of safety.

She let out a slow breath. *I wish someone would tell me these things sooner,* she told the Ghost quietly.

Lucian and Chance alike are stubborn and afraid. They both think they must conceal the fear, present a strong face for the other.

I know. And thanks for warning me about Ayliad. Eria drew up her legs and rested her chin on her knees. More than ever, right now, she wished for her mother. *If spirits really do linger after death, why can't the ones we WANT to see find us again?*

By nightfall, they were outside the forest and rumbling down a long stretch of desolate land. Dust filtered through the seams into the back of the truck, a faint haze that hung in the air and lightly coated everything. The Ghost pulled over for everyone to stretch their legs and take care of other necessities.

"Should we start a fire and make dinner?" Eria asked.

"No." The Ghost's tone was curt. "Get food from the supplies and we'll keep going."

"We aren't even stopping for the night?" Quicksilver groaned.

"No. Bone men sometimes lurk around this area, despite Lucian's efforts to eradicate them," the Ghost answered.

"This close to Forest Town?" Eria asked in concern.

"We're not as close as you might think—we've been driving all afternoon," the Ghost said. "And they have learned not to enter the forest. The Guardian turned a great many of them into fertilizer until they finally accepted they are not welcome."

They ate and climbed back into the truck. After a brief argument with the Ghost, Chance settled into the driver's seat. Looking into the back, he told Eria, Quicksilver, and Tieln, "Get some sleep if you can."

"You know where we're going?" Eria asked, looking at her father and the Ghost both.

"As promised, Yazah left markers. You might sense them, if you look," the Ghost answered.

All elves could, to some degree, sense the lingering aura when another elf used magic, especially if the magic affected the ground or plants in some way. Not many elves, though, honed that sense as precisely as Chance or Lucian had.

Eria found a stack of blankets in one of the cubbies and handed them around, then wrapped one around her shoulders. She lay down on one of the benches and closed her eyes, focusing her thoughts and seeking any sense of magic near them.

She didn't detect anything at first, but finally, a faint pulse tugged at her mind. It grew gradually stronger as they neared it, until it grew clear. Eria's heart sank. She recognized the feel of that pulse, immediately knew the elf who had left it. Despite everything said at Forest Town, she'd clung to a faint, irrational hope that somehow, the humans had been mistaken, and the elf who'd announced himself as Shiranak's heir was not Yazah. But she was intimately familiar with Yazah's magic, and these beacons, left to lure them to Shiranak, radiated that magic.

She shivered, pulling the blanket tight around herself. *Maybe, when we find him, I can talk to him. Understand why he would do this.* Eria let out a long breath. *Who am I kidding? When we find Yazah, we won't have heartfelt monologues or questions regarding his motives. Uncle Lucian will be trying to kill him. And I don't know whether or not I should try to stop him.*

She slept fitfully. The movement, sounds, and smells of the truck were all unfamiliar, constantly jolting her from rest with a surge of adrenaline-fueled alarm. When they stopped, sometime still well before dawn, she roused from her doze. *Dad? What's wrong?*

Nothing's wrong. We're just stopping here for the rest of the night. Go back to sleep, he answered. Weariness laced his mind-speech.

The truck remained still, and she finally fell into a deeper sleep.

Eria woke early and slipped out of the truck for fresh air and a little privacy. Chance had parked in the shelter of some tall rocks worn smooth by the elements. Eria stretched and stepped around one of the rocks to see the landscape.

Barren land stretched away on all sides. A faint shimmer on the south-western horizon caught her eye. She squinted, trying to decide if it was just a trick of her eyes in the early morning light. Frowning, she searched for handholds on the rocks to get a little height and maybe a better view.

"Are those lights?" she asked softly.

"They are lights."

Eria jumped, looking around quickly, then finally up. Lucian… the Ghost sat atop one of the taller rocks, gaze on the distant point. "Stars! I didn't realize you were up there, Uncle Lucian."

He glanced down to her, one eyebrow rising in question at her use of Lucian's name. "We are, give or take, about three hundred miles from Forest Town. The beacons have been growing stronger—more recent."

"We had enough fuel to drive three hundred miles?" she asked in surprise.

He simply nodded. "Using the spare cans stored with the truck. However, we do not have enough to drive all the way back without restocking. Assuming that Shiranak and his people have methods of refining fuel."

"Are you sure the town ahead belongs to Shiranak?" she asked.

"Yazah's trail leads straight to it. You think an elf with Creatures in tow will walk into just any human town?"

"I don't think many humans would be stupid enough to *stop* an elf who did so," she countered. "But… you're probably right." Eria looked toward the distant lights again. "So, what are we going to do?"

"Walk straight in and ask where he is."

After no little argument, the Ghost relented from his intentions of swooping into the town and demanding answers from the inhabitants, but only under the condition that Chance not enter the town either. Tieln agreed, dubiously, to stay with them and the truck while Eria and Quicksilver gathered information.

The first couple of miles, Quicksilver carried them both with levitation, just barely above the surface of the ground, but faster than walking. As they got close enough that someone might see them, Eria and Quicksilver tied scarves around their heads to conceal their pointed ears and walked. No defined roads marked the approach, but the ground was bare and flat. Dust clung to their clothes. A breeze stirred up clouds of dust and tossed it about.

Quicksilver broke the silence. "What if Yazah is here, in this town?"

"If he is, I want to talk to him first," Eria said. "And if possible, convince him to leave before Uncle Lucian comes after him. The rest of the people living there don't need to suffer for Yazah's actions."

Quicksilver nodded, eyes on the ground. "I'm still not sure I believe Yazah would do this. Side with Karishan, I mean. Work with Ravys. Lead an *army*." He sighed. "He was my friend. What happened to him?"

"I don't know, Quick," Eria said quietly. "I've been asking myself why I didn't notice anything, what I missed, or whether I could have turned him away from this path. You know that he and I…"

Quicksilver nodded. "I know you were lovers. And if he could even fool you, I'm a little scared to think how crafty he really is. You have a keen sense for lies and deceit, Eria."

She gave him a thin smile. "Not all the time, I'm afraid."

"Often enough that I'm glad to have you with me right now," he said soberly.

As they drew near the town, Eria saw stone walls around it, but no obvious sentries. The beacons of Yazah's magic led them straight to the open gate. A woman stood guard there, a long spear leaning against the wall beside her.

"Hello, travelers," she greeted them. Her voice held a smoker's rasp. She wore a leather tunic dyed a fading green, and her brown hair was pulled back in a braid. "What brings you here?"

Quicksilver gave the woman one of his infamous charming smiles. "Hello. We're looking for an old friend, and had word he might be in this area. If you would be so kind, what's the name of this town?"

She looked at him, then Eria, and chuckled. "You don't either of you look old enough to be having *old* friends. This is the town of First Rest, gateway to the Kingdom of Our Great Lord, Shiranak. Who are you looking for?"

Tell the truth, or lie? Quicksilver asked Eria.

Eria threw caution to the ever-blowing wind and answered the woman. "Yazah."

The guard froze for an instant, her eyes growing wider. "Oh. I see. I beg your pardon, and take back my assumptions about your ages. You are, of course, welcome here. Whether you wish to travel openly or not is entirely up to you."

Eria stopped cold as the implication of the guard's words hit. "What?"

The human woman raised a hand to touch her own ears. "If you wish to remove the scarves and travel openly among us, you are welcome to do so. Or not, of course—you are free to do as you please here. Lord Shiranak does not demand that any reveal more of themselves than they wish."

Eria sucked in a sharp breath. *She knows, or thinks, we are elves. How? Simply saying Yazah's name was enough? Are there enough elves in Shiranak's domain that having a couple show up on your doorstep is normal?*

"Erm, thanks, but I think we'll just stay as we are," Quicksilver said, recovering his wits. "Habit. So, is Yazah here?"

The guard shook her head. "I'm afraid that Lord Yazah and his retinue left several days ago. Though I do not know for certain, I believe they were bound for the capital, Lightharbor, about three days' walk south from here."

The woman's tone had grown respectful, almost obsequious. *Because we're elves? Or because we claim to know Yazah? Does she expect something from us?*

Quicksilver's smile lit his face. "Thank you so much, ma'am. What was your name?"

"Siuna, sir."

"Siuna of First Rest," Quicksilver repeated. "I'll remember that, and mention your help to Yazah when we catch up with him."

Siuna saluted him. "Thank you, sir! Do you need anything in town? We would be honored to offer you supplies or whatever else you might need."

Quicksilver hesitated, clearly tempted.

We have supplies, Quick, Eria reminded him.

We could see if they have gas, Quicksilver said.

I don't want them to know we have a truck, and I don't want to accept any gifts from devotees of Shiranak. And the longer we're gone, the more likely the Ghost and Chance are to lose patience and come here themselves.

While the first argument might not have convinced him, the second was certain to do so. Quicksilver answered aloud.

"Under other circumstances, we would be happy to accept. Unfortunately, duty calls."

"Of course, sir, ma'am. Safe travels to you, and Shiranak's blessings upon you."

Eria suppressed a shudder. Shiranak's blessing was the last thing she wanted. "Thank you. Before we go, though, how many were in Yazah's retinue?"

If Siuna thought it an odd question, she hid it well. "Lord Yazah was accompanied by Councilor Ravys, nine Creatures, and a young woman whose name I did not catch."

Ravys and Yazah together, accompanied by Creatures. Even I can't deny how damning that sounds. Why, Yazah? Why have you joined our enemies? "Thank you. You've been most helpful, Siuna."

The woman beamed. "It's my honor to assist friends of Lord Yazah."

Eria and Quicksilver walked south until they could reasonably expect to not be seen before circling back to the truck. Knowing they were in Shiranak's territory, neither Eria nor Quicksilver were willing to take the risk of calling to Chance, the Ghost, and Tieln through mind-speech. There was far too much chance that an elf loyal to Shiranak might be close enough and powerful enough to overhear. Eria didn't know of many elves who had honed their natural mind-speech magic to the point where they could listen in on other's private conversations, but she would not be surprised to find such spies here.

They got back to the truck early in the afternoon. Tieln met Eria and Quicksilver just outside the camp with obvious relief. "Did you learn anything?"

"Yeah, we did. Yazah's not in this town, but he came through here, and we know where he's headed," Quicksilver answered. "Things okay here?"

"As well as they can be, I think," Tieln answered. "The Ghost and Chance argued over whether to follow you, and who should go if they did. Since neither would agree with the other going, neither left, but if you hadn't returned soon, I think the argument would have begun again."

"Either that or one of them would have just left, and the other would have followed," Eria said. "It's a long-running question as to who is more stubborn: Uncle Lucian or my father. And the Ghost isn't known for patience either."

They followed Tieln back into the small camp. To Eria's relief, both the Ghost and Chance were still there, neither slipping off while Tieln's back was turned. Both men rose at the same time.

"Where is he?" the Ghost demanded.

"Lightharbor, three days' walk south," Eria answered. "It's Shiranak's capital. And I'd rather you *not* burn the city to the ground, Uncle Lucian."

He scowled at her. "I am the Ghost, Eria."

"And you've said you decide when Lucian comes back in control of himself. I don't want you to let that happen until we are actually standing in front of Yazah. The humans who live here don't deserve to be murdered just because they're under Shiranak or Karishan or Yazah's rule."

The Ghost scowled, but didn't argue.

"Are we walking or driving?" Quicksilver asked. "How much fuel do we have?"

"The truck is running low," Chance said. "If we leave it here, we'll have whatever fuel is left to get us back across the waste toward Forest Town."

"Anyone could find it," Tieln warned. "It might not be here when we return."

"It'll be here. Get what you need from the truck. We'll leave it," the Ghost said.

They quickly collected gear and supplies. The Ghost extended the rocks to encircle the truck, concealing it and effectively preventing it from being moved except by someone with rock-shaping or levitation. Without another word, he set off south.

Quick, would you take Tieln and follow him? Eria asked. *Dad and I will catch up.*

Quicksilver nodded and tugged on Tieln's sleeve, then set off at a steady stride after the Ghost. Tieln followed, though he cast a questioning look back to Eria and Chance. Eria waved him on.

Once the others were far enough ahead they couldn't easily overhear, Chance turned to Eria with a raised eyebrow. "What is it?"

She helped him settle his pack across his shoulders. "You're still angry at the Ghost. Why?" She saw no reason to dance around the question.

His expression darkened. Chance gazed at the distant figure. "Because the Ghost is wrong."

"About?"

"Lucian can handle this himself. I know he's furious, but that doesn't make him an uncontrolled time bomb."

Eria remembered the earthquake when Lucian learned of Cylin's abduction. She remembered her terror at the depths of pure rage she'd sensed. "I don't know. I would think the Ghost would be in a good position to assess that."

"No." With that clipped, angry word, Chance started walking after the others. "I know Lucian. He has anchors to steady himself, just as Lonewind does. They keep him stable."

Eria bit her lip as she kept pace with her father. "In your absence, Dad, Forest Town *was* his anchor. The only one he had."

Chance shook his head. "He had Cilvi, Tash, and Sun."

Dad was in a coma for decades. I've told him how many years it's been, but to him, the losses are still recent, the memories of Mother and our friends still something he can cling to. Her voice was quiet. "No, he didn't. Dad, would you expect Lonewind to be stable and on balance if he was separated from Cahron for fifty years?"

Chance stopped cold. "What are you saying?"

"*Think* about it," she said. "Cilvi died within two years of us being separated. Lucian lost Tash and Sun within a year after that. He's been *alone* since then. I'm sure he clung to their memories for balance as long as he could, but that wasn't enough. The forest and the people in it have been his only anchor. Now Karishan and Yazah have threatened and defiled it, and taken one of his people." Eria swallowed hard. "Dad, Lucian reacted just about how he would if they'd attacked and taken *you*."

"The Ghost didn't take control when I was abducted," Chance countered.

"And did Lucian leave anyone alive when he came to rescue you? Or did he slaughter them all?" Eria asked.

Chance's silence answered the question.

"I'm worried," Eria said quietly. "And I'm afraid of what might happen, what Lucian might do. I'm afraid of the Ghost being right."

For a long moment, Chance said nothing. "I won't let him fall, Eria. We won't lose Lucian."

"Just… be careful, please," Eria told him.

All her life, she'd known that her father and Lucian relied and depended on one another. As a child, she'd assumed that all adults had someone they depended on utterly and completely, someone who they would do anything to protect. She'd not understood until much later that the bond between Lucian and Chance was forged by their shared pain—the abuse, betrayals, and tortures inflicted on them both by Willow, Ayliad, and Chance's sadistic father, Moonfire. It was a bond that could only be created at a time when neither of them had anyone else they could trust. It was the only thing that kept either of them from being shattered by all that had been done to them.

Chance picked up both himself and Eria with magic and flew after the others. The group skirted around First Rest and headed south, alternating between walking and flying. Quicksilver and Chance took double duty during the times of flying, carrying Tieln and Eria, respectively. Lucian would have remembered neither of them had levitation, and would have taken part in carrying them, but the Ghost simply didn't think about it.

They camped well after sunset, ate, and slept with little conversation. On the second day, they steadily encountered more signs of habitation and civilization. Maintained roads led between villages. Eria noticed tufts of grass and small shrubs, even what she thought must be farms.

"Is the ground clean here?" she asked.

"Cleaner of the toxins that render it sterile than most places," the Ghost answered. "But the Guardian feels very thorny. We're in Karishan's territory, and Karishan loved experimenting with corrupted magic. I wouldn't recommend eating anything grown here."

"Um… Guardian? Thorny?" Tieln asked cautiously.

"That's… an explanation for another time," Quicksilver told him. He paused. "Although, since you have Tree magic too, we'd better not put it off *too* long."

Tieln gave him a long look, as if he could will answers from Quicksilver. Finally, he said, "Everything was far simpler before I met all of you."

"Yeah, that's the way it usually goes," Quicksilver agreed. "But, on the other hand, if you hadn't met us, you might still be stuck back in Springvale, or worse."

Tieln's jaw tightened. His head jerked in a short nod of agreement. He might have still been stuck in Springvale. Or he might have been sold to the bone men along with the children he protected.

Too many people walked the roads to make flying inconspicuous, so they walked. Eria noticed that most people traveled on foot, and the few vehicles were drawn by animals rather than motorized. She wondered whether the absence was a lack of industry or an intentional suppression of technology by those in authority.

A few polite questions confirmed that the road they followed would bring them to Lightharbor. Eria hoped they were being successful in not drawing too much attention, but the Ghost put little effort into blending in aside from the head covering to conceal his ears.

They made camp off the road in a small patch of trees. Eria had just set out a pot to make dinner when Tieln sprang to his feet, hand dropping to the butt of his pistol. "Who's there?"

The elves all looked up in surprise, neither hearing nor sensing anything approaching. However, at Tieln's challenge, a figure rose from the tall grass, hands spread open in a gesture of peace. "My apologies. I did not mean to disturb your repose."

"No, you meant to spy on it," Chance said dryly. "Who are you?"

"Well, it is rare to see someone choosing to camp when they could avail themselves of the comforts of an inn and civilization," the stranger replied. "I am Tras, warden of this district." He pushed back the hood of his cloak, showing dark brown hair, tan skin, and weathered features, and sharp edges worn down by time and trial. A tattoo wound up the side of his neck, its once vibrant colors now faded. Gold rings pierced the length of both his long, pointed, decidedly elven ears.

If Tras expected surprise at the revelation of his race, he was disappointed. "And do wardens usually take it on themselves to lurk in shadows and spy on travelers?" Chance asked coolly.

"As I said, it's unusual to see travelers choosing the open over beds and a hot meal," Tras replied.

Quicksilver raised an eyebrow. "What, it's *that* unusual for people to be broke? I mean, sure, a bed sounds nice, but not nice enough to spend my last, um…" He paused to look into his pocket and pull out bits of random junk. "My last matching nut and bolt, along with two washers and a broken nail."

Tras's eyebrows rose briefly in surprise. "Oh? Did you not come here by invitation?"

"That depends on what you mean by invitation." The Ghost's voice was flat, and his eyes followed Tras's every move.

Tras started to speak, hesitated, then instead used mind-speech. *You… are all elves, aren't you?*

Not all of us, Chance answered in the same. He didn't elaborate.

But you did come here in answer to Lord Shiranak's call, yes? Tras asked.

Shiranak's call? What does that mean? Eria shifted uneasily.

Yazah extended an… invitation, the Ghost said.

"Lord Yazah invited you?" Tras asked aloud. His brow furrowed. "I am sorry, he must have neglected to tell you this. All of our people who answer Lord Shiranak's invitation may partake in a night of lodging and a meal in any town, free of charge. Lord Shiranak has already arranged to cover the cost."

"Is that so? No, Yazah failed to mention that," Chance said. "Nor did he mention wardens or, it seems, many other pertinent details."

Tras frowned at them with more suspicion. "Your names?"

The Ghost's eyes narrowed, but Quicksilver spoke first. "I'm Tammin. That's Tieln over there, the lovely lady is Lyric," he gestured to Eria, "and then Kell and Raven." He indicated Chance and Lucian in turn.

Eria was surprised and a little impressed at how easily the false names fell from Quicksilver's lips. Tras still looked uneasy —doubtless due in no small part to the hostility radiating from both the Ghost and Chance. "I see. Then, Tammin, as a representative of Lord Shiranak, it is my duty to see all of you safely to the lord's palace in Lightharbor."

"While kind, that's really not necessary," Quicksilver began.

"I must insist," Tras said, his voice growing hard.

Movement shifted the grass behind him, and Eria glimpsed the hunched form of a Creature. While she had no doubt their group could handle one disciple of Shiranak and a few Creatures without much difficulty, the threat implied that Tras might have other resources to call on as well.

Eria cast a pointed look to her father and the Ghost. "Lightharbor is our destination and, I understand, not more than another day's travel. I'm sure you can help fill in some of the gaps in our knowledge of Shiranak and his kingdom."

Tras relaxed ever so slightly. "It… would be my pleasure."

In a closed, tight message to the rest of the group, Eria said, *I don't like this idea any more than the rest of you, but if we start fighting now, we might not *reach* Yazah without exhausting our magic and resources. Let's just try not to make him any more suspicious than he already is, learn what we can, and find Yazah.*

No one argued with her, though Eria sensed that the matter was far from settled. She turned to Tras. "I was about to make dinner. I hope you'll join us." *Where we can keep an eye on you.*

"Thank you," Tras accepted.

"And your backup there in the bushes can do the same," Chance added. "If they want."

Tras's expression twisted into a tight smile. "Ah, no, they will forage for themselves." He gestured, and the movement withdrew. Eria wasn't foolish enough to think that he'd dismissed all of them, though.

She set the pot over the small campfire and added a little oil. "So, Tras, what are the first five things any elf should know about being in Shiranak's lands?" If he was talking, he wasn't asking them questions.

He cleared his throat. "The first, I expect, is that we speak of Lord Shiranak and his immediate court with respect."

Okay, I should have expected that one. Stars, I do NOT want to put any honorifics on Karishan's name. "Sorry. We'll try to remember that," Eria said. "What else?"

"Lord Shiranak believes that the laws must apply to all equally. We're not exempt from them, nor are we punished any less should we violate those laws," Tras continued.

"Are his laws documented somewhere?" Tieln asked. "How would someone know if they were in danger of breaking one?"

"Yes, of course!" Tras assured him. "They are inscribed on the walls of the town halls, and anyone who has questions need only speak to the local magistrate or a teacher. Schooling is available to all, and all the teachers ensure their pupils learn the laws along with their other studies."

Privately, Chance said, *Control the education, ensure the next generation learns just what you want them to learn.*

"The third, I should think, is that our kind are welcome here and free to travel openly," Tras continued. "The majority of the humans worship Lord Shiranak, and extend devotion to those of us who trail in the shadow of his majesty."

The 'shadow of his majesty'? Quicksilver repeated. *Is this guy serious?*

He's deadly serious, Chance responded. *And he would gut you for mocking his god.*

Quicksilver shifted uncomfortably. Tras cast him a questioning look, but Quicksilver waved his concern aside. "We're not *required* to travel openly, though, is it?" he asked. "I kind of like staying under the radar."

Tras's eyebrow rose. "I haven't heard *that* expression in a long time. But no, it's not required. However, the longer you're here, the more comfortable I hope you'll become with the idea."

"Are there any restrictions on travel?" Quicksilver asked. "I know elves go around to other areas to spread the word of Shiranak, but I don't know that I've ever met anyone other than them who identified themselves as coming from here."

Tras looked genuinely puzzled. "Why else would anyone want to leave? Here, we have food, water, shelter, and a just ruler who treats his subjects fairly. Out there, people starve, are murdered, or scrape by under the thumb of a warlord who might just one day decide to take everything they possess."

"Some of us would rather have the option, and make the decision for ourselves rather than be told we must stay somewhere for our own good," Eria said quietly.

"We aren't forced to remain here," Tras assured her. "We do so by choice." He said it so sincerely, he probably believed it.

Eria stirred the mix of grains stewing in the pot and shaved salted meat into the mash. "I see."

Undeterred by her neutral response, Tras continued. "The last two things, I think would be to not anger Councilor Ravys, and not to expect to meet Lord Shiranak in person."

"What is Councilor Ravys's role?" Tieln asked. Eria tried not to shudder at the name of Karishan's second-in-command. She remembered Ravys as a Creature—one who still retained his individuality and intelligence, while being fanatically loyal to Karishan. The descriptions given by Devin and Doctor Kinnel implied that he'd disguised or removed his more obvious Creature characteristics, but she couldn't imagine anyone feeling comfortable around Ravys.

Tras shifted uncomfortably. "Councilor Ravys is without a doubt the most devout and loyal of Lord Shiranak's inner court. His influence is without question. However, he is also… responsible for administering the harshest of punishments that can be meted in this land."

"He's Lord Shiranak's executioner?" Tieln asked warily.

Tras looked even more uncomfortable. "No. He is… gifted with the skill to transform others into Creatures." He spoke quickly. "It's a punishment reserved only for the worst of crimes—treason, murder…" He trailed off with a shiver.

Yet those crimes apparently occur often enough for Shiranak to have an army of Creatures. Eria glanced to her companions and wondered how many of them harbored similar thoughts.

"Have you seen Shiranak in person?" Chance asked.

Tras's relief at the change of subject was strong enough that he didn't chide Chance for omitting the honorific. "Me? No, no, I've not been worthy of such an honor. I have only heard his voice."

Chance's eyebrows rose. "Oh? Do tell." He leaned forward slightly, conveying interest.

"It was about seven years ago, before I came here. I was attacked by a band of humans who proclaimed themselves 'demon hunters.' They would have killed me had Lord Yazah not heard them and come to my aid. At that time, he traveled alone, but he was far more powerful than any elf I had met before. The humans were no match for him. I was… badly injured, and could offer little assistance. Once he'd dealt with the hunters, he healed me without asking any compensation, not even that I listen to Lord Shiranak's call. I was ignorant then, blindly and foolishly believing I had no need for the guidance of an Ancient." Tras shook his head and continued.

"While Lord Yazah healed me, Lord Shiranak spoke to me. He… he called me by name. He knew who I was, what I had endured, and he offered me a place. A home. A refuge, where not only I, but any who sought him could find safety and rest." Tras closed his eyes, expression growing reverent. "I swore into his service then and there, and he has fulfilled every promise he made."

Tieln listened intently, but he shifted uneasily at the description of Tras's first encounter with Shiranak, and he glanced to the others to judge their reactions. The rest of the group, however, kept their masks of interest or indifference firmly in place.

Eria hesitated a moment. A skilled healer could cause hallucinations. "Have you heard his voice since then?"

Tras smiled, as if understanding the intent of the question. "I have, several times. Sometimes directly to me, other times when he addressed a larger group."

Eria dished up food. If she was moving, it wasn't as obvious that her hands shook. *Is Karishan's spirit returned from the place of the dead? Is he building a new empire? Are all his elven followers this devout?* She handed a plate of mash to Tras. "Thank you for sharing your experience with us."

He smiled at her and accepted the food. "I have no great powers, but whatever lies within my meager abilities, I will do to bring Lord Shiranak's vision into being. A land united under a fair, just leader forever."

She made herself smile in return, but said nothing, instead continuing to hand around plates. When she came to the Ghost, she said in tight, focused mind-speech, *You've been very quiet tonight.*

He glanced to her. *Chance emphatically encouraged me to not speak to Karishan's devout lackey.*

A good idea, Eria agreed. *Thanks.*

I do not object to the thought of reaching Yazah over the corpses of his underlings, but doing so would slow us. And you already expressed a desire to avoid unneeded bloodshed. So I say nothing to the lackey.

It was the best she could expect from the Ghost, but the thought hung with Eria for the rest of the night. Her sleep was filled with unsettling dreams of Yazah, with his familiar charming smile, explaining to her how this was the way things should be, while torturing nameless and faceless prisoners.

Eria woke before dawn. Quicksilver, on watch, waved when she got up. She walked over to his post. "All quiet?" she asked in a low voice.

"Other than the Creature lurking around the edge of camp, quiet," he agreed. "And it hasn't been doing anything, just keeping its own watch. Making sure we don't leave without our guide, probably."

She looked into the light morning haze, but didn't see any lurking forms. Eria shivered and sat beside Quicksilver, taking comfort in her friend's presence.

Everyone else roused at dawn. After a breakfast of leftover mash, they set out. Tras took the lead. He commented a few times on locations of interest as they passed, but otherwise their journey passed with little conversation.

By early afternoon, Eria caught hints of an acrid stink in the air. Her gaze swept the horizon, but she didn't find a source. "Tras," she called, "what's that smell? It's sort of a burning rubber, industrial odor."

Tras frowned a moment, sniffing. "I'm afraid I don't smell it yet, Lyric," he said, calling her by the pseudonym Quicksilver had given. "But it's probably coming from the facility outside Lightharbor. Another of Lord Shiranak's projects. They conduct research and work to revive or recreate some of the technology lost during the war. I'm afraid it does sometimes get a little pungent downwind of the facility."

"What sorts of technology?" Eria asked. "I noticed on our way in that people rely on animal power both for transport and farming. Have combustion engines not been reintroduced?

Especially for farming, the increased efficiency would improve the people's lives by leaps and bounds."

"My understanding is that they are still working to develop a reliable, efficient renewable fuel source," Tras answered. "I'm not privy to the details of the research, however. My aptitude doesn't lie in the sciences. But they have produced seeds capable of producing untainted fruit even in areas of corruption. Lord Yazah even indicated the plants could hasten the breakdown of the corruption."

"Impressive," Eria agreed with more enthusiasm than she felt. *I don't believe Karishan would develop a method to cleanse the corrupted magic from the land. Not when he was always so adept at manipulating it.*

After another hour of walking, everyone could smell it. Tras looked apologetic. "It's not usually quite this strong."

"I'd hope not!" Quicksilver said. "No one would ever get the smell out of their clothes."

Clouds of dark smoke rose in the distance. Tras pointed to them. "The facility is over there. Lightharbor lies upwind, and receives very little blow-back from it."

When the road forked, Tras turned up the northern branch. The stones that paved both roads showed the ruts of much travel. People they passed nodded respectfully to Tras, who made no effort to disguise his elven nature. Traffic in both directions steadily increased.

A pair of tall, delicate spires rose in the distance. A little further on, they saw the distant walls of a city. The afternoon sun shimmered off both the spires and the walls, casting radiance across the surrounding plains.

Quicksilver whistled softly. "Okay, I'll admit it, I'm impressed."

Tras turned to them and raised his hand toward the city. "Lightharbor, home to Lord Shiranak, and the ever-beating heart of our kingdom."

The Ghost spoke for the first time all day. "Where is Yazah? The spires?"

Tras shook his head. "*Lord* Yazah resides in the palace. The spires stand as a memorial to those lost in the war."

The Ghost fixed a cold, unblinking gaze on Tras. "I changed Yazah's diapers. I'll call him whatever the waste I want."

"You… uh…" Tras glanced to the rest of them for confirmation of the claim.

Quicksilver shrugged. "Well, he did."

Tras gaped a moment, then quickly looked aside. "My apologies for presuming, sir. I did not mean to offend."

Without further comment, Tras quickly led them toward the gates of Lightharbor. Eria guessed that he'd not given much thought previously to the age, or potential power, of their group. She guessed him probably younger than five hundred years. Any one of them, except Tieln, was ancient compared to him.

All right, be honest, Eria. We're all ancient compared to most elves on the planet. It's no wonder Tras finds the thought unsettling. He undoubtedly assumed we were of his generation.

Guards armed with high-powered rifles stood at the gates, accompanied by half a dozen Creatures. One of the guards held a hand to stop them. "No weapons are allowed within the city walls. Please step aside and submit to a search."

Tras shook his head quickly. "That isn't necessary." He leaned close, speaking rapidly to the guard. The other man's eyes grew slowly wider. Tras nodded.

The guard turned his attention to them again. A sheen of sweat glistened on his brow. "Pardon me, please. I was mistaken. By all means, please enter. Welcome to Lightharbor."

"You are a wise man," the Ghost told the guard as they passed.

The guard did not look reassured. Eria didn't blame him.

Tras gave them little time to look around, weaving quickly through the crowds in the courtyard inside the city gate, and turning onto side streets before they entered the main commercial district. Most of the buildings stood one or two stories, and the silver spires dominated the skyline.

Their route skirted the spires. Between buildings, Eria glimpsed a massive open area filled with people standing in lines. Tras explained. "As I mentioned, the spires are monuments to those lost in the war. Almost every day, humans come to pay homage to their ancestors. Even those who have accepted Lord Shiranak as their true god wish to pay respect to their ancestors and maintain the traditions of their heritage."

"How seriously was this area affected by the war?" Chance asked suddenly.

"I don't really know," Tras admitted. "My family and I lived much further south when the attacks came. I never even knew who launched the bombings that flattened the city where we lived."

Eria frowned. When she thought back to the chaotic aftermath of the bombing of Briarhaven, she realized she'd heard a great many rumors as to who launched the attack, with most people eventually settling the blame on a warmongering smaller nation, which had itself been bombed into obliteration early in the war. But their involvement had never been actually confirmed, so far as she knew.

"The ground here doesn't contain the same levels of toxins," Chance continued. He glanced to the spires. "I would say they came out better than most."

Chance didn't have any skill in shaping or sensing stone, but the Ghost had said something similar before they met Tras. Carefully confining her message just to Chance, Eria asked *Dad, what are you thinking?*

Only a suspicion, right now. Something I intend to ask Yazah.

She worried when he kept suspicions to himself. Experience had taught her that her father's suspicions held some truth more often than not, and the ones he opted not to share often revolved around something truly dangerous or traumatizing.

Less than half an hour later, they reached the palace. While it lacked the towering height of the spires, the structure practically glowed with magic. The strength of the magic radiating from it told Eria it couldn't be more than two decades old; probably less. Metal, stone, and wood fused and melded together in a manner that even humans would know no mere craftsman could achieve. Reliefs of elves shaping stone and plants, healing wounds, or flying danced across the walls, the artwork so realistic they seemed to move as the shadows fell across them.

As Eria stared at the structure, Quicksilver turned to Tras. For once, his expression and voice were entirely serious. "You've done us a great service to guide us this far, Tras, but now you should return to your duties as a warden."

Tras opened his mouth to object. Quicksilver shook his head. "You'll be happier going back. It's for the best." His expression remained serious, but sympathetic.

"But you will need me to make introductions at the palace gate—," Tras began.

Quicksilver smiled wryly. "I doubt that, to be honest. At the very least, they should be expecting him." He nodded to the Ghost.

Tras looked to the Ghost. The Ghost gazed back at him, and Tras's mouth, on the verge of forming new objections, snapped shut. Their guide looked away, nodding finally. "All right."

Eria hoped it would be enough to protect him from Ravys,

or whoever else might attempt retribution or some form of justice. She watched Tras walk away, his head downcast.

Quicksilver hissed in alarm, and Tieln drew a sharp breath. Eria spun to see the Ghost striding into full view of the guards at the palace entrance. She started after him, but Chance caught her arm and shook his head.

"Yazah expects Lucian. He may not know the rest of us are here."

"That's well and good, Chance, but what's your plan for getting inside?" Quicksilver asked urgently.

The guards ordered the Ghost to stop. He ignored them. Chance glanced their way once, then said, "I expect the way to be open momentarily."

"I thought you and the Ghost were still fighting," Quicksilver said. "And that you objected to his plan."

"I don't have to like it or agree with him to know what the Ghost will do or to use the distraction he creates," Chance said.

The guards pointed guns at the Ghost. The Ghost raised his hands. Gun barrels twisted and warped, curling up to point back at their wielders. In a cold, clear voice, the Ghost said, "Where is Yazah?"

To their credit, the guards only gaped momentarily at their ruined weapons. They also didn't make any further move to threaten the Ghost. "Lord Yazah is currently overseeing a project at the facility south of Lightharbor, sir. I can see if someone else is available—"

"No." The Ghost rose into the air. "I'll find him there."

"Well… shit," Quicksilver whispered. "He could at least have asked if Cylin was here."

"If she's being used to draw Lucian to a location of Yazah or Karishan's choosing, she'll be where Yazah is," Chance said. "Quicksilver, take Tieln."

Eria felt her father's magic wrap around her, then she rose

from the ground with him. Quicksilver followed, carrying Tieln as they set in pursuit of the Ghost.

The facility was impossible to miss. High walls topped with razor wire surrounded the complex, and each gate was heavily fortified. The Ghost was no longer in sight, but evidence of his passage remained. Not surprisingly for a facility operated by elves, the guards actually watched the sky. The northern gate had been equipped with a turret. At least, Eria assumed that the twisted hunk of warped and tortured metal had been a turret less than half an hour ago. Uniformed figures scrambled about frantically.

A shout of alarm rose, and someone pointed toward the four of them. Guns rose immediately.

Chance snapped a curse. Eria touched his arm. *Put us down outside the gate, Dad.*

He gave her a sharp look, but carefully alighted on the road outside the northern gate. Quicksilver and Tieln followed suit, though neither of them looked comfortable with the idea. Guards rushed out, weapons at the ready, but paused when they saw no threatening moves from the group.

Eria put on her best reassuring smile. "I'm sorry, have we come at a bad time? I was told I could find Yazah here, but knowing this is a research facility, I didn't want to contact him through magic and potentially interrupt some delicate experiment."

The lead guard stared at her as if trying to make sense of her words. "Um… I beg your pardon?"

"We came here to speak to Yazah," Eria repeated. "It's rather important."

"This is… not a good time," the man managed.

Eria's eyes narrowed. "And that is exactly *why* we must speak to him *at once*."

Chance stepped up beside her and caught the man's eyes. He held out a blank piece of scrap parchment. Eria sensed the flicker of magic as her father impressed on the man's mind what he wanted the other to see. "I trust our credentials are sufficient to secure entry."

The guard looked at the paper and drew a sharp breath. "Of course! At once, sirs, ma'am. Please allow me to escort you."

The rest of the guards looked puzzled for a moment, but whatever signal their new guide gave, it sent them hurrying back to their duties.

What did you make him see? Eria asked.

I strongly suggested that he see proof that we have both the right to enter and the rank to see Yazah immediately, Chance told her. *I don't know how well that will hold up once we're inside, though. We may need to be rid of our guide quickly.*

They entered what appeared to be the main building, their guide waving them through the initial security and led the way down one flight of stairs. Eria glanced to her father. *Yazah and Ravys both ought to know that an elf with the right skills could fool human guards. Why wouldn't they protect against that? Or… have they, and we just don't know how yet?*

The floor trembled, accompanied by a distant crash. Their guide jerked, head whipping toward the sound. He seemed to shake off a daze, but hesitated a long moment in indecision. "What… wait…"

Eria rested a hand on his shoulder and pushed a gentle pulse of healing magic through him. The man's eyes rolled back and he slumped. Quicksilver sprang forward to catch him, then looked around the long hall.

"Where do we leave him?"

Chance pointed at a door labeled "Men." "Shove him in a stall. It'll be good enough for now."

Eria fidgeted. "Where are all the people? I don't hear anyone." She moved to the nearest door and pressed her ear against it, then shook her head.

Tieln had said very little since their abrupt departure from Lightharbor. Now he looked up and down the hall, considering. "This isn't the direction Lucian is going."

"I don't suppose you can find someone you haven't met, can you?" Quicksilver asked. "Like Cylin?"

Tieln shook his head. "I need to know what I'm looking for."

Quicksilver grimaced, then drew a sharp, startled breath. "What about magic? Could you find something crafted by Lucian's magic?"

"I… don't know," Tieln said cautiously. "Why?"

"He made a bracelet for Cylin. She wore it all the time. If you can somehow find that…" Quicksilver trailed off hopefully.

Tieln's brow furrowed. "Look for something that has the same feel as the forest…" He bit his lip, pensive. "Anything else? Design, inscription? The very large glow just over there is hard to sense past." He pointed in the direction the crash had come from.

"Oh, will that help? Yeah." Quicksilver looked around, then turned to Chance. "Can I borrow that paper for a minute?"

Chance handed the parchment scrap over. Quicksilver found a pencil nub in his pocket. Eria had no idea when, where, or why he'd found one and pocketed it, but somehow, she wasn't surprised he had.

She peered over his shoulder at the words he wrote, then raised an eyebrow at him. "Really?"

"Really." Quicksilver offered the paper to Tieln. "That's the inscription."

"The pattern is very elegant. Are they words?" Tieln asked.

Chance looked at it, snorted, and shook his head. "I need to hear the story behind this one. Yes, they're words, and it says 'Welcome to the fucking family.'"

Tieln blinked. "Oh."

"The short version is, Lucian did something that pissed Cylin off enough that she yelled at him and stormed off. I sarcastically told Lucian he ought to commemorate the occasion, and he actually did, making the bracelet for her," Quicksilver said.

Tieln only nodded distractedly. "There's an inscription matching that one in the building." He started walking slowly. "It's not the direction Lucian's going, though."

"The Ghost has never been particularly good at long-term planning," Chance said, following Tieln. "I expect the only 'plan' he has right now is wreck everything in his path until he either finds Yazah or Cylin."

Unfortunately, Eria suspected that her father was right. Vibrations ran through the floor again, accompanied by the sense of Lucian's magic.

Really, Lucian? I heard you the first time. And you know, you could have knocked on the front door instead of tearing out the wall. We've been expecting you. The voice spoke in an open broadcast, audible to any elf within range. Yazah's tone carried a mix of amused exasperation.

The Ghost broadcast his reply as well, voice flat and chill. *Your guards shot at me.*

They did, Yazah acknowledged. *And you ripped a turret off the wall and dropped it on them, saving me the need to discipline them. I'd say that makes us even—wouldn't you agree?*

Where is Cylin?

If you stop trying to impale every person you see, one of them can show you to her, or to me, Yazah replied. *I assure you, Cylin has been treated with all the courtesy and comforts due to an honored guest.*

"Was that Shiranak?" Tieln asked warily.

"That was Yazah," Eria told him. "I don't know if he realizes we're here as well, so if we can find Cylin before he notices us…"

She wasn't quite sure how to finish that thought, but Tieln nodded as if he understood. "This way."

The continued absence of people on this floor continued to worry Eria. The back of her neck itched as if something watched or followed them, but when she looked back, she saw no one.

They turned a corner and Tieln stopped short, hand dropping to his gun. Eria looked past him in time to see three Creatures turn toward their group. The trio stood guard in front of a heavy iron door. All dropped into predatory crouches, baring teeth and flexing savage claws. Blood pounded in Eria's ears and her breath stuck in her throat. She remembered all too well the rough feel of their armored skin, the low growls of those who had once been people, twisted and tortured until they were reduced to little more than animals.

She took a step back, then another. Chance gripped her shoulder, and she stopped. The Creatures didn't advance, didn't lunge at them. One turned and scratched at the door they guarded. Eria grabbed Chance's arm and the edge of Tieln's shirt, pulling them back around the corner. Quicksilver scrambled with them as the door hissed open.

"Do we have a visitor? A rat that shouldn't be poking around uninvited?"

Eria and Chance both stiffened at the cold voice from around the corner. It didn't have the coarse, throaty rasp of a Creature, like she remembered, but Eria could never forget

Ravys's voice. Her pulse raced and her breath came too quickly. *He knows we're here. He's coming for me.*

Ravys continued. His footsteps rang loud in the quiet hall. "You should not be here, girl. My lord does not abide trespassers, even if they are guests. You should be with Yazah, quiet and out of the way."

For a moment, Eria was certain he was talking to her, chiding her for not staying with Yazah as his lover rather than following her wanderer's nature.

A sharp female voice answered from down the hall, and Eria realized that Ravys assumed his Creatures were alerting him to someone else entirely. "Go fuck yourself, Ravys. Or do you only get off on torturing whoever your lord's annoyed at today?"

Quicksilver's eyebrows flew for his hairline. Tieln looked around quickly in search of the source of the voice, but it came from the opposite end of the hall, further past the door that the Creatures had been guarding.

"I do not 'get off'," Ravys retorted stiffly. "Find the rat and bring her to me. Alive and as undamaged as possible."

Claws scraped on stone as the Creatures scrambled to obey, moving away from the small band of elves. Eria waited anxiously for the sound of the door closing again before she peered around the corner.

The Creatures guarding the door were gone. The door was closed, and Ravys was not in sight, hopefully having returned to the room. She'd never been so glad that, Ravys aside, Creatures didn't speak, and that they followed orders without question, even when they knew other intruders were close. Eria looked to Tieln and whispered, "Can you still find her?"

Tieln nodded, but eyed the closed door uneasily. "We will make less noise if we fly."

Chance cut that thought short with a sharp shake of his

head. "The chance of Ravys sensing magic right outside his door is far higher than the risk of him hearing us."

Tieln swallowed hard and nodded. One hand resting on the butt of his gun, he cautiously advanced, stepping as lightly as possible. Quicksilver followed and Chance started after. He paused, looking at Eria, who hadn't moved. He held a hand out to her.

"I won't let Ravys hurt you again," he promised.

Eria drew a deep breath and gripped his hand. Even with her father's steadying presence, she had to force herself to pass the door. Every moment, she expected to feel Ravys's claws sink into her shoulder and drag her into his torture chamber. She didn't breathe until they rounded another corner and she had the illusion of concealment once again.

Ahead, she heard the sounds of the Creatures' claws scraping on the floor. A moment later, the same female voice snapped, "Yeah, and fuck you too."

Tieln drew his gun and ran toward the sound. The elves rushed after him. They found an open doorway leading into a break room. The three Creatures moved to surround a young human woman in her late teens or early twenties. She held a gun, but wasn't aiming at any of the Creatures yet. Her gaze flicked past the Creatures to the elves, and her eyes narrowed.

"Don't shoot!" Quicksilver said quickly.

Two Creatures spun to face them. Chance grimaced and made a swatting gesture, flinging both of them against a counter with enough force to daze them. Instinct and adrenaline took over. Eria sprang to the downed Creatures and laid her hands on their scaly skin.

"Sleep." Her magic pressed against their wills, forcing them unconscious. For a moment, Eria held their lives in her hands. With only a thought, she could stop their hearts. End their tormented existence.

She jerked her hands back, unwilling to murder the helpless. She wasn't sure whether she was sparing or condemning them.

Quicksilver tossed the third Creature back into the wall. It sprang back to its feet, snarling. Chance grabbed its arm and drove it unconscious like the others.

Quicksilver turned to the young human woman. "Are you all right, Cylin?"

Cylin straightened and holstered her gun. Her blond hair was pulled back in a braid to her shoulders. She wore sturdy denim pants and a long-sleeved green top. A pack hung on her shoulders. "I've been worse, that's for sure. Who's everyone else?"

"Chance, his daughter Eria, and Tieln," Quicksilver introduced. "Guys, this is Cylin." Quicksilver frowned, studying her face. "Your scar's gone."

Cylin touched her cheek, though Eria saw no indication that a scar had ever been there. "Yeah, I know. Bit of a story there. I'll tell it later. I assume from all that crashing up above that Lucian's here?"

"Yeah. And Yazah strongly implied that you were with him, wherever he is," Quicksilver told her as he made a quick search of the room, pocketing satchels of tea and instant coffee.

"He probably thinks I'm still where he left me. I wasn't interested in playing bait any longer than I had to, so I left." Cylin looked to Eria and Chance. "Hi. Nice to meet you. Glad Lucian found you and you're not comatose any more, Chance. We gonna find Lucian now?"

"Yes." Chance studied the human, then stepped into the hall and looked both ways. "Where did you get the gun?"

"It's mine. Part of the agreement I made when I agreed to go with Yazah. I said that since we were 'all friends' now, they shouldn't object to me bringing my gun. For self-defense, of course." Cylin's expression grew sour. "Yazah countered that since we were 'all friends', and I was his guest, he was responsible for keeping me safe, so I shouldn't object to bringing only one magazine."

"Tieln, can you find Lucian?" Eria asked.

Cylin raised an eyebrow in question at that. Tieln simply nodded. "Already done."

They filed out of the break room, but got only a few steps before Ravys spoke from behind them. "Ah. I should have known. My Creatures are not usually so incompetent that they cannot catch a single human."

Eria spun. A man stood at the corner, flanked by half a dozen Creatures. He stood straight, though his shoulders betrayed a tendency to hunch. His hair was cut close to his scalp, and his ears were unexpectedly round rather than elven pointed. The sleeves of his shirt were rolled up, and Eria saw no hint of scale or armor on his flesh. His face, though, and his eyes—his cold eyes, devoid of mercy—those she knew, even though his form had changed. He might not have the appearance of a Creature any longer, but she knew she looked at Ravys.

"What is this all about, Ravys?" Chance demanded. "Karishan is dead. And you, it seems, have given up his handiwork."

Ravys's lip curled in anger. "This appearance is a temporary necessity before I can restore the true form given me by my lord."

"Do you expect me to believe that Karishan made plans for *this* far beyond his death?" Chance scoffed.

"My lord guides us," Ravys said. He looked them over. Eria felt him dismiss Cylin and Tieln alike. "And he is pleased to that some of your clan still remains. As I only sense Lucian making all the noise upstairs, I must conclude that Lonewind is… indisposed in one way or another."

Tieln hissed a warning. Eria glanced toward the other end of the hall and saw more Creatures blocking that route. She made her voice hold steady. "Lucian doesn't need his father's help to deal with you, Ravys."

"So confident, are you?" He smiled, an expression that looked just as wrong on his human face as it had when he had the visage of a Creature. "Even so, he's not here to help you right now, is he?" Ravys gestured at the Creatures. "No doubt you could inflict casualties if we fight here, but as I recall, none of you possess any talent with stone. I have the numbers to overwhelm you."

So why isn't he just doing it instead of talking? Quicksilver asked Chance and Eria.

Chance's eyes narrowed. "What do you want, Ravys?"

"My lord Karishan knows you have skills that would be of great use to him, as does Lucian. He would discuss an alliance with your clan." A loud crash sounded from somewhere above. Ravys continued. "However, such conversation must wait until Lucian is more disposed to talk." The Creatures slowly advanced from both sides. Ravys gestured toward the break room they had just left. "Until then, I simply want you to wait in there. No unnecessary injuries. I won't even insist that your pet humans give up their weapons."

Eria saw at least two dozen Creatures now. Ravys was right; he could overwhelm them by sheer numbers, and that didn't even take into account Ravys himself. "Why would we want to ally with *you*?" Her pulse raced.

Ravys snorted a laugh. "To rebuild the world as it should be. The humans seek strong leaders. They seek new gods. They seek *us*. We will guide them, teach them, and rule over them. Is Lucian's village in the forest so different?"

"Yes, it is," Cylin snapped. "You just want to replace the human warlords with yourselves. Lucian doesn't give two shits about being a god."

Chance's gaze stayed fixed on Ravys. "Rebuild the world in Karishan's image, is that it? And you just patiently waited for the humans to destroy themselves so you could come in after-wards to save them?"

Ravys's smile showed sharp, Creature-like teeth. "Creating a new, better world sometimes requires removing the old and the flawed first. Now, I have many things to take care of." He gestured toward the break room again. "So, do you go in there without a fight, or do I drag you beaten and unconscious into the dungeon? I am *more* than willing to accommodate if you chose the second."

Eria swallowed hard and looked to her father. Chance's jaw was set and his eyes grim. She knew he'd already assessed their chances, just as she had. *Dad, Quick?* Eria asked.

I don't like playing into his hand, Chance said. *But against the alternative, it gives us time to plot and to tell Lucian what's going on.*

He motioned for Tieln and Cylin to retreat back into the break room. Ravys smiled as he watched the three elves follow the pair inside. "A wise decision, Chance."

"That remains to be seen," Chance growled.

"You will find some amount of food within the drawers, and have access to clean water." Ravys rested his hand on the doorway. Stone bars rose from the floor to the ceiling, blocking the doorway. Eria's stomach tightened. *Ravys couldn't shape rock before, could he? How is he doing this?*

"Now, you must excuse me. My lord requires my service, and I have preparations to make." Leaving only a pair of Crea-tures to stand guard on their prison, Ravys departed, leaving them caged inside.

Cylin paced around the room. "Sorry. I should have shot that ass when I had a chance."

"I'm sorry to say it might not have worked," Chance told her. "Ravys is like a cockroach, and just as hard to kill. We've certainly tried to do so ourselves no few times."

Eria shivered and sat in one of the chairs. "He spoke like Karishan is still alive and giving him instructions."

Tieln cleared his throat. "Or, perhaps, like Karishan continues to give him orders regardless of whether or not he is alive? He didn't deny it when your father said Karishan is dead, but he did continue to speak as if he's receiving instructions regardless. And his words didn't seem to indicate those instructions came from Yazah."

"I know," Eria said quickly. "And that scares me."

"Well, first thing to do is find a way out of here," Cylin said. She started opening cupboards.

Quicksilver looked up the wall at the vents and sighed. "Only in the movies do villains' lairs have ducts large enough for random intruders to crawl through."

"The obvious solution is to tell Lucian we need help," Chance said. "And I suspect Ravys prepared for that possibility well before he proposed this as our prison."

Perhaps you'd accept an alternative source, then.

Everyone but Cylin turned abruptly toward the doorway. Eria didn't see anyone, but the voice was vaguely familiar. *What source would that be?*

She heard steps in the hall. One of the Creatures guarding the doorway growled in warning. The person who approached growled back. The Creature drew back in surprise. Chance took the opportunity to reach between the bars to touch the Creature's shoulder. It slid to the floor, unconscious. The other Creature dropped as well, though Eria couldn't see the cause.

She did, however, recognize the elf who walked into view and stopped outside the bars, out of reach of any of them. "Tras."

The elf nodded. "Miss… Lyric, wasn't it?"

"Eria," she told him, seeing no need for the pseudonym now. "What do you want?"

"I can release you," he said.

Quicksilver eyed Tras dubiously. "Right, I'm going to immediately trust the guy who was, last time we talked a couple hours ago, firmly of the opinion that Karishan is god and Ravys is his prophet."

Tras's jaw tightened. "Last time we talked, I didn't know that my 'god' murdered my family. My wife and my daughter were killed by magic-tainted bombs." Hate burned in the glare he cast down the hall where Ravys had gone.

"That mean you're going to help us out of here?" Cylin asked.

"Will you bring down Shiranak?" Tras asked.

Eria wondered if he understood the enormity of that task. They'd fought Karishan before. Last time, they'd even thought they'd won. And this time, they didn't have Lonewind or the other older members of the clan.

"We will," Chance told Tras. "It won't be clean, and it won't be pretty, but we will."

"Good enough." Tras fixed his glare on the stone bars. They melted into the floor.

"Uh, Chance?" Quicksilver spoke quietly. "Do you have a plan for how to kill someone who's already dead?"

"I've always heard that for the dead to linger in this world, they must have some sort of anchor," Tieln offered. "But I don't know if that is different for elves."

Chance stepped into the hall, where Tras waited. The others followed. "I don't know, Tieln. If he does have an anchor, we need to determine what it is. What object might hold enough value to Karishan to serve that purpose." He looked to Tras. "Ideas?"

"Karishan is another name for Shiranak?" Tras asked.

"Other way around, but yes." Chance waited.

"I have only heard him speak, as I told you earlier. I don't know of any item that would serve such a purpose." Tras's brows pinched.

The only thing Karishan ever seemed to value was… A chill ran down Eria's spine. "Ravys."

Everyone turned to her. "What about him?" Cylin asked.

"The only… thing that Karishan valued was Ravys. And Ravys always viewed himself as an extension of Karishan's will. I know he looks like an elf or human now, but his 'real' form, the form Karishan gave him when he tortured and twisted Ravys into the person he is now, is a Creature."

"But if we kill Ravys, how do we ensure that he and Shiranak… Karishan don't attempt to find another to fulfill that role?" Tieln looked warily up and down the hall, alert for enemies.

"I don't believe either Karishan or Ravys could form a connection that strong with another person or object," Chance said. "Eria's theory is good." His eyes narrowed. "And I want Ravys dead whether or not he's Karishan's anchor. But if we're taking on Ravys, we need Lucian."

"That's been him crashing around up above, hasn't it?" Cylin asked.

Chance simply nodded. "Tras, lead the way upstairs."

Tras's mouth curled in a dark smile. "Don't trust me yet, hmm?"

"I trust you enough to have you leading the way," Chance retorted. "*I* don't know the nearest staircase."

"Oh, right." Mollified, Tras headed up the hall, away from Ravys's lair.

Do you trust him, Chance? Quicksilver asked.

I don't trust any near-stranger who just happens along at the right time with a convenient grudge.

Okay, just making sure. Quicksilver followed Tras.

"I don't really know my way around here either," Tras said. "I've only been here once before, and I don't have any more authorization to be down here than you do. I saw you all fly out of Lightharbor rather suddenly, and guessed this was the most likely place where Lord Yazah would be found. There was a great deal of confusion outside, and I took the opportunity to slip in."

"And you came down here instead of heading toward the source of the crashing and chaos?" Eria asked.

"I thought if I'd misjudged your purpose and you were trying to gain access to either confidential research or if you were trying to find someone who'd been sentenced to transformation, all the chaos might have been intended as a distraction." Tras paused, then turned left down a short hall to a door marked with a stenciled "Exit." "I heard what Ravys said about removing the 'flawed, old' world to make way for Shiranak's new design." His fists clenched. "I thought I was honoring my family's memory by helping restore order. Instead, I've been aiding their killer."

What's more dangerous than a zealot? A zealot who discovers he's been betrayed. "Karishan and Ravys are experts at manipulating people, Tras. They've had thousands of years of practice." Eria wasn't certain if her words would offer any comfort, but she knew it wasn't his fault he'd believed the honeyed lies and half-truths.

They climbed a metal staircase, their feet clanging on the worn steps. Scrapes and scratches from clawed feet showed that many Creatures had used these stairs over the years. A lingering chemical odor hung in the air, stinging Eria's nose. They passed the door to the first floor, climbing to the second, then the third. Tras opened the door cautiously, looking all around before stepping into the open.

The exterior of this door proclaimed it an emergency exit. Its blocky lettering and utilitarian design stood at odds with the rest of the room, an open, comfortable looking lounge. Sunlight flowed through massive windows, though filter film obscured the view. On some windows, the film had been printed to show alternate scenes—forests, mountains, a sandy beach. Leather chairs and couches invited visitors to sit and relax. Potted plants filled the room with a fresh fragrance. Here, in this space, Eria finally felt Yazah's touch in the choices of décor and the attention to comfort. Hearing a relaxing sound of flowing water, Eria turned around slowly until she realized what she'd first thought to be a realistic image of an aquatic scene was actually a massive nine-foot tall fish tank that served as a dividing wall. The fish within all appeared to be narrow in width, but roundish in shape.

She frowned, stepping closer to look at the fish. Her eyes narrowed. "Seriously, Yazah? Not only do you have this ridiculously extravagant, self-indulgent fish tank, you filled it with *piranhas?*"

Cylin followed her. "Is that what they're called? Yazah just said I shouldn't stick my hand in the water, because the fish bite. Said he likes to have them around to remind visitors who the biggest predator in the room is."

"They're notorious for how quickly they can strip flesh from bone," Eria told the human.

Cylin shrugged. "I told him it looked like he was trying to compensate for something. He laughed at that."

"Yazah does not need to compensate for anything," Eria said before she thought about it.

Cylin raised an eyebrow. "The voice of experience?"

"You could say that." Eria met Cylin's eyes and spoke in a low voice. "Cylin, have you been mistreated in any way while you've been with Yazah or Ravys?"

Cylin shook her head. "No. Seems they're both pretty serious about maintaining appearances and that whole 'rule of law' thing. No mistreatment, no advances—though from what I saw, Yazah would be the only one who might make advances. Pretty sure Ravys doesn't know what his cock is for."

"Creatures don't have sex drives. It's an 'unneeded distraction.' Also, from what I know, Karishan himself was asexual."

Eria supposed Cylin didn't really need to know that, but it was knowledge that had given her comfort so many years ago, when she'd been Karishan's captive.

Cylin grew pensive. "Can I tell you something, Eria?"

"Of course. Anything."

"I know Shiranak or Karishan or whoever does some nasty shit, and being on his bad side gets people turned into Creatures. But I saw some of the towns on our way here, and most people are… happy. They aren't afraid, they aren't starving, and they aren't wondering when the local warlord is going to drag off their wife or daughter to rape them in the town square. If I hadn't found Forest Town first, I could have been happy in a place like this."

"I can understand that," Eria said slowly.

"Yeah, but what I'm trying to say is… look, I know Lucian wants to kill Yazah. And I think he *should* kill Ravys—or someone should. But if we don't leave someone behind to keep things running, a lot of people are going to lose everything. I think Yazah has the likeability and presence to hold shit together without Ravys. And if I had to pick one to leave in charge, I'd pick Yazah." Cylin shifted from one foot to the other, glanced toward Chance and Quicksilver, then added even more quietly, "Even if he is banging Ayliad."

"He's *WHAT?*" Some words should never be said together. Eria paled. "Is she here?"

"She said she was going to wait for Lucian," Cylin said. Her fingers rose to run down her cheek. "Creepy bitch."

Eria swallowed hard. *How could you, Yazah? You know what she and her mother have done to us. Even if I could somehow forgive you following Karishan, Ayliad is going too far.* She spun to the others. "We have to find Lucian *now.*"

"What happened?" Quicksilver scrambled over.

"Cylin says that Ayliad's here. With Yazah."

The color drained from Chance's face. His legs folded

under him, and he sat with a hard thump. "She's *here*?" His eyes darted around the room as if Ayliad might appear in their midst. His breath grew sharp and rapid.

"Who?" Tieln started to ask.

Before Eria could even begin to formulate an answer, Cylin said, "Lucian's crazy sister. Come on. I haven't heard anything break in a while, and that worries me."

Quicksilver pulled Chance to his feet, asking him something in a low, worried voice. Chance shook his head sharply, but panic still gleamed in his eyes. Tras kept his peace, uneasy. Eria drew a deep breath, waited for the others to regroup, and took the lead from the lounge down the carpeted hall to a pair of frosted glass doors. *Uncle Lucian, where are you?*

Facing Yazah. The response quivered with barely restrained fury. Not the Ghost, but Lucian. *He claims to have all of you and Cylin trapped by Ravys.*

So the Ghost meant it when he said he would get Lucian to Yazah, then relinquish control. I hope that really was the best idea. *They did trap us briefly. We're free now, and almost to you. Don't kill Yazah before we get there, please? Just… stall a bit. Is anyone else with you?* *Please, stars, don't let Ayliad be in there with Yazah.*

Half a dozen dead or dying Creatures. Did you kill Ravys?

No, sorry. Cylin's with us. She's safe.

Despite the fury that gripped Lucian, Eria sensed his relief at the news. *Good.*

She also told us that Ayliad is here.

Lucian didn't answer, except that Eria felt a spike in his rage.

She pushed open the glass doors. A breeze ruffled her hair, blowing through the gaping hole in the wall where, presumably, Lucian had entered. The bodies of Creatures hung impaled on spikes jutting from marble pillars. Some still twitched. Though smaller than the lobby, this space was also furnished as a waiting area, reinforcing to visitors that they were not the most important person in the room and that Yazah's time was far more valuable than theirs. Just in case the piranha tank hadn't made that clear enough. Vines and climbing plants trailed out of planters around the room, some of them winding up the pillars.

The thick wooden doors at the far end hung ajar. Eria couldn't see into the room, but voices carried to her.

"I don't see that you left me many alternatives to arrange this meeting, Lucian," Yazah said. Though he sounded calm, Eria picked up an undercurrent of stress in his voice that told her the conversation wasn't going as well as he'd hoped. "I didn't know when you might return or how long you would be gone. We could hardly just sit around and wait forever. This way, your humans are unharmed, and we can sit down and have a conversation like *civilized* people."

Wood splintered. Lucian spoke in a low, furious growl. "You came to my home, threatened and abducted my people, and you expect to have a *calm, civilized* conversation with *me*?"

"Stars, Lucian, they're just *humans*! In another century, they'll all be dead and gone."

Whatever else he might have intended to say was lost. The door shattered into splinters and Yazah flew backwards out of the office, skidded across the floor, and tumbled to a stop against a pillar. A black and purple bruise swelled on his jaw. He picked himself up with a wince and dusted off his suit jacket. Eria had to admit that even scuffed up and bruised, his red hair coming loose from its braid, Yazah cut a handsome figure in a three-piece suit. "You are being so unreasonable right now, Lucian."

"Seriously? What the fuck did you *expect*, Yazah?" Cylin asked.

Yazah spun, seeing them for the first time. For a moment he looked startled, then his expression shifted into a wry smile.

"I told Ravys you wouldn't stay put for long. It's been too long, Eria. Good to see you, Quick, my friend. And Chance, I'm glad to see you awake and aware." He gave Tieln a brief frown, nodded to Cylin, and fixed a chill look on Tras. "Well. Tras. I would not have expected to find you in such company."

"Rather like how we would not have expected to find you following in Karishan's footsteps, Yazah," Chance retorted.

Lucian strode from the office. He stopped, seeing the rest of them, and slowly let out his breath. The tension in his back and shoulders eased some.

Yazah braced for another attack, but smiled. "And here we all are now. Maybe now we can actually discuss the reason I wanted to meet with you, Lucian." He looked back to Tras, seeming annoyed to find the other elf still in the room. "Still though, why is he here?"

"You..." Eria stormed up to Yazah and punched him with all her might.

He fell back, catching himself against a pillar. "What was *that* for?" A new bruise promised to shortly join the one Lucian had already dealt his jaw.

"Tras joined us because he heard Ravys tell us that Karishan is responsible for the magically corrupted weapons that started the war." She glared at Yazah. "Making Karishan responsible for not just the deaths of Tras's family, but that of my mother, your father, Cilvi, Tash, Sun, and stars only know how many other elves and humans. All so he could remove the 'obstacles' that civilization and established governments and infrastructure posed to his own vision of this world." Eria looked Yazah in the eyes and repeated, slowly, "You killed my mother."

"We have all made sacrifices for Lord Karishan to bring his vision to reality." Ravys appeared from a concealed passage. Creatures swarmed after him, their eyes wide and wild. Ravys himself looked far more Creature than man now, walking in their characteristic half crouched stance. Long claws tipped his fingers, and armored hide shielded much of his exposed skin. He cracked his knuckles. "And now that vision is near enough at hand that my lord has finally restored me to my true form."

Tras roared in fury and lunged at Ravys. The decorative stones set in the floor rippled with him, forming into long, slender spikes. Tras gathered the spikes in a sweep of his hand and stabbed at Ravys.

Several snapped against Ravys's hide, but three pierced through, drawing blood. Ravys didn't even flinch. One hand ripped into Tras's gut, claws shredding deep gouges. Tras screamed, stumbling and falling to his knees as he clutched at the wounds. "Such betrayal of Lord Karishan deserves only one fate," Ravys proclaimed in a voice cold as winter.

A Creature grabbed Tras. At the crack of gunshots, it reeled back, bleeding from two bullets to the chest. Tieln and Cylin trained their weapons on the rest of the Creatures, waiting for the next to take aggressive action.

"Really, Ravys? I was trying to *avoid* descending into total violence just yet," Yazah protested.

"With all due respect, Lord Yazah, there is no point in attempting further conversation," Ravys said. He jerked the spikes free and tossed them aside. "Lucian will no more join Lord Karishan without force that his father would."

"To be honest, I didn't expect him to," Yazah said, grinning far more than the situation warranted. "We don't get the first claim anyway."

Lucian's magic snatched one of the Creatures accompanying Ravys and flung it at Yazah. Yazah ducked and sprang aside quick as a cat. The Creature slammed into a wall with the crunch of breaking bones.

Eria glimpsed movement. Vines from the planters uncurled from their pillars and struck like serpents, seizing both Lucian and Chance. Chance gasped in alarm, jerking back and trying to break free. A tall elven woman with flowing blonde hair stepped out of the passage Ravys had used. "No, first claim on my dear brother and his delectable cousin belongs to me."

Ravys shot her a glower. Eria just stared. Her own past encounters with Ayliad had been mercifully brief, and she'd not seen the other woman in centuries. She'd forgotten the breathtaking physical beauty that hid Ayliad's vile heart. No one else moved for several agonizing heartbeats.

Lucian tore free of the plants, amber eyes burning with pure hate. "Ayliad."

"So good to see both you and Chance in the flesh this time," she purred. Raising a hand to her mouth, she blew Lucian a kiss.

Eria sensed both Lucian's and Chance's magic fling Ayliad back down the passage she'd come up. Chance struggled loose from the plants holding him. Lucian flew after Ayliad, flinging aside Ravys and the Creatures in his path without a second glance.

Lucian! Chance shouted, fear making his mental voice sharp.

Lucian didn't slow, vanishing into the passage. Chance swore, looking from the passage to Ravys.

Eria swallowed hard. *Go with Lucian, Dad. We'll handle this.* She wasn't sure *how* they would handle it, but letting Lucian pursue Ayliad alone was even worse.

Be careful. Chance threw a handful of Creatures out the hole in the wall as he flew after Lucian.

Eria swallowed hard, eyes fixed on Ravys. Several Creatures started to follow Chance, but Ravys called them back with a sharp gesture. Tras managed to rise to his knees, one hand pressed against his bleeding abdomen. Cylin and Tieln pulled him back to the relative shelter of a pillar. Quicksilver stood beside Eria, gun in hand.

"What does Karishan intend?" Eria demanded, breaking

the moment of stillness. She edged toward Tras, hoping for an opportunity to heal the wound before he lost consciousness.

I intend to rule this world. And you will not stand in my way.

Eria froze, breath catching in her throat. Some voices she would never forget, no matter how hard she tried. Karishan's was one.

She huddled in the cell, knees drawn up against her body, eyes squeezed shut as if she could shut out the torture she'd just witnessed. She didn't even know what the elf's name had been. He'd begged and screamed as Ravys began the process of converting him into a Creature. Karishan had stood beside her, not letting her look away until the victim finally lost consciousness.

Outside her cell door, Karishan spoke. "You have great talent, Eria— talent I can use. Join me, and your clan will be safe. Continue to refuse, and you will see them suffer the same fate as that unfortunate rebel."

Quicksilver squeezed her shoulder, breaking her from the memory. Eria swallowed hard, head jerking in a quick nod to acknowledge him. "I will not stand down, Karishan." Her voice wasn't as steady as she would have wished. "I didn't stand down before, and I won't now."

A pity to waste such potential. Fortunately, Ravys is quite convincing.

Creatures lunged at Eria and Quicksilver. She knew what Karishan would do—he would capture them both, then torture Quicksilver until either she yielded, or he was converted into a Creature.

I won't let that happen!

She didn't have flashy magic like Lucian. She couldn't fly like so many of their clan could. She was a healer, a mender of wounds. She brought comfort and hope to those in need. She didn't use her magic to cause pain or twist and warp living flesh as Karishan and Ravys did.

But that didn't mean she didn't know how.

A Creature's clawed hand closed around her arm. Eria's healing magic flowed into the limb and severed the nerves. It looked confused rather than hurt as its arm fell limp, hanging uselessly.

Beside her, Quicksilver threw back several Creatures and muttered, "Now would be good."

"What would be good?" Eria hissed.

In answer, a whirlwind of white fur and slashing claws appeared in the midst of the Creatures. Snow yowled in anger and tore into Karishan's minions with all the fury of an outraged panther, taking full advantage of his surprise teleportation into their numbers.

"What the—Snow!" Yazah burst in surprise. "Stop!"

Eria couldn't imagine that he actually expected his younger brother to heed the command. Yazah stepped as if he intended to grab Snow. A gunshot cracked, and Yazah staggered, his leg buckling.

"Oh look, you didn't redirect *that* one," Cylin said. Eria abruptly realized that she had all but forgotten about Cylin and Tieln. To judge by the surprise on both Yazah's and Ravys's faces, she wasn't the only one. Yazah grimaced in pain.

Quicksilver seized advantage of Yazah's distraction, directing the plants to bind him. Despite herself, Eria hoped Yazah came through this conflict alive.

Tieln fired at Ravys. Ravys sprang aside, taking the hit in his shoulder. He bared fangs at the half-elf. Rock spikes flowed from the marble pillars, and this time Eria sensed the hand wielding the magic. It wasn't Ravys's power that molded the stone. It was Karishan's. Tieln dodged them with a startled curse.

Forehead wet with sweat, Tras pushed up to his feet. His eyes squeezed shut and his hands clenched in fists. The growth of the spikes slowed, then stopped as he fought Karishan for control of them. Eria dashed toward him, but Ravys moved faster. His backhand threw Tras into one of the planters, shattering it. Soil and vines spilled across the floor. Ravys bared his fangs again and raised a hand to strike.

Without thinking, Eria grabbed Ravys's arm. Her magic gathered and flowed into the corrupted elf, instincts urging her to strip away the Creature elements, restore him to the form of an elf.

His healing magic surged in reaction, rejecting hers. Ravys spun to face her. His hand closed around her arm, holding her when she jerked back. He leaned close, face close enough that she felt the heat of his breath. "You think *you* can defy us? You think *you* a match for *me*? You're not worthy of the blessings my lord would give you."

For an instant, she was that young woman in the cell again, with Karishan standing in the doorway, telling the place she could have in his empire, telling her that none of her family or clan had to suffer further if she joined him. Eria's pulse raced and fear gripped her as firmly as Ravys's clawed hand.

"I don't want your lord's blessings." The words came out hoarsely. She tried again. "I don't want your lord's blessings! Everything Karishan stands for goes against all I believe." She fixed a hard, cold glare at Ravys. "He perverts and corrupts everything he touches. Especially you."

You remain willfully blind, foolish child. She heard the sneer in Karishan's voice.

A gun fired. Ravys snarled in pain and fury, for a moment distracted from Eria. Already his healing magic was knitting the wound, but while it did, it wasn't as effective at blocking her. She poured exhaustion into his veins, forcing sleep on him. Ravys sagged to his knees, teeth still bared, fighting her.

"Even if I fall... Lord Karishan... will raise me... again."

That's impossible. There's no coming back from the dead. If Karishan could have come back in a body, he would have.

"Shut up and sleep!" Eria snapped.

With a final surge, her magic overwhelmed his defenses. Ravys slumped in a limp heap on the floor. Eria sucked in deep breaths and stepped toward Tras.

"That's not going to help as much as you might think," Yazah said. He'd healed his leg, but remained tangled in the vines Quicksilver had used to bind him. Tieln kept his gun trained on Yazah, while Cylin watched Ravys for signs of movement.

Ravys sprang to his feet and slapped the gun from Cylin's hand. She fell back with a startled, indignant yelp. Ravys's eyes were still closed, and when he wasn't moving, his breathing fell back into the slow, deep rhythm of sleep. Yet his lips curled in a cold smile. He stood between Eria and Tras, blocking her path to heal him.

Yazah gave Eria a shrug with an almost apologetic smile. "Karishan. He doesn't actually need Ravys to be conscious."

"Enough, Yazah." The voice came from Ravys's mouth, but the inflections were all changed.

Yazah shrugged again. "As you wish, my lord." He glanced to Eria. *Karishan's spirit lives in Ravys's body. Even if you try to kill Ravys, Karishan will heal him faster than you can kill him.*

Why should I believe you, Yazah? Why tell me this? she demanded.

Because I'm an ambitious asshole who's ready to actually claim my inheritance.

While far from a flattering statement, she had to admit it was more convincing than any appeal he might make to their shared clan allegiance or their personal relationship. Eria sidled back from Ravys, not looking at Yazah. *You'd better give me more to go on than what *won't* work if you expect me to do anything useful.*

You have to sever the connection. And that requires a soul healer.

Icy fear prickled down her spine. One of the last places she ever wanted to be was inside Ravys's mind. *Well that's great, Yazah. How do you expect me to manage that? Ask him nicely to sit down and relax for a bit?*

Cylin and Tieln both shot Ravys. He staggered momentarily, but as Yazah warned, the wounds closed quickly.

You're as brilliant as you are beautiful, Eria. I'm sure you'll figure something out.

Eria's jaw tightened. *Fuck you, Yazah.*

Anytime you want to, my dear.

This is a terrible plan. Eria waited for Cylin and Tieln to shoot again, then seized hold of Ravys's arm again. "Keep him busy!"

In response, Tras pulled rock up around Ravys's ankles, pinning his feet in place. The wounded elf was pale. Eria ached to rush to his side and heal him, but to do so would be to release Ravys. She sensed Tras and Karishan fighting for control of the stone around them. Her breath hissed between her teeth, then she shut out all distractions, everything outside, and sent her spirit into Ravys's mind.

Eria stood in a straight, unadorned hall. The walls were carved stone blocks, each precisely the same. The air was still and silent. Her steps whispered on the smooth floor, as if something muffled all sounds. Everything she saw was sterile and oppressively orderly.

Every mind was unique, the settings within reflections of the individual. A skilled soul healer could learn much about another simply by interpreting the scene, before they ever reached the soul of the individual. The emptiness of this place, though, sent chills crawling down Eria's spine. Branching passages lay at equal, predictable intervals, leading into more identical stark halls.

With a strong will and strong magic, a soul healer could sometimes impose their will on the mind of another, change the scene to bring them to where they wished to be. Eria hesitated to try, far too aware that if she attempted to do so, Ravys or Karishan could, in turn, manipulate her destination to one of their choosing. Instead, she walked. Time here passed more quickly than in the real world—what felt like hours to her might only be a handful of minutes outside—but she still had no time to waste. Her body was defenseless; she had to trust Quick, Tieln, and Cylin to protect her out there and hope that Ravys didn't gut her.

She heard voices. Eria froze a moment, then cautiously moved closer. She sensed the first change from the uniform halls when she smelled cloves and jasmine. The scents immediately reminded her of Karishan. She'd all but forgotten how they clung to his clothes.

She peered around a corner and saw a throne room. Swooping stone arches supported a high ceiling, and a woven carpet in blues, golds, and greens covered the floor. Three braziers around the room produced fragrant smoke. The throne was shaped from stone and polished wood, and on it sat Karishan.

The ancient elf leaned back comfortably on the throne, narrow eyes gazing at something distant. His face was pinched and thinner than she remembered. His hair hung in a long black braid down his back, and he fingered a pendant on a plain leather cord. Eria couldn't see the pendant, but the leather cord struck her as oddly plebeian for him.

Ravys, in his monstrous Creature form, sat like a loyal dog at Karishan's feet. He even wore a jeweled collar—and not much else aside from a loincloth. She also saw he was missing the pinkie finger on his left hand. She was sure he'd had all ten digits in the physical world. Any deviation between the spirit and the physical meant something, but what did this one tell her?

Ravys looked up abruptly, turning toward the doorway Eria peered from.

"My lord, we have a visitor."

Karishan's eyes narrowed. "Go. Hunt."

Ravys rose, bowed to Karishan, and stalked toward the doorway. Eria swallowed hard and drew back, ducking down the nearest hallway, heart pounding. Behind her, Ravys's claws clicked on the stones in deliberate, measured steps. He paused a moment to draw a deep breath.

"Foolish little girl. I smell your fear."

She was surprised he didn't hear the pounding of her heart. The bare halls offered no shelter.

I can't hide. I didn't come here to hide or cower in a corner somewhere. The real question is who do I fight: Ravys or Karishan?

"I will make you suffer," Ravys hissed. "Your screams will be a hymn to my lord."

Ravys first, then Karishan. I can't hide. That's not why I'm here. I don't have time to waste.

Eria spun to face him. Ravys's eyes narrowed. He sprang, claws extended to rake at her. Eria flung out one hand, willing the air before her to become solid. She felt momentary resistance to her manipulation, then the air molded to her will.

Ravys slammed into the unseen but solid barrier. He clawed at it with a scream of wordless fury. She'd caught him unprepared, but Eria knew that the same trick wouldn't work twice. He'd be prepared for her to manipulate the environment next time. Even now, she struggled to maintain the barrier against his assault, and Ravys's claws slashed far closer than she liked.

Her barrier splintered. A claw opened a gash on her cheek. Eria hissed at the sharp flare of pain, but grabbed hold of

Ravys's left arm. His magic fought hers, trying to amplify her pain. She pushed back, trying to find the link between him and Karishan.

Eria sensed the connection, envisioning it like a shimmering cord. Instead of one, though, she found two—one that ran from Karishan to Ravys and curled around Ravys's neck in the form of the jeweled collar, the other running from Ravys's missing finger back to Karishan.

A blinding burst of pain made her jerk away from Ravys. He tackled her. Eria hit the ground hard, breath knocked from her. Fresh pain assaulted her as Ravys's magic continued to attack. His claws sank into her shoulder. She grabbed at his neck, fingers hooking onto the collar. Ravys snapped at her face. She twisted aside and pulled hard on the collar.

Ravys growled and seized her wrist trying to pull it away from his neck. Eria hung on and focused all her will on the collar. *Come loose! Release!*

The force of will holding the collar in place pushed back, intent on denying her this goal. Closing her eyes, forcing back even the pain of Ravys's attack, Eria focused only on the collar. On the fragment of Karishan's power wrapped around Ravys's throat.

She felt a sliver of weakness in the metal, a tiny imperfection. Eria focused everything against it, demanding that it yield. She felt it expand, becoming a crack even as Karishan fought to mend the damage.

Eria screamed in determination. Ravys jerked back from the ear-piercing shriek.

The collar snapped.

A roar of fury shook the halls. Not Ravys's voice, but Karishan's. Ravys's hand rose to his neck, then he looked at the jeweled collar in Eria's hand with a mix of disbelief and outrage. "You dare!"

She scrambled to her feet. "I dare."

"I'll gut you and make *sure* you live through it."

Eria spun and ran down the hall, Ravys close on her heels. The world twisted and shifted around her. She tripped over a long crimson carpet. Breath hissing between her teeth, Eria looked up and found herself in the throne room. With Karishan. Doors slammed shut, cutting off any escape route, but also, for the moment, cutting off Ravys's access as well.

Fury twisted the malevolent elf's stern face. "Do you have *any* idea what you have done?"

Eria straightened. "I've broken part of your connection with Ravys." *And the other half hangs around your neck.* Her gaze moved to the leather cord Karishan had been holding earlier. His hand no longer obscured the pendant. A scaled, clawed finger hung from the leather. She swallowed bile. *Was it your idea or his to sever his finger?*

Karishan rose and descended the two steps from the dais. His cold eyes never left her. "You will not banish me so easily. Give me the collar."

Eria gripped the collar tight. Her thumb rubbed over one of the jewels, and it shifted in its setting. She worked the stone free and threw it toward the back of the room. "There's part of it."

"You…!"

She got another loose and hurled it in another direction. "I'd have thought that you'd put more effort toward quality in making a token for your favorite pet, Karishan."

She wasn't sure what reaction to expect, but Karishan remained in control of himself, even with the anger burning in his eyes. Rock spines burst from the floor, stabbing her in the legs. Eria cried in pain and fell.

"Ravys knows and accepts his place. You have yet to learn yours." Karishan loomed over her. "You don't have the power to defeat me, Eria."

She looked up through tears of pain. Karishan, the elf who

had a plan for every contingency he could imagine. Who had defied death. Who had hurt her before, and promised to do so again until he had broken her to his will. The elf whose greatest flaw lay in his overconfidence.

She forced herself up on her bleeding legs. In one desperate lunge, Eria dropped the collar and grabbed hold of the mummified finger hanging around Karishan's neck.

Dead flesh did not respond easily to healing magic. As Karishan wrestled to free the pendant from her grasp, Eria pummeled the severed digit with her magic, draining tiny pockets of moisture and preserving minerals from it. Karishan hit her in the face. Eria fell back. Ravys's finger crumbled to dust.

Karishan stared at her. His hand moved to the leather cord where the finger had hung. She waited for him to say something, do something, attack her. Karishan's eye bored into hers, then, he was gone.

Ravys's scream of rage and grief shattered the stone halls. Eria stumbled to the ground, but all around, she saw nothing but empty darkness. Then Ravys was charging at her, expression twisted in horrific fury. She cried in fear. Nowhere to hide, and only one escape open to her. As Ravys lunged, claws and fangs stretching for her, Eria jerked her spirit back into her own body. She stumbled two steps back from Ravys before he whirled, murder in his eyes.

The room was a cacophony of noise and movement after the sterile stone halls of Ravys's mind... or Karishan's influence on Ravys's mind. She couldn't focus on any of it, and didn't dare take her attention off Ravys.

His voice was barely more than a primal snarl. "Give him back."

"I don't have him." The words stuck in her throat.

"You took my lord. Give him back, or I will tear him from your soul."

Eria fell back another step. "I don't have him. He's gone, Ravys. Karishan is dead."

"Give him back!" Ravys screamed, eyes wild and crazed. He sprang.

Someone slammed into Eria from the side, throwing her out of Ravys's path. A second scream joined Ravys's. Eria hit the floor and rolled onto her back to see what was happening.

Tras had shoved her, and took the vicious strikes meant for her. Ravys's claws rent bloody gouges through his flesh. Despite them, the elf's expression bore a pain-twisted, cold smile. His hands fell away from the stone lance that pierced through Ravys's chest and out his back.

"This… is for my wife… and my daughter… you murderous monster."

Eria pushed to her feet, reaching for Tras and calling her healing magic once again, though she wasn't sure she had enough strength to save him. Ravys slashed at her with a wordless howl. His eyes, wild and crazed, fixed on her with feral rage. He threw Tras aside like a broken toy and lunged at her again. His claws ripped bloody gouges across her stomach.

She ducked under his next swing and hit the butt end of Tras's rock spike, driving it deeper and tearing back open the wounds Ravys had instinctively healed. Ravys staggered and looked down, as if only now becoming aware of the impaling spike. It only distracted him for a moment, then he was trying again to attack her.

A moment, though, was all Cylin and Tieln needed. Two gunshots cracked, one after the other. Blood blossomed across Ravys's chest, then flowed from his head as the shots slammed into him.

Somehow, he still tried one more time to tear into Eria. Even as he finally crumpled to the floor, claws outstretched toward her, with his final breath, Ravys hissed, "Give him back."

Eria sucked in a shaky breath. Her stomach bled from Ravys's claws, but she scrambled to the limp form of Tras. He lay too still, not breathing. She sensed a fading spark of life in his broken body. *Tras, can you hear me?*

The spark stirred. *Are they gone?*

Yes. Karishan and Ravys are dead.

Good. Then I can join my family in peace.

Eria shook her head. *I can help you. I'm a healer; I can—*

She felt the spark dim. *I want to go. To be with them. Please.*

Her eyes stung. She wanted to argue, wanted to drag his spirit back from the brink and push him back into life. But she didn't have that right, and the heavy weariness in his voice pierced her to the heart.

Sometimes, the hardest thing any healer can do is to accept the wishes of their patient. She swallowed hard. *Rest with them in eternity's embrace, Tras.*

No words answered her, only the sensation of gratitude. Then, silence.

Eria bowed her head, silent for a long moment. The magic she'd drawn up knit her own wounds. She rose slowly and turned to her friends.

The remaining Creatures now stood behind Yazah. He'd freed himself from Quicksilver's entanglement and healed his leg, and now, Cylin, Tieln, and Quicksilver all had their guns trained on him. Snow stood beside Quicksilver, hackles raised as he glowered at his brother and the Creatures. Yazah, in turn, watched Eria.

"I knew you could defeat Karishan," Yazah told her.

"Seriously, Yazah?" Eria glared at him. "You did not abduct Cylin and threaten Lucian's village with the goal of getting *me* to go into Ravys's head to break the connection between him and Karishan's spirit."

"No, I had another goal in mind then, but this worked out better overall," he said. He gestured, and the Creatures shuffled back, out of the hall and into the lobby, leaving Yazah without visible backup.

"Better for who?" Quicksilver snapped. "You? Because it wasn't better for Cylin. Certainly not for Tras over there. And it sure wasn't for Lucian or Chance! And with that, *what the fuck* are you doing with *Ayliad*?" His expression twisted in disgust. "And no, that doesn't mean I want to know *anything* about you and my *mother* screwing."

Yazah raised his hands in a gesture of peace at Quicksilver's outburst. "Ayliad and I were allies of convenience that just happened to include some side benefits. And at least I'm not actually related to her. She and her bone men offered resources that Lord Karishan needed."

Everyone stopped cold. "*Her* bone men?" Eria repeated.

Yazah nodded. "Bone men are Ayliad's followers. Most of their experiments are aimed toward drawing essences from other humans with the intent of using those essences to perfect themselves—make themselves the most beautiful, flawless men in the world. They're also trying to find ways to extend their lifespans, so they can be the perfect mates for Ayliad forever."

Cylin made a noise of disgust. "So *that's* why she acted affronted about my scar?"

Yazah shrugged. "Yep."

The bone men who took Tieln's wards and Father... they served Ayliad. Does he know? Did Lucian know? Eria's hands clenched. "You disgust me, Yazah. Serving Karishan, allying with Ayliad, then using me when you were ready to be done with Karishan. I know Lucian will be more than willing to smash this place to the ground, and you with it. Can you give me one good reason we shouldn't let him?" They needed to find Lucian and Chance as quickly as possible, but Yazah still had to be dealt with one way or another.

"If I'm dead, Shiranak's empire will crumble," Yazah said. "And all the people living in it will suffer."

Cylin scowled. "Sadly, he's right, much as I hate to say anything nice about this ass wart. Like I told you, Eria, from what I saw, this isn't that bad a place to live. Without someone in charge, bandits and warlords will make life utter shit for the people."

"There, you see?" Yazah said. "Even Lucian's human thinks—"

Cylin shot him in the shoulder. "Shut up before I change my mind. Just because you're the best of a bunch of shitty options doesn't mean I *don't* want to put a bullet between your eyes."

Yazah sank to his knees with a grimace and pressed a hand to his bleeding shoulder, but said nothing. Eria glanced to Quicksilver, who gave her a small smile. *Remember back when I said that if we didn't return to Forest Town, I was pretty sure Cylin would hunt me down and shoot me? This is why,* he told her.

"Lucian and Chance should have some say in whether we're leaving Yazah alive. We must find them," Tieln said. "And that woman."

"Unless Yazah intends to intervene on his lover's behalf," Cylin said darkly.

The wound on his shoulder was closing, but Yazah made no move to rise. "Absolutely not. I may follow the Rule of Law, but the Rule of Lucian supersedes that. And Rule of Lucian is that if it has to do with Lucian and his mother or his sister, they are on their own and I'm staying out of the way. That staircase heads down into the basement. Ayliad was checking the results of one of our joint research projects."

Quicksilver eyed Yazah suspiciously. A fresh growth of vines crawled across the floor to wrap around Yazah's ankles, then pin his arms against his body. "I'm sure Lucian still has a few things he wants to say to you," Quicksilver told him.

"No doubt," Yazah said.

Eria walked to the door and stepped onto the staircase. Without turning, she said, "Let's go. Goodbye, Yazah."

"Until next time, Eria."

"No. There will be no next time. We won't meet again. Goodbye." She had little doubt that by the time they returned, he would be gone, Quicksilver's restraints notwithstanding.

The others followed her down the stairs. As Eria neared the bottom, she sensed Lucian's magic in contention with another she didn't recognize. Behind her, though, Quicksilver hissed Ayliad's name, and Snow growled.

A short hall at the bottom of the stairs split in two directions. The fork to the right ended at an open door. Seeing movement, Eria looked inside.

Whatever "joint experiments" Yazah had been working on with Ayliad, they apparently required an elegantly furnished bedroom with a large four-poster bed and planters overflowing with morning glory and other vine plants. Perhaps he'd meant that experiments took place in the room beyond—Eria did see another closed door at the far end of the room.

In the center of the room, Lucian and Ayliad fought. A wall of vines encircled Ayliad, lashing out at her will. Lucian attempted to wrest control of the plants from her. The floor writhed with plants shifting and wriggling like snakes. Vines pinned Chance to one of the bedposts. One thick vine seemed to be trying to worm its way into his mouth. Eria could see the panic in her father's eyes as he twisted his head away from the vine.

"Help Lucian!" she told Quicksilver.

He nodded, and she raced to Chance and drew her knife. The vines cut easily, but for every one she cut, another replaced it. Chance struggled, lips pressed tightly closed against the persistent vine. The plants slithered across Chance, teasing under his clothes. Taunting him. Mocking her efforts to release him.

Snow bounded to Eria's side, looked at her, then looked at Chance. She attacked the vines holding his wrists. She freed her father's hand just enough that he could grab the scruff of Snow's neck. Snow teleported to the entryway, bringing Chance with him. Chance collapsed, shuddering and gasping for breath.

Ayliad turned toward him, then scanned the rest of the room. "Done with Yazah already? A pity. I suppose it's time I take my leave of you, my dear brother."

"I'm not letting you get away!" Lucian snarled.

She smirked. "Shall I take you with me, then? You can join Dash at my side."

Eria sucked in a sharp breath. Lucian's younger brother, Dash, had been missing since the war. Centuries ago, though, well before Eria's birth, Dash, like Lucian, had been seduced by Ayliad.

"You lie." Lucian grabbed a fistful of vines and ripped them away from Ayliad.

Dash, show yourself to your brother, Ayliad responded.

All around the room, blight spread through the vines, turning them black as death. Thorns pierced out of the delicate tendrils. Eria scrambled back, retreating to the relative safety of the doorway. A wave of corrupted magic radiated through the room with the blight. Only a circle directly around Lucian remained clear.

Shadows drew into a shape in the corner of the room. Darkness shrouded its features, but it stood a little shorter than Eria. The shape lifted its head and opened amber eyes. Black vines roiled and curled around it. It advanced one cautious step, then another toward Lucian and Ayliad. The amber eyes fixed on Lucian.

Help me.

Lucian stiffened. "What have you done, Ayliad?"

"Me? I have fed him. Cared for him. I have given him what he needs so he's not consumed by the corruption and running rampant." Ayliad smiled like a spider to her prey. "I have helped him, when you did nothing for him." She held back a hand to the dark figure.

Black vines coiled down the figure's arm as it rested its hand in Ayliad's, but its gaze never left Lucian. *Help me.*

The sense of corrupted magic intensified. Lucian made a sound of pain, clutching his head.

Ayliad smiled and held her free hand to him. "Come with us, my beautiful brother. Come and see the wonders we have created."

Lucian staggered back a step. "No. Dash, get away from her!"

Help me. The dark figure stared intently at Lucian. *Lucian... help me...*

The black vines wrapped around the figure and Ayliad, then sank into the floor. The rest of the vines slithered after, leaving behind only shattered stone and the stench of rot and decay. Lucian screamed in rage and frustration. "Come back here, bitch!"

Faint and distant, only Dash's plea answered. *Help me.*

~

INTERLUDE FOUR: HOMEWARD

When Cahron rested a hand on the smooth stone wall of the passage, he wondered whether he only imagined that he could feel the chill of the void beyond seeping through. The walls of their vessel were thick, and this close to the heart of it, no windows peered into the darkness. Even so, sometimes he was sure that endless cold crept in. With a shiver, he let his hand fall again.

At his side, Arrel cast him a look of concern. "Are you cold?"

Cahron shook his head. "No, I'm fine." His mouth twisted in a wry smile. "Or as fine as I can be, all things considered."

Arrel's smile was equally wry. "True enough." He considered the marble wall blocking their passage, its mirror-smooth whites and pinks at odds with the reddish stone walls to either side. "But if anyone can talk to Lonewind, it's you."

"And we all know it. *Especially* Lonewind. I'm fairly sure that's why this is here." Cahron gestured at the wall blocking the passage before them.

Arrel chuckled softly. "If Lonewind *really* wanted to keep us all out, he'd find a way, I'm sure. Or he could have inscribed 'Keep out' on the wall or something."

Arrel was by far the oldest elf in their vessel, having at least five centuries on Lonewind, and more than that over the rest of them. He had at least some skill in almost every magic known to elves, though he occasionally lamented his inability to shapeshift or teleport. Despite that, he was one of the most relaxed and easygoing people Cahron knew. Even now, faced with the very clear evidence that Lonewind didn't want to talk to anyone, Arrel was calm and confident that whatever the problem, Cahron could resolve it.

Putting off the coming conversation a moment, Cahron asked, "Do you have a sense of how far we are from… home?" He wasn't sure what else to call the planet where he'd been born. Where all of them had been born.

Arrel shook his head. "I can roughly estimate our location when we're moving at a constant velocity, but Lonewind keeps pushing our vessel faster." He shook his head. "Lonewind's the only man I know who can calculate astrophysics and telemetry in his head."

Cahron chuckled. "He's tried to explain it to me a few times, and claims it's really just a matter of applying a dozen relatively simple formulas. I just trust he knows what he's talking about."

Arrel touched his hand to the wall and opened a passage. "Speaking of talking to Lonewind…"

"Wait here. I'll let you know if I need your help convincing him." Cahron stepped through the opening and down the passage to the heart of their vessel.

A stable, steady rotation created the illusion of gravity, up and down, but the closer Cahron moved to the center of the vessel, the less that force held him. No engines propelled their shell of shaped and hollowed rock, only elven magic. In theory, whoever was guiding the vessel could do so from anywhere within, but Lonewind had designated the center of the vessel as the proper location from which to do so.

And for the last three days, he'd blocked the passages that accessed the heart of the vessel and refused to answer anyone's questions to him through mind-speech.

Cahron ran a hand through his sandy brown hair and sighed. If Lonewind wasn't talking, Cahron was the only one who stood a chance of getting the reason from him. He truly hoped he could get the answer from Lonewind, rather than venturing into Lonewind's mind and speaking directly to Lonewind's soul. He would if necessary, of course. That was what a soul healer did, and Cahron knew Lonewind's soul well.

He caught himself on a handhold where the passage opened to the heart of the vessel. In the middle of the chamber, Lonewind floated, long auburn hair spread like a wave around his head. The glow of light in the chamber shone on his bronze tanned skin. His eyes were closed, and he didn't respond to Cahron's entrance.

"I know you know I'm here, Lonewind." Cahron kicked off the wall and floated across the chamber.

"I'm fine, Cahron." Lonewind didn't open his eyes.

"Of course you are. That's why you closed the passages, won't come out, and won't talk to anyone. Because you're fine, and there are no problems at all." Cahron glanced around the room. At least he knew Lonewind had water and food in here.

Lonewind finally turned to him. Cahron looked into the haunted amber eyes. If Lonewind had slept in the last several days, it had been no more than a few hours at a time. Dark shadows ringed his eyes and lined his face. "We have to go faster."

Lonewind was always a man of strong emotions, with a tendency toward obsession. Though he kept it in check relatively well, threats to two particular people sparked that trait to its full intensity. People for whom Lonewind would drive himself beyond exhaustion without a second thought. Cahron was one of them.

Though there was no one else to hear, Cahron spoke quietly. "What happened to Lucian?"

Lonewind shuddered. "I don't know. I went out into the spirit realm to tell him we're close."

Cahron nodded. Even as powerful as Lonewind was, the distance between their vessel and the planet meant he'd been able to do little more than assure himself that Lucian was, in fact, still alive. Now that they were closer, though, he could devote more of his magic to piercing through the wails and shouts of tormented souls. "Did he hear you? Did he answer?"

"The Ghost answered."

Cahron stiffened. "What did he say?"

"He said, 'Come faster. Lucian needs you.'"

That explained everything. Cahron drifted to Lonewind and rested a hand on his arm, trusting Lonewind to use his magic to stop Cahron's momentum and maintain his own position. "How far are we from the planet?"

"Too far," Lonewind said.

"Let Arrel help, Lonewind. At the least, he can maintain this velocity while you sleep for a couple hours." Cahron sensed the exhaustion radiating from Lonewind. It would take only a touch of magic to push him from waking to sleep.

"There's no time for me to rest, Cahron! Lucian needs help!"

Logic wasn't going to get him far, but Cahron still tried it. "I know you're worried, Lonewind, but there's still only so hard you can push yourself, there's only so fast we can go, and there's only so far you can bend the laws of physics."

"Laws were made to be broken."

I'll need you to take over propelling the vessel in just a moment, Cahron called to Arrel.

He sensed Arrel's acknowledgment. Lonewind's eyes had drifted closed again. Perspiration beaded his forehead.

"Sorry, Lonewind," Cahron murmured. "You can be mad at me later." He called his healing magic and sent a gentle pulse into Lonewind. Lonewind's tense shoulders eased as sleep took him. "Lucian will understand."

PART FOUR

GUARDIAN

GUARDIAN

The heavy stench of acrid smoke hung in the air. A thick black column rose from the fires burning around Shiranak's research facility. Tieln wasn't certain how many were intentional, and how many were the result of the facility guards firing heavy weaponry at a very angry elf, only to have their ordinances flung back into their faces… and into their stores of ammunition. Orders or not, in the guards' place, he would have immediately ceased fire after the first shot came slinging back to the weapon that released it.

From the dozen smoldering piles of melted slag on the walls, the guards here had not been so quick to grasp that lesson.

Cylin walked up beside Tieln. "No sign of Yazah. I'm not surprised."

The young woman was eighteen or nineteen years old, with shoulder-length blond hair, a keen gaze, and an acerbic wit. She was also the only fully human member of their group—a label that Tieln would have applied to himself as well only a month ago.

By most people's standards, Tieln looked no more than a

year or two older than Cylin. He kept his dark hair short, after the style of the guards at the city of New Watch, where he'd served several years before Shiranak's forces overran the city. He'd spent years learning ways to make himself look older, trying to disguise his perpetual youth, with varying degrees of success. Until he met Lucian, Chance, Eria, and Quicksilver, he'd never known the reason for his unnatural failure to age. He still didn't know what to think about learning that he was half elf. He had even less idea what to think about discovering his father, and learning he had an entire family he'd never known.

"It doesn't appear that anyone else expected to find him still here either." Pulling his thoughts from the conundrum of his existence, Tieln nodded toward the clump of four elves and one massive white feline—a panther, if he correctly remembered the picture books of his childhood. The elves conversed in low, worried voices as they walked down the road. "I don't think he's their main concern at the moment, either."

They joined the others. Lucian, raven-haired leader of the elves, stopped mid-sentence, brushed past Eria and Quicksilver, and grabbed Cylin in a quick, fierce hug. "Were you hurt?"

She shook her head. "I'm fine, Lucian. No, Yazah didn't hurt me, neither did Ravys." She returned the hug, then stepped back. "But I'm glad to see you."

Lucian touched Cylin's cheek. "What happened to your scar?"

She brushed his hand aside. "I'll tell you later. So, where are we headed? Back to Forest Town?"

"You should go back there," Lucian answered. His amber eyes swept over the rest of the group. "You all should. It's safer there."

"There is *no fucking way* I am letting you go after her alone, Lucian." Lucian's cousin Chance glared. "Don't even think about it."

Both Chance and Lucian were on edge, tense and expecting an attack. Grass swaying in the wind drew sharp, wary looks from both of them. Tieln felt as if everyone understood some threat that remained invisible to him.

"You intend to pursue that woman, sir?" he asked Lucian. The "sir" was reflexive, from a lifetime working as a guard or soldier in towns and cities around the wasteland.

"I won't leave my brother in her clutches," Lucian growled. "And I'm not leaving her to slither back into the shadows, to taunt us at her leisure. I will end this."

"Then you need backup," Tieln said. "Especially because she has an ally." He didn't add that the beautiful blond woman had already proven capable of holding her own against both Lucian and Chance at once even without the aid of the shadow-shrouded figure.

Lucian looked him in the eyes. Tieln didn't flinch from the intense gaze. Lucian spoke directly into Tieln's mind. *You'd do better to get as far away as you can and never look back. It would be better for you. Safer.*

Though he could hear the elven mind-speech, Tieln didn't know how to answer in the same. Aloud, he said, "No, it would not."

Lucian's jaw tightened. *This family is cursed, Tieln, and that curse is my mother and her legacy. You should leave before it sinks its claws into you as well.*

"Is that an order, sir?" Tieln said.

Lucian finally broke his gaze, releasing a long breath. "No. Stars know you're probably as stubborn as the rest of us, and wouldn't obey if I tried to make it one."

"Good. Then I don't have to disobey. Do you know where to find this woman?"

"I know how to find her," Lucian said.

"Back to the truck, then?" Quicksilver asked. "And can we leave before anyone from the city comes to see what happened here? We're not going to get a friendly reception for trashing the place."

"Back to the truck," Lucian agreed. "We'll fly."

Not all elves could fly, but those who could also could lift other people. Tieln didn't know which elf's magic picked him up, but he soon found himself hanging thirty feet off the ground with nothing under his feet and the wind whipping through his short dark hair. The sensation was more than a little unsettling. He swallowed hard and tried not to think about how far he would fall if the elves dropped him.

Flying was faster than walking, but even so, it couldn't traverse multiple days on foot in an afternoon. When the sun hung low, they landed well away from the road, on a wide ledge halfway up a rocky slope. While it was a defensible location, it wouldn't be a comfortable one.

Before Tieln could voice the thought, Lucian leaned wearily against a large stone. "Figure out watches without me."

The rock curled away from him, opening a cave in the hillside. Lucian staggered two steps inside, sank to the ground, and closed his eyes.

Cylin stepped inside and nudged him with her toe. "Not the best place to sleep, Lucian."

"He's exhausted," Chance said. "The last of his magic went into making the cave."

"But Cylin's right that it's not the best place for him to sleep." Quicksilver gestured. Lucian's limp form lifted slightly from the ground and floated to the back of the small cave. The white-haired elf was the youngest looking member of the group. Sometimes Tieln forgot that even Quicksilver had seen over a thousand years.

Eria scanned the land. "No fire tonight. It would be too easy for someone to spot the light."

Tieln did a quick count of their number. "Where is the panther?"

"Snow?" Eria asked. "He's probably off hunting somewhere. He'll find us when he wants to." Seeing Tieln's puzzled but uneasy expression, she added, "Snow's an elf. He can shape-shift, and he likes the form of a large cat. He's… Yazah's younger brother, actually."

Tieln blinked. "Oh."

Eria handed him a thick piece of jerky, dried fruit, and flatbread. Tieln waited until everyone was served before sitting to eat. Everyone ate quietly, wrapped in their own thoughts. He hesitated to break the silence, but an important question lingered, unanswered.

He cleared his throat. "The woman who was with Yazah, who we fought. Who is she?"

Everyone stopped cold. After a moment, Cylin said, "That was Ayliad."

"And who is Ayliad?" Tieln asked. Everyone else seemed to understand the danger this person posed.

Quicksilver and Eria both looked to Chance, but Chance didn't answer. After a long moment of expectant silence, Cylin spoke. "Honestly, it ought to be one of them telling you, but since it doesn't look like they will, I'll tell you what I know, and someone else can correct whatever I get wrong."

Still none of the elves spoke. Tieln gave Cylin a grateful smile and nodded for her to continue.

"So, I've got to start this before Ayliad." Cylin pursed her lips, considering. "You know much history, Tieln? Human history, I mean."

He nodded. "I learned some when I was young."

"You've heard of the Black Witch?"

He nodded again. "She was said to be one of the most manipulative and cruel people to ever gain control of the early empire."

"That's the one. Except that she wasn't human; she's an elf, and she's *much* worse than our history says."

"She *was* an elf," Chance cut in. "Her name was Willow, and she is dead."

Cylin nodded. "Yeah, and she was Lucian's mother."

The Black Witch was my grandmother?

Cylin continued. "Willow seduced Lucian's father, Lonewind, held him against his will, and at some point in there had Lucian. Lonewind escaped with his son and got far away from her."

Briefly, Tieln wondered what Lucian's childhood had been like, living on the run. In the enclave where he grew up, he'd seen mothers and children who'd fled from abusive spouses or rapists. So many of those children carried dark shadows of fear with them.

"Willow wasn't willing to give up on getting them back, but because she was an elf, she took some forty years to actually put her plan in motion," Cylin continued.

Chance interrupted again. "During which time my father, Moonfire, joined them. The clan crossed an ocean and had an unpleasant encounter with Karishan. I was born, and after that, we crossed another continent."

Cylin waited a moment to see if he would add more. When he didn't, she said, "I don't know, and don't want to know, details about the second time Willow caught Lonewind and Lucian. Really, the important thing you need to know about that is that they escaped her again, and she didn't tell them that she got pregnant again. This time, she had a daughter, Ayliad, by Lonewind."

Chance shuddered. A hard lump of dread formed in Tieln's gut. He'd seen Chance as aloof and distant. Watching the elf's reactions, though, he wondered what had actually happened to him. *How much lies unspoken?*

"About a century later, Willow sent Ayliad off to go find and seduce Lucian," Cylin continued. "Because, psycho bitch that she was, she still hadn't given up on getting Lonewind and Lucian back."

"She never gave up on that goal," Eria said quietly. "Willow died pursuing it, and nearly destroyed us all."

Tieln listened quietly, hands folded in his lap so no one could see how his fingers dug into his palms. "Ayliad seduced her own brother?" *Do I want to know?*

"Brothers," Chance corrected. "She and Lucian were together for decades, but she was not exclusive with him. At that time, we lived in a large community of elves. Meeting strangers wasn't unusual or suspicious. We knew her as Morning Glory then. On the side, she had a relationship with Lucian's younger half-brother, Dash, who was born while we were there. I know she had engagements with several other attractive men in that community." His expression darkened. "She also pursued me. Thanks to my own… experiences with Willow, I had no interest in a sexual relationship with anyone at that time, let alone my closest friend's lover. Ayliad did not appreciate being told 'no.' Sadly, she wasn't stupid, either, which means that when she did rape me, she set it up so that it wasn't clear whether it was a mutually consensual encounter between two drunken people that just went sideways, or if *I* had assaulted *her*." Chance's hands trembled, and he firmly folded them together. "I couldn't remember what happened. She'd drugged me."

From Cylin's expression, she hadn't known that detail. Eria rested a comforting hand on her father's shoulder.

Tieln cleared his throat. "I… think that gives me some idea what this person is like. If you want to stop there."

Chance raised his head. His intense amber eyes bore into Tieln's. "No. You should know *all* of it. And it gets *much* worse."

For a moment, Tieln regretted asking the question, and resented Cylin for answering it when the elves clearly would have preferred not to. He knew of warlords, male and female alike, who abused and tortured their subjects, but the fear he sensed from Chance, Eria, and Quicksilver lay deeper and older than anything he'd known before. "What did she do?"

"The community where we lived was a relatively safe place. We'd all begun to let down our guard. Ayliad talked Lucian, me, Dash, and our friends Tash and Sun into leaving—go out and see more of the world. Careless… I was careless. She lured us straight into Willow's reach. Tash and Sun were left marooned on an island, where they could be used as hostages to demand our cooperation. Willow had no strong feelings of spite toward either of them. Lucian, Dash, and I, on the other hand, each woke alone and isolated, imprisoned in Willow's underwater Coral Palace. She used magic to give Lucian and Dash the ability to breathe underwater. I wasn't so… lucky. Both Willow and Ayliad wanted to be certain I stayed where they put me."

"If it was underwater, how could they keep you alive without such an ability?" Tieln asked. The more he heard about elven magic, the more unnerving it became, with so many ways to twist and alter not only the world, but other people as well.

"My cell was airtight and filled with plants to refresh the oxygen," Chance answered. "My restraints didn't allow me to reach the water passage that accessed it, otherwise I would have either swum to find my friends or drowned trying." He closed his eyes and drew a deep breath. "Willow tortured us. I don't think that she raped either Dash or Lucian." His jaw tightened. "She was saving that for Lonewind." In a very low undertone that Tieln barely heard, Chance added, "And me."

If anyone else heard, they pretended not to. Tieln tried to imitate them.

Chance continued. "She left Dash to Ayliad, mostly. On

Lucian, however, she inflicted mental tortures, causing him hallucinations until he couldn't tell reality from her 'games.'"

Cylin drew a startled breath. Heads turned to her. "Her games. That's what he calls it. That's where Lucian thinks he is when he's having an episode. He kept saying that everything was part of 'her games.'"

Chance paled, but continued. "Ayliad revealed her true identity to me, and to Lucian as well I'm sure. She didn't torture like her mother, most of the time, but any time she entered my prison, I knew she was going to take me. I struck a bargain with her: sex for answers." He shivered, shoulders hunching. "I didn't know what, if anything, I could *do* with the information she gave me, but it gave me some meager illusion of control."

"Why would she accept such a bargain?" Tieln asked. He could think of reasons that warlords he had encountered would do so, but hoped maybe it wouldn't be quite so bad.

Chance's gaze bore into Tieln's. "She could use her healing magic to force my body to respond to her lusts, but she drew far more satisfaction from having me in position of choosing to fuck her voluntarily. She wanted the power, the control. She wanted to humiliate and break me."

I was wrong. What Ayliad did was worse than any warlord I've known. "How long were you prisoners?" Tieln asked, catching a tremor in his own voice.

"As close as any of us can guess, somewhere between a year and a half to two years," Chance said. "Willow wanted Lonewind, but she also did not allow any of us to slip loose with a plea for help until she was well and truly certain she had all of us subdued."

Horror left Tieln speechless. Two years of rape and torture, with no escape. And this woman was one of those responsible for it. No wonder Lucian wanted her dead.

"Willow trapped Lonewind when he tried to rescue us.

That took some of her attention off me, but Ayliad more than filled in that absence. She got pregnant, and told me that I was the father. Evidently brothers proved a little *too* closely related for a viable pregnancy." Chance had drawn up his legs and wrapped his arms around them, though he didn't seem conscious of doing so. "I attempted to strangle her. I failed, and things grew… much worse. If rescue had not come when it did, there would not have been much to rescue."

"Who rescued you?" Tieln asked. "Did Lonewind somehow?"

Chance shook his head. "Other allies, elves from outside of our clan. A friend of Lucian's who I'd never really liked or trusted. He and his people got us all out of Willow and Ayliad's clutches. And while they helped and guarded our shattered few back to safety, Willow attacked repeatedly from the spirit realm. Except… for the time she came to whisper in my ear that Ayliad had given birth, and named her son Lynx."

"Wait, she only told you about Lynx?" Quicksilver cut in.

Chance nodded.

"Oh. Shit. That's twisted."

"Why?" Tieln asked.

"Well, technically, Lynx is the oldest, but… Okay, Lynx and Echo are twins," Quicksilver said. "They're Eria's half-brothers on their dad's side, and…" He sighed. "And my half-brothers on their mom's side."

Tieln blinked, taking a moment to absorb that. "I… see."

"Fortunately, my father was one of Ayliad's pretty boys, and *not* related to anyone else," Quicksilver added. "And lucky for me, Ayliad was out of the picture for other reasons when I was young. I ended up with this side of the family by accident, but it turned out well enough for me."

"And the twins?" Tieln asked.

"They're elsewhere," Chance said. "Beyond Ayliad's reach."

"I see." Tieln didn't ask more. He glanced to Lucian's sleeping form. *So this is what you meant when you called your mother a curse on your family.*

He took the last watch of the night, hoping for a chance to speak to Lucian before the rest of the group woke, but Lucian slept until well after sunrise. When he did rouse, he said little to anyone but Chance.

They flew again through most of the day, skirting around towns and villages. Sometimes people on the ground noticed them and pointed or waved. Quicksilver usually waved back, though no one else did. Tieln was just glad no one shot at them.

How quickly will word of our attack on Yazah and the research facility travel? Will the common people learn of it, or will that knowledge be concealed as much as possible? In Yazah's place, I would choose to conceal. He certainly won't want word of Shiranak's fate getting out.

The sun had sunk below the horizon, leaving only fading twilight, when they returned to the place where they'd left the truck. The vehicle remained undisturbed behind its shielding stone wall.

Cylin raised an eyebrow when she saw it. "You drove?"

"Doctor Kinnel suggested we take one of the trucks," Quicksilver told her. "Got us here a lot faster than walking."

"And some people in Forest Town said we'd never need them." Cylin nodded with a self-satisfied smirk.

"We'll stay the night here," Lucian said. "Leave in the morning."

"Not much fuel left," Chance warned. "We'll be on foot before long."

Eria scavenged kindling and built a fire. Quicksilver helped her prepare dinner. Tieln's instinct was to take a guard post, but the stone walls rendered that task irrelevant.

Lucian joined him. Tieln nodded to him. "Sir."

Lucian gave him a thin smile. "You're not going to stop calling me that, are you?"

"It seems far less awkward than calling you 'Father'," Tieln responded.

Lucian grimaced. "True." He rubbed his eyes. "I didn't know."

"I believe you." He didn't understand everything that the others seemed to know about the Ghost, but he understood that it was an awareness distinct from Lucian's. He'd once served a warlord who claimed, at various times, to be at least three different people, and none of them had shared full awareness of each other's actions.

Lucian let out a heavy breath. "There are so many things you need to know, and I don't know where to start." He gazed at Tieln. "And that's not at all fair to you, either. Here I'm trying to think what to tell you about us when I still know so little about you."

Tieln shifted uncomfortably. "I have spent many years perfecting ways to avoid talking about myself."

"I'm sure." Lucian's expression was sympathetic and a little guilty. "Would you tell me about your mother?"

Tieln settled on the bare ground. "Her name was Jinh. She was in her early thirties when I was born. We lived in a community run by the survivors of a military brigade. The commander took in a lot of widows and orphans. My mother… she was kind to everyone, even the women who mocked her claim that she'd been visited by a spirit." Tieln gazed at a point on the wall, carefully not looking at Lucian.

"Did she say that often?"

"Every night, she told me the story of how she had wandered lost and despairing in the wasteland after her husband's death. A spirit found her, gave her hope and a new life. He guided her to safety, but would not stay himself." He caught himself falling into the familiar cadence of his mother's voice and stopped to collect himself. "No one else there really followed the Old Faith. By the time I was twelve, I'd decided that spirits weren't real, and that her tale was a delusion she'd convinced herself was true." He paused and glanced to Lucian. "I decided that she'd been raped, and this delusion was her way of coping with that."

Lucian flinched. "I didn't—"

Tieln shook his head quickly. "I don't think that you, or the Ghost, did. But it was the explanation that made sense to me then. I never doubted that she loved me, and if that delusion was a part of that, I was never going to tell her that I didn't believe it."

"Why would it be tied to her loving you?" Lucian asked.

"Some of the other women had gotten pregnant by rape. I saw how some of them struggled not to project their feelings toward their attacker onto their child."

Lucian looked horrified at the idea. "I can't… I don't want to imagine what that would be to a child, knowing their parent could not love them." His jaw tightened. "I know now that my mother never loved me or saw me as more than a tool to control my father, but he concealed that from me when I was young."

Tieln wasn't sure what to say in response. Rather than attempt an insufficient platitude, he continued. "By the time I was fifteen, it was obvious I wasn't physically maturing as quickly as the others my age. But I wasn't the only child with oddities, and mine was deemed relatively… minor compared to some of the others." A shiver ran down his spine. Some of the radiation mutations had been truly horrific. "We were all taken care of, though, even those who would have been killed anywhere else. Those of us who were fit were trained by the soldiers. That training earned me a lot of work as a guard in other towns after I left."

"Why did you leave?" Lucian asked.

"My mother died. Pneumonia. Without her, I realized that place didn't offer the life I wanted. I… wasn't sure what life I *did* want, but I couldn't find it where I was."

"I understand."

"I traveled to other communities. With my training, it was pretty easy to find work as a guard. After a few years in any spot, though, someone would always start wondering why I never looked any older." Tieln's shoulder rose in a half-shrug. "I found ways of disguising it, but it always became a problem at some point. Either because I looked too young, or because I looked too… pretty."

Lucian winced. "I'm sorry. The looks are… well, whether you call them a blessing or a curse depends very much on whose attention they attract."

"Someone like Ayliad."

Lucian nodded, tensing at the name. "How much do you know?"

"After you went to sleep last night, Chance told me about who she was and how she seduced, then betrayed you and him to your mother."

"Chance told you?" Lucian looked surprised, glancing toward his cousin.

Yes, I did, Chance responded from the other side of their shelter. *The events up through the Coral Palace.*

Tieln flushed, realizing their conversation wasn't nearly as private as he'd thought it. Realistically, he shouldn't have been surprised. The campsite wasn't that large, and he hadn't been focused on keeping his voice soft. "I do have a question about that."

"Only one?" Lucian asked with a thin chuckle and a wary expression.

"Only one at the moment, at least. How long ago was that? The Black Witch was said to have been killed hundreds of years ago. Is the Coral Palace when she died?"

Chance laughed darkly and answered aloud this time. "If only she'd died then. No, the abduction I described took place nearly two thousand years ago. She had *plenty* more time to toy with us."

"So you weren't telling me the end of your torments at her hands, but the beginning." Tieln shivered. *Those who worship elves as gods call their long lives a blessing. Chance and Lucian might call it a curse.*

The thread of conversation trailed off awkwardly. Eria declared dinner ready, and everyone sat to eat. Only once food was consumed did discussion begin again.

"How do we track Ayliad?" Eria asked.

Quicksilver rubbed his left arm. "That part's easy. Between her and Dash, they're somewhere between strenuously inviting and outright demanding through the Tree."

Tieln's own left arm had been tingling most of the day, but he'd been trying to ignore it. Before he could ask, Lucian's voice murmured in his mind. *All my father's offspring carry a fragment of a powerful magical entity we call the Tree.* Accompanying the name was an image of a broad-limbed leafy tree large enough to hold the population of Springvale in its boughs with room to spare. Glowing fruit hung from its branches, and swaying vines moved without wind. *It's the reason you have those markings on your left arm. Ayliad is my sister, and Dash is my half-brother, and both are using their connections to that Tree magic to pull at me and Quick. I don't know how much you will feel it.*

He nodded, acknowledging the message. He wished he knew how to speak mind-to-mind as the elves did. "If they are drawing you toward them, it's reasonable to assume it is a trap."

"No doubt about it." Lucian leaned back on his elbows, gazing into the fire. The shadows cast by the flickering light aged his features. "I don't know what else she might have lurking in wait for us."

"A lot of extremely loyal human women," Cylin said. Heads turned to her. "She met with Yazah while we were on our way to his city. While the two of them were off having sex, I chatted with her harem boys. They told me all about what life is like there. A nice place, if you're female. Less so if you're not."

"Did she know that?" Tieln asked.

Cylin snorted. "She invited me to make whatever use I wanted of them. I decided that what I wanted was information, so I taught them a card game and we talked. Thanks for teaching me to play Shadow Ladies, Quicksilver."

Quicksilver blink. "Uh… you're welcome. Not what I expected you to say, but glad to have helped."

"We must also expect bone men," Tieln said.

Lucian looked at him sharply. "Why?"

"While you and Dad fought Ayliad, Yazah told us that she's in charge of the bone men," Eria said. "And that their goal is to transform themselves into perfect mates for her." She shuddered.

Chance did as well. "If that's true, some of the things they said when I was their captive make more sense."

"That bitch," Lucian hissed.

They packed everything and slept in the bed of the truck that night.

Tieln jerked awake when the engine rumbled to life. A quick headcount inside the truck showed only Lucian absent. Sitting up, Tieln spotted black hair and a pointed ear through the window between the bed and the cab. He picked his way to the window to confirm that Lucian sat in the driver's seat. Outside the truck, the land remained dark.

He slid the window open. "It's pretty early to start, isn't it sir?"

"All our supplies are packed and we know where we must go. Why should we not leave now?"

"Because you need sleep." Tieln glanced to the elves and Cylin, wondering why none of them had roused.

Lucian turned, but it wasn't Lucian. In the glow from the truck headlights, Tieln saw that the hair he'd thought was black was actually a dark green, with leaves growing amid the locks. However, it was the eyes that startled him most. Like Lucian's, they were intense and piercing, but had no whites, only two black pupils in the amber. The presence that watched him through those eyes was no elf, nor human, but something alien.

Tieln's hand dropped to the butt of his gun. "What and who are you? Where is Lucian?"

"We are the Guardian. We are the aspect of the Tree that dwells within Lucian. And a piece of us grows roots within you. A sapling with great promise."

"Where is Lucian?" Tieln repeated, never taking his eyes from the stranger that took Lucian's shape.

"He sleeps. As do you, sapling."

"If this is supposed to be some 'wake your sleeping magic' shit—"

"No, Sapling." The Guardian didn't blink. "You sleep. You lie on the bed of the truck, wrapped in a blanket. Lucian lies closest to the entrance, ready to wake and lash out should any come with intent to harm. You are asleep, and we are speaking to you while you sleep."

"I'm *dreaming* this?" Tieln demanded.

"After a fashion. Our presence can enter your sleep because you are Lucian's sapling… offspring. We came to judge your worth."

Tieln's eyes narrowed. "My worth?"

"The Fruit controls the Branches and wills that he become a Dark Tree."

"Talk sense," Tieln said coolly. "Or get out."

"We call them by the names of their aspects." The Guardian's brow furrowed with effort. "The Fruit, the sister, Ayliad, controls the Branches, the brother, Dash. She would bend the corruption that takes root inside him. She wishes to control it for her own purposes. Her hold on Lucian and on Chance runs deeper and stronger than either knows. They may be unable to defeat her. But you are untouched by her." The amber eyes narrowed. "You must grow, Sapling, so that your roots run deep and your branches reach high, and you have very little time in which to do so."

"How am I supposed to do *that*?"

"Your blood runs true and the power sleeps within. Wake it and learn."

"*How*?" Tieln demanded.

The truck shuddered as the engine rumbled to life. Tieln jerked up, head whipping back and forth. The blanket slid off his shoulders. Around him, the others yawned and stirred. The window between the truck bed and the cab was closed, and in the cab, Lucian and Chance spoke. Tieln still sat where he'd gone to sleep, and early morning light filtered in from the mouth of the truck.

His left arm ached. Tieln rubbed it, trying to figure out how much had been dream and how much truth.

He glanced at Lucian and Chance again. *If they can't defeat Ayliad, what hope do I have?*

~

The truck finally sputtered to a halt late in the morning. Tieln had no idea how far they were from Shiranak's lands, or Forest Town, or their destination. The elves employed their magic to form a cave and fly the truck into it, then seal the entrance once more. The supplies were distributed between the members of the group, and they set out on foot.

The ache in Tieln's arm had risen to a dull throb. After a time, he stepped up beside Quicksilver. The silver-haired elf looked younger than he was, but Tieln knew the other had seen a millennia. Still, he projected an air of welcome and greeted Tieln with an easy smile.

"What's on your mind?"

"Does your arm hurt?" Tieln asked.

"My… Oh." Understanding flashed in Quicksilver's eyes. "You feel that, huh?"

He nodded.

Quicksilver shook his arm and flexed his fingers. "It doesn't *hurt* to me, but the pull of the Tree is definitely there." He frowned. "Maybe I'm only feeling it through Ayliad, and you're feeling it from both Ayliad and Dash. I don't know, though." His brow furrowed, then he shook his head. "I just realized that we're cousins. That is… weird, for some reason. Anyway, do you have questions about the Tree and all that?"

"Who or what is the Guardian?"

"The Guardian is what happens when magic goes and develops sentience," Quicksilver answered. "I know, that's a weird answer, but something happened with Lucian, way before I was around, that caused his Tree magic to become aggressively opposed to other sources of corrupted magic. From there, it slowly developed an awareness. And, because it's inside Lucian, it built its own personality based off his and shares a lot of his characteristics."

"*Other* sources of corrupted magic?" Tieln cut in. He cast a suspicious look at the markings on his arm.

"Erm, technically speaking, the Tree magic is corrupted magic too," Quicksilver admitted. "Or it was when it infected Lonewind. But it's changed as it passed on to his children."

"Are all of them like the Guardian?" Tieln asked.

Quicksilver shook his head. "Not at all! The Guardian is unique in that it's the only one to become self-aware and distinct from its host. It's given names to all the other elves who have Tree magic, though. Lonewind is the Heart, for example. Ayliad is the Fruit, while Lynx and Echo are the Thorns and Shadow, respectively."

"And you?"

Quicksilver shrugged. "I'm a Sapling—the perpetually young one, I guess. Possibly the Guardian's way of saying I lack ambition, or that I've mostly neglected my plant magic. Both of which are true."

The Guardian had called him a sapling as well. But it hadn't felt dismissive. More an acknowledgement that his magic, assuming he actually had any, wasn't mature yet. "This event that happened to cause the Guardian to develop awareness—could that happen to others with the same magic?"

"It's possible, I guess," Quicksilver said. "But each of us interacts differently with the magic, so there's no guarantee that any one of us, put in the same situation, would get the same results."

You wouldn't want to be in the circumstances that started it, Lucian told Tieln from the front of the line. *It was a bad situation all around.*

Tieln nodded in silent response to both elves, though he thought he was the only one who'd heard Lucian. "How do you discover that you have a particular magic? How do you… make it work?"

Quicksilver shifted uncomfortably. "Someone else want to take this one? Because I honestly have no idea how to answer that."

"Now just a minute," Cylin cut in. "Unless humans have suddenly started to be able to do elf magic, there is something you guys haven't told me about Tieln."

"Tieln is my son," Lucian said. "A fact that both of us learned quite recently. His mother was a human woman I met sometime in the period after Tash and Sun died, and before I created the forest."

"Oh. Okay, that's not the answer I expected, but that makes some things here make sense. So he really can use elf magic."

Tieln glanced to her. "I maybe can use elf magic. If I have any, and I can figure out how to make it work."

"Your ability to locate items and people is elf magic, Tieln," Lucian said. "But a more subtle skill than levitation or some of the others. You probably don't remember how you discovered you had that talent."

Tieln shook his head. He still didn't think of the knack for finding things as magic. "I don't remember. But if there are other abilities that I can use, I want to know how to call on them. Our enemies wouldn't expect elven magic from a human."

"Ayliad will probably dismiss you as a threat," Chance said. "I don't know about Dash."

Lucian gestured in the direction of Shiranak's territory. "Dash focused on me back there. He needs the Guardian's help." He turned to Tieln. "As for magic, my experience is that we tend to discover our magic when we need it. Some abilities come more easily than others. Levitation came easily to both Chance and me—just imagine a toddler whose response to being told not to climb the bookcase is to float to the top of it instead."

"That young?" Tieln asked, feeling an unhappy twist in his gut. If he hadn't demonstrated any magic in his childhood, did that mean he didn't have anything but what he already knew?

"I didn't figure out that I could do it until I was older, though," Quicksilver said. "I climbed a lot before I finally got the hang of flying. But I think you've probably been successful at affecting plants at least once."

Tieln frowned. "Why?"

"Because you have the markings on your arm. Mine didn't appear until the first time I used plant magic."

Tieln looked at his arm. When had the marks appeared? Had they always been there? He didn't think so—he remembered scrubbing at them in the tub until his skin was raw, terrified because they wouldn't come off. "They appeared after I left the enclave where I grew up. I'd been taken in as a guard in a town, and we were on patrol. Mutated animals attacked us. I don't remember exactly what happened—it was all very fast. We only lost one man, and there were thorns... everywhere. I found the marks on my arm that night." He shook his head. "The others on patrol with me were certain I'd done *something*, and they weren't at all sure that it was a good thing. I didn't stay long after that. Especially not once they spread their version of the story around town."

He'd packed his belongings and escaped that night, before the mob gathered enough momentum to storm the barracks so they could drag him outside the walls and burn him. And he'd kept the markings on his arm hidden ever since.

"Huh, I heard a story about something like that once," Cylin said. "But I don't know if it was the same place. I heard plenty of outrageous stories on the road."

"It would have been... a long time ago," Tieln said. "I'm... older than I look."

"I figured."

"You've had to conceal your abilities from normal humans," Chance said. "It might take you a while to overcome the instinct to suppress your magic."

I've been holding myself back. Captain Ollen always told me not to hold back. I always thought he was harder on me than he was on the others. Did he know what I was? Did he believe Mother's tales about her meeting with a spirit?

When they made camp, Tieln sat away from the others. He let out a deep breath and closed his eyes.

I can't keep holding back.

What can elves do?

What can I do?

When he was finding something, he formed a picture of it in his mind, and sought something that matched its characteristics in the world. Perhaps he could make other abilities work through the same method. Tieln pictured a small patch of green grass in a ring around him. He focused on the image, willing it to be true. He wasn't sure if he was pleading or demanding.

He opened his eyes to see only bare, barren dirt, unchanged for all his wishing. He tried again, and again, without results. His hands clenched in frustration.

Why won't it work? What am I doing wrong?

Tieln gazed into the twilight. Maybe there just weren't any plants here to answer him. What else could he try?

He listened to people move around, envisioning where each one was. He caught something like a murmur of voices, half-heard mind speech between Lucian and Chance. All the elves could use mind-speech, and he could hear it. Didn't that mean he should be able to speak in it as well?

Can you hear me? He pictured Lucian, imagined himself saying the words to Lucian without opening his mouth. *Can you hear me?*

His eyelids sank closed. He concentrated on that simple question, and on the idea of sending it to Lucian. To… his father. His fingers curled around the hem of his shirt, gripping, holding, digging through the cloth into his palm.

Just hear me, damn you! Hear me! Answer me! His breath hissed between his teeth. The voice of his thoughts grew younger, angrier, more afraid. *Why won't you answer me? Why didn't you ever come back for us? Was I not good enough? Were you ashamed? Disgusted by your half-human son? Mother said you would return. She died saying that you would come back! Why did you abandon us? ANSWER ME!*

Something snapped. A thousand wailing, screaming voices smashed into his mind. Tieln reeled, clutching his head. His scream was lost in the maelstrom. He looked around frantically. Nothing looked as it should. The ground shimmered with a faint sickly green glow, with a few tiny spikes of healthier green around the spot where he… lay sprawled on the ground.

He was looking at himself. At his body.

The air above the camp teemed with ragged, ghostly forms. They tore at each other with savage claws and teeth. Their cries rose in deafening chorus. Several dove at him. Tieln swung wildly, trying to drive them back. Fangs sank into his arm. He screamed again.

Bright shapes rushed to his body. They glowed like the fires in a watchtower, almost too brilliant to look at. Tieln's attackers snapped at them, but something prevented them from piercing the brilliant glows. They turned back to the easy prey, biting again at Tieln.

The chaos of sound, sensation, and pain left room for nothing but panic and the need to flee. He scrambled back from the cruel assault, desperately seeking escape.

A firm hand seized his wrist. He struggled desperately, but the grip drew him down into the midst of the brilliant light. He squeezed his eyes shut, but no further assault followed.

I've got him, Chance said.

Is he all right? Tieln, are you all right? Lucian demanded.

He heard them, but their voices didn't drown out the shrieks and wails that buffeted him. He blindly scratched and clawed at the hand holding him.

Stop struggling, Tieln, Chance ordered. *I'm going to help you. Stop. Let me help.*

The voice was stern, but not unkind. *Help,* he pleaded.

He's stopped fighting me for the moment, Chance said. *He might know who I am.*

A sharp wave of panic and despair hit Tieln. He'd spoken. He was sure he'd spoken. Hadn't he? *Can you hear me?* He tugged at the hand, not fighting for release, but begging for an answer.

I can hear you, Chance answered. *I'm going to help you return to your body.*

Return…?

Chance drew him to the prone body. *This is going to feel strange. Don't fight me. You understand?*

I won't fight, Tieln said.

The elf rested a glowing hand on Tieln's chest. Light flowed through his hand into Tieln's body. Then the light wrapped around Tieln and pulled him in with it.

His eyes snapped open. He lay on a pallet in the barracks. The smell of venison stew lingered in the air, but he didn't hear any shouts from the yard or sounds of anyone moving around. Tieln pushed himself up.

Pain stabbed through his arm. He gasped and looked at the limb. Blood seeped through his sleeve, staining the cloth.

"Let me see," Chance ordered.

Tieln's head whipped around. He stared at the elf. "You… what… how…"

"Your arm, Tieln. Let me see how much of a chunk those wraiths took."

He shook his head. "No, what are *you* doing *here*? How did you get here? How did I get back here?"

"We haven't gone anywhere. We're inside your head—this is the landscape of your mind. I assume this must be someplace of significance to you." Chance pulled up Tieln's sleeve. "And these are wounds to your spirit, not your body."

"What… how?" Tieln looked at the jagged bite.

Chance held his gaze. "You sent your spirit out of your body. Even at the best of times, that's reckless and foolish for someone with no experience. Right now, with the chaos in the spirit realm, it's flat-out stupid. What the fuck were you trying to do?"

Warmth spread thought his arm, and the pain eased. Tieln tried to make sense of Chance's words. "I was... trying to speak. Mind-speak."

Chance's stern expression softened. "And you found out how to send your spirit out of your body instead."

"What was that place? What were those things?" He shuddered.

"Spirits driven mad by the corrupted magic unleashed in the war. You were in the spirit realm. Fortunately, I was able to catch hold of you before anything managed to take a larger chunk out of you." Chance frowned at the wound. "You'll feel some pain from it for a while, though. Wounds to the spirit act differently than wounds to the body."

Tieln looked around the barracks. Everything appeared exactly as he remembered it. "How are we... inside my mind? If I left my body, how did I return?"

"Some healers can enter another's mind. If they have hold of a spirit at the time, they can bring that spirit with them."

Tieln shifted uneasily. "What if the spirit they hold doesn't belong in the mind they're entering?"

Chance's expression made him regret the question. The elf answered in a low voice. "Then the healer is a sadist, and both the one whose mind they violate and the trapped spirit will suffer." He drew a slow breath and focused again on Tieln. "What were you trying to say to Lucian when this happened?"

I don't want to know what happened to Chance to put that look of fear and hate in his eyes. He took the change of subject gladly. "I was asking 'Can you hear me?'"

The question echoed through the barracks, but with it, lingering in the undertones, Tieln heard the angry cries of a young man he thought he'd put behind him. *Why wasn't I good enough? Why didn't you come back? Why did you abandon us?*

"Mind-speech is all but universal among elves, but most of us learn to use it when we are still children," Chance said. "As we mature, we learn to control it, but this magic, at its heart, is an act of exposing your spirit and your inner thoughts to others. You can't lie in mind-speech, and sometimes the truths that come out are those we'd rather not reveal."

Tieln said nothing for a long moment. "So, I can't even manage something that any child can do."

The words were harsher than he meant. Chance, however, responded, "Not on your first attempt, no. Unless you're planning to make that your only attempt."

Tieln shivered, pulling his injured arm from Chance's hold. "And how am I supposed to—"

"Right now, you and I are using mind-speech, Tieln. You want to use it, then *you* need to speak." Chance jabbed a finger to Tieln's chest. "Your spirit must be the one speaking, not your mouth."

I don't know how! He opened his mouth, but he heard the frustrated cry echo faintly in the air. And if he could hear it, he was sure Chance could as well.

"When you do find the way to do so, then you can start learning how to close your thoughts as well. We're fortunate to learn as children. Most children learn how to close their minds before they experience enough shit in this world to have truly painful echoes."

"Even you?"

Chance snorted in dark amusement. "I learned early. And the man I call father was very skilled in such things." His expression darkened. "Fortunately for me. He prepared me to stand against my actual father, who sided with Willow and Ayliad."

"Everything comes back to Ayliad," Tieln said softly. "Doesn't it?"

"Everything comes back to Willow," Chance said. "Ayliad is

the last living legacy of Willow's reign of terror over our clan." He stood. "And I am not going to talk any more about that here. You should wake up as soon as I leave."

Tieln pushed to his feet. "Wait, what do you mean—?"

Chance vanished. A heartbeat later, Tieln found himself on his back, small rocks digging uncomfortably into his back and legs. His head pulsed with pain, and his arm throbbed. He blinked his eyes open and tried to speak, but only managed an inarticulate mumble.

"Easy, easy." A hand touched his shoulder, then helped him sit. "It's all right, you're safe."

His eyes focused on Lucian, and he nodded. "I'll be okay." He coughed and winced.

"You scared me," Lucian told him. He squeezed Tieln's shoulder. *I just found you. I don't want to lose you now.*

"Not planning to try that again anytime soon," Tieln managed. "Was trying to…"

"Trying to make your magic work?" Lucian finished quietly.

Tieln nodded.

You'll find it. I know you will. Lucian gave him a small smile. *Next time, though, maybe warn us ahead of time?*

"I'll try."

Lucian helped him up. "Eat something, then sleep. Trust me, after that, you need it."

~

Tieln hadn't ached so much or felt so exhausted since his first week of training. He'd slept deeply despite the lingering images of ghostly forms with long, sharp teeth that he saw when he closed his eyes.

Lucian watched him with concern as they walked. "How are you doing?"

"I'm fine, sir." The answer came as reflexively as if a commanding officer had asked.

No, really, Tieln. How are you doing?

I feel like something tried to eat me. "Sore. And tired."

Lucian frowned. "What was the first thing you said?"

Tieln frowned back at him. "Sore?"

"No, before that."

"I… didn't say anything before that," Tieln said slowly.

"It was very quiet," Lucian told him. "But I'm sure you did. And since I don't read minds, if I heard your thought, it's because you projected it, at least a little."

Tieln blinked. "I didn't… I wasn't *trying* to." He paused. "Are there some elves who *can* read minds?"

"There are. It isn't a common magic, fortunately, and most of those who do have it aren't able to look very deep," Lucian told him.

"Most?" Tieln repeated warily.

"Most," Lucian agreed. "Those who can look deeper into the minds of others… well… their mental stability depends on what sort of guidance they had and how old they were when they focused on developing that power."

"And it's a rare magic, which means what, that only half the members of your family can do it?" Tieln asked.

Lucian grimaced. "Only one. And he left with my father and those of our clan who went to the stars."

Tieln blinked, then shook his head. *Elves make no damned sense to me.*

We make no damned sense to anyone, Tieln. It's not just you.

His head jerked up and he met Lucian's amber eyes. *What?*

It's quiet, but you are projecting your thoughts. Or some of your thoughts.

Tieln groaned and put his hand to his forehead. "So I *can't* do it when I'm trying, and can when I just want to be rude in the privacy of my own head?"

Lucian's mouth quirked in a smile. "If it helps, I didn't think that you were particularly rude."

Tieln just looked at him, then shook his head.

Lucian clapped a hand on his shoulder. "Yeah, I didn't figure." In a lower voice, he said, "Chances are good this is an after-effect of your trip into the spirit realm. Doing that may have weakened some of your internal barriers."

"But if I can't control it," Tieln began.

"You will," Lucian said firmly. "Or else you'll learn how to block it away again. Magic is in your blood, yes, but your elven heritage isn't your *only* heritage. You've lived as a human. You could continue to do so."

He shook his head. "I… don't think I can. I didn't really live as a human. I… lived as someone pretending to be a human." He didn't realize how true it was until the words left his mouth. "But I don't know if I can be an elf, either, or if I'll be… pretending again."

"While you're with us, you don't need to pretend to be anyone or anything else," Lucian said. "Even if you need some time to figure out what that means for you."

You say that, but we don't have time to wait.

If Lucian heard, he didn't answer.

Tieln jerked awake, swiping at whatever was crawling over him. Still pulling his mind from the fog of sleep, he rolled to his feet and looked around the camp, ready to stomp on whatever scorpion or vermin he'd felt.

He froze. In the faint light from the fire, he saw snakes. Hundreds of dark, sinuous forms slithering through their camp. He raised his booted foot to crush the nearest, but he couldn't find its head, only the long, unending body.

Then he saw the thorns.

Tieln jerked away as one of the dark vines began to wind around his ankle. *What's going on? Who's on watch?*

He looked to the edge of the camp. Someone slumped on a rock, vines curled up their legs and chest. Around Tieln, the others lay asleep as the vines advanced.

Is this real? Am I dreaming?

"Wake up!" His voice sounded unnaturally loud in the still night air.

Someone shifted with a confused mumble. Tieln stepped to them, grabbing a shoulder and shaking the other firmly. "Wake up!"

The other jerked and swung at him. Tieln sprang back. The knife they clutched nicked him, but the cut wasn't deep. He identified the sleeper as Cylin when she shook back her hair with a mumbled, "The fuck?"

"Wake up," Tieln repeated urgently. He moved to the next person and shook them.

Only a faint noise of protest answered him. Tieln hissed and pulled at the vines that slithered over them like a blanket. That drew a sound of pain, but not waking.

"It's late. Going back to sleep," Cylin muttered fuzzily.

"*Vines* are attacking the camp!" Tieln snapped. "I need help!"

Finally Cylin blinked blearily at their camp. Then she stiffened and shoved to her feet. "What in drifters' bones?"

Tieln drew a knife and slashed at vines. "Build up the fire." He thought the elf he was trying to wake was Quicksilver. As he severed more vines, the elf started to stir a little more.

Light flared as Cylin added kindling. Tieln heard her curse and looked over quickly. She was looking around the camp, far more awake and alert than she had been. The additional light showed Tieln that the black vines covered the ground and cocooned the other two sleeping elves, as well as whoever sat on watch. Thorns prickled the surfaces of the vines, and they left welts of blood when he peeled them off Quicksilver's arm.

Quicksilver shuddered and groaned, then swiped wildly at the air. The vines withdrew around him, leaving a tight outline of bare ground around the elf. Tieln waited a moment, but Quicksilver didn't rouse further, and the vines didn't assault him again.

"What is going on?" Cylin demanded. She cut a path to the next elf and began slashing through the vines.

"How in blight would I know?" Tieln retorted sharply. "I woke up to these things crawling over us."

Don't fight it. Come with me. Stay with me.

Tieln's head jerked up and he spun around. "Did you hear that, Cylin?"

"Hear what?"

"A woman's voice saying not to fight."

"Nope. But if it was a sultry voice that made your skin crawl, I'm gonna bet it was Ayliad." She ripped a vine loose. "Dammit, wake up, Lucian!" She shook the limp elf. For every vine she tore away, another took its place. "Crazy evil bitch! Ow!" She pulled a thorny tendril off her hand.

This isn't working. We're under attack, and I don't know how to fight this enemy. What can I do against something the elves can't stop?

Cylin slapped Lucian's pale face to no avail. "I don't know how to get them out of her hold, so if you've got ideas, I'm listening."

"My only idea is reckless and probably foolish," Tieln said.

"Magic? Damn—I can't help with that."

"Try to rouse Quicksilver and Eria," Tieln told her. He hoped, at least, that Ayliad had less interest in those two elves.

"Got it." Cylin stood. "Good luck."

He had no idea how to enter another person's mind, but

his instincts told him that the battle they faced was taking place in a realm beyond the physical. Lucian had heard his thoughts before; perhaps that could help him find a path. Tieln rested his hand on Lucian's forehead.

I'm here. I will help you however I can. Show me how to reach you.

He sensed a presence coiled around Lucian like a constrictor. He felt it take notice of him. A thick vine whipped around his arm. Thorns pierced deep into his flesh. Something reached into him and pulled hard. Tieln instinctively tried to pull back, but it was too strong. It dragged him into darkness.

Tieln staggered. Soft sand shifted under his feet. The warm, damp air smelled sweet with the perfume of flowers. He heard a rhythmic rush of water, like the sound of waves hitting a beach from the movies they had watched on holidays in his youth, when the enclave still had enough power to operate such devices. They had always been a welcome break from training. He looked to the left and saw where the sand met the sea, and beyond, an endless stretch of water.

Something tugged on his arm. A slender vine curled around his sleeve. Pink flowers with star-shaped white centers bloomed up and down it. The vine was stronger than it looked, insistently tugging on his arm, but at least it didn't have thorns.

Where am I? What is this vine? Why am I wearing my dress uniform?

He glanced down quickly and confirmed that he was, in fact, wearing the brown trousers and jade green coat of his enclave's dress uniform, the colors sharp and vivid as a photograph, unfaded by time or sun. On his left hip hung the ceremonial sword, and on his right, the less ceremonial and far more functional handgun.

The vine tugged again, and he allowed it to lead him. *I must find Lucian.*

The vine led him off the beach past a jungle of unfamiliar plants with broad leaves and fragrant flowers, to the bleached white bones of some unknown leviathan. Massive ribs jutted from the ground to claw at the sky. The vine released its hold and slithered to the bones.

He approached an elongated skull taller than a two-story house. Even the smallest of its fangs was longer than his arm. Vines draped across the skull and hung from the empty eyes like tears. Smothering stillness pressed down on Tieln. Hearing noises from within, he circled around to the open end.

Masses of black vines, like those that attacked the camp, carpeted the ground and crawled up the interior of the skull like smears of ash. Tieln stepped past the vines, and staggered as a wave of conflicting magics crashed over him. When his vision cleared, he saw Lucian, Chance, and a woman with long blond hair that hung to her knees. Black vines curled around her feet like fawning puppies.

Lucian stood against the side of the skull, arms and legs pinned spread-eagle. His eyes burned with rage as he thrashed against the vines that held him. He was gagged, and a vine hung loosely coiled around his neck. Chance was in the air, trying to get to Lucian, but several vines gripped his limbs.

The woman turned to face Tieln. She was all but nude, wearing only a filmy skirt and no top. Her smooth skin was tanned bronze, and her frame slender and muscular like a dancer. Her eyes were the same amber color as Lucian's, and they looked Tieln up and down lasciviously.

"Well, well, what have we here?" she purred, stepping toward him.

"No one of significance, ma'am." He shifted uncomfortably. She moved with an awareness of her body that drew his eyes to every curve. His trousers felt uncomfortably tight.

She tutted disapproval. "No need to be so disparaging of yourself. You're quite handsome for a human. There's no need to compare yourself to them." She gestured toward Lucian and Chance.

Tieln's gaze slid toward them. Ayliad seemed to be paying her brother and cousin no mind, and if he could keep her distracted, perhaps they could take advantage.

The plants hung still. Chance dove to Lucian. A vine lashed at him. He jerked to the side, narrowly avoiding it.

Tieln swallowed. "No, ma'am, I don't compare myself to them. That would be like judging a rowboat's usefulness by comparing it to an airplane. But I am no one of significance, and certainly not worthy of the attention of a lady such as yourself." He hoped that sounded like flattery, and she didn't question what "a lady such as yourself" actually meant.

Chance reached Lucian and began to free him from the restraints. Then the floor erupted with movement. Vines seized Chance's limbs and slammed him hard to the ground. Lucian strained against his bonds with a muffled sound of helpless anger. Chance's cry cut off into a choking gasp.

Ayliad didn't even turn around. "Poor, foolish Chance. You know I won't let you go. You and Lucian are mine." Her full red lips curled in a smile. "Now, pretty little human boy, you must be terribly warm in all that. Come, take off your coat and make yourself comfortable."

Lucian and Chance both struggled. The vines crept over them like taunts, mocking the elves. Cloth ripped as the plants began stripping their captives.

Tieln made himself look back at Ayliad. "I am… quite comfortable," he managed. "I, uh, prefer to stay in uniform."

"It does suit you very well. And a man in uniform does have a certain appeal." She stood so close, he smelled the flowers in her hair. "But those pants are definitely too tight right now. You should take them off."

The more he breathed her scent, the more he wanted to comply. When he didn't move, she reached down and unbuckled his belt.

He jerked back, stumbling three steps back. Her eyes narrowed in warning. The only response that Tieln could muster came from military protocols learned long, long ago. "Please, ma'am, it is inappropriate for a soldier to fraternize with a member of the nobility or the equivalent thereof, per Section 7, Clause 8, Paragraph 3 of the Doctrines of the Jadeheart Regiment."

She actually stopped, head cocked slightly as she made sense of his rushed babble. "Your superiors are not here, boy. I am."

He backed away another step. She followed. "I am afraid you are incorrect, ma'am. And even if you were not, I must maintain the honor of my regiment."

"Are you refusing me, *boy*?" she demanded, sultry voice growing colder and harder. "No man refuses me." She gestured toward Lucian and Chance. "*They* know what happens when someone tries to reject my invitation."

At any moment, plants might drag him down, pin him as they had Chance, so that Ayliad could have her way with him. But right now, it seemed she wanted to toy with him, to make him give in rather than claiming her prize by force. Tieln tried to play on that, delay her longer, though he had no idea if there was anyone to make use of that delay.

"Ma'am, under no circumstances would I refuse your wishes, or deny you that which you seek from me. But I must maintain my post, and no matter what my desires, while I am on duty I cannot engage in such acts."

Her eyes remained dangerously narrow, but they also held a gleam of wicked mischief. "Is that so? I suppose, if I must, I can exercise a little patience. But only under one condition."

Tieln shifted uneasily. "Ma'am?"

She stepped close, invading his space once more. One hand grasped his coat, holding him close. Her other hand slipped into his pants and down to his groin. Tieln's breath caught as her fingers explored and massaged. She smiled, then her lips brushed his.

"I'm quite looking forward to you being off duty, my pretty little soldier boy."

He swallowed hard. "I…" If he had to breathe her scent much longer, he wouldn't have any resolve left. "Yes… ma'am."

She gave him a caress, then withdrew her hand and stepped back. Tieln looked past her to Lucian and Chance, hoping desperately that they had found a way to break free. The vines had stripped the clothes from both elves. They'd also pulled Chance upright against the wall beside Lucian. Tieln couldn't be sure if he was gagged, or if the vine had actually slithered into his mouth and down his throat. Ayliad turned away from Tieln and walked back to her captives.

I can't let her do this! I have to stop her, but I don't have magic that can fight this.

His right hand fell automatically to his hip, then closed around the grip of the gun he'd forgotten rested there. There was nothing honorable about shooting a naked woman in the back, but honor, as Captain Lonze used to say, was worth less than shit if it meant you lost. He drew and fired.

Something jerked his arm, throwing off his aim, but not enough that he missed completely. Ayliad screamed in pain and fury, bright red blood flowing from her shoulder. She whirled on him with murder in her eyes.

The world shook violently. Tieln tumbled to the ground, clinging to his gun. Black vines swarmed toward him, but beyond them, he saw Lucian break free and raise his hand. The vines stopped just short of Tieln, twisting and writhing.

Ayliad pushed to her feet, her beautiful face twisted with

anger. "You can't stop me! Lucian is *mine!*"

"You will not touch him. We will not let you take him or Chance." The voice wasn't quite Lucian, but that of the Guardian. "Nor will we allow you near that one." He gestured at Tieln.

Ayliad's lips curled back in a snarl. "You're weak. You won't win."

The Guardian raised his hand again. Power radiated from him, and the black vines around him crumbled to dust. "Challenge me now, then."

She hissed a curse, pressed a hand to her bleeding shoulder, and vanished.

Tieln pushed unsteadily to his feet and staggered several steps. The Guardian spun to Chance, pulling away vines by magic and bare hands alike. Chance crumpled to the ground, coughing and gagging, then he vomited.

Tieln hurried to them. "Are you hurt? Did she…?"

Chance shook his head, still fighting for breath. "She didn't… this time." He grabbed Tieln's arm and used it to pull himself to his feet. His gaze moved to the Guardian. "Return Lucian."

"The Fruit's mindscape crumbles, and her corruption withdraws. Lucian does not need us to remain in control." The Guardian's tone implied it was agreeing with Chance.

"How do we leave here?" Tieln asked.

"That will happen on its own," Chance told him. "Then we'll wake up and figure out how the fuck we ended up here in the first place."

"I assumed that happened because of the black thorn vines that invaded our camp," Tieln said, confused.

"The *what?*" Chance and Lucian said in unison.

Tieln had just enough time to realize that they didn't actually know what had occurred in the camp. Then the world shattered like glass, and he was falling.

"Tieln?"

"A minute," he mumbled, waving away whoever was speaking to him.

"Guess that means you're back, at least."

He blinked away grit and opened his eyes. Cylin crouched over him, worried. When he focused on her, she relaxed. "A vine grabbed you," she said. "Wasn't sure if that's what you meant to do, so I didn't cut it. You all right?"

Tieln groaned. "Not quite my plan, but it got me where I needed to be. The others awake?"

"Just Quicksilver. He was conscious enough to keep the vines from attacking me, but that's it. He's out again. The vines all crumbled a minute ago." Cylin offered him a hand up, and he accepted her help.

Plant debris littered the camp, dark and dry. Quicksilver lay curled by the fire, his breathing slow and deep. Cylin had moved Eria over there as well. Chance's daughter stirred and murmured groggily.

Almost in unison, Lucian and Chance jerked awake. Chance swiped at the remains of the vines hanging over him, shuddering. Lucian helped him up, then moved to the fire, scanning the ground for any movement from the desiccated plants.

"Are you all right, Cylin? Tieln?"

"Creeped out but not hurt," Cylin answered. "What about you? We tried to get you and Chance loose, but the plants weren't nearly as willing to let you go as they were Quicksilver and Eria."

"Been better," Lucian told her. He looked to Tieln. "How are you?"

"Unsettled," Tieln answered. "That was… difficult." The word was completely inadequate to encompass his experience.

Lucian's expression was serious. "Thank you, Tieln. Without you, things would have gone much worse."

Chance crouched beside his daughter and tried to rouse her. His gaze remained on her, but he said, "Yes, they would have. You managed to be better prepared than either of us." His hands clenched. "I should have been prepared for her to attack us."

"I woke before the vines caught me," Tieln said. "That gave me the opportunity to realize we were under attack. I was able to free Cylin, but after that, they had grown too quickly."

"We got Quick loose too, but I had to work hard to wake him at all," Cylin added. "We tried to get you out, Lucian, but had no luck."

"Chance and I were her targets," Lucian said. "The rest of you were incidental."

Tieln shuddered. He could still feel the touch of Ayliad's hands on him. The arousal that her touch had woken disturbed him at least as much as everything else. "Is that what she is like?"

"That is what she's like if you don't refuse her," Chance said. "You're fortunate that she accepted your answer."

"I have a little experience in handling... Persons in Authority who don't like being told no." Tieln's mouth twitched in a small, wry smile that faded quickly.

"It served you well." Lucian picked up Quicksilver, who mumbled groggy protests. "How's Eria?"

"She'll be all right, but whatever drug the plants injected in her is not responding to healing." Chance lifted her. "Let's go."

"Go? Go where? It's the middle of the night!" Cylin protested.

Lucian looked at her. "I'm not getting any more sleep. Certainly not here. Are you?"

She grimaced and collected their gear. "Just remember I don't see in the dark."

Tieln helped her with the gear and snuffed the fire. "How do we protect our camp from her attacks?"

Chance used magic to carry his share of the gear, and kept hold of Eria. He looked to Lucian. "Normally, we would receive some warning of an attack by plants. Why didn't the Guardian react sooner?"

Lucian slung bags over his shoulder and carried Quicksilver. "Let's go."

Chance's eyes narrowed. "Lucian."

Tieln thought Lucian was going to leave without answering, but finally he said, "I don't know."

Chance stiffened. "What do you mean, you don't know? Ayliad has never been powerful enough to actually suppress the Guardian. How could she do so now?"

"I don't know." Lucian's voice was tight. "The Guardian won't answer me."

"It won't answer you now, or it has not been speaking to you?" Tieln asked. He thought back to his own conversation with the Guardian.

Lucian turned and gave him a long look. "This may surprise you, Tieln, but I don't tend to have conversations with the voices in my head unless they belong to other people."

Tieln's brow furrowed in confusion. "What?"

Lucian shook his head. "Never mind. The short answer is that I don't usually talk to the Guardian, and it tends to communicate to me through other means. Normally, if it hasn't communicated with me, that's because there's nothing that needs communicated." He started walking.

The others followed. Tieln frowned as he guided Cylin. The Guardian had spoken to him shortly after they left Shiranak's lands. He wasn't certain whether he should mention that dream or not.

Before he made up his mind, Chance said, "So you don't know for sure how long the Guardian has been unresponsive.

Did Aiyliad do anything during the confrontation at Yazah's laboratory? Or did Dash?"

"You said that some drug in the plants isn't responding to your magic," Cylin interrupted. "Maybe it's affecting the Guardian too."

"I don't know," Lucian said slowly. "If that were the case, I don't know that the Guardian would have been able to react when Ayliad was distracted."

"It didn't react when Ayliad was distracted," Chance said. "It reacted after Tieln shot her." He looked back at Tieln. "And I am still wondering how it is that actually worked."

"I… had a gun. I fired it. Is there a reason that shouldn't have worked?" Tieln asked.

"We were inside a mindscape of Ayliad's creation. She was in control of it. Despite that, you managed, somehow, to bring in and use a weapon that could hurt her."

"You shot her? Nice! Wish I could have seen that," Cylin said.

Tieln made a helpless gesture. "I don't know how magic and mindscapes work. I know how guns work. I think she didn't view me as a threat, and didn't think to guard against the weapons I might have."

Chance looked at Lucian, then back to Tieln. "Perhaps. Our fights with her are more likely to involve magic than physical weapons."

Conversation trailed off. Tieln thought back over the encounter, uncomfortable though it was. He couldn't count on the same tactic working a second time, nor on Ayliad dismissing him as harmless again. *I need to understand her. How she thinks. What she's capable of.*

He helped Cylin over a large rock. The night was quiet, lit by a sliver of the first moon and the half-full second and third. Stars glittered above them. Everything felt vivid and real… yet, so had the mindscape.

"How do you know when you're in a vision of someone else's making, and not in the real world?" he asked of no one in particular, breaking the silence.

Cylin yawned. "Is it not obvious?"

"It wasn't to me. Everything felt real—smell, touch, all of it. And it didn't even seem odd that I was in an entirely different location." Tieln looked to Lucian, then Chance, hoping for a simple, straightforward answer that pointed out the clues he'd missed.

Lucian's gaze remained focused ahead. His voice was quiet. "Sometimes, you can't tell the difference. Especially not if the vision was crafted by someone skilled who intends to trap you."

"Then how do you get out?" Tieln asked, a chill crawling down his spine.

"If you're trapped, then either you have to make it through the situation with some part of your spirit and sanity intact, or someone else pulls you out," Chance said. "Even recognizing that it's not real isn't enough to free you. Though it may help you on the 'keep your sanity intact' aspect."

Cylin shivered. "Don't like the sound of that."

"You shouldn't. Especially if you are dealing with anyone close to Willow's skill." Chance was deadly serious. "I don't know how much she taught Ayliad. I can only hope it wasn't a lot."

"They can be… more realistic than that skeleton?" Tieln asked.

"That was only a setting," Chance told him. "Willow crafted entire storylines, with enough left undefined that her victim's mind could fill in details she might not know, for added authenticity. You could feel like years passed, living in her vision of the world." He shuddered.

"Enough talk about it." Lucian's tone brooked no argument. Tieln's gaze moved to him, and he read tension in Lucian's tight voice and stiff posture.

I hope I never experience anything that terrifies me as much as Willow's mental traps terrify Lucian.

They stopped when Cylin couldn't keep to her feet any longer. Tieln was sure he wouldn't be able to sleep, but once he finally sat down, his head drooped and his eyes kept drifting shut.

Get some sleep, Tieln, Lucian told him. *Chance and I will keep watch.*

That should be my job. I should be guarding our camp.

You're not some hired mercenary tasked with protecting us. You're one of us. Part of the clan. Part of the family.

His eyes sank shut. *Ah, rot, I'm projecting again, aren't I?*

Lucian moved to his side and laid a hand on his shoulder. *You're exhausted. Rest now. Worry about the rest later.*

Two days later, they came to a small fortified outpost. Wary, but in need of supplies, the group approached. Tieln kept a hand near his gun as they neared the closed gate. He was certain they'd been seen and were under surveillance, but no one challenged them.

Lucian banged a fist on the thick wooden gate. After a moment, it opened partially, and a male voice said, "A rare day, when strangers come knocking on our door."

The speaker stepped into view. He was tall, with short brown hair and features that might have been cast from a mold —a little too still, a little too perfect. Tieln gripped his gun. He'd seen that face before, the same too perfect features on other bodies.

Bone men.

Chance shot a sharp glance to Tieln. He hadn't been trying to project the thought, but he hadn't exactly been trying not to, either.

You're sure? Chance asked.

He has the same face. They all have the same face, and it always looks... not quite right.

When none of them spoke, the bone man continued. "What brings such esteemed visitors to our door?"

Lucian's jaw tightened. "Nothing. We don't need anything from *you*."

The man opened the gate further, smiling. "We would be honored to offer you provision."

Lucian made no move to enter. He folded his arms, gaze not leaving the man. "Who are you?"

The man dipped a bow. "My name is Reth. Please come in to our humble home."

"Not a chance." Lucian didn't break eye contact with Reth. *Tieln's right. He has the same look as the bone men at Springvale.*

Didn't you see them, Chance? Tieln tried to focus the thought to Chance alone.

I was drugged most of the time. What I thought I saw was... not this. Chance's hand rose to rub the back of his neck.

Reth flashed them all a smile that could have been seen half a mile away. "You have no need for concern. We will gladly give you the supplies you need, so you may continue on your way."

As Lucian grew more tense, his voice grew more curt. "No. We're leaving."

"Our lady will know of your passing whether you accept the gifts she bid us give you or not," Reth said.

Lucian's hands clenched. "I want nothing from you."

A bag flew over the wall and landed with a heavy thump on the ground beside Lucian. He sidestepped away from it. Reth still smiled. "She wants you to reach her palace whole and in good health."

The bag hurtled into Reth, knocking him back inside. The gate slammed shut. "I said no," Lucian growled.

Tieln waited, gun drawn, for any retaliation from within the outpost. None came, not even taunts. When Lucian stormed away, Tieln followed, keeping an eye on their rear and his senses alert for ambush.

Cylin caught up with Lucian. "What in drifters' bones just happened?"

"Those were bone men," Lucian said, voice tight with anger.

"Bone men?!" She cast a look back. "And we're walking away?"

"We don't know how many they have," Tieln said. "Or what defenses."

"Ayliad expected me to attack them," Lucian said. "She likely left something very unpleasant for us to find there."

Tieln shivered. "What is it the bone men do that Ayliad wants? They experiment on people, living and dead. They steal children. They take flesh as currency, but no one understands *why*. What do they do that benefits her?"

"You can go back and ask them, if you want," Lucian said darkly.

"It's a good question, though," Quicksilver cut in. "She wouldn't use them if they didn't provide something she wants or needs."

Cylin frowned. "My parents used to tell stories about how in the war, people used weapons that didn't kill right away, but released some sort of poison designed to cause specific effects."

Tieln nodded. "Biological and chemical weapons. I learned about some of the more common ones and how to recognize their effects."

"Well, back when the vines attacked us, you said that the poison in the vines didn't respond to your magic, right Chance?" Cylin continued.

"Yes."

"And you didn't think Ayliad was powerful enough to do that with magic. But what if the bone men can make something that would do that for her?"

"A biological weapon tailored to resist magic?" Eria shivered. "That's horrifying."

"It could even be tailored more precisely," Tieln said, "if they have the means. It could be meant to affect only you—certain genetic keys. Perhaps one to target the Guardian specifically?"

"Regardless of what else bone men do, if they could make something like *that*, it would be no wonder Ayliad would use them," Quicksilver said.

Lucian and Chance both listened to the conversation closely, but neither spoke in a way Tieln could hear.

When they stopped for the night, Lucian used magic to create a cave for their shelter. The narrow entrance could easily pass for a natural crack, and they obscured their tracks. The group ate a small, cold dinner, set watches, and retired for the night.

Soft movement woke Tieln. His eyes scanned the darkness for vines, but everything looked as it should. The only movement was someone slipping out the cave entrance. Tieln slowly slid out of his bedroll, taking a count of his companions. Lucian was absent. He could have stepped outside to relieve himself, or to keep watch, but Tieln was uneasy. He wondered whether he was awake, or if this was another dream.

Cautious, he edged outside. He didn't see anyone at first, until the light of the moons briefly caught a figure flying back in the direction they'd come from.

"Lucian?" Tieln whispered. "What are you doing?" *Rot, I should follow him, but someone needs to keep watch, too.*

A deep purr rumbled from the darkness. Tieln spun, grabbing his gun. On a small ledge just above the cave entrance, a massive white panther gazed down at him. It raised one huge paw and began grooming.

A voice as coarse and rumbling as the purr spoke. *I keep watch. Lucian asked.* The cat paused in grooming and looked in the direction Lucian went. *You should follow.*

The panther... could use mind-speech. "Who... what are you?"

Snow. Yazah-brother. Friend. Follow Lucian. The panther yawned, showing an impressive mouth of sharp teeth. *I guard.*

Tieln gazed at the panther, then nodded. "Thank you. Do you know where Lucian is going?"

Didn't say, but I think, the house of bones.

Tieln nodded, checked his gun, and set in pursuit of Lucian.

Lucian was well out of sight. Tieln instead focused on the sense of where Lucian was compared to him, and followed it. Briefly, he considered returning to the camp to wake the others, but he suspected that if they knew of Lucian's departure, they would try to stop him. Tieln didn't want to stop Lucian, especially if he intended to wipe out the bone men outpost. Tieln did, however want, even need, to know what Lucian was doing and what he would find.

He alternated between a walk and a jog. Lucian, not hampered by terrain or other considerations, continued to extend the distance between them. After several hours, though, Lucian slowed, his movements becoming concentrated in a confined area. Tieln pushed himself harder. At a steady jog, he reached the outpost less than an hour later.

The wooden gate hung open, the doors askew on their hinges. Tieln drew his gun and cautiously entered. Lucian was close.

The smell of blood hung in the air. Two figures slumped against the stone wall just inside the gate. A quick check confirmed that both were dead, their skulls cracked from impacts with the wall. Another man sprawled on the ground, a metal spike driven through his back.

The outpost consisted of half a dozen shacks and one central stone building. Tieln checked each shack and found bodies within. Several corpses held handguns, and one clutched a long knife. Blood streaked the blade. Tieln gathered what ammunition he could find, knowing that if it didn't work for his weapon, he could find plenty who would trade for it. The knife worried him—Lucian had already acknowledged that he had no healing magic.

The door of the main building stood open, inviting him to enter. Tieln warily accepted, stomach sinking at the thought that he might be entering another bone men laboratory. He entered a large, open room with several long tables. The back of the room held a kitchen area. Tieln found more bodies, men killed by wooden spikes and hurled objects. He also found spots of blood on the floor around the entrance, where no bodies lay. He guessed the freshest corpse to be less than five minutes dead.

How many manned this post? The shacks aren't meant to house more than a couple people apiece, and I've already seen more corpses than would comfortably live in them. Did Lucian enter a trap?

His sense of Lucian's presence told him the elf was above him. Tieln climbed the stairs, but paused before he stepped out of the stairway, listening.

He heard heavy breathing, then Lucian's voice. "I hear you. Hiding won't save you."

"Sir, it's Tieln." He stepped into view cautiously, ready to spring aside if spikes flew at him.

Lucian stood alone in the middle of the room, narrowed eyes watching the stairway. Only three bodies sprawled on the floor. Behind Lucian stood the bone men's laboratory, mostly empty except for some long tables and tall metal cabinets. A metal box stood on one of the tables, and it appeared that Lucian had been about to examine it when Tieln arrived.

"What are you doing here?" Lucian demanded.

"Following you, sir." Tieln didn't blink. "I would have said watching your back, but it seems I was too late for that." He looked pointedly at the bloodstain on Lucian's side.

Lucian's jaw tightened. "I'll be fine."

"Unless the blade was poisoned."

"They weren't trying to kill me."

"Only disable you," Tieln said flatly. "Or poison you with something that resists magic and cannot be removed by healing." He walked past Lucian to the box on the table. "Is this what you came here for?"

"I came here to kill the bone men," Lucian said.

Tieln picked up the box. If it was what Ayliad wanted Lucian to find, he was certain the contents were a trap of some sort. It was about the size of a military ammunition box, with a hinged lid. The latch slid open when he pushed it.

Lucian tensed as if he meant to snatch the box out of Tieln's hands. Tieln swung the lid up and pulled aside the cloth that padded the contents.

A sealed glass jar and an envelope lay within. Wary, Tieln picked up the envelope first. Flowing script read "For my dear brother."

Tieln looked to Lucian. "Do you want to know what she left? Because I'm very willing to take this box and burn everything in it, sight unseen."

Lucian hesitated. "What does the message say?"

"The envelope is addressed to 'my dear brother'," Tieln told him.

He saw the struggle in Lucian's eyes. "Open it. What does it say?"

This is a bad idea.

"Yes, it is, and I know it is," Lucian said, voice tight. "Just read the damned message."

Tieln broke the wax seal on the envelope and pulled out the sheet of paper it held. "I knew you couldn't stay away, Lucian. After all the work you put in to getting here, you deserve a reward. I'm giving you back something of Chance's. Of course, he's a skilled enough healer that you probably didn't even know he'd lost it, did you? And I know he wouldn't have told you if he had a choice. Do tell him we've made good use of everything my bone men extracted. It gave them all they needed to personalize a few special surprises."

A sick, sinking sensation twisted in Tieln's gut. He glanced at the jar still within the box and tried to locate Chance. He sensed the distant presence of the elf he desperately hoped was still sleeping. He also sensed a dimmer, fainter sense of Chance from the jar.

"What else is in there?" Lucian's voice hissed between his clenched teeth.

"A jar." Tieln didn't move to pick it up.

"What is inside it?"

Tieln closed the lid on the box and slid the latch shut. "You don't actually want to know, and neither do I."

The sides of the metal box peeled away like paper. The glass jar sat exposed, a container full of a faintly yellowish liquid, presumably some type of preservative to prevent the severed finger floating within from decaying. Tieln swallowed back bile.

Lucian stared at the jar, knuckles white as his hands clenched in fists. "She's lying," he hissed through clenched teeth. "There's no proof."

Tieln had no intention of volunteering that he could tell the finger belonged to Chance. "Are we done here?"

Lucian looked at him. For a moment, Tieln was afraid he'd

projected his thoughts, but Lucian only jerked his head in a nod of agreement. "We're done."

Tieln folded the letter and tucked it into his belt pouch. He left the jar on the table. "You're still bleeding."

"I'll manage."

"That's beside the point. Chance *will* notice a large blood-stain on your shirt that wasn't there when you went to bed. Let me see how bad it is."

Lucian scowled at him, but gingerly peeled the bloody cloth away from the wound. Tieln took the waterskin from his belt and wet a handkerchief to clean the gash. "A slash rather than a stab—that's good. Not too deep. It shouldn't need any stitch-es." He checked his belt pouches until he found a roll of bandages.

Lucian watched him. "Do you normally carry an apothe-cary with you?"

Tieln raised an eyebrow. "Needle, thread, and bandages is hardly excessive, sir. Especially when one doesn't possess healing magic." He folded one bandage and pressed it to the wound. "Hold this here."

Lucian complied. Tieln wound another bandage around Lucian's abdomen to hold it in place. Lucian pulled his shirt back down and headed down the stairs. Tieln followed. As he neared the bottom of the stairs, he heard glass shatter upstairs. His head jerked toward the sound.

"That was me," Lucian said. He didn't look back. "What-ever she meant about 'making good use' of what was in that jar, no one *else* will do so."

Once they left the hall, Lucian's magic lifted them both off the ground. Tieln reflexively tensed when his feet found nothing beneath them. To distract himself, he asked, "Will you tell Chance what you found?"

"Absolutely not," Lucian said.

Tieln looked to the sky. Strange how it didn't seem any

closer when they were flying, even when the ground lay far below. "Even flying, we won't be back to the camp before the others wake."

"I expect it will be a surprise to approximately zero percent of our clan that I went back. The others are more likely to be surprised that you left than that I did." Lucian considered him. "Why didn't you wake anyone else when you left?"

"I assumed they would attempt to stop you," Tieln said. The anger he'd seen in Lucian while they were inside the outpost seemed to have dissipated. "If you had wanted them to come with you, you'd have woken them yourself. I thought that, as a soldier, I could be more help to you in a fight than…" He paused, considering how to frame the thought. "Civilians."

That startled a laugh from Lucian. "Civilians? Well, Quick, Eria, and Cylin might be considered civilians, but never assume that Chance is. If I were to put it in military terms, I suppose that I'd be classified as 'special ops.' Chance would be the intelligence department, in all its 'we were never there and had nothing to do with the mysterious death of that dictator' implications."

"I see." Tieln considered. "But he would still have tried to stop you from going back to the bone men."

"Either that or he would have insisted on going with me." Lucian's eyes narrowed. "Ayliad wrote her letter with the hope that he would be there to hear it in the moment."

Another reason to believe she was telling the truth. Tieln shivered. The bone men who'd abducted Chance and Tieln's wards from Springvale had held them for no more than half a day, but he didn't want to consider what terrors and tortures those hours had contained. He hoped that the children had been spared that.

The darkness of night had begun to recede when Lucian set down beside a stream. He shucked his shirt and washed it until he got most of the blood out.

Tieln walked up the stream bank a little ways and knelt to investigate the small plants that grew between the rocks. Growing up, he'd always seen plants, both in the gardens and in the wilds. He'd never realized how fortunate they were to have clean land until after he left and discovered how rare plants were to find outside of carefully cultivated areas.

Lucian found him. "Ready?"

"Yes." Tieln stood. To distract himself from the bone men and their tortures, he asked, "Lucian, when you brought my mother to the enclave, did you clean the ground there, like in your forest?"

"I… don't know." They rose off the ground. "I might have done some there, but I suspect it didn't need much help. I wouldn't have taken her to somewhere that wasn't safe. The Guardian is extremely attuned to corruption in the ground. It would have known if that ground was poisoned." Lucian shrugged. "Of course, you might have helped it yourself. That magic is in your blood."

Tieln shook his head. "The marks on my arm didn't appear until much later."

"You could still have plant magic that's not tied to the Tree. Or the Tree could still have been at work in a very subdued state to provide a healthy environment for a young 'sapling' to grow up."

Tieln sighed. "Every time I think I understand elf magic, something complicates it more."

The sun had crept several fingers over the horizon by the time they reached the cave. Chance sat at the entrance, waiting for them. Snow lay curled against his side. The panther opened one eye and rumbled a purr of greeting. Chance stiffly rose, looking from Lucian to Tieln, then back to Lucian.

"Well, at least you had enough sense not to go alone," he said by way of greeting. "They're dead?"

"They're dead," Lucian said.

"What did she leave?"

"A taunt." Lucian stepped toward the mouth of the cave. "And no, I didn't bring it with me."

Chance stepped aside to let him enter. When Tieln followed, though, Chance stopped him. *What did he find?*

"Nothing I want to describe," Tieln answered in a low voice.

Tell me.

Tieln was certain Lucian didn't want him discussing this with Chance, but he was more afraid that not doing so would leave Chance without vital information he needed to defend himself. "A letter that implied some tortures the bone men might have inflicted while they held you prisoner."

Chance stiffened. He spoke aloud, very softly. "What did she say they did to me? I was drugged, and I can't be sure which events were real and which were hallucinations she inflicted on me."

Tieln glanced down to Chance's hands. Both appeared intact, five digits apiece with no indication that any had been amputated.

His gaze wasn't subtle enough. Chance followed it, then paled. He folded his arms across his chest, tucking his hands under either arm protectively. "Did she say why?"

"If what she wrote was true, her bone men severed your digit to extract something from it that they could use to craft what I presume would be a weapon or means of attacking that will target you specifically."

Chance shivered. Without another word, he walked into the cave. Tieln followed, realizing their conversation had taken barely long enough for Lucian to set a kettle of water to heat. Cylin, Eria, and Quicksilver were all awake and up, but as Lucian had said, none of them acted surprised to find Lucian returning from an unannounced nighttime excursion.

Eria came to Tieln's side and rested a hand on his arm.

The aching weariness he'd begun to feel from an active night and shortened sleep lifted. She smiled at him. *Thanks for going with Lucian. I'm glad he wasn't alone.*

He nodded. *What did you do?*

Muscle fatigue and general tiredness respond to healing magic. It doesn't work as well for mental exhaustion, and shouldn't be applied as a long-term way of avoiding sleep, but it's a great way to stave off the effects of a long night.

"Thank you," he murmured.

Eria smiled. "Just try not to be out too many nights in a row." She handed him a strip of jerky.

Tieln noticed that neither Chance nor Eria offered to heal Lucian's weariness, nor did Lucian ask for anyone to do so.

They left camp only a little later than usual. Their trek was mostly quiet. Tieln thought on the problem that Ayliad posed, and the unknown threats she held in reserve for them. Somehow, during the course of the day, he found himself at the head of the line.

"Um, when did I take the lead?" he asked, confused.

"About the time you started turning west when everyone else was going straight," Cylin said. "You seemed pretty focused."

"You… could have just pulled me back in the right direction," he said.

"I would have, except that Quick and I figured out you *were* going the right direction, according to the pull of the Tree," Lucian said. "But you picked up the change before either of us."

Tieln shifted uneasily. "I think I might have unintentionally focused on finding Ayliad. I can stop."

"You can, but focusing on finding her might get us where we need to be faster," Quicksilver said. "On the other hand, I completely understand not wanting to focus that much attention on her, so, it's your call."

"Can you tell how far away we are?" Chance interrupted.

"A little more than a day. Less than two," Tieln told him.

Chance drew a deep breath and nodded slowly. "All right. We'd better assume that she knows we're close."

"So watch for more vines tonight?" Cylin asked.

"Depends what sort of entrance she wants to make," Lucian said. "But… yeah. Watch for vines." He looked to Chance. "Be careful."

"You're one to talk," Chance muttered. "She wants you at least as much as she wants me."

Tieln looked between the two elves, and realized what neither of them wanted to say. *Ayliad may want them equally, but she also knows that the best way to get at one of them is to get her claws into the other. And all of us know it.*

At nightfall, Lucian made another cave, and they set a subdued camp. Tieln sat gazing into the fire, watching the bright flames flicker and dance. Letting none of his thoughts creep into projection, he let them chase a thousand paths. They all came together in one conclusion.

This is my family. This is where I belong. And I can't allow Ayliad to take either Lucian or Chance. I can't allow her to destroy this family that I have finally found. And that means I must stop her, whatever it takes. Whatever it costs. He closed his eyes and tried to find that place within his mind where he and Chance had spoken. *Captain Ollen said that one thing a master of combat should fear is a true novice, because the novice is too ignorant to know what they cannot do, and the master cannot predict them.*

Tieln opened his eyes. He sat on his bunk in the barracks, wearing his dress uniform. He stood and walked to the equipment locker. All the gear and clothes within were fresh and clean, no patches or wear, no dull, faded colors. He shed the dress uniform and pulled on grayish tan combat fatigues. The pockets and pouches were already stocked with spare ammunition and quick rations. He belted a handgun and knife around his waist, then slung his rifle over his shoulder.

He walked outside. A tree grew in the middle of the training grounds. The trunk was slender, and it stood twelve feet tall, still a sapling. Broad green leaves unfolded to drink in the sunlight. Tieln walked to it and rested his hand on the smooth bark.

At his touch, the tree changed, drawing into itself until it had a humanoid form. It turned, and Tieln looked into a mirror of his face, cast in wood.

"We are… awake?" Its voice was the whisper of wind through leaves, faint and uncertain. It cocked its head at Tieln, forehead wrinkling in confusion. "Should we be awake? Should not saplings sleep until they are grown?"

"I don't know," Tieln said. "It's all new to me too, so I've got to make it up as I go. But whether we're supposed to be doing this or not, Ayliad is going to destroy my family if I don't stop her. If… we don't stop her. So, are you in?"

The sapling reached out and touched twiglike fingers to Tieln's face. "We… you and us, we must fight the Fruit, to protect the Guardian?" The tone still held a question, but was gaining confidence. "We must stop the Fruit. Yes. Because she will not expect us. Because we are young, and should not be awake, but we are, and we can reach the Guardian, because that is our progenitor." The sapling straightened to attention, and Tieln could all but feel it becoming more… him. The sapling smiled. "We are in. We will protect our family."

Tieln nodded. "Then let's get ready for war."

～

As they traveled through the next day, Tieln was vaguely aware of a second presence in the back of his mind, watching everything he saw with youthful interest and curiosity.

Even though he'd invited it, the sensation was still disconcerting.

No one commented on his distraction, but they had concerns of their own. Neither Lucian nor Chance slept well, to judge by the dark shadows around their eyes. Cylin projected restless energy that exacerbated everyone else's stress. Eria and Quicksilver seemed the best off, but even Quicksilver was subdued, and Tieln didn't hear a single quip from him. Snow started the morning with them, but before midday, the cat had somehow disappeared, and despite how he scanned the landscape, Tieln couldn't locate the massive white feline.

They avoided the few clusters of houses they saw, until they saw a structure on the horizon. It shimmered in the sun, painful to look at directly. Tieln shaded his eyes, trying to get a better view.

"What *is* that?" He squinted. "It's not a skyscraper, but it shines like it's made of glass."

"It doesn't radiate magic," Chance said, but his tone was wary.

"Probably Ayliad's palace," Cylin said. "Her pretty boys told me about it. Something about her finding some fancy building that survived the war and making it even more eye-catching. She's also got a school there for the girls and young women she takes from slave traders."

Tieln's eyebrows rose. "A school?"

Cylin shrugged. "Yeah. She claims to be big on helping other women."

"That actually makes a sort of sense," Eria admitted. "She's always believed that women should be in power over men. The idea of equality doesn't fit anywhere in her worldview."

"And that's where she is?" Lucian cut in, pointing to the structure.

Tieln nodded. "That's where I sense her presence."

"Then that's where we're going."

To Tieln's surprise, Lucian didn't set off toward the structure. Instead, he scanned the landscape, frowning. The flat land held little in the way of vegetation or other cover.

"Not many ways to make a stealthy approach," Chance observed.

Tieln looked to the structure, then turned to Cylin and Eria, brow furrowing in thought. "If we can't approach by stealth, what about misdirection instead?"

Cylin raised an eyebrow. "You got an idea?"

"The start of one, at least. If she proclaims her support for other women, some must hear and come to find sanctuary here," Tieln said. "What if Cylin and Eria took the lead and we simply... walked in? They could be coming as women seeking this place, and we would be coming as their... companions."

All the elves started to protest. Cylin's expression grew thoughtful. "You know, for just getting us inside, I think it could work."

"Ayliad would not believe it for a second," Lucian said.

"She doesn't have to, sir," Tieln said. "I'm not concerned with fooling her. I'm concerned with fooling her guards, who *don't* know us." At least he hoped Ayliad hadn't filled her palace with elven guards who could recognize Lucian and Chance.

"That's not a bad point," Quicksilver allowed. "We do have to get past whatever guards she has. And we can do some things to disguise ourselves."

"Yes, but... we're talking about my father, my uncle, and my cousins. I don't know if I can pretend that any of you are my... sex slaves." Eria shuddered.

"The more effort you put into trying to pretend, the less believable it is anyway," Cylin told her. "What you have to do is just walk in acting like *of course* everyone will accept your right to be there with your entourage. If you act like you have to convince them, people start to wonder what you're trying to convince them of and why. Just act like you're already in charge, and *lots* of people will assume you wouldn't act like that unless you really were in charge, and they'd better get in line before they find out what authority you hold over them."

"The movie star walk," Quicksilver said. "The one that says 'If you don't know who I am, you're not worth my time'."

Eria pursed her lips, but nodded slowly. "Dad, Uncle Lucian? What do you think?"

Neither spoke for several long moments. "I don't like the idea, but I don't have a better one," Chance said. "Lucian?"

"She'll know we're coming, as will Dash, whatever route we take. Tieln's plan gets us inside." Lucian glared at the structure.

The elves began discussing ways to disguise themselves to be less obvious. Tieln kept watch on the approach to the structure. As night fell, he noticed that traffic to it increased rather than decreased. At first he attributed it to late arrivals trying to get inside before full dark, but as the night progressed, the flow did not abate.

He didn't hear the rumble of trucks, but the lines of bobbing lights told of caravans of some sort. Bone men? Slave traders?

"We can send our roots near?" The voice whispered in his mind like a breeze through leaves.

Tieln started. Realizing the source of the voice after a moment, he shook his head. *"Lucian and Chance say that elves can sense magic. Ayliad would know if we did that."*

"The Fruit is more powerful than us," the Sapling said glumly.

"Yes, but she doesn't know about you, and she doesn't know much about me. That's our advantage." Tieln's gaze followed the line of lights as they gathered around the structure. Lights glimmered

within the structure as well, though he couldn't guess how many people dwelt within.

He sensed the Sapling's attention shift elsewhere. Tieln sat and continued watching the caravans.

Steps came up behind him. He glanced over his shoulder and nodded in greeting to Cylin. "How are the preparations going?"

"They're figuring it out. There was a lot of talk at first about whether or not to use magic to alter appearances, but they've mostly agreed that cosmetics and clothing is the better method for now. Weird to hear anyone talking about actually changing their bone structure like it's... a normal thing to do, though." Cylin sat beside him and peered into the darkness. "Anything happening out there?"

"Night caravans," Tieln told her. His dark vision had always been better than the average human. "Could be bone men reporting on the slaughter at the outpost, and who knows what else."

Cylin's jaw tightened and she rubbed her cheek. "Lucian rescued me when the guy who owned my debt decided he was going to carve off my ear to sell to the bone men. Left a good scar down my face. When I first met Ayliad and said something about it, she used magic to remove the scar. I don't think it was guilt or anything like that behind her doing that, but knowing now that she controls the bone men, I'd rather have the scar." She turned to Tieln. "Are you okay with going in there pretending to be a pet?"

"Are you okay with going in there pretending that I am?" he asked. "I've been a lot of places, and I've had to play a lot of roles. It was easy to get work as a guard, but there aren't a lot of good warlords out there. I've had to work for a few, male and female alike, who cared more about how pretty their guards were than how skilled they were. So I'll take pretending to be a pet over being expected to be one."

"I always thought guards had it easy—you got food and shelter, and got paid to scare the locals and harass drifters and scavengers," Cylin said.

Tieln laughed softly. "I didn't think drifters had it easy, but I did envy them sometimes. They, at least, had the option to pick up and walk away when things got bad. Deserters got hunted down and shot."

"Okay, that part sucks. Why did you keep doing it? Sounds like you had chances to leave, if you were a guard in more than one place."

"Because I could protect people. Sometimes, I was protecting them from the dangers outside, sometimes I was protecting them from those in authority. But if I didn't protect them, who would?"

She considered that. "I didn't see many guards who thought like you. Makes me like Forest Town even better."

"I didn't get to spend much time there, but the people I met seemed genuine," Tieln said. "I hope I can return and stay there for a while."

"Yeah." Though she didn't say it, Tieln was sure that like him, she'd silently added, "assuming we make it back."

Eventually, they both rejoined the elves, who apparently had no intentions of actually sleeping. Tieln let them keep the watch, and rested while he could.

In the morning, they set out for the structure. Quicksilver had dyed his silver hair a dull brown. Strategic application of ash and dirt gave Lucian the appearance of unshaven scruff. He couldn't do much to alter his short black hair other than let it hang loose rather than pull it into a tail, but overall, the effect made his face seem less narrow. Chance had taken the opposite tactic, emphasizing the dark shadows and hollow cheeks, giving himself an appearance more gaunt and haunted than usual. Tieln wondered, but didn't ask, how much was cosmetic, and how much genuine.

For himself, Tieln changed very little in his attire, focusing instead on stance and bearing. It was easy to fall back into acting like a guard, as if Cylin and Eria were the lords he was responsible for protecting. Inside his mind, the Sapling watched nervously.

As they got closer to Ayliad's palace, the Sapling whispered, *"The Fruit is not alone. Another Aspect is with her."*

"I know," Tieln said. *"Lucian's brother Dash is there too. Didn't you know that?"*

"Your thoughts have focused on the Fruit, not on the other Aspect. But the other is the corrupted Aspect, not the Fruit. Is that not the greater threat?"

He supposed the Sapling wouldn't understand the threat of rape and violation that Ayliad posed any more than Tieln understood the threat posed by a corrupted Dash. *"I don't know. But the elves believe Ayliad is the greater threat, and that Dash doesn't want to hurt them."*

"But the corrupted Aspect will do harm whether it wants to or not."

"It's a matter of intentions," Tieln explained. *"Dash will do harm because he can't help it, whether he wants to or not. Ayliad does not have to do harm; she does it because she wants to. She'll continue to do harm whether or not there's a reason for it, because it's what she wants."*

"We do not understand."

Tieln considered a moment. *"It's like… if a wildfire was burning, that would be dangerous, but not intentionally so. It burns because that's what it does. I might have water to put out the fire and stop it from spreading. But if Ayliad were there as well, she would try to push me into the fire. I can't stop both the fire and her at the same time—I have to stop her first, then I can stop the fire."*

"The Fruit would use the corrupted Aspect as a weapon against us?" the Sapling asked in horror.

"That seems likely," Tieln said.

The Sapling shuddered. *"We do not like the Fruit."*

"You're not the only one."

They reached the packed dirt road then, and Tieln focused on their surroundings more closely. They'd been walking for several hours, and someone had certainly noticed their approach by now. Now that they were closer, he saw that the palace was built from the shell of a pre-war structure, repurposed and reconstructed. Metal and glass gleamed in the sun. Most if it struck Tieln as decorative rather than functional, adding an imposing air of power to an otherwise serviceable large four-story building that might have once been a factory or warehouse. A tall wooden wall surrounded the palace, gates closed.

As they approached the gates, one opened, and a pair of women stepped out. Both wore swords and full sets of leather armor. They studied the party, frowning slightly. Tieln automatically adopted a blank expression and positioned himself to protect Eria and Cylin as necessary. Cylin didn't hesitate, striding to the women as if she had every right to be there.

The guards stopped her, but didn't adopt aggressive stances. The taller woman said, "None of the caravans mentioned any late arrivals planning to join them here. What brings you to the House of Morning Glory?"

"Ayliad invited me," Cylin said.

Both women stood straighter. "The Lady invited you personally?"

Cylin nodded. "She spoke to me in a little town on the edge of Shiranak's lands." She gestured in the general direction they'd come from. "But I didn't want to come without my sister." She indicated Eria, who nodded.

Though the elf and the human bore not even a trace of familial resemblance, the guards seemed to accept the explanation. They looked to the men, and when Cylin didn't offer any explanation, the shorter woman asked, "And your other companions?"

Cylin blinked. "Aren't we allowed to bring them? I thought that was what I understood from the Lady."

The guards relaxed further. "Of course, so long as they are with you." They opened one of the gates. "Enter the House of Morning Glory."

Tieln stepped through first, cast an assessing look around, and nodded to Cylin, stepping aside to let her pass. Quicksilver, Lucian, and Chance followed, then Eria, as if ushering them inside.

The area between the wall and the palace was crowded with wagons, either built from salvage or the shells of motor vehicles converted to be drawn by draft animals. The smell of fresh manure drew Tieln's notice to a pen of oxen and horses jostling each other to reach the food and water troughs. Around the wagons, the traders bartered with each other. A good half wore full-length robes, the hoods raised. He suspected those were the bone men.

"It's very busy," Eria said.

The taller guard nodded. "The caravans arrived last night, but we don't usually get all of them at once. They'll be leaving tonight, once they've finished trading stock amongst themselves. Our Lady already made her purchases."

Catching a view inside one of the wagons, Tieln saw several thin young men seated on narrow benches, their ankles shackled to the floor. *Slavers.*

The Sapling stirred restlessly, sensing his anger. *"They are willful poison, like the Fruit? We destroy them?"*

"They are, but we must deal with Ayliad first. Destroying the slavers now will alert her to our presence."

"Too many rules," the Sapling complained, but didn't press the matter.

"I'll send for someone to take you to the Lady," the taller guard said, scanning the crowd as she led them toward the palace.

A young man, sixteen or seventeen years old, stood against the side of the palace, watching the caravans with the gaze of one more than a little worried that someone might rush out and drag him into one of the wagons. He was bare-chested with a fit physique and handsome features. A gold collar ringed his neck, and gold armbands adorned both his arms. He glanced toward them, then his gaze found Cylin and his expression brightened.

Abandoning his watch of the caravans, he scrambled over to them. "Miss Cylin! You're here!"

"You know her, Balin?" their guard asked.

The young man nodded quickly. "Yes. From the Lady's last trip. Miss Cylin spent an evening with us."

"Did she? Good. Show her and her sister, with their companions, to the Lady." Her mission accomplished, the guard returned to her post.

Balin's voice dropped low. "Have you come to see the Lady?"

"Eh, sort of," Cylin told him. "You want to show us inside? You and the rest of the guys might be able to help us out a bit."

Balin looked to the rest of them, uncertain, but nodded. "Okay." He motioned for them to follow him.

They circled around the palace, entering by a small side door rather than the main entrance. Tieln expected a narrow, dim set of servants' halls, but Balin's door brought them into a well-lit hall with polished marble floors and clean walls painted with decorative patterns of vines. Tieln discretely ran his finger over one to assure himself that it was paint and not a real plant. He noticed Chance doing the same.

Balin checked both ways, as if he was doing something he shouldn't, and set a quick pace down the hall until he reached a wooden door decorated with carved blooming flowers. The flowers' elongated stamens struck Tieln as oddly obscene. Balin opened the door and waved them after him.

The smell of cologne and sex hit Tieln as he stepped inside. Silky curtains in greens and blues hung on the walls and covered doorways. Instead of chairs, the airy lounge had reclining benches and piles of cushions for sitting or other activities. Eight young men around Balin's age or a little older sat around the room. All of them stopped and stared when the group followed their guide in.

"Balin, what... who... did the Lady say...," one began.

Another got the same delighted expression Balin had when he saw them outside. "Cylin!"

"Hey guys." Cylin walked into Ayliad's harem with a smile. "How've you been?"

Two thirds of the men in the room clustered around her, talking excitedly. Tieln looked to the elves, and saw expressions of surprise that mirrored his. "Cylin?" Eria asked.

The harem boys fell quiet at the unfamiliar female voice, looking from Cylin to Eria, then to Tieln and the other new men. "Uh, Cylin? We're... not really supposed to associate with companions who don't serve the Lady."

"Oh, that's okay. They aren't companions. They're my friends," Cylin said. "She didn't say anything about that, did she?"

The young men looked at each other. "She said not to be rude to guests," one said finally.

"And she also said, back when we first met, that you should fulfill my desires, right?" Cylin asked. "Did she ever set a time limit on that?"

Another round of uncertain glances. "No...," Balin said cautiously.

Cylin gave him a bright smile. "Then there's no problem, right?"

Clearly, not all were convinced, but they hesitated to openly argue or contradict Cylin, and she was more than willing to use that to her advantage.

"Where's Orteth?" Cylin asked.

"I'll get him." A young man jumped to his feet and scrambled through one of the doorways.

A few moments later, a new man stepped out of the doorway. Like the rest, he was shirtless and handsome, but he was noticeably older than the rest, a few years over twenty. His brown hair hung in a long braid down his back, and three emerald studs adorned his ears. He gazed at them for a long moment, then spoke. "Cylin. I didn't expect you to come here."

"Hi Orteth," Cylin greeted. "We were in the area. Thought I'd stop by and ask if you've thought more about what we talked about."

As vague as her statement was, Orteth obviously understood it. His gaze swept the room. "Back to what you were doing," he told the rest of the harem. "Come on, Cylin. Bring your friends."

As Orteth strode back through the doorway, Tieln leaned over to Cylin. "Who is he?"

"Orteth is kind of in charge over the rest of Ayliad's harem. Met him the same time I met the rest of the guys I know here," she whispered back.

Orteth shooed a few lingering young men out of a sitting room and settled on a cushion in front of a low table. Cylin walked to the cushions across from him, but didn't sit immediately. "What's safe?"

"Those cushions are clean. No one's had sex there since the last time they were washed," Orteth told her. "As is the pile over there, if your friends want to sit."

"I'll stand, thanks," Lucian said, voice flat.

"Suit yourself." Orteth leaned back on his elbows. "What makes you think my answer has changed, Cylin?"

"There's a lot of caravans outside," Cylin said. "How many new pretty boys did she buy?" She looked him in the eyes. "How many did you have to pick to leave?"

He winced and glanced aside. "Three. It would have been more, but she broke several of her Toys recently, so they took spaces I might otherwise have had to fill."

Cylin's eyes narrowed. Her voice was quiet but firm. "You have to decide which of Ayliad's pretty boys get sold off to the slave traders to make room for the new ones. You know they're going to end up dying of some nasty disease in a filthy whorehouse. You really think my suggestion is *worse*?"

Orteth folded his arms, gazing at her once again. "How, exactly, do you propose we leave? And go where? Do what? It's not like any of us can go back to whatever shithole we came from, and it's not like any of us have skills outside of knowing how to please a woman. We could run away, and then what? Become someone else's whores?"

Cylin leaned forward, about to speak, when Lucian interrupted. "You want to bring them to Forest Town, Cylin."

"Well, yeah," she said. "You wouldn't turn them away, would you?"

His jaw tightened, but he studied Orteth. "No, I wouldn't turn away anyone who escaped Ayliad."

Orteth frowned, suspicion in his eyes. "What is this place, and why should it be better than here?"

"It's Lucian's town." Cylin gestured at Lucian.

Orteth jerked to his feet. "*You* are Lucian? One of the men the Lady's been waiting for?" He glanced to Cylin. "And you came *with* him? Do you *know* what she wants to do?"

"I know that we are going to really piss off Ayliad, and if you can be not here when that happens, things will be a lot better for you," Cylin said. "I know you guys have somewhere you can hole up for a while that the guards don't know about."

He ran fingers through his hair and started pacing. "Shit.

We do, but we need to move fast. I'll send Balin to collect the new boys, and someone else to grab those scheduled to leave with the caravan. I'm the only one who can get to the Toys, and I'll have to get as many of them out as I can."

It was the second time he'd mentioned "Toys." Tieln suspected the meaning, but asked, "What do you mean by toys?"

"Up here, in these rooms, you'll find her 'good' boys, the ones who do what she says. The Toys are the ones who keep fighting back. She uses them until they break." Orteth's voice was tight.

Despite his knowledge of Ayliad, Tieln had hoped, somehow, the term might not mean what he thought. Orteth's answer crushed that hope. He nodded understanding. "Where will we find her?"

"Top floor. Take the door at the end of this hall," Orteth said. He looked to Cylin, then the rest of them. "Good luck."

As they walked down the hall, Tieln said, "You've been planning to do that since we came in sight of this place, haven't you?"

"Ha! I've been wanting to get them out of here since I met them," Cylin said. "Ayliad invited me to visit the portion of her harem that she's brought along while she and Yazah were off fucking the night away. Since my alternative was to spend the time stuck with Ravys, I visited them. Taught them to play Shadow Ladies, and we played cards all night. Partway through, I figured out that I was the first woman in a long time to treat them like people rather than just penises with pretty faces. Orteth and I talked a while over cards, but he wasn't convinced he'd be better off somewhere else."

"There is a point when you become convinced that the abuse you know, however crushing it may be, is the best you deserve, and anywhere else could only be worse," Chance said. "Especially when it's all you know."

The door Orteth directed them to opened into a staircase. As they climbed, tension grew within Tieln. The Sapling jittered restlessly. He smelled the fragrance of flowers in the air, growing more powerful the closer they came to the top.

"This place reeks of the Tree," Lucian said. "And all of it is wrong. The Guardian is very, very thorny. Don't know how I couldn't sense it from outside."

"Corrupted magic?" Tieln asked, remembering what Quicksilver told him about the Guardian's formation.

Lucian nodded. "You and Cylin should stay back, Tieln."

"Yeah, sure, *that's* going to happen," Cylin said under her breath.

"I can't protect my family if I'm hiding around a corner," Tieln said.

Quicksilver cautiously opened the door at the top of the stairs. The smell of flowers hit Tieln like a wall, staggering him. He shook off the moment and followed the elves inside.

Long, slender tendrils of flowering morning glory covered the walls, wrapped around metal trestles. The pink and blue blossoms weren't the source of the scent, though. That came from the tree that grew up through the floor, its roots somewhere far below. The undersides of the tree's leaves glowed with a gentle phosphorescence. Its branches drooped, heavy laden with oval-shaped crimson fruit. Just looking at the fruit made Tieln's mouth water.

"*No no no no no!*" the Sapling shrieked at him. "*Corrupted! Bad!*"

Tieln shook his head to clear it. The heady perfume muddled his thoughts, but the Sapling kept yelling in his mind until he looked more carefully at the tree. Its bark was cracked, oozing dark sap down the trunk. Beneath the perfume of the flowers, he caught an undertone of sickly sweet decay.

Lucian headed straight toward the tree. "Dash, I know you're there. Come out. Let the Guardian help you."

A long, oozing crack in the tree's bark began to peel apart, opening wider until Tieln thought he glimpsed a figure within.

Doors burst open on either side of the room. Bone men rushed out bearing darts and needles. Tieln snatched his gun from the holster and fired. A bone man rushing at Lucian's back tumbled and sprawled to the ground. Lucian spun around, lips curling in a snarl. A sharp wave of his hand sent bone men flying into the walls.

Tieln ran forward, checking for Chance, Eria, and Quicksilver. Cylin came in behind him, gun raised and ready. Chance stood near Lucian, rapidly assessing their situation. Quicksilver and Eria dodged around bone men, striking at them as they could. The bone men tried to jab them with their darts as they pressed toward Lucian and Chance.

Another door opened, admitting Ayliad. Golden blond hair hung past her waist. Every movement oozed sensuality, from the precise placement of each step to the sway of her hips and bust. Jewels gleamed in her long pointed ears and hung from her necklaces and bracelets. She wore a flowing skirt with a halter top and bare feet.

Tieln raised his gun and fired at her.

A tree branch snapped down. The bullet splintered wood, but didn't pierce through to Ayliad. She smiled. "So, you're the soldier boy. As handsome in person as in spirit."

Four bone men rushed to guard her. The rest attacked the elves again. Tieln shot into their ranks. Lucian threw more into the walls hard enough that Tieln heard bones crunch. Chance also flung bone men aside, moving toward Ayliad.

A gnarled hand coated in dark sap reached from the crack in the tree and seized Lucian's arm. Lucian whipped around to face the tree and the figure emerging from it.

Help me. The figure's scream rang through Tieln's mind. Tieln staggered, but Lucian stood firm. With his free hand, he grasped the other's arm. Tieln felt a surge of the Guardian's presence from Lucian.

Two darts hit Lucian in the back. The Guardian howled in fury. Abruptly, its enraged cry cut off. The sense of its presence vanished like a popping soap bubble. Lucian staggered. Tieln shot the bone men who'd flung the darts, but too late.

Lucian tore free of the figure in the tree. Along the walls, the metal trellises warped and twisted at his gesture. "Whatever you think you're doing, bitch, you didn't stop my magic, even if you did somehow silence the Guardian."

She smirked. "But my dear brother, silencing the Guardian is all I needed to do. Dash, show Lucian proper hospitality."

The sap-covered figure emerged completely from the tree and wrapped its arms around Lucian. Tieln aimed at it, but multiple elven voices shouted *No!*

Tieln winced and fired instead at Ayliad. Again the tree branches shielded her, even with Dash focused on Lucian.

Lucian and Dash struggled. New branches pushed from the tree to tangle around Lucian's legs. Chance lunged at Ayliad. Tieln didn't hear what she said, but he saw her laughing.

The vines on the wall ripped from the trellises and swarmed the room. They grabbed indiscriminately, tangling the bone men as they drew back. Tieln sprinted across the room, jumping over fallen bone men and dodging vines. A stab of guilt pricked him as he passed Lucian locked in struggle, but he didn't stop.

Vines wrapped around Chance's legs, dragging him back from Ayliad. She reached up and plucked a fruit from the tree. Before Tieln could reach them, she took a large bite, the juices running from her mouth. Chance grabbed for the knife on his belt. Ayliad stepped close, grabbed Chance's shirt to pull him against her, and kissed him. Chance pushed against her, trying to force her back. Freeing his knife, Chance stabbed her in the side. Ayliad jabbed a dart into his thigh and released him.

She put a hand to her bleeding side, and the wound knitted shut. She'd never lost her smile, and now it grew cold and malicious. *Remember all the good times we had together, Chance. Savor each memory as I do.*

Juices from the fruit trickled from Chance's mouth. He stumbled, eyes open but glazed. The knife fell from his fingers. Tieln reached him just as Chance crumpled. He caught the elf, but Chance was a limp weight. Tieln glared at Ayliad. "What did you do to him?"

She licked her lips. "I reminded him of the last time we were together. And with a little help from my bone men's work, he'll stay there, remembering and reliving each moment. And what are you going to do, Soldier Boy? What does a mere human think he can do against his gods?"

Chance convulsed with a strangled scream and a burst of images and sensations through mind-speech. A room with walls of some unfamiliar, porous material similar to stone, its only exit blocked by water. Being pinned to the floor, limbs restrained by plants. Ayliad on top of him, using her magic to stimulate him so she could rape him.

Tieln's breath hissed between his teeth. In those brief images, he also felt Chance's anger, his fear, his torment, the betrayal he'd felt when Ayliad revealed her true self. "Let him go."

She laughed. "Why? Chance needs to remember his place —I'm simply reminding him. And you have nothing to offer in exchange."

"I wouldn't trust you to keep a bargain even if I did." Tieln heard movement behind him, but didn't dare take his eyes off Ayliad.

"I've got him," Quicksilver whispered. Chance's weight lifted from Tieln's arms.

"Well, my little Tammin," Ayliad purred. "You've grown to quite the handsome man."

"You're my mother, and that's disgusting," Quicksilver snapped.

"And *you* aren't taking Chance." She moved faster than Tieln anticipated, shoving him aside and catching Quicksilver's arm.

Quicksilver shrieked in pain, arm falling limp. Chance dropped to the floor. The vines swarmed over him.

"Lucian! Chance needs help!" Tieln yelled with both his voice and his thoughts.

He heard wood splinter. The tree shook. Lucian flew across the room, eyes alight with anger. "Don't touch him, bitch!" He slammed into Ayliad, throwing them both against the wall.

Tieln tore vines away from Chance and picked up the elf. The thin tendrils of morning glory curled rapidly around his legs, and more of them still clung to Chance than he liked. He cast a look around to find his companions.

Eria pulled Quicksilver to his feet and back from Lucian and Ayliad. The bone men that had eluded the vines made their escape, and those who remained were entangled in cocoons of green. Cylin watched the tree, gun ready. Tieln didn't see the figure Lucian had been fighting, though broken and splintered branches covered the ground.

Moving before the vines tangled him in place, Tieln stumbled to Cylin. "Can you take Chance?"

"What?"

"Whatever Ayliad did put him out of the fight. Can you get him out of this room, out of her reach?"

Cylin looked to Eria and Quicksilver. "I don't have magic to protect him, you know."

"I know. You also don't have magic to feel the memories he projected earlier."

She hesitated a moment, then holstered her gun and lifted Chance from Tieln's arms. "I'll do what I can, but I'd really like backup."

He nodded and ran to Eria and Quicksilver. "Cylin's guarding Chance. One of you go with her."

I will, Quicksilver said. *Eria has healing. She'd better stay with you and Lucian.* He hurried after Cylin as she retreated to the stairs.

Chance released another burst of images and sensations. Tieln shuddered at the wave of terror that accompanied the image of the tall woman with long black hair who smiled down at him... at her prisoner. He saw something of Lucian in her features, and something of Ayliad, but she radiated an air of age and power beyond either of them. Then he saw Ayliad again, taunting, playing with her victim before she forced herself on him again.

"Oh stars," Eria whispered in horror. "How... she's forced *those* memories on him? That was before I was born, when Ayliad lured Chance, Lucian, Dash, and Tash into Willow's trap. She held them captive for... for far too long."

Lucian screamed in rage. The metal trellises that had held the morning glory warped and twisted into spikes on the walls. He threw Ayliad at them. A combination of tree branches and vines caught her before she hit, though one spike tore a gash on her hand.

She raised her hand, blood trickling down to drip to the floor. "Such anger, Lucian. It's going to get someone you care about hurt one of these days. Oh, that's right, it already has, hasn't it?"

A shape leapt from the tree branches. Tieln grabbed its arm before it reached Lucian. Some of the black sap had been scraped off, exposing patches of pale skin an unhealthy color of yellow. The elf was short and compact, and the smell of decay clung to him, or to the sap that covered him. Amber eyes fixed on Tieln.

Guardian.

"*Corrupted!*" the Sapling screamed at Tieln.

Dash, we can help you. Let us help you. Don't fight us, please, Eria said.

It burns. It burns! Help me!

Lucian and Ayliad still fought, and whatever poison had coated the Bone Men's darts still stopped the Guardian from acting. Tieln's hold on Dash's arm tightened. *"How do we purge the corruption?"*

Dash snarled suddenly, his free hand slashing at Tieln's face. Tieln dropped his gun and caught the elf's arm, holding the clawing fingers inches from his eyes. "Can you knock him out, Eria?"

She slapped her hand against Dash's back, but Dash continued to thrash. "He's fighting it! Dash, please! We're trying to help you!"

Dash jerked away from her, dragging Tieln with him back toward the gash in the tree. Tieln tried to brace himself, but his feet found little purchase, slipping on the juices of crushed vines. Dash's hands shifted so that he gripped Tieln's forearms as well as Tieln held his.

He means to drag me into the tree with him! Tieln strained, but the wiry elf was stronger than he looked. Dash got one foot inside the gash, making contact with the tree.

The Sapling gasped, then shrieked as another presence shoved it aside and invaded Tieln's mind, sharp, angry, and bristling with thorns. Tieln screamed in pain. The invading presence seized control of his body, but Tieln could still see and hear.

Dash froze, staring at him. *Guardian.*

The Dark Tree must be destroyed. The voice of the presence within Tieln sounded similar to Lucian. *We will purge the corruption.*

You... how? Tieln tried to form a coherent thought.

He felt it looking at him. *We are part of the Tree, and can use it as a pathway—even through a twisted, corrupted growth like this Dark Tree. Even if the Fruit can cut us off from our host, she cannot sever our connection to the Tree. And she did not sever the connection she did not know—that between us and the sapling within you. We cannot destroy the Dark Tree through our host, so we must use our sapling's host.*

Power flowed through Tieln far beyond what he'd imagined himself capable of. It burned in his veins, and he learned that even though he couldn't control his body, he could still feel pain. He felt the Sapling's cries as well, ringing in his mind. The Guardian forced magic through Tieln's body and into Dash's, and Tieln could see the power moving through Dash, attacking the corruption. Dash shrieked in pain that matched Tieln's, as if they had both been set on fire.

Flashes of lucidity grew in Dash's eyes, but as they did, the corruption fought back. Dash dragged Tieln close, teeth bared in a snarl. Then he spun and shoved Tieln into the gash in the tree.

The bark closed around him. Something pierced his skin and began pumping the black sap into his veins. Tieln writhed, but the darkness swallowed his cry as corruption raced through his body.

The Guardian, full of thorns and fury, surged to meet the invading magic. As Tieln convulsed, the Guardian ruthlessly forced his body to channel more power. Tieln pulled back within himself, into the core of his being, seeking relief from the torment.

Even in the depths of his soul, the corruption pursued him. Tieln stood in the barracks, but before he could move, lashing black tendrils burst through the floor, whipping wildly about. Tieln tried to dodge them, but there were too many, and every blow they landed seared his skin.

He staggered outside. Wicked thorns overran the training ground. They held the black tendrils at bay, but tore Tieln's arms and legs when he struggled through them. He found the sapling wrapped in thorns, its branches broken and its bark scarred and torn. Pain radiated from it, and he felt the Sapling growing weaker.

"No. You can't. No. Stop." He stumbled to the young tree and pulled at the thorns as if he could tear them away. "You're killing him!"

The Guardian didn't manifest in humanoid form. *The Dark Tree must be stopped at all cost. The corruption must be purged, even if a sapling is lost.*

"No! I won't let you!" Tieln tore at the thorns again.

The thorns peeled back enough to let him reach the sapling. He pressed against it. "Hold on. You have to hold on."

If you will not sacrifice the sapling, then you must be the channel for the Tree, to purge the corruption from the vessel that the Fruit has made, the Guardian warned.

Tieln closed his eyes. "Will I survive?"

Probably. But you will also be taken in, made part of the Tree. It will become part of your body, and you will become part of its. The Guardian sent an image of Tieln's blood turning to sap, his body melding with that of the tree. *You have no healing and no means to dull the pain. It will hurt.*

"Will the others be safe from this corruption? Can I protect them?"

Yes.

He didn't open his eyes. *I'm sorry, Lucian. I wish I could have known you longer. I wish I could have known more about what it is to be an elf. I wish I could go back to Forest Town and see my wards grow up.*

He let out a trembling breath, opened his eyes, and looked at the thorns.

"Do it."

INTERLUDE FIVE: SHATTER

Ayliad's plants wrapped around Lucian's legs, and the Guardian still wouldn't, or couldn't, answer him. She stood smirking, confident and smug. He flung her back toward the spikes again.

Once again, he drew blood, but her plants protected her from more serious damage. *You just don't know when to stop, do you, Lucian?* she purred. *Even when Chance is screaming for your help, you just keep fighting.*

Don't try to blame me for what you've done! He tore from the vines and lunged at her.

The plants grabbed at Lucian, but failed to stop him. He got his hands around her neck and squeezed.

Her voice spoke in his mind like the brush of a lover's fingers. *It's been too long since we were this close, my dear brother. Don't pretend you don't miss it.*

He tried to ignore her cloying scent or the sickening, unwanted memories of a time when he had loved her. *I'm going to kill you.*

Magic flared behind them. Dash screamed. Ayliad kicked

Lucian and broke free in his moment of distraction. She didn't press her advantage, though, looking to the tree. "What are you doing, Soldier Boy?"

Before Lucian could react, the Guardian's magic erupted in the room. Lucian's head jerked around in time to see Dash shoving Tieln into the split in the tree. He had no idea how, but the Guardian's magic radiated from Tieln. He took a step toward the tree, but the Guardian still didn't respond to him.

*What's this? Why, Lucian, is that little human *yours?** Ayliad laughed, catching his arm and turning him around to face her. *You had a child with a *human?* I'll be reminding you of this for *years.**

"You'll be *dead* before you do!"

Images—Chance's memories—slammed into him. Ayliad. Willow. Torture. Rape. A desperate, hopeless bargain that could only end in more torment.

Hear him calling to you, Lucian. Hear how he screams. And here you are, thinking you're free. Playing Mother's game and thinking that you can win. Ayliad smirked. Her hands closed on his shoulders, pulling his mouth to hers. *You don't think you ever actually escaped the Coral Palace, do you?*

Her kiss was sweet with the juices of the fruit, tingling on his lips. She pushed an image into his mind: himself, bound in chains of bone to a wall of coral, gaunt, naked, and unconscious.

No. No, that isn't possible. This is real. I'm not there. This isn't one of Willow's games. It can't be.

He pushed against Ayliad, but she didn't release him. Her tongue sought entrance to his mouth. *Do you know how long Chance has fought to reach you? How he strained to pierce Mother's game enough to cry to you for help?*

You're lying! He flung her back with his arms and his magic both.

The plants rose to catch her, but they weren't enough.

Ayliad slammed into the wall of metal spikes. Her chest heaved as her blood spilled to the floor. Somehow, she still gave him a final, mocking smile, and her laughter rang in his mind.

Foolish, beautiful brother. Now you have no way out. No escape. No one to pull you out of the game. You're trapped here, and Chance will be mine forever.

Chance screamed in his mind again with an image of Ayliad's healing twisted his limbs while she whispered to him of the tortures she inflicted on his friends.

Lucian staggered, falling to his knees and clutching his head. He still tasted the fruit in his mouth, her lips on his. The world rippled around him. He was gasping for breath on the floor of Ayliad's palace.

He was bound with chains of bone, pinned to a coral wall.

The sickly sweet stench of the fruit and the flowers choked the air.

He was underwater, and every breath tasted of salt, until he could taste nothing else.

Ayliad hung dead on the wall, pierced through by metal spikes.

Ayliad ignored his useless struggles, pinning him against the wall of his cell and raping him.

He felt something crack in the depth of his soul. A wall he'd built centuries ago, then forgotten. Chosen to forget.

No.

The crack spread, the wall no longer enough to hold back the weight that pressed against it.

No.

Someone grabbed his arm, trying to pull him to his feet. "Uncle Lucian, what are you doing? Stop! You're going to bring the whole building down!"

His eyes fell to the floor. Cracks radiated out from him across the floor, up the walls. Chunks of the ceiling fell loose and rained down around them. He looked up, and the entire roof flew away, tearing chunks of wall with it.

It's not real. None of it is real. It's all her game. All of it. Everything. The only place that's real is there. The Coral Palace. We never escaped.

I'm still there.

Lucian screamed, and the walls shattered around him.

PART FIVE

PRINCE

PRINCE

Chance couldn't breathe.

Where is Lucian?

Weight pressed down on his chest. He struggled. His hands closed around rough chunks of stone, too heavy to move. But he wasn't restrained. No vines snaked down his throat. He pushed with magic, and the rubble shifted. The weight on his chest eased. He gasped a breath and pushed again.

No vines. No water. I can breathe. She isn't restraining me.

Stones tumbled away. He sucked in another deep breath. Dust choked the sunlight and filled his lungs. He crawled to his feet and looked around, trying to figure out where he was.

A doorway choked with rubble stood to his left. The wall around it remained intact, but the roof looked like it had been ripped off by some violent force. A tree grew up through the floor, and several figures lay around its trunk. Branches curled down protectively over them. Vines of morning glory carpeted the floor. Chance jerked away, but they remained inert.

He steadied himself as a tremor shivered through the building. *Ayliad's stronghold. We're on the top floor of Ayliad's stronghold.*

Rubble shifted near him. "What the fuck did those fucking fuckers do?" muttered a female voice. "Ah, shit!"

Chance lifted the rubble, revealing Cylin, a human woman in her late teens, her short brown hair disheveled and her face smeared with dust. A cut on her forehead bled sluggishly. "Lucian?" she asked, blinking grit from her eyes. "Oh—hey Chance. Glad you're back with us again."

"Back with…" he started to ask, but before he finished, he remembered.

She answered anyway. "The crazy bitch did something that took you out of the fight. Tieln pulled you out here and Lucian attacked Ayliad. Things kinda went to shit after that."

Where was Lucian? Chance looked around urgently for his cousin, his closest friend. *Lucian! Where are you?* At least the dust couldn't interfere with elven mind-speech.

I'm coming. Lucian's mental voice was strained and exhausted.

Though it didn't answer Chance's question, it was reassuring. Still, it left a nagging question of why Lucian had left and where he'd gone.

He moved slowly toward the tree. His gaze moved around what remained of the room and found the far wall. He froze.

Ayliad hung on the wall, impaled on dozens of metal spikes that bristled from the wall. Her eyes were open, but glazed in death. She'd died with a smile on her lips, mocking, taunting, carrying secrets into her grave and beyond.

He still felt her hands on him, heard her whispers in his ears. He was shaking. The memories she'd drawn up to drown him lingered too near the surface still, ready to pounce. He passed the tree and came closer, until he could reach out and just make contact with her arm. At any moment, he expected her eyes to focus on him, her hands to reach up and drag him into her embrace.

His magic confirmed what his eyes told him. She was dead.

A little of the tightness in his chest eased as Chance tore his gaze away from his dead tormentor and approached the tree.

The tree's branches curled low, drawing close to shelter those pressed against its trunk. Chance counted three figures, and felt a moment of relief that aside from Lucian, they were all accounted for. Then he realized he was wrong.

His daughter Eria and her cousin Quicksilver picked themselves up, wincing. The third, however, wasn't Lucian's half-human son Tieln. He was a short elf, skin coated in viscous black sap, and he lay curled in a tight ball. Chance knew him—Lucian's younger brother, Dash.

Eria looked at Chance with relief. *Dad. Are you all right?*

Been better. What happened?

Quicksilver looked down at Dash, then at the tree, and color drained from his face. "Oh no…" He whirled to Chance urgently. "Chance, do you know how to pull someone back out of the Tree? You have to, right? It's happened before to others in the clan. You know how, don't you?"

"What?" Chance demanded. "Is Lucian…?"

Quicksilver shook his head, if anything, more panicked. "Not Lucian. Tieln. He was fighting Dash. Dash pushed him into the crack in the tree. And somehow… Tieln was channeling the Guardian. Not his own Tree magic… it was the Guardian."

"That's not possible." Tieln could barely manage mind-speech. There was no way he could have harnessed a power like the sentient, strong-willed manifestation of Lucian's Tree magic.

"I know. It shouldn't be possible," Eria said. "But I felt it too, Dad. The Guardian's magic came from Tieln."

How? Why? Chance forced the questions back. "I need you to open the tree, Quick. Can you?"

"I… yeah. I can."

"Sooo… not to interfere with your wise and elfly stuff, but

you think this will work if we do it from the ground floor?" Cylin asked. "I don't know about you, but I don't like the way this floor is shaking."

"We have to get Tieln out of the tree before we go anywhere," Chance snapped. He knew he shouldn't be short with her, but his every nerve was on end. "Eria, how's Dash?"

"Out cold," she said. "I'm glad he has healing; the Guardian was merciless in scouring the corrupted magic out of him."

Quicksilver pressed his hands to the trunk of the tree. Physical contact wasn't necessary for most magic aside from healing, but from Quicksilver's pale face and trembling arms, he needed the tactile connection to focus on the task.

The dark scar in the tree's trunk split open, as it had when Dash crawled from it at Ayliad's order.

A hand reached out from the opening. Eria grabbed it and tugged. Tieln spilled out and collapsed on the floor. Tendrils from the tree pierced the skin all over his body, pumping sap into his body and turning tan skin a sickly yellow hue. The amber hue bled into his wide, pain-filled eyes. Chance tried to remember the last time he'd seen someone being absorbed alive by the Tree. It had been… centuries.

Tieln's hands opened and closed as if he was trying to reach something. His entire body jerked. He screamed.

Chance pressed his hands to Tieln's chest, calling his healing magic. What it told him was worse than he'd feared. The Tree could absorb an elf, its own magical essence allowing it to alter an elf's body enough to survive, though it was a horrible, agonizing experience. But Tieln was only half elf. His human blood rejected the Tree's magic, and the Tree's invasion was killing him. Killing him slowly and in utter agony.

Across from Chance, Eria poured magic into Tieln. Her eyes met Chance's, frightened by what she saw happening in Tieln. She swallowed hard. "We can't move him. Not like this."

Cylin stared at Tieln. "Oh shit. That's… what…" She stared, then looked away, and finally turned her eyes to the sky. "What the fuck?"

If Tieln was aware of them, he showed no sign. He writhed and screamed.

Chance wanted to close his ears. Too many screams rang through his memories—most of them his own. Ayliad hung dead on the wall, still smirking at them. Lucian was still not in sight. Tieln was dying. And, when Chance raised his head and followed Cylin's gaze, he saw the fiery blaze of a meteor scorching across the sky toward them.

He watched its approach with detached fascination. *After all this, all our struggles and battles, is this how it ends? A rock falls from the sky to obliterate whatever's left?*

Somewhere on the ground far below, people screamed. Chance felt waves of heat as the meteor plunged closer, but he couldn't muster the energy to be afraid.

Then, defying all physics, the meteor simply stopped. The red-hot exterior skin sloughed off to hang in the air radiating heat like a miniature sun. The meteor gently landed on the remains of the floor. Rock flowed down from it, creating a more stable landing site, reinforcing the rest of the building at the same time.

The shell opened. Like an ancient deity descending from on high, Lucian's father Lonewind stepped out, long auburn hair flowing in a rush of wind. He stood tall with unconscious grace and dignity, surveying his surroundings as if to claim ownership of everything he saw.

After him came a second elf, far less dramatic or eye-catching, but in the moment, the most welcome sight to Chance.

Cahron! I need your help!

Before Lonewind could say a word, Cahron was sprinting to Chance. As Cahron knelt beside him, Chance dumped everything he could about Tieln's condition into the older healer's mind.

One thing Chance had always admired about Cahron was how he wasted no time. He didn't ask how or why the Guardian had used the youth, or where they were, or why Chance's mind-speech verged on incoherent babbling. He just took charge with calm confidence that radiated from him like cool, soothing water.

Quicksilver, we need your help, Cahron said.

What do I do? Quicksilver scrambled closer.

Plant-shape as I tell you, Cahron said, as if he'd extracted people from the Tree dozens of times.

Considering some of the more difficult periods in their clan's history with the Tree, he might have.

Chance followed Cahron's guidance, more relieved than he wanted to admit to have someone with experience take charge. Under Cahron's direction, Chance and Eria healed as Quicksilver drew out the invasive plants. Lonewind asked questions urgently. Cylin was speaking, but Chance focused only on saving the life of Lucian's son.

Deep in the healer trance, he lost any sense of time until Cahron said, *He's stable.*

"He'll be all right?" His voice rasped in his dry throat. Chance blinked gritty eyes.

Cahron gripped his shoulder. "Tieln will live, with rest and care."

Chance let out a trembling breath and nodded. He wanted to collapse and sleep for days. Instead, he tried to stand.

Lonewind loomed anxiously over them. "Chance, where is Lucian?"

"He's..." Chance looked around, dread growing in his gut. *He said he was coming. Why isn't he here?* *Lucian? Lucian! Where are you?*

An answer came, distant and faint. Further than he had been before. *I'm coming back.*

It should have encouraged him, but this time Chance heard the despair in Lucian's voice, the wail of a broken soul.

Lucian, where are you? Chance staggered several steps. Lonewind caught him before he collapsed.

I'm coming back.

"Chance."

He looked up at Lonewind. "He says 'I'm coming back,' but I don't know where he's talking about, because he doesn't mean here, or he'd already *be* here."

"He answers you, at least. I tried, but he didn't respond." Lonewind's gaze moved over the destruction of the building again. He stiffened. Chance followed his gaze. Lonewind had seen Ayliad. "What happened?"

"Ayliad happened," Cylin said.

Chance flinched. He'd pushed the images back while healing Tieln, but they swarmed through his thoughts as mercilessly as Ayliad's hands on his bare skin.

Cahron was at his side in a heartbeat, taking him from Lonewind. *Chance, did she force you?*

Not… this time. She didn't… have the opportunity. His heart raced. *Instead she used all my memories of other times.* His body ached as if he'd relived the rapes physically as well as mentally.

The others were talking to Lonewind, but their voices were meaningless noise. Chance looked at Tieln. *Tieln and Lucian fought her. I couldn't do anything. I couldn't stop her.*

Cahron gripped his arm tightly. *There's some kind of drug in your blood, Chance. She may be to blame.*

Chance simply nodded. His eyes found Ayliad again. Looking at her smirk, he thought of the despair in Lucian's voice. *What did she do?*

"We have to find Lucian," he whispered, clutching Cahron's arm.

"We will." Cahron's words left no room for doubt. "But first, we should leave this wretched place."

"Do we need the humans for anything? I hear quite a few scratching around below us."

Chance's head snapped toward the new voice. In the midst of everything going on, he'd somehow missed the third member of the clan who accompanied Lonewind and Cahron.

He wasn't the only one caught by surprise. Cylin burst a startled "What the fuck? One of Shiranak's Creatures?"

The elf turned milky, blind eyes toward her and snorted in disdain. "Hardly. I am what Karishan's mindless rabble could never dream of being." He flexed his hands, extending and retracting razor sharp claws.

Quicksilver cleared his throat. "Uh… that's Lynx. He's… my brother. Half brother."

"And here I thought I couldn't learn anything that would make me think your family was *more* messed up," Cylin muttered.

Like a Creature, thick, bony ridges and heavy scales armored Lynx. He walked upright, without the typical hunch of a Creature. And none of Karishan's Creatures dared speak with Lynx's acerbic sarcasm. "You don't even know the half of it, human girl. And Eria is my sister as well. By half, as Quicksilver says."

Cylin shot Chance a look that said, even without mind-speech, "You spawned this?"

"The humans," Lynx repeated. "Many are fleeing. Some are hiding. Do we need any of them?"

"Orteth and the rest of the guys with him," Cylin said. "I promised we'd take them somewhere safe.

"And they are?" Lynx asked. Then, cocking his head as if

listening to something, he nodded. "Ah. Mother's pretty boys. Fine, I'll fetch them."

"Uh… how are you going to find them?" Quicksilver asked.

Lynx snorted. "They're Mother's pretty boys. I'll just follow the smell of sex."

Chance glanced at Cahron. *Please tell me you didn't bring Echo down here as well.*

No, Echo is still safely in orbit. Even he agreed that getting him any closer to the chaos happening in the spirit realm on this planet would be a disaster.

Lynx and Echo, the twin sons Ayliad had birthed shortly after Lucian, Chance, Lonewind, and the rest were freed from Willow's Coral Palace. Lynx was blind, and Echo deaf, both from birth. Lynx was brawn, raised to be his brother's keeper and protector. Echo was a mind-reader, raised to have none of the mental barriers a mind-reader needed to avoid being overwhelmed by the thoughts, emotions, and personalities of those around him, and none of the moral compunctions against manipulating the thoughts and emotions of others. He'd learned both, to a degree, but Lynx was the only person he obeyed with any reliability.

"Be quick about it," Lonewind said. "We have to find Lucian." He turned to Chance. "Where do we start?"

"Forest Town. We should start there."

"Is that where the rest of the clan is?" Lonewind asked.

Chance stared at him blankly before understanding hit. *He doesn't know.* His throat tightened, choking the words. He tried again, forcing them out. "This is the clan, Lonewind."

"What about Tash? Sun? Ahmea, Cilvi?" Cahron stared at him in disbelief.

Chance shook his head.

In the sudden silence, Eria spoke. "The humans went to war with each other. Mother died in a bombing, and Dad was badly injured and fell into a coma. Quick and I got him out, but we were separated from Lucian and the others. We found a place where we could make shelter and take care of Dad. Tash, Sun, and Cilvi were with Lucian. I know they were killed, but I'm not sure of the details. Forest Town is the place where Lucian eventually settled. The Guardian made a forest there. At some point, humans moved in too and made a town."

"I can tell you a little more—what Lucian told me," Chance said softly. "But not now. Not… here."

Cahron drew a deep, trembling breath and closed his eyes, head bowed.

Lonewind stood unmoving for a long moment, silent, unreadable. Finally, he nodded. "You can also tell me later how a human boy nearly got assimilated by the Tree."

Chance didn't have the strength to carry Tieln, but he could summon enough magic to levitate him. "His name's Tieln. He's Lucian's son."

Lonewind stopped short, his gaze snapping to Tieln. "Lucian's son." A heartbeat later, Lonewind's magic pulled Tieln from Chance. Not harshly, but with possessive demand. Chance let him. He was too exhausted to argue.

Between Lonewind, Chance, and Quicksilver, they all got down to the ground. Ayliad's guards, minions, and the caravans had fled, either when Lucian ripped the roof off the building, or when Lonewind landed a meteorite on the remains.

Lynx herded a clump of terrified young men toward them. Dirt smeared their faces and what little clothing they wore. Cuts and scrapes abounded. Several limped, and Orteth cradled his arm against his body. Chance recognized most of them from their brief visit to Ayliad's harem. The three he hadn't seen there, he immediately identified as Ayliad's Toys—the sex slaves who fought back. He saw himself reflected in their suspicious glances, their closed stances, the metal collars around their necks.

Lonewind gave the humans a brief, dismissive look. He waved his hand, and the collars and chains fell away. While Ayliad's slaves gaped, he asked, *Where is Forest Town?*

Find the largest concentration of the Guardian's magic, Chance told him. *Please be there, Lucian.* The fear welled up again. He closed his eyes and drew slow, deep breaths until he could focus again.

The meteor freed itself from its landing site, absorbing stone from the surrounding structure to expand enough to fit their increased numbers. Lonewind entered, carrying Tieln and Dash. Cahron stepped in after him, motioning for the rest of them to follow.

"No reason to stay here longer than we must. Come on."

"Get into *that*?" Cylin whispered.

"Unless you want to walk to Forest Town." Chance stepped into the hollow interior.

Lonewind had shaped seats and benches into the stone. Tieln and Dash occupied two of the benches. Chance sank down beside Tieln. He rested a hand on the young man to reassure himself that Tieln was still stable.

Lynx ushered the released slaves in, and Cylin, Eria, and Quicksilver followed them. The shell closed after Quicksilver. Stones set around the top of the stone shell glowed, illuminating the interior. Chance sensed Lonewind's magic more than he felt actual motion as they rose and flew toward Forest Town.

After a few minutes, Quicksilver said, *Wow. We're moving… really fast. I didn't know anyone could fly this fast.*

We could go faster if I didn't have to account for air resistance, Lonewind responded.

Cahron snorted softly. *I'm not sure if Lonewind actually

broke laws of physics to get back to the planet, but he certainly proved they can bend a lot further than I expected.*

Why did you come back? Not quite how Chance intended the question to sound, but he was too drained to rephrase it.

Lonewind glanced at him. *Lucian needed help. Needs help. So I returned.*

To be fair, we've been on our way back ever since Lonewind visited and encountered the utter chaos that is the spirit realm around this planet, Cahron interjected. *We just started moving a lot *faster* when the Ghost told Lonewind that Lucian needed him.*

You've been checking in on us?

Trying to, Lonewind corrected. *The Ghost answering me was the first time I'd been able to push far enough through the spirit realm to reach Lucian. Before that, I'd only been able to confirm that he was alive.*

Not for lack of trying, Chance was certain. Lonewind would do anything to see Lucian safe.

Chance rested his head against the stone wall and closed his eyes. *Please be in Forest Town, Lucian.*

He didn't want to fall asleep. He didn't want to venture into dreams, where Ayliad waited in his memories, ready to pounce. Exhaustion, however, nibbled away his defenses until his head slumped and he sank into the embrace of darkness.

Ayliad's mouth pressed against his as she pinned him down, binding his limbs with her plants.

Dad! Wake up!

Chance jerked awake, gasping. Tremors shook him. Sweat ran down his face. He shuddered and drew up his legs against his body.

Ayliad's slave boys stared at him, though most quickly turned away. Only her Toys met his eyes. They understood.

He hated it.

The space was too quiet. People shifted, breathed, rested, but no one talked. The silence strangled him. He wanted to break its hold, but he couldn't find any words.

Maybe Cahron sensed his silent plea, or perhaps he found the silence as oppressive. The elder healer looked to the humans. "In the rush of everything, we failed to make introductions. My name is Cahron. I'm a healer, if any of you need aid. And this is Lonewind. You have met Lynx, though he may not have introduced himself."

"I told them enough to convince them to move," Lynx said.

"And you are… all elves?" Orteth glanced uncertainly at Lynx.

"We are," Cahron said. "Part of the same clan as Lucian, Chance, Eria, and Quicksilver."

"And the Lady?" Orteth asked.

"There was a time when Ayliad claimed to be a part of our clan, but she never was," Cahron told him.

"We… belong to her," Orteth said uneasily. "She won't permit us to leave."

Chance found his voice. "She's dead."

They all looked at him. One of the Toys spoke, his voice raw. "Are you sure?"

"I have never been more sure."

"Does that mean… we belong to you?" asked Balin, the young man who'd led them to Ayliad's harem at Cylin's request.

"You don't belong to anyone," Eria said. "You're free."

"You can stay in Forest Town until you decide what you want to do," Cylin said. "You'll be safe there."

Some of them looked reassured, others dubious, but none argued. Not when a woman spoke.

Chance looked away from them, to Tieln and Dash instead. He knew Ayliad's harem boys needed help and guidance from someone who understood what they'd endured, but he couldn't give it to them. Everything about them—the way they moved, the way they spoke, the way they cowered from those they perceived as holding power—burned like salt in the raw wounds in his soul.

I can't help them. I can barely help myself. And whatever she did, I have to help Lucian.

~

The sense of Lucian's forest pulled Chance from his half-asleep haze. He briefly wondered what Lucian's humans would think of a huge rock soaring through the air and landing in their midst.

"Lucian has a cave just outside the village. Maybe land there?" Quicksilver suggested.

"The trees are too thick for anywhere else to be convenient," Lonewind agreed.

Vibrations ran through the vessel as it landed, then it opened. Chance blinked in the sunlight. He had no idea what time it was. Quicksilver and Cylin hopped outside, and Chance followed, stiff and aching.

He heard voices shouting Lucian's name. Hope rose. *He's here.* *Lucian, where are you?*

No answer.

"Lord Lucian! You're back!"

Chance shaded his eyes and saw a human young man, a few years younger than Cylin, scrambling up a dirt path toward them. He remembered the boy—Devin. One of the humans in charge of Forest Town in Lucian's absence. He was as devoted to Lucian as any human was to their gods.

"Devin!" Cylin rushed forward and grabbed him in a hug. "Drifters' bones, it's good to see you again! But isn't Lucian here?"

Devin blinked at her. "No. Isn't he with…" His voice

trailed off and his eyes opened wide as saucers when Lonewind descended. "Who…?"

Sometimes Chance forgot the impression Lonewind could make on those who didn't know him. His bronze skin, defined muscles, and lean build showed no hints of excess body fat. His piercing amber eyes and stern expression rarely softened around strangers. Long auburn hair flowed down his back. He carried himself with a poise fit for any deity of human legend, and Devin's awestruck reaction was far from unique.

Then there was Cylin, who brooked no fools and showed herself to be no respecter of persons. She glanced back and said, "That's Lucian's dad."

"Oh," Devin squeaked. He swallowed hard. "And… Lord Lucian isn't with you?"

"No. We were hoping that he'd come back here," Cylin said.

If Lucian isn't here, we should leave the humans and go, Lonewind said.

Go where, Lonewind? Cahron asked. He rested a hand on Lonewind's arm. *We need a plan before you rush off.*

Much as Chance agreed with Lonewind, he knew Cahron made a good point. *Tieln can locate people and objects. When he wakes, he can help us find Lucian.*

Quicksilver herded Ayliad's boys outside and was explaining their presence to Devin. Down at the bottom of the path, more humans from the village gathered, gaping up at the massive rock now attached to the hill in which Lucian made his home. Chance looked around until he found the cave entrance.

You can bring Tieln and Dash in here, he told Lonewind and Cahron as he entered the cave.

Inside, he let out a trembling breath. Too many eyes on him outside. Too many people watching, expecting something from him. Chance leaned against a stone wall and closed his eyes until he sensed Lonewind behind him.

Lonewind entered, Tieln and Dash floating with him. He looked slowly around the cave. "How long did Lucian live here?"

"I don't know. At least thirty years, maybe longer," Chance answered.

Lonewind's eyebrows rose. "You don't know?"

"I was in a coma from the time Ahmea died until a few months ago." Chance walked down the passage until he found Lucian's bedroom. "Eria and Quick took care of me. Lucian was here alone." He caught himself. "Well, not *alone*. The humans have lived here for some time. But no one else from the clan."

Lonewind laid Tieln on the bed, and Dash, the smaller and more compact of the two, on the couch. "I didn't know how bad things were here. If I had, I would have pushed us faster."

Chance ignored the table and chairs, instead sinking down on a rug. "I don't blame you for any of this, Lonewind."

Lonewind eyed him, understanding in his gaze. He sat facing Chance. "Just yourself?"

"No. Maybe. A little." *Lucian needed me and I wasn't there.*

"Tell me what happened."

Chance took a deep breath and let it out slowly. "Fifty years ago, the humans went to war with each other, using weapons that not just killed, but poisoned both the ground and the spirit realm. We thought that the effect on the spirit realm was unintentional, but given some things we learned in the last months, it wasn't an accident." He walked through the last fifty years, history pieced together from things told him by Quicksilver, Eria, and Lucian, stories told by Cylin and other humans, and the revelations given by Yazah and Ravys. Lonewind's face contorted with fury at times, but he didn't interrupt.

Chance got to the confrontation with Yazah and Ravys, but stumbled when he reached the point where Ayliad joined them, and he and Lucian pursued her. Just saying her name made him start shaking.

Lonewind rested a hand on his shoulder. Chance drew a deep breath, and the panic receded enough for him to continue. He told Lonewind about Tieln's attempts to break the mental barriers that blocked his magic, and only stumbled a little over Ayliad's assault with the vines that invaded their camp. When he got to Ayliad's palace, though, he couldn't make himself go on.

When it was clear that Chance wouldn't say more, Lonewind spoke. "Whatever happened there, we will find Lucian."

She must have done something to him, like she did to me. What did she do? "We need Tieln."

Lonewind stood. "Then we aren't leaving until he wakes. Get some rest."

"No, I…"

Lonewind was already walking out of the room. Chance gazed after him. He thought about following, but couldn't summon the energy. The fur rug was soft and warm. He sank down and closed his eyes.

He woke with the awareness that someone sat nearby, watching him. His chest grew tight and his pulse raced. Part of him needed to open his eyes and see who was there. The rest of him was certain he would find Ayliad or Willow smirking down on him.

He opened his eyes. Eria sat at the table. She turned to him when he shifted, and smiled. "Sleep all right?"

"Better than I expected." Chance sat up slowly. "How are Tieln and Dash?"

"Both stable, but still out. I checked on them a little while ago. And Cahron was in here keeping an eye on things before me. You slept through the afternoon and all last night. It's about an hour after sunrise now."

His stomach growled. Chance pushed to his feet. "How's the village?"

"The humans still aren't sure what to make of all of us, but Cylin's done a lot to reassure them. I can't tell how much she believes what she says, but her attitude of 'Yeah, Lucian isn't with us right now, but we just have to go pick him up' has put a lot of the other villagers at ease. I don't think Devin or Doctor Kinnel are convinced, though." Eria watched him, mouth tightening in worry. "Did Lucian give you any hints about where he was going?"

"Only if 'I'm coming back' is a clue," Chance told his daughter. "I think it is, but I don't know *where* he's going back *to*."

"We'll figure it out. You'll figure it out," Eria said confidently. "Go get breakfast. The villagers brought up food."

He hadn't gotten much opportunity to look around Lucian's caves the last time he was here. As he walked further in, Chance caught himself expecting, at any moment, that Lucian would step around a corner, or call for him to wait up. When he found the kitchen and saw only Lonewind within, he fought disappointment.

Platters of smoked meats, bread, and fresh fruits and vegetables awaited on the table. Chance took a seat and grabbed a sausage.

"Lucian's humans are quite accommodating," Lonewind said.

"Lucian's humans are probably in their homes, offering prayers to you at this very moment, Lonewind," Chance said dryly.

"Better than having them declare me a demon," Lonewind said.

Chance shrugged. He'd never experienced that degree of animosity from humans, but Lonewind was much older than him and had, at times, experienced far more extreme reactions.

"I've been considering ways we can locate Lucian," Lonewind said. "The spirit realm is almost untraversable right now. Quicksilver is trying to use the Tree magic, but had no success so far."

Lynx strode into the kitchen and helped himself to bread and sausage. Lonewind eyed him. Chance knew Lonewind had never been fond of either of the twins. Sometimes he was surprised that Lonewind had agreed to take them when he left the planet.

Lynx leaned against the table, seeming to be waiting for one of them to speak.

"Can Echo find Lucian?" Chance asked.

Lynx smiled, showing his fangs. "We wondered when someone would ask."

Chance's fists clenched. *If you have the means, and have been withholding it just because no one ASKED…*

"He can't, not the way you mean," Lynx continued. "Echo could tell you exactly what Lucian sees, hears, smells, feels, thinks at this moment. He can't tell you how far Lucian is from here or which direction."

"And what *is* Lucian thinking?" Chance was sure he wouldn't like the answer.

"I should have known."

"Should have known *what*?" Chance demanded, slamming his fist on the table and pushing to his feet.

"You asked what he was thinking. At that moment, that's what he was thinking," Lynx said.

"No games, Lynx," Lonewind warned.

Lynx cocked an eyebrow. "Actually, games are exactly what Lucian calls them. Willow's games."

Color drained from Chance's face. He fell back into his chair. "No."

"He thinks himself in such a game—that everything that's happened since you were all rescued from the Coral Palace has been one of Willow's mind games. He believes that you, Chance, are still there, and still being tortured and raped by Ayliad and Willow.

Chance shook his head. "No." His pulse raced.

"He thinks that nearly two thousand *years* have been an illusion?" Lonewind demanded. "Years that included her death?"

Lynx turned to Lonewind with a bland expression. "Do you really think Willow *wouldn't* do so, had she had the chance? How much more satisfying to crush someone when they have spent so long thinking they were free?" He turned, and his blind, milky eyes seemed to fix on Chance. "As she was dying, Ayliad convinced Lucian that the memories you projected were actually your attempts to reach him through Willow's barriers —that you were piercing through the 'game'."

Chance shuddered. When they were captives in the Coral Palace, he'd succeeded in mentally reaching Lucian a few times. Sometimes he'd caught glimpses of the mental tortures Willow inflicted on her son. Willow had been powerful enough to block most attempts at communication through mind-speech.

Lynx continued. "Then she claimed that by killing her, he'd destroyed his means of ending and leaving the game, and that he'd trapped himself inside it, knowing it was Willow's torture, but lacking the means to escape."

I'm coming back. Lucian's words and the tormented anguish Chance had heard in them gained a terrifying meaning. "He's trying to return to the Coral Palace."

"Impossible," Lonewind said. "Even if something remains, it's miles out to sea and deep underwater."

Chance turned haunted eyes to Lonewind. "You think *that* will stop Lucian? Would it stop *you*, if Willow had Lucian or Cahron?"

Lonewind didn't answer, but he didn't have to.

Fear sat heavy in the pit of Chance's stomach. He felt cold, and his fingers tingled. He wanted to get away from everyone. The feeling of dread grew until it threatened to overwhelm him.

Then, as if someone had thrown a muffling blanket over his rising panic, the sensations eased. He could breathe again. The fear and dread remained, but muted, no longer crushing him.

Lonewind gave no indication that he'd noticed Chance's lapse. "I'll call everyone together. If you're right, we need a plan."

Chance simply nodded and waited for Lonewind to leave. When they were alone, he glared at Lynx. "Did you tell Echo to do that?"

"No. But I haven't told him to stop. Did you *want* to have a panic attack in front of Lonewind?"

Chance gritted his teeth, hands clenching. "Stop toying with my emotions, Echo."

No. As always, Echo's mental voice sounded far too young, like a child younger than Cylin rather than Lynx's twin.

"Echo, stop. Now," Chance ordered.

"Echo, do as he says," Lynx said.

It's not a good idea.

"You and I know that. He doesn't. So do as he says."

An unhappy sigh answered. The smothering blanket tore away. Jagged, raw emotions crashed into Chance like a thousand shards of glass.

He doubled over with a strangled cry. Panic. Anger. Fear. Despair. Horror. Dread. He couldn't breathe. He saw Ayliad standing over him, shoving him into warm salt water and holding him down as he choked and drowned. She pulled him up only long enough to rape him, then forced him under again. He heard her whispers mocking him, telling him that Lucian belonged to her. Telling him that no matter how he tried, he couldn't save his cousin.

He tried to flee, but someone blocked the doorway, cutting off his escape. He retreated to the far corner, pressing his back against the wall as he curled in on himself, shaking.

The worst of it finally released him. Sweat drenched Chance's shirt and trickled down his face. He was out of breath and his muscles ached as if he'd been running for miles. His palms bled from small, crescent-shaped cuts where his nails had dug into his skin.

Lynx stood at guard just inside the kitchen doorway. *And that is why Echo has been suppressing your emotions.*

Chance's hands still trembled. He pushed unsteadily to his feet. *I can't put them to rest if I can't feel them.*

You haven't put your fear of Ayliad or Willow to rest in two thousand years. You and Lucian both learned how to bury it instead. So why object when someone else helps you bury it again? Lynx leaned against the wall, folding his arms.

*I *object* to you, Echo, or anyone else deciding they know what's 'best' for me, whether or not I want it. If I do, as you say, bury these fears, it will be by my choice, no one else's.* Chance glared at Lynx.

A curious thing, choice. Tieln chose to merge with the Tree—Echo felt it. You went against that when you dragged him out of it. What about his choice? Lynx countered. *Would you put him back, if he insisted?*

Chance opened his mouth, then closed it, at a loss. Finally, he said, *No one would *want* to go back into the Tree like that.*

Just like no one would want to live in constant, paralyzing fear of their tormenters or be at the mercy of their own memories? Lynx asked. Before Chance could answer, he turned and walked out of the kitchen. "Lonewind has called a conference in the sitting room. Everyone else is there already."

Chance washed his face in the sink basin. He healed the cuts and took slow, deep breaths until his racing pulse calmed.

As collected as he could be, he left the kitchen and made his way to the sitting room.

He found not only the elves, with the exception of Dash and Tieln, but also Cylin, Devin, and Doctor Kinnel within. Lonewind stood in front of the empty fireplace. Cahron and Doctor Kinnel were engaged in spirited discussion. Eria and Quicksilver talked with Cylin and Devin, and Lynx lurked.

"Sorry to keep you waiting," Chance said, sinking into a plush chair.

"Don't worry, it hasn't been long," Cylin said. "We had a lot of stuff to get sorted out down in the village."

Lonewind waited only a moment for everyone to wrap up their conversations and sit. "Chance thinks Lucian is trying to reach the Coral Palace."

A chorus of startled exclamations answered him. Eria spoke up over the others. "Why would he go there? Does it even exist anymore?"

"Somehow, with her dying breaths, Ayliad convinced Lucian that he's currently trapped in one of Willow's mind games, and that he, Dash, and I are still prisoners there," Chance said.

Cylin and Devin both jerked up straight in their seats. "You mean, he's having an episode, but unlike others, he's not pulling out of this one," Cylin said.

"An episode?" Lonewind looked at her sharply.

"Not frequently, but at times, Lucian fell into a delusional state where he believed that everything he experienced was actually a hallucination inflicted on him by his mother to torture and torment him," Doctor Kinnel said. "Those that he experienced in Forest Town rarely lasted longer than eight to ten hours, and once he woke from them, he retained no memory of the event."

Cahron frowned deeply. "I don't like the sound of that."

"I can hardly say that any of us *liked* them," Doctor Kinnel said. "Unfortunately, I studied to be a surgeon, not a psychiatrist, and I'm not at all qualified to render mental health treatment to anyone, let alone an elf. I did as much as I felt I could without causing more harm than good, but..." He shook his head.

"So now Lucian's trying to get back to the Coral Palace because... he thinks he can break out of the hallucination there?" Quicksilver asked.

Chance closed his eyes. He hated the answer he found, and hated it more because he understood it. He'd felt it too many times. "No. He's going there to surrender. If Willow manipulated all of this, let Lucian think he had his freedom, a wife, a life without fear of her and Ayliad, and then she ripped everything away, and let him discover it had all been a lie, it would crush Lucian. It would crush... anyone."

"How do we get Lord Lucian back?" Devin asked urgently. "How do we convince him that this is real?"

"And what in drifters' bones are the Ghost and the Guardian doing about it? Why isn't one of them taking over?" Cylin put in.

"They're busy fighting Lucian's inner demons," Lynx said. "Perhaps one of them could take control, but those inner demons would overrun the other and tear Lucian's soul apart."

Chance looked to Lynx, and the fear and dread churned in his gut again. He clenched his fists. *Focus. Don't panic, focus.*

"First, we have to find Lucian," Lonewind said in a tone of command that silenced everyone. "Then, it will be up to Chance."

Chance nodded. It would be up to him to venture into Lucian's mind and break the curse of Ayliad's final vengeance.

"Do you know how to find Lucian?" Quicksilver asked. "I've been trying to sense the Guardian, but no luck there." He turned to Lynx. "What about Echo?"

"No, he cannot, and you're not the first to ask," Lynx said, though he answered with less disdain than he had Lonewind and Chance earlier. But Lynx did tend to treat his siblings better than he did other people.

"So we'll need Tieln's help, then," Eria said.

Chance nodded. "Cahron, when do you think he'll wake?"

"Physically, he could wake any time," Cahron said, a note of caution in his voice. "I'm more concerned about the state of his mind."

"You said he would be all right!" Chance protested.

"I said he would live," Cahron corrected. "But you know as well, if not better, than I do that having the Tree invade your body and mind is traumatic."

Chance didn't respond immediately, remembering Lynx's statement about Tieln's choice. Finally he said, "Yes, I do."

Cahron looked at him sympathetically. "I'm sorry to place this burden on you as well, Chance."

"Hold on, what burden?" Cylin interrupted.

"Entering Tieln's mind and drawing him out," Cahron said. "I do have a great deal of experience in that area, but healing a soul requires trust on the part of all parties. Tieln doesn't know me, and has no reason to trust me."

"He knows me, though," Eria said. "I can go."

Chance shook his head. "You don't have the experience with the Tree, Eria."

She shot him a glower. *I can handle the Tree.*

I know. But I don't want you to get hurt.

Eria made a sound of exasperation, but said, "I'll be ready to back you up, then."

"Thanks." He hoped he wouldn't need help, but, as Cahron warned, he didn't know what to expect in Tieln's mind after the youth's experience with the Tree.

~

Chance sat on the edge of Lucian's bed, beside Tieln. The youth didn't stir. His color was better, and his breathing slow and steady in sleep. Chance rested a hand on Tieln's shoulder and sent himself into the youth's mind.

The barracks he'd seen during his first visit to Tieln's soul lay in shambles. Something had torn the floor to splinters and crushed bunks, chairs, and tables. Chance slowly picked his way through the wreckage, not seeing Tieln anywhere within. Smothering silence hung over everything.

Outside, a wall of brambles, brittle and dry but armed with wicked thorns, ringed a practice yard. He grabbed a branch to pull it aside, careful to avoid the thorns.

An echo of the Guardian glowered at him, thorny and threatening.

"Get the fuck out of my way," Chance snarled.

Dry creaks filled the still air as the brambles slowly peeled back, opening a narrow gap. Chance edged through.

Tieln lay in the middle of the yard, curled protectively around a stunted, drooping sapling. Chance walked to him, stepping over debris from the brambles. "Tieln."

Tieln slowly raised his head and turned to Chance. His brown eyes had turned amber, like Lucian's. For a moment, his gaze felt all too much like Lucian's. Then he shuddered and closed his eyes.

"Am I in the Tree? The Guardian said I would become part of the Tree." His voice was low and hoarse.

"You were in the Tree. We pulled you out," Chance told him.

"I don't hear the Guardian anymore."

"You aren't in the Tree any longer, Tieln." Chance wasn't sure if Tieln heard or understood him, or if the youth was even talking to him.

"I wasn't in the Tree when the Guardian took control,"

Tieln said, looking at Chance again. He laid a hand on the trunk of the battered sapling. "It was killing my Sapling."

Chance stepped closer. He could see gouges in the trunk now, and not all the fallen branches here came from the bramble wall.

Tieln rested his head against the trunk. "Talk to me. Please. Why can't I hear you?"

Chance knew the youth wasn't speaking to him this time, but he answered anyway. "If your sapling was injured, it might need time to heal before it can answer." And he had no idea just how long that might take.

Tieln's fists clenched. "He tried to shield me from the pain. He shouldn't have. I agreed to do this. To become part of the Tree."

It was a rare day when Chance thought Dash might have more success than he would talking to someone. But Dash understood the Tree in ways Chance never could.

I can't wait for Dash to wake up, though, and I don't know what state his mind will be in either.

He touched Tieln's shoulder. "We're in Forest Town. Ayliad is dead. The Tree is under control."

Tieln didn't respond.

"We need your help, Tieln."

Tieln looked at him with hollow eyes. "Why? I'm just some half-human screwup who can't protect anything I care about."

Chance shook his head. "That's not true, and none of us believe that of you. And we need your help because you can do things the rest of us can't." He drew a deep breath. "Lucian is missing."

Tieln gazed at him, unblinking, unmoving. "And that's all that matters, isn't it? Lucian. That's all that mattered to the Guardian, why it would have sacrificed me and my Sapling both. And it's all that matters to you."

"What?" Chance stared at him. "No, that's not true."

Tieln sneered. "I thought you couldn't lie in mind speech."

"I'm not lying," Chance said.

Tieln slowly rose to his feet. "You wouldn't even be here if you didn't need me to find him. You don't care what happens to me, or whether I or the Sapling needs help, just as long as you get a compass."

"That's not true!"

"Get out of my head." Tieln's voice was cold as ice, hard as the Guardian.

Chance didn't move. "This is not just about Lucian, Tieln." *Is it?*

Tieln drew the pistol from the holster on his belt. "Get out."

Chance backed up a step. "I came here because you haven't woken yet, and we all worried about how you fared after your encounter with the Tree." He needed to make Tieln listen. To make him understand that he needed to wake up, that they wanted to help him.

Because you want to use him to find Lucian, whether he's in any condition to use his magic or not. The insidious whisper in his mind was his own voice, scorning him for claiming altruistic motives. *You're going to use him as a tool, just like Willow and Ayliad used Lynx and Echo. Not even people, just tools.*

Chance staggered. "No. That's not... I'm not..."

"Get out." The pistol hammer cocked.

Chance fell to his knees, clutching his head. The world wavered around him. For a moment, he saw bare white walls, a bed, chains... and Willow.

No. No, I can't inflict that on Tieln's mind. He couldn't hear Tieln anymore, only Willow's sultry, mocking whisper.

"Did you think you could escape me, slave?"

With a cry of horror and fear, Chance broke the connection with Tieln's mind. He was falling, falling...

He hit the stone floor hard. Dazed, he couldn't make sense of the urgent voice speaking to him.

"Dad! What happened?"

He shied away from the hands that touched his shoulder. "Get Cahron," he managed.

Maybe minutes, maybe hours later, someone ran into the room. Chance lay curled on the floor where he'd fallen. He flinched when the steps stopped beside him.

I'm here, Chance, Cahron said. *Do you hear me?*

"Yes," he whispered.

Can you tell me what happened?

He couldn't gather himself enough to respond in mind speech, and his thoughts shied away from considering why. He whispered, and sensed Cahron lean close to hear. "Tieln is in pain. Angry. Afraid. His sapling was badly wounded when the Guardian fought Dash's corrupted Tree. I… don't know how to help it. If I can help it." A tremor shook him. "When I told him we need his help, he said I just want to use him, that I only care about Lucian. Told me to get out of his head."

And then? Cahron prompted gently.

"Tried to tell him he was wrong. He wouldn't listen. Said I was lying. I wasn't lying. I… I wasn't… Then, I… left."

Cahron rested a hand on his shoulder. Chance flinched, but didn't jerk away. *And what else, Chance?*

He knew Cahron was offering him a choice, a chance to preserve a little privacy, but he couldn't force himself to take it. "Nothing else."

He felt Cahron enter his mind, and the healer's magic pulled his awareness with it, inside, to a place he knew too well. A place he knew, and hated, and feared.

T he room had no doors, no windows. No way in or out. The off-white walls held no adornments, nothing to catch the eye or give the mind a distraction. Only a single piece of furniture occupied it: a four-poster bed. Chance, naked, lay on the bed, his limbs drawn spread-eagle, each chained to one of the bedposts. A gag muffled his screams of terror.

His eyes darted frantically around the room. He was alone. Willow wasn't here. He struggled against the chains. Tears of fear and despair ran down his cheeks.

You deserve this. The whisper spoke with his own voice. *You're no better than Ayliad or Willow. Using Lucian's son. Abandoning him to his pain. You earned these chains.*

Chance squeezed his eyes shut, shaking his head in denial of the accusations. Not this. Not here. He didn't deserve to be trapped once again in this room that Willow had created in his mind, where she had imprisoned, tortured, and raped his soul until he could take no more.

"Chance!" Cahron's shout was muffled, distant. Then Chance felt Cahron pitting his will against his own.

Not against Willow's will. Against Chance's. Against the part of his mind that demanded he be punished. Chance tried not to resist. He desperately wanted Cahron to free him, even more than he desperately feared what Cahron would think, seeing him in this room, these chains. Cahron had freed him from this room more than once. Willow had taken great, sadistic pleasure in trapping Chance here time and again when she sought to crush him and make him into her slave.

It was hard not to fight, even knowing who sought to influence his mindscape and why.

The world shifted around Chance. He heard the soothing splash of a burbling fountain. He stood in the enclosed courtyard of his father's home, surrounded by shaped rock formations, sheltering trees, and pools fed by the fountain. His limbs and mouth were free. Chance shivered and closed his eyes, willing himself to be clothed. His wrists and ankles bled from his struggles against the shackles, but the linen shirt and trousers that materialized on him hid the abrasions.

Steps approached. "Chance?"

"Here," he answered Cahron.

The older soul-healer looked no different in the spirit than in the flesh, but his spirit had an unmistakable aura of power that went unseen in the physical world. Cahron sat on the rim of the fountain and looked around. "It's been many centuries since I last saw Aisling's caverns."

"It's been a long time since you were here, either," Chance said quietly.

"True." Cahron gave him a long, steady look. "What happened?"

"I did not try to wake Tieln just to use him to find Lucian! I was worried about Tieln as well, and how the Tree might have affected him. I wanted to be sure he was all right."

"Is he?" Cahron asked.

The question hung in the air. Chance looked away from Cahron. "No. And the fragment of the Tree magic inside him, his sapling, isn't either. I should have been able to offer him some kind of help. But I didn't. He accused me of using him and not caring what happened to him." Chance paused a moment to collect himself, but his voice still trembled. "When he said that, all I could think was that it was no different from what Ayliad and Willow did to Lynx and Echo. Used them as tools for their own desires." He shuddered.

"There's a world of difference between seeking the aid of someone who can help you find Lucian, and systematically, deliberately shaping children into weapons," Cahron said.

"Is there, though?" Chance turned to him again. "If I'm willing to use *Lucian's son* as a tool when I *know* that he's hurt and wounded, how can I claim to be any better?" His voice fell to a whisper. "How can I claim that I don't deserve to be punished?"

Cahron rose and set a hand on Chance's shoulder. "Whether or not you're right, you do *not* deserve any punishment of Willow's creation. You don't deserve to be trapped in that room again."

Chance squeezed his eyes shut and sank to the floor, trembling. "I don't know how long since I was last there, but it was like nothing had changed. I was in that room, and I was just… her plaything again. Her… her slave. I couldn't get out."

"You're not there anymore, Chance," Cahron said. "You're safe."

I'm never safe. Willow and Ayliad taught me that. "I wasn't prepared. I should have been. I should have been able to resist when Ayliad manipulated my memories. I should have anticipated how she would attack Lucian. That's what I *do*! Learn everything, prepare for everything so they can't take us by surprise again. And I failed. Again."

"Yet now Ayliad, like Willow, is dead, and you are not." Cahron sat beside him. "Neither is Lucian."

"I should have stopped her before she got to Lucian."

"We'll find him, Chance. Ayliad won't win this time." Cahron patted him on the shoulder. "You should rest."

"There's no time," Chance began, turning to Cahron.

"You can rest, or I can make you rest," Cahron told him. "You have the best chance of drawing Lucian out of his delusion, but you can't do that if you've run yourself dry."

Protests lay on his lips, but finally Chance bowed his head, conceding. "I'll try."

Before he said more, he sensed Cahron's magic lulling him toward sleep. "Good."

Chance shot the older healer an exasperated look. "I said I'd try to rest." He lay down on the marble floor, resting his head on his arm.

Cahron just smiled gently. "I know. And this way, you actually *will* rest. Sleep well, Chance."

~

Despite his objection to Cahron's method, Chance admitted that he'd needed the sleep. Five hours of rest for his mind as well as his body cleared his head. But it still didn't tell him what to do now.

He made his way back to Lucian's room. Cylin sat at the table, idly doodling on a scrap of paper. She turned to him. "Oh, hey Chance. Tieln and Dash are still out cold. Hardly seen either of them even twitch."

Chance sat across from her. She seemed calm, but Cylin kept her emotions tight to herself. "Are you worried about Lucian?"

"Of course I am! He's wandering around out there somewhere in the middle of an episode that he can't get out of. I'd be stupid not to worry about him."

"You've spoken of his 'episodes' before. What do you know?" Chance asked her.

"I've only seen one of them," Cylin answered. "He thought he was stuck in one of Willow's mind games. At first he thought I was one of her pawns in the game. When I finally convinced him that I wasn't, he thought I must be someone else inside his head, which makes a little more sense now than it did then." She considered. "When he did think I was someone else, he wanted me to find and free you first."

Chance listened, silent.

"When I told him I didn't know where you were, I expected him to start raging again, but it actually calmed him down." She gazed at Chance. "It calmed him down a *lot* to think that you weren't Willow's prisoner. So I think that right now, Lucian thinks that she and Ayliad have you."

Chance shuddered and nodded. "It's always been like that —me trying to protect him, and him trying to protect me."

Cylin looked at the bed where Tieln slept. "During the episode, when Lucian finally lay down, he created a stone lattice barrier around the bed. At the time, I thought it bizarre that someone as powerful as him would be afraid of me. I understand now. In the morning, he made a joke about the barrier. He didn't have any memory of the episode, but I'm sure he knew exactly why he'd put the wall between us."

No memory of the episode. Lucian had said that as well. Did he truly not remember them, or did he bury those memories deep within his soul? Had they been lurking there, festering, until Ayliad opened a path for them to break free?

Chance rose and walked to Tieln. "I'm going to try to wake him again."

"Anything I need to do?" Cylin asked.

"If you see me start to convulse, break my physical contact with him," Chance told her. He sat on the edge of the bed and rested his hand on Tieln's chest. "Then start yelling for Cahron."

Cylin's eyebrows rose, but she just said, "Good to know. Good luck."

∽

Tieln sat beside his sapling. His eyes followed Chance, but otherwise he didn't move.

Chance approached within easy speaking distance. "I did everything wrong last time I came. I came with my needs and ignored yours."

Tieln said nothing.

"I don't know if I can help your sapling, but if you are willing, I'll try."

"Who was that woman?"

Chance froze. "What woman?"

"The one who appeared just before you left. Black hair, black dress." Tieln turned to face him.

Chance flinched. "Willow."

"I saw glimpses of her in the images you projected after Ayliad disabled you. You're afraid of her."

"Yes."

"Is Lucian as well?"

"Lucian hates her with every fiber of his being." The words seemed insufficient to describe the fiery rage Lucian felt toward his mother. "His hate leaves little room for fear."

"But Lucian's afraid now," Tieln said. "Afraid that Willow has somehow deceived him, and he's still her prisoner. Right?"

Chance stared at him. "How do you know that?"

"I can still hear," Tieln said. When Chance continued to look at him, baffled, he said, "When you all talk with your minds, I hear it. There are some voices I don't recognize. One of them is especially worried about Lucian." He frowned. "And apparently about me as well."

"You can hear Lonewind speaking to Cahron," Chance said, stunned.

"Why is that strange?" Tieln asked.

"Lonewind wouldn't discuss that sort of thing openly, and most people can't overhear private mental conversations. It's like being able to hear what someone's saying when they're whispering two rooms away." Chance frowned, wondering whether Tieln had always had such a talent, or if it was a new development. "It's possible to develop one's skill in mind-speech to the point where someone can eavesdrop, but the only elf I know who could do so at will was… Willow."

Tieln digested that in silence. Finally, he stood. "You need my help to find Lucian."

Chance looked from Tieln to the damaged sapling. "I'll try to help your sapling whether you locate Lucian or not."

Tieln rested a hand on the trunk. "He wants to find Lucian too. He told me so." He faced Chance. "We're ready."

"Are you sure?"

"I hope I don't have to point a gun at you again to convince you that I am," Tieln retorted.

"You don't. But I want to be sure this *is* what you want, and not simply what you think you have to do."

Tieln's hand remained pressed against the trunk of the sapling. "The Guardian gave me a choice. It was going to destroy the corrupted Tree either way, but I could either let it channel that power through my Sapling, or through me. If it used my Sapling, the Guardian's power would destroy the Sapling. If it used me, the Guardian said I would become part of the Tree, and while that probably wouldn't kill me, I would be trapped forever. But it said that if I did, I could protect the rest of you from the Tree." He looked into Chance's eyes. "If I was willing to accept *that* fate, do you think I'd do less to stop Ayliad and Willow?"

"I think that you were justified in telling me to get out and leave you alone last time," Chance said. "And that if you choose to prioritize your own needs, you have every right to."

Tieln shook his head. "Not worth the price. That will come later."

A stab of guilt jabbed Chance. Just like Lucian, pushing back his own needs because he thought someone else's were more important. "You are indeed part of this clan," he said softly. "Stars help us all."

Chance drew a deep breath and straightened, lifting his hand from Tieln's chest.

"No convulsions," Cylin said. "That's good."

Chance turned to her, to find that Cahron, Eria, and

Lonewind had joined the human. Lonewind's expression was hard to read, but Eria looked worried and Cahron scowled. Cylin continued. "You didn't mention that you weren't supposed to be doing stuff like that, though."

"No one said I couldn't," Chance said.

"Clearly an oversight on my part, thinking that good sense would override such impulses," Cahron said.

Behind Chance, Tieln shifted and rolled onto his side, facing toward the voices. "Thought good sense went against the rules of being an elf."

"No, but ignoring it tends to come with being part of this clan," Chance said. He turned and offered Tieln a hand. Lucian's son waved it off and slowly sat up.

Something about Tieln's eyes bothered Chance. It took him a moment to realize that their color had changed. Before the Tree, they had been brown. Now Tieln's eyes, like Lucian and Lonewind, were amber in the waking world as well as in the mindscape. Tieln's gaze found Lonewind and Cahron. "I don't know you."

"This is Cahron. He's the greatest soul-healer I know," Chance began. "And this is—"

Lonewind swept across the room. "I am Lonewind. Lucian is my son, and you are my grandson."

Tieln blinked and stared at the forceful presence standing over him. He seemed unsure what to make of the possessive declaration. After a moment, he collected himself enough to say, "I thought you were exploring the stars."

"I returned when I learned of the situation here," Lonewind told him.

"Oh." Tieln carefully pushed to his feet.

Lonewind steadied him. "Chance told us that you are able to find people and things."

"Lonewind, he *just* woke up," Cahron chided. "Let Tieln get his bearings."

"No, it's fine" Tieln straightened and closed his eyes. "I can find Lucian." He wavered, then steadied himself. "He's… quite far away."

"But you can find him?" Lonewind pressed.

Tieln nodded. "I can sense him."

Chance released a breath he didn't remember holding. "Then we just have to reach him."

Cylin jumped to her feet. "Great. When do we leave?"

"Immed—" Lonewind began.

Cahron cut him off. "As soon as we decide who is coming with us and who is staying here. Dash hasn't woken yet, and he will need someone who knows how to handle him when he rouses."

Eria's lips pressed into a thin line. "Well, obviously Dad needs to go. And you're going with Lonewind, Cahron. So as healers go, that leaves me." She let out a heavy breath. "I *want* to go with you and help Lucian, but if one of us needs to stay with Dash, I'm the only reasonable choice."

Hurried steps rushed down the hall, followed by an equally swift, but more even set. Quicksilver entered the room, with Lynx a little behind him. "Lynx said Tieln's awake, and we need to plan?" Quicksilver asked.

"We're deciding who needs to stay here with Dash," Eria told him. "And all in all, that should be me."

"Oh." Quicksilver looked around the room. Chance could all but see the thoughts racing through his mind. "I'll stay as well. I can help with the Tree aspect for Dash. Also, the humans we rescued from Ayliad's lair will do better with a few familiar faces."

Lonewind looked around the room. "Then Eria and Quicksilver will stay here, and I'll take Chance, Cahron, Tieln, and Lynx to Lucian."

"There is no fucking way you're leaving me here!" Cylin folded her arms and glared at Lonewind.

"Why not?" Lonewind asked.

Cylin raised her arm and turned it so that the bracelet faced Lonewind. "Because I'm part of the fucking family. Lucian said so."

Lonewind looked at the bracelet, then at Cylin. "Very well."

~

Lonewind bypassed any argument with other residents of Forest Town by simply not talking to them at all. The four elves, Tieln, and Cylin left Lucian's cave without fanfare as evening drew near, carrying their gear and a supply of dried food scavenged from Lucian's cave. Chance was concerned about Tieln, so recently returned to consciousness, but Tieln waved it away when Chance mentioned it.

Since landing the meteor at Lucian's cave, Lonewind had reshaped the stone. Rather than a shapeless hunk of rock, it now clearly held the form of a vessel. Knowing that Lonewind had been born and raised on a tropical island, and knowing his innate love of water, Chance wasn't surprised to find that the craft now resembled a sailing ship, including twin masts and stone sails. The hull was textured to imitate wood planks held together by iron nails. Stone struts extended from the hillside to support the ship.

Lynx sprang ten feet from the ground to the side of the ship, his claws finding purchase to climb the rest of the way aboard. Chance levitated himself, Tieln, and Cylin aboard, while Lonewind brought Cahron with him.

Tieln's gaze followed Lynx. In a low voice, he asked Chance, "Why is there a Creature with us?"

Chance grimaced. "I told you about Lynx and Echo, my sons by Ayliad."

Tieln nodded.

"That's Lynx. No, he wasn't born looking like that. He's always been blind, but he was born looking like an elf. After an encounter with Karishan, Lynx decide that the claws and armor of a Creature were ideal physical enhancements, to better protect his brother."

"He did that *voluntarily*?" Tieln eyed Lynx warily.

Lynx flexed his claws. "As Chance said, this form is ideal for keeping my brother safe from harm."

"Right." Tieln tore his gaze away and looked around the ship. He turned to Lonewind. "You didn't travel the stars in this, did you?"

"No," Lonewind answered. "Our spacecraft is still in orbit, with the rest of the clan aboard." He gestured toward a doorway. "Bunks are below."

"I brought some furs and blankets from the cave," Cahron added. "You don't have to sleep on bare stone."

Lonewind's magic wrapped around the ship. The mooring struts melted back into the hillside and the stone ship floated in the air. Lonewind turned to Tieln, who stepped up to the helm. The wheel actually turned, Chance noticed. The rudder probably did as well, though neither would affect the direction of the vessel.

Tieln pointed. "That way."

The ship moved smoothly up and away, flying south-west. As they went, Lonewind manipulated the stone to create wind shields. Cylin stood by the railing, not even trying to disguise her amazement as she looked down.

Night crept across the land. Cahron eventually went below deck to sleep. Chance sat near the bow of the ship and looked up to the stars. Without lights from cities, the night sky was deep and dark. Two of the moons were waning crescents, and the third, half full, hung low on the horizon. He picked out a glint of light moving across the sky, and wondered if that was the shell that held the rest of the clan.

Lonewind, if you want me to take control of this ship so you can rest, tell me.

I'll rest once we've found Lucian, Lonewind answered.

Chance doubted that. Once they found Lucian, Lonewind would pace until his son was safely freed from the prison of his mind, or until Cahron used magic to knock him out as he had Chance.

Without meaning to, Chance dozed. He jerked awake several times in the night, thinking he heard someone calling his name, but each time, it was only the wind. When he looked to the helm, he saw Lonewind standing like some ancient maritime captain, the wind sweeping back his long auburn hair. The first time, Tieln stood beside him, but later in the night, only Lonewind remained.

When morning dawned, they flew over barren hills. A river carved between the slopes. In the distance, Chance saw trickles of smoke from a village. He made his way over to the helm. Lonewind stood with one hand on the wheel, gazing into the distance. Tieln lay at the base of the mast, a blanket wrapped around him.

Not wanting to wake Tieln, Chance asked, *How much further, do you think?*

We're less than a day from the coast, Lonewind answered.

Tieln shifted in his sleep and raised one hand to point in the direction they were going. Chance blinked and looked to Lonewind with unspoken question.

Lonewind spoke quietly. "Since he lay down, that's been his response when I asked him in mind-speech which direction to go. Though I didn't know he would also hear conversations not directed to him."

"That seems to be a new development," Chance said. "His magic has manifested somewhat haphazardly. I don't know how his encounter with the Tree have affected it, either."

Lonewind looked down at Tieln, then bent and tucked the blanket around him. He straightened and turned his gaze to the horizon once more. "Whatever may happen, Tieln is part of the clan now. My grandson."

Tieln didn't wake until mid-morning, well after everyone else was up and moving around the ship. By then, the landscape had changed to flatland studded by craters where bombs had impacted. Chance saw no sign of current habitation by humans, and not even a hint of green on the brown and gray ground.

Chance brought Tieln a meal of dried meat and flatbread. As Tieln chewed on the jerky, he said, "Lucian has stopped, for the moment. And we are much closer than we were in Forest Town."

Lynx dropped down from the mast he'd been climbing. "Lucian has reached the shore where you were all captured and taken to the Coral Palace."

A chill ran down Chance's spine. Lucian must have been driving himself to exhaustion and beyond. "He can't swim to the Coral Palace."

"Echo is working to convince him of that," Lynx said. "He's focusing Lucian on the idea of waiting on the shore until Willow's minions come for him instead."

That wasn't much better, to Chance's mind, but it might at least prevent Lucian from drowning himself. "How fast are we going, Lonewind?"

"Faster than an automobile, not as fast as a jet," Lonewind answered. "Cahron forbade me from breaking the sound barrier."

"Certainly not in an open-air vessel with passengers," Chance said.

"My calculations already accounted for that, Chance," Lonewind told him with an expression of mild exasperation.

"I'm not even going to ask what all that means," Cylin said from her post by the railing.

Tieln shook his head and joined her. "No idea."

Cahron settled on a bench and looked over the rail, gaze distant. "I keep expecting to see green fields and herds of game animals below, not this barren, empty land."

"There is still green in some areas of the planet," Lonewind said. "Mostly further south—jungle areas. The coast is also in better condition. I noticed while we were in orbit."

"Well, that's good to know," Cahron said.

Cylin flopped down beside the older healer. "You're one of those elves who can go into other people's heads, right?"

Cahron smiled. "Yes, although I've never tried entering a human's mind before."

She raised her hands, shaking her head quickly. "I didn't mean me! But you're going with Chance to pull Lucian back, right?"

"Ah." Cahron looked to Chance, then back to Cylin regretfully. "No, this isn't something I can help Chance with—not at first, at least."

"Why not?" she demanded. "I understand why you couldn't with Tieln, but Lucian knows you. So why won't you help him?"

"I wish it was that easy," Cahron said quietly. "There's a strange and delicate balance to working with the soul, Cylin. I knew from Chance that Tieln had little experience with elves or magic. A stranger entering his mind would have caused more turmoil and alarm. I would have done so if it were necessary, but both Chance and Eria had an established relationship with him."

Cylin nodded slowly. "Sure, but how does that relate to *not* going into Lucian's head?"

"It's about understanding the situation. I would much rather enter Lucian's mind myself, or at the very least accompany Chance, but the truth is, Lucian would be *more* receptive to an unknown elf, so long as they bore no resemblance to Willow or Ayliad, entering his mind that he would be to me."

Chance winced slightly, regardless of the accuracy of Cahron's words.

Cylin's brow furrowed in confusion. "Why? Doesn't Lucian trust you?"

"His conscious mind does. His unconscious, though…" Cahron sighed, but gave her a small, wry smile. "To his unconscious mind, I am too much his father's soul healer. When you look at Lonewind, you see a father who would do anything, make any sacrifice for his son."

Cylin looked back, and Chance followed her gaze to Lonewind—stoic, determined, and focused. Cylin nodded slowly and looked back to Cahron. "Are you about to tell me something that reveals this clan is even more messed up than I already knew?"

"If you don't know, then yes, probably. And if you have already heard the tale, you've probably only heard it in part, because there are some aspects that the younger generation doesn't know as well.

"Great." Cylin let out a long breath. "Okay, let's hear it."

"I don't know how much you know about Lonewind's past, so forgive me if I repeat things you already know. Lonewind was born and raised on a tropical island. His father was not a native of the island, and was the most powerful elf any of that tribe had ever seen. As a leader, he apparently did well enough, but as a father, he was aloof and distant. Once Lonewind came to the mainland, one of the questions he carried with him was what had made his father the way he was. In those early years, we were a fairly nomadic little clan, and eventually, we came upon a small, isolated community of powerful elves. Their leader, a beautiful and powerful woman named Willow, welcomed us, and we learned before long that this was the place from which Lonewind's father had come."

Cahron sighed. "When you're immortal, isolated, and powerful enough that nothing external can threaten you, boredom and ennui become the new enemies. Lonewind's father had been caught in an internal power struggle with Willow, and when he lost, he fled for fear of her retaliation. Most of the members of our clan weren't of great interest to Willow, but Lonewind, the powerful son of her former rival, drew her like a magnet. She seduced him, then held him prisoner when he tried to leave. He escaped before he knew she was pregnant, and had to return to steal his son from her. We —the rest of the clan—didn't let Lonewind go back there alone, much as he wanted to keep us safely away from Willow. Once he had Lucian, we fled back toward our home.

"Willow sent some of her followers in pursuit, but she was by far the greater danger. She didn't attack us in the flesh, but through the spirit realm. She was a good eight hundred years older than Lonewind, with the power to show for it." Cahron gazed toward the horizon. "She was furious that Lonewind had slipped from her net and taken Lucian with him. Not out of any great love for Lucian, sadly, but because he was a pawn she could use to manipulate Lonewind. Her target was Lonewind, but the times that he resisted her relentless attacks, she turned her focus onto the rest of us. Lucian, fortunately, was very young; he doesn't remember."

Not consciously, at least. Chance was less confident than Cahron that some fragments didn't linger in Lucian's nightmares.

Cahron looked at Lonewind, then back to Cylin. Tieln had drifted closer to listen. Lonewind gazed into the sky beyond the ship, but Chance was sure he heard every word. Cahron spoke more quietly. "Lonewind knew Willow was merciless. To protect the rest of us from her, he offered her a deal. If she would agree not to attack his friends and companions, they… we, in turn, wouldn't attempt to interfere with her visiting Lonewind or Lucian through the spirit realm."

Chance winced. The bargain. Even understanding why Lonewind had made it, hearing about it always made him feel sick. He wasn't sure if that was despite his own deal made with Ayliad and Willow, or because of it.

"You *agreed* to that?" Cylin demanded.

Cahron gazed at her. "At the time, I was barely keeping myself together. If Willow wasn't targeting Lonewind, her next most likely victim was me. She was eager to weaponize my guilt over encouraging Lonewind to enter a relationship with her in the first place, as well as the more straightforward mental and magical attacks. I didn't like the deal—none of us did—but I wasn't in a condition to attempt to stop Lonewind."

"You took a child into the spirit realm?" Tieln cut in, aghast.

"What? No!" Cahron shook his head quickly. "Absolutely not. Willow traveled through the spirit realm to visit him. But for the rest of us, it meant that she might show up any time, and if we interfered, she could and would retaliate."

"She had two kinds of visits," Lonewind said, looking into the horizon. "Those that happened during the day, when Lucian was awake, when she kept up the pretense of a caring mother, and those that happened at night, after Lucian was asleep. Those were the visits when she tried to break my will and crush my spirit, so that I would return to her."

Cylin's frown deepened. "So she could come and go as she wanted, as long as she didn't touch anyone other than Lonewind or Lucian?"

"Yes." Cahron spoke in a quiet but steady voice. "And there was one more piece to it. If Willow abided by the deal, Lonewind swore that he wouldn't poison Lucian against his mother. He hoped that Lucian, at least, could have a better relationship with his mother than Lonewind ever did with his own father. Willow didn't care about protecting her son's innocence, but she knew that Lonewind did, and they both knew she could, and would, use it as a weapon."

This time, Cylin spun and looked at Lonewind. "How the *fuck* did you expect *that* to work out well?"

"I trusted Lucian," Lonewind said. "When he was old enough, I knew he would be able to see the truth for himself."

"And in the mean time, everyone had to pretend she wasn't an evil, manipulative torturer? No wonder he said there's no such thing as an innocent lie to tell a child."

"Lucian was almost fifty when he finally learned the truth," Cahron said.

Tieln, nearly fifty himself, shifted uneasily, perhaps thinking about his own experiences with having his understanding of the world torn to pieces.

Cahron continued. "The clan had migrated to a new continent and made our home on the coast in a subtropical climate. One day, while Lonewind was teaching the boys to sail, Willow appeared in the flesh. She'd altered her body to breathe underwater. She snatched Lonewind from the boat and dragged him into the depths.

Chance closed his eyes. He vividly remembered the look of shock and fear on Lonewind's face, the terrified cries in the boat, the confusion and hurt in Lucian's eyes as his mother stole his father from him and ignored him completely.

"We also learned then that Chance's birth father, Moonfire, had been her spy in our midst," Cahron said. "While the rest of us still reeled from Willow's abduction of Lonewind, Moonfire gave Lucian the ability to breath underwater and brought him to Willow." Cahron closed his eyes. "I don't know what Lucian saw there, or what Willow told him."

"She told him that it was time to build our perfect family, as it always should have been." Lonewind's voice wasn't loud, but it carried to all of them. "She claimed that if not for the rest of the clan, I would have returned to her with Lucian long ago. Always, there was enough twisted truth that she wasn't lying. She could both overhear and block mind speech in her lair. I couldn't refute her claims, and I couldn't speak to Lucian without her knowing. I could only hope he would see the truth through her deceit. Eventually, he did, or at least he doubted her enough. He freed me, and we escaped."

Chance shuddered, glad eyes were on Cahron, not him. His first encounters with Willow had happened when he was in the spirit realm, helping guide Lucian and Lonewind through the depths toward shore. At their first meeting, she had been amused. The next time, though, Willow, already angry over her son's defiance, lost her patience. She'd trapped Chance's spirit and violated him. With a whispered warning about what happened to those who 'interfered', she'd released him to flee back to his body.

Fighting to block out that memory, he missed some of Cahron's words. His attention snapped back when Cahron said, "As we all gathered on that beach around Lucian and Lonewind, everything fell together for Lucian. In that moment, he understood that every adult in the clan knew the truth about Willow, and had known it for his whole life."

Another moment burned into Chance's memory.

Lucian's eyes moved from one person to the next. Sea water dripped from his clothes and hair. "You knew. All of you. You knew." His chest heaved in rapid breaths. "You lied to me. You never told me the truth."

"What truth, Lucian?" Cahron asked, kneeling beside Lonewind's prone form.

Lucian's face twisted in rage. "That I'm nothing more than an unwanted byproduct of my mother raping my father."

Cahron continued quietly. "We all, at points, had to play a part in concealing that knowledge from Lucian, but I'm the one who was most intimately acquainted with the tortures

Willow inflicted on Lonewind. I'm the one who entered his mind to heal the horrors she inflicted on his soul. Lucian trusted me to tell him the truth about his father, and with the bargain in place, I chose to follow Lonewind's wishes rather than tell Lucian what Willow had done."

"Oh." Cylin digested that.

"We'd hidden the extent of her destruction from Lucian better than I knew. Chance understood, I think, but for a long time, Lucian didn't understand that the bargain wasn't just about deceiving him; it was the only way Lonewind could protect the rest of the clan from her." Cahron let out a heavy breath. "She excelled at drawing out information from people. She knew how to attack us, whether physically or mentally, in the ways that hurt the most."

"What, you didn't think that was a little important for him to know?" Cylin cut in.

Cahron gave her a sad smile. "It's easy to think that what's clearly obvious to you should be equally obvious to someone else. But that's why Lucian's soul won't accept me, and why it must be Chance who enters Lucian's mind."

When neither Cylin nor Tieln said anything, Cahron stood and climbed the steps to the upper deck and spoke quietly with Lonewind.

Several more hours passed before Tieln suddenly said, "More south." He pointed.

The ship smoothly swung in the direction he indicated. "Is Lucian still stationary?" Lonewind asked.

"He's sticking in one area," Tieln said. "I just hadn't realized we'd angled too far west."

"And the distance?"

Tieln's gaze grew distant. "We're getting close."

Another hour, and Chance saw the ocean. He shivered. As a youth, he'd loved the ocean—swimming, fishing, sailing, and all the other joys it held. Now he couldn't look at the waves without thinking of the dark evil that had lived beneath the waters.

Lonewind followed the coastline south, passing over several small fishing communities. Humans gaped at the sky, pointing wildly at the flying ship. If anyone called to them, they were too high to hear.

The air was warm, but a cold lump of dread grew in Chance's gut. He didn't understand why until he realized that he recognized this stretch of coastline, a memory buried and nearly forgotten.

Laughing, Ayliad splashed through the surf, her golden hair streaming behind her. Lucian ran after her, laughing as well, and they both tumbled into the water, kissing passionately. Chance rolled his eyes. Beside him, Dash, grinning, offered, "I could convince some seaweed to get caught in all the wrong places, you know."

A memory of joy, of pure happiness and innocence, made hard and bitter by the truth. Chance closed his eyes against stinging tears.

Does Lucian remember that? Does he think about those memories now, while he waits to be dragged back into the depths, into a prison he cannot escape?

Several people spoke, but Chance didn't hear until Cahron gave him a mental nudge. He opened his eyes and turned to the others. "Sorry, what?"

"Do you know this area?" Lonewind asked.

"It's… familiar, to a point," he admitted.

"We're close enough to go overland the rest of the way, and I agree that approaching Lucian on foot might be better than landing this ship in front of him," Lonewind said.

Lynx nodded firmly in response to that. "It would not convince him that this is reality, certainly."

The vessel sank to the ground, Lonewind shaping the stones in the earth to hold it upright and provide support. Once they were securely grounded, he formed a ramp so that those without levitation could disembark. Chance floated off the ship, but couldn't quite convince himself to set foot on the land, as if it might hold memories of its own from that time. They'd landed out of immediate sight of the ocean, but the air carried the scents of water, salt, and the plants that thrived nowhere else. Stiff grass grew in uneven clumps, and sea birds circled to investigate the intruders.

Tieln took the lead. His stride was confident, unburdened by the fears and memories that gnawed at Chance. None of the others had been here before either. Did they know the significance of it?

"This is where we made our winter camp," Chance said quietly. "We were going to stay here until spring, then make our way back home. It was a time when everything... seemed right. Peaceful." His hands clenched. "And it was all a lie."

They climbed a hill and saw the ocean. Waves lapped at an expanse of yellow sand studded with clumps of the hardy grass. Strands of dry seaweed, tossed ashore by some storm, lay strewn about.

A lone figure with short black hair paced in the surf, taut with barely restrained impatience. His gaze was fixed on the ocean, as if he could will it to obey his command. His clothes were torn and ragged, and his feet bare.

Chance flew toward him. *Lucian!*

Lucian froze. His eyes remained on the water, but when he found nothing, he finally, slowly, turned. His eyes met Chance's. In their depths, Chance saw a moment of hope, then soul-shattering despair. Lucian looked away. "No."

Chance landed beside him and reached out to him. "Lucian."

Lucian stumbled back away from him. "No. No! No, you can't do this to me! I won't! I'll never give him to you!" His eyes darted madly around, searching for something or someone. "You can't have Chance!"

Fear drenched Chance like a deluge of ice water. "She's not here, Lucian. She's dead. She can't reach either of us now."

Lucian continued to retreat, shaking his head. "No, no, that's the lie. That's what she wants me to think. That's how the game works. Make me lure you into her reach. Make me… watch…" He stumbled, but caught himself. "Not this. Not Chance." He raised his eyes to the sky. "Isn't it enough? You've taken everything else! Isn't it enough?"

Chance stepped toward him. Lucian ran from the surf onto the beach. He stumbled over a piece of driftwood and fell to his knees. Rather than push back to his feet, Lucian crumpled, shoulders shaking with sobs of despair.

Chance caught Lucian's arm. "I wouldn't lie to you, Lucian. I swear to you, she can't reach us now."

"Why is my pain never enough for you? Every time I think I can't take any more, you twist the knife deeper. What do you *want*?" Lucian screamed.

Chance had asked Willow that once. She'd laughed, then raped him.

He called on his healing magic. Lucian didn't resist the push that sent him into sleep. His cries faded, and he lay still.

Chance didn't look up as other steps hissed through the sand toward them. "We need some sort of shelter."

Lonewind's hand gripped his shoulder briefly. "You'll have it."

No one else spoke. Chance almost wished they would, and give him an excuse to lash out.

Up here, Chance, Lonewind said.

Chance slowly pushed to his feet. His magic lifted Lucian's limp form as he climbed from the beach back to stone and dirt. Lonewind drew walls from the ground, forming a shack. It wasn't extravagant, just four walls with a doorway and windows, and beams for a roof.

"I'll get blankets from the ship," Cahron said. "Cylin, Tieln, gather reeds and grass for a roof."

Chance carried Lucian inside and lowered him to the ground. His cousin was cut and bruised. His face was lined with exhaustion. Even without using healing, Chance could tell Lucian hadn't eaten in several days, and probably hadn't slept in that time either. His clothes were ripped and caked with dirt.

Lonewind stood in the doorway. Chance turned to him. "I'm going in."

Lonewind nodded. "Bring him back."

Chance lay down on the bare ground and rested his hand on Lucian's arm. Before he sent his spirit into Lucian's mind, he heard Lonewind quietly say, "If we lose one of you, we will lose you both. Be careful."

~

C hance stood alone on a beach. The wind was chill and sharp, tossing sand in the air and flinging it about haphazardly. Lightning flickered between clouds overhead, and white-capped waves smashed against the shore.

"Lucian."

The storm swept his voice away, drowning it in the roar. Rain began to fall in icy sheets, soaking him in an instant.

"Lucian!"

In the darkness and the blinding rain, something brushed against him. Chance spun toward it, but saw nothing.

"Lucian! Where are you?"

The presence brushed by him again. Then long, slender fingers gripped his shoulders from behind, nails digging into his skin. Warm breath teased across his ear as Ayliad whispered, "He's mine now."

Chance tore free and spun, swinging at her. His attack met only mist. "Where are you? Where's Lucian?"

The ocean surged, a massive wave sweeping over the entire beach. The water dragged Chance with it. It filled his nose and mouth, and he couldn't find the surface. Panic clawed at him.

This isn't real! I'm in Lucian's mind. I'm not going to drown! He squeezed his eyes shut and tried to focus despite his burning lungs. He had to adapt, or he had to change the mindscape and risk losing whatever path it might be opening to Lucian. He willed himself to be able to breath underwater.

A sharp stab of pain on his back made Chance gasp, but he didn't drown. The waves tossed him like another piece of flotsam, and the light from above grew dim and distant. He flailed, trying to regain some control over his movement, his direction, anything.

In the depths, a light glowed. The current swept toward it, and the closer Chance came, the more he felt waves of dread pulsing from it like a heartbeat. Jagged growths formed walls and spires. He'd never seen the structure from the outside, but he knew what it had to be.

Willow's Coral Palace.

The water flung him through the open front doors. The doors slammed shut behind him. Momentum carried him nearly to a wall full of jagged edges ready to cut his skin. Chance swam as close to the wall as he dared, keeping it at his back as his eyes darted around the vast chamber.

He saw no sign of Willow or Ayliad. No sign of any living creature in the water-filled palace. Wary, he swam toward one of the passages leading out of the chamber. The weight of fear and oppression weighed down on him, casting a sinister pall on the beauty of the structure. Something within the coral produced light in some passages, while others lay dark and threatening. Chance paused, considering his options. The light might lead him to Lucian. On any other venture in Lucian's mind, he would follow it. But this wasn't any other venture into Lucian's mind.

He turned into a dark tunnel. Despair and pain nearly bowled him over. Forcing himself to swim deeper, Chance searched the shadows. He didn't see anything moving, but whispers teased at the edge of his hearing. Most he couldn't understand, but some were far too clear.

"He's mine now. Nothing you do will save him," Ayliad purred.

Willow murmured, "My beautiful, perfect son. You cannot fight me. You cannot stop me. Chance is already mine, and soon, Lonewind will be as well."

Chance shuddered. "Don't listen to them, Lucian. Don't listen."

Somewhere ahead in the darkness, Lucian screamed.

"Lucian!" Chance surged toward the sound.

It led him through twisting passages amid the coral deeper into the palace depths. The walls contorted and warped around him, the elegant beauty taking on hideous and monstrous shapes. Something grabbed at Chance, opening a gash on his leg. He twisted away with a gasp of pain, but didn't stop to see what it was.

The tunnel ended in a dimly lit chamber. Lucian's scream radiated from the very walls, not from the lone figure hanging in chains. He was young—younger even than Lucian had actually been when they were prisoners here. Perhaps as young as Lucian had been when he discovered the truth about his mother. The boy Lucian lifted his head and saw Chance, and his expression twisted in terror.

"No, no! You have to get away before she finds you!"

"I'm getting you out of here, Lucian," Chance promised, swimming closer.

Lucian was naked, his skin bruised and abraded. Ribs showed against his skin. His wrists and ankles were raw from struggles against the bone chains. He flinched back from Chance, eyes wide with panic.

"No, don't! She'll come. If you free me, she'll come. She'll hurt you. She'll put me back in chains and make me watch." He huddled back as far as his restrains allowed. "If I don't fight, it doesn't hurt as much."

"I'm not leaving you here, Lucian." Chance caught one of the boy's hands. Lucian whimpered in terror.

This isn't right. Lucian never cowered. He never stopped fighting, even when he had nothing left to fight with. Even when we found him on the beach today, when he thought he'd lost everything and that Willow was going to take me, he kept fighting.

He released Lucian's hand, looking at the youth again. *Is this Lucian or not?*

The boy lunged at him. The chains released, and he grabbed for Chance's arms, trying to pin them. "Won't be fooled again," he hissed.

Chance tried to throw him off, but the gaunt youth was stronger than he looked. "Lucian, stop! It's me! It's Chance!"

The youth just bared his teeth, twisting in the water and trying to force Chance back toward the chains. Chance heard Willow's voice whispering in his ear, the words not quite audible. Desperate, Chance flung his will against the scene around them. Anywhere but here.

Chance and the youth hit dry, dusty ground. Before Chance could stand, the youth was attacking him again. He barely looked like Lucian now, his limbs too long, tipped with savage claws, and his mouth filled with sharp teeth. His head elongated, taking an animalistic shape like a perverted combination of dog and elf. Long, spindly limbs wrapped around Chance. He kicked and struggled, but the creature didn't let go.

"Lucian! Stop!"

"Mine," the creature hissed. It opened its mouth wide to tear into him.

Chance glimpsed movement, a looming shape behind the

creature. Something grabbed the creature and ripped it off Chance, flinging it back. The creature shrieked in fury and lunged again. Chance's rescuer grabbed it by the throat and held it aloft, ignoring the thrashing limbs and slashing claws.

"Back where you came from," he said in a cold, flat voice.

With a final shriek, the creature vanished. Chance pushed to his feet. "Lucian."

The other turned to face him, expressionless, and Chance saw the Ghost. He looked almost exactly like Lucian, but there was no warmth, no passion in his eyes. "That was a nightmare. Lucian is deeper within."

"I was in the Coral Palace," Chance began.

"A nightmare," the Ghost cut in. "One of many. Be wary of their traps."

They stood on a barren, dusty wasteland. For miles, Chance saw nothing but rocks and dirt under a dull grey sky. "Where's Lucian?" he demanded.

"Deeper," the Ghost repeated. "He's withdrawn to the depths of his soul, beyond the reach of the Guardian or me. And even if we could reach him, doing so would give a path of escape to nightmares such as the one you found."

Chance looked around the barren landscape. "Is this your solution? Level everything?"

"This is where I dwell," the Ghost answered. "It's the land that formed me into what I now am. It is the barrier I hold between the nightmares and Lucian."

"I've been in Lucian's mind many times. It's never been splintered like this. How long has it been this way?"

"I have known it no other way. Ask the Guardian."

Chance's eyes narrowed. "Lucian hasn't been out of reach in the depths of his soul the entire time."

The Ghost met his gaze evenly. "The core of his self took refuge there when Tash breathed his last." The landscape rippled around them.

Chance saw the detritus of a camp—a dead campfire, three packs with their contents spilled haphazardly across the ground, rumpled and bloodstained bedding. Just beyond the scattered belongings, two stone cairns stood.

Pain twisted in Chance's heart. He closed his eyes and turned away. Tash, steady, grounded, always dependable. Before Chance's birth, Tash had been Lucian's closest friend, but he'd never shown any jealousy or regret when Chance slid into that role. He'd accepted his own endless duty of trying to be the voice of reason to both of them.

"Did you bury them?" Chance managed, voice choked.

"Yes. I sensed the need from the fragments of Lucian's soul that lingered. Then I departed."

"But Lucian returned from those depths," Chance said. "In the forest where he made the village. He came back from that dark hiding place."

The Ghost gazed at him. "Think that, if you wish."

Chance glared. "Lucian returned then. He'll do so again. I'll make sure of it."

"If any can draw him from that darkness, it will be you," the Ghost said. He pointed beyond the camp. "Follow his path."

Without another word, Chance started walking in the direction the Ghost indicated. *I'm going to find you, Lucian. I promise.*

He sensed the scene shifting around him and tensed. *Where now?*

A babble of voices surrounded him, the sounds of people talking, going about their everyday life. Laughter, cheers… a celebration. Chance closed his eyes, and when he opened them, he stood on a packed dirt street. Night crept over the sky, but the bonfires cast more than enough light to make up for the sun's absence. He breathed in the scents of fresh pastries, cooking meat, and generous draughts of alcohol. It took him another moment to realize that everyone in the crowd was an elf.

The Ingathering. Fall Festival.

The clan had lived here for many centuries—the largest community of elves Chance had ever seen before or since. Its leader had been a powerful man whose greatest ambition was to bring together as many of the scattered elves as possible, create for them a refuge, a place of safety. That hadn't been Lord Alosian's *only* ambition, of course, but the politics and inner workings of his court had not often infringed on Lonewind's clan.

Lucian had been carrying so much anger during the early years here. He'd still been reeling from recent revelations about his life. He'd learned that his mother never loved him, never saw him as anything but a weapon against Lonewind. He'd learned that the rest of the clan, with the exception of Tash and Chance, had known the truth and never told him. He'd learned that Chance's birth father, Moonfire, had betrayed them. Everything he'd thought he'd known had been turned upside down, and Lucian hadn't known who to lash out at: his mother, his father, his clan, or himself. It was hardly a surprise that he'd embraced his own rebellious streak and railed against Lord Alosian's rulership.

Which Fall Festival is this? What happened this night that keeps it living in Lucian's memory?

Chance scanned the crowd. Then he froze, blood running cold. "No."

She wove and danced with the music, the light of the fires shimmering on her body as she deftly dodged the groping hands that sought to pull her close. She circled around to Lucian and greeted him with a long, passionate kiss. He laughed, dancing with her until they both stopped to quench their thirst.

Chance couldn't move, couldn't speak, couldn't cry out the warning that screamed through his mind.

Off to one side, observing but always a little withdrawn stood a young man with dark hair and watchful gray eyes. He was thin—he'd always been slender, but in those days, he'd been underweight even for his build. He never, ever drank spirits, even at the festivals. Never willing to risk giving up control or inhibiting his faculties. The youth nursed his mug of unfermented cider, always keeping one eye on Lucian, and one eye alert for danger. Because even here, there was danger.

Chance tried to speak, tried to warn his younger self, or Lucian, but no sound came. He watched Ayliad collect three drinks—two alcoholic, one not. He watched her, and saw the moment she slipped the mugs around, pressing the powerful, fermented cider into the young man's hand, keeping the safe drink to herself.

The young man drank, frowned slightly, then shook off his concern. Chance remembered thinking the cider tasted a little different, but with the scent of alcohol heavy in the air all around, he hadn't distinguish the smell of it within the mug.

With great effort, Chance took a step toward his younger self, then another. But the young man drank deeply, and the alcohol hit his unprepared system quickly. Ayliad was there, teasing him lightly when he stumbled drunkenly. Lucian was talking to an acquaintance, and thought nothing of Ayliad talking to Chance.

She took Chance's younger self by the arm to lead him back to the house. Chance tried to follow, but he couldn't, because this was Lucian's nightmare. Lucian, who hadn't noticed the moment when his lover stole away with his cousin. Lucian, who continued to dance and laugh and drink while Ayliad, cold, calculating, and not at all as drunk as she pretended, attempted to seduce Chance then, when that failed, took what she wanted anyway. Lucian, who wouldn't realize anything was wrong until he felt Chance's incoherent, panicking screams.

"Lucian! Turn around!" He finally forced his will through the nightmare, and his words found voice.

Lucian started and looked around, wondering who called to him. He saw Chance, but no recognition lit his tipsy gaze. "Uh… what do you want?"

He longed to tell the truth, but here and now, he had to lie if he wanted Lucian to listen. "Aramis sent me." That was a name Lucian would know and trust, a man who had become a father figure during a time when Lucian was too angry to allow Lonewind to take that role. "Chance needs help. Someone drugged him."

Protective fury flared in Lucian's eyes. "Who? Where is Chance?"

"Last saw him stumbling back home," Chance answered.

Lucian barreled through the crowd, shoving and elbowing people out of his way without apology. Chance ran after him, taking advantage of the path he opened.

Somehow, Lucian got ahead of him, and the crowds pressed close. The more Chance tried to push through them, the more they blocked him. Frustrated, he tried to will them to open a way for him. This time, the nightmare pushed back, unrelenting.

Lucian's cry of horror and rage tore through the crowded street and the scene dissolved around Chance. He caught a glimpse, impossible though it should have been from this distance, of his younger self cowering on the bed, naked, hands tied to the bedpost with one of Ayliad's scarves. She loomed over him, intentions obvious, when Lucian burst into the room.

Then that image too dissolved, swallowed in darkness.

INTERLUDE SIX: ECHOES

Lynx sat against a palm tree, listening to the rest of the clan. Lonewind paced. Cahron lingered nearby, sometimes speaking quiet reassurances. Tieln rested in the grass. Lucian lay in the shelter as if peacefully asleep, an illusion as inaccurate as Chance's apparent calm healer's trance.

He needs help. With Lynx, and Lynx alone, Echo didn't revert to his child-like tones. But Lynx alone knew that his twin had finally grown up despite every impediment Ayliad and Willow had laid on him.

Of course he does, Lynx answered. They both spoke their private language in mind-speech. *He doesn't believe it, though. Chance is stubborn.* And sometimes, Chance's stubbornness served him well—like when he'd worked to convince Lynx that Echo would be safer as a part of Lonewind's clan than as Willow's tool. Other times, it was just stupid.

Echo projected distress. *Tell them. They can help.*

You could do the same thing without them.

Not as well, Echo argued.

Lynx sighed and rose. Echo wouldn't stop pestering him

until he made some effort to help Chance and Lucian. He walked to Tieln and nudged the boy with his foot. *Follow me.*

"What?" Tieln asked, confused, but he complied.

Lynx made for Cylin. The human sat on a rock looking over the ocean, far enough from the others for a private conversation. Echo could have shown him the entire scene through both Tieln and Cylin's eyes, but Lynx didn't need sight to hear the human turn toward him.

"What do you want?" she asked.

"You both want to help Lucian," Lynx said.

Instantly, he had their attentions. "Damn right I do!" Cylin said. "And if I had magic, I'd be there too." Her voice challenged him to argue.

"If I had magic that would let me, I would as well," Tieln agreed. "But I don't, so why bring it up?"

Neither were cowards, and both were aware of their limitations. Lynx appreciated those traits. While the first wasn't an issue in this clan, the second was a different matter. "There is a way you can enter Lucian's mind."

"What? Why didn't anyone else tell me?" Cylin demanded.

"No one else told you because they don't know how and don't have the means to do it." Never mind that neither Lonewind nor Cahron would consider sending these two into Lucian's mind. And they certainly wouldn't agree to using Echo to facilitate such an intrusion.

Lynx smelled Tieln's unease. "Everyone's been quite sure only Chance can bring Lucian back."

"Probably true," Lynx agreed. "But to do that, he has to reach Lucian, not wander lost in Lucian's nightmares. I doubt you'll be able to do anything once he finds Lucian, but you *can* make sure that he gets that far."

"How?" Cylin was wary. Smart girl.

"You've undoubtedly heard about my brother Echo and his mental skills," Lynx said. "Among other things, he can look far beyond the surface of others' thoughts, and he can project directly into the depths of the mind."

Cylin shifted, crossing her arms. "How about you try saying that again in a way normal people can understand?"

He turned toward her. "Lucian adopted you into the clan. 'Normal' doesn't even share the same continent as you any more, if it ever did. However, what I am saying is, at its essence, that Echo is able to act as a conduit of sorts between your minds and Lucian's. You can think, feel, and act as if you sent your spirits into his mind like Chance. And you will have a greater ability to influence the mindscape because you will be drawing on Echo's power, not your own."

"Your brother, who is still in orbit around our planet, can send us into Lucian's mind, just like that?" Tieln snapped his fingers. "What's the catch?"

"You will not actually be in Lucian's mind. Your awareness will be, but your soul will still be in your body. And there are places in Lucian's mind that Echo can't reach—such as wherever Lucian's soul has retreated to. You can help Chance reach it, but it's unlikely that you'll be able to enter with him." Lynx scratched a claw along the edge of a loose scale. "The catch? You might go insane. Your body might not be able to handle the strain, and your heart or other organs might fail. Echo might become overwhelmed by Lucian's mind, and cause you to receive the brunt of the feedback. And of course the risk that any soul-healer faces, that you'll unintentionally, irreparably screw up something in Lucian's soul."

"Wow, that's not really encouraging," Cylin muttered.

"So this isn't just dangerous to us, it's dangerous to your brother as well," Tieln said. "Chance said that protecting him is your strongest driving motivation. So why take that risk?"

"Because I know what the risks really are," Lynx told him. "You see this as a matter of 'Chance succeeds or Chance fails.' The stakes are much, much higher than that. If Chance fails,

Lucian is lost. If Lucian is lost, Chance is lost. You know that much already." He leaned toward them. "If Lucian is lost, *Lonewind* is lost, or nearly so. Cahron might keep him contained, but the wound will not heal. You've seen a form of Lucian's Ghost. You have never seen Lonewind give way to his inner demon. Pray you never do." Lynx shook his head. "Also, Echo has been very persistent in telling me to speak to you about this. For whatever reason, he's taken a liking to the pair of you."

A moment of long silence followed. Finally Cylin said, "Lonewind and Cahron don't know about this, do they?"

"They know it's possible for Echo to do. They haven't thought about it in this context."

"I'll go," Tieln said. "I'll accept those risks to help Lucian and Chance."

"Well, yeah," Cylin said. "Of course we're going. When do we start?"

Chance walked in darkness.

He'd been in Lucian's mind many times and seen it in many states, but he'd always known how to navigate it. He'd always known how his friend thought. Whether walking forest paths or stone corridors, he'd always found Lucian.

Chance was lost.

The Ghost has warned him about Lucian's nightmares. He hadn't warned Chance that Lucian's mind was splintered. Perhaps he hadn't known to.

"Lucian!" Chance shouted. "Where are you?"

The silence swallowed his voice. This emptiness should have been filled with a sense of presence, a sense of Lucian.

The Ghost said Lucian's soul retreated into the depths after Tash died. But Lucian came back. He lived in Forest Town. He found me. He killed Ayliad. That wasn't just some shell that acted like him—that was Lucian.

"Lucian! I'm here. Answer me!" He closed his eyes. "Please. Answer me."

Something tugged gently on his pant leg. He jerked away and looked down. A tree root, glowing with a faint green light, stretched through the darkness. The tip of the root curled up, beckoning him to follow.

Chance kept a wary distance between himself and the root, though it probably wouldn't do much good if it attacked him. It could be the Guardian, or it could be a manifestation of Ayliad, but he followed the root back toward its source.

Crossing an invisible borderline, he left darkness and stepped into a dense forest. Chance blinked until he adjusted to the sudden light. The air smelled fresh, clean, and full of life. He turned sharply at the sound of movement. He wasn't alone, and the company was not who he expected.

Tieln and Cylin looked around in confusion. Tieln's expression hardened and his eyes narrowed as he looked at the vibrant growth. Cylin just walked over to Chance, eyes darting around warily. "So this… is the inside of Lucian's head?"

"This is the Guardian," Tieln said, voice chill.

Cylin glanced to him. "You sure?"

"I have *never* been more sure," Tieln told her, voice unchanged.

"What are you… *How* are you here?" Chance demanded.

"Ask your son. It was his idea," Cylin said.

"My… Echo." Chance's jaw tightened. *This is no place for them, Echo.*

It's exactly where they need to be, and where you need them to be, Echo said.

Chance winced slightly. Receiving mind-speech from outside while he was in someone else's mind always felt strange, and the whispers that lurked on the edges of Echo's mental voice only made it worse. "And Lynx agreed?" he asked Tieln and Cylin.

"Lynx told us about it," Tieln said. "Lonewind and Cahron don't know, though."

"Of course not—Cahron would never agree to you doing something this foolish." But he couldn't force Echo to leave or to pull Tieln and Cylin out. "I can't believe that you two would either."

Cylin folded her arms and scowled at him. "What, like you're the only one who gets to save Lucian from himself?"

Tieln ignored the argument and strode into the forest. Chance snarled a curse and followed him, Cylin on his heels.

The Guardian waited for them beside a looming tree of a species unfamiliar to Chance. The branches stretched far toward the sun, and glowing fruit hung from them. The Guardian stepped away from the trunk. His green hair hung longer than Lucian's, and his skin was rough and brown like bark. His eyes had no whites, only amber orbs with piercing black pupils. But like the Ghost, he had Lucian's features. He cocked his head curiously at Tieln and Cylin.

"We did not think the Sapling could enter, and we are certain the human cannot."

"Don't ask," Chance told him sharply.

Tieln stormed to the Guardian. "You lied to me."

"We did not lie. We didn't present all the possible outcomes to your decision, but we did not lie." The Guardian waved a hand. "Chance was disabled. We could not pierce the Fruit's barrier to interact with Lucian's body. The Dark Tree had to be purged. Should we have told you that, under some circumstances, you could be extracted from the Tree once more? Would telling you such have changed your decision?"

Tieln's jaw tightened. "No," he said finally.

"Where's Lucian?" Chance demanded.

"In the depths," the Guardian said. "Deeper than my roots run."

"Why is his mind like this? Fragmented?"

"In your absence, Cilvi and Tash held him together, and he clung to them. When he lost them, Lucian lost the anchors that kept his mind stable and focused. The Ghost took form and took control of his body, then set a wall between himself and the chaos within."

Chance's eyes narrowed. "The Ghost implied that Lucian never returned from the depths of his mind. If that's correct, how could he have been lord of Forest Town? How could he have gone in spirit form and woken me?"

"The Ghost is wrong." Four seats rose from the ground. The Guardian sat. "The Ghost needed to focus on survival— that is one thing the Ghost does well. He looked outward, and not inward."

Even though he could sense a "but" coming, the tightness in Chance's chest eased a little. He was right. Lucian had come back.

"With time, Lucian's wounded soul began to heal and he

began to emerge." The Guardian focused on Chance. "But Lucian left a portion of himself in the depths, in the darkness —the pain and despair he couldn't yet bear. The Ghost incorrectly interpreted that to mean that Lucian's true self remained hidden."

"That doesn't work," Chance said quietly. "Trying to lock away your pain and hide it behind walls doesn't work." *You should know that already, Lucian. You should know it from having seen all the times I tried.*

"It worked to a point," the Guardian said. "It allowed him to function, to build his village and collect his humans. But it was not perfect, and the pain slipped loose sometimes. Our forest could prevent the Fruit from reaching him, but it could not prevent his fears and memories from overwhelming him, leaving him lost and questioning whether the world was as he saw it, or an illusion woven by another to ensnare him."

"Yeah, most of us noticed that," Cylin said. "Why didn't you stop it?"

The Guardian cocked his head at her. "The Ghost is but a fragment of Lucian, an echo with limited ability. We are an aspect of the Tree, but we dwell within Lucian; we do not control him. Seizing control from him requires great effort, and retaining it requires yet more. We didn't stop the darkness from overwhelming him because we cannot. We reserved seizing control only for instances where he could not easily be isolated."

"Why?" Tieln asked, still wary of the Guardian.

"Because when Lucian doubts reality, he grows less cautious and more destructive. He feels less restraint when he believes his actions are unlikely to have real consequences."

"You're not taking control now, either," Tieln snapped. "When his 'real consequences' might mean drowning because he tries to swim to where he thinks Willow is waiting."

The Guardian gazed at Tieln. "You should know better than most that we have limits, Sapling."

Tieln's jaw tightened.

"We cannot fix what's broken in Lucian, only limit its impact," the Guardian continued. "We are a barrier to the horrors and nightmares rising from the depths. Those that escape us, the Ghost hunts and eliminates before they take root. But neither of us can reach the source."

"How many of those nightmares and horrors center around Willow and Ayliad?" Chance already knew he wouldn't like the answer.

"Many. Those that do not focus upon them often center around him destroying or killing those he loves, or failing to protect them from other sources of pain and death."

Chance closed his eyes and drew a slow breath. "I should have seen it before." *I knew something was wrong from the moment I found him, thrashing and screaming in his nightmare of Ayliad. I shouldn't have believed him when he claimed that everything would get better now that I was awake and he wasn't alone.*

"You were weak when first you found Lucian. You were not ready to delve into the depths of his mind then. Drawing him out of the Fruit's nightmare exhausted you. By the time you had regained that strength, his soul had begun to heal. We thought the need not as urgent, and believed that once all returned safely to our forest, you could complete the healing that had already begun." The Guardian shook his head, tossing a scattering of leaves to the ground.

"But Karishan got there before us," Chance said quietly. "And the Ghost refused to let me enter Lucian's mind."

"We cannot judge whether the Ghost was right or wrong in that refusal." The Guardian glanced to Cylin. "But allowing you to enter then would have left Cylin longer in the hands of both Yazah and the Fruit."

Cylin shifted uncomfortably. "And Ravys," she added.

But if I'd done it anyway, maybe Ayliad wouldn't have been able to reach him. Maybe she would have found no purchase for her claws. Even as he thought it, Chance knew she'd have found a weakness. If not this, then something else. Like finding a way to abduct Chance.

"You say you're stopping his nightmares from escaping. Does that mean they still stand between us and Lucian?" Tieln cut in.

"It does."

Tieln checked his pistol, then turned to Chance. "Can we go?"

Chance nodded, then paused, eyeing him. "Can you 'find' Lucian here?"

"Everything here feels like Lucian. But… yes, I can sense a stronger presence."

"Go," the Guardian said. "Beware the nightmares. Those we have held in are worse than those that escaped to the Ghost."

Chance sensed a push from the Guardian, and the forest was gone. He stood with Tieln and Cylin in a wide, well-lit cave passage. Glowing crystals on the walls cast warm illumination. The floor and walls were smooth, the work of stone-shaping. Chance started walking.

The other two followed. "Is this a nightmare?" Cylin asked. "It doesn't look or feel like one."

"No, this is a pathway of Lucian's mind," Chance answered. This was what he'd expected to find when he entered, and he was relieved to finally find it. "When you enter someone's mind, how it manifests depends on the person. My mindscape reflects my father's home. Tieln's takes the form of a barracks. This is a version of a place our clan lived for many years." *A place where Lucian finds peace and comfort. A place where he feels safe. That's what the manifestation of our minds should be.*

"Huh. Wonder what mine would look like. Maybe Forest

Town," she mused. "Can't think of anywhere else I'd call home."

The walls rippled around them. Chance tensed, but the passage had nowhere to turn aside, nowhere to go but forward or back.

Blinding despair crashed into him, dropping him to his knees. Blood pounded in his ears. He couldn't breathe.

"Chance!" Cylin grabbed him by the shoulder. "What in drifters' bones… Tieln?"

"I'll be all right," Tieln gasped. "Think it hit Chance harder."

Cylin's free hand fell to her gun. "*What* hit him?"

"Pain… loss. Despair." Chance grabbed her arm to pull himself up.

She lifted and steadied him. "I don't feel anything."

"Count yourself lucky." Chance leaned against her and let the world come into focus.

They stood on an empty stone street. One and two story houses shaped from wood and stone lined the street in either direction. A stone dome high overhead told Chance they were underground, but the air smelled fresh and carried the scents of plants. He didn't recognize this place.

The oppressive weight of Lucian's despair didn't relent, but its source wasn't immediately clear. Chance pushed one foot in front of the other, grateful for Cylin's support. The town lay silent, no residents in evidence.

"I failed…" Lucian's voice whispered. "I couldn't protect you…"

Chance's head jerked up, but he saw no one else. "Did you hear that?"

"Yeah, I heard that," Cylin said. "Was that Lucian? He sounded… broken."

Tieln held up his hand for quiet. "I hear someone else. A woman."

A chill of terror crawled down Chance's spine.

Cylin nudged him with her elbow. "Don't worry. If it's Ayliad or Willow, Tieln and I will shoot her."

He managed a small smile in response. "Good to know."

Tieln motioned for them to continue. A moment later, Chance heard the murmuring voice. Equal measures of relief and grief washed over him. "That's not them. That's…" His voice choked. "That's my wife."

Her voice drew him like a lodestone. From the cadence, Ahmea was reading aloud. He wanted to run to her, hold her in his arms, and tell her how much he loved her.

"I should have saved you," Lucian whispered. "I'm sorry… I'm sorry…"

The street opened into a small park, an oasis of green. Ahmea sat on a stone bench, an open book in her lap. Her dark brown hair hung in three looped braids. He wanted to loose the ties and run his fingers through her locks. He wanted to kiss her and never leave her again, but Cylin gripped his arm tightly. Finally, Chance tore his eyes away from his beloved and saw the other person with her.

The other sat slumped in a wheelchair, facing Ahmea. He was thin and limp, held up by straps. His skin had the sallow yellow of someone who was linked to the Tree, and when he looked carefully, Chance saw slender vines wrapped around the other's exposed arm, piercing into the skin like intravenous needles, providing nutrients, keeping the major organs functioning. Keeping the body alive. He saw the slack face, the open, empty eyes that saw nothing.

He couldn't breathe. He couldn't look away. He could only stare in mute horror at himself. A vision of himself kept alive by the Tree long after his spirit had fled.

"I couldn't save you, and I couldn't let you go," Lucian whispered. Finally, an ephemeral image of Lucian appeared, kneeling beside the wheelchair, head bowed. Ahmea continued reading, unaware of him. Lucian reached toward one of the limp hands resting on the arms of the wheelchair, but let his hand fall again. "I'm sorry. I can't ask you to forgive me. I can't even bring your torment to an end."

Then Lucian threw back his head and screamed.

The nightmare shattered.

They stood in the halls of Lucian's mind again. Chance pulled away from Cylin and sagged to the floor. He cradled his head in his hands, shaking.

He heard Cylin and Tieln sink down beside him. One of them rested a hand on his shoulder. They didn't ask questions, but he had to say something; he knew he did.

"If she could have seen that, she would have laughed, and known she'd gotten what she always wanted. Me, crushed, broken... nothing." He wrapped his arms tight around himself.

"Ayliad?" Tieln asked.

"Willow. The last time, she all but succeeded. A little more and... that would have been me." His voice broke. *That would have been me, and it would have destroyed Lucian.*

A moment of long silence, then Cylin spoke. "Lucian's nightmares and your nightmares aren't much different, are they?"

He raised his head, staring at her. Such a simple statement, with so much profound truth. "No, they aren't."

Slowly, he pushed to his feet and began walking. Footsteps behind him told him that the other two followed. Cylin spoke. "I'm still not convinced that it wouldn't be better for Cahron to be here too."

"Then I hope we don't find a nightmare that proves why you're wrong," Chance said. He didn't want to see that moment again. Didn't want to hear Lucian's rage, his screaming accusations, the final destruction of his tattered innocence.

Chance stopped at a door—the first he'd seen. He hesitated, then cautiously reached out and pushed it. It yielded smoothly.

A line of blood trickled along the floor toward the door. His eyes followed it back to the source. Blood. A key, lying on the floor, now stained with the red liquid. A knife, resting beside a limp hand…

Chance jerked the door shut, breathing far too fast. Tremors shook him. He remembered Willow's voice when she dropped both the knife and the key to his collar in front of him. *"You're no more use to me, Slave. You're nothing but a burden to me —as you are to everyone. Begone."* She started to walk away from him, then paused without looking back. *"Of course, you could always do everyone a favor and use the knife instead. I'm certainly not going to waste the magic to bring you back."*

He remembered the utter despair that her words brought. The moment when his wounded soul had believed her, believed that he had nothing left to lose. A moment when Lucian had almost been too late. "Don't open that."

"Definitely not planning to," Cylin said. Her hand pushed gently but firmly against his back. "So let's keep walking."

He let her propel him on, but couldn't help rubbing his wrists. No scars remained, but he couldn't get the image out of his mind now. He'd been unconscious by the time Lucian found him. He didn't know what must have happened in the chaos of that last battle against Willow. She'd captured him and Cahron, then tortured and abused them both to destroy Lonewind and Lucian.

She'd almost succeeded.

"Perhaps this is a foolish question," Tieln said, "but does Lucian hold *any* happy memories?"

Despite himself, Chance laughed. "He does. Many of them."

"So where are they? These halls reek of despair and pain."

Chance paused mid-step, wondering if that was Tieln speaking, or Echo through Tieln.

"Maybe he decided to bury them, like he did with the painful ones," Cylin said.

"Many are probably not down here. Neither the Guardian nor the Ghost would have reason to block the good and pleasant memories," Chance said.

The hall opened into a chamber with a crystal fountain. The walls glowed and the polished marble floor reflected the light. This place, at least, Chance recognized as one of the mental healing wards in the Ingathering. He'd spent over a year here receiving treatment for trauma. He couldn't recall Lucian ever seeking similar treatment, though.

I never pushed him to do so, either. I knew that I needed help, but somehow, I always thought that what I could give Lucian would be enough. I thought he didn't need anyone else's help.

"No! Let go of me!" Lucian's shout broke the silence.

Chance, Cylin, and Tieln bolted toward the sound.

Four ward attendants surrounded Lucian. Two pinned his arms behind his back, while the others were either trying to calm him or drug him. Lucian thrashed and kicked with increased urgency. "Let go of me!"

A crack of gunfire rang in Chance's ears. One of the attendants in front of Lucian fell with a startled cry. Cylin fired again, but missed, striking the stone wall to the left of the other attendant. Tieln shot at one of those restraining Lucian. Lucian tore free of the other, and Chance threw all the attendants, injured or not, against the wall with levitation.

Lucian dashed to Chance, eyed wide and wild. He wore the simple shirt and trousers of a ward patient. His wrists and ankles bore bruises from the padded restraints the ward attendants sometimes used to prevent patients from harming themselves or others. This version of Lucian was young—maybe two hundred years old.

Lucian grabbed Chance's arm and clung to him desperately. His breath came in short, rapid gasps. "Help me, Chance. Please. Please don't leave me here. You believe me, don't you? I'm not insane."

"I believe you, Lucian."

Lucian sagged in relief, still clinging to Chance. He gave no notice to Cylin or Tieln. "They won't listen. They don't believe me. They keep me locked in here and they won't stop her!" His eyes pleaded with Chance. "Get me out of here. Please. We can go anywhere. We can go to Aisling's! Aisling will believe me. Won't he?"

"Aisling will be able to tell the truth. He'll believe you," Chance promised, trying to make sense of Lucian's wild ravings. He wrapped an arm around his cousin. "Come on."

He turned to lead Lucian out of the ward. They'd gone only a few steps when Lucian froze with a strangled sound of terror. Chance looked ahead. Ayliad stood in the mouth of the exit.

Her face pinched in an expression of concern that looked almost genuine. "Oh, my dear Lucian, what are you doing? You need to stay here. The healers will take good care of you. And Chance, I know you're worried about him, but you know Lucian needs this. It's not good to encourage these delusions of his."

She stepped forward. As one, Cylin and Tieln raised their guns and shot Ayliad. She staggered but didn't fall.

"Don't listen to her," Lucian begged. "She's lying."

"I know she is," Chance said. "I believe you, Lucian." He raised his hand and slammed Ayliad into the wall with magic.

Tieln and Cylin kept shooting, and the bullets came faster than Ayliad could heal herself. She kept trying to push away from the wall and reach Lucian and Chance, but finally she slumped to the floor, blood splattering the wall behind her. Chance half carried Lucian out of the ward.

"She can't reach you any more, Lucian."

Lucian stared at him and whispered, "You *do* believe me."

"I'll always be here, Lucian. Believe that. I won't let you fall."

They stepped out of the passage into daylight. For a moment longer, Chance felt Lucian clinging to him, then the nightmare dispersed, a fraying dream put to rest. They stood in the corridors of Lucian's mind once more, and Lucian was nowhere to be seen.

He turned to Cylin and Tieln, who both still carried their guns drawn. "Thank you."

Cylin looked over her shoulder to double-check that Ayliad wasn't crawling up behind them. "Was that a memory?"

"Not a real one," Chance said. "It was a memory of one of Willow's 'games.' Lucian told me about it once. In it, we were rescued from the Coral Palace—all of us. Including Ayliad. She played the role of the frightened victim and convinced everyone that she was innocent, no matter how much Lucian insisted that she was Willow's daughter and that she'd been responsible for our capture."

"She convinced even you?" Tieln asked dubiously.

"Willow was controlling Lucian's hallucination, Tieln. She could make everyone in it believe the sun rose in the north if she wanted. The rescuers became convinced that Lucian was mentally unstable, and he was confined in the ward for treatment. Ayliad could visit him whenever she wanted, and Lucian's cries that she used her visits to rape him were dismissed as indications of a deteriorating mental state."

"And did what we just do in there help him?" Cylin asked.

"Yes." It was a small step, but it was a step. A nightmare put to rest.

Something had changed. Chance couldn't pinpoint it, but

he sensed it in the air. Somewhere in Lucian's mind, a path had opened.

The corridor branched. Chance paused a moment, but Tieln turned to the left and kept walking. "This way."

"Where are you, Lucian?" Chance whispered.

If Lucian heard, he didn't answer.

The corridor continued, but the further they went, the more Chance felt Lucian's mind pushing back against him, as if to stop their advance.

Don't do this, Lucian. Don't push me away. Don't shut me out. He pushed back, even as it felt like he walked through tar.

The walls of Lucian's mind resisted. Chance gritted his teeth and pushed harder, a battle fought with no visible manifestations. Ahead of them, the corridor ended in a stone wall. Tieln stopped before it, frowning, his head cocked to one side.

"We didn't pass any doors or other turns. My sense of Lucian says that he's beyond this." Tieln rested a hand on the wall as if hoping it was an illusion.

Chance tried to reach the wall, but the force of Lucian's will fought back. Cylin steadied him. "What's wrong?"

"Lucian doesn't want me getting closer," Chance growled. He gripped her arm and tried to push forward.

"So we're getting close, and he doesn't want to be found?" Cylin wrapped her arm around his waist and half walked, half dragged Chance to the wall. Tieln stepped back and helped her. Cylin shook her head. "Okay, yeah, *something* is pushing back. Wonder why it doesn't stop me and Tieln, though."

"Because you aren't really here," Chance said. "Echo's manipulating Lucian's mind to make it seem like you are. But Lucian *knows* that I'm here."

"Is it that?" Tieln wondered. "Or is something beyond this wall that he doesn't want you to see?"

Chance looked at him, startled. "What?"

"If his nightmares are your nightmares, and the worst are

those locked in the deepest, darkest places of his mind…" Tieln trailed off.

"They're between us and him." Chance fixed his gaze on the wall. "I'm not leaving without you, Lucian." He pressed his hand against the stone.

Another moment of fierce, determined resistance. Then cracks spidered across the wall and slender vines of morning glory forced their way through from the other side. The wall crumbled under the assault, and everything went black.

Chance stood in the hall of the house he, Lucian, and Tash had shared in the Ingathering. The house was still and dark with night. To his left, the door to Lucian's room stood slightly ajar. He stepped toward it, feet silent on the wooden floor.

"What's wrong, Lucian?"

Chance froze at the sound of Ayliad's voice.

"It's… I'll be all right," Lucian said.

A shift of movement on the bed. "You don't have to lie to me, Lucian. Your thoughts have wandered far away."

"I'm sorry. It's just… being down at Lonewind's place today, seeing everyone, it's just…" Lucian sighed. "Sorry. Sometimes, it's just hard to act like everything's okay."

"Shhh." She kissed Lucian. "Just close your eyes. Rest. It's over now. Sleep now, my sweet prince."

A sudden, startled movement, and Lucian said sharply, "What?"

Ayliad made a sound of confusion. "What do you mean? Sweet prince? It's a term of affection in my tribe."

"Sorry…," Lucian said again. "It just… sounded like something else."

The Prince. Ayliad and Willow called Lucian that—if Willow was the ruler, then Lucian was the prince, her son, a constant reminder that she was his mother, and nothing he did could change that. Chance shuddered as Lucian's memory faded away around him.

In the darkness, whispers of Ayliad and Lucian's voices

continued. Mundane conversations, intimate conversations, wordless cries of passion. With each memory, Chance felt Lucian's emotions. Not the horror and revulsion that they brought now, but the pure joy, the love Lucian had felt then. He'd truly loved the person he'd thought Ayliad to be, just as Lonewind had as deeply and as passionately loved the woman he thought Willow was.

And like Willow's betrayal of Lonewind's love, Ayliad's betrayal had crushed Lucian.

A whispered memory brushed against Chance, and he recoiled, feeling dirty and sick before he knew why. Ayliad's soft, sultry voice never changed. "Do you know what I'm going to do now, Lucian? I'm going to Chance. He offered me a deal: he'll give himself to me willingly if I go to him instead of forcing you." She laughed. "Of course, he has no way of ensuring that I'm upholding my end, now does he?"

"Stay away from him!" Lucian screamed, voice raw.

"My dear brother, Chance is selling his body and his soul alike to try to protect you. Why would I deny him his wish?"

Chance doubled over, gut twisting. He'd always known he had no way of knowing whether Ayliad kept her end of the bargain, but he'd somehow, foolishly, naively, hoped that she wouldn't tell Lucian about it.

Someone seized his arm and jerked hard. Chance felt himself pulled through a resistant barrier, then he landed, gasping, on solid but unseen ground. Tieln and Cylin crouched beside him.

"Back with us?" Cylin asked.

Chance nodded and pushed to his feet. When he raised his head, he saw an opaque bubble. "You pulled me out of that?"

"Tieln did," Cylin said. "That 'finding' trick of his is really handy."

Tieln eyed the bubble warily. "What is that?"

"It's a bundle of memories that Lucian doesn't want to remember," Chance said quietly. "About Ayliad."

"About her abusing him?" Tieln asked.

Chance closed his eyes and shook his head. "No. Most of them were… about him loving her. Loving the person he thought she was, before she revealed the truth." *He thought he'd finally found the woman he would spend the rest of his life with. It was more than a century after the Coral Palace before I met Ahmea and allowed myself to love and trust someone so intimately. But it took decades beyond that before Lucian dared let another woman into his life in anything more than a superficial relationship.*

Neither of the others spoke. Chance stared into the darkness a long moment, then started walking. The next memory bubble pulled him in before he realized it was there.

"Mama!" squealed a delighted boy. He was safe and warm in his father's arms, content.

His mother brushed her spirit-form fingers through his hair. "Hello, Lucian. Have you been good?"

Chance shuddered, wrapping his arms tight around himself at the sound of Willow's voice. Even Lucian's innocent love for his parents couldn't counteract the horror and terror her voice woke in Chance.

Lucian's voice was a little older in the next memory, but he was still a child. Still innocent. Still hoping that one day, the two people he loved most in the world could resolve whatever mysterious adult stuff kept them apart, and they could all be a family together. "Mama, sometimes Daddy gets really sick after you visit. Could you… maybe not visit for a little while? Until he gets better?"

"But how can I see how you are doing if I don't visit, Lucian?" Willow asked, as if her visits were anything more than opportunities to torment Lonewind.

"I'll visit you!" Lucian said eagerly. "In the spirit, just like you visit us!"

"You're able to do that already, Lucian? My, such a talented child you are. All right. You can visit me instead."

Tears trickled down Chance's cheeks. He hadn't even been born when Lucian was this young. The purity in Lucian's thoughts cut to the core. A child shielded from the horrible truths of his own existence.

The next one wrapped around him, and even before he heard Willow, Chance felt Lucian's confusion and doubt, the sense that something shook him to the core and made him question everything he believed.

"Why did you leave me?" Lucian asked. "Why did you take Dad and leave me in the boat?"

"I knew Moonfire would bring you here safely, my dear son," Willow answered. "If the others had known I was near, they would have stopped me. They forced your father to leave me in the first place, Lucian. If not for them, our family would never have been separated. Isn't that true, Lonewind?"

"Yes." Lonewind's voice was barely a whisper of despair.

"But…" Lucian's emotions swirled in confusion. "But they're his friends."

Another gap, then a moment of memory sharp in its clarity and its emotions. Lucian raised his head, sensing Willow's spirit approaching to torment them once again. The surface of his mind seemed dead and emotionless, but behind the mask burned a rage so hot and so deep, nothing could extinguish it. A rage so hot it could, it would consume everything, even its host.

"I hate you."

Chance fell to the ground, curling around himself and clutching his head. Once, he'd hated Willow with that same fierce fury. She'd crushed him. Broken him. Enslaved him. Destroyed him.

The memory passed, and a new one followed.

Lucian stood, hands clenched, panting for breath. All

around him lay broken glass and the warped, twisted remains of metal tools. Chance recognized it as Lonewind's shop in the Ingathering, and knew he must be seeing when Lucian vandalized his father's shop, the finale of his increasingly brash efforts to get Lonewind to break the silence between them.

"Don't ignore me," Lucian hissed to the silent shop. "Don't you *dare* ignore me." His emotions roiled and twisted. Chance expected the frustration and anger, but under them, he was surprised to find fear. He knew that Lonewind's reluctance to reach out to Lucian had been born from the fear that Lucian would reject him and declare his hate for his father, as he had for Willow. But he'd never recognized the fear that Lucian kept buried under his anger: the fear that Lonewind's love was as much a lie as Willow's had been, and that Lonewind hated him for being the child conceived by force.

Someone grabbed Chance and pulled him from the memories. He didn't move, didn't raise his head.

"Chance?" Tieln asked.

He bit his lip and nodded. "I'm… here."

"Was it more Ayliad?" Cylin asked, pulling him to his feet.

"No. It was his childhood, and the loss of innocence. It was… betrayal. Both sets of memories hold the worst, the deepest betrayals done to him."

Cylin kept hold of his arm, and he leaned against her. The battering of Lucian's emotions against his spirit left him shaky. Tieln draped Chance's other arm over his shoulder. "Can you keep going?"

Chance nodded. "I have to." He forced himself to walk.

Memory wrapped around them. The world turned to blood. Haunted eyes that saw only pain, despair, and emptiness looked up from a blood-streaked face. Chance heard his own agonized plea.

"There's nothing left, Lucian. She's taken everything. Why won't you let me go?"

"Oh *hell* no!" Cylin tore him out of the memory. "Oh no, we are *not* going there."

Chance gasped, slumping against her. His other hand gripped Tieln's shoulder, his fingers digging in tightly. He couldn't breathe. Between Cylin and Tieln, they carried him through the darkness until it finally gave way to light.

He raised his head and freed himself from his companions' support. They stood on a cobblestone path under the light of a warm spring day. To either side, crumbling walls fought a losing battle with creeping plants, moss, and weather. They passed through the remains of a stone archway, the capstone long gone, into an overgrown courtyard filled with statues. Those nearest the entrance had succumbed to the elements—a pair of legs on one pedestal, on another, only legs and trunk remained, the rest lying in shattered fragments across the ground.

A few steps further, Cylin stopped. Her eyes scanned the statues. "Is it my imagination, or is every single one of these Lucian?"

"It's not your imagination," Tieln said.

They were right. Every statue depicted Lucian in some activity, and Chance saw at least a hundred scattered about the courtyard. It should have felt ridiculously self-aggrandizing. Instead, the cold stones radiated self-loathing and despair, each a monument to failure.

Beyond the courtyard, a central building loomed, its façade cracked and crumbling. "Tieln, where's Lucian?"

Tieln pointed to the building. "He feels very close." They picked a path over rubble and debris toward the structure. "This place looks like it used to be beautiful."

"It may have been, once," Chance said. "But this place isn't familiar to me."

As he said it, something nagged at him, some fleeting,

unpleasant twinge that this ruin was not so unknown. He shivered.

"You okay?" Cylin asked.

Chance answered with a curt nod. "Let's find Lucian."

He climbed the crumbling steps and crossed the threshold. An icy chill, like a hand on the back of his neck, raced through him.

He heard Cylin and Tieln climb the steps, then sounds of surprise and alarm, followed by silence. Chance spun around to see the stones of the doorway flow together, blocking the path outside.

Chance stared at it a long moment. *Is this truly the depth of Lucian's mind, or have I walked into another trap?*

Wary, he took the only route open to him and walked deeper inside the building. The walls were pale stone, smooth and seamless. Light flowed in from the gaps in the walls and ceiling. He could see his reflection in the polished marble floor —a gaunt, haunted figure, too thin, face lined with pain.

The entry hall opened to a throne room. Chance froze as unthinkable dread pierced him through. This room… he knew this room. His breath stuck in his throat. Unbidden, his eyes sought the throne, fearing who he would find seated on it. His hand rose to his neck, more than half expecting to feel a collar there, just as he expected to see his Master… to see Willow on the throne waiting for him.

The center throne stood empty. A little tightness in his chest eased. To the left of the primary throne stood a second on a lower tier—an addition Chance had never seen to the throne room. Lucian sprawled on it, one leg swung over the arm. His clothes harkened back to ancient days, when elves could call themselves gods and expect worship and tribute. The finest of silks, perfectly cut to his figure, rich with embroidery and jewels. Somehow, though, their perfection was as marred as that of the statues in the courtyard, as if Lucian wore them as a mockery of… something. One sleeve was pushed up, and he drew on his arm with a pen or quill.

"Lucian."

Lucian didn't look up, and didn't answer.

Chance forced himself to step forward, to set foot inside the room that haunted so many of his nightmares. "Lucian. What are you doing?"

"Isn't is obvious?" Lucian slowly raised his head and looked at Chance. "I'm surveying my kingdom."

"You're… what?"

Lucian raised his hand, gesturing expansively. Chance realized that what he'd first mistaken for a quill was instead a knife. "The Prince, surveying his realm. The glorious empire of broken hopes, shattered souls, and endless pain that his mother left him."

Chance made himself take another step toward Lucian, though he felt like he was moving through tar that grabbed at him and threatened to drag him down, never releasing him. "That's not who you are, Lucian."

"Isn't it?" Lucian's voice grew quiet. "You're the one who told me that it didn't matter what words we used to try to make it palatable. They can't change what we are."

Chance flinched. He remembered that conversation from so long ago, a time after one of his imprisonments and tortures by Willow's sadistic and merciless hand. A time when he'd been unable to think of himself as anything but her slave. "And you told me that was bullshit."

Lucian settled back in the throne and resumed drawing on his arm. "Which was such an *effective* argument, wasn't it? So *convincing*."

Chance winced. "No, it wasn't. But that doesn't mean you were wrong then, Lucian."

A trickle of blood followed the knife's passage. "Look around, Chance. You see the ruins. The monuments to my failure. A kingdom of nothing. The legacy of a broken prince with the shattered remnants left after his mother's destruction."

"That's enough!" Chance snapped. "She's gone, Lucian. She lost. We picked up the pieces and put them together again. We won." He stepped closer. "*You* won. Do you remember *that?* Remember how even when my spirit was shattered, when I thought that all I had left to claim as my own was death, you refused to yield. You would have challenged death itself to bring me back and make me see that I had not lost everything."

Lucian raised his eyes again, and his gaze was hard. "I remember. And I remember how you stabbed me in the chest when I wouldn't let you turn that blade on yourself."

This time, Chance didn't flinch. He didn't dare show Lucian how painful, how horrifying that memory remained. "I know."

Lucian never broke eye contact with Chance. "Then let me finish what you started." He lifted the blade and slashed a deep gash in his arm.

Chance flew to him, his fear of the room forced aside. He reached Lucian in time to see the savage wound knit itself closed and vanish without a scar. Lucian turned his arm one way, then the other. "Not today, it seems."

Chance's jaw tightened. "You knew what would happen."

"I knew it probably would. But some day, some time, she'll slip."

"You wanted to see me react."

Lucian's left arm was covered with thin cuts where he'd drawn with the knife. They bled sluggishly, and unlike the gash, didn't immediately heal. Chance moved to set his hand on them. Lucian seized his wrist, squeezing hard.

Chance hissed in pain. "Let go."

"Why?" Lucian countered. "Do you think covering the marks will make them go away? Or do you just want to not see them? If you can't see the pain, it doesn't count, right? Cover it over, stuff it away someplace where it won't *inconvenience* anyone."

"No," Chance said quietly. "It doesn't work that way. I would know—I've tried. Tried too many times. It always comes back."

Lucian released his arm and shoved Chance back. "Why are you here?"

"Because there's nowhere else I can be, Lucian."

Lucian's lip curled. "Nowhere other than *here*? In Her throne room?"

"Here, where you are," Chance said. "Here, in the depths of your mind. Here, where your soul has retreated."

"There's nothing here!" Lucian slammed the knife into the arm of the throne. "Nothing! This? This is what she wants— her good little Prince who will sit quiet in his corner and keep his fucking mouth shut. A proper son who does as he's told." His eyes bore into Chance's. "Isn't it?"

Before Chance answered, Lucian continued. "So why *not* let me open my veins for you, *Mother*? I promise not to bleed out on the rug. Just pose me as you want. Jab that dagger into my back to hold me upright and watch me smile at your court. What does it matter to *you*?"

"Lucian." When Lucian didn't respond, Chance stepped back onto the dais and caught Lucian's face in his hands. "Lucian. Look at me."

Lucian's hand closed around the hilt of the knife, but he didn't pull it free.

"She's dead, Lucian. Willow is dead. Ayliad is dead."

Lucian's expression twisted, ugly with rage. His eyes narrowed, and his voice fell just above a whisper. "And why the fuck do you think that makes any difference, Chance? Did *that* matter when you saw Ayliad in my memories? When you heard

Willow speak? Did you tell yourself 'they're dead' and walk away?"

Chance said nothing.

Lucian jerked away from him and rose. "It doesn't matter, Chance. Like you said, what we are never changes." He strode across the throne room and threw open the doors to the balcony.

Chance followed him and stepped outside, relieved to be free of the throne room for a little while. The balcony overlooked the courtyard and its statues. Beyond, he saw only darkness. "And what do you think you are?"

"Pain." The word fell flat and hard from Lucian's lips. He remained standing in the doorway. "My birth… my very *conception* was intended to bring pain. To torture Lonewind." His jaw tightened. "And I've been so *good* at it, haven't I? I didn't even know then that I was stabbing him in the heart every time he looked at me and remembered how my mother took what he never wanted to give."

"Yet he loves you," Chance said. "Calls you the one perfect thing to come from it all."

"Perfect." Lucian laughed, a hard, cold sound. "Yes. Perfect at hurting everyone around me. Perfect at destroying every good thing I ever had." He waved at the courtyard. "See my *perfect* life!"

The statues twisted into grotesque forms of themselves. Leering faces and clawed hands loomed over the courtyard like demons.

"You saved me," Chance said quietly. "You pulled me back, even when I thought I had nothing left to hold onto."

"Did I, though?" Lucian asked as quietly, eyes on the courtyard. "Or did I only save myself, demand that you survive for my own sake?"

"No. It was never just for your own sake, Lucian, no matter how it seems right now."

Lucian gripped the edge of the door, and it crumbled under his grasp. He raised his hand and let the dust trickled down between them. "Pain and destruction, Chance. A fire that consumed everything in its path. That's what I am."

"No, Lucian. That's not even close to who or what you are. A fire, maybe. A fire that lights the way, a fire that the rest of us know we can rely on to keep us warm, to protect us when we're wounded, to pick us up when we fall, to show us the way back when we're lost."

"I abandoned my own son!" Lucian screamed. The world trembled.

"You told me once that the only way you saw to protect the children of our clan from Willow was to leave them somewhere they would be safe, far from us," Chance whispered.

Lucian whirled on him, eyes burning with anger, but Chance looked into the darkness beyond the courtyard and continued. "Maybe it wasn't the right answer. But you tried to protect him the only way you could, Lucian."

"And for what?" Lucian demanded bitterly. "For the Tree to consume him instead."

"Tieln is free of the Tree. Dash is as well."

"No thanks to me."

Chance was silent. He knew that trying to force the matter, trying to make Lucian see was a sure way to trigger his friend's rebellious nature. He had to let Lucian think. At least it seemed that his soul knew reality from Willow's mind games. Then he remembered Lucian's rant earlier, and wasn't so sure.

Is that why he lashes out? Because he doesn't think this is real? He doesn't think that I am real?

Lucian spun and strode away from him. Chance turned to follow, but stone bars rose from the floor, blocking the doorway. "Lucian!"

Lucian didn't look back or respond. He climbed back up to the lower throne and slumped into the seat. Chance hissed a curse and scanned the building for another way in. Lucian picked up the knife and began drawing on his arm once more.

Don't do this, Lucian. Don't shut me out. Please.

Several windows let light into the throne room, but they were all too small to squeeze through. Chance flew from the balcony around to the front of the building, but that entrance remained closed as well. He circled the structure. Small windows, walled off doorways, no openings large enough for an elf—not even one as underweight as Chance. He landed on the balcony again.

"Lucian, let me in."

Lucian's grip on the hilt of the knife tightened. "You don't want to be in here."

"Why are you keeping me out? I didn't fight through everything your mind threw at me just to give up now," Chance said.

"I didn't ask you to come."

"You should have."

The knife bit deeper into Lucian's skin. Blood dripped to the floor. "There's nothing you can do. Nothing left but pain. Eventually, even that will be gone."

"Lucian, let me in!" Chance demanded. He pushed his will against the stone bars, but they refused to yield.

Lucian raised his head and looked across the throne room. His gaze met Chance's. "How does it feel to be the one on the other side, Chance? To be watching someone you love destroy themselves in front of you?"

Chance's throat tightened, but he didn't look away. "I'll answer that if you tell me first: does it make you feel better to attack your friend, the person trying to help you? Because I can tell you, doing so only made me hate myself more."

Lucian said nothing.

"I'm going to find a way to reach you, Lucian."

Lucian still said nothing, but broke eye contact and looked back to his bleeding arm.

Chance made a second, more thorough inspection of the exterior. Even so, he almost missed the window. It stood high on the wall, set back and mostly hidden by an overhang. The angle meant that it wouldn't let much direct light inside, but it looked large enough to squeeze through. He floated cautiously to it, expecting the stone to shift and close it at any moment. Alighting on the sill, he peered inside.

While his eyes adjusted, he picked out a wardrobe, a couch, and a large bed that left him inexplicably uneasy. Chance leaned further inside, looking for anyone else in the room. He saw a closed door that presumably led further inside. The room lay in a state of mild, lived-in disarray, with the wardrobe slightly open and the covers rumpled.

Light glinted on something on the bed. His eye found the object. The world froze around him.

A metal collar rested on the bed, a chain running from it to one of the bedposts.

He knew this room. He'd woken here, naked but for that collar around his neck, the final time Willow captured him. The time she'd crushed him completely.

Chance flung himself backwards out the window. Panic clawed at him, but behind it rose anger.

He rushed back to the balcony. The stone bars didn't yield when he levitated a large rock from below and slammed it into them, but inside, Lucian raised his head and turned toward him. His expression was unreadable.

Chance trembled with a twisting mix of fear and fury. Breath hissed between his teeth. "Is this your idea of some sort of sick test, Lucian? Trying to see how far I'll really go? Trying to make me *prove* that I mean it?"

Lucian didn't blink. "I don't know what you're talking about."

Chance's eyes narrowed. "Don't you? The *one* way into this place is through *that* room. The room where Willow raped me.

Tortured me. *Killed* me and brought me back again and again until she broke any resistance I had left!"

Color drained from Lucian's face. He started to stand, but his legs buckled and he crumpled to the floor clutching his head. "No. No, no, I can't. Anywhere but there. Don't make me hear the screams again." He curled in on himself, tears running down his cheeks.

Chance wasn't sure what reaction he'd expected, but Lucian's collapse was not it. "Let me in," he said quietly.

Lucian closed his eyes. "Just leave me alone. Haven't you done enough? You've taken everything. I can't go there. Please…"

"I'm right here, Lucian. Just open these bars." Chance reached between the bars toward him.

"I *can't!*" Lucian turned anguished eyes on Chance. "There's only one way out… I can't go into that room… hear the screams…" He shuddered and squeezed his eyes shut. "Please stop. What do you want from me? What haven't you already taken?"

The bars, the sealed doors, they aren't just to keep me out. They're to keep him in. But how? Is this a trap left in his soul by Willow that somehow lay undetected and untriggered until now? Or is Lucian caged by his own pain and guilt?

Chance reached out with his magic and pulled Lucian toward him. Lucian didn't resist, even when Chance rested a hand on his shoulder. He felt Lucian shudder.

"Look at me," Chance said quietly, crouching at the bars.

Lucian turned and met his eyes for a moment, then looked away. "I know you're not really here. I know this is all… Willow's game." His voice cracked. "She makes me hear your screams, your pleas, when she tortures you. I've tried to leave, but the only way out is through that room, and every time I try… she hurts you and makes me see what she's doing to you.

I can't…" Tears ran down his face. "And all she leaves me is pain."

"No, Lucian. I'm here. Me. Chance. No games, no lies. This is your soul, and I am here."

"She destroyed you because of me."

Chance shook his head. "Willow was determined to destroy me because I refused to bow to her. Because I fought. Because she couldn't *bear* the thought that anyone could stand against her, no matter what she did to destroy them. You're not the reason she destroyed me, Lucian. You're the reason she failed to do so." He gripped Lucian's hand through the bars. "Even when I thought she'd taken everything from me, you pulled me back, even when I didn't think I wanted to be pulled back." His jaw tightened. "And I will *not* let her crush you."

"But she knows that to crush me, all she needs is you," Lucian whispered.

"Lucian. Do you remember Forest Town?"

Lucian nodded, a faint movement of his head.

"Quicksilver found you there, told you that he'd show you the way to me, so you could wake me from the coma I'd fallen into since Ahmea's death. Do you remember that?"

"Yes." Lucian's voice was very quiet.

"And what happened when you couldn't bear to wait any longer?"

"I went into the spirit realm to reach you," Lucian answered.

"In my dreams, Lucian, I was here, in this throne room. Willow was taunting me. She meant to put the collar on me once more." Chance looked into Lucian's eyes. "Then you came. You drove her back, and you gave me the strength to crawl out of those dark dreams and into the light. You fought her. You stopped her. She doesn't have me, and she never will again. So don't let her claim a battle she's already lost. You can't stay here."

"Yes, I can," Lucian said softly.

"I won't let you."

"But you're not here."

Trying to argue his own reality wouldn't convince Lucian. Chance let out a weary breath. "If I'm not, then I must be a conjuring of your soul, Lucian, because you know Willow would never allow a vision of me as anything but her slave."

That, at least, reached Lucian. He pushed up on one arm, and his other hand gripped Chance's. "Either you're real, or I want you to be real, and whichever it is, she isn't controlling you."

"That's right." Chance rose slowly, tugging on Lucian's hand. Lucian pushed himself to his feet, never letting go of Chance. "Can you open these bars, Lucian?"

"They won't let me out."

"Maybe not, but can you let me *in*? The bars weren't here before, and the front entrance didn't close until after I'd gone through it."

He felt Lucian trying to assert control, but the bars didn't even twitch. Lucian rested his head against the stone. "I'm sorry. I can't even do this…"

"'Even this'? Lucian, I know it's not a small thing I asked," Chance said.

"But it should be. Shaping stone should be as easy as breathing."

"If you can't let me in this way, then we have to go to… that room."

Lucian paled and shook his head. "I can't."

Chance let out his breath slowly. "If it's the only way out of here, then one way or another, we have to."

"We? No, you must stay away from that room, Chance. If she's there, if she's waiting for you—"

"If she is, I *will* need your help, Lucian," Chance interrupted. He looked into his friend's eyes. "I know you won't let her hurt me again."

Lucian looked away. "How can you say that, when I've failed to protect you so many times?"

"I can say it because I know you," Chance said. "I know that every time I fall, you'll be there to pick me up again and keep me safe until I can stand again. Even when you aren't sure what's real and what's not, even when you're in pain and lashing out blindly, I know that if I cry for help, you will answer. And because of that, I know that when you need me, I'll be there. Even here."

"I've fallen so many times, Chance. I don't know if I remember how to pick myself up, much less anyone else."

Chance gripped his hand. "That's why it's my turn now, Lucian. Trust me, like I've always trusted you."

"I trust you, Chance."

"Meet me at that bedroom," Chance said. "I'll be there. I'll be waiting for you."

Lucian shuddered, but he didn't argue. Chance released his hand and stepped back. He waited until Lucian turned and slowly walked across the throne room toward the interior door. Once he was sure Lucian wasn't going to turn back, he flew around the building again until he found the hidden window.

Chance perched on the sill and closed his eyes, drawing slow, deep breaths. Despite his words to Lucian, this room terrified him even more than the throne room.

What was it Cylin said? Lucian's nightmares and mine are the same, through different eyes.

I'm here, in the hall outside the door, Lucian said.

I'm sitting in the window, Chance told him. *I don't see anyone else here.*

He heard the door to the outer chamber open and Lucian's hesitant footsteps as he entered.

A scream of horror and anguish rent the air. Lights flared

to life in the room. Chance jerked, gaze flying to the bed. It no longer simply held rumpled sheets and the empty collar. He saw a vision of himself, limbs bound to the bedposts and the collar ringing his neck. Willow stood over her terrified, screaming captive, her lips curling in a smirk that Chance knew all too well. Her long black hair hung loose down her back, and she wore the flowing silver dress that had been her trademark when the humans had known her as the Black Witch.

"Ah, my foolish son, you just don't learn, do you?" she said over the cries. "You think you can be free? Very well. Claim your 'freedom.'" She looked back to the vision of Chance in chains. "All you have to do is walk past and leave him with me."

This is the cage. This is what holds him here.

I'm here, Lucian. That isn't me.

Lucian didn't answer, but Chance heard footsteps stagger through the outer room. Finally, Lucian sagged against the doorframe, trembling.

"I won't… let you… hurt him." Lucian panted for breath, as if fighting for every step.

"You?" Willow laughed. "My dear son, my little prince, you hold no power here. Everything is under my control."

"Not everything." Chance flung himself at her. "You don't control Lucian, and you don't control *me!*"

He slammed into her. For a heartbeat, his soul recoiled at touching her. Her fingers bit into his shoulder, the nails piercing skin.

Then Lucian was at his side, flinging Willow back. Chance pushed to his feet. On the bed, the phantom of himself faded and was silent. Chance's throat was tight, but he made himself speak.

"You're dead, Willow. You'll never touch me again. And I won't let your memory destroy Lucian or anyone else. Go back to the abyss where you belong!"

"Insolent, arrogant slave," she hissed, wiping a trickle of blood from her mouth. "I know your every shame, your every fear. You will beg me for mercy, and I will laugh." Her gaze moved to Lucian. "And there's nothing you can do to stop me."

Tremors of fear raced under Chance's skin. She could do as she promised and more—he knew that far too well.

Lucian straightened, lips curling back to bare his teeth. His eyes met Willow's, and he gave a short, sharp laugh. "'Nothing' I can do? That's where you're wrong. You used Chance to keep me caged. You used our friendship as a weapon, just like you used Lonewind's love for me. But you could never understand that it's not a weakness. It's the only thing that will always give me strength. And you'll never understand, because you only know how to hate." He steadied Chance, gripping his arm. "You've lost, Willow. You're dead. You have no more power over us. So *get the fuck out!*"

"You dare." Her eyes narrowed in cold fury.

"I dare." Lucian threw up a hand, and she slammed into the far wall.

Chance felt the rage building in Lucian, a blind anger that could be as dangerous as his despair. "Let's go, Lucian. Let this illusion collapse and take her with it." He nodded up at the window.

Lucian never took his eyes off Willow, but he flew with Chance up to the window. Chance slid out the opening and held his breath, desperately hoping that the palace wouldn't prevent Lucian from leaving. Lucian hesitated, as if asking himself the same thing. Then, with one final glare at Willow, he swung himself out.

Chance caught Lucian's arm and drew him further from the palace. Lucian slowly looked over the building, then the courtyard, and finally the darkness beyond. He whispered, "Chance, is this real?"

"We're in your mind, Lucian. This is where you retreated after we fought… after you killed Ayliad."

Lucian closed his eyes. "I remember that. You were screaming, and I kept seeing flashes of you in the Coral Palace, with Ayliad and Willow."

"She triggered those memories somehow." Chance shuddered.

"As she was dying, she told me that it was all one of Willow's games, a hallucination, and that you and I were still in Willow's clutches." Lucian opened his amber eyes and held Chance's gaze. "So tell me, please, one more time… Is this real?"

This is real, Lucian. Everything that's happened. Willow's death, Lonewind and the rest of the clan going into space, the war, the deaths of Ahmea, Cilvi, Tash, and Sun, the birth of Tieln, your creation of Forest Town, you drawing me out of my coma; it's all been real. The good and the bad alike.

Lucian drew a slow, shuddering breath. "All of it." He looked at the palace and courtyard. "But not this."

"As a manifestation of your guilt and pain, it's real enough," Chance said quietly.

Lucian winced. "I said things… Things meant to hurt you."

"You did," Chance agreed. "But on the whole, they weren't really untrue, either."

Lucian cast him a sidelong look. "Gee, thanks, Chance. 'Oh, sure, you threw in my face a bunch of things that happened in the worst period of my life, Lucian, but they were true, so don't feel like shit about that.'"

Chance couldn't help the small chuckle that slipped out. With it came a wave of relief to hear Lucian talking like himself, no matter how inappropriate the moment. "Well, I'm not saying I might not bring it up sometime in the future."

Lucian's shoulders shook with a silent laugh, but he grew

serious all too soon as he looked into the darkness. "All the walls are cracked and broken. There are so many things that should be behind them. Things I don't want."

"Hiding them behind walls doesn't make them go away, Lucian. It lets them fester until something breaks and the walls won't hold them any longer." Chance sighed, "Trust me on that one."

"I don't want the pain again," Lucian whispered.

"None of us can hide from it forever. I would know."

Lucian looked at him and finally said, "I know you do. But how do you put it back together when everything's fallen apart?"

Chance gazed past the palace toward the clusters of Lucian's memories. "I asked much the same of Cahron once, when I couldn't see any end but surrender. He said that sometimes, you don't. Sometimes, you leave the pieces to fall where they will, and build something new from them."

"Cahron said that?"

"And a lot more. Sometimes we forget just how much shit he's been through with Lonewind, both before Willow and after."

"I wish he was here," Lucian said.

"He is. Not in your head, but he's here," Chance said.

Lucian stared at him. "What?"

"Lonewind, Cahron, and the rest of the clan returned. And my understanding is that Lonewind somehow managed to shove about five years worth of the trip into the last month. He's probably been pacing anxiously since I went into your head."

"I have to go back, don't I?"

"I can't say that I'd recommend a forty-year coma," Chance told him. "But if you aren't ready, if you want to face some of this first… I know it won't be fast. It won't be easy. But however long it takes, when you're finally ready to come back and open your eyes, I'll be there. Just like I always knew you'd be waiting for me."

Lucian took a deep breath and shook his head. "Putting it off won't make it easier. So I guess… it's time to wake up." He looked at the palace, then turned to Chance. "Thanks. See you on the other side."

"See you on the other side," Chance agreed quietly. Then, forcing his mind to reach back to his distant body, he lifted his hand from Lucian and broke the connection.

LUCIAN

The world was full of sharp edges stabbing into his senses. Warm, damp air prickled across his skin. Stiff muscles throbbed. His dry tongue stuck inside his mouth.

He smelled salt water, crushed grass, freshly exposed stone. Chance's magic clung to his skin, and Lonewind's magic radiated from all sides. Beside him, someone quietly shifted positions with a faint, stiff groan. Further away, a rhythmic pattern of steps told him that someone paced. Further yet, he heard a voice, too far away to understand the words, but the tone clearly indicated that Cahron was Very Disappointed in someone. For half a moment, he thought that Tash must be the recipient of one the healer's legendary reprimands.

Then he remembered.

Lucian drew a trembling breath and curled in on himself, tears spilling free.

A hand touched his shoulder. "Lucian."

He reached up and gripped Chance's hand. "You're here." His throat was raw, and speaking hurt like metal shavings tearing at his insides.

"I told you I would be."

Why did I think I had to wake up now again?

"Because you were afraid that if you didn't do it now, you'd stay hiding in your mind and never emerge."

Chaos and pain lay in those depths, exposed and raw. *Oh, right.*

He peeled open gritty eyes. A simple stone structure thatched with grass sheltered him and Chance. His cousin looked wan and weary, heavy shadows ringing his eyes. If he looked how he felt, Lucian suspected he didn't look much better. Outside, tall stalks of grass waved in an ocean breeze.

This is real.

He tried to sit up. Chance steadied him, then helped him stand. Leaning on his cousin, Lucian shuffled outside into the sunlight.

Less than two heartbeats later, Lonewind snatched him in a fierce bearhug. Raw, unfiltered emotions rushed through Lucian, a tangled knot of relief, a child's love for his father, old pain, respect, and joy. For only a moment, he felt the buried, secret fear he'd never told anyone, that his father hated him for how he'd been born.

Lonewind pressed his forehead against Lucian's, never letting go of him. *I came as fast as I could. I should have been here sooner. Forgive me.*

Tears again ran down Lucian's cheeks. *It's not your fault. I forgive you, Lonewind.* He closed his eyes. *For everything.*

Lonewind drew a small, startled breath, then embraced Lucian tighter. *I don't deserve that. Thank you.*

He released Lucian and stepped back. Cahron, Tieln, and Cylin gathered around. A little past them stood Lynx. Lucian looked at all of them. "You're safe. What about Eria, Quick, and Dash?"

"Back in Forest Town," Cylin said. She wiped at a trickle of blood running from her nose and frowned at it.

"The Guardian freed Dash of the corruption," Tieln added. Dark circles ringed his eyes, but he stood straight.

"The Guardian?" Lucian had a sudden, horrifying memory of feeling the Guardian using Tieln as a conduit, and Tieln being pulled into the Tree. "Are you all right?"

"Not an experience I'd care to repeat, but I came through with all parts intact," Tieln told him.

Cahron slipped past both of them and gave Lucian a hug. "Welcome back, Lucian."

"Shouldn't I be saying that to you?" Lucian asked with a laugh. "It's good to see you, Cahron."

Cahron leaned close and spoke quietly. "In case you didn't know, I feel obliged to tell you that your son is at *least* as headstrong and stubborn as you. And your human friend is no better."

Lucian looked to Tieln and Cylin. "Uh… just what did you guys do while I was indisposed?"

The two exchanged looks. "I'll tell you later," Cylin said. Tieln raised an eyebrow at her, but didn't volunteer any further answer.

"Great. That's not going to worry me at all." Lucian looked around, taking stock of their surroundings.

He stiffened, realizing just *where* they were and why this stretch of beach felt familiar. Chance steadied him, and Lucian was sure his cousin understood the fear that gnawed at his mind. "Can we leave?" Lucian asked.

"Are you sure you're ready for that?" Cahron asked in concern.

"I'm sure I don't want to stay in this place."

"We can go wherever you want, Lucian. Anywhere," Lonewind said. In mind-speech, he added, *Whether in this world or another.*

What right do I have to decide that? What right do I have to any of this?

From the depths of his soul, among the nightmares, memories, and phantoms of the past, an answer came.

The Ghost, curt, blunt, and practical said, "You need them, and they need you."

The Guardian's voice was a whisper of wind through leaves. "Who bestows that right on you, if not them? Go. You know where you belong. They will lift you when you fall; they will plant you in fertile soil under the sun. And when you have need, you will find us always. But for now, you are safe, and we may rest."

Lucian looked from Lonewind to Cahron, then Lynx, Tieln, Cylin, and Chance. His clan. His family. "Let's go home."